MOST VALUABLE PLAYERS

A COLLEGE SPORTS ROMANCE COLLECTION

I0649482

USA TODAY BESTSELLING AUTHOR

REBECCA JENSHAK

You know those stories where the smart girl tutors the dumb jock?
This isn't it.

Blair

What's the probability of insulting the one guy on campus I need to help me pass statistics? If I knew, I wouldn't be standing in front of Wes Reynolds begging him to tutor me.

Basketball player, sexy, arrogant, always sleeping through class . . . these are the things I knew about him. What I didn't know is that he is a seriously smart jock.

Wes

What's the best way to get rid of the peppy and unrelenting girl that keeps asking me to tutor her? If I knew, I wouldn't be staring at her tan legs and attempting to teach her statistics.

Sorority girl, fine as f**k, determined, ball buster . . . these are the things I knew about her. What I didn't know is that she is all the things I didn't realize I wanted or needed.

Or that one semester with her would change everything.

PROLOGUE

Blair

Three Years Ago

"Who run the world?" Gabby and I scream the lyrics at the top of our lungs. Top down on her cherry-red convertible, music blaring, hair blowing across our faces, we pull out of the high school parking lot with the first day of classes behind us.

"One more year, Blair. One more freaking year, and we're out of this place," she says when Beyoncé stops singing.

"You don't think you'll miss it? Even a little bit?"

She shoots me a look that questions my sanity. "No. We're going to Valley U, we're going to study hard, party our asses off, and then, when we graduate, we're going to start some fabulous female only business and end up on the cover of *Forbes* or *Vanity Fair*. You and I are meant for more than Suck Hill."

Her enthusiasm is contagious. I want all those things, truly, but it's Gabby who is counting down the days until we can leave our small town of Succulent Hill, which Gabs lovingly renamed Suck Hill. I've always liked the community and friendliness of living in our hometown. Not Gabby. She's been dreaming of moving to Valley and attending the university there since we were in middle school.

Bringing the car to a halt at the four-way stop just outside of our neighborhood, she turns the radio down. There aren't any other cars as far as the eye can see, but we continue to idle in place. I meet her serious gaze. "What's wrong? Are we out of gas again or something?"

"Promise me we're getting out of this town."

I laugh off her words. "I promise."

She grabs my wrist and pulls on the friendship bracelet I made in eighth grade. The ratty thing made of purple thread from my mother's sewing kit still hangs on my arm. A matching one dons her wrist. It's become a symbol of our relationship and the promises we've made. "I mean it, Blair. You and I are getting out of this place. We're going to make something of ourselves. Run companies, have someone fetch us coffee, live in fabulous downtown apartments, and have brunch dates after Pilates on the weekends."

"I know. We've only been talking about it forever."

I don't understand the sudden urgency of her words. We should be enjoying our last year and planning what we'll wear to prom or what we'll put in the senior time capsule. College is a year away and there's so much to do before then.

"Swear it. Swear you're going to do it with me."

Gabby's perfectly styled blonde hair blows in the breeze like a commercial for Vidal Sassoon. It's easy for people to laugh off her ambitions as the rambling of a pretty girl whose been handed everything her entire life. She *is* beautiful, and she *has* been handed her share of privilege, but only I know how strong her desire to rule the world is. I don't believe in my own dreams nearly as much as I believe in hers.

I nudge her with my elbow. "I swear, Gabs."

My faith in myself is shaky, but I believe in Gabby, and with her by my side, I know we're capable of anything.

Dark clouds off in the distance warn of a monsoon storm rolling in just as Gabby parks in front of her house and closes the convertible top. "Sure you don't want to come with me tonight? Rachel's back to school pool party is going to be epic."

"Can't. We're going out to dinner to celebrate my dad's birthday."

Outside of the car, I breathe in the smell of rain in the distance. The wind has already picked up, and I'm looking forward to the heavy gusts and downpour that won't be far behind. When Gabby and I were little we'd talk on the phone through storms, anxiously waiting for the puddles that would be left behind so we could splash and play before the dry desert ground soaked up all the water. I shuffle toward my house, just three houses down from Gabby's. We've been neighbors our whole life, best friends too.

"You could sneak out after." Her sea-blue eyes light up with mischief.

"No thanks. I'm not risking getting grounded two weeks before the pep rally."

She kisses the air. "Fine, loser. I'll text you later."

"Later, Gabs."

I send her a wave over my shoulder and make my way home. Thirty minutes later, I'm sitting at my desk, watching the rain trickle down the window of my second story bedroom, when I see Gabby's car pull away from the curb. With a sigh, I pull out my history textbook and turn to the assigned reading.

If my best friend could see me now, she'd roll her eyes and call me an overachiever. I'm probably the only person sitting at home tonight instead of attending Rachel's party. Tomorrow everyone is going to be talking about it, and all I'll have to contribute to the conversation is the formation of the Provincial Congresses during the American Revolution.

I struggle to focus on the words as my brain tortures me with daydreams of how much fun everyone is having. Still, an hour passes and I'm almost done with the first chapter when my mom knocks on my door.

"Blair, honey."

I stand and stretch. "Come in."

I grab my purse, prepared to celebrate my dad's birthday. My brother and his new wife are meeting us. It should be fun. Although, it doesn't really compare to a pool party with all the coolest kids at SH High.

When I open the door, mother's face is not of happiness or celebration. My stomach drops, and my body tenses in preparation of receiving bad news.

"Mom, what's wrong?"

"Honey, it's Gabby."

People talk around me. My brain catches and fixates on single words. Hydroplaned. Unconscious. Critical. Brain Trauma.

I don't care about any of it. I just want to see her. I want to march back there and see Gabby pop up out of bed and tell me it was all a big joke to get me out of the house for the night.

But it's two long days and nights of sleeping in the waiting room before they let me into her room in the intensive care unit. I've been warned about the trauma of the accident, internal and external, but when I see her lying in bed bruised and covered in bandages, I run to her side and grab her hand. It's only relief and happiness that brings the tears to my eyes as she tries to smile around the cuts on her face.

"Gabs."

She opens her mouth and then closes it, frowning. "I . . ."

"What is it?"

A single tear slides down her face. "I can't remember your name." More tears fall, and each one breaks my heart a little more. "I know you're important. I can feel it in here." She slowly lifts a casted arm to her chest and taps. "But I can't remember who you are."

A nurse in blue scrubs enters the room. "Gabriella, I need to take you downstairs for a scan."

The use of Gabby's full name opens the floodgates, and every emotion I've felt in the past forty-eight hours assaults me at once.

"I'll come back, Gabs." I squeeze her fingers lightly and then flee like a coward out of the room.

Tears blurring my vision, I stumble into the small sanctuary of the hospital and let the sobs wrack my body. I curse God and then apologize and send up a quick prayer. I'm not sure where I stand on God, but this doesn't feel like the right time to snub divine intercession.

A small head pops up in the front row, and I halt two rows back, leaving a respectable distance between us. A girl, no more than ten, turns and offers me a small smile. I wipe my face and nose and give her a half-hearted wave before settling into the pew. The wood creaks beneath me, and I gaze forward to the huge cross nailed to a cement block wall.

Little feet skip down the side of the room and a mass of blonde ringlets bounces beside me. "Hi, I'm Sunny."

Of course she is. She exudes light and cheer, which is saying something in this shitty excuse for a house of worship.

"Hi, Sunny. I'm Blair."

"I like your bracelets." Her eyes track my arm as she studies the colorful adornments with wide-eyed wonder.

"Thank you. They're friendship bracelets." My voice breaks and I swipe at new tears.

"It's okay to cry," she says with reassurance. "Momma says we gotta cry out all the sadness to make room for hope to grow. Positive thinking attracts miracles."

The door to the chapel opens and a woman looks in, finds Sunny and motions for her. "That's my mom. Gotta go." Sunny doesn't wait for my good-bye, she runs into the arms of her mom. I watch as the frail woman hangs her head low and clings to the bundle of sunshine.

It's too much, so I turn forward, giving them privacy and letting Sunny's words take root. Positive thinking attracts miracles, huh? I close my eyes and say another prayer because, devoted believer or not, I'm willing to call in favors just in case, and then I push away all negative outcomes and only allow myself to imagine the future with Gabby by my side.

ONE

Blair
Present Day

"Well, that pretty much seals my fate." Vanessa flashes her test, showing off the red F at the top of the paper. "Wanna come with me to get a drop slip?"

"No. Don't leave me alone in here, V. It's only the first test. We can do this." My attempt at a pep talk fails miserably. Probably because I'm simultaneously suppressing a groan at my own hostile red letter. Circled and underlined for emphasis. As if I needed more than the large D staring up at me as an indication I hadn't done well on our first statistics test.

We wait for our classmates to filter out of the large auditorium, and judging by the grim expressions and mutterings about the evil professor, we aren't the only ones who did poorly. A small comfort, I suppose.

So much for my perfect GPA, and so much for winning over Professor O'Sean. He's the program coordinator for the accelerated MBA track that I'm applying to next year. It's just a hunch, but I don't think failing his class will help me get in. College hasn't been exactly what I envisioned when Gabby and I planned our futures all those years ago. Actually, that's too bland a statement. It hasn't been all bad, but so far, this semester royally sucks. I feel guilty for even thinking those words. It'll all work out. I just need to buckle down and study harder. Think positive.

Vanessa nudges me while we trudge up the stairs. She leans in to whisper, "My last chance to ogle the man candy."

I follow her slight head nod to the back row, which is occupied by three members of the university's basketball team. I'd like to think I would have noticed the trio, built like the nationally ranked athletes they are, even if Vanessa hadn't pointed them out each and every class. But the last month has been a haze of homework and studying. I'm not sure I would have noticed them even if they'd sat beside me. If it doesn't involve classes, caffeine, or sleep, I don't have time for it.

Their skin tone varies from light to dark, as does their hair color, but each one is tall and muscular. Decked out in athletic gear, they look like they walked off the set of a Nike commercial.

The one on the end closest to the aisle has his foot propped up on the seat in front of him, a black walking boot covering it completely from just below the knee on the right leg. His arms are crossed over his chest, and the blue Valley basketball shirt he's wearing is bunched up around his muscular arms and pecs. A baseball cap is pulled low so it's covering his eyes, but it doesn't matter—it's obvious whatever lurks below is as good as the rest.

"Why is the line moving so slow?" I step to the right to see what the holdup is. I have places to be, and it's lunchtime. What's the hold up?

"Slow down and appreciate the view with the rest of us," Vanessa retorts.

I glance ahead and behind, seeing nothing but necks careening and eyes darting to the back row. The line out of the class moves at rubberneck speed. Has this been going on since classes started three weeks ago? How had I not noticed the ovary explosion they caused? I'd assumed it was just Vanessa being well, Vanessa. Apparently, no one was immune to their beefy muscles and chiseled jaw lines. Except me.

I would be proud of that fact if my grade backed up the time I'd spent not noticing hot guys. I've actually been paying attention to the professor. I need this class. Correction. I need an A in this class. Now, I wish I'd used my time more wisely like V.

"Everyone is staring at them."

"Duh, look at them. They're the best part of this class," Vanessa says loud enough that the girl behind us snickers.

She's right about that. Each one of them is stop-and-stare worthy, but my eyes are pulled back to the guy on the end. The top half of his face is a mystery—covered by a white university hat. But his lips are fantastic and full in a way that no lip injections could replicate.

I'm still starting at him when his teammate, the one sitting closest to him, reaches over and flips up the baseball hat, revealing a pair of heavy lids. He rights his hat and then reaches for the paper on his desk. My eyes follow his long fingers and bulge at the big red letter A that is underlined and circled just like mine. The underline and circle treatment of my D seems a lot less hostile now, so that's something.

But what the hell? This guy is sleeping during class and still gets an A?

"Why does he even bother coming to class if he's going to sleep through it? There's no way he earned that grade without help. How are the rest of us supposed to compete with the private tutors and special treatment that's afforded the student athletes?" The words spill from my mouth before I can censor and spin them in a more positive way.

We push out of Stanley Hall and join the rest of the students bustling between classes at Valley University.

"Bitter much? What happened to your peppy optimism and we-can-do-it attitude?"

I wear my positivity like armor. Smile on and words of wisdom on deck, I'm always the first person to look at the bright side to hide the insecurities and fears I don't dare speak.

"It just had a heavy dose of reality. Even the jocks did better than we did," I say as I stare down at my yellow chucks.

When I look up, she gives me a sympathetic half-smile and shrugs. "I don't know about the basketball team, but Mario says the baseball guys get ridden pretty hard about grades."

"I'm sure they get ridden hard, all right."

Vanessa's eyebrows disappear under her long bangs. "That is the weirdest thing you've ever said. Never repeat it."

She's effectively lightened my mood, and I hip check her playfully. "Speaking of riding them hard. Where is Mario? He's usually waiting like a puppy out here."

On cue, Mario comes into view. He's jogging to get to V as quickly as possible, as if it's been days since he's seen her instead of fifty minutes.

"We're going to lunch at University Hall after I stop by the registration office. Come with?"

Not even a full month into the semester and my roommate has already managed to snag a boyfriend. Mario may be a jock, but he seems different. He doesn't have any of the asshole, holier-than-thou narcissism I'd expected. He's pursuing V hard, walking her to and from every class, bringing her flowers, and taking her out on date nights, the works. I'd knock his adoration and classify him as a stage-five clinger if he weren't so handsome and sweet.

Wearing his practice clothes—a cutoff T-shirt and baseball pants—accentuates the whole all-American, tan, blond-hair, blue-eyed, good-guy thing he has going for him. Bonus points that Vanessa is completely smitten. I know this because she's trying way too hard to convince me otherwise. Case in point, inviting me to tag along on their lunch date.

"Can't save you from love today. I'm heading to the library to study."

"That sounds positively boring," she says over her shoulder as she skips off to meet him halfway. They come together, hugging and kissing, completely oblivious to the people shoving around them.

Gross.

Except it isn't. It's actually really sweet.

As skittish as I am about the opposite sex these days thanks to the last guy I trusted, Mario has given me no reason to doubt his intentions. And I refuse to let one asshole taint my view on every other guy for the rest of my life.

Speak of the devil.

My phone vibrates in my pocket, and I fight back the urge to press Ignore.

"Hello?" I answer cheerfully as if the man on the other end isn't the absolute worst.

"Where are you?" He wastes no such effort on niceties.

"I'm on my way," is the only thing I say before I hear the line disconnect.

With a heavy sigh, I head to the library. David paces the front entrance. His dark hair is tousled perfectly and emphasizes the crisp white dress shirt. He stands out among the other students who are dressed more casually. I used to like that about him, how he stood out amongst the crowd. Now, it's just another thing I despise.

"You have it?" he asks before the double doors have even closed behind me.

I bite back every mean and awful thing I've thought about the man in front of me. Polished and handsome on the outside. Horrible and ugly where it matters.

I hand over the folder, keeping my mouth closed.

He opens it, absolutely no regard for its contents. He can't fathom his actions having consequences, and he's made me all too aware of the ramifications of every single action I've made.

"Jesus, David, you could wait to inspect it until you get back to your room. It's all there. I wrote the answers on a blank piece of paper, so you can fill the worksheet in with your handwriting."

"We aren't in fucking high school, Blair. The librarians aren't sitting around looking for suspicious activity. As long as you keep your mouth shut, no one will ever know."

I grind my back teeth.

He snaps the folder shut and holds it in one hand at his side. "Professor Shoel assigned a five-page paper on a classical music composer. It's due next Monday, but I need it Friday so I can go over it and make sure it sounds like me. The last one you wrote sounded too girly."

Because a *girl* wrote it.

"How much longer are you going to do this to me? I'm failing my own classes, I can't keep up."

Desperation clings to my voice as if I could be anything but desperate.

He sneers, turning his handsome features cold and sinister until the outside matches the inside. "Would you rather I share your nude selfies with the world? Maybe that's what you wanted all along, for me to pass them around and give everyone a little taste."

My stomach twists with shame and regret. "Those pictures were for you, my boyfriend. You know I never meant for anyone else to see them."

"I'm sure you tell that to all the guys, but I'm not buying it." He leans in close, and I hold my breath as if not breathing in the scent of his expensive cologne and mint gum could take back everything. "When I feel like you've learned your lesson, then we're done. You got a problem with that, Blair?"

I hate that I'm in this position. Hate that he put me here. But, mostly, I hate that I don't have the balls to knee him and tell him to go to hell.

"No problem," I mumble.

TWO

Wes

Joel pulls the Tesla into the garage and Z and I pry ourselves out of the tiny sports car. The rest of the team is already here and the splashing and music from out back filters through the house. It's a hundred and eight degrees in Arizona today. August was worse, but we're nearing the first day of fall, and I could literally fry an egg on the hood of the car. Shit isn't normal.

I miss the Midwest humidity. Never thought I'd utter those words.

Sometimes, I'd like to come home to a quiet house instead of the craziness of our non-stop party house, but I get why our place is the hang out.

The White House, which is what it was dubbed because it's white, it's huge, and it was purchased by the university president. Our house is only a few blocks from campus and right across the street from Ray Fieldhouse, making it ideal to walk just about anywhere we need to go—not that we had to thanks to my gimp foot and handicap parking. The only perk of being injured.

The White House is nicer digs than anyone else has. Fuck, this house is nicer than the one I grew up in. The only place I've seen that's nicer than this house is Joel's parents' estate. Estate as in it's too fucking big to just be called a house.

But the pool is really why they're all here. Well, that and the stocked fridge.

I swipe a cold water and head out to sit under the mister. Z grabs a protein drink and follows, taking a seat next to me off to the side and away from the pool hangers.

"Welcome home, roomies," Nathan calls from the pool. He has a cigarette dangling from his mouth and a beer in hand. It's barely noon. On a Monday.

I shake my head at him. I'm not pissed he's drinking and smoking. I'm pissed he's doing it in front of the young guys. He can handle himself. I'm not sure about the freshman.

I turn my attention to Z. "Getting in today?"

He grunts something in response. I've never seen Z get in the pool. We give him shit about it, but I honestly have no idea if he doesn't like getting into the water because it's usually filled with lots of people or because he can't swim. I can't imagine there's anything he can't do.

Quiet. Grunting. Out of the limelight. That pretty much sums up Z off the court. On the court, he's a whole different person. People who have never seen him play assume all kinds of dumb shit about him solely based on his mammoth size, or as he would put it, a big, beautiful black man. The fact that he walks around wearing his headphones oblivious to the world and rarely speaks more than a word or two at a time also doesn't help.

Once people see him play, though, it's like seeing someone in their natural habitat. He's smart, quick, and loud. Dude doesn't shut up on the court.

Shaw tosses one of the ball honeys—Charlene? Charla? Carla?—into the air, and her high-pitch squeal makes me want to cover my ears. There's a whole posse of girls standing in the shallow end, being careful to keep their hair and makeup water free. I wish I were a bigger asshole because I'd really like to go dunk the whole lot of them and watch the chaos that would ensue. Lucky for them, I only think this. Also, I'm not doing a lot of swimming these days with the boot and all, so I just sit back and admire the view. I'm annoyed, but I'm not blind.

So yeah, I'm a grumpy asshole. I haven't always been, but getting injured senior year—the year I was supposed to take the team all the way. Yeah, that would make even the nicest guy go a little douchebag.

The rest of the team mills around, swimming, lounging, drinking, eating all our damn food.

I drain the water bottle and drum the plastic container on my leg.

Bored.

Restless.

Joel appears at my side and flings himself down, cracking a beer open in the process.

"Rookie is out of control. I can't wait until you're back. Freshman needs to be put in his place."

My eyes go back to the freshman rookie who is front and center in the pool, tossing girls up and lavishing in the attention.

"Three more weeks. Fingers crossed."

"Good because we're screwed if we're depending on Shaw to get us the ball. I know it's supposed to be some big damn deal that he's playing two sports, but shit just makes me nervous. Twice the risk of injury and half the amount of focus."

I nod in agreement. "I'll talk to him and to Mario. I'm sure the baseball team has the same concerns."

"Wanna have a little fun with them?" Joel's attention is focused on the pool and pure mischief coats his expression.

"What did you have in mind?"

"Remember my freshman year when you guys made us crash parties and run plays?"

A chuckle rumbles in my chest. Being a freshman sucked in so many ways. My rookie year, the upper classmen mostly just made us do things like carry their gym bags and act as water boys. Fuck, I'd been so glad to be a sophomore and for a new crop of guys to take the heat. Joel and his class had been an obnoxious batch of freshmen and we'd increased the torture to knock down their huge egos. Come to think of it, Joel's class was a lot like this year's rookies.

"You thinking of taking them out tonight?"

"Yeah, but I think we should elevate—take it to the next level."

Shake my head. "We have practice in the morning, so don't elevate it too much. Coach'll kick our ass if we show up with a bunch of hungover rookies. Exhibition is coming up, and he's chewing Tums like candy."

"Live a little, Reynolds. It's your senior year. We're doing it up right."

"We're? You still got another year."

"Yeah, but it isn't gonna be the same without you and Z. This feels like the last year of something great. Something none of us will ever forget."

Shit. He's right. The season is shaping up to be the best year of our lives, and I'm itching to get out of this damn boot. It's making me cranky.

"Yo, Shaw." My voice booms across to the pool, and he lifts his head slowly, taking his damn time. A chin tilt is the only acknowledgment I get.

"Get me a beer."

Joel cackles. "My man, you don't even drink during the season."

"Rookie doesn't know that."

"No. No. No. Come on, guys. That's sloppy."

Sitting in a plastic chair on the sidelines with my booted foot propped on another, I bounce the ball back and forth under my knee. Back and forth, back and forth. I can't tell if it's making my nerves better or worse. I don't need to be here. It's torture, but there's nowhere else I'd rather be. This is my team. I may be injured, but they're still my responsibility.

"Fifty free throws and two miles on the treadmill and call it a day. We have a big week coming up. Talent only goes so far. Focus. Repetition. Heart.

Already having about a gazillion shots in for the day, I head to the weight room. I can't remember the last time I did leg day, and I've never wanted to squat and dead lift so much in my entire life. I pass Mario and a few of the baseball guys leaving as I enter.

Athletes have our own weight room, but we share it between all the different sports. It's huge—easily big enough for three or four groups to be in here at any one time, but we've all got our own styles. Football guys can't be in here without grunting and talking smack. The swimmers spend more time gossiping like old ladies than lifting. The basketball team likes the music turned up so loud there isn't much of an option to chat.

"Reynolds. Still gimping around, huh? When's the cast come off?"

Mario's guys keep going with a nod in my direction.

"Three weeks. Can't freaking wait."

"Thank the fuck. Those chicken legs of yours are getting damn near embarrassing."

I take his jabs in jest. Mario and I have been leaving our blood, sweat, and tears in this room for years, and we both know I have fucking great legs.

"Give me a few weeks, and I'll be squatting your pansy ass under the table."

"We'll see." He wipes his forehead with a towel and tosses it on his shoulder. "We're having a party at the house next Thursday. Be cool if you guys stopped by, haven't hung out in a while."

"Yeah, I'll let the guys know. Speaking of the guys, how's Shaw doing? Team's worried about him splitting his time. I am, too, if I'm honest. We're gonna need him to sub in some this year. Need him to be ready."

"I hear ya. I don't like it, either, but he's the best damn relief pitcher we've had in years. I'll keep an eye on him as best as I can while he's with us."

"Ditto."

Fucking freshman has two babysitters and almost fifty teammates between the two sports, and he's still shaping up to be the biggest pain in the ass I've seen in my four years.

THREE

Blair

Three days out of the week I work at the small campus café in University Hall. In addition to the café, University Hall houses the university bookstore, a mini convenient store, and a sub shop. Untying my blue apron, I lean on the counter completely exhausted after the lunch rush.

Coffee and a pastry totally counts as lunch in college making it our busiest hour. College kids—we're nothing if not lazy creatures of convenience.

"Hey, Katrina." I let out a sigh as my replacement arrives, signaling the end of my shift.

"Rough day?"

"The worst," I admit. She places a hand to her forehead and then swipes a strand of hair out of her eyes. Katrina is the same age as me but has a total mother-hen vibe. Maybe because she *is* a mother. She brought Christian in with her once. He is adorable, but he's also the best birth control ever. Katrina has her hands full between classes, working, and raising a little man by herself. Puts my own crap in perspective.

"It's nothing I just failed my first statistics test."

"Oh, that sucks. I'm sorry."

"Thanks."

She looks up to the ceiling. "What's the quote you're always writing about failure?"

"We learn from failure not success." I roll my eyes. "I know. I know. But

I don't have any clue how I'm going to get an A when I'm already struggling a month into the class. The first month is supposed to be easy."

"You get what you work for not what you wish for." She recites another one of the quotes I often write on the to-go cups.

"It feels more like a suck it up, buttercup kind of day."

She pulls a cup from the counter and fills it with our house brew before handing it to me. "For the road."

I shake my head but grab a sharpie and write the quote on my to-go coffee.

"Another night of disappointed faces when they realize the quote girl isn't here."

That makes me smile. I love that I've been able to add a little bit of positivity. We've all got our struggles and I want to be someone that builds up other people.

The quotes were my idea. A random scribbling when I would notice someone looked like they were having a bad day or seemed stressed. Eventually they became something people looked forward to and I started writing them on every cup. It really isn't so hard to tell who needs tough love or an inspirational pick me up based on their demeanor or tone when they order. The quotes on the sides of the cups have become a part of the café, and it's a legacy I'm proud of.

I trek back to the sorority house with determination and resolve. I won't just ace statistics, I'll destroy it.

Suck it up, buttercup.

Two days later as I'm preparing for class, my inspired mood is appropriately deflated. Another late night of studying and homework leaves me pessimistic and petulant. I hate who I'm becoming. I've worked too hard and have come too far to crumble under pressure.

I decide to dose myself in positivity. Maybe if I feel good about how I look, some of those good vibes will soak into my attitude. I pull on my favorite yellow sundress and matching chucks. With a nod at my reflection, I'm off.

The large auditorium is made up of a semi-circle of three sections that face the podium, which stands front and center. Since Vanessa dropped the class and left me alone in my misery, I opt to sit in the back on the far right.

At exactly one minute before class begins, the eye candy arrives. Kudos for getting my head out of my ass to notice the trio of jocks. Vanessa would be proud. Honestly, what has my life become that I'm so overwhelmed with schoolwork that it took so long for me to appreciate hot guys without Vanessa to point them out?

When Professor O'Sean takes his position behind the lectern, I sit straighter in my seat and attempt to give him the kind of attention I usually reserve for the first week of class, jotting down nearly every word that exits his mouth and tallying the number of times he pushes his glasses up with his middle finger. Is he trying to flip us off or is it just a happy coincidence?

I'm able to focus on independent and dependent events for six minutes and fifteen seconds before I find my gaze wandering across the top of the lecture hall. My eyes go directly to the jocks. One in particular. Foot propped up on the seat in front of him, baseball hat pulled low. His teammates are next to him looking bored out of their skulls, but at least their eyes are open.

Honestly, how did this guy get an A? His tutors must be amazing.

When class is dismissed, I hurry out and then pace the sidewalk.

I can do this.

I *have* to do this.

I turn and face the massive fountain that sits in the center of the quad and take three deep breaths. When I turn back to Stanley Hall, it's just in time to see the three basketball players finally emerge. Statistics is the first class I've had with any of our college's nationally ranked team. They seem to stick together, though, always travelling in groups.

"Hi, excuse me." I smile brightly and step directly into their path.

They exchange a confused look but slow down instead of trampling over me like a bug, which they could very much do.

All five feet and three inches of me stands taller. I make eye contact with each of them, trying to look friendly and not at all intimidated, which I'm not . . . nope, not at all, and then lock my gaze with the sleeper's. He's the shortest of the three, but the intensity of his navy blue eyes makes it hard for me to find my voice.

"I'm Blair, we have statistics class together." I wave toward the building behind them in case they don't even know what class they just came from. Apparently, I am still bitter about the grade.

"Wes," he says as he shrugs his backpack up higher on one shoulder. "This is Joel and Z."

"Nice to meet you." I look to each of the guys and then back to Wes again, silently communicating he is the one I want to speak to. They don't get the memo. "Wes, can I talk to you for a minute?"

"We'll meet ya at the car," Joel pipes in, and he and Z leave me alone with Wes. It's only slightly easier to think without all three of them staring at me with rapt interest.

"What's up?"

"I was wondering if you could tell me who does tutoring for the team? I noticed your test grade the other day, not that I was trying to see it or anything. Sorry, that sounds horrible. I just happened to glance down as I was walking by your desk. Honest mistake. Honestly."

Deep breath, Blair.

"Anyway, I didn't do so well, and I really need an A in this class. Does the team have someone specifically, or do you guys use the tutor center?"

His eyebrows pull together, and he shifts his weight to his left side, making me conscious that standing here talking to me is probably causing him pain.

Join the club. This whole interaction is excruciating.

"I'm lost. You want information on the tutor center?"

The hot Arizona sun shines bright and sweat trickles down my back. "Just information on the tutor or tutors you're using . . . for statistics."

"You think I have a tutor?"

"I'm sorry. I wasn't trying to be rude, but it's just you're sleeping through class."

He crosses his arms over his chest in a silent challenge. The neckline of his shirt pulls down, revealing a hint of tan chest underneath. Annoyed is a good look for him.

"You don't have a tutor?" The question is no more than a mumble. Or maybe I just can't hear it because my pulse is pounding in my ears. I open my mouth several times and then promptly close it when I can't find the words to apologize. He smirks as he watches me grapple with the realization that I've made a very wrong, very humiliating assumption.

Uncrossing his arms, he takes one step in the direction his friends went. "Tutor center is on the first floor of the library." He points in the direction of the campus library, making me feel about a foot tall. "I'm sure someone there can help."

As I watch him walk away, admiring his gait that's somehow sexy and confident even with the boot, I wonder—statistically speaking, of course—what are the odds that the guy sleeping at the back of the class could not only pull off an A but also manage to get that grade without help?

I have no idea, probably because I'm failing statistics. My guess, though? Not good.

I arrive back to the scene of the crime, aka statistics class, with a cup of coffee, a new pen to inspire better note taking, and a determination to hide from Wes and company. I slip in five minutes early so I can grab a seat and be wholly enthralled when they show up. I don't fancy myself important enough that they'd seek me out, but my humiliation has big plans of cowering and hiding for the rest of the semester.

As if my body is now connected to my mortification, I feel the exact moment they enter the classroom.

Wes Reynolds, Joel Moreno, and Zeke Sweets are quite a trio. Yep, I looked them up. I'm calling it research, but in reality, I just wanted to have all the information on the guy I'd thoroughly insulted. They sit in the middle section at the very top, giving them a bird's eye view of the entire class. If Wes's eyes were ever open, would have been nearly impossible to be out of his line of sight. I'm not invisible, but it's as far away as I can get.

Zeke pulls his red headphones down and rests them around his neck as he squeezes his large frame into the seat. According to everyone I asked (more research, of course), Zeke is already rumored to be going pro after this season.

Wes wears a glare that would frighten small children . . . or grown ass women because I slink down in my seat as I continue to watch him. I have a hard time looking anywhere else, glare be damned. He's unbelievably gorgeous. Hell, they all are. Even Joel, who hasn't looked up from his phone, is strikingly handsome with his black hair and bronzed skin.

When Wes glances around the class and his blue stare lands on me, I become very interested in my notes from the last class, reading over them with a fervor I should have tried before the last test.

When we're dismissed, I hang back, waiting for the last row to leave before making my way up the stairs, but when the auditorium is nearly cleared out and the three musketeers haven't made any move to leave, I'm left with no other choice but to suck it up and hope they don't notice me.

Joel nudges him as I approach. Nothing gets past that guy. It's as if he's Wes's eyes and ears. As Wes's dark blue eyes land on me, I plaster on a big smile and decide to be the bigger person. "Hello."

Wes stands, awkwardly making his way to the aisle and holding on to the back of the chair for support. A flash of pain crosses his handsome features as he meets me on the stairs.

"Ball Buster Girl."

"I'm sorry about the other day. I just assumed . . ."

"That I was a dumb jock who couldn't possibly get a passing grade without the help of a tutor or tutorsss?" He emphasizes the plural version with a hiss as he trails me out of the auditorium. As we come to the door, he steps close and pushes the handle, swinging it open and holding it with one large hand. A gentleman. Interesting.

"To be fair you haven't made much of an effort to look like someone who is trying to get a good grade."

We stop on the sidewalk, and I'm aware of Joel and Zeke hanging back and giving us space. Wes adjusts his hat, lifting it so I get a glimpse of the dirty blonde hair matted down like he'd slept in the damn hat. Right, he had . . . just now.

"I could ace that class even if I never showed up."

"That's an awfully bold statement for the first month of class."

He shrugs. "Any luck finding a tutor?"

"Not yet, but I'm sure I'll have no problem finding someone who passed statistics with their eyes open."

His lips part, and his straight, white teeth peek out. "Good luck with that."

I shove my ear buds in and put on my favorite podcast and head toward the library. By the time I get to the tutor center located on the first floor of the campus library (already knew this without the help of Wes, thank you very much), I've turned my humiliation into focused anger.

Okay, so I jumped to conclusions too quickly, but if he can get an A with his eyes closed, surely, I can manage with a whole lot of determination and a tiny bit of help.

I'm still bristling at the way his indigo eyes laughed at me. He could have politely set me straight instead of acting as if I'd personally attacked his intelligence. Okay, maybe I had, but I mean, how was I supposed to know that the guy sleeping at the back of the class somehow magically aced the first test without help, which I'm still not entirely convinced he did.

A text from Gabby momentarily pulls me from my foul mood.

Gabs: Still coming down next Wednesday?

Me: Of course I am! It's your twenty-first so we're going out!

She doesn't text back, which tells me she isn't exactly on board with my plan to celebrate her twenty-first but knows me well enough to know I'm not going to take no for an answer.

I tuck my phone away as I walk to the tutor center's front desk.

"Hey, Blair, what are you doing here?" Molly, a sophomore sorority sister, asks from behind the sign in area.

"I have a question for you." I lean against the counter and pull out my ear buds.

"Shoot." Molly places both elbows onto the counter.

"What can you tell me about tutors for the athletic teams on campus?"

She scrunches her nose and tilts her head to the side. "Are you interested in being a tutor?"

"No, no. Nothing like that. I just wondered if you could tell me who tutors the athletes. Do they have their own private tutors, or do they come here for help?"

"I'm not aware of any tutoring services specific to the teams on campus. I suppose they could have personal tutors, but I've never heard of it. Why?"

"So, they come here?"

"We don't get a lot of athletes in here despite the assumption they need it. I mean, no more than any other group."

Great, I really am a profiling bitch.

Molly rattles on, "There's a few guys from the football team that come in regularly. Baseball team, softball team, wrestlers . . . yeah, I guess as far as I know the ones that need help come here."

"What about the men's basketball team? Do any of them come in for tutoring?"

She brings her thumb to her mouth and bites on the pad of it while she considers my question carefully. "Not that I can think of."

Damn.

"Do you guys have anyone for statistics?"

She grimaces. "Must be rough if you need help."

I nod. "D on the first test."

"Ouch," she says as she flips through papers hanging on a clipboard. "We have Sally and Tom in today, they both tutor math. I think they mostly do algebra and calculus, but I could put you in the schedule and you could meet with one of them and give it a try. Interested?"

"Sure. Why not? Got anything now? I'm done with classes for the day, and I don't want to come back to campus this afternoon if I can help it."

"Looks like Tom is free after his current session. You can hang over there." She nods to a section of chairs and couches pushed to one side of the room. "He should be done in ten minutes or so."

I stop short of the waiting area, spying the men's basketball schedule on the wall with a picture of the team decked out in their uniforms. The guys stand stoic and unsmiling, and my eyes drift first to Wes. He stands in the back row, wearing jersey twelve. His legs are hidden by the guy standing in front of him, which makes it impossible for me to see if he's wearing the boot. My research didn't pull up any information on his injury, so I don't know if it's recent, what he did, or even if he'll be out for the season. I'm suddenly very curious about Wes Reynolds.

In truth, I've paid very little attention to any of the jocks since arriving at Valley. Freshman year, I'd barely looked at anyone who wasn't in a fraternity. Greek life became a home away from home, and there was something exciting about finding a guy who had the same sort of passion for his fraternity brothers as I had for my sisters. And, of course, fraternity guys love nothing more than they love freshman pledges.

By the end of sophomore year, the guys at socials and parties started to blend together and Vanessa and I'd stopped choosing our weekend activities based on frat parties. We plan on moving out of the sorority into an off-campus apartment next year. I'll always treasure my years at the sorority, but I'm ready to have my own space.

David had been the quintessential frat guy, and I'd fallen for his charm and good looks before I'd realized what a monster he is beneath the shiny facade. Too little too late. It isn't as if I think all frat guys are douchebags based on one bad experience, but it's like getting food poisoning at a restaurant. Even if it was the cook's fault, your brain associates the restaurant itself with a horrible experience and you aren't likely to go back anytime soon.

When Tom finally waves me over, I'm so hopeful I could burst. But my optimism only lasts a few minutes. I'm not an idiot. Far from it. I get the basic principles of business statistics. I've read the book and memorized definitions. It's the real-world application that is just out of reach. Math word problems were the devil in sixth grade, and they haven't gotten any easier no matter how much I study.

Molly catches me on my way out. "Any luck?"

"No." I exhale a deep breath. "There has to be someone on campus who tutors statistics."

"Did anyone at the house have O'Sean last year?"

"I asked around. Nothing."

"I'll see if anyone here knows anything," she offers. "Someone has to have something on him. Old quizzes or tests. I've heard he's old-school and still does everything on paper."

Of course. Why hadn't it occurred to me sooner? Wes must have gotten his hands on tests from someone who'd taken statistics last year. O'Sean seems exactly like the type of professor to re-use the same material every year. That has to be the answer. Wes isn't sleeping through class and magically learning by osmosis. He already has the answers.

FOUR

Wes

"Rise and shine," Joel says as he nudges me. I'm not asleep. I wish I were. My eyes are closed, hat pulled down, but there's no sleep to be had.

"She's coming back for more." The tone in his voice is almost inspired.

I don't have to look up to know who he's talking about, but I do anyway. She's the most entertaining thing about this class. Open my eyes and lift the hat, turn it backward so my view isn't the least bit blocked.

Today she's wearing little pink shorts that show off tan legs, yellow tennis shoes that don't match but somehow work, and a bracelet with a little charm around her left ankle. It's too small to make out, but I stare anyway. Her brown hair is pulled up in a high ponytail, and she has a megawatt smile plastered on her face. A big bow on top of her head is all she'd need to look like head cheerleader of my high school fantasies.

"Wes, hey, can I talk to you for a second?"

"What's up?"

I'm hella impressed by the balls on this chick. She's put her foot in her mouth, not once, but twice, and damn near insulted the entire student athlete population, but she keeps coming back. She has determination and grit. I admire that about her.

I also am not in the least bit offended by her assumption that I'm a dumb jock. I'd be lying if I said I wasn't surprised she came right out and asked who my tutor was, but I know exactly what it looks like. I've fed into the stereotype for years, doing nothing to make it seem otherwise. Well, nothing but get straight A's.

"I have sort of a favor."

"What's up?" I stand to walk with her out of the class.

"The tutor center was a bust. I know you said . . ." She looks like she's choosing her words carefully. "Do you have old study notes or tests from previous semesters?"

"Still convinced I'm not capable of passing on my own, huh?"

"I'm sorry, really, no offense. I just want in on whatever study materials you're using. I can't afford to fail another test. What's your secret?"

The secret? I'm fucking smart. Photographic memory smart and statistics is my whole world, but I can't resist messing with her.

"You know, saying no offense doesn't make whatever you're saying less offensive. It just makes you feel better about saying something offensive."

Joel snickers behind me. I just can't resist fucking with her. She's making it too easy.

"Sorry. I'm really so sorry. What about the other guys on the team? Anyone have any awesome math tutors who aren't available to us non-jock students? I can pay."

"Couldn't say for sure, but I don't think so. Most the guys hold their own academically." I lean in catching a whiff of her hair. It smells good—like sugar cookies or candy canes or something sugary sweet that I want to sink my teeth into. "Shocking, I know."

Her shoulders slump in defeat, and I can tell she's finally accepted that I have no answers for her. At this point, I almost wish I knew of someone to send her to. I don't exactly travel in circles that clue me in on secret study sessions and underground tutor societies.

"Thanks anyway." She gives a little wave with the hand clutched around the strap of her backpack.

Joel catches up to me, and we watch as she crosses the campus toward the library. "Dude. That chick . . ."

"I know," I say, and we continue to stare after her completely awe stricken.

"Quit gawking after the poor girl and let's go. I'm hungry." Z's voice pulls at me just as Blair disappears from sight.

When I turn, Z's grinning like he heard the entire exchange, despite the fact he has his headphones on. Sometimes I wonder if he even has music playing or if he just uses them as a deterrent. I don't have the heart to break it to him that he's intimidating as fuck and probably doesn't need another reason for people not to engage.

Back at the house we sit around the television watching ESPN and devouring the chicken pasta shit that Joel's mom dropped off earlier. She has taken it upon herself to keep us fed and our pantry stocked. Several times a week we come home to find casseroles in our fridge, index cards with cooking instructions taped to the top of the tin foil.

"Why do girls insist on using eight emojis for every text?" Joel asks without looking up from his phone. His fingers tap at top speed on the damn thing.

"I dunno," Nathan says from the floor. He's alternating sets of push-ups and sit-ups. That's Nathan for you. One minute, he's cramming nicotine and alcohol in his system, and the next, he's doing bonus workouts. I guess it evens itself out. "It's up there with using text slang when it isn't any shorter. Using the number two in place of the word to saves what? Like a half second?"

"I deduct two IQ points for every text acronym or abbreviation," I say around a mouthful of pasta.

"This is why you haven't gotten laid in six months," Joel quips, still not looking up.

"Fuck you. It hasn't been that long."

Close.

I've been busy.

Busy sulking. First a soul crushing loss to end last season and then an injury that's kept me sidelined.

And I'm real tired of girls throwing themselves at me for the thrill of sleeping with a jock. Or in some sort of misplaced show of support to heal my fragile ego. Pity fuck? No thanks.

I know, I know. I got uptown problems.

"What happened to Sarah?" Nathan says as he stands and starts to jog in place.

"It was Tara, and last time I saw her, she was giving a big Valley welcome to a freshman soccer player."

Joel looks up. "God bless her dedication. She's single-handedly welcomed nearly every jock to campus in her short time here."

"Yeah, she's a real Mother Teresa." Z rolls his eyes. He's adamant about not messing around with girls in college so he can focus on ball and his quest to the NBA, so he thinks we're all petty assholes.

He isn't wrong.

An hour later, I'm in hell. Practice is shit. Shaw has talent, but he's all over the fucking place, trying to prove his worth by taking risky shots and hogging the ball. My nerves are shot. I can't do a damn thing but wait for this boot to come off.

"Reynolds, my office," Coach calls to the sideline when he's done giving orders for the guys to work on shooting drills.

I take my time, already knowing what he's going to say.

He's sitting behind his desk, and though I've seen him in his office before, it always strikes me how weird he looks perched upright like he's working a nine-to-five desk job. Some men just weren't meant for that kind of life, and coach falls squarely in that category. "Come on in, son. Have a seat."

I take the old chair in front of his desk. Thing looks like it's been here since the university opened in the fifties.

"How's the foot? Cast comes off in two weeks?"

"Yes, sir. I'm anxious to get back on the floor."

"And we're anxious to have you back, but the trainers say you may not be back fully for another two to four weeks after the boot comes off. We have the exhibition in two weeks and then our first game the week after. I know it isn't what you want, but have you considered a medical red shirt?"

I grind my back teeth to keep from speaking exactly what I'm thinking. Even knowing this was what he was going to say, it still pisses me off. Hell no, I don't want to redshirt my senior year. Sure, I take the redshirt and I'm still eligible to play an extra year. We get five years to play four seasons, but next year Z will be gone. I'll be done with my degree. It's an option. But it isn't one I'm willing to take.

"I'll be ready. Whatever it takes."

He nods. "Once you step out onto that floor, it gets a hell of a lot harder to take it back. You're sure about this? You can take some time and talk to your folks about it."

Right, like they give two shits about my ball career.

"Positive."

I can tell he's torn. He wants me to play and wants me to take the year to heal properly. I get it. I do. It's risky, but I'm prepared to do whatever it takes to be ready to go and to lead my team to a national championship. We were so close last year. Top four in the nation is good. Most people would be happy with that.

I'm not most people, and I want that national title.

FIVE

Blair

Three more statistics classes pass in the same fashion. I sit, feverishly taking notes, as Wes sits in the back sleeping. Today I've given up the pretense of stellar note taking. My scribbles don't even make sense to me as I write them. It's more about keeping my hands busy and my attention trained forward.

I'm doodling hearts and flowers along the margin of my notepad when Professor O'Sean's monotone stops. The lack of noise is deafening.

"Mr. Reynolds," Professor O'Sean's voice booms off the walls of the room, and every person in the room, including me, duck and pray for invisibility to avoid being the next victim of public shaming in the form of being called on in class.

I keep my head low and peek up to the top row just in time to see Joel elbow Wes. Slowly, he lifts the hat and sits straighter.

"Mr. Reynolds, can you tell the class the probability of the example on the screen?"

I wince for him. Despite my glee that he's been caught sleeping, no one deserves to be grilled in front of the entire class.

"The probability is three-eights. It's a binomial distribution with a sample space size two to the third equaling eight. Would you like me to list the events?"

My mouth gapes. Wes wears an arrogant smile and boyish charm that makes the guys in class laugh and the girls swoon. Professor O'Sean has a begrudging look as he shakes his head to indicate the answer is sufficient. I'm inclined to be on his side. How dare Wes sleep through class and still know the answer? Here I am, taking notes and hanging on every word, and I still have no idea if I could have provided more to the answer than the scribblings I'd written down in my notes.

Glance at my neatly printed letters. The collection of all possible outcomes of an experiment is called a sample space. Yeah, that isn't helpful. All I've done is copy the definitions.

Without responding to Wes, Professor O'Sean moves on. At least I wasn't the only one who assumed the guy sleeping at the back of the class had no idea what was going on.

I dare another peek at the back row, stilling when I find Wes's gaze on me. He smirks as if mocking me instead of the teacher. My cheeks warm, and I turn quickly and keep my eyes forward for the rest of the class.

"There'll be another short test in two weeks that will cover the material in chapter three. The midterm is only one month away, and it makes up thirty-five percent of your overall grade. These tests are a taste of what will be on the midterm, so I suggest you prepare for them accordingly. Have a good weekend."

Good weekend? He's just ruined any possibility of my doing anything but studying from now until the test. I trudge up the stairs with a pit in my stomach, and a foreboding feeling that I'll be lucky to eke out a C in this class. So much for my stellar GPA and so much for getting into the highly competitive MBA program.

At the top of the stairs, I look up to see that Joel and Zeke wear worried expressions. Ones that I'm sure match my own.

Zeke scrubs a hand over his massive jaw. "Man, I don't think I can learn this shit by then."

Joel nudges him. "Sure you can. Wes could teach this stuff to children."

"Isn't that what I've been doing?" the man himself states dryly.

As I approach, he stands and meets me on the stairs.

"Blair." He says my name like a challenge.

"So, you're what some sort of statistics genius?"

"Your words."

"And in your words?"

"I already told you in my words, I could pass this class even if I never showed up." He shrugs as if it's no big damn deal.

I hold back an actual growl. "That's infuriating."

He grins wide. "And impressive?"

"Maybe, but more infuriating than impressive." I point toward his teammates. "And those two, *you're* tutoring them?"

"What? No, nothing like that."

Something tells me that's exactly what's happening. He looks almost embarrassed by the prospect. I don't know why it hadn't occurred to me before. I don't need to find a tutor; I've already found the best man for the job. I just have to convince him to help me.

The excitement of my idea must be written all over my face.

"Oh, no. No. I'm not a tutor."

"I know, but you obviously know your stuff."

"I'm sorry. I don't know the first thing about being a tutor, and even if I did, I don't have time. Between practice and homework . . ." He offers another shrug. "There's a reason I sleep in this class."

Nodding, I swallow the lump of disappointment in my throat.

I have no idea how I'm going to convince the statistics God to help me. I don't have anything to offer him. And my schedule is as insane as his until I get David off my back.

Between classes and practice, I don't doubt Wes is strapped for free time. And then there are the parties and the ladies. I'm no fool. I know how girls throw themselves at jocks. Vanessa's told me what it's like. She's ready to throw down every time a girl so much as looks at Mario. And they do a lot more than look.

So far, they seem to have gotten the memo V isn't one to mess with because I guarantee the first time one lays a finger on him—innocent or not—she'll be walking around campus with a black eye or half her hair pulled out.

I digress . . . how do you get a man to do something he doesn't want to do for someone who insulted his intelligence and has absolutely nothing to offer him?

I mull over this question on the two-hour drive to Succulent Hill as I sing along to an old high school playlist. When I pull up to Gabby's house, I haven't managed to come up with any solutions, but I'm in better spirits anyway.

Gabby's mom, who had taken a job that allowed her to work from home after the accident, greets me at the door before I can ring the doorbell.

"Come in, honey. Gabby is upstairs." She rolls her eyes and shakes her head, smiling as if it were totally normal for her twenty-one-year-old daughter to be hiding away.

"Knock, knock," I call as I enter Gabby's room. Unsurprisingly, I find my best friend behind her laptop with eyes squinted behind thick glasses. My life has changed so much since the accident, I moved to Valley and did all the things we'd promised—pledge a sorority and major in business. I even force myself to go to Pilates occasionally.

I got my miracle that day. Whether it was thanks to God or the power of positive thinking, I'll never know for sure, but that day changed me forever.

Gabby's memory returned, but the fun-loving and determined girl I grew up with was lost during the crash. She stayed in Suck Hill, refusing to move away and basically hiding out in her parents' house. Deep down, her ambition hasn't changed. I know this because I almost always find her in front of her computer, studying or doing homework for her many online classes. She's a Valley U student, too, but taking classes online isn't the same as being on campus.

"Come in," she calls without looking up, and then as if just registering my voice, her eyes find mine and a big smile spreads across her face. "Blair."

I make the two-hour trip to Succulent Hill at least once a month to see Gabby and have dinner with my parents. Today, though, is just about Gabs.

"Happy birthday!" I squeeze her tightly and then step back to examine her outfit of yoga pants and tank. She looks fabulous, but she isn't exactly ready for dinner at our favorite local restaurant and pub. "You aren't ready."

She bites on her lip. "I thought maybe we could just hang out here."

"Uh-uh. You cannot celebrate your twenty-first birthday at home."

"But going out is so"—she sighs and then plops back down onto the bed—"soul crushing. I don't want to deal with the pity smiles or stares."

I try to see her as a stranger might. She has two long scars on the left side of her face that cross in an X. I think it makes her look badass, but I can't say I haven't noticed the looks she gets when we're in public.

"I promise to verbally attack anyone who dares to look at you the wrong way." She doesn't look convinced. "Come on, please?"

After a few more minutes of pleading, and twenty more minutes for her to change, Gabby and I head to dinner.

"How are classes going?" she asks as we're seated into a high-top table near the bar. She fidgets and keeps her gaze turned down, basically ducking out of anyone's line of vision.

"Mostly good. Statistics is a bit of a nightmare."

"You'll manage. You always do." Her voice is proud, almost motherly.

"I actually made quite an ass of myself trying to get a tutor," I admit. I like to fill her in on bits and pieces of college, but I almost always underplay the good and leave out the truly terrible—such as David blackmailing me. Somehow, it makes me feel less guilty about being the one pursuing our dream and hopeful that she might join me someday.

When I've finished telling her how I wrongly assumed Wes was a dumb jock, she is hysterical with laughter.

"It isn't funny," I say but join in laughing anyway. "I was a total ass, and now, I need to convince him to tutor me."

"You're going to have to grovel," she says decidedly. "Try food. Men love with their stomachs."

"I think that ship has sailed. I'll go with helpful acquaintanceship."

As she drinks her first legal adult beverage, I fill her in on Vanessa, who is always a favorite topic. Vanessa's life is way more entertaining than mine, and though, they've only met once, I think Gabby likes to hear our college escapades. And I'd never deny her that.

I've tried on more than one occasion to get Gabs to Valley, but she maintains she's perfectly content at home. I think she's hiding scared, but can I blame her? I'd like to think I'd be able to get out of bed each day and ignore the questioning looks, but I don't know if I'm that brave either. Still, I sometimes wish I could trade places with her. It's her dreams I'm living every day, and I can't help but think she deserves it so much more.

"Oh, hey, I made you a new bracelet to match mine." She lifts her arm and points to an orange bracelet. It's one of about twenty on her arm, but it matches the one she's slid to me across the table. "Another year of friendship."

I tie the bracelet around my wrist and then run a hand over my matching bracelets as I smile. "You know, Valley has a really great arts program, including jewelry and fashion design. You—"

"Not this again."

"Yes, this *again*. Gabby, you should be with me at Valley."

Before I can pitch her my best argument on all the reasons she should be at university, two guys approach our table.

They aren't bad-looking and are dressed as if they just came from work, but they look at least thirty-five. "Can we buy you ladies a drink?"

"Sure. Actually, it's Gabby's twenty-first birthday."

Gabby shifts, letting her hair fall over her face, and stares hard at the table top.

"Oh yeah? Happy birthday. Birthday shots are on us. What's your poison?"

It's silent for two long seconds before she looks up and meets his gaze. She flips her hair back, deliberately drawing attention to the scars. Both men drop their eyes.

"Fire ball," she says and finishes the drink in front of her in a long gulp.

"Coming right up." The men recover from their surprise and scurry off, presumably to get our drinks.

"*That* is why I can't go to Valley. I'd rather hide away in my parents' house than spend all day, every day, watching people react to my face."

"Ignore them. Those guys are idiots."

"It isn't just them," she insists. "Last week, a kid in the dentist waiting room cried when I sat beside him. He *cried*, Blair."

"Your scars are not that bad." I cringe at the way it sounds, but honestly, I don't see her the way she must see herself. She's still stunning. The scars didn't change her obvious beauty—only her confidence. "And anyway, college is different. I promise. No one cares. There's a guy in two of my classes who never wears shoes. He has these dirty, calloused feet, and he just owns it, and no one says a thing."

"Not to his face, just over drinks with friends."

The guys return, cutting our conversation short, and set four shots onto the table.

"What are we drinking to?" The guy closest to me asks.

I grab two shots, hand one to Gabby and lift the other in the air. "To Gabby. Happy twenty-first birthday to the most amazing chick I know. Love you, Gabs."

"Love you too," she says with a smile before we clink glasses and throw back the fiery cinnamon liquid.

Shortly after we've thanked them for the drinks, the guys seem to get the memo that we aren't interested and return to the bar. Gabby and I sit and chat about anything and everything. With each glass we finish, Gabby acts more like the confident and happy girl of the pre-accident days.

"So, Vanessa is still dating the baseball guy, any prospects there for you?"

"I don't know," I admit. "I haven't met any of his teammates."

"Vanessa is dating a hot jock, and you haven't scoped out his friends? What's wrong with you?"

"I've been studying." I point a finger at myself. "Failing statistics a month into the semester."

"Lame. You need to get back out there." I resist the urge to throw the advice back at her. It's too good of a night to ruin.

But Gabby isn't done doling out the advice. "Seriously. You haven't dated anyone since David. What's up with that?"

"Nothing is up with that. I've just been busy."

She gives me a no nonsense look that has always caused me to cave under her peer pressure.

"All right fine. I'll scope out the hot baseball guys."

Satisfied, she smiles. "And report back."

SIX

Blair

I haven't seen much of Vanessa since she dropped statistics. She's taken to staying at Mario's most nights, and during the day, our class schedules keeps us out of sync. It goes without saying that when I find her rummaging through our closet singing along to K-pop the next night after work, I'm caught completely by surprise.

"What are you doing here? I thought you were staying at Mario's again tonight?" I ask as I set my backpack down at my desk. Four hours of working at the café has left me with sore feet and a kink in my neck. Not to mention, splattered with the sticky sweet syrups I can't seem to wash off my hands and always manage to smear in my hair.

And worst of all, my quotes went completely unappreciated tonight. I usually get at least one smile or thanks. So much for putting good out into the universe and getting it back.

"I am, *but* the guys are having an after-hours party and *you're* coming with me."

I attempt a smile that I'm sure looks more like a grimace. "Tonight? Shoot, you know I'd love to hang out, but I'm exhausted and have a class at eight tomorrow."

"Who signs up for eight a.m. classes past sophomore year?" She shakes her head. "And that was your excuse the last two weeks. You're coming."

"It was the only time advanced econ was available."

Vanessa pulls out a red tube top and shakes the hanger at me.

"No, not that one. Last time I wore it, I kept pulling it up all night afraid I was going to flash the entire bar."

"Would have made the night more interesting and maybe you wouldn't have ended up back here alone."

"How do you know I ended up alone that night?"

She raises two perfectly arched brows.

"Fine, I came home alone." It isn't that I'm a prude, but picking up a guy at a bar or party seems so freshman year. Is it too much to hope that a nice guy might notice me in the daylight, completely sober?

"Ever since that asshole David, you've been hiding away all this awesomeness." She waves a hand in front of me and waggles her eyebrows.

"I have a lot on my plate this semester." Vanessa doesn't know that my workload is double what it should be because David is blackmailing me into doing his work. I've considered telling her everything a million and one times, but I know Vanessa's reaction would be to march right over to his frat and kick him in the balls. It's exactly what I want to do every time I think about it, but I won't risk pissing him off and having him expose me in front of the entire college . . . *or worse, wind up on one of those revenge porn sites.*

I move past her, and I know I've already given in when I find myself scanning the clothes on my side of our tiny walk-in closet.

When we leave thirty minutes later, I've managed to shower and make myself presentable. I let Vanessa talk me into a short black dress that leaves none of my curves to the imagination, but I refused the high heels in favor of my chucks.

Vanessa has practically been living at the baseball house, and when we walk in, she's greeted enthusiastically. The two-story house is small, old, and borderline condemnable, but the upper classmen baseball players don't seem to care as they mill around.

The bars haven't closed yet, so the party is still small, mostly baseball players and their girlfriends and the many single girls vying for the guys' attention. A keg sits in the dining room, and an array of liquor bottles clutter the kitchen counters. Mario already has Vanessa's drink and is walking it over to her when we cross the living room.

"Hey, babe." He hands her the cup and drops a kiss to her temple. He puts an arm around Vanessa and addresses me. "What can I get you to drink?"

I don't even have to think about it. The smell of anything fruity or sweet makes my stomach roll after serving mochas and caramel macchiatos. "Vodka tonic. I don't suppose there's any lime in there?"

He shakes his head apologetically. "No tonic, either. How about Sprite?"

I nod my approval. I bet if Vanessa wanted tonic and limes he'd not only make sure there were limes but also he'd plant a tree out back.

"He is in love with you," I say when he disappears back into the kitchen.

A panicked look crosses Vanessa's face. "Don't be ridiculous. We've been dating for three weeks."

No one dates the first few months of a new school year. It's all the excitement of new students and different situations. Guys especially, but it isn't just them who reserve the first few months of the semester for hookups and having fun. I'd probably think he was in love with her regardless of the time of year by the way he caters to her every whim, but the fact that it isn't even October yet makes me certain.

Before I can detail out all the reasons why I believe it to be true, Mario is back with my drink.

"Thanks, Mario."

We stand, chatting and drinking, until the house begins to fill. Vanessa and Mario and two other couples claim spots on the couch, sitting on laps and watching the Phillies play the Diamondbacks. Neither being around happy couples or watching baseball are on my top one hundred ways to spend a Thursday night, so I venture downstairs where a makeshift DJ booth has been constructed from a card table and a sheet of plywood. The rest of the dingy unfinished basement has been cleared, and I find a few girls from my sorority holding red cups, shaking their butts, and singing way too loudly. The universal sorority girl version of dancing.

But I don't care that I can't dance for shit or that this basement smells of mold and cheap beer. For the first time all semester, I let it all go. All the worry about grades, David, Gabby . . . *it's all pushed aside as I give in to the rhythm of the pop mix booming from two large speakers. This is what college is supposed to be—exhilarating situations without real-world stipulations. After we graduate, we won't be able to go out on a random Thursday night and let the night lead us wherever we want. We'll have jobs and careers to obsess over. Bills and responsibilities. With David on my ass, I've had a taste of what it might be like to have a prick boss breathing down my throat, and I'm not eager to enter that world yet.*

"I need air," I yell over the music after the fifth song. Physical exertion has warmed my body and my soul. I move out of the circle, and the remaining girls close the space as I make my way up the stairs. I'm still moving to the beat of the music as I spot some of the basketball players, including Zeke and Joel. They stick out in this cramped stairwell, hunkering their tall frames down so they don't bang their heads on the ceiling.

Joel notices me first, and we pause on the stairwell, holding up traffic on both sides.

"Hey it's stat girl."

I chuckle at the nickname. It'll be flunked stat girl pretty soon if I don't pass this next test.

"What are you doing here?" I ask, genuinely surprised. I assumed the athletes didn't mix much outside of their own houses, and I can't remember ever bumping into any of the basketball team before. I'd like to think I wasn't so frat boy crazy that I wouldn't have noticed.

"Same thing you're doing here," he quips, and we both start to move on as the people behind us get impatient.

I look over the other guys and give them a brief nod. They're staring at me intently, and it's way too much attention for my poor underappreciated lady parts.

Mario and Vanessa are gone from their cozy spot in the living room, so I slip out the front door. The baseball house is sandwiched between two other houses, presumably for other sports teams. All the jocks live nearby, giving them close access to the training facilities across the street.

I follow the wrap-around porch to the side, hugging myself and enjoying the cool air whipping through my hair. September days in Arizona are still disgustingly hot, but the nights are the best. The sky is clear, and there is just a touch of heat in the air.

I inadvertently stumble upon a couple making out on the back side of the house, catching dark figures embraced so closely makes it hard to make out two distinct forms, but I see enough to know I should turn around and walk away. Reminders are everywhere I look that happy coupledom can exist in college. Or maybe it's just happy one-night stands. Honestly, I'm almost desperate enough to consider either as a step up from my current situation.

I quietly return to the front of the house, giving myself a silent pep talk to go in and have fun. Enjoy my carefree college years and ignore the stack of homework I need to finish. If only for one night.

"No way. *You're* at a dumb jock party?" Wes somehow manages to skip up the steps onto the porch.

Placing my hands on my hips, I give him a playful smile filled with attitude. "I never said all jocks were dumb."

"Just me."

Mario and Vanessa emerge from the shadows, looking rumpled and surprised to see people outside. That shock is quickly wiped away when Vanessa realizes it's just me and Mario calls out, "Wes, man, you made it."

They meet in the middle, slapping hands and doing that one-arm hug thing guys are so fond of.

"You two know each other?" Vanessa asks, stealing my thoughts.

The guys exchange a look that clearly says they think we are the idiots for not knowing they are friends.

"Wes is the only guy at Valley who spends more time at the fieldhouse than I do."

"Yeah, I'm gonna beat your deadlift weight just as soon as I get this thing off my foot," Wes says, nodding his head down to his booted leg.

"In the meantime, what do you say we get you a drink?"

The four of us make our way through the living room. Slowly. I hadn't thought of Wes as a big man on campus, but clearly, I missed the memo. Wes Reynolds—big damn deal.

As if my humiliation hadn't been bad enough before.

Guys yell out to him, slap his back, or ask about the foot. And the girls? If desperation has a smell, I am inhaling it now, and it reeks of flavored vodka and self-tanner. Hanging back, I glance around the room, paying particular attention to the way girls move so they'll be in his line of vision. Even the ones who aren't brave enough to come forward seem to be biding their time until he looks their way.

I grab Vanessa and pull her into the kitchen.

She careens her neck backward as if she can't bear to look away. "Did he get better looking since I dropped statistics, or have I been with one man for too long?"

I roll my eyes. "He puts me on edge. He has this arrogant charm that makes me want to kiss him and punch him at the same time. And I really need him to pass statistics, so I cannot make an ass of myself . . . again."

"Isn't it great? All that muscle and confidence and who would have guessed—brains!" Vanessa fills two cups with vodka and a splash of Sprite Zero and hands me one. "God bless smart jocks."

I play hide and seek with Wes for the rest of the night. To be fair, he has no idea we are playing any such game, but every time he comes into view, I duck out of the room. My theory is that if I don't talk to him, then I can't put my foot into my mouth. I still haven't figured out how I am going to convince him to tutor me, but I have a hunch that getting drunk and begging isn't the way.

Well after two in the morning, I drag myself outside and call the sober driver to take me home.

"You know, it seems you were practically invisible tonight." His voice sends goose bumps racing over my skin.

"Yeah, weird, I didn't see you either. Guess we just kept missing each other."

"You waiting for a ride?" He places both hands into his pockets, which forces me to really look at him. Dark jeans, a gray T-shirt that fits tight across his chest and arms, and tennis shoes . . . *well, one tennis shoe.*

The look suits him. I can't picture him in a dress shirt or loafers, my usual preference, but he works this look.

"Yeah, one of the girls should be here in a few minutes."

"One of the girls? Roommates?"

"Sort of. Sorority sisters. The sophomores take turns being sober drivers during the week."

"Smart idea."

"You guys don't have some sort of similar set up?"

"Nah. We can usually walk."

"Must be nice to be a guy sometimes and not have to worry about walking home alone in the dark."

He glances down at his body, pulls his hands from his pockets and runs one from his chest to his abs, which is where he lets it rest before pulling up the hem of his shirt just enough to tease me with the hard lines and a promise of a six pack. "I totally understand. I swear that every time I walk home, old ladies are honking and yelling out the window for me to take my shirt off or get in the car."

My mouth waters as I openly check him out. He's joking, but I have zero doubt that what he says is true.

He lets his shirt fall back into place. "Why don't you make the freshman do the sober driving?"

I shake my head and force my eyes back up to his face. "Excuse me?"

"Well, it makes more sense that you'd put that sort of crap job on the newest girls—sort of a rite of passage. I thought it was freshman who got hazed."

"Our freshman girls get the red carpet laid out for them. You don't gain loyalty and sisterhood by hazing."

"No?"

"People are more loyal when they respect and trust you. Respect and trust come from treating people well. A positive first year makes loyal sisters."

"Yeah, but if you put them through hell right away, then you know who will really be there when times get tough."

I consider this. "Fair point, I guess, but we aren't marching to war. Sisterhood is supposed to be fun."

"F-U-N," he says dryly.

The sober driver pulls up to the curb, and we say goodbye. As I walk away, I bite back the temptation to turn and ask him to reconsider being my tutor. I need to figure out what it is he wants or needs, and then I need to strike a deal.

SEVEN

Blair

I stop by the café before statistics Monday morning and then navigate to class carefully with a drink carrier full of coffees and a bag filled with muffins in my backpack. I'm running late thanks to the long line, but it works to my advantage when I spot Wes and crew already in their seats at the back of the auditorium.

"Good morning," I chirp.

"Stat girl," Joel calls out, giving me an easy smile.

Zeke nods, and Wes adjusts his hat just enough to reveal his eyes.

"Coffee?"

Joel and Zeke lunge for the drink carrier. Several girls sitting nearby flash me dirty looks, obviously thinking I've resorted to caffeine bribery to win them over, which is only partly true. They don't even look mad. They look more jealous that they didn't think of it first.

I pull my own drink free and then nudge the last coffee toward Wes. "Coffee?"

He eyes me warily but takes the drink.

"I have muffins too," I say conspiratorially as I take the seat in front of Wes and pull the brown paper bag from my backpack before handing it to an eager Joel. He and Zeke make quick work of the pastries. They don't offer any to Wes, and he doesn't even glance in their direction. He's laser focused on me.

"What are you up to, Blair?" he asks just as Professor O'Sean starts in on the lecture.

Shooting a playful smile, I swivel in my seat.

Halfway through the class, I turn my head slightly to get a glimpse of Wes, certain he'll be sleeping again, but I am surprised to find him staring at me. Our eyes lock, and I offer a small wave. He lifts a brow as if he's still trying to figure out my angle, but I just smile sweetly and return my focus back to the front.

When the class is over, I take my time packing my things.

Wes waits until the class has filed out and steps down a stair so he's very much in my way. "What's your play? Coffee and muffins just because?" He narrows his eyes.

"I work at the café on campus." I don't meet his gaze.

"You worked before class?"

Looking up hesitantly, I admit, "Well, no, but it was on my way."

Wes shakes his head. "Thanks for the coffee. I actually managed to stay awake for once."

He gives me a salute with his cup before he shuffles away.

"Wait," I call. Before his steely blue eyes have a chance to regard me in that arrogant, calculating way, the words spill from my lips. "One score makes happy *one* player. An assist makes two happy."

"Uhhh, what?"

"The quote on your coffee." I can feel my face warm and know I'm beet red. This is humiliating. Did I really use coffee and a cheesy basketball quote to win him over?

He lifts his fingers and turns the cup until he can read the words I scribbled.

I hang my head. Might as well go all in at this point. Too late to pretend this never happened. "I was wondering if you wanted to get together sometime this weekend to study? I can work around your schedule."

"Aww man, you mean I drank bribery coffee?" He looks down at the cup in his hand and curls his lip, eyes still smiling.

"Not bribery," I protest. "Friendship coffee. Come on, I need help. Just one time. Let me join you guys the next time you study, and I'll never bother you again."

It'll be easier to ask for more help once I've shown him what a quick learner I am.

Joel nudges him as he tips his head back finishing his coffee. When he's drunk every drop, he speaks, "You know Z and I are going to need to talk it out a bit more, let her join. Plus, girl used a Tony Kukoc quote. Mad props for that. Wait are you the café quote girl?"

I bite my lip and nod.

Wes shoots him a look to zip it, to which Joel just shrugs. Zeke just watches silently, but there's the slightest upturn to his lips.

"Fine. Be at the house at four this afternoon."

"Yes!" A victory smile breaks out on my face, and I don't even care if I look as ecstatic as I feel.

I hold on to those good feelings until I meet David at the library. He's disheveled, clothes wrinkled, hair mussed like he's been running his fingers through it. I hold back questions about how he's doing because, frankly, I don't care if he's having a rotten day.

"We had a pop quiz in computer programming," he says as I take the seat across from him.

It's the only class he didn't shove off on me because most of the work is done in class. You'd think he'd be able to manage one freaking class on his own, but apparently, he can't. I pass over the folder filled with the latest assignments he gave me without saying a word.

"I convinced Professor Reilly to let me do some extra credit to make up for the grade."

"Un-fucking-believable," I mutter as he hands me the paper with directions for the additional work. "I don't know shit about programming, David."

His lip twitches on one side, and he takes out a heavy textbook and plops it down between us. "Thought you'd say that."

I'm still staring at it baffled when he stands. "Need it by Tuesday next week."

Awesome. Add programming to my list of classes this semester, why the hell not?

I read the directions five times. Yep, five. I give up and shove it in my bag. I'll deal with it this weekend.

My shift at the café ends at three thirty, so I reek of coffee and whipped cream as I walk up the sidewalk toward a house I can't believe belongs to anyone I know.

It's only a block from the baseball house so I guess it's fitting—most the jocks live near the fieldhouse. But this isn't like any other off campus house I've seen. It's huge, and the lawn is manicured with shrubbery and flowers. It's obviously landscaped professionally and often.

I check the address three times. It's only when I hear the faint sound of a basketball bouncing from inside that I believe I'm in the right spot.

Wes's instructions were not to knock, so I disregard all manners and push open the door and hold my breath, preparing for anything.

Standing in the entryway of the massive place, I gawk. The room I share with Vanessa would fit inside the foyer.

Zeke comes down the stairs, sans shirt, a pair of long shorts slung low on his hips. I try not to stare but I figure it would be a crime not to admire all that muscle. A series of tattoos trail from his left shoulder all the way down to his fingers. He nods to me and attempts a small smile. His gesture makes me take a deep breath and relax.

"Hey, Zeke," I pause. "You know where I can find Wes?"

"He's in the gym upstairs."

"The gym . . ." My voice trails off as he continues past me walking toward an open room with a large television mounted on the wall. Unsurprisingly, it's tuned to ESPN and a couple of guys are lounged back in big armchairs that look like theater seating.

"You aren't coming?" I call after him. Joel mentioned they'd need help too.

He shakes his head and keeps going without saying any more.

Oh-kay. I walk up the stairs, the sound of basketballs leading me to the court. It's a half-sized version of the one at Ray Fieldhouse and even has the roadrunner mascot painted on the sideline.

Three guys are positioned around the hoop, a ball cart full of basketballs between them, but Joel and Wes huddle together on one side. A shirtless Joel stands with his hands on his hips, watching Wes carefully. Wes has a basketball in one hand and uses his other to emphasize whatever he's saying.

I walk slowly toward them as I take in Wes's focused and determined face and the way he so effortlessly holds the ball, dribbling it occasionally or palming it with one large hand, fingers splayed out to cover what seems like half the ball. It doesn't look like he is even aware he is doing it. The ball is an extension of his hand.

Joel nods slowly, as if a light bulb is being switched on in that pretty head of black hair. He holds both hands out, asking for the ball as he cuts to the top of the three-point line. Wes passes, a crisp fast move that has the ball in Joel's hands before I can be thoroughly impressed with the way he moves. The ball arches to the net and in. The guys move toward each other happy smiles on both their faces as they exchange some words I can't quite hear.

"Hey." I hang back a few feet, giving them room for their bro moment.

Joel and Wes turn to me in unison.

"Stat girl," Joel says with a smirk. "You're just in time. We're just finishing our study session. He's all yours."

Joel has the sort of charisma and good looks that convince girls to do dumb things like make out with their friends or follow him to his room.

Or send nude photos.

I shake away the negativity and give his sweaty forehead and chest a once over. It doesn't look like much studying has taken place, but I'm not about to argue that point.

Joel lifts his head to Wes in acknowledgment. "Thanks, man." He bounces the ball to Wes and tips his head to me. "Catch you later."

"It's just the two of us?" My voice is a screech, but I'm too nervous to care. "I thought Zeke and Joel were joining us."

"They had some stuff they needed to do this afternoon, so we studied early. They're good, so that just leaves you."

We stare at each other for a moment. Well, I stare. He is probably trying to figure out what is wrong with me while simultaneously devising a plan to get the crazy, gawking girl away from him. He has to be used to that by now, though, right?

"You ready?" Wes finally asks.

"Sure. Yep. Great," I manage with more confidence than I feel.

"We can study downstairs in the television room, but I think some of the guys are down there hanging out, or we could go to my room."

"Your room," I blurt too quickly and then fumble to cover my slip. Great, now I sound like I just want to get him alone. "I mean, the quiet would be good."

"Cool." He motions for me to go before him, and I backtrack out of the gym and into the hallway.

"This way."

I let him take over, and I follow him past open bedrooms while I openly admire the living arrangements these guys have. I've counted three bedrooms already. Each one is large and set up almost in a dorm format with the same bed frame, desk, and large flat screen mounted on light yellow walls. And the bedding and décor isn't bachelor style mismatch stuff picked up from Target. It's all in team colors, and the roadrunner mascot makes an appearance in much of it.

"This is me."

His room looks exactly like the others, but I still scan it from floor to ceiling, looking for clues that make it different. Make it solely his.

"This is your room?" I turn and grin. "What no balcony or bathroom?" I say sarcastically.

"Joel has the master since his dad paid for the house."

My attention snaps to Wes, and the wheels turn as I piece together what I've read about the team and his last name clicks. It should have since it's plastered all over campus. "Joel Moreno. He's a Moreno, like, Moreno Hall and—"

"The president of Valley University? Yup."

Wes grabs the statistics book and a pair of glasses from his desk before taking a seat on his bed.

"Chair's yours if you want it, or you can sit up here. Big bed." He slides his glasses on and then flips open the book, and I swear it's like someone turns on a wind machine. The black rimmed glasses take him from hot jock to hot *smart* jock, and I know this must be what it's like for guys watching a supermodel eat a double cheeseburger. It seems all wrong, and yet, it is sooo right.

"You have specific things you want to go over? Questions? I'm not a tutor, so I don't really know the right way to do this."

I take a seat on the edge of the bed. My heart rate spikes just being this close to him. "Joel and Zeke seem confident enough so whatever you taught them in the past few hours seem to contradict your modesty."

He scrubs a hand over his jaw. "Yeah, all right. How about we start with measuring variation in data sets?"

For the next thirty minutes, Wes basically recites the book as I ask questions and pour over the notes I've taken in class. He never looks at the book before he answers. He flips through it a few times when I mention something in reference to a chapter number, but he seems to be an encyclopedia.

His effectiveness, though . . . I mean, I have read the book on my own, but I'm not even remotely close to understanding a fraction of what he does.

Zeke walks in and then freezes. "Sorry, didn't realize you two were still studying. Practice in ten."

Wes takes off the glasses and sits back on the bed, resting his large frame against the wall. He clears his throat like all the talking has made him lose his voice. I suppose lecturing to a person for an hour could do that.

I gather my notes and shove everything into my back pack as I try to lift the fog that has settled over my brain. This is worse than the confused and drugged feeling I have when I leave Professor O'Sean's class. I'm more confused than ever. Between the glasses and his general hotness, I barely registered a word he said.

When someone likes the way a person's voice sounds, they often say they could listen to them read the phone book. Yeah, that's basically what just happened. He read me the stat book and his smooth voice and handsome face mesmerized me, but I learned absolutely nothing.

I stand and shift toward the door. "Thank you for the, umm . . . help. See you guys on Monday."

Wes follows me to the door with a scowl on his face. "Sure. No problem. Hope you got what you needed. I'm sorry to cut out, we have late practice tonight."

"Practice on Friday nights, huh?"

"Every day. We have an exhibition game coming up."

I nod and shift one foot farther as I consider asking if I can come back for more help just to see him put the glasses back on. It wouldn't help my grade, but it'd certainly brighten the day. "Thank you again."

I spend the rest of Friday night finishing David's music appreciation paper and Saturday alternating between trying to figure out this stupid computer programming assignment, trying to study for statistics, and figuring out what I'm going to do when I fail the midterm and have to drop the class with an incomplete. I'm taking four classes this semester. That isn't counting the four classes David is enrolled in but passing along to me. I'm drowning in assigned reading, research, and assignments.

As the quiet sorority house starts to buzz with excitement of girls getting ready for a Saturday night out, I finally give up any pretense of absorbing any more information.

With no other plans for the night, I find myself back at the baseball house. I shoot Gabby a text to let her know I'm back and scoping out the hot jocks. She replies with about ten smiley faces. I'm standing with Vanessa,

Mario, and a freshman named Clark, who hasn't left my side since I walked through the door unattached. He's funny, charming, and cute, but I have one eye aimed on the door as he trails on about his first months in the Arizona heat. And if my pulse accelerates at the sight of Joel and Zeke entering the party . . . *well, I'll blame that on the alcohol and not the blip of hope that another player might not be far behind.*

"I didn't realize the baseball team was tight with the basketball team," I say to Mario and Clark, trying for nonchalance. "Aren't you guys supposed to have some sort of rivalry or something over gym time and national titles?"

Clark pipes in. "Basketball team is cool. It's the soccer guys we don't like."

Mario gives Clark a glare. "We don't have beef with any of the jocks."

A steady stream of guys I now recognize as basketball players follow in behind Joel and Z. It looks like the whole team is here . . . sans one. Maybe Wes is busy memorizing more of the statistics book. How does someone get that sort of knowledge? I consider myself bright, but he has some sort of effortless genius. Or it appears effortless anyway.

I wave to Joel and Zeke as they look out over the crowd but resist the urge to go hang out with them and ask where Wes is. Maybe he's just late like last time. I don't know why I'm hoping for the latter, but as I let Clark attempt to dazzle me with more conversation, my nerves start to fray a bit more each time the front door opens.

"Listen to me go on and on, tell me about you, Claire."

His inability to even remember my name annoys me and snaps me out of my trance. "You know what? I think I'm gonna go home and study. I'm failing statistics, and I'm stressing and . . . *well, I won't bore you.*"

I turn without waiting for his reply and curse the heels that are pinching my feet with every step. I knew I should have stuck with my guns and worn my chucks, which make much better getaway shoes.

"Wait, can I get your number?" I hear him call but hurry my pace and don't stop until I'm a block away and it's clear Clark has given up the chase. I laugh to myself. Did I really think a guy who couldn't even remember my name was going to follow me to get my number?

I keep walking, waiting to call a sober driver, telling myself it's because it's still early and it is a nice night to walk a bit, but when I arrive at the front of Wes's house, I stop and look up at it for signs that he's inside. The faint sound of a basketball being dribbled catches my attention, and I smile, imagining

Wes inside hard at practice. Maybe it isn't even him, he has another room-mate I haven't met, and Wes did mention that all the guys on the team hung out here. Still, I want to imagine it's him practicing and that's what kept him from a night out with his friends.

I take another step down the sidewalk and pull out my phone to dial the sober driver when I realize the sound I'm hearing is outside. It's the echo of a basketball hitting pavement and not the gym floor inside. Curious, I ig-nore every single girl horror story thing I've learned about trespassing and being out alone at night and I walk toward the noise. The parking garage for the house curves around the back, and in the far corner, they have a basket-ball hoop set up. The rusted backboard and chain look out of place with the immaculate house. It's funny to me that anyone would be out here playing when they have such a nice court inside.

In the darkness, I can't make out his face, but the movements are all him. Even without the cast, I think I would be able to pick him out of a sil-houette lineup of athletes.

I cross the lot, taking advantage of the view. He's tossed his shirt on the ground and wears a pair of athletic pants that zip at the ankles but are open on the right leg around his cast. The late summer night has cooled, but sweat beads up and shines in the light the streetlights cast around him.

"Hey, Reynolds. Didn't anyone tell you it's Saturday night?"

He stops under the hoop, but he doesn't stop dribbling as he stands to his full height. "Best time to be out here. Got the whole court to myself."

"And no spectators to appreciate the view."

"If you build it, they will come . . ."

"How's that?"

He palms the ball and extends his arm toward me. "You're here."

"I'm not much of a spectator." I close the distance between us and take the ball from him. I turn the ball over in my hands and then dribble it twice, hyper aware that he is watching me. I stop a couple of feet in front of the hoop and shoot the ball.

"Yes!" I call out when the ball rattles around the rim and goes through the net.

"Nice shot." He catches the ball and passes it back to me. I shoot it again, but the basketball gods are fickle, and it bounces off the rim.

"Try again."

He passes it back to me, and I take my time lining up and concentrating at the free throw line. The ball sails up, and I hold my breath until it swishes through the net. Gabby and I played one whole year of junior varsity basketball before we determined we were not cut out for competitive sports.

"Two out of three. You have a spot for me on the team?"

"Sixty-six percent would have you riding the pine."

"What about you? You gonna be ready to play this season?"

He looks down to the cast and grimaces. "Comes off next week, but I won't know what sort of shape I'll be in until then."

"What'd you do? If you don't mind my asking."

"I don't mind," he says and dribbles the ball slowly. "Stress fracture. I hurt it in practice about a month back. Just came down on it wrong and that was it."

"I broke my arm once. Missy Thomas pushed me off my bike. My cast was pink, though."

He looks down at his black cast and then pushes his bottom lip out in a pout. "They didn't give me that option."

"Too bad."

He tosses the ball to me almost as if he's forgotten I'm me and not one of his teammates.

"So, really, why are you out here on a Saturday night and not out with the guys? I saw Joel and Z and a bunch more of your teammates at the baseball house. Were you busy memorizing more textbooks?"

He arches a brow.

"I took a guess. The way you know statistics, I assumed you spent your spare time memorizing it."

He chuckles. "Photographic memory. Plus, statistics is my life."

"How do you mean?"

"Well, say I get fouled taking a shot and get two free throws. Each shot has two outcomes: make or miss. So, there are four possible outcomes. I could miss both shots. Miss the first shot and make the second. Make the first and miss the second."

"Or make both."

He grins. "Exactly."

I stare at him as he moves around the court, and I process what he just told me. "Oh my God. This is how you've been tutoring Joel and Z."

He shrugs. "Not tutoring, just explaining it in terms they understand.

They're smart dudes, but ball is our life. So, by giving them examples about shit that doesn't mean anything to them is a lost cause."

"Wes, that's genius. Can you show me more? Explain it like you've been doing for Joel and Z?"

Scrubbing his hand over his jaw, he studies me carefully. "I don't know how much sense I'm going to make talking ball stuff with a chick in a dress and heels."

"Don't let the outfit fool you. I can keep up."

"That so?"

"Yep. I'm not some prissy sorority girl."

He gives me a once over that sends a shiver through me.

"Okay, well, I am, but it isn't *all* I am. I've played basketball before."

"Yeah, how long ago was that?"

"It was a while ago," I admit. "Come on, please?"

"The sorority girl wants the dumb jock to tutor her? It's pretty funny, really."

"Sorry I assumed you were a dumb jock."

"You're only sorry because you need my help."

"I'll play you for it."

"Play me for what exactly?" He cocks his head to the side.

"More of your tutoring services."

"You think *you* can beat *me*??" He raises a brow as he spins the ball around in his hand. He's showing off, but I'm very much enjoying it.

"Not one-on-one." I hold my hands out, and he bounces it to me. I moved to the side of the basket, dribble once and pull up and shoot. As the ball goes through the net, I turn to him. "We'll play PIG."

One side of his mouth tugs into a half smile, but he retrieves the ball and dribbles it to where I stand. I hold my spot, so he moves behind me, the warmth from his body swallowing me up. He leans down so that his lips are a hair's breath away from my neck. "I'm seventy-five percent from the left wing. You sure this is your play?"

I turn my head to meet the arrogant glint in his eye and nod. "I'm not intimidated."

That's a lie, but I'm not about to show any more weakness in front of this guy.

Without taking his eyes from mine, he raises the ball over my head and shoots. The sound of the ball swishing through the net is the only indication it went in. That, and the swagger and cocky athleticism that ooze from him as he retrieves the ball.

And so it goes. I take shot after shot, taking my time and concentrating like I haven't since the SATs, and then he makes the shot while watching me. It's infuriating. And seriously hot.

When I miss, he takes over, picking spots all over the court and moving back a foot each time. Miraculously, I manage to capitalize twice, and we're tied, both having P-I.

"Only one more letter."

"Don't count your chickens before they're hatched." Lining up at the free throw line, I turn away from the basket and hold the ball with two hands. I hear him snicker, but I keep focused on the shot. Trying not to overthink it, I toss it up and over my head and then crane my neck around to watch as it rattles through the net.

"You got trick shots," he says, sounding more impressed than anything.

"Trick shots? Does it somehow count less this way?"

He chuckles and shakes his head. "Fair enough."

He lines up in my spot, peeking over his shoulder once before facing away from the basket and tossing the ball up into the air. The ball hits the front of the rim and bounces back to him.

"Yes! I did it! I beat the conference assist leader."

"Seems you do know my stats."

Heat floods my cheeks. "I might have looked you up. I won! I won!"

"You got lucky. I demand a re-match."

"Nope. I won fair and square." I walk off, grabbing my purse and phone from where I left them.

"You're leaving?"

"I know when it's time to walk away. Tomorrow at two work?"

I don't look back, but I can feel him smiling after me. "See ya then, baller."

EIGHT

Wes

"All right, the probability of success remains constant for all trials. In other words, the probability of me making a shot is always fifty percent no matter how many times I shoot."

The words fall out of my mouth without thinking, which is good because all I can concentrate on is how fucking adorable she looks as she lines up at the free-throw line in her short shorts and Valley T-shirt. Eyes focused on the hoop, she dribbles three times and then pauses with the ball up to her face before shooting. Fucking adorable.

And I'm not the only one who is taken with Blair. The whole team is here, hanging on Sunday afternoon, and she won them all over the minute she waltzed in with paper bags. It looks like she wiped out their entire pastry counter, but she waved off any notion that it was a big deal as she'd tossed the bags onto the counter with no need or want for thanks or acknowledgment. The gesture gained her both.

It isn't just the food, though. Only two type of girls come over to hang at the house. Type one is the ball honeys who have only one objective— landing a basketball player. Those girls are tossed around and become frequents lounging in the house at all hours willing and ready to be used for the bragging rights that she landed a ball player. I stay far, far, like outer space far away from those girls. The second type is girlfriends and those are far and few between. Zeke's made it very clear he isn't dating until he's signed an NBA contract. Nathan parties too much for any girl to take him seriously, and Joel refuses second dates like he's afraid it binds him contractually to marriage and kids.

But Blair isn't either of those things. She isn't settled down with any of the guys, and she most definitely isn't a ball honey. Right now, though, she looks like a cross between the two—hotter than both but taking the best of each. Being all domestic and feeding and taking care of us but looking too hot to be in a relationship. No sane dude would let his girlfriend wear what she has on right now in a house full of other guys.

Joel and Z shoot around us. Joel pipes up when he thinks of something to add. He's smarter than people give him credit for. He just doesn't like to make a big show of it. Z stays quiet like he always does, but he's listening. He's always listening.

"Sounds like you have it down," I say reluctantly. As much as I didn't want to tutor her, I'm clinging to our time together. What I feel borders on disappointment that it's over so soon. "How about a rematch?"

"PIG again? You sure you want me to embarrass you in front of the guys?"

My teammates have trickled in from around the house and the pool and mill about, but they don't intrude, just linger on the sidelines watching.

"Nah, one on one. First to three points. I'm at a distinct disadvantage here with the boot and all."

"You're like a foot taller than I am," she squeaks and waves her hand, gesturing from my feet to head.

"I'll even give up my good hand." I put my right hand behind my back and walk the ball to her. She looks up at me with a cocky grin that is sexy as hell. I can see the hesitation as clearly as I can see her determination.

Pulling her bottom lip behind her front teeth she looks like she is in deep concentration as she tries to figure out her next move. I hold the ball out to her, and she reaches for it. I'm faster and move it out of her grasp as I shake my head. "If I win, I want no mention of last night's loss to anyone. I have a reputation to uphold."

Her brown eyes sparkle. I push away the thought that I just referred to a girl's eyes as sparkling as she speaks. "Buying my silence?"

I nod.

"What do I get if *I* win?"

"I'll keep tutoring you."

I'm not even sure I've been all that helpful. She's a sharp chick, she'd have figured it out on her own. I wonder if she can see through my weak attempt to see her again.

"Give me the ball, hotshot."

Ball in hand, she telegraphs her every move, giving me a distinct advantage even with only one good leg. She has no poker face and when she fakes left while looking right, I'm already prepared for her to make a move. What I'm not prepared for is Joel standing in my damn way.

"What the hell, man?" I ask as I nearly trip over him while Blair dribbles undefended to the basket and tosses up an easy shot just under the basket.

"Sorry," Joel gets out between chuckles, clearly amused at my expense.

Nathan calls out the score from the sidelines. "You're rusty, Reynolds. Weak defense."

Blair saunters back to me, swinging her little ass side to side as she dribbles like she's just walked on to the team. She dribbles the ball right up to me. Her hair is pulled up into another high ponytail, and it flips from side to side. "One to zip."

"You got lucky."

I take the ball and palm it in my left hand, dribble side to side, front to back. She tracks the ball with a focus that makes me want to keep showboating. Thank you, Pistol Pete. I spent an entire summer doing ball handling drills until not having the ball in my hands felt like the loss of a limb.

The guys around the gym have stopped any pretense of minding their own damn business and all eyes are glued on us.

"Show off," and "Steal it, Blair." ring out in steady succession. It's clear who they are routing for, and it aint me.

Traitors.

I make my move to the basket, spinning around her as best I can with the boot weighing down my right foot. Z steps forward just as I'm preparing to pull up and puts his big body between me and the basket. No way am I getting around him with a bad leg. Even with two good ones, he would still be a wall that is hard to break through. I get the shot off, but he's thrown me enough that it rattles around and bounces out without going through the net. Z rebounds and tosses it to Blair.

"What the hell?" I stop and glare at my center just as Blair whizzes by me again and makes another short shot.

"This is sabotage," I mutter as I watch Z and Blair high-five.

To be clear, I want her to win . . . but I don't want to get my ass handed to me.

My teammates are very squarely on her side. She brings the ball back to me with a smile so sweet I want to kiss it off her . . . and then beat her. Girl or not, I have my pride, and the more she taunts me, the harder it is to let her win.

While she stands there waiting for my reaction or for me to make a move to the basket, I decide not to risk it and shoot the ball from where I stand at the top of the three-point line. The surprise on her face turns to a frustrated, and maybe impressed, frown as the ball swishes through the net.

The gym erupts with boos. I turn to the guys sitting around the sidelines and nod toward them. Wise guys, the whole lot of them. I meet Shaw's gaze. No surprise that he's the loudest heckler. "You keep at it, and you won't see the ball all year, Rookie."

He pipes down, but the rest of the guys continue to let me know how much they want her to hand me my ass.

"Aww, come on, don't be a poor sport," Joel says as he shoots a wink to Blair and beckons her over to him.

My "friends" huddle around her, leaning down so they can . . . fuck, I dunno, come up with a game plan?

"What the fuck? I'm only using one hand and I have a boot on my foot."

Silence. They ignore me and keep whispering until finally Blair nods frantically and smiles. She takes her spot at the three-point line and then holds her hands out for the ball. I'm nervous and maybe a little pissed that I'm going to lose like a chump. There's a big difference between letting someone barely eke out a victory over you and whatever the hell is going on right now.

I'd be lying if I didn't admit I'm also a little turned on watching her strut around all dark hair and long legs in a tight little petite package. It's all very confusing.

"You ready for your whole team to watch you lose to a girl?" she taunts as she dribbles twice and then dares to crossover to her left hand right in front of me. She's goading me, trying to get me to make a move, and my hands tingle to oblige.

"Your win is going to be tainted in lies."

"A win is a win."

She steps closer, putting her right hip into me and keeping the ball on her left side. She's surprisingly good with her weak hand. The long strands of her ponytail tickle my arm and chest as I put pressure on her side. The air between us shifts and maybe that was her plan all along because she doesn't seem nearly as affected as I am. I wrap my left hand around her tiny waist, nudging her backward. I hadn't planned on getting this handsy or aggressive, but she's making it hard to remember this is a friendly game. A friendly game that I wanted her to fucking win.

"You smell good," she says on a breathy whisper so quiet I'm sure no one else can hear.

The statement catches me off guard, but I manage to get out a weak thanks.

"I guess you aren't used to your opponents noticing things like that."

"If they did, they definitely wouldn't say it."

"They're probably too busy trying to keep up with you to notice. You're a really good ball handler. Some of the things you can do with the ball in your hands is just insane. Where'd you learn to do all that?"

"I, uh, well . . ." I clear my throat while I try to figure out how to respond to that, but it's too fucking late. She pulls a spin move that wouldn't fool a preschooler toward my bad foot and is off. I turn just in time to see her pull up and make another damn shot just under the basket. No block, no assist—all her. I lost to a fucking girl. A hot girl, but a girl none the less.

Z and Joel laugh their asses off, and the rest of the guys rush toward Blair. They have her up in the air on their shoulders before I can even hobble over and rebound the ball.

"You played me," I yell to her over the noise. I doubt she can even hear me over the guys, but I don't miss the triumphant smile plastered on her face and surprisingly I think my smile is almost as big . . . just not victorious.

NINE

Blair

After my victory, the guys take over the court for their own game, leaving me, and much to his obvious dismay, Wes, on the sidelines. "Come on, we can finish studying in my room where my teammates can't get in the damn way."

If I were a better person, I'd let him off the hook tutoring me since I clearly had help beating him. But now that he started teaching me like one of the guys and shown me what a good tutor he is, I'm not about to pass up the opportunity.

Also, he's hot. I mean I'm not shallow enough to only entertain the idea of hanging around hot guys, but when they're hot and fun to be around *and* they can help me get a better grade? Yeah, I'm grabbing the opportunity any way I can.

In his room, I pull out the Chewy Sprees tucked away in the side pocket of my backpack and reward myself with two. One for learning something and one for beating him.

He doesn't bother grabbing the statistics book this time as he sits on his bed and winces as he props his foot up on a pillow.

"You all right?"

"Yeah, just gets sore if I don't elevate it every few hours. You want to cover covariance next?"

"Sure."

"All right, let's do the definitions first and then we'll go into scenarios."

He fires off terms and I reply, parroting back the information I've read and memorized from the text.

At each nod from him, indicating I have the right answer, I pop another candy into my mouth.

He raises a brow. "I can't remember the last time I saw someone eating Sprees."

"Want one?"

"Dear God, no." He looks absolutely horrified at the idea.

"Come on. Have one. Live a little." I wave a red candy in front of him, and he grimaces, pulling his lips into a tight line.

His refusal only eggs me on, and I lean on my knees to get closer and press it into his lips as he tries to keep me from getting the candy into his mouth. I swear you'd think it was poison the way he fights.

"Come on. One piece."

His lips part slightly, and I drop the candy in and sit back. I watch his face carefully. The grimace turns to intrigue and then pleasure.

"That's good," he says finally. "Give me another."

I hand him the pack and he tosses a handful of colorful candies into his mouth.

"Hey, that's all I have left." I swipe my precious Sprees back and frown at the two remaining. "Now how am I going to study?"

He shakes his head. "I could rub behind your ears and tell you good job."

"Just ask me the next question," I grumble and hold my candy tightly.

He gives me a scenario, and I fumble to remember anything we've just covered.

"You know the parts, just put them together."

"Ugh, I suck at this part. The essay questions kill me." I close my eyes and focus. Negativity isn't going to get me anywhere. "Stay positive. I can do this. I've already come a long way. I know more today than I did a week ago. I just need to keep putting in the effort. *I can do this.*"

"Uhh . . ." He cocks a brow, and I realize I've been muttering aloud.

"Sorry, you weren't meant to hear that last part."

"What the hell was that?"

I'm sure I turn a hideous shade of red as he stares at me like I've officially lost it. "A pep talk. When I'm feeling down about something, I try to flip it, phrase it to better represent my achievements instead of focusing on the things I can't control. Positive thinking attracts miracles."

"You're weird," he says but winks and goes back to drilling me.

We continue long after the Sprees are gone, and my eyes start to glaze over. "I need a break," I finally admit when I can't take it any longer. "All the definitions are jumbling in my mind."

"You want to stop for the night or . . ."

"I just need a short break. You ate all my rewards, and I'm losing focus." The loss of focus might be in part due to the way he's sprawled out on the bed, making me picture all sorts of scenarios that involve fewer clothes.

He snickers. "I'm afraid we don't have any candy in the house."

"Of course, you don't." He probably fills his sculpted body with carefully proportioned meals meant to fuel the long hours of practice and training. Not pure sugar.

A knock at the door snaps my attention toward it. Joel's face appears, hand covering his eyes. "Everyone decent in here?"

"We're studying, asshole."

Joel stands to his full height and lets his hand drop. "I know. Just messing with ya. It's six."

"Again, we're studying."

"Take a break then." Joel turns, and I'm looking between them, trying to figure out what is so important about six o'clock. "Movie starts in five. Nathan said to tell you he wants extra butter on the popcorn this time."

Wes looks sheepish as he explains, "It's movie night."

"Yeah, I got that." I chuckle. Standing, I begin to gather my things. "I can finish studying at home. I've taken enough of your time today."

"Nah, stay. We can go over it again after the movie."

He must read my hesitation. "It's cool. It's just the roommates. We kick everyone else out for movie night." He pauses. "You don't talk during movies, do you? Nathan demands silence."

"And buttered popcorn, apparently."

"You in?"

I drop my bag. All that awaits me at home is reminders of David and the shitstorm he's made of my life. "Why not?"

Wes takes me by the movie room while informing me he's on snack duty for the night. "Popcorn? Soda? Beer?"

"Soda'd be great."

"Save me a seat. I'll be back in five."

Joel arrives as I'm trying to decide where to sit. "Yo, Blair, you met Nathan?"

I shake my head and stretch out my arm to take the elusive fourth room-mate's hand. "Good to meet you."

"Nice work on the court today. I thought our boy was gonna lose his shit." Nathan's hair is longer, hanging about chin length, and he tucks a strand behind his ear as he speaks.

Joel plops down in a one of three seats in the front row and Nathan hovers next to him. There's one seat left in the front and four in the back. I take a step to the back row and then hesitate.

"Your boy usually sits in the back by himself. Lucky him. I'm thinking this was his plan all along—leaving room for pretty girls to sit beside him."

My face flushes at Joel's playful flirting. Z and Wes enter the room, and I sigh a breath of relief. Wes, for all his arrogance, has a presence that puts me at ease. I'm starting to trust him.

Wes cradles three huge bowls of popcorn. He hands one to Nathan, places one on the empty seat that is presumably Zeke's, and then tucks the other at his side. Z has five sodas stacked up in his large hands and tosses them to the guys and then walks one back to me with a shy smile. The whole thing is so casual and homey that, when we settle into our seats, I grin at the whole charade. Who would have guessed this is how they spend a Sunday night?

I learn the pick rotates each week, and tonight it's Zeke's choice. Nothing could have surprised me more than him picking a Tom Cruise ro-mantic comedy, *Knight and Day*.

"Seriously?"

Joel tosses popcorn in Zeke's direction. "Z's working his way through all of Tom Cruise's movies and taking us along for the ride."

"I've never seen this one," I admit.

I recline the seat and curl up. I'm sitting next to Wes Reynolds watch-ing a movie. No big deal, just a Sunday night Netflix and . . . well, there's no chill, but a girl can pretend.

TEN

Wes

I sleep through movie night ninety percent of the time, but there's a zero percent chance of that tonight.

Cameron Diaz should have my eyes glued to the screen, but she pales in comparison to the intrigue I have for the girl beside me. I don't know what Blair's story is. All I've been able to determine so far is that she's a sorority girl, driven, and sexy as hell. So, basically, nothing that every other dude at campus couldn't have figured out with a cell phone and social media account.

Blair yawns and stretches her hands over her head. The movement lifts the hem of her shirt and exposes the creamy, flat skin of her stomach.

I need to get laid before our next study session or I'm likely to embarrass myself with a boner that has nothing to do with my love of probability.

As Tom and Cameron fill the screen, Blair is riveted. It gives me a chance to study her better. Her dark brown hair is pulled up in a ponytail that falls past her shoulders. I like when she wears her hair this way giving me an unblocked view of her small features and delicate neck. The tank she wears shows off her rack, which is the perfect size for her body. They aren't so big she looks like she'll fall over but plenty for me to palm in my large, skilled hands, which is as likely to happen as Tom Cruise somehow *not* ending up with Cameron Diaz at the end of this movie.

I don't have to ask her to know she isn't up for a one-night stand. She has complicated and relationship written all over her. And I don't have time for that. I don't even have time for the study sessions I now owe her.

I shift in my seat and slam the back of my head into the chair to get my thoughts off sex, catching Blair's attention in the process.

"You okay?" she whispers.

"Yeah, just wondering when Tom's going to start kicking ass." It's the first thing I can think of, but she buys it.

"Shh." Nathan's shushing is louder than our talking, but I don't point that out. Guy is serious about movie night, and I'd be lying if I said I hadn't grown to love our weekly ritual.

"Want some popcorn?" I lean over the arm of the chair to whisper the question.

She nods, and instead of handing her the popcorn, I lift the armrest and scoot closer so I can place the bowl between us. Nathan shoots a dirty look over his shoulder at the noise from our shuffling, and I kick his chair. "Calm your tits, man."

The rest of the movie is spent in silence. When Cameron and Tom cross the border into Mexico and the end credits roll, Joel jumps up to turn the lights on and the television off. We have early practice on Monday mornings so we don't usually waste any time hitting the sack after movie night.

"How many left on the list?" Blair asks Z.

He grins. "Everything he's done since. I'm watching in order."

Joel groans. "The early years were the worst."

"I enjoyed *A Few Good Men* and *Risky Business*," Nathan says.

"And *Interview with a Vampire*," Blair adds. "*Jerry Maguire*."

"Girl knows her Tom Cruise." Z looks positively impressed.

"You wanna cover probability theory one more time?" I'm gonna be tired as hell for six a.m. practice if she says yes but I'm thinking it might be worth it to spend a little more time getting to know her.

"Actually, I'm exhausted, and my brain is mush. I feel good about what we covered today, though. I think I have it."

We head up the stairs with the guys, and Blair says good night to them all like they're tight now. In my room, she grabs her things, and I lead her back down and outside. She unlocks her car and places her backpack in the passenger seat. "Thank you for helping me. You really don't have to keep—"

I cut her off before she says something stupid like I don't have to keep tutoring her. Of course, I do. It's the only way I'm going to figure her out, and that's become as important as my need to see her succeed. "I have weight training in the afternoon tomorrow, but I could meet you at the library say around seven?"

She looks relieved at my offer. "That'd be great. What's your major anyway?"

I think about giving her my quip about the Final Four being my major. That's all most people really want to hear about anyway. But the fact that Blair sees beyond my stats makes me want to be honest. "Officially, it's business, but basketball is the only thing I've ever seen for my future." I could leave it at that, but I don't. I keep going. "I'll deal with the real world when the season is over, find some bullshit job if I have to. What about you? What are you going to be when you're all grown up?"

"Oh, man, I don't know." Her eyes light up, and I feel like I'm seeing my first real glimpse of Blair. "I have one more year and then hopefully my MBA. My end goal is to be an influencer, an entrepreneur, a badass female boss. I want to inspire people and work beside others with the same sort of passion."

She stops rambling and ducks her head as if she's just realized how much she's said. "Anyway, something business related, which is why I need an A in statistics. O'Sean is the program coordinator for the accelerated MBA track, so I need him to like me."

I nod. She's given it a lot of thought, and I haven't allowed myself to think about anything beyond March.

"Thank you for your help. I really appreciate it, and you're a good teacher. Maybe you should consider that when you start your bullshit job search."

She slides into the car seat, and I close her in. She rolls the window down and tilts her head to look up at me, a playful smile sitting on her lips. "And, for the record, you really do smell nice."

ELEVEN

Blair

"Sorry. Training ran late," Wes apologizes as he takes a seat across from me in the library.

I wave him off. It's only two minutes past, but I'd been so buried under the newest assignments David shoved off on me I hadn't even noticed.

"No worries. I was just finishing some homework."

He grabs the programming book in front of me and flips through it, holding my place with a finger. "You're taking a computer science class? I thought you were business?"

Shit.

I take the book back and shove it into my backpack. "Most businesses run on computer science."

I think I heard David say that once, so there's a slight chance it's true.

"So, I worked through the practice questions in chapter six. I think I showed my work right, but can you take a look?"

He nods as he rummages through his bag, unzipping every pocket and dumping the contents onto the table—two mechanical pencils, a notebook, a folder, and a bottle of Icy Hot. The bag is clearly empty, but he keeps riffling through the pockets.

"You forget something?"

"I, uh, was hoping I had a granola bar or a forgotten pack of trail mix. I didn't have time to eat."

Extra points for skipping food to hurry to meet me. The tally is somewhere in the millions at this point.

I check the time and close my laptop. "University Hall is open for another thirty minutes."

His eyes light up at the prospect of food. "You don't mind?"

"Nah, I need to stock up on Chewy Sprees anyway. *Someone* ate all mine."

He sweeps everything back into his backpack as I do the same, albeit much more carefully.

The sun is setting as we walk, disappearing behind the mountains and taking the daylight with it. The colors that paint the sky with its descent take my breath away. I used to hate sunsets. Hate the signal of another day ending without accomplishing everything I wanted. I preferred the sunrise and the prospect of a new day filled with possibilities.

It was David who made me fall in love with them. He'd told me that sunsets were meant to be shared. That, unlike sunrise, which was about individual reflection, they were a gathering and celebration of a day spent with people you cared about. I'm sure it was a line he heard somewhere, or worse, made up on the spot to win me over, but even if everything else about my time with him had been a lie, the idea of sharing sunsets stuck.

"You lost?" Wes interrupts my thoughts and motions toward the University Hall, which I nearly passed.

I point toward the horizon. "I was just admiring the sunset. Arizona has the best sunsets."

"Better than wherever you're from?"

"Well, no. I'm from here."

He laughs. "So, your data point is one?"

"I don't need to go anywhere else to know *that* is the best sunset."

He looks up as if he's really seeing it for the first time. "It's pretty good. I'll give you that. Better than any I saw in Kansas."

"Kansas, huh?"

He nods. "Yep."

"Ruby slippers, Dorothy, tornados, the Wicked Witch, and Toto . . . that is literally everything I know about Kansas."

He chuckles. "Not a lot else we're known for, I guess. *The Wizard of Oz* and the Jayhawks."

"The what hawks?"

"University of Kansas Jayhawks. One of the best college basketball teams in the nation." He looks at me like his explanation should jog my memory. I'm not about to tell him I know next to nothing about college basketball, let alone which teams are the best.

"Why'd you decide to come to Valley instead of being a Jayhawk?"

"According to my father, I did it purely to piss him off."

"Did you?"

He smiles sheepishly. "No, not entirely, but it was an added bonus."

"So why Valley?"

He holds open the door for me as we enter University Hall and runs the other hand over his chin. "Got Z to thank for that. I played against him my senior year of high school in an AAU championship. Coach Daniels recruited Z hard, everyone did. When he signed with Valley, he put in a good word for me. Never even talked to the guy off the court. Anyway, I owe him. It's been incredible playing alongside him. Players like Z don't come around very often. He has the kind of talent that people will still be talking about in twenty years."

"I heard he's going pro next year."

"Yeah, definitely. He should be a first-round pick, but it depends on how the season goes. If I can get us to the final four, he has a shot at a top five spot. Joel could go, too, if he doesn't screw it up with the partying and women. He has another year yet, though."

"What about you?"

"Nah, doubtful. I could maybe get drafted in a late round, probably spend some time on their minor league teams, but I'm just focused on the next five months."

"I'm surprised," I answer honestly. "I can tell how much you love it, and you're obviously talented enough to play with guys who are going pro, why wouldn't you want to go for it or at least try? You might be surprised, and worst-case scenario is that you don't make it and you can fall back on your business degree."

He grins, which is not at all the reaction I am expecting. "You have spunk. I like that. I just need to focus on getting the team to that national championship. Z and I have been working toward it for four years, and it's so close I can taste it."

We go our separate ways to get supplies for our study session and then settle into a table where I sip coffee and Wes devours a sandwich and chips.

He quizzes me on binomial distribution between bites, and I find I mostly know the answers. I'm picking it up faster now, whether because it's clicking or because Wes is that good, I don't know. I'm leaning toward the latter.

I'm able to concentrate more too. It isn't that his looks don't affect me anymore, he's still mind jumbling hot, but as I learn more about him I realize the outside isn't even the sexiest thing about him. He's intelligent and polite and just . . . nice.

When they dim lights at University Hall signaling closing time, I'm reluctant to leave but I know Wes has other things to do. Guilt for tricking him into helping me gnaws at my conscious. I should probably let him off the hook now and tell him I can finish preparing for midterms on my own.

"Same time tomorrow?" He asks as he scrolls through his phone and then taps out a message.

"Uh, yeah, sure. I work at the café until four, but I'm free after that."

"Shoot," he says and stops on the sidewalk.

"What's wrong?"

"Joel has a late class tomorrow night."

I stare at him trying to figure out how Joel's schedule impacts his.

"He's my ride," he finally says as he stares down at his phone. "I can't drive yet with the boot."

"Oh, right. I'm sorry. I completely forgot. I could come to the house again if that's easier?"

"Yeah, that'd be great."

"How are you planning to get home tonight?"

He shrugs. "Joel's coming to pick me up."

I laugh, something about Joel playing chauffeur makes me adore their friendship even more. On cue, Wes points to a black sports car pulling into the parking lot behind the library with no regard for the speed limit. Joel pulls up to the curb and grins up at us through the open window. "I feel the need . . ."

Wes shakes his head, but I don't miss the big smile on his face as he finishes the quote. "The need for speed."

He looks over sheepishly. "*Top Gun.*"

"I should have guessed."

"You need a ride, stat girl?"

"Nah, it's a short walk." I point in the direction of the sorority house.

Both men look at me stubborn and hard. "You are not walking across campus at night by yourself."

Valley isn't exactly a hub of violent crime, but I can see any retort I could make would be in vain. They aren't letting me walk.

Wes holds the door open for me, and I slide in to the back of the car that still smells new and expensive. It fits Joel, who I haven't gotten a good read on yet. He's flirty and playful and seems to be so different from Wes and Z, but they're close. I can tell their friendship goes beyond ball.

"What kind of car is this?" I ask as I run my hands over the soft leather. A large screen rests in the middle of the dashboard and Joel taps it to set the music for the drive.

"Tesla 3." Joel turns to me, mischief in his eyes. "Ever gone zero to sixty in three seconds?" The way he says it sounds positively dirty.

I shake my head slowly, afraid what my answer means.

Joel's eyebrows raise, and he smiles wickedly. Before I can brace myself, he speeds off so fast I forget to breathe. Holy shit. Wes careens his neck back to check my expression, and the wolfish smile he gives me only speeds up my already racing pulse. Zero to sixty. Yep, I'm falling just that fast.

TWELVE

Wes

I barely get the threadbare Valley basketball T-shirt pulled over my head before I hear Blair walk up the stairs toward my room. Her footsteps are tentative and soft, a definite distinction from the heavy ones of any of my roommates.

She knocks on the doorframe as she peers in. "Hey."

"Hey." I take in her tan legs and the tiny white shorts that cover places I want to see and taste.

I squeeze my eyes shut to try to erase the thoughts. I recite the presidents backward in my head and then open my eyes to find Blair bent over in front of me to get something out of her bag. An innocent act, but the way her T-shirt gapes open and gives me a view of her rack? Not so much.

She stands straight all business and pep. "I spent some time going over the first two tests to try to determine what this one might look like."

We settle onto my bed, sitting so close her hair brushes against my shoulder. "I think I'm good with the short answer questions, but the essay killed me last time. What do you think he might ask us to do for this one?"

I take her last test and read the essay question and her answer. Then re-read twice because my head is not in it.

"I think he'll have us compute probability of events."

We take turns coming up with scenarios and then computing the probability. She chews on the end of her pencil in thought, and I'm mesmerized by the way her lips part and her teeth rest gently on the rubber end. This woman is going to kill me a slow, achingly painful death.

"Every single example you used was basketball related," she says looking back over our scenarios that she's carefully written in her notebook.

I shrug. "It's what I know."

She raises both eyebrows as if she's daring me to think beyond ball. I clear my throat. Only two things currently occupy space in my brain. Ball and . . .

"The probability of you letting me kiss you." My throat feels like gravel as I continue. "Possible outcomes include allowing and not allowing. Each outcome has a probability of point five."

Her eyes widen, and she shifts uncomfortably. Her voice is quiet and throaty. "No."

The sting of rejection hurts. I thought I'd seen interest in the way she looked at me. And not just my brain and what I could do to help her or my status as a jock for some sort of ego boost. Interest in *me*. I flip open the textbook, hiding my disappointment and giving my fingers something to do. "It was just—"

She rests her hand on top of mine. The G-rated touch sends X-rated thoughts. "That example doesn't work because not allow isn't an outcome."

Her words register, and my fractured ego repairs itself and then alley oops a beautiful lob that ends with my mouth capturing hers. Slam dunk.

Fuck, I don't even care that the thoughts going through my head are screwed-up ball references. I can usually compartmentalize the aspects of my life that don't revolve around my jersey, but this girl's lips against mine feels like the sweetest victory.

Our tongues tangle, and she grows bolder, running her hand up to my chest before fisting my shirt as if she's afraid I might run away before she's ready.

Baby doll, I'm not going anywhere as long as you're touching me. I keep the thought to myself but do my best to show her that truth by placing a hand at her hip and deepening the kiss. I smile into her mouth when I taste the lingering sweetness of Sprees and something that is uniquely Blair. Damn, I had been curious about kissing her and assumed it'd be nice, but now that I've kissed her, I don't wanna stop.

The door swings open, "Hey, man, I invited some girls—"

Joel stops short when he catches Blair scrambling away from me and placing the back of her hand to her lips.

"My bad. Looks like you already have plans for the night." His grin makes the stiffy in my pants deflate. Fucking Joel.

"Ever consider knocking?"

"Ever consider locking the door?" He throws back.

Blair scoots off the bed. "He's all yours. I have to finish a paper tonight anyway."

Joel backs out of the room, leaving me alone with this girl who has my head spinning. I half-hoped kissing her would cure my interest, prove that she was just like any girl, but it didn't. I want to do it again.

"Sorry about Joel."

"It's fine." She waves me off. "I really should get going."

I shove my hands deep into my pockets. "Okay."

I walk her downstairs and past the noise of the party forming out back.

She stops just outside the door and peers back at me. "So, I'll see you in class tomorrow?"

"Actually, no. I'm getting the boot off late tomorrow morning. Professor O'Sean is letting me come in during his early office hours to take the test."

"There goes my idea of cheating off you."

I chuckle and run a hand through my hair. "After that stunt you pulled on the court Sunday, I wouldn't put it past you, but you don't need it. You're ready."

"I hope so. I need to pass this class. No, I need an A in this class."

"I'll get you your A."

And I know I will. I've taken on her grade the same way I've taken on Zeke's first round pick. I don't know what it means or even why, but I can see the possible outcomes, and I know the probability of walking away is the least likely of them all.

THIRTEEN

Blair

When I arrive at class the next morning, I take the seat in front of Joel and Zeke and wordlessly hand them the muffins and coffees I grabbed from the café. They both turn the cups straight to the quotes and smile.

Professor O'Sean walks up the stairs to begin passing out the tests, so I offer them a nervous smile and wait, tapping my pencil against the desk and praying that I've retained some of the knowledge that came out of Wes's beautiful mouth. Thoughts of his mouth lead to dissecting the kiss that still burns my lips, which is pretty much all I've been doing since it happened.

The first person stands and takes their completed test to the front with five minutes remaining. O'Sean's tests are no joke—long and arduous. A minute later the room becomes a hub of energy as the whole class finishes or maybe just gives up. I wait for the last possible minute, going over each question, re-thinking my answer, and ultimately changing nothing. I know this stuff.

Joel and Z wait for me just outside the classroom.

"Longest test ever," Joel mutters.

I nod as Zeke elbows Joel and points behind me.

"I'll be damned. He's back!" I hear Joel and Z share their excitement with some sort of hand clapping, but as soon as I look over my shoulder, it all becomes background noise. Wes is walking toward us. The off balanced gait I've grown accustomed to in such a short time is replaced with a strong, sleek elegance.

"Hey, how'd it go?" he asks, a genuine smile filled with trepidation like he's afraid I've failed and his tutoring didn't help.

I'm very aware that his eyes rest solely on me. "Good. I think."

He wraps his arms around me, taking me completely by surprise. "Knew you could do it," he mumbles and then just when I'm about to swoon from the feel of his hard body wrapped around mine, he ruffles my hair like a big brother might do to his annoying little sister.

He pulls back quickly and steps toward the guys.

"You're back?" Joel asks looking down at his foot. "Please tell me you're back."

Wes's face lights up as he does a little dance side to side. "I'm back, baby."

Z grabs Wes in a bear hug and then pulls back. "With me." He lifts his hand up to his head. "Without me." He drops the hand to his waist. "With me," Z repeats and smiles as he lifts his hand back up.

Wes chuckles. "Definitely with you."

The three of them grin and chuckle as they share their Tom Cruise movie quote moment, but I can't peel my eyes off Wes.

Oh no.

I'm totally falling for him. First, I let him kiss me, and now I'm getting all mushy inside watching him have a bro moment. Making out with a jock is one thing, falling for one? That spells disaster, and I can't stomach any more relationship disasters.

"Let's grab lunch at The Hideout to celebrate all the things. Another statistics test done and the boot is off! It's a damn good day," Joel interrupts my thoughts and just like that I find myself back in the small sports car with enough testosterone to power it Flintstone-style.

The Hideout is the most popular restaurant and bar near campus. The décor is sports themed and judging by the warm welcome they receive as we slide into a booth, I'd say the employees are fans.

Wes and I sit across from Joel and Zeke, who are deep in debate mode over whether Coach should start Nathan or some rookie who neither Joel or Zeke seems to like. Wes angles his body toward me and nudges me under the table with a knee.

"Tell me honestly, did you use basketball references in your essay?"

"Nope," I say proudly.

"No? All my good basketball examples went to waste?" His eyes light up. "Wait, did you use my kissing example? Please say yes!"

I flush, and my eyes fall to his lips, remembering the way they felt against mine. "I took your examples and flipped them to football terms instead. Professor O'Sean prefers football."

"He does?" Wes tilts his head to gauge my seriousness.

I nod. "He used the Cardinals as an example twice last week during the lecture."

"Well, I'll be damned. Maybe I shouldn't have slept through class."

He winks, and my heart does a little pitter patter.

"How's the foot feel?" I ask as the waiter brings our food.

"I'm cleared for practice today."

"Wow, just like that, huh?"

He nods. "Exhibition game is on Friday, so I don't have a lot of time to get my guys ready."

"Your guys?"

"I'm the point—the leader on the floor. Z and I have been playing together since freshman year, Joel and Nathan a year later, but we have younger guys who aren't meshing as well as I'd like yet. Takes a lot of time together."

"I'm impressed."

He waggles his eyebrows. "Oh yeah?"

Joel and Zeke get quiet as they start piling food into their mouths. I eye the food in front of Z. Two sandwiches, chips, and a milkshake. I don't comment. He has to be close to two-hundred and fifty pounds, so it's probably a drop in the bucket.

"I can't wait for practice." Joel chews, and his body practically bounces with excitement. "Coach letting you play the exhibition?"

"He'll let me play." By the tone in his voice, I venture that Wes is used to getting his way on the court. And probably off it.

"What about you? Are you coming to the exhibition?" Joel asks, stealing a chip from my plate.

I swat playfully at his hand. "What exactly is an exhibition?"

The table goes silent. Even their chewing stops.

"Wait a minute. Have you ever been to a Valley basketball game?"

I bite my bottom lip and try my best to look sweet and innocent. "No."

"Never?" Wes drops his sandwich and stares at me.

"Well, I watched last year's tournament on television."

He shakes his head. "The exhibition game is like a scrimmage or practice game where we split into two teams and play each other."

"When is it again?"

"Friday night at seven," Wes answers.

Joel steals another chip, and I pretend not to notice. "And there's a party at the house after."

"Cool. I'll see if I can round up some of the girls."

"You're a sorority girl?" It's more of a reminder than a question. "Yeah, bring some friends."

I pull my plate back as he reaches for another chip. "My friends are too good for you."

Turns out a lot of the girls from the house already made plans to see the exhibition game.

"I had no idea people came to these," I whisper to Vanessa.

"They didn't until they started making it to the Final Four."

The cheerleaders and Ray Roadrunner, our lovable mascot, dance in the center of the floor to Magenta Riddim, but I'm too nervous to follow any of it with any real focus.

"You're gonna have to stop bouncing your leg like that you're shaking the whole row."

"I'm sorry. I'm just so nervous."

"Why are you nervous?" Vanessa asks with a smirk.

"I don't know."

"You like him."

I shoot her a look as the crowd around us erupts. Turning my attention to the floor, I watch as the team runs onto the court. I spot Wes right away even in their matching warm ups and shoes.

But it's Joel who steals the show by joining in with the cheerleaders and doing the ridiculous dance perfectly in step with them. If Wes is cocky, Joel is an attention whore. He eats up the female screams and shouts as he shows off his dance moves.

Vanessa and I stand and cheer with the rest of the student section.

"I can see why you like him. The man is seriously fine. He really knows how to rock the whole hot athlete thing."

"That he does." I motion with my head toward Mario, who is standing on the other side of Vanessa and talking to one of his buddies from the base-ball team. "So, does Mario. He's hot and nice—the total package."

She checks to see if he heard our conversation and then hushes me. "Don't say that shit where he can hear you."

"You're spending every night with him, I think he knows you're into him. Give it up, V. You aren't playing this cool."

She scoffs but smiles. Turning my attention back to the team, more specifically to Wes, I'm completely transfixed by the way he moves—quick, confident. He oozes athleticism, and—crap, I'm totally into a ball player. No, not just a ball player. *The* ball player. Do they even date?

Obviously, they kiss girls in their bedrooms.

After a short warm up, the guys split up into two teams: white and blue. Wes and Zeke don the home team jerseys while Joel and Nathan are on the blue team.

I'm lost in all of it, in all of him. Sure, I've seen plenty of games between high school and the NBA games my brother made me watch when we were kids. I mostly know the rules and the lingo, but I've never been so invested. I wring my hands every time he shoots the ball. I scream like a total fan girl every time he makes a shot, but I'm keenly aware of how badass he is lead-ing his team. They trust him. They look to him. They follow him.

Z's also surprising. The quiet guy I've come to know is a total trash talker on the court. I can't hear him, but his mouth moves constantly while the ball is in play. On defense, he mumbles what I assume is razzing com-mentary to his opponent. And on offense, he calls out for the ball, pumps up his team with pep talks and attaboys.

Joel's personality is exactly the same on the court. He's arrogant, but he backs it up by leading his team in points and looking good doing it. The cheerleaders yelling just a little louder for him doesn't go unnoticed, and I have a sneaking suspicion he's earned their favoritism with a lot of sexual favors.

I don't have a read on Nathan yet, but his game face is as intense as his desire for silence during movie night. His longer hair is pulled back in a nubby ponytail. If I'd passed him on campus, I never would have pictured him a jock. He has a grunge style that I thought died with Kurt Cobain.

The game ends with Wes and Z's team on top. Joel and Nathan look pissed but still accept fist bumps from Z as they walk off the court.

Part of me wants to hang around and wait for Wes, but I have no idea how long he'll be or what his routine is like. I don't even have his number. And if I did, I wouldn't know what to say. I mean I guess we're friends, but it isn't the friend in me who's anxious to see him again. The girl he kissed last night, on the other hand, is ready to stalk him into a dark corner and demand a repeat performance to verify it was as mind-numbingly good as I remember.

"You ready?" Vanessa asks as the people around us start to clear out. "Mario says everyone is going straight to The White House."

"Sure." I watch Wes until he disappears completely into the tunnel that leads to the locker room. "Let's go."

FOURTEEN

Wes

"Nice job out there," Z says as he removes his headphones from his locker and places them around his neck.

"You too. You keep playing like that, and you'll be a top-round pick for sure."

He grunts, but I don't miss the smile. I take his future as seriously as he does. It's my job to get the ball to him, so if I fail, then he fails. That isn't gonna happen.

"See ya back at the house," I call after him. When the rest of the guys go, I unwrap my foot and hobble to the shower. Pain throbs as I wash quickly, leaning on the wall to take some of the weight off it. I'm supposed to be easing into it, but I only have one mode—all out.

"How's the foot, Reynolds?" Coach asks as I step out of the shower with a towel around my waist.

"Sore, but good. It felt strong out there."

He nods and eyes me carefully. When he seems convinced I'm telling the truth he nods again. "All right. Take it easy tonight. I know you guys are celebrating, but make sure you ice it before bed and check in with the trainers first thing tomorrow before practice. Need you strong out there."

"Yes, sir."

"And, Reynolds? Spend some time with Shaw. He has potential."

Just the mention of the rookie irritates me. "He's a hot head."

"So were you." He pushes open the door and taps the doorjamb twice with a fist. "Nice work out there tonight. Good to have you back on the floor."

When the door closes behind him, I slink down on the bench and flex my foot to try to loosen it up a bit.

I'm back.

The party is loud, and people are everywhere when I get back to the house. I push through to my room and throw my bag onto my bed. I'm not really in the mood to party, but I am hoping a certain brunette will show up. I spotted her at the game, which might have had something to do with my refusal to ask coach to pull me even after my foot started throbbing.

"Fifteen points, three assists, and either two or three steals. I lost track trying to keep count of all of it." The object of my thoughts stands in the doorway of my room. "And I can't believe Zeke."

"He's pretty incredible."

"I meant the talking. The guy never shuts up out there. Who knew?"

I laugh. "Yeah, he saves it all for the court."

She steps into the room and holds out a beer. "Drink?"

I shake my head. "I don't drink during the season."

"I don't think Joel got that memo. He's halfway through a bottle of Jack downstairs."

She moves to sit on my bed, and I take a seat at my desk.

"Your foot hurts." A crease forms between her brows, and she speaks with certainty.

"A little sore."

"You should probably have it elevated." She moves into action, looking around the room before zoning in on a chair propped up on the other wall. She pulls it across the room and then motions for me to put my leg up. "You have any ice in here? Or is it heat that you need?"

"Shit. I should have grabbed an ice pack from downstairs."

She bites her lip and looks as if she is considering leaving to go get it. She's gone into full-blown mama bear mode. It's hot, but I don't want her to leave.

"Hand me that beer."

She obliges, and I place the cold can against the side of my foot just above the top of my shoe. I should really take it off and ice it properly, but I don't want to give her any reason to rush off. "Guess I did need that drink after all."

She shifts as if she doesn't know what to do—or worse, as if she might leave.

"Sit, please. You're making me nervous pacing around."

She does, and we study each other with the bass from downstairs vibrating the floor below us. "Did you enjoy your first game?"

"I did."

I'm not convinced. "You don't sound very sure."

"I was a nervous wreck. I don't know how you do it. Every shot, every pass . . . I'll have an ulcer by the end of the season."

I like that she's already planning on going to more games. Like that I popped her ball cherry. Hell, I even like that having her there made me work that much harder.

I swing my foot down off the chair and stand. "Move over."

Before she can protest, I sit on the bed next to her and scoot until my back rests against the wall. My feet still hang off the edge, though. A detail that doesn't go unnoticed.

Blair moves so she's facing the headboard and I angle myself to face her and move my legs onto the bed. Without a word she places her still mostly cold beer against my foot.

Her phone pings, and she sits forward to retrieve it from her back pocket giving me an eyeful of cleavage. A gentleman would pretend not to notice, but there's no part of her covered flesh I haven't already imagined in vivid detail.

"It's Vanessa. She and Mario are leaving."

"Already? Party just started."

"I think they're far more interested in being alone than a party with half the university."

She pulls the beer away from my foot and lets her legs hang off the edge of the bed. "I should go. I rode over with them."

"I doubt they want a third wheel for what they have in mind. Stay. I'll get you a ride home later."

"You sure I'm not keeping you from your adoring fans?"

"Got my number-one fan right here."

She cocks a brow. "I'm your number-one fan? I'm not sure what that says about you, considering I've only been to one game."

"I guarantee you're the only one here who tracked my stats tonight. It was three steals, by the way." I wink, and she blushes. Truth be told, it's fucking hot that she watched me close enough and cared enough to keep a tally.

"So, I surmise there's no boyfriend. If there were, he'd have tracked you down and kicked my ass by now."

"Was that a question?"

"Yeah." I laugh out the word. "Is there a guy?"

The tiniest shake of her head is my answer. "And you aren't dating anyone and on top of the list for every girl downstairs. I'm actually surprised I'm the only one who thought to come upstairs."

"Smart girl." I worry a little about the talk she might have heard. I haven't dated anyone since freshman year when I realized I didn't have the time or energy for that while playing college ball, but I'm not ignorant to the rumors and talk that have me sleeping with or paired up with a different girl every week. Not true, by the way. Girls are too exhausting to go through them like Joel does.

She rolls her eyes. "I just wanted to check on you. I saw you favoring the leg as you went up the stairs.

"I'll be all right. Feels better already. So, why no boyfriend? I haven't heard any chatter, but I'm not blind."

"You have the weirdest way of asking a question that feels like it isn't really a question."

I cross my arms behind my head and wait for her to answer.

"I've dated a little, but nothing serious."

I'm content to keep her to myself in my room. Hell, I didn't even want to party before she showed up, but Blair isn't an easy nut to crack. Maybe the atmosphere downstairs and another drink or two will loosen her up. And I don't mean that in a crass way. I'm more interested in learning something about her than getting in her pants. At least for tonight.

"You ever seen a six-six guy do a keg stand?" I ask as I stand and hold out my hand to her.

She puts her delicate hand in mine. "No."

"Let's go find Joel then. It should be just about showtime."

I wrap an arm around her shoulders and make sure to lean some weight on her so she feels like she's helping me. Part of me does it to claim her, self-ish man that I am. Mostly, though, I just want an excuse to touch her.

Joel is exactly where I expected him to be—the center of fucking attention on the back patio. Girls hang off either side, and he's telling one of the five stories he tells every damn time he gets drunk. He stops mid-sentence when he spots Blair and me.

"Reynolds!" He calls out my name and lifts the bottle in his hand. "About time that you two lovebirds decided to show your faces."

I grin but feel Blair shrink a little in my arms. Fucking Joel. "Don't be jealous that I got the hottest girl on my arm."

It's a dick thing to say, considering the two on his, but I'll trade their annoyance to make Blair feel less unsure. I nudge us through to an outdoor patio set. "Shaw, wanna give me and Blair your seats?"

He growls at me and doesn't budge.

"Come on man, I need to get off my foot."

He nods to the girls next to him, and they leave slowly, taking their damn time as he glares at me.

"They always do what you say?" Blair asks when we are seated.

"I wish. The freshman are the worst. Takes half the season to get their egos in check."

"Who keeps yours in check?"

"Ball busters like you."

I pull her closer so she's all but on my lap. She doesn't resist, and my dick starts making plans. A girl stumbles past us, covering her mouth like she is about to puke, and Blair and I watch in combined horror and fascination as she moves like lightning into the house.

"Not exactly how I pictured our first date."

"This is a date?" Her voice borders on panic.

"Kinda feels like one. We're hanging out together, and I plan to try to kiss you at the end of the night."

"No," she states adamantly and turns to face me. "You don't fall into a date. A date is planned . . . intentional."

"That right?"

"Yes." She leans back into me. "Now, ask me on a real date."

I chuckle. "Ball buster."

She shrugs, telling me she isn't budging on the subject. Not that I mind, exactly, but I haven't been on a real date since . . . well, I can't remember, but it probably involved high school and a dark movie theater where I could try to cop a feel.

"Go out with me."

It's her turn to laugh. "Was that a question or a command?"

"Blair Olson, will you go out with me?"

She shrugs again. "Yeah, I guess so."

This girl. "But, uh, even though this isn't a real date, I'm still kissing you later."

"Promise?" She turns her head to face me, bringing our lips inches apart.

I stare at her mouth as she moistens her lips like she's waiting for me to make a move. Instead of answering with words, I capture her face with both hands and pull her to me. What I'd planned to be a quick kiss—a taste of the promise I made—turns serious fast. There's nothing quick or innocent when it comes to my response to this girl. She hums into my mouth, and I deepen the kiss, not giving any fucks about making out in the middle of a party.

My dick aches as she molds her body to mine and wraps her arms around my neck. We're as close as we can get without lying down on the floor and going at it. I weigh that scenario out in my head before breaking the kiss. "Think we should probably go back upstairs if you want to continue this."

Please say yes. Please say yes. Yep, I'm cool as a cucumber on the outside but straight up begging on the inside. Her eyes dart from my mouth to the party, taking in what we've done and where we are. She looks more stunned than embarrassed, but then she pulls away and runs shaky fingertips across her lips.

"I should go."

Well, hell.

"But pick me up tomorrow night for our date?"

FIFTEEN

Blair

"He's here." I read the text saying as much and smooth my dress down. I do a final turn side to side to see myself in the mirror from every angle.

Vanessa lies on her bed, watching me obsess. "Want me to go downstairs and ask him what his intentions are?"

I laugh, easing some of the nerves that have taken over my shaky hands. "As entertaining as that would be, maybe we should wait until at least the second date to scare him off."

Or until I get laid. I know it's probably a terrible idea to sleep with the guy who holds my statistics grade in his hands, but a girl can only be expected to have so much restraint.

"Better to know now before you waste a perfectly good Saturday night."

Most people I know don't even go on real dates, let alone on a Saturday night. Weekend nights are pre-filled with frat parties and nights out at the bar. The rare occasions I've been asked out on a real date, it's always been something mid-week. A Monday night coffee date, a Tuesday dinner, sometimes even a Thursday out together at The Hideout. Fridays and Saturdays are reserved. I'm willing to risk missing a party to go on a date with Wes. One almost certainly ends with me coming back alone, but the other . . . has possibilities.

The sorority house is a two-story home with bedrooms on both floors and a basement with a kitchen and dining room, laundry room, and our chapter room where we hold meetings. Vanessa follows me down the stairs from our second story room and into the first-floor entry way/living room. Men aren't allowed beyond the entryway unattended, so essentially it serves as our "suitor waiting area." It doesn't see a lot of suitors for all the previously mentioned reasons.

Hostess duty is a real thing in the house, a chore shared between all of us, and it seems Molly has jumped at the opportunity to play hostess. She hasn't only let Wes in, she's proceeded to fawn all over him. I hold back a giggle as I watch him lean back away from her as she tries to snake a hand up his arm. An arm that leads to those hands I admire so much. He looks up as I appreciate my first glimpse of him in date attire—a black T-shirt, dark denim jeans, and tennis shoes—a different pair from what I've seen him wear before, and I'm suddenly curious how many pairs of sneakers this guy owns.

I stop at the bottom of the stairs and Vanessa pushes ahead of me. She waltzes up to Wes and eyes him carefully.

"You gonna give me the talk, maybe show me your gun collection before you let me take our girl out?"

"Nah, I don't think it's necessary to tell you I'll either personally kick your ass or pay someone to do it for me if you hurt *my* girl. I'm sure it's also not necessary to tell you that a badass chick like Blair deserves a gentleman. Where are the flowers? Chocolate covered strawberries?"

I groan, and Wes looks embarrassed. V, however, keeps going.

"I expect that, for the rest of the evening, you bring you're A game. I'm talking door-opening, attentive, no-looking-at-other women, hold-her-hand, chivalrous shit."

"Okay." I step in front of Vanessa and take Wes's arm. "I think we have it from here."

Wes chuckles and lets me lead him to the door. I give V a small wave over my shoulder. Her intentions are good. She knows enough about the shit David pulled to understand why going out with someone new is both nerve-wracking and exciting. We've almost made it outside when Wes stops abruptly and turns. V still stands in the doorway watching us.

"Don't worry about our girl. I'm well aware of just how badass she is."

Wes leads me to a small black SUV and opens the door for me. I flush, assuming he's following V's orders. "Don't let Vanessa get in your head. She's—"

But my protest is cut short. He winks and leans in. "Would have opened the door for you either way. It gives me more time to check you out. You look amazing."

"Thank you. You too."

Wes drives us to a small bistro on the outskirts of town. It's well out of the three-block radius that most university students venture out of, and I wonder if it's a coincidence or if he's purposely taken me somewhere we won't be seen.

"I've never been here," I say as he helps me out of the car. A blue awning welcomes us, and inside, I'm surprised to find the décor a mix of local sports memorabilia and amateur artwork. Canvases are hung artfully around the small space with the artists' names boldly displayed on gold plaques underneath. Jerseys ranging from tee-ball size to high school are lined up on one wall like a walk through a lifetime of an athlete. It's a bizarre design, but it feels welcoming none the less.

"Hey, Wes Reynolds." A man with a mess of unruly gray hair that makes him look like a mad scientist appears from behind the counter. His smile falls, and he pauses. "Did you get the days mixed up? Game is next week."

"Nah, came here to eat." Wes places a hand at my back. Those long fingers splay out across my lower back. The heat of the contact makes me feel secure and possessed all the way down to my toes. "Cal, this is Blair. Blair, this old man is Cal."

"She's with you?" Cal gives Wes a shocked look and then tosses a wink in my direction. "Honey, he didn't kidnap you, did he? You're free to go. I have a bat under the counter here and I'd love an excuse to take some practice swings."

Wes snorts and lifts his foot. "The boot is off, old man. You can't catch me now."

Cal's expression softens, and he rounds the counter, zeroed in on Wes's leg. "You're really back? Coach letting you practice and everything?"

Wes nods. "Yep, all the way back. Even let me play the exhibition game last night."

"Well, I'll be damned. Don't tell Mason or he'll be pissed we missed it." He looks to me apologetically. "Sorry for the language. My boy loves to watch Wes play. Thought we were gonna have an angry teenager on our hands this season, and trust me, that would have been good for no one."

"Those your son's jerseys?" I ask, pointing to the multi-colored, multi-numbered shirts.

"Sure are. Mason's a baseball player, but he loves watching basketball."

"Kid's gotta wicked curve ball," Wes adds.

Cal beams with pride. "Your table is open." He nods toward the small seating area.

As Wes leads me to *his* table, I ask the obvious questions. "You have a table? What is this place?"

Wes throws his arm over the back of the booth, looking as comfortable as if this really is his table. "Cal's wife owns a cleaning service and does some work for Joel's family."

He looks up sheepishly.

"Which means she cleans The White House." I connect the dots.

He nods. "She started bringing by food, got us hooked on the grilled cheese and homemade pies. Z and I started coming here to get our fix. So, yeah, I have a table."

He winks, and I'm a total goner. Instead of trying to impress me by taking me to a restaurant where we would have maybe shared a bottle of wine and asked about the daily specials, he brought me to a hole-in-the-wall bistro that requires him to drive off campus and where he has his own table. This feels so much more real.

Cal brings us menus and a pitcher of iced tea, which Wes pours for both of us before almost draining his own glass.

"Best damn iced tea this side of Kansas."

I must be staring at him with a perplexed expression because he looks around and then asks, "What? Got something on my face?"

"No. I'm just trying to figure you out. What's the game he mentioned?"

"Mason has a home game next week."

"And you're going?"

"Wouldn't miss it."

"So, you help your teammates study, you tutor failing students in your spare time—"

"That one was not my choice, if I remember correctly," he points out.

"You attend high school baseball games and support local businesses . . . you're like a decent guy under that arrogant, egotistical exterior."

He holds a finger up to his lips. "Shh, not so loud."

"No, honestly. It's hot."

His mouth pulls into a big smile. "Well, if you put it that way."

"What's your family like back in Kansas?"

He visibly stiffens, but the smile only falls for a second before it's back. "If I tell you we had Sunday dinners every week and I call my mom every day is that going to get me extra points?"

As if he needs them.

"Depends on if it's true."

A tall kid with shaggy hair desperately in need of a haircut brings our food to the table. Wes stands to shake his hand. "Mason, how's it going? How's the arm?"

Mason bobs his head and cradles his arm protectively. "Good. I'm starting next week."

"I'll be there."

Mason's face shows his excitement, but he gives a one shoulder shrug like he's too cool for school.

"Mason, this is my friend Blair."

I offer a wave. "Nice to meet you. Good luck next week."

Mason does some sort of blush, nod, wave before he disappears into the back.

"Good kid," Wes says as we dig into our food. "Parents too. They're at every game, home and away. I know it can't be easy working the hours they do, but they make it work."

"Do your parents make it to many games? Must be hard being so far away."

He doesn't look up as he answers. "They'll be there if we make it to the Final Four."

All right, that seems to be a touchy subject. I let him lead the conversation after that, which includes him asking me the most random questions about myself.

How the coffee shop quotes came about, my favorite songs and books and television shows. I can barely get in a question back as he fires them off one after the other. It's surface-level stuff, but one thing I learn for sure about Wes Reynolds is that, despite the lack of information he gives me about himself, he's damn good at making me feel special and wanted.

Wes

I drive back to campus after dinner, but I'm not ready to end the night, so I park at the house and then usher her across the street to Ray Fieldhouse. Going inside would only lead to me kissing her, and trust me, I want that, but I promised this girl a date.

"Tell me something about yourself that has nothing to do with basketball."

I gape. Something that doesn't pertain to basketball. What does that leave? And when was the last time anyone asked about me without mentioning basketball? It became part of my identity somewhere along the way and separating it from me leaves . . . *someone I don't recognize.*

"What were you like in high school? What are your parents like? What's your favorite color? What do you want to do after college?"

"That's quiet an interrogation. I'll give you one. My favorite color is orange. I like the new addition to your bracelets, by the way." I pull at the orange string tied around her wrist. One of about twenty on her arm. All of them are different colors, and some are faded and frayed, but the orange one looks new.

"Thank you."

"What's up with the bracelets? Do they stand for something?"

"A friend makes them for me. For us. Friendship bracelets. It's sort of our thing. I started making them for us in middle school, and we've worn them ever since."

"Girl friend or guy friend?" I ask, feeling insanely jealous at the prospect of her having that sort of attachment to some other guy. It's ridiculous because whatever we're doing is casual. That's all I have time for right now, no matter how cool of a chick Blair is or how much I wish I had more time to really get to know her and date her like she deserves.

Vanessa was right about one thing—Blair deserves all of it, all the romance, and I'm not that guy. Maybe after the season, but nothing can get in the way of getting back to the Final Four.

"Her name is Gabby. Wait, how did this get turned around? You're supposed to be telling me about you."

"I'd rather talk about you."

"A question for a question then. Where in Kansas did you grow up?"

"Just outside of Kansas City. You?"

"I'm from Succulent Hill, it's a couple of hours south of here. You have any siblings?"

I shake my head.

"I have an older brother. He lives in Phoenix and is married with two adorable kids."

"What's your greatest fear?"

She balks, thrown by the deep question. I can almost see the answer on the tip of her tongue, but she holds back. "I don't know."

"You don't strike me as someone who isn't self-aware. What scares you?"

"Failing." Her voice comes out quiet, barely a whisper. "And letting people down."

Silence falls between us. I get that fear because it's tied so closely to my own. What if I can't get the team whipped into shape? What if Z is looked over for a big NBA deal because his team lets him down? Yeah, I get the fear of failure. Guilt washes over me for being such an ass about helping her with statistics. It obviously is as important to her as basketball is to me.

"Come on, let me show you something."

The gym is empty and dark. I love it this way. I love it packed full of people on game day, too, but no athlete gets that without a lot of days and nights with only the echo of the ball bouncing off the wooden floor.

I lead her up the stairs to the very top and we sit on the blue plastic seats so we can take in the darkened gym.

She's quiet and pensive, as if maybe she's trying to figure out why we're here. Or maybe she is counting down the seconds before she can make a run for it. Bringing a girl to a deserted gym probably is not on the top one hundred best first dates.

"This is my greatest fear." I lift my arms on either side.

"Bad seats?" she jokes.

"Being a spectator and watching the game from up here, smart ass. It's my final year, and I'm not ready for ball not to be the center of my life."

It's terrifying, actually. No, terrifying doesn't seem like a strong enough word. Anxiety wracks my body when I think of being one of those guys watching from the sidelines, talking about the good ole days. As a kid, it felt so far away, but every day, I get closer to it all going away, and I don't know what that looks like. Don't even want to think about it yet. One final season. This is it. This is my moment to soak it all in. I can deal with the rest later.

"Have you thought at all about what you'll do next year?"

I shrug. "Not really. I know I should be thinking about it, making a plan, but I just can't. I need to focus on the season and the season alone, and when it's over, I'll figure out what's next. Speaking of, I don't know any way to say this that doesn't make me sound like a conceited prick, so I'm just going to say it."

She raises both eyebrows but nods for me to continue. "Dating isn't really an option for me right now. Vanessa is right, you deserve more than anything I can give you."

"So, this is our first and last date?" Her voice is filled with humor. Not what I expected.

"I like hanging out with you. I'd like to see more of you, but I can't make any promises beyond that."

"Vanessa means well, but what she wants for me and what I want aren't the same thing. I've dated guys who promised me the world and didn't make good on it. I appreciate your honesty, and I get it." She grabs my hand and interlaces our fingers. I've avoided touching her too much tonight, because I'm finding that, with Blair, each touch only makes me want her more. "You have an incredible gift. I don't know if I've ever loved anything as much as you love basketball, and I can't pretend to understand your fear, but I know the things I'm most scared of tend to be the things that push me the most. No risk, no reward. So that's how I'm choosing to look at whatever this is between us."

"You're smarter than you look."

"That's the nicest thing you've ever said to me."

I shake my head. I don't know what I'm doing on a real date, acting like a gentleman and talking about fears and life goals, but the time I spend with Blair feels so much more substantial than even the best of fucks I've had with other girls. "No. *This* is the nicest thing I've ever said to you. I think you might end up being the best thing that ever happened to me."

She blushes, and I wonder if I've put my foot into my mouth or scored points. I stand and offer her my hand. "Come on."

With her small hand cupped in mine, we walk back to the basketball house. It turns out this dating thing isn't so bad. I've almost even forgotten about sex while I've learned more about what makes Blair tick. Nah, that isn't true, but I did enjoy myself more fully clothed than I ever imagined I would.

Joel bounds down the stairs dressed to go out when he spots us. "Hey, it's Bless."

We share a confused look.

"Blair and Wes. Bless. You know, it's like your couple name."

Blair giggles. "I guess it could be worse, our couple name could be Weir."

Joel slaps me on the back as he passes us on his way to the door.

"Don't get into any trouble," I warn. "We have practice in the morning."

"Yes, Dad," he calls and then, as if just remembering, he calls out, "Oh, hey, Blair, how'd your test turn out?"

She looks shell shocked, and I shoot Joel a glare.

"Don't worry, I'm sure you did great. Z and I both passed."

He leaves, and Blair turns to me. "Grades are up? Up where? How do you know?"

"O'Sean posts them on the student portal before he hands them back."

I lead her to my room and hand her my iPad so she can log in and check her grade.

Tension hangs heavy in the room while she pulls up her grade and then sighs. "I got an A," she says like she almost doesn't believe it. "Oh my God, I really got an A!"

I smile and say a silent thank you to the math gods. Then nix that because I did this. Props to myself. "Congratulations."

She hands the tablet back to me and eyes me warily. "You weren't going to tell me grades were up, were you?"

"I was planning on mentioning it about the time I dropped you off."

She punches my arm playfully.

"I had faith in you . . . well, and in my excellent tutoring."

I toss the iPad onto my bed and wrap my arms around her waist, drawing her against me.

"You were okay, I guess," she says, her voice husky and tight as it travels straight to my balls.

"Admit it." I lean down and let my lips linger just over hers. "Admit I'm a good tutor."

Instead of answering, she closes the space between us and brings her mouth to mine. I consider pulling back and making her say it for all of a second before her soft tongue brushes against mine, I'm lost and exactly where I should be all at once.

She threads her arms up and laces them behind my neck, forcing her up on her tiptoes and putting her flush against me. Not daring to break away from her, I mumble, "I'm taking your non-answer as confirmation."

She chuckles into my mouth in response and then pulls back, breathless and flushed and sexy as hell. "If I admit you're a good tutor, will you wear those sexy glasses again?"

"You think my glasses are sexy?" She drops onto the bed, and I grab my reading glasses from my desk. If I'd known that tidbit sooner, then I'd have been playing it to my advantage already. "You mean, these glasses?"

Her eyes light up and her tongue darts out to wet her lips. She gives the faintest nod before sitting up on her knees and reaching for me. "You're like the best of both worlds—hot jock meets hot nerd."

"All I just heard was you calling me hot."

She rolls her eyes. "Don't act like you don't know it."

"Oh, *I* know it." I brace myself over her and look into her brown eyes, which dance with amusement. "I'm just happy to hear you agree. Makes my next play a little less risky."

I kiss her and tumble us back onto the bed. My glasses are getting in the way. I've never made out with a girl while wearing them before, but then again, I've never had one react like this to my need to see clearly. Most girls are far more interested in the jock side than the nerd side. Or maybe I just never let anyone see anything but the jock. Until Blair, I wasn't exactly winning girls over with my *brain*.

Eager limbs and mouths tangle together. Neither of us wastes any time giving into the electrical pull between us. I run a palm up and down the leg she's draped over me, ankle to thigh and back. Blair hums as her breasts rub against my pecs, hard nipples poking through the material of her little black dress.

An angel and a devil sit on either side of my shoulder, or more accurately a little Vanessa and a little me. Vanessa's warning about Blair deserving a gentleman isn't lost. Sure, I've cleared my conscience by letting her know I can't commit to anything serious, but she isn't the kind of girl you sleep with and never call again.

Our kisses are frantic, and her hips rock into me, beckoning me to do something with the raging hard-on pressing into her. Trailing my fingers back up her leg, I let them slide under her skirt and to the lacy material of her underwear. No wait, it's a thong. Christ, this girl. I cup her ass and growl. *Mine.* Serious or not, I'm *serious* about this ass.

When my fingers slide under the scrap of material covering her pussy, she falls back onto the bed, arching her whole body into my palm. Her eyes flutter open and lock onto me. "Oh God, I think I might come just watching you. The way you're looking at me right now and with those glasses."

She sighs, emphasizing how close she is, and my chest shakes with a silent laugh as I move one finger inside her. "Just watch me then."

She does exactly that as her body trembles under my touch. I'm mesmerized by this girl. Her heart hammers in her chest, and she whimpers and pants, squeezing around my fingers and moaning loudly as she finds her release.

Her eyes close behind dark lashes, and she whispers my name on a sigh.

"That was the hottest thing I've ever seen," I say, hearing the wonder in my own words. Damn.

"Ditto," she mumbles without opening her eyes.

Music starts to play from another room, and the bass vibrates the wall. "I think Z might be trying to drown out your sex sounds."

Her eyes pop open, and she pushes up onto one elbow. "Oh my God, he can hear us?"

I shrug. "Well, I can sure as shit hear his music, so it goes to reason . . ."

"You could have warned me or, I don't know, gagged me."

A gag? As hot as that sounds, no way I'd want to miss out on hearing the way she responds to my touch. "I'll remember that for next time. Speaking of, when can I see you again?"

She buries a smile into the crook of my neck. "Will you wear the glasses again?"

Hell, I'd forgotten I was wearing them. "Any time you want."

SIXTEEN

Wes

"Shaw take Reynold's spot."

My foot is killing me, but I still resent the substitution. I take a seat on the sidelines next to coach.

"How's your foot?" he asks, keeping his eyes glued forward watching the guys run through our plays against a full court defense. Our season opener is Sunday, and the team isn't where I want it to be. Coach's face tells me he feels the same.

"It's fine," I grit out.

"Doesn't look fine out there. You're favoring it. Stay off it, ice it, check in with the trainers." He finally looks at me, taking his eyes from the action on the court. Concern, or maybe just disappointment, etches his features. "We need you ready."

"Yes, sir."

Coach blows the whistle, and the guys stop as he starts barking at them about lazy defense.

Hanging my head, I welcome the pain in my foot. It reminds me that I have one season left. This is it. I don't have delusions about playing in the NBA. Maybe I could make it as a late pick, but it just hasn't ever felt like the right path for me. There are better, faster, and stronger point guards out there. My mental game is what's kept me competing at this level. That, and a whole damn lot of dedication. Guys that make it beyond college, though? They have it all—mental, dedication, and raw talent. Guys like Z.

The man himself takes a seat next to me and wipes a towel across his shaved head. I know he's here as a silent comfort, but I can't bring myself to feel anything but anger and self-pity.

"This fucking sucks." I sound like a bratty teenager, but Z only nods with a grim acceptance of what I'm saying.

"Did you see that behind the back pass Shaw tried to pull off? Crazy kid is gonna cost us games out there trying to be the next Jason Williams."

I hear the question in his statement. "Fuck. I'll work with him. He has talent. He's just trying to force too much too fast."

Z tosses the towel and stands. "The guys are going to Theta house tonight. You in?"

"Nah. Blair and I are going to watch Mason play. He's starting pitcher tonight."

The big center grins, which is a rare sight on his serious face. "Another date with Blair. She sleeping over this time? Do I need to make myself scarce to avoid your headboard banging against our shared wall? I could stay in Joel's room."

"I think the theater room couch is a more sanitary spot than Joel's room."

We both laugh and cringe at the same time because Joel getting the master on the other end of the house was probably the best for all the roommates. No one wants to be within hearing distance of his room. The guy's room is a revolving door.

"You're a lucky man." The words hang between us and the irony isn't lost on me that we both seem to be coveting the other's life. I never imagined Z wanting anything other than ball. "Blair is great. I'll find somewhere else to stay tonight so you don't have to worry about me listening in. Enjoy the night with your girl. Hers is probably a much better shoulder to cry on right now than mine, anyway."

"I don't know, big guy, I think I might feel much safer in your big beefy arms." I bat my eyelashes at him and the tension lifts.

"You're the best point man I've ever played with."

He walks off, and I'm glad he doesn't try to tell me everything will be okay or some other cheesy cliché. The game is a few days away, and I'm having serious doubts that my foot can hold up through forty minutes of play.

When I get to the house, Blair is already there. She's on the sofa, bare feet pulled up and crossed, she's the picture of comfort. I could get used to coming home and finding her here. I love that she feels at ease with my friends, it's just another way she positions herself above the rest.

Joel stands in the middle of the living room, turning with his arms held out to his sides like he's a princess twirling in her fancy new dress. Except this Latino princess holds a basketball in one outstretched hand.

"What the hell is going on in here? A fashion show?"

He tosses the ball at my head, which I catch because I've got reflexes like a cat.

"Blair is helping me pick a shirt for tonight."

Ball in hand, I take a seat next to Blair and pull her closer before delving any further into whatever messed-up, dress-up game is going on.

"Why the obsession over attire tonight?"

It isn't that Joel doesn't always dress nice, but he's never asked me, or anyone else I know, if we approved of his outfit. Dudes don't do that. He'll be asking if his butt looks big next.

"He struck out getting a number this afternoon and is now all bent out of shape." Nathan's voice is filled with humor and judging by the death glare Joel shoots him, I know it's true.

That makes me smile. "Aww, you poor, poor schmuck."

"That isn't what this is about. It was one girl. One girl." He flashes his index finger, but he sounds so desperate and whiny we burst into laughter.

"Fuck you all," he says but smiles. He runs his hands down the shirt and rolls the sleeves up on either side. "So, this one is good?"

Blair nods. "You look hot. Black is a good color for you. It gives you the whole dark and mysterious thing with your skin tone and dark hair."

"Easy, now." I pull her fully onto my lap.

Joel winks at her. "*Muchas gracias, linda.*"

"Yeah, definitely do that." She bounces with excitement. I don't think she knew he spoke Spanish, and she's obviously a fan. As is the rest of the female population when he busts it out.

"Do what?"

"Talk in Spanish. Not all the time . . . but drop it in casually. Accents are sexy."

"All right, all right." I squeeze her waist. "I think your work here is done."

She kisses me on the cheek as she stands. "Actually, I just stopped by to see if I could rain check on dinner. I need to finish a paper before Mason's game."

This girl's dedication to schoolwork is insane. "Sure. I'll text you before I head over."

She winks and gives a little wave, and I watch her fine ass until the door closes behind her.

"Soo . . ." Joel's tone reeks of a loaded statement on deck. "You and Blair . . . *things getting serious?*"

"What? No, it's just . . ." I don't know how to finish that statement.

"If you're having sex, then it's getting serious. You wouldn't be mixing business with pleasure unless it's serious."

"I'm not mixing—you know what? I'm not even gonna go there."

"Wait, wait, wait. You haven't slept with her?"

"Is that really so ludicrous? I've only known her a few weeks." Fine it's bonkers that I've spent so much time with her and we still haven't had sex, but I don't want to admit that it's a big deal.

"Uh-huh. Uh-huh." He scratches his chin and wears a shit-eating grin. "So, does that mean tonight is the night?"

"We're going to a high school baseball game, not looking to do jail time for indecent exposure."

"Don't bullshit me. Tonight's the night." Joel practically sings the words as he dances around.

Nathan draws a heart with both index fingers. "She completes you."

"Fuck off, both of you."

"I gotta shower." Nathan stands and hustles toward the staircase.

"Hurry up. I'm leaving in fifteen, and I need to make a stop for condoms," Joel yells after him and then looks to me. "You good? Need me to put some in your nightstand?"

My answer is to lob the ball at his head.

"Okay, fine. I'll lay off. You probably need to go take care of business anyway. Since she bailed on dinner, you have time to rub one out before and after your shower."

I groan. "For the love of all that is holy."

"What? Please tell me you aren't planning to show up to the game without clearing your head?" His shocked expression makes his eyes go ridiculously wide, mouth gaped open. "Dude, you go in there without taking care of business, and you're gonna embarrass yourself and the whole male population."

I shake my head and let it hang down between my knees. Is this how a panic attack starts? I seriously need new friends—the kind who don't interfere in my damn business.

SEVENTEEN

Blair

"**S**o how does it work? Do you remember everything you've ever heard or read?"

Wes shakes his head, eyes focused on the pitching mound where Mason warms up. "No, not everything. Some things I remember more easily than others, same as everyone else."

"You just recited all the US and French presidents in order. That isn't the *same as everyone else*," I mock his blasé tone.

"The way I remember things is different. I see it in more detail. I can recite the presidents because I spent a year in fourth grade staring at a time-line banner the teacher posted above the white board. My memory allows me to remember it more clearly than other people, that's all."

"So annoying and hot at the same time," I mumble under my breath.

"What was that?" He takes his eyes off the field and leans in. "Did you say I was hot again?"

"Your brain is hot. The rest of you"—I let my gaze rake over him and I purse my lips—"is okay, I guess."

"What if I told you I can recall in vivid detail every outfit you've ever worn."

I narrow my gaze. No way that's possible. Do guys even notice clothes beyond the amount of skin they show?

He takes my silence as a challenge.

"It's true. The day you called me a dumb jock you were wearing a yellow dress. Your hair was down, and you looked fine as fuck pacing the sidewalk and practically stomping your feet to pry information out of me."

I cover my face. "That's so embarrassing."

"Wanna know what else I've committed to my amazingly hot memory?"

By the way he says it, I have a few guesses that make my heart lurch. "What?"

He leans in until our sides touch from shoulder to knee. He looks at my mouth and brings the pad of his thumb to the corner. "The sounds you make when I touch you. When I kiss you here, you make this adorable little hum."

The noise sings from my throat on command.

"And when I touch you here . . ." Long fingers wrap around my thigh and move up until his palm stretches from hip to the bundle of nerves, which is throbbing at the prospect of what his magnificent mouth and hands can do.

"Wes." His name comes out sounding more like a plea than a warning.

He grins and moves his hand back to a more appropriate spot on my knee. Damn appropriateness. "You say my name in the sexiest way."

We're still staring, holding each other hostage with that promise of an end to the sexual tension banging between us, when the umpire calls out, "Let's play ball."

We watch Mason pitch six innings before he's pulled to rest his arm. Six excruciatingly long innings, where I spend more time tracking touches and glances than the strikes thrown from the pitching mound. I meet Maria, Mason's mom, and we make our apologies to her and Cal as we duck out before the end of the game.

"Can I convince you to stay tonight? We have early practice tomorrow before we leave for our game up state. I won't be back until Sunday night."

Convince me? Is this guy serious?

"Okay." I one word it to avoid the squeal that threatens to embarrass me.

"Can we swing by the sorority house on the way? I need to at least grab a toothbrush and a change of clothes."

"All right, but I'm coming inside with you. I want to see your room." He turns the car in that direction, and his excitement about our impending sleepover makes my insides tingle.

"You know you aren't technically allowed in my room," I say as I walked us to the side entrance, which is the closest one to my room and hopefully the easiest to sneak him in. "So, be quiet and try to blend in." I wave a hand in front of him and then giggle because there is no way he is going to blend in.

Thankfully, the house is empty since it's a weekend, and I shut the door, closing us into the safety of my room. I busy myself grabbing the essentials for a sleepover while Wes roams around my room taking it all in. He looks absolutely ridiculous in my and Vanessa's ultra girly room with the low ceilings and purple walls.

"Who's this?" He lifts a frame, my and Gabby's faces pressed together as we smile into the camera. It was taken right after the accident, and the fresh scars on her face would make me hate the picture if it weren't for the big smile on her lips. It was the first genuine one I remember seeing after the accident.

The pity in his voice makes me irrationally defensive, and I take the frame from him and place it back onto my desk. "My best friend Gabby."

He looks guilty at my reaction. "The one who makes the bracelets?"

I nod. "She was in a car accident senior year. That is how she got the scars."

"I'm sorry."

I can hear the sincerity in his voice. "Thank you. She's actually why I want to rule the world. It was her dream for us to be lady bosses."

"She here at Valley?"

"Sort of. She takes online classes and lives back in our hometown."

He places a kiss on my forehead and takes the bag I dropped onto the floor. "Ready?"

"Yep."

"Bless is out," he says and winks.

There are those tingles again. I secretly love that he uses our ridiculous couple name. Bless is out. Bless ready to get it on.

EIGHTEEN

Blair

The White House is empty when we return. Wes tells me we have the place to ourselves for the night, and we settle into the theater room, legs and bodies intertwined. The television is on, but I have no idea what we're watching. I'm lost to him. His kisses, his hands, his words.

"Why'd you start playing basketball?" I ask as his calloused palms caress my calves and move up, higher and higher but never quite reach the apex of my desire before moving back down. My hands have taken on a mind of their own, tracing the lines of his stomach and arms. If he doesn't tear off my clothes soon, I'm going to combust. I can feel how much he wants me—it's pressing against my stomach, but he makes no move to take off my clothes. I thought sleep over was code for sex.

"Girls, obviously."

I swat at him. "Seriously."

"I don't know. I can't really remember a time I didn't play. My parents worked a lot, so they overcompensated by putting me in every extra-curricular activity possible from rock climbing to piano to origami . . . you name it, I tried it."

"Origami?"

He nods, a big proud smile on his face. "Yep, but basketball was the first thing I was really good at. I guess it sounds lame, but basketball was something that got me attention. My dad was always working long hours, coming home about the time I was getting ready for bed at night, and then all of a sudden, he was around more, getting home in time to shoot hoops outside and coming to practices. He was proud of me, and I wanted to keep that feeling. I loved it, don't get me wrong, but I loved it more because of the way people treated me. The attention didn't last, of course, I mean not from my parents, but the way other people praised me filled that void."

"I don't think I was ever that good at anything," I admit with a small laugh. "I was okay at sports, got decent grades, but it must be really incredible to have a true talent for something."

"I have other talents." His fingers trace up and down my sides in slow movements that leave me equal parts wanting more and wanting just this. "These origami fingers can do magical things."

"I may have already noticed how good you are with your hands." My voice is filled with want and desire even to my own ears.

He dips his head, his lips finding my collarbone. "It isn't just my hands that are talented."

I respond with something witty and sexy, I'm sure, but the words don't register above our combined sighs.

His phone vibrates in his pocket, and I'm so keyed up I nearly groan at the hum of pleasure against my hip. "Let me just make sure it isn't one of the guys needing a ride or something."

I pry myself off him reluctantly, and Wes fishes out his phone. "Fucking Joel," he mutters and stands before he adjusts himself—no shame. Wes lets out an audible sigh. "Give me five?"

"Everything okay?"

"Yeah. I just need to take care of something."

Wes leaves me, and I sit, tapping my toes and impatiently waiting for him to return. I do a swipe under my eyes in case any eye makeup has smudged, run my fingers through my hair, check the bra and panty situation to make sure they aren't all twisted. I've been wearing my best lingerie for weeks now just in case.

Minutes pass, and I listen for any indication of what he's up to. What in the world could he possibly be doing?

The answer should be me. He should be doing *me*.

An idea forms, and I hesitate for half a second before bounding up the stairs to Wes's room and grabbing my overnight bag.

There's no sign of Wes. Maybe he went to Joel's room for something? I quickly pull the shirt I'm wearing off and then pull on the Valley jersey.

Without a mirror, I can't properly check my reflection, but I have a feeling Wes is going to enjoy seeing me wear his name and number.

I'm contemplating removing my shorts and just making my intentions ultra-obvious, but he appears in the doorway. He's holding his phone and tapping away like he's sending a text. When he sees me, he stops short, fingers still over the screen. "Holy shit."

"You like?" I turn so show off the back and, yes, my ass because I know it looks fantastic in these shorts.

"Come here."

We meet in the middle, and I give myself over to him. His touch, his kisses, the smell of him . . . I breathe him in. Everything moves slowly, he's taking his time as if there's no rush when I'm so keyed up I might die if things don't move faster. I'm forcing myself to let him take the lead, and it's as if his restraint is something of Gods and not mere mortals like myself.

I whimper when he finally brings two rough palms up under my shirt, but just as his hands graze the bottom of my lacy bra, he pulls back and lets his hands fall to my hips.

The restraint I've been holding on to snaps. "You're either some sort of saint or you just aren't as into me as I'm into you."

He laughs, a deep throaty sound that I feel shake his chest. "I promise you I'm no saint and I'm definitely into you."

"Then what is it? I have my sexiest lingerie on and I'm practically throwing myself at you. Can we please get naked now?"

He groans and pulls at his hair with both hands. "Fucking Joel."

The mention of Joel catches me by surprise. Seems like a weird time to chat about his friend. Maybe their friendship really does know no bounds.

"Did Joel do something? Say something?"

"He just gave me maybe the worst advice ever."

I wait for him to say more, utterly confused.

"This is embarrassing, but I guess I'd rather risk humiliation then have you think I'm not into you. I'm *so* into you—so much so that I took fucking Joel's advice."

"I—"

"Joel lives by the motto that you shouldn't show up on game day without getting your head in the right place." He says it so quick that I'm pretty sure I heard him wrong.

"I'm sorry, what?"

Why the hell are we talking about basketball right now?

"You know . . . clean the pipes, buff the wood, polish the rocket?" He uses both hands to point to his junk. "Joel jerks off before—"

"Ewww, okay. TMI. I do *not* need to know about Joel's pre-game rituals."

"No. Fuck. I'm going to kill him." He takes a deep breath and lets it out. "Joel told me I should jerk off before we had sex. It's been a while, and he was worried about me making an ass of myself." He continues muttering under his breath, but I'm doubled over in laughter.

He finally joins in, and it only eggs me on. I'm laughing so hard tears are streaming down my face while simultaneously wondering if it is the end of romance when you find out the guy you want to have sex with is taking matters into his own hands . . . literally.

"So, just now . . . while I was downstairs?" I motion at his crotch, which sets me off again.

He scrunches his nose like he knows he's said too much. "Fuck, this is humiliating."

I try to rein in my laughter. He's clearly embarrassed. "Guys really do that? You jerk off before having sex for . . . what reason exactly?"

"I know it sounds dumb as fuck now, but Joel was convincing."

"Joel seems like the last person to take relationship advice from."

He runs a hand through his thick hair in frustration. "I really fucking like you, Blair."

"I like you, too, but why does that require . . ." I wave my hand in front of him. There's no way I can bring myself to say it again.

"I panicked. Joel got in my head. I wanted tonight to be perfect. So, yeah, I listened to my douchebag roommate, but don't think for a second that my restraint has anything to do with not wanting you. I fucking want you so much I listened to *Joel.*"

"That's oddly sweet, but I think I'd prefer come in your pants to this jerked off version that has me ready to hump your pillow. I want the perfect, can't-keep-his-hands-off-me, afraid-of-embarrassing-himself-because-he-might-explode-at-any-moment guy I'm falling for. Just you."

"Fuuuuck." He drawls out the word and closes his eyes.

I slide my hands up his chest and link my arms around his neck. "Okay by you?"

He nods and just as I'm feeling fully in control, he has me on the bed and is braced above me. His muscular arms press into the mattress, caging me in as he stares down at me like I'm everything.

He stands and pulls his T-shirt over his head before lying back beside me. Hooking a finger into the V of my shirt, Wes tugs just enough to show a bit more skin. "I really want to see what's underneath, but damn, you look good wearing my jersey."

"The whole point of putting it on was for you to take it off."

He grins and slides his hands to the hem and slowly inches it up as if he wants to delay the surprise underneath. "So beautiful."

As he stares down at me and his navy eyes darken, I fall a little deeper under his spell. He's everything I never knew I wanted or thought to fantasize about. Smart, fun, loyal, and smoking hot. His muscular body moves with elegance and confidence that is as hot as it is commanding.

I'm not nearly as patient as I scramble to get naked and then free him of his jeans and boxer briefs. Maybe I should have aspired to the Joel Moreno life motto, because the sight of Wes's naked body is nearly orgasmic on its own. His penis is the kind of perfection that romance novels are written about.

"Need to study this gorgeous body," he murmurs against my lips. The heat of his gaze rakes over me. True to his words, he looks at me as if he wants to memorize every detail as he trails kisses down my body. He places one at my belly button that sends a tremble down my spine.

"Can you study later . . . or maybe during?"

His smile is slow and cocky. "So impatient."

One long finger trails up my inner thigh and slips inside me, causing my hips to rock into his palm. He fucks me with one finger and then two, circling my clit with his thumb. I open my eyes to find his gaze still hard and studying.

His hands are magic. As my moans fill the silence of his bedroom, his lips find the pulse in my neck, and he sucks hard. My orgasm tears through me at rocket speed, and I call out his name as I shatter.

"Perfection." He dusts kisses down my body, places a kiss on my hip, and then trails back up. "I want to hear you say my name like that again."

He reaches to the nightstand and pulls out a condom, and I watch on greedily as he slips it on. I'll happily say his name any way he wants, as many times as he wants, if he makes me feel like that again.

I stare hard at his beautiful penis as he fists it and guides it to my entrance. I'm mesmerized as our bodies join. He stretches me gloriously, and I let out a sigh of complete contentment.

"You good?"

Good? No. Fan-fucking-tastic.

"Super," I say as I reach up and rub both breasts.

His size and strength and endurance make me realize what I've been missing out on, and I suddenly comprehend the devotion of the jersey chasers.

His eyes stay on me as he pumps in and out at a delicious pace that promises another bone-melting orgasm. I struggle to keep my eyes open, but the way he looks at me, as if somehow this is a big deal even though we've said from the start that this is casual, is as hot as the rest of him. He has promised me nothing but has given me everything.

I push away all thought, letting the sensations overwhelm and pull me under.

"Wes," I say as my lids close with the pressure of my second orgasm.

He slams into me harder grunting out my name as he shudders through his release.

The next morning, I wake to an empty bed. I miss the heat of him immediately. I open my eyes and stretch my limbs, feeling the soreness of last night and bask in it. Wes is gone, which I knew he would be, and the house is quiet. I sit up in his bed and spy my name written on a note on his desk. Pulling the blanket around me, I stand and walk over to it. I pick it up and turn it over, but the note says nothing else. I frown until I spot what's resting behind it—a paper rose folded intricately and perfectly. I lift it and clutch it carefully to my chest. Damn, he really is good with his hands.

NINETEEN

Wes

W e're on a high after winning our first game of the season and end up at The Hideout when we get back to Valley. It's packed, especially for a Sunday night. Blair sits on my lap, and Z and Nathan are across the table from us, arguing over who is getting the next round from the bar.

"I'll get a round. I want to go say hi to Vanessa, anyway."

I let her go, watching as she pushes through to the other side of the bar where Mario and Vanessa sit with a group of baseball guys, including Shaw, who is still on my shit list. Rookie had two turnovers in the six minutes he was on the floor. The same six minutes I sat on the bench and watched in combined frustration and pain.

Nathan's phone rings, and he silences it as he shakes his head. Z glances over and smirks. "Don't ignore your momma, boy. What the hell is wrong with you?"

"I'll call her later," Nathan insists.

Zeke reaches over and picks up the phone, answering it before Nathan can stop him. "Hello, Mrs. Payne. It's Zeke."

Nathan grumbles and reaches for the phone, but Z moves the phone to the other ear. "Thank you, ma'am, I appreciate it. The team played well today. Yeah, your son is right here. Good to talk to you, Mrs. Payne."

He hands the phone over to an angry-looking Nathan.

Jealousy eats at me. I absently check my own phone. Nothing. I feel a bit like a sullen child who is sitting around and wishing his parents would call or text or in some way acknowledge that he had a game today. I know they're a thousand miles away and it isn't like I expect them to make it to every game, but a *good job* or *I'm proud of you* text once in a while would be nice. I guess a hardship of being the parents of an elite athlete is that it gets old watching your kid win trophies and travelling to games every week because somewhere along the way, my parents totally checked out. They probably assumed they'd told me enough times they were proud that they could just stop.

"I think I'll help Blair."

I see the pity in Z's eyes. Nothing gets past him, and I may not express my disappointment in my parents, but he knows me too well not to pick up on it.

Mario slides off the bar stool as I get near. "Congrats on the game. How's the foot holding up?"

"It's getting there," I tell him. It's my new canned answer since it's the only thing people want to hear.

I look past him to Vanessa but missing in action is Blair. Did I pass her? Where'd she go?

"Hey, Vanessa." She eyes me warily, clearly still not convinced that I'm not gonna drop kick her friend's heart. Kiddie gloves are on with Blair. All the way on. I'm doing my best not to screw this up. She's a cool chick, and I like spending time with her. "Where'd our girl go?"

"That douche canoe David grabbed her." She points to the corner of the bar where Blair is talking to a guy I don't know but instantly don't like. He's backed her into a dark space and leers over her in a way that sets all my alarm bells off.

"David?"

"Her ex-boyfriend," Vanessa says. Blair and I haven't gotten into the specifics of our past dating life. She mentioned she dated, but she played it off like it was no big deal. By the way Vanessa looks at me, it's clear Blair left some important things out.

I step toward them, trying to keep an air of calm while I'm nothing but a knot of defensiveness as I approach.

"Everything okay?" I ask, leaving a few feet of space between myself and the back of the prick talking to my girl. Yeah, my girl. I'm regretting not laying down a claim.

Blair's demeanor changes when she sees me. Her shoulders sag in relief but then stiffen as if she feels some weirdness about being caught talking to her ex. David turns with a scowl and gives me a once over.

"Mind your own business. We're having a conversation that doesn't have anything to do with you."

Aww, hell no. I place myself between David and Blair. "My girl looks upset. I'd say that's my business."

His lip curls. "Your girl?" He looks to Blair for verification. I don't bother checking her reaction because I can practically feel anxiety roll off her in waves.

"Wes." I extend a hand, and the bastard glances at my palm and then dismisses it. Dismisses *me*.

"I'll call you tomorrow." With a final patronizing glance, David turns and disappears into the crowd.

I wait until he's completely out of sight before I turn to Blair. "You okay?"

Her hands shake in front of her. "Yes. I'm fine. You didn't need to do that. We were just talking."

I cross my arms and study her. I'm calling bullshit, but I can't decide if she's playing it off because he's an asshole or because she's embarrassed I caught her in a dark corner with another guy. "Friend of yours?"

"We dated last year. He was just asking about classes. I'm sorry if it looked like it was anything."

"No reason to be sorry. You looked upset, and I wanted to make sure everything was good."

"So, that wasn't you peeing all around me?" Her lips pull into a knowing smile, calling me out for referring to her as my girl.

I rub a hand over my jaw. "Might have been a little of that."

"Don't worry." She closes the space between us and throws her arms around my neck. It's her go-to move, and I love the way it presses our bodies together. The contact immediately sends communication down below. Red alert, hot girl is touching you. Yep, I'm fourteen years old again. "I have zero interest in David. He's a total . . ." She waves a hand at my ear like she's grappling for the right word. "Douche canoe."

"You ready to get out of here?" Ex-boyfriends, reminders of parents who don't give a fuck? Yeah, I'm ready to bounce.

She places her hand in mine and tugs. "Bless out."

TWENTY

Blair

"Blair, what is all this? Your bag weighs a ton." Vanessa struggles to move my backpack from the small table at the library so she can sit.

I barely look up from my laptop. "I have a paper due in econ, reading for American literature, and about a million other things before my shift at the café this afternoon."

"You stay at Wes's last night?"

"How do you know? Did you go back to the house?" Screw my paper, if Vanessa knows I wasn't at our place, it means she wasn't with Mario.

"Yeah, I just needed a night off from Mario." She says it flippantly, but the perfectly curled hair and extra makeup speaks volumes.

She's overcompensating.

"Oh no, why? I like Mario." I've done my best to keep my opinions about Vanessa's boyfriend to myself because nothing scares her more than approval, but Mario seems great. I've never seen Vanessa happier.

"It's just too much. *He's* too much. I keep waiting for all his scary flaws to appear. I mean, no man can possibly be as perfect as he is. Seeing David last night reminded me that perfect on the outside hides a whole bunch of crazy on the inside."

Great. The aftermath of Hurricane David continues to unveil more damage. "Mario is nothing like David."

"Or maybe Mario is just good at hiding his crazy like David is."

"What's this really about? David and I have been broken up for months, you've dated other guys since my break up."

"I . . ." She pauses and twists the gold ring she wears on her thumb. "I like him," she says quietly.

I hide my glee that she's finally admitted it. "Then, please, for the love of God, don't let David be the reason you don't trust Mario."

"I was worried you were going to fall back under his spell when I saw you two together. What did he have to say at the bar last night?"

I consider telling her the truth, but if she knew just how calculating and horrible David really is, then she might see that as a sign to steer clear of men, and I don't want that for her. David is an asshole, but he doesn't represent every guy. I sure hope not, anyway.

"Not much. Wes walked over, and David took off."

"I saw that! I was so freaking glad when Wes got between you two. I only wish he'd punched him."

I laugh, mostly because I'd wished that too.

"You aren't thinking of getting back with David then? Because you're finally starting to seem like the old you."

I'm starting to feel like the old me as well. "No, I'm absolutely not getting back together with him. What's more important is when you're going to tell Mario how you feel."

She stands, clearly the interrogation has gone beyond her comfort level because we're talking about her feelings, and V doesn't do feelings. "Why would I do that?"

After she leaves, I spend the next three hours in the library and then hustle over to the café to relieve Katrina. She's beyond frazzled and knee-deep in supplies as she restocks everything.

"Everything okay?"

"My sitter just bailed, and I have to pick up Christian at daycare in ten minutes."

"Go. I have this."

She looks around at the mess, hesitating. I know she'd do the same for me in a heartbeat, so I place my hands on my hips and smile. "Seriously, go. It's no big deal."

"I owe you," Katrina says, hopping over the box and untying her apron.

Monday afternoons are slow after the lunch rush, but Monday evenings are not, so I enjoy a bit of down time stocking shelves and singing along to the cheesy nineties' music playing over the university station.

My mood is high until David walks through the door. His demeanor makes it clear he's here to see me and knew he could catch me alone. I hate the way my body responds like it's a fight or flight moment. I desperately want to be emotionally detached enough for his presence not to send me into panic mode.

"What do you want, David? I'm at work."

"Tall house blend." Black like his soul. "And put one of those inspirational quotes on there for me, would you?" He has the audacity to wink.

I remind myself that killing him would only get me thrown in jail while I get his coffee and write "Choose kindness" onto the cup. "Here ya go."

He looks down at the quote and smiles.

"You're banging the basketball team now, huh?"

Arizona has the death penalty.

Arizona has the death penalty.

"My life isn't your business anymore, David."

"Oh, but it is. Especially if it interferes with our arrangement."

"I've done everything you've asked."

"That bullshit paper you wrote on Chopin got me a B. You're distracted, and it's fucking up my GPA."

"I'm distracted because I'm doing two people's homework."

"I need this one on Friday." He slides me a piece of paper with the details. David's been careful to leave no electronic paper trail. Only paper copies that we both know would easily be dismissed if I ever went to anyone and tried to tell them what was going on. "It better be an A paper, Blair. I'd hate to have to embarrass you in front of your new boyfriend."

The thought of Wes knowing about any of this makes the muffin I ate fifteen minutes ago feel like a brick in my stomach. Trapped and angry, I watch him walk out of the café and vow to end this somehow, someway.

TWENTY-ONE

Wes

Blair and I sit on the floor of the gym while we wait for Z and Joel so we can all study for our next statistics quiz.

"You play over Thanksgiving break?" she asks, clearly surprised by this revelation that we have a tournament the weekend after Turkey Day.

"Yep, it's one of our busiest times. With no school, we get to focus solely on ball. Christmas break is the same."

"So, you don't get to see your family?"

I shake my head but don't meet her eyes as I say, "We get a full week off for Christmas. I'll see them then. I usually go to Joel's house for Thanksgiving. Mama Moreno invites the whole team and anyone else who doesn't have anywhere to go."

She lets out a little huff that's her adorable version of being appalled. "My family is ditching me this year. My brother and sister-in-law invited my parents on a Disney cruise. I think I'm gonna go home to see Gabby, though. Plus, it'll be good to get away for a week." Her tone has bite, and I wonder why she's so anxious to go home to an empty house.

I can't bring myself to feel too sorry for her. Judging by her annoyance, I'd guess this is the first time she hasn't seen her folks during a holiday break. I was probably like that the first time my parents bailed too. Now I'm just indifferent. Well, I'm trying to be. After years of my parents planning vacations that in no way work around my schedule, it's clear they don't care if they see me for Thanksgiving or Christmas.

"Let's do this," Joel calls out as he and Z enter the gym. "I have a date in an hour."

The stuff we're going over tonight doesn't lend itself that well to my usual basketball analogies, but it's good to be on the court with my boys and my girl. When Nathan shows up, clearly bored and looking for something to do, we give up statistics altogether and start running through plays. Blair fills in the place of our power forward, Malone. She's about a foot and a half shorter and a buck fifty lighter, but she's way better to look at.

Damn, it feels good. Nah, feels *right* to be playing around with my roommates and to have Blair here.

"You guys wanna hit The Hideout?" Nathan asks the rest of us as Joel hustles off the court to get ready for his date.

"Negative ghost rider," Z says and shakes his head.

"We could have a pool party," Blair pipes up, looking beyond excited at the possibility. "I've been carrying my swimsuit in my backpack for weeks waiting for an opportunity to get in that pool."

"Pool party it is." Nathan claps his hands together. "I'm gonna invite a few people."

"I'm out." No surprise that Z isn't interested in swimming.

"What about if we set up the projector, put on a movie poolside?"

Z narrows his gaze. "My pick?"

Chuckling, I rack the balls. "Yeah, you can pick."

He hustles off the court, and I reach for Blair so I can wrap my arms around her. "Twenty bucks says we're watching something with Tom Cruise."

She laughs and then we head up to my room to change, and she slips into a hot pink bikini that makes me hard on sight. I don't know how word got out so fast, but when we get down to the pool it's already filled with people. Nathan is in the pool, a cigarette hanging from his lips and a beach ball raised above his head. Z's taken up residence in one of the lounge chairs pulled up in front of the projector and has attracted a circle of girls who are faking interest in *Mission Impossible*.

I lead Blair to the shallow end of the pool, and she wriggles her butt into my crotch and leans against me. We're more spectators than active members of this party, which suits me just fine.

"Last year, where would you have been right now?"

"With V. Before Mario, we were inseparable."

"And what sort of trouble would you two have been getting into on a night like this?"

"We'd have been at one frat party or another." She sighs. "I dated David for most of last year, so we usually went to Sigma."

"Dude seems like an asshat, how'd you two get together?"

"He can be very convincing when he wants something. He showed me what he wanted me to see, and I gobbled it right up. He was sweet and charming at first."

"And then?" My chest tightens with all the shitty things he might've done to my girl. I saw a glimmer of what he was like pissed, and I didn't like it. "He didn't hurt you or anything, right?"

"No, he was never physical. It was little things like he talked shit about everyone, even guys he was tight with. He got mad when I so much as said hello to another guy, and he didn't like me going out with V if he wasn't there, stuff like that. When I'd try to talk to him about it, he made me feel like it was my fault."

"I'm sorry."

She shrugs and turns to face me, wrapping her arms around my waist. "I don't want to waste another second regretting my time with him. I can't take it back, any of it, but I would if I could."

There's more hurt than she's shared, judging by the dark look in her eyes, but far be it for me to push her to relieve her painful past. "Come on, let's dry off and then grab some food. Joel's mom brought by enchiladas and she made me a gallon of sweet iced tea."

"You can't make your own tea?"

"I can; just don't." I pat her ass as she steps out of the pool in front of me.

She grabs her towel and drops onto a lounge chair as she wrings out her hair. Her nipples salute me through her top and when she realizes what I'm staring at, she quickly wraps the towel around her chest. "Perv."

Instead of grabbing my own chair, I pick her up and sit down, placing her between my legs. She leans back against me and then startles when she feels the bulge in my board shorts.

"Your fault," I murmur in her ear and brush a kiss against her shoulder.

Turning, her eyes focus on my crotch as she bites on her bottom lip. She drapes the towel over my lap, and I watch, amused by what she might be planning and a hell of a lot turned on at the endless possibilities.

She slides her hand up the leg of my shorts and curls her fingers around my shaft. I exhale through gritted teeth as my balls draw up tight. It isn't the first time a girl has given me a hand job in public, but it's the first time one did so without the hope of being seen. The way Blair looks at me, it's about me—us. She doesn't want to be caught. She just can't keep her hands to herself, and God, is that hot.

No one is paying us any attention, but I sit upright and pull her closer to better block us just in case. She pumps and squeezes at a pace that already has me teetering on blissful release. She's so beautiful like this. Blair deep in concentration and filled with determination and pep for the task is breathtaking. Her lids are heavy with lust and her breathing labored even though I haven't even touched her. I won't out here. I'm a selfish guy and want her pleasure to remain mine alone.

My hips thrust forward, and a knowing smile pulls at her lips. She hums as if my pleasure were hers, and that little sound is all it takes. Ecstasy jolts through me, and I come with her name on my lips.

Between practice, games, and Blair, the weeks pass in a blur. A blissful blur. Team is playing well and starting to mesh like I knew we could. Even the rookie is annoying me less. Bus rides back from away games are tense when we lose, but tonight, the mood on the bus back from New Mexico State is light. We only get two days off for Thanksgiving break, but it's the most we'll be free from now until the end of the season.

"You're heading home with Blair tomorrow, huh? Does that mean you two have made your relationship official?" Joel tucks his phone into the seat back pocket in a clear sign that he isn't going to let the conversation end with a yes or no answer.

"It isn't like that. She knew I wasn't going to be able to make the trip to Kansas and she felt bad. Her parents aren't even going to be there. They're on some Disney cruise."

As I replay the conversation in my head, I'm sure that part of what I've said is true. She did invite me because she felt guilty I couldn't be with my own family, and she probably felt some sense of obligation to include the guy she's banging.

My reaction is the one that has me worried. I've never been to a girl's house for a holiday. I've been invited, sure. But I always turned them down with some sort of lame excuse such as not wanting to intrude or needing to catch up on schoolwork or claiming I had extra practice. I can usually just throw out the words ball and schedule to get out of anything I don't wanna do.

I've never wanted to go, therefore, I haven't. When Blair asked, I surprised us both by saying yes.

"Mama Moreno is going to be disappointed you aren't coming to our house again."

I smile. "Mama Moreno. How is she? Still doing the barre classes?"

Joel's eyebrows disappear into his hairline. His mom is seriously hot. Not like hot for a woman her age, either. She's just hot. Everyone gives him crap about it, myself included. His reaction is just too much not to screw with him.

"Don't try to change the subject to my mom to get out of talking about Blair. You like her. She's the first girl you've dated in the three years I've known you. You are smitten kitten."

"Sure, of course I like her. She's great."

"But?"

I shrug. "Why does there have to be a but?"

"You tell me."

"There doesn't. I really like her."

"Wooooo." Joel covers his mouth too late, the noise carries, and the guys around us are looking. "Wes likes a girl."

"Pipe down or I'll tell them I'm dating your mom."

I pull out my own phone to busy myself and avoid Joel's questions and am pleased to see a text.

Blair: You were amazing. I watched the game with Vanessa and Mario. Fifteen points, seven assists, one steal. My man is on fire.

Me: You missed my most important stat: four.

Blair: What stat is that?

Me: The number of orgasms I plan to give my girl when I get back.

A text from my mom flashes in my notifications.

Mom: Great game tonight. Your dad and I caught part of it in

the airport. We're boarding soon but wanted to tell you Happy Thanksgiving!

Me: Thanks, Mom. Enjoy your trip.

Mom: Love you!

Another text from Blair pops up.

Blair: Ooooh, in that case. I better finish my school stuff. See ya soon!

Me: I love you.

My hands freeze after I press send. Oh shit. "Shit."

Joel looks over and cocks a brow. "Problem?"

I scrub a hand over my face. "I just told Blair I loved her instead of my mom."

"You're gonna have to explain that."

"I was texting my mom and Blair at the same time. I meant to send it to my mom."

His eyes widen. "What'd Blair say?"

I wake the screen, "Nothing. She went silent."

Joel sucks in air through gritted teeth, grimacing and putting a sound to the panic strumming through my pulse.

"What do I do? Oh my God, what do I do?"

"I dunno. This one is out of my league. I don't tell girls I love them, and if I somehow screwed up and did, they wouldn't believe me anyway."

"Your player status is not helping me right now. What do I do? Do I tell her it was an accident or just hope she doesn't see it? Can you recall text messages like email?

"Well, do you?"

"Do I what?" I stare at the screen. This little device is going to destroy me.

"Do you love her?"

"What kind of question is that?"

"Oh, come on, it isn't that ridiculous of a notion. You're spending all your spare time together."

Oh my God. It's been three minutes with no response. Did she block my number? Is she gonna ghost me? Holy fuck.

"Still no response?"

I slam my head back into the headrest. "Nothing. She's probably busy changing her number."

"Okay, calm down. Tell me this, if she responded right now and said it back, how would that feel?"

I consider that for a moment. Her reaction—or non-reaction, as it currently stands—aside, how would it feel to have Blair love me?

"It'd feel good. I guess. Fuck, I dunno. It's too soon. I don't have time for love."

"Love don't give a rat's ass if you have time."

I'm taken aback by that sentiment from Joel. "When did you start waxing poetic on love?"

He shrugs and stands, turning his body so he can place one hand on the headrest of his seat and one on the seat in front of him. "Yo, boys. Our point man needs a little girl advice. Anyone got any experience with texting blunders? Specifically telling your girl that you love her for the first time over text?"

The bus erupts with noise. Some cheers and words of encouragement and some heckling me as if I were on the opposing team.

Coach, who sits two rows in front of us, moves to the aisle and the bus quiets. His suit jacket is unbuttoned and hangs open. He's a commanding man, and not just because he's our coach. We respect him beyond that.

"Sit down, Moreno. You're the last person who should be giving Reynolds advice."

A collective chuckle waves through the bus and Joel sits.

"Good game tonight, guys. We're going to take tomorrow and Friday off." Applause rings out, and Coach lifts a hand. "But I expect you all to be back Saturday ready to practice hard."

The bus comes to a stop at the fieldhouse. "And, Reynolds," Coach says as I stand and move past him in the aisle, "for the love of God, don't text anything else. Some things are meant to be said and heard. Go tell her in person."

I practically run from the bus to the locker room, where I deposit my gear. I shower quickly, pulling the plain white T-shirt over my head while my skin is still damp.

Z puts a hand on my shoulder before I can sprint off. "The guys and I are heading to the Moreno house tonight. Happy Thanksgiving man."

I know them staying at Joel's tonight instead of The White House is for me, and I would kiss his bald head if I could reach it. "Happy Thanksgiving."

Shaw notices my urgency. "Might want to slow your roll. Too eager, and you'll scare her away. Chicks smell desperation like dogs smell fear."

I don't dignify his remark with a response, but as I walk up to the front of the house, I do make a point to take my time, slow my breathing, and get my shit together.

The house is quiet—almost eerily so. I take the stairs to the second level two at a time, unable to restrain my desire to see her any longer.

The light in my room is on, and Blair sits at my desk, earbuds in and a notebook in front of her with a pen poised in one hand. She stares straight forward in deep concentration.

I cross the room quietly, taking in the number twelve jersey she wears with my name printed across the back and the cut-off jean shorts that are inched up, showing off those legs that I can't get enough of.

She's stunning.

I tug on one of the earbuds, and she startles, letting out a little squeal and pressing a hand to her heart.

"You scared me." She pulls out the other earbud and uncrosses her legs. "I can usually hear you three coming from a mile away."

Her eyes dart past me like she's expecting to hear or see signs of my roommates.

"They decided to stay at Joel's parents' house tonight so they could sleep in and then roll out of bed in time for Thanksgiving dinner."

"No such luck for us. I promised Gabby we'd stop by to see her in the morning and then stay for lunch with her family. I hope that's okay. She's dying to meet you."

"You mean to grill me?"

What is it with girls always wanting to interrogate the guys who date their friends? I've never once considered inserting myself into one of my buddy's relationships. Hell, if I did, I'd be more likely to tell them to run away than to warn them against hurting my friend. Perhaps that's the root of the problem. My buddies, my teammates, and I are typically stereotyped as the ones breaking hearts.

In the case of Joel and some of the other guys on the team, that's probably true. But I'm not looking to break her anything. I don't have time for games. The life that Joel lives doesn't interest me. He uses women as a distraction from his time off the court, a rush to tide him over until the next game or practice. Not me. Distractions are expensive.

My edge on the court is that I've studied and prepared better and harder off the court. Allowing a woman to have that time is like giving away some of my edge. And she's the first girl I've ever even considered doing that for. A smidge of edge for more of Blair.

"I can't wait to meet her," I say and mean it.

I stare at her, wondering if she's going to say more. If she's going to mention the love-bomb I dropped. She doesn't.

I should be relieved, but the way she's avoiding it makes me realize I *want* to talk about it. I want her to acknowledge that this thing between us is something important.

Petty as it is, I want her to voice that my loving her, real or not, is a big freaking deal. If she weren't in my life, I'd spend the night reflecting on the game and my performance and looking for areas to improve.

But, now, I just want to focus on her.

"So, listen about my text—"

She waves her hands in front of her. "No explanation needed. Your iPad was displaying the text notifications from your mom. I put it together that you meant it for her."

I glance down at the desk where my iPad is docked. Well, that was easy. Way too easy. "Right. Okay then."

I force a smile. Her notebook lays open to where she's been taking notes. With a head nod in its direction, I ask, "What were you working on?"

She hesitates and nips at the bottom of her lip before responding. "It's nothing. I was just listening to a podcast on goal setting."

I'm intrigued. What college girl spends a night before a holiday listening to podcasts and taking notes?

"May I?" I reach for the notebook, eyes on her. I won't tease or taunt her, and I won't look if she doesn't want me to, but I really hope she lets me. It's a rush when she finally nods and my fingers brush against the paper she's scribbled onto. I read through what she's written, keenly aware of her discomfort. Her hands clasp in front of her stomach, and she studies her cuticles with an intensity that they don't warrant.

"This what you're always listening to between classes? Business podcasts?" I'm not sure if she can hear the pride in my voice, but I am proud. She's hella smart, and this makes her more attractive to me in some way like I've discovered her weird matches my own. Numbers and ball are my poison, looks like hers is business.

"Not *all* the time. Sometimes I listen to music."

"It's really cool." I hand her back the notebook. "You really are going to take over the business world."

She shrugs. "I don't know. I listen to them more hoping it'll spark some inspiration on a career path than anything else."

"I thought you were decided on being a boss lady and all that."

"I have, but I don't want to spend my life climbing the ladder at some fortune 500 company. I think I might like the idea of a career as a business woman more than the life of actually being one. I can't figure out where my skills will be best utilized."

"You'll figure it out."

"I guess so. It feels like everyone else already knows exactly what they want, and I don't. And I desperately want to feel that kind of passion for something."

"You want passion, huh?"

I'm rewarded with a smile and playful glint to her eyes. "Doesn't everyone?"

After sliding my hands around her waist and down the curve of her ass until I reach smooth legs, I glide my fingers around the hem of her shorts.

"You look good wearing my jersey." I want to buy her one for every day of the week so she'll walk around with my name and number like a brand. She belongs to me not because I want to own her body and mind—although, I'm a dude with a pulse so of course I want that—but because she wants to belong to me. I can see it in her eyes and in the way she studies me. I don't need her to say she loves me. She's mine, and that's enough. Still, I press her. I want to hear the words come from her mouth.

"Does this mean you're mine? I can brag to all my buddies that I got the hottest girl at school?"

She snorts as if to blow off the compliment, but I don't let her get away with it that easy. I slide my hand up inside the leg of her cutoff shorts until the tips of my finger brush against lace. She stills, and her eyes flutter closed for an instant. My lips find the corner of her mouth and stop before making contact. I can feel her breath, warm and shallow, on my face. "You are hot. Gorgeous, smart, sexy as fuck. Own it, Blair. Thinking you're anything less than that is an insult to me. You think my girl is ugly?"

Her lips part and pull into a smile. "No, your girl is fine."

"Fine as fuck," I mutter and capture her mouth.

TWENTY-TWO

Blair

I s being someone's girl the same as being their girlfriend? I'm contemplating the differences as we drive to Succulent Hill. Wes is driving, and I'm sitting in the passenger seat exhausted and satiated. He made good on the sex stats last night and this morning, not resting until my limbs were weak and my mind mush.

I could just ask him, but I'm a little afraid of the answer. I know he *likes* me. Suddenly that doesn't feel like enough. And if being his girl is really his way of calling me his girlfriend, then why is the word so hard for him to say? What we're doing doesn't feel any different from what I've done with other *boyfriends*. Except, it kind of does.

I push back my disappointment, the niggling voice that wishes he would have stormed through the door last night and told me, accident or not, he does love me. Stupid, I know.

If Wes hasn't been clear on labeling what we mean to each other, he has been loud and clear on basketball being number one in his life. His life revolves around the sport, and even with as much time as we spend together, I know that I'm the other woman, so to speak. The mistress when he's away from his true love. And even as I allow myself to think this, I know how dumb it sounds.

Wes is who he is because of his passion. Taking ball away from him would take a piece of him that I love. I admire his dedication, but I can't help but wonder what it would feel like to have that kind of passion directed at me. Is there any room for him to love anything else the way he loves basketball?

Ugh, my mind circles around my insecurities, and I stew, too afraid to voice any of it. Every guy wants a desperate girl begging for love and attention. Yeah right.

I need to just focus on the things I can control, like my career path. I've been searching for my purpose since I arrived at school. I love business, but I haven't found my place in a field that encompasses so much. After throwing myself into the cause with books, podcasts, vlogs, inspirational blogs, the only thing I've become passionate about is my quest for passion.

Wes puts the cruise control on and shifts so he can flex his foot.

"Your foot still bothering you?"

He waves me off with a shake of the head as he rests one hand on my leg. "All good."

I turn toward him to revisit a conversation from last night. "Gabby won't grill you. She isn't like Vanessa. Actually, no she's a lot like Vanessa— or she used to be. I should warn you, though, she is really sensitive about her scarring."

He nods, and his eyes go thoughtful. After a moment of silence, I stare ahead, watching the familiar sights of my hometown come into view. When he finally speaks, we're pulling up in front of my parents' house.

"We all have scars we're trying to hide. Gabby's are just more obvious. I'm excited to meet her. She's important to you, she's a part of you, and I want to know all of you."

His words are a promise, and I hold on to them as we step out of the car and walk to Gabby's house.

Whatever fears I had about Wes meeting Gabby are short lived. They embrace like old friends, and as we sit in the living room after lunch, college football on the television as background noise, they chat like little old ladies at the hair salon. My face hurts from smiling even as my most embarrassing moments have become the topic of conversation.

"Blair always fails to mention that the reason Missy Thomas pushed her off the bike is because Blair was showing off. She was the first to get rid of her training wheels, and she rode up and down the street, ringing her bell and rubbing it in all our faces."

"I did not. I was just excited and my parents would only let me ride in our cul-de-sac." My attempt to defend myself falls on deaf ears. Wes and Gabby are in stitches, paying no attention to my rebuttal.

Traitor, I mouth to my friend and tug on the end of one of the bracelets on her arm.

"Oh, I almost forgot." Gabby reaches into her pocket and pulls out two matching bracelets of blue and yellow. She hands one to me and the other to Wes. "I made them with twelve strands of thread to represent your number."

"Matching bracelets?" I stare at her a little dumbfounded. It's one thing to wear best friend bracelets but a matching bracelet with my sort of boyfriend who is keeping me firmly in the I-like-you zone is a whole different thing.

Wes wraps the braided thread around his wrist and holds it out, indicating he wants me to tie it. "You embarrassed to match me?"

I roll my eyes and tie it securely before reciprocating and holding mine out to be tied with the others that don my arm. He shakes his head and nods to the other arm. He wants me to wear it on my right arm. It's bare, and a shiver takes my whole body as I pull my left back and extend my right.

He seems to understand the significance of wearing it separately from the others because a playful smirk rests on his lips, but his eyes are dark and serious.

As he ties the knot snugly, my heart squeezes with possibilities and hope. I search for meaning in the gesture as my eyes flit to the many bracelets that adorn my other arm. The colors vary from vibrant to dull, but as a whole, they complement each other to create beauty. Years of friendship are living art that I wear daily as a reminder of years gone by and dreams that are still unfulfilled.

This new bracelet, shiny and colorful without the grime and dirt of the real world to mar it, represents a new dream that I hadn't realized I wanted until I met Wes. A life shared with new hopes and dreams. Like the others, I know it will soon be tested for durability and strength, but I feel certain of one thing as I stare at our matching jewelry. I'll strive to hold on to Wes and our time together with the same passion and intensity that I've strived to hold on to Gabby and the plans we created when we were just kids. Bottom line, if he decides he suddenly doesn't have time for me, I'm going to be crushed. I'm in deep.

As we stand to hug Gabby and say our goodbyes, she wipes tears from both cheeks. Wes hangs back as I embrace my friend.

"What's wrong? Why the tears?"

She shakes her head and pulls back. "Ignore me. I'm just so happy for you. And maybe a little jealous too. You really did it . . . the whole college experience we always talked about. I know I'm not supposed to be ungrateful or sit around wishing things were any different from how they are. I've mostly made my peace with it. I don't want you to think I resent your happiness, no one is more proud of you. I promise. But—"

"Gabs, of course. You're allowed to feel that way. You can still have all those things. You just have to decide you're ready."

We share a sad smile, having spoken truths we usually leave unsaid. She turns to Wes and cocks her head at him. "Take care of her and promise you'll come back. I want to hear more about how amazing she's doing. She underplays it."

His eyes slide to me and back to Gabby. "I bet she does."

After more hugs and promises to return, Wes and I walk down the street toward my parents' house. At the front door, he cages me in by putting both hands around my hips and pressing my back against the door.

"Thanks for letting me come. Gabby is something."

"She liked you too."

"I get it now. I see the way she drives you."

"She was always the one who wanted to rule the world. I just wanted to be by her side while she did it." The words taste bitter.

"That doesn't make you less worthy."

"Maybe not, but it feels that way."

He's quiet for a beat before he responds. "There are two types of ball players. Those with more talent than heart and those with more heart than talent. You'd think it'd be the ones with the most talent who perform the best, but it isn't."

"This coming from the guy who was sleeping through statistics. Where was your heart?" I tease.

"I've been running stats for myself and my teammates for as long as I can remember. That class is cake because I studied it early on in order to understand basketball."

"And none of that is talent or brains?"

"Sure, of course. Listen, Joe Schmoe off the street who's never touched a ball before isn't likely to be able to beat Lebron, but when you're talking players of a roughly equal talent spectrum, heart wins out. Sure, the most talented guys make some shots, pull off things I couldn't dream of, but they never really become a part of the team. When it comes game time they never mesh, and we're a team out there. We practice seven days of the week, year-round, and it rules our lives. Talent burns out before heart."

I consider his words and how it relates to me. Am I all talent and no heart?

"You have as much heart as you do talent," he says as if reading my thoughts. "You show it in everything you do. I've never met anyone with more heart than you. You're holding on to dreams of your best friend long after most would have abandoned all hope. When you figure out what *you're* passionate about, you'll be unstoppable. It's time to decide what your dreams are. As shitty as it is, Gabby may never be ready to stand by your side running a company, so whatever plans the two of you had back then have to be shifted some. Why are you holding on so hard when she's making it clear she just wants you to be happy?"

"Because I can't give up hope that, someday, she's going to be ready. I just won't let myself believe that's a possibility. She's the most deserving person I know. At first, I thought I could somehow make up for her absence by doing everything we planned like nothing had changed. And I guess I wanted to honor the dreams we made. I still want those things, and I want her beside me. The scars and the emotional toll of the accident changed her, but she has grit and determination hidden away somewhere deep inside. You two are a lot alike—well, Gabby before the accident."

"I'll take that as a compliment. I liked her a lot."

I nod toward his bracelet. "I'd say it was mutual. I'm a little jealous, actually. You're the first person besides me she's ever made one for."

"Yeah?" He looks positively elated. "In that case, I'm gonna have to get a wristband so I can wear it during games."

I roll my eyes, but it makes me happy he's going to make a point to wear it even if no one else can see it.

TWENTY-THREE

Wes

"You're dragging ass, Reynolds. Shaw take Reynold's place while he rests the foot."

"Coach."

He lifts a hand. "Don't bother. You're off. I'd rather you be rested and ready."

My foot is killing me, but I keep my face neutral, not giving in to the grimace that begs me to grind down on my back molars to distract from the throbbing radiating up my leg. I sit on a chair at the end of our row, leaving a half dozen seats between me and anyone else. Cursing Coach and Shaw, I wipe my face with a towel and then toss the terrycloth onto the floor in front of me. I know it's no one's fault but my own, but I'm pissed anyway.

I'm off my game, and I don't know if I can blame it on just my foot. I'm not as focused. I spent the past two days with Blair and hardly thought about ball. I'd even put off coming back last night, convincing her to leave at the ass crack of dawn this morning to get back in time for practice. A good break before the crunch of the season was what I'd told myself when guilt crept in for not getting in my drills and daily run. Maybe I shouldn't have been so eager to have time off. I'm not where I should be, and I have only my lack of concentration to blame.

Coach takes the chair next to me as the rest of the team runs through the plays with Shaw on point.

"How many more weeks of physical therapy?"

"Two more weeks. The foot is fine, coach. It bothers me when I push too hard. They said that was to be expected."

"I'm switching up your workouts. Until further notice, I want you and Shaw working together. Everywhere you go, he goes. Everything you do in this gym, he does."

I open my mouth to object, close it, and think through my words before I say something I can't take back. "I'll be ready. I won't let my team down."

"I know. You always leave it all on the court, but your team needs you to take it easy. Even if you were at your best, we would still need a strong six man. I think Shaw can be that."

I nod. I don't like the thought of anyone taking my spot. Least of all the guy who has one foot on the court and the other on the field. What happens if he decides he just wants to play baseball? Or gets hurt? It's ironic, I realize, worrying about someone else getting hurt while my foot screams. I rationalize it away because I hurt myself playing the sport I love, not the one I'm splitting my time playing.

"All right."

"The guys look to you, and I depend on you. I've never had to ask you to do anything because you've always just done. I'm asking this for me, for your team. We need Shaw ready to go sooner than later."

Blair calls as I'm changing out of my sweaty practice jersey into a clean-ish T-shirt for weight lifting and drills.

"What's up?" I ask, my voice less grumpy than I feel.

"Heading back to Succulent Hill. I forgot my cell charger and my back-pack in our rush out. Got time to entertain me while I drive?"

"Got five."

"I figured it out," she says, and I can hear the excitement in her voice. "I have you to thank, really. I can't believe it didn't occur to me on my own, but what you said about heart and talent finally hit me today while I was unpacking. The thing I'm passionate about is other people's goals."

I cock a brow. "Your dream is for other people to achieve their dreams?"

"I know that sounds like a cop out. Hell, even I thought that, which is why I've had such a hard time pinning it down. But hear me out. Think about all the people who have had an impact in your life. Those who helped you get closer to your goals. With social media and a myriad of goal-setting re-sources, there's an entire market out there for helping people achieve their goals. Live streams, vlogs, blogs, books, podcasts, life coaching, the list is endless. That's what I want to do."

"The lady boss that creates more lady bosses."

"Exactly." While I'd love to pretend it's all about me, I can tell she's really excited about the idea. She's a bundle of excitement that's contagious even through the phone. "I'm meeting with my advisor this week to see if there are opportunities in the career resource center."

"You're really something, you know that? You're willing to dedicate your entire life to helping others, and I'm bitter about helping one dude on my team."

She's quiet for a beat, and I picture the adorable way her brows scrunch together when she's trying to figure something out. "Why? That isn't like you."

"This guy just gets under my skin. He has talent, but I'm not sure about heart."

"What makes you say that?"

"He's a multi-sport athlete, which means he plays two sports—basketball and baseball."

"Oh yeah, Tanner Shaw. Mario mentioned him. It's kind of impressive that he's playing both sports."

I roll my eyes. "It's a giant pain in the ass for everyone."

"So, you think because he isn't solely dedicated to basketball that his heart is less than his talent?"

"How could it possibly be otherwise? I can't imagine playing another sport, trying to juggle between two different games, and then comparing that dedication to someone who only plays one. You see what it's like, how basketball takes like a thousand percent of my time."

More silence that makes me feel like a prick.

"Maybe his path is different, but I don't think it's fair to question his heart. You said yourself that the test of heart comes with how well a guy meshes with the team come game time. You're only a few games in, and he played less than six minutes of the last game."

"Keeping stats on the rookie? Should I be jealous?"

"No, I was keeping stats on you, dummy. When he was playing, you weren't."

Those words, which were meant to be reassuring, cut deep. Is that why I'm being a giant baby? I've never had a problem giving other guys the limelight. Fuck, it's what makes me a good point man. I'm not greedy. I take my shots, but I don't force it. I always do what's best for the team. Until now.

"It's my last year," I say and wonder how such a bland statement can hold so much weight. "My foot is slowing me down, and if someone is going to take my spot, I want that person to give everything for the team. Someone like . . ."

"Someone like you?"

I nod, aware that she can't see the movement but unable to speak.

"Give him a chance to prove you wrong. Maybe he just needs someone to help in his journey. Someone smarter and wiser. Someone with experience leading a team. Someone with heart and talent." Her voice is sugary sweet, and I let her words heal like a salve to the open wound of my ego.

"Someone who understands what it takes to be great."

I'm eager for more. The way she believes in me almost has me convinced I'm capable. But she doesn't say anything else.

I can do this. For my team. For myself. I can live up to the standard that Blair believes I'm capable of.

Damn, she's good.

The locker room door opens, and a few other guys stop in to change before hitting the weight room. "Gotta go. See ya later?"

"Sure, text me later. I need to do some school stuff for a few hours."

Damn, this girl spends more time studying than anyone I know.

I find Shaw in the weight room as he's finishing a set of squats. By the annoyed look he shoots me, Coach has already informed him that we're going to be working together from now on.

He moves to pull all the weight off, but I shake my head. "Another set."

Shaw glares but silently adds another ten pounds to each side of the barbell.

"You need to build up your leg strength and endurance. When you're leading the point, your legs have to be as fresh at the end of the game as the beginning. Forget about what the rest of the guys are doing," I say as he looks around the room, envy clear in his eyes. "You have to be stronger, faster, and smarter out there."

He takes the weight on his back and squats out eight reps. When he finishes and faces me, breath ragged, the glint in his eye is determined. I hide my approval.

Every exercise is the same. I push him harder than he wants, but he doesn't back down.

"All right, let's hit the gym for some ball drills and then we'll join the team for the run."

His jaw flexes. As we walk out onto the court, I grab two balls and pass one back to Shaw. "I usually start with some half court runs, switching off every turn. Left up, right back, and so on until I feel warm."

I take off, and a split second later, he's beside me, pushing me faster. I lose track of how many times we've gone up and down the court after ten.

"All right, now, suicides with the ball. Stop and touch the line with your free hand and then switch over to the other hand."

Again, we turn what should be a light warm up into a race. The only sound in the gym is the steady drumming of the ball hitting the hardwood and our sneakers squeaking as we pivot at each line on the court. We stop after each one is complete, only resting as long as the other will allow. My foot throbs, but I don't dare let him see me weak.

Sweat pours down my face, my back, my arms. After the fifth, rookie cracks a smile. After seven, I join him, my lips curling of their own accord. At ten, a laugh that is filled with tension, relief, and hope escapes from my chest, and the sound is like the first crack in a dam. It grows and builds and then is joined by Shaw until we collapse on the floor completely exhausted, probably delirious, but I've gained his respect. And him, mine.

And Blair was right.

Nathan's birthday is the following week and as much as I don't feel like going out, I can't deny the man a proper twenty-first birthday celebration. Joel elbows me and lifts a hand. I turn my attention to the door to see Blair entering The Hideout. I swear the guy has girl radar and one eye always trained on the door.

My girl couldn't make it until after she finished studying. She's starting to make me feel guilty for my big brain with all the time she spends at the library. Not that I don't ever need to open a book, but I only have to a couple of hours a week tops. Whereas it's all Blair seems to do.

I meet her halfway and pull her into a hug. "Hey, you made it."

She goes limp in my arms, leaning her head against my chest.

"So tired," she mumbles as she pulls back.

"We don't have to stay long. The birthday boy is one more shot away from passing out." I slide a hand into the back pocket of her jeans and guide us back to the bar.

Nathan is propped up on a stool, eyes glazed and wearing a drunken smile. "Blair, you made it."

He makes a move to get off the stool and stumbles, setting off a domino effect as he crashes into guys on the team, who in turn bump into the people around us.

Z helps a totally clueless Nathan back up onto the chair. "Don't move," he instructs.

Blair goes to Nathan and embraces him. "Happy birthday. Can I buy you a drink?"

He winks at me over her shoulder and sniffs her hair. Fucker is messing with me, but I'm not scared. He knows I'd kick his ass if he made a move on my girl. Still, I move closer just in case he decides to test me.

"Hell yes," Nathan responds and pulls back. That's right, dude, hands off.

She orders two shots of Fireball at his request and Nathan slurs the same toast he's been shouting all night, "To love and basketball."

That seems to put him over the edge, thank God, and Nathan voices his desire to go home and pass the fuck out. Joel and Z help him stand, and Blair and I trail behind. We're almost to the door when someone steps in front of her.

"A word," David says, teeth clenched and jaw flexing.

My hand tenses in her back pocket, and I tug her closer. "We're on our way out."

The glare that David shoots me further pisses me off, but I feel Blair cower next to me. Instead of telling him to get lost, she pulls away from me. "Go ahead with the guys, I'm right behind you."

The fuck? I start to protest, but she leans up and presses a kiss to my lips. I relent. "Five minutes."

"Five minutes," she repeats with a nod.

I'm bristling as I walk outside.

"Something doesn't feel right." I pace behind the car as Z gets Nathan in and Joel starts the car. "Maybe I should go back in and get her. I'm gonna go back in."

No one is listening to me as I work this out aloud. David looked angry, and as tough as Blair is, and as much as I don't want to be the kind of guy who acts like a jealous asshole, this just doesn't feel right.

"I'm gonna go get her," I repeat, louder this time so the guys can hear. I get the faintest head tilt in acknowledgment.

My eyes scan the bar when I step back inside, and my pulse quickens when I don't immediately see Blair.

I push toward the back, where I found them last time, and it seems this is David's go-to spot for cornering women. I'd only meant to check and make sure she was okay, but the tears in Blair's eyes push me to action.

"I can't keep doing this. I've barely slept all week. Do what you have to do, David, but I'm done helping you." Blair's voice quivers, but I'm damn proud of her for standing up for herself, even if I'm hella confused about what's going on.

"Blair," I say her name just loud enough to be heard but don't move to put myself between them. I get the feeling that she needs to fight this battle on her own. I'm just back up, and I want fuck face to know it.

Instead of the anger I'd expected from David at my approach, he looks downright gleeful. "Do what I have to do, huh?"

There is panic in Blair's eyes as she looks between us. He steps toward me, and she reaches for his arm. *The hell?* He rips his arm away from her and continues until we're chest to chest. He isn't a short dude, but I have him by several inches.

"Don't worry, bro, she's all yours. I got what I wanted from her, including some mementos to remember her best assets." He winks, which is the final snap to my barely contained rage. Don't know where the fuck this guy gets off, but I don't like the way he suggests he still has any ties to her.

I shove him, and he staggers back. Before I can advance, I'm being pulled backward by Z, who I hadn't realized followed me back inside. "Should get out of here, man."

Blair's crying fills the silence of the parking lot as we're ushered out to Joel's car. Z pushes us into the back with Nathan, who's already passed out.

"What the hell?" Joel asks, getting a look at our faces.

"Just drive," Z says as he slams his door shut.

I sit, stunned, as Joel takes off to the house. What the hell just happened?

"Dude." Joel's eyes find mine in the rearview mirror, and he nods toward Blair. Right, I'm meant to be comforting my girl.

"Come here," I murmur and pull Blair into my arms. She falls into my chest and sobs harder. She tries to speak, but I run a hand through her hair and tell her we'll talk later.

I need to get my emotions in check before I deal with hers. I'm pissed, and only part of my anger is at David. I'm also mad at myself for losing my cool. I mean, he totally deserved it, and I'd do it again in a heartbeat, but I've never been in a bar brawl. In fact, the only time I've ever gotten into any kind of physical altercation has been on the basketball floor. It's the only place that has ever gotten me riled up enough to want to throw a punch. Until now. Until Blair.

Her crying quiets as I lead her out of the car and up to my room. She crawls onto my bed and kicks off her shoes. "I'm so sorry."

"Hey." I slide in next to her. "What are you sorry for? You didn't do anything wrong."

That seems to set her off again, and her chest heaves with new tears. I hold her until she cries herself to sleep, and then I slip downstairs.

Joel and Z are in the living room watching television.

"She okay?" Joel asks when I plop down onto the couch.

I nod. "Yeah, I think so. Guy was a total ass to her. Never expected her to react like that, though," I admit. "She's sleeping now."

"What the hell happened in there to make you haul off and hit the guy?" Joel asks.

"I didn't hit him, just shoved a tiny bit." Okay a lot, whatever. I fill them in the best I remember and include the bits that Blair has told me about the way her relationship ended with David. At least the parts I don't think she'll mind me sharing.

"She was really shaken. It doesn't add up. You know the guy?" I ask Joel.

"Know of him. Not any more than what you told me, though. He's a Sigma, and he's a tool."

"I'm gonna text Mario. Let Vanessa know what happened and see if she knows anything."

"I'll text Mario," Joel interjects. "You need to chill out before you do something stupid."

TWENTY-FOUR

Blair

I wake in the darkness, but voices carry from downstairs. My head aches from the bawl fest, and I'm filled with humiliation as I wonder what Wes must think. Or what he'll think if I tell him everything. I've played out this scenario a hundred times, how I'd tell Wes if it ever came down to it. Admittedly, I never planned on it unless my hand was forced.

Fucking David. I spent two hours waiting for him to show up at the library so I could give him the latest assignments and he blows me off then has the gall to show up at The Hideout.

What's worse than being blackmailed by your ex-boyfriend? Your new boy-whatever finding out exactly why you're being blackmailed in the first place. I have no idea how I'm going to explain myself. Wes deserves the truth, but oh God, the truth is horrifying.

I force myself out of his bed, inhaling his scent and praying it isn't the last time I'm allowed in said bed, and then I head downstairs. I know there will be questions about what went down and why I reacted the way I did, and I'm having a hard time finding the words even as I try to sort them in my mind.

"What are you doing here?" Fresh tears fall down my face as I run toward Vanessa.

She offers me a sad smile as she stands from her spot on the couch next to Mario and embraces me. "Checking on my best girl. Come sit, tell me what happened."

Wes, Mario, Joel, and Z watch us carefully. It's clear whatever I have to say, they want to hear it too. "I ran into David at The Hideout. He was an asshole, per the usual."

"Blair, honey, you need to stop giving him face time. No more letting him pull you aside. The douche canoe knows he screwed up royally, and he's trying to get you back."

"That isn't it." I look at my hands as I say the words. "He doesn't want me back."

"No guy corners a girl in a bar unless he's trying to get in her pants." As Joel speaks, I look to Wes. His expression is guarded, and I wonder how much he's already guessed. It seems laughably obvious at this point, and Wes is a smart jock.

"He cornered me tonight because we were supposed to meet up."

Wes's eyes widen slightly and then he slips the cool and collected mask back into place. I look to Vanessa, unable to watch him while I finish explaining. Vanessa raises her brows, prompting me to continue.

"I've been helping him with his classes. No, not helping. I've been doing his class work."

"Why would you do that? You hate him." V's shocked voice makes me regret the months of keeping it from her.

"Because he has pictures of me. Naked pictures. He threatened to post them online, around campus, basically ruin me." I exhale once I get it all out.

The hand that V rests on my leg squeezes. "That rat bastard."

I peek up at Wes, who has placed his head between his legs. Shame and humiliation force me to look away.

"Baby doll, every girl on campus has nude photos." Joel sits forward in his chair. "Check this out, these are just from tonight."

I cover my eyes as Joel pushes his phone in front of my face and I get an eye full of boobs.

"Jesus, that isn't helpful." Wes stands. "V, can you stay here with Blair for a bit?"

"It's fine. I can go home." My bed sounds great. A private place to hide and cry for a day or year. I can't bear to guess what Wes must think of me now.

He crosses the room and threads his hands through my hair, tilting my head up to meet his gaze. "Stay. I'll be back as soon as I can."

"Where are you going?"

"To Sigma."

"What? Why? There's nothing else to say. I told him tonight I was done. It's over."

He drops a light kiss onto my lips and pulls back, but then he growls as he crashes his lips to mine. This kiss is hungrier. Desperate and hard and steals the air from my lungs before he steps back.

"Let's go," he says, and I watch in fascination as all the guys file out of the house.

I can't stop the anxious giggle that bubbles up and escapes from my mouth. "Did they all just march out of here like some sort of soldiers going to battle?"

Vanessa smiles. "Yep. Off to fight for your honor."

I groan.

"Sit," she orders. "Tell me how this all happened?" She holds up a hand. "Actually, let's go upstairs and wash your face. I refuse to let that ass hat be the cause of your makeup running down your face."

Leave it to V to be concerned about my smeared makeup at a time like this.

Wes

"What's the plan? We can't just waltz in there and roam the halls until we find him."

There's a group of guys outside the Sigma house, kicked back in chairs and drinking beer. I spot David as he stands and lifts his chin in a silent dare to step on to his pad.

"Not necessary," I grit out and quicken my pace.

We're welcomed by the group of guys joining David and lining up across the small patio, puffing out their chests and pulling their hands into fists at their sides. No doubt, David's already filled them in on what happened, so our appearance doesn't seem to shock them. It doesn't make them happy either. Having four big, athletic dudes who are clearly pissed strolling up on them makes me almost feel sorry for them. Almost.

"This is private property, Reynolds. You've already given me enough ammunition to press assault charges. Get lost, or I'll have the cops here in five, and we'll add trespassing to your rap sheet."

"Maybe before you start slinging accusations you should know that blackmail and extortion are felonies. I have the Valley president on speed dial, so we could add cheating and sexual harassment to that list as well." Joel looks at David with a smirk on his face.

Joel doesn't like to use his family to fight his battles, so I acknowledge his willingness to call up dear old Dad with a nod in his direction before I step toward David. "I want every single picture you have of her, every emails, texts, or scraps of paper she wrote on gone. Delete it. Burn it. Erase her from your life."

He laughs, and I fight back the urge to pummel him. First, I need to be sure he's going to do what I ask before it comes to blows.

"And if I don't, what is it you think you're going to do about it?"

"Whatever I have to. You're a sick fucker blackmailing a girl to do your schoolwork. Tell me, are you too stupid to pass your own classes or are you just holding on to her anyway you can?"

"Holding on to Blair?" He bends at the waist as he lets out a deep laugh. "That slut was annoying as fuck, all positive vibes and doing things for others." He rolls his eyes. "And a lousy lay on top of it."

My fist connects with his cheek, causing him to let out a grunt as his head cracks to the side. It's chaos as guys charge and punches are thrown. David's a pussy, no shocker there, and after I land a gut check, he collapses to the ground and holds up a hand for mercy. His signal breaks up the fight, but I still bend and get right in his face.

"Delete everything. Tonight. And stay the fuck away from her. You see Blair, you walk in the other direction. She's mine, and I protect what's mine." I straighten and pull out my phone. "Say cheese, asshole." I snap a picture of him lying on the ground, lip busted, and then flip him off for good measure. It isn't the same as a dick pick, but for a dude like David, I'm gonna guess a leaked photo of him looking like a pussy would be just as humiliating.

I'm still fuming when I get back to the house, but when I push open my bedroom door and see Blair curled up on my bed sleeping, it dissipates.

"Sweetheart, wake up."

Blair lets out a little groan as her eyes flutter open. I drop a kiss to her lips and pull her against me. Damn, I'd do anything for this girl. If I had any question about that before tonight, they are gone. I'm in love with her.

"Is everything okay?" Her voice is tentative.

"Everything is perfect. I'm sorry I left you alone while you were upset. You doing okay?"

"I'm so embarrassed," she says as she buries her face against my chest.

"What are you embarrassed about?"

"For all of it. Sending him the pictures to begin with, being too mortified to stand up to him, letting him use me, getting you involved. I'm especially sorry about that. Are you going to get into trouble because of this?"

"Nah, he's too much of a coward to tell anyone. Besides, it was worth it. You're worth it."

Because I freaking love you. I love you.

"The stupidest part is I didn't even want to send him the pictures. I know lots of girls do it, and that's cool. I totally respect a woman's right to sexy pictures without labeling her a slut, but I did it for all the wrong reasons. He was really possessive, and I was trying to prove that I cared for him and that there was no reason for him to play the jealous boyfriend card all the time. We were fighting a lot, and I thought, 'hey maybe this will show him.' Sounds really dumb now."

"Not dumb at all." I squeeze her a little tighter. "You were fighting for something you believed in."

"Yeah, like I said, incredibly dumb."

"Stop talking about my girl like that. She's smart, gorgeous, caring, and she didn't deserve what he did to her."

"I know."

"Do you?" I lift her chin so I can see her eyes. "You didn't deserve what he did. Even if you'd been the worst girlfriend on the planet, which we both know you weren't, you didn't deserve to be exploited and blackmailed."

The war in her eyes tugs at my emotions, which are bouncing around like a ball in a pinball machine. I want so badly to tell her how I feel about her and make her promises I have no business making. Promises to protect and love.

Tonight isn't about my feelings, though. It's about hers.

As I roll over on top of her, I kiss her tenderly, taking my time and expressing everything I can't say with gentle caresses and strokes. When I'm finally inside her, I look deep into her eyes and wonder if she can feel the shift between us or if it's just me who's careening into the unknown.

TWENTY-FIVE

Blair

I slide into my seat after having pushed and clawed my way through the crowd at Ray Fieldhouse. Vanessa scoots down, making room for me, and Mario gives me a small wave from the other side of my friend.

"What took you so long? The game is about to start."

You'd think it was her boyfriend who was getting ready to play instead of mine. I'm not worried about the game. Wes has been on fire all season. He's playing amazing, the team is winning, and he's even helped bring Shaw into the group; although, he still doesn't seem thrilled about that last part.

Tonight is the last home game before Christmas break. Wes and the guys only get a week off. I'm heading to Succulent Hill to spend my break binge watching holiday movies, eating too many sugar cookies, and sleeping with no fear of missing class and no grueling study sessions keeping me up to all hours.

To be fair, the grueling study sessions usually ended with me naked in Wes's bed, so I can't really complain too much about that. And since I've been managing only my own course load, the semester had flowed along nicely.

"I was waiting for my final stat grade to be posted."

Vanessa pries her eyes away from the court where both teams are taking the floor. "Well? Did your private tutor make it worth your while?"

My face warms. Did he ever. "Grades aren't up yet."

"I'm sure you pulled an A. Even if you only studied a quarter of the time you two were together you should have been able to ace the final."

He's been insatiable this week, and I've been happy to provide stress relief in the form of letting him use my body as a distraction. It isn't as if I'm not getting mine as well. If I'm honest, it's been a good distraction for both of us. I've not seen or heard from David, but I'm still looking over my shoulder expecting him to pop up out of nowhere.

Arizona State wins the tip off and the game begins. The energy in the room is bursting. The pep band works through their material, the cheerleaders are dancing along, and the fans are on their feet. The student section, enthusiastic as ever, is overflowing with students who are burned out on classes and ready to see our team win one before we head off to see family and visit hometown friends. But the game is a back and forth, both teams playing hard and not giving an inch. As we go to halftime, the score is tied and my nerves are shot.

Determination and sweat drips off him. I stare hard at him as he follows the team off the court, willing him to somehow find me amongst the crowd. He doesn't look up. He's in whatever fog or bubble he creates to stay focused and not let the fans, the other team, or even amazingly hot girls distract him.

"I'm gonna go get some popcorn," I say to Vanessa and Mario. "Want anything?"

They shake their heads and make the exact same scrunched up face to indicate no. They're freaking adorable, but I keep that to myself. Vanessa would just roll her eyes if I said so. She's been unable to stay away from him, but I know she's still skittish, and I'm not giving her any reason to back off. Mario is good for her.

The line to the concession is long, and I slide in behind a couple of high school girls. I would say they were freshman, but even freshman know better than to wear *that* much makeup or skirts *that* short.

"Joel Moreno is definitely the hottest player," one of the girls says and fans her face. "And his family is like super rich. My sister had English with him senior year, and she said he wore a different pair of Jordan's every month."

I've seen Joel's many pairs of shoes strewn around the house and can confirm he has enough for that statement to be true.

The other girl chirps in after showing her amaze and wonder with an actual jaw drop. "Joel is hot, but Wes Reynolds is my favorite. Have you noticed he started wearing a sweatband on his right wrist?"

Her friend shakes her head, but I smile. I have to force myself from butting into their conversation to politely inform her that he started wearing the blue band to hide the bracelet Gabby made for him.

"Watch him when he shoots free throws. He kisses it before each shot for good luck or something. I wonder what it means. Think someone died or something?"

He does?

The girls keep talking. I vaguely hear them speculate between it being a death in the family or an injured teammate who passed it down, but it's background noise to the reel in my head analyzing his free throw ritual. All the guys have them. Some dribble two or three times, count to two, and a million other variations. No matter the intricacies, it's the exact same every time. Wes's ritual is burned into my memory. Breathe out, spin ball with both hands, one dribble, count to two, shoot.

I exit the line and make my way back to my seat.

"What happened to popcorn?" Vanessa asks.

"The line was too long."

The team is back on the floor, and I follow Wes's every move watching and waiting for him to step behind the line to practice free throws. He doesn't, and the coach calls them over before I can confirm the ramblings of my boyfriend's high school fan.

I pray to the basketball gods that Wes gets fouled taking a shot. Not my proudest moment, but I'm desperate to see if it's true. Has he somehow incorporated me into the ritual? What else could it mean? I'm glued to the action, holding my breath every time Wes has the ball and practically growling every time it leaves his hands.

When he's finally fouled driving to the basket, I jump and cheer so loudly Vanessa side-eyes me. I don't pay her any mind. Wes lines up to take his shots, and the rest of the men on the court take their spots along the outside of the lane and at half court. The ref bounces the ball to Wes, who then begins his ritual.

Breathe out, spin the ball with both hands, dribble. And just as I've decided the girl in the concession line must have been mistaken, he brings the ball up to jaw level and touches the sweatband to his mouth. I could almost believe he's just wiping his mouth it's so quick. So quick and fluid that I don't know if I ever would have seen it on my own.

"Oh my God," I whisper and grin like a fool as he takes the shot and it swishes through the net. I cheer along with the rest of the home-team fans, but I'm already giddy as I wait to see it again. With the ball in his hands, ready to take the second shot, he restarts the process and just like last time, the quick kiss of his right wrist before he shoots is unmistakable.

"I think he's in love with me," I say, turning to Vanessa as the crowd cheers the point made.

Her mouth quirks up. "Duh."

"Oh, you're one to talk." I nod to Mario, and as if on cue, he turns and gives Vanessa an adoring smile.

"So we're freaking in love." She rolls her eyes, but I can read her well. She's happier than I can ever remember her being.

"Are you gonna talk to him about it?" Vanessa asks, both our eyes glued back to the court. There's a time out and the cheerleaders wave their pom poms in front of us screaming about Valley pride.

"I don't know. He's been pretty clear that whatever we're doing isn't serious."

"He's made that clear or you're too chicken shit to ask him and assume that's what he thinks?"

"Okay, fine, I've been too chicken to ask, but his schedule is insane and is just going to get crazier. The season goes until April, if they're lucky, and then he graduates in May. After that, there's no telling where he'll end up. Meanwhile, I'm going to be here."

"You're spinning. Take a breath. Just talk to him about it. You two have managed to make it work for this long, and it's been an eventful semester."

"No kidding."

Arizona State has possession of the ball after the timeout. Wes is guarding their point man, giving me a view of the serious and determined look on his face as he provides a barrier between the opposing player and his teammates. His opponent has him on height and size, but my man is faster. The guy fakes right and passes left, but Wes gets his hand on the ball and sends it sailing toward the half court line. Both players take off as fast as they can, but Wes gets there first.

The crowd is on their feet, screaming Wes's name and jumping like the basket has already been made. But the other team isn't giving up that easy. Wes drives to the basket, power and confidence. He explodes up toward the rim, the ball safely tucked in one of those big hands of his. The defense is tight against him, a step behind, but so close that the crowd holds their breath as the ball leaves Wes's hands.

I follow the ball as it goes up and into the net. A whistle is called, and the ref signals a foul on the play, granting the basket and giving Wes an opportunity to make it a three-point play. I'm lost to the explosion of cheers around me. There's a commotion on the floor. Wes and a player in a red jersey are lying in a heap on the floor from the contact. His groan is the first signal something is wrong. Wes's face is angled down, his body curled into a ball, but he reaches for his foot and my stomach drops.

Everything happens in slow motion. The coach and some other guys wearing Valley University polos circle Wes, making it hard for me to see what's going on. I grab on to Vanessa's arm at some point, holding on to her tightly because I don't trust my legs to hold me.

There's movement, and he stands with the help of three other guys. The crowd cheers around me, but I'm silent. He's favoring his foot, holding it in a way that hurts my heart and sends a million what-if scenarios shuffling through my head. There's some back and forth between Wes and the coach, but he hobbles to the free-throw line, making it clear he's going to take his shot.

Z steps up behind Wes, and his lips move, but I can't make out what he says. Wes nods once, his mouth set into a grim line. All but two players from the opposing team move back. I hate them for even considering that he might not make the shot, even knowing they're just doing what makes sense.

Still, sensibility has nowhere to sit in the crowd of emotions pushing around inside me.

Wes has the ball. A calm sense of routine eases the hard lines of his face. Breathe out, spin the ball with both hands, dribble once . . . but the kiss of his right wrist is lost. He completes the sequence like it never changed. There's no indication in the rhythm or his features that says he's missed a step. It's as if it were never part of it at all and I just imagined it. The ball leaves his hand and bounces around the rim before slipping through the net.

Coach Daniels calls a timeout, and Joel and Z flank Wes, leading him off the court.

TWENTY-SIX

Wes

"I'm afraid the news isn't great, son."

No shit.

I don't look up at the doctor as he slaps my x-ray onto a lighted screen. From my peripheral, I can see he's pointing, but I don't need to see it to know it's broken. I knew it the second it happened.

"You've re-broken the fifth metatarsal."

"How long will I be out? Same recovery time?"

He hesitates, and I grind my teeth impatiently. "This is much more serious. The bones have displaced this time."

"How long?" I growl, not caring that I sound like an asshole.

"You'll need surgery. Three months, maybe four until you're—"

"Three months? The season will be over in three months. My college career will be *over* in three months."

His eyes are solemn. "I'm sorry, Wes. I know it's crap news."

"What if I don't have the surgery? I could wear a boot for a few weeks, finish the season and then have the surgery." It sounds crazy even to my own ears.

"You need the surgery. The bones aren't sitting properly. Even if you wanted to grin and bear it, this is just going to get worse every time you put pressure on the foot. You aren't going to be able to play competitively with this type of injury until you've had the surgery and healed properly. I'm sorry."

The doctor leaves and a nurse comes in to get my signature on a stack of papers. I sign them without reading the fine print. What the hell could it possibly say that would make this any worse?

Coach steps in as they prep me for surgery. I've taken off my jersey for the last time, and it sits awkwardly between us in a clear plastic bag. He shuffles from one foot to the other. It's obvious he has no idea what to say, but I'm glad he doesn't try to pacify me with words of hope and encouragement. We're two quiet men, each stewing with his own version of this nightmare.

"The team is out in the waiting room."

"I don't want to see anyone right now."

"I figured as much, but I wanted you to know they're here just the same. There's a pretty brunette out there pacing the floor too. That the girlfriend?"

Blair.

I nod.

"She has the stubborn look of a woman who isn't leaving until she sees you."

"That sounds like her." A small smile cracks and then falls. "Tell her to go home. Tell all of them to go home. They aren't doing me any favors by being here. I just want to be alone."

"I'll tell them," he says and backs out of the room, stopping with one foot in and one foot out. "Won't be responsible for kicking anyone out who doesn't want to go, but I'll tell them."

As his steps echo down the hall, I lie back and close my eyes. I embrace the pain. I'd embrace it every day if it meant I could keep playing and see this season through.

I can't think about what's next or what tomorrow will bring . . . what I'll say to those people in the waiting room. My request may scare off some of my teammates, but I know when I wake up, Coach, my roommates, and Blair will be waiting for me. Waiting to reassure me and pamper me. I don't want any of it. I want to crawl into a hole and fixate until I've come up with a plan to rewind time or gain another year of college eligibility with Z.

This was our year.

It was our fucking year.

I crack one eye open, then the other. Reflexively, I close them both. The light in the room makes the fog in my head swim. There's movement beside me and then her touch. I'd recognize it anywhere—even drugged and pissed at the world, apparently.

"What are you wearing?"

"What?" Her voice is shaky and quiet like she's talking to an invalid. Guess that's me.

"I asked what are you wearing? Leather skirt maybe, halter top, sexy nurse? Give me a visual."

"Jeans and your jersey," she says with a hint of humor in her voice. "I'm sorry I'm not dressed like a puppet from your teenage wet dreams."

I peek out at her beautiful face and let my eyes wander to the jersey she wears, the one I'll never put on again. I close my eyes to squeeze away the pain. "I'm pretty sure my teenage wet dreams always included chicks wearing my jersey."

I joke with her, even though I don't feel like being funny. I'd really like to send her away and drown in misery, but I think I'm more likely to get her to leave if I pretend I'm okay instead of a man who has lost a piece of his soul.

I open both eyes slowly, letting them adjust to the light and finding her face. Looking at her heals and breaks me. I'll never be the same, and whoever I was when she met me? He's gone. Maybe she knows it, maybe she doesn't. Her eyes give nothing away as she tries a hesitant smile.

Regardless of how I've changed, I still want her. She's maybe the only thing I've ever been certain about besides basketball. But even as I realize this, I know my actions won't back up my feelings. Sometimes, we make bad decisions not because we aren't aware but because it feels good to cause pain. That's how I feel as I plan to break her heart and mine.

"Shouldn't you be in Succulent Hill by now?"

"I wanted to see you before I left."

I raise my arms to the side. "You saw me."

Her hands go to her hips. "You didn't really expect me to go without checking on you first, did you?"

I hadn't. Hoped, maybe, but I knew she'd be here.

"Go, be with your family. My parents are on their way, and I'm heading to Kansas with them."

"You are?"

I can tell she didn't anticipate this. I wasn't supposed to leave Arizona until the week of Christmas. What the hell did she think I was going to do? Ride along with the team? Roll myself in a wheelchair to the games? Sit on the fucking sidelines and have everyone look at me with pity? Yeah, no thanks.

"But what about . . ." She fidgets with the bracelet on her arm. The one that matches mine.

"I'm out for the rest of the season, Blair. I'm done." The words physically hurt. I don't feel done. I haven't finished what I set out to do. I've failed them. Failed Z. It's his last season too, and what if he doesn't get drafted because I couldn't get him the ball? I owe him my whole college career and I've failed him.

She nods. Everyone seems to be doing that a lot lately. Silent bobble-heads, unsure of what to say. "I could stay until you leave. I'm just going to be sitting around by myself. Both my parents are working next week."

She sure as shit is not making this easy.

"Nah, go. I just want to be alone. Finally catch up on sleep and all that."

She bites her lip, clearly torn between making a stand to stay and honoring my wishes. Reaching into her purse, she pulls out a box wrapped in red-and-white stripes with a huge green bow on top. "Merry Christmas, Wes."

She pushes the present into my hands and I open my mouth to speak. "I—"

She cuts me off. "It's okay. I wasn't expecting anything."

What I'd been about to say was that I'd left her present at the house where we'd planned to say goodbye before the break. I lift the box, shaking it gently like I'm trying to guess what it is. She doesn't smile. She's no longer fooled by my playful charades. She sees through me. Sees me. Always has. I wonder what she sees now, a broken man?

"Merry Christmas, Blair."

TWENTY-SEVEN

Blair

I unlock my phone, checking for the hundredth—no, thousandth—time for a text or phone call that I've somehow missed.

Nothing.

Wes's texts have been few and far between and only in response to my messages, so I shouldn't be surprised. He didn't even reply back when I told him I'd gotten an A in statistics.

A man who falls short of his dream is sad. Wes is something else entirely. To call him sad is a compliment to the word and an insult to the void in his eyes. I'd been jealous of his passion, and now I realize how much that made up his identity.

It isn't as if I care about him being a ball player because of the hype around him or the jealous looks shot my way when we were together. I can admit it felt good to be on the arm of a man who sits on top of the social ladder, though. He could call me right now and tell me he was going to dedicate his life to origami, and if it filled him with as much hunger as basketball did, I'd be just as happy. It isn't the what—it is the fire that burns inside him because he is doing something he loves. He is oxygen to my own small blaze, and without him I'm afraid my flame will die out too.

It's a helpless and hopeless feeling that I remember well from Gabby's accident. The sitting around, feeling sad. The silent fury at the world. The helplessness.

Another person I love has watched their dreams slip away.

Maybe when a person's dreams are big like Gabby's and Wes's, their failures are that much more traumatic. Love lost is still love. Are dreams lost still dreams? Is there still an overarching lesson in having a dream and failing?

Dragging myself from the couch to the dining room table, I stare at the stack of books I brought home. Each title and tagline promises inspiration and steps to setting and achieving goals. How can I possibly throw myself into career planning when I've failed, twice now, to help two of the most important people in my life?

It feels like a test. I finally decide exactly what I want to do with my life, and then fate throws another bump in the road. Although, this bump is really more of a boulder in the form of a sulking man who has just had his dreams crushed. Everything he ever worked for is gone. How do I spin that into something positive and push him to make new dreams?

They say those who can't do, teach. I never liked that. The most inspirational and knowledgeable people are those who have lived it. But maybe those who can't help the people they really want, set out to help everyone else.

I grab my purse and phone and head for the front door. After slamming it shut behind me, take that world, I walk with purpose down the street. The purpose being I need my best friend to save me from my thoughts.

I find Gabby sitting at the small desk in her room, an array of color thread laid out in front of her. I pull a chair to the side and grab the three spools closest to me, unwinding it until I have a good length for a bracelet.

I haven't done this in years, but my fingers remember, and I work at a good pace until I reach the end and tie it with a knot. It isn't perfect. In fact, the imperfections are glaring as I smooth a hand over it and place it next to the two Gabby has made in the same time.

"Can I ask you something?"

She sits back and smiles. "Sure. What do you want to know?"

"Do you ever resent the fact I'm living your dreams while you're still here in Suck Hill?"

She starts to respond, eager to tell me no way, I'm sure. I don't want whatever practiced, positive spin she's about to say.

"Honestly. I mean I know you love me and want nothing but good for me, but do you ever resent me for it? I'm doing all the things you planned for us. These were your dreams not mine. I just wanted to do whatever you did. You're the one who made me promise we'd rule the world."

"I think you're remembering that differently from how it went down."

I shake my head as I think back to all our conversations about what we wanted to do when we graduated and left Succulent Hill. "No, your dreams were always so much bigger than mine."

Gabby takes my hands. A white scar runs across the top of her hand, and I focus on the reminder of pain that has healed and hope that even in the worst of times people survive.

"You gave me permission to have those crazy dreams. My family, my teachers, even our classmates thought I was nuts. You never did."

It's true. She was, no *is*, special. I'd always known she was capable of anything.

"Your love and friendship are the reasons I dreamed big. You let me believe I could have everything I ever wished for. Even now, I don't know if I'd be able to get out of bed every day if it weren't for your voice in the back of my head telling me I can."

"Gabs." My voice breaks, and I squeeze her hand tightly. "I don't know how to be that for him. He's lost everything he ever wanted."

"Give him time. When he's ready, you'll know, and then, just be you."

"He's pushing me away."

"Don't take this the wrong way, but what do you expect him to do? His identity has changed. You still see him as the same guy, but everything he ever thought he was has been flipped upside down. He has to deal with that before he can let other people back in. I can see how much you want to run to him and fix it."

I open my mouth the deny it, but she gives me a knowing smirk. "It's written all over your face. Remember how you used to storm in here and get me out of bed? Lord, I wanted to toss you out of here some days when you'd pop in all chipper and bring me magazines or books. You're lucky we're neighbors or I'd have ghosted you too. The first time you brought the yoga mats, I thought our friendship was over for good. I could barely look at myself in the mirror and you were spouting inner peace bullshit."

I hold a hand over my mouth to suppress a giggle. "I never knew that."

"You're the strongest person I know, Blair. You don't have to hold on to my dreams, or his, but you do because you desperately want to see everyone have everything they could ever want. You're a little dream maker. You always have been. You sell yourself short for not wanting big things, but you want big things for *everyone*. Your dreams are not only bigger than mine ever were, they're more important. You're going to do amazing things. You're going to inspire and help so many people."

"Speaking of helping people." I pull out the spring semester Valley course catalog from my purse and hand it to her.

Surprise makes her eyes widen. "Blair, I can't."

"You can." I leave no room for argument. "Just think about it. It will probably be hard at first, I don't dispute that, but you can't sit up here for the rest of your life. And I promise to be right by your side."

She drops the catalog and hugs me fiercely. Her voice is quiet and shaky when she whispers, "Still letting me dream big."

TWENTY-EIGHT

Wes

"You're back!" Joel stops short after he spots me lying on the couch in our living room.

"Was there some doubt about my return to school?" I ask dryly. I'm being an ass, but I want no part of all the questions and small talk now that I'm back. I've only managed to avoid it to this point because I've ignored texts and calls like it was my job.

"Classes don't start back for another week," he says by explanation.

I let out a sigh. "I couldn't handle my parents hovering over me, checking the clock like I was keeping them from their usual holiday festivities. Happy?"

Joel laughs. "No, not really, but I'm glad as shit you're back. Z has been quieter than normal. In fact, if it weren't for the shit he says on the court I'd think he'd gone mute."

As if on cue, the big man walks through the door. A smile spreads across his face and then falls. "You're back."

Before I can brace myself, I'm lifted and squeezed like a teddy bear in the desperate clutches of a child.

"Fuck, Z," I wheeze out and chuckle. "I missed you too, big guy." I pat his back a few times, and he eases me back down to the couch.

Joel plops down in the armchair with a big goofy grin on his face as if nothing has changed. Fuck, I missed being here. Even more than I hated the idea of coming back and being the only one not running off to practice. Coach told me I was always welcome in his gym and encouraged me to come be his eyes and ears, continue working with Shaw and all that. I told him hard pass.

"We going out to celebrate tonight then?"

"No," Z and I say in unison.

"Aww, come on. You don't have anything going on tomorrow." Joel points to me before swinging his attention to my right. "And, Z, we have late practice tomorrow and our next game isn't until late next week. Come on, you pansy asses. I'm texting Nathan, he'll be in."

Something about his plea or the idea that we could have a night out just like the old days touches something in both of us, I guess, because we're both nodding and making plans before I realize what's happening.

We head to The Hideout and grab a table where I can sit and prop up my leg. The pain is better every day, but too much time upright, and I'm gritting my teeth and sucking down painkillers.

The bar and grill is quiet, but then Joel has to open his mouth.

"Blair coming?" he asks as he puts a beer in front of me and takes a seat across the table.

"Think she's still in Succulent Hill."

"You think?" He pauses, beer resting on his lips.

"We haven't talked much over break. Been kinda busy," I grumble, pointing to my leg.

"Bullshit. Busy feeling sorry for yourself."

Joel takes out his phone, and I drain half the glass in front of me, thankful for once Z is quiet.

Nathan and a few more of the guys from the team trickle in, and Joel waves them over as he puts the phone to his ear.

Tables are pushed together, and pitchers are placed in the middle so we can fit everyone.

"Blair, hey, it's Joel."

My ears perk up at her name, and all the blood rushes from my head to a pit in my stomach.

"What. The. Fuck?" I grit out.

"You back in town? We're at The Hideout. Wes was just crying about how much he misses you, why don't you come down so he'll stop pouting."

I grab for the phone, but he pushes back and stands, walking out of ear shot. I pull out my own phone and open my and Blair's text history. The last thing I said to her was "Okay" in response to her asking me how I was feeling. That was two days ago. She finally got the message that I wasn't up for idle chitchat about my wellbeing and here Joel is, meddling in my shit.

He walks back to the table, a shit-eating grin on his face. "She's on her way. You're welcome."

My phone vibrates with a new text, but it's from Mario, not Blair.

Mario: Angry chick alert. Heading your way with Vanessa and Blair. Guard your good leg, V is pissed you ghosted Blair all break.

I don't respond before I tuck my phone away. Maybe I can act surprised when they arrive. Z is beside me, and I hide behind him a little. Call me a coward all you want, fucking Vanessa is scary.

Seeing Blair again after my less than warm behavior over the past three weeks makes something ache in my chest. She stays firmly planted to Vanessa's side as the trio walks up to the table and says hello. Empty space at the table and chairs scattered around the place go untouched as the girls make their excuses and head to sit at the bar. It's like she came just to make a point she didn't want to see me. Makes zero sense, but here she is, looking hot and angry and hotter because angry looks good on her. Fuck.

"Ouch," Z says, eyes watching Blair. "What the hell did you do to have Blair giving you the shrug off? Must've been something bad, it isn't like her. Girl doesn't know how to be cold."

"I was an ass all break," I admit quietly. "I haven't been returning her texts or calls."

"Why the fuck not?" It's a response I'm not prepared for. Z doesn't insert himself into relationships, and he certainly doesn't take sides when neither side is his.

"I was dealing with shit."

His expression tells me he thinks I'm in the wrong, but he doesn't say any more.

More and more guys from the baseball and basketball teams join us as the night goes on. Blair doesn't so much as glance back at the table from her spot at the bar. Vanessa, on the other hand, glares at me every chance she gets.

Mario and Clark, a freshman baseball player, stand behind the girls at the bar. Blair laughs at something Clark says. Her shoulders shake with the movement and the strap of her dress slips off one side. My eyes dart to the bare skin at the same time Clark reaches out and pushes the strap back into place.

I see red and move faster than I thought possible. I'm pushing my way between them before rational thought has a chance to intervene.

"The fuck, man," Clark says as he catches himself on the stool next to Blair.

"Hands off if you want to keep them."

Clark steps forward, not the least bit tempted to give my punk ass a pass even if I have a gimp leg, but Mario steps between us. "Take a walk, Sinclair."

Clark doesn't budge. His nostrils flare, and his hands curl into fists.

"I said take a walk." Mario's voice is even and calm.

Clark shrugs off, his displeasure at being called down clear on his face. "I think you should probably take a walk too."

"Don't get in my way, Mario," I warn. "I just want to talk to Blair."

He doesn't move, but I see his resolve crumble. "Just trying to look out for her. I'll move when she says it's okay, but not before."

He glances over at Vanessa, who looks at him like he's her hero.

"It's fine, you two," Blair says, hopping down from her chair and placing a hand on Mario's arm. "Can you give us a few minutes?"

Vanessa side-eyes me as Mario leads her away.

"You want to sit?" Blair reclaims her spot at the bar.

I don't know what I expected after I crossed the bar, got in some guys face for touching her, and then treated another guy that I've been cool with for years like shit, but it isn't civility from her.

"Sorry about that," I say as I sit. I'm not sorry in the least, but there's a laundry list of shit I've done in the past few weeks that needs apologizing for, so it feels like a good move to start groveling right off the bat.

"When did you get back?" A seemingly simple question made treacherous by her tone.

"Today. I was going—"

She holds up a hand. "Save it."

"You look good." At least that's the truth. She's wearing a silver dress that shows off her toned shoulders, and her hair is pulled up and away from her face in the way I like. I don't know if the effort was for me, but it doesn't go unappreciated. She looks all shiny and new, and I feel all tarnished.

"Thank you." She lets out a breath as if she's preparing for battle. "How is it being back?"

For some reason, I don't give her my rehearsed line. Maybe it's the way she asks like she cares or understands. Maybe I just want to be real with someone. Maybe it's just her.

"Tough, but it's better than watching my mom walk around with a Kleenex in her hand, wiping her eyes like I died or something."

"Blair, we're gonna head out." V hovers off to the side.

She stands and pulls her purse strap to her shoulder. "Well, I should get going. I have work tomorrow."

"The café is open over break?"

She shakes her head. "No, I quit my job at the café. I got a job with the campus career center. I'm going in tomorrow to get things set up."

Joel appears at my side and pulls Blair into a hug. He's drunk and completely oblivious to the moment he just barged in on.

"Blair, it's so good to see you. You coming back to the house? We're having some people over for a little after party."

I grind my teeth. "We are?"

"No, sorry. I was just telling Wes I got a new job teaching workshops on goal setting and choosing a career path."

"That's a thing?" Joel asks with a confused expression on his face.

"It is. It's an optional workshop taught once a month by an upper classman. I'll also be occupying a table at the tutor center for one-on-one sessions and tips on setting and achieving goals."

"Who would go to something like that?"

I elbow him in the ribs. "Sounds"—I search for the words, any words but the ones that are coming to mind—"interesting."

"Yeah, well, let's hope others think so."

"Good to see you, Joel."

She faces off with me. "Wes."

She takes a step, and I grab her arm. The heat and spark between us surprises me, not because my feelings have changed but because I haven't felt anything in weeks. How does this girl break through my walls without even trying?

"It was good to see you, Blair."

"Take care of that foot. And maybe give your mom a pass this once. She's crying because of your loss—not hers. It is a hopeless feeling to watch the people you love go through tough times with nothing to do but hope they'll accept whatever support you offer."

She breezes past me like she didn't just cut me down at the knees.

And the fuck . . . she didn't say it was good to see me too.

TWENTY-NINE

Blair

"It's gonna be incredible, V. I have my own little cubicle at the tutor center, and I bought this letter board so I can post inspirational sayings or quotes so everyone that comes in can get a little bit of positivity added in their day."

She chuckles but throws her arm around me. "I'm proud of you. Tossing inspiration around like confetti while your boyfriend is being an ass."

"He isn't my boyfriend," I grumble. "We were a casual thing, and now it's over I guess."

"Mm-hmm. Spin it however you want, but I saw the way he looked at you the other night."

"Well, regardless, it's been a week, and I haven't heard a peep from him."

Vanessa gives me a reassuring smile.

"It's fine." I shake off the sting of rejection. "On a happier note, Gabby is coming up next week to meet with an advisor and scope out the campus. Fingers crossed it goes well and that senior year the three of us can get an apartment off campus together."

"Now you're talking."

Her phone beeps, and she gets that look on her face that tells me it's Mario, which is confirmed when she says, "Mario says the guys are having a party tonight. What do you say we go celebrate surviving the first day of a new semester and your awesome new job?"

"I dunno."

"Come on. The basketball guys are at an away game, so you don't have to worry about running into them, and I'll tell Mario I'm spending the party hours with my best girl. I promise I will not leave your side." She sticks out her bottom lip, pouting and looking ridiculous.

"All right, all right. It's better than sitting around here feeling sorry for myself."

There are more people than I've ever seen crowded into the small space. Looks like everyone is looking for a way to celebrate the beginning of a new semester. "This is insane."

"I know, right?" Vanessa says as she pushes through the living room. "Mario is probably downstairs. Let's get a drink and say hello."

With plastic cups filled with vodka and Sprite, we move toward the music pumping downstairs. Unlike the last time I was here, the basement is so packed that I can't even tell it's a dilapidated shithole.

We skirt the edges of the dance floor, holding hands so we don't lose each other. "I see Clark and some of the other guys on the other side, maybe Mario is with them."

I sip my drink and sway to the music, following V. It feels good to be out and not to be obsessing over if or when Wes might call.

A row of couches are pushed back against the far wall and people are smushed on them, girls on laps of guys I recognize. Clark is holding on tight to a busty redhead, and another guy I recognize as one of Mario's room-mates is leaning back, letting a petite blonde rape his face. She's using so much tongue that I cringe and look away.

But what I see next stops me in my tracks. His lap is currently playing host to a beautiful brunette who has her hand affectionately resting on his chest. He's drunk, that much would have been clear even if he didn't have a tequila bottle in his hand.

"What the fuck, Wes?" It's Vanessa's voice, not my own, that gets his attention.

When his eyes find mine, they're filled with regret and pain. He sits forward like he's going to get up, but I'm not interested in talking to him. Not now. Maybe not ever again.

I turn and flee the way I came, pushing through the crowd as best as I can with my eyes blurred with unshed tears.

I make it all the way to the porch before Wes catches up to me. He puts his big body in front of me. "Wait, damn it, woman. Hold up."

His breathing is labored, and he grabs ahold of the railing like he needs the support.

"What are you doing here?"

"Hanging with Mario and the guys. Nothing happened with that chick. She just sat down. I didn't do anything."

Nothing happened? God, if that isn't the guilty man's anthem, then I don't know what is. Laughter bubbles in my chest. "I meant why aren't you in California with the team?"

He shrugs. "Didn't feel like it."

He reaches out and caresses my cheek, brushing away a tear before he leans in bringing a waft of alcohol with him. I step back.

"You're free to do whatever or whomever you want. You've made it very clear that whatever we were, we aren't anymore. Just leave me alone."

He looks conflicted about my words, but I mean it. I don't want to talk to him when he's like this. I knew standing by while he dealt with his shit would be hard, but this is too much. "Please. I'm begging you. Not here. Not tonight."

He nods and tucks his hands into his front pockets before turning back to the house. I sag against the railing when he's gone and let all the tears fall. I don't even know why I'm crying. Despite the cliché, I believe that nothing happened between him and the chick downstairs. Not yet anyway. And I guess that's what wrecks me—he is going to move on, and man, does it sting to picture him with other girls.

"Aww, don't tell me the happy couple broke up?" David's voice is like adding insult to injury. He walks out on to the porch with a beer in hand.

"I don't have anything to say to you, David. What are you even doing here?"

He shrugs. "Looks like the whole university is here tonight."

"Go away." I bite back the horrible words I want to say. "Please."

David smiles cruelly. "Reynolds cut you loose, huh? Maybe we should work out another agreement." He leans in. "You didn't really think I deleted all the pictures just because you got your boyfriend to threaten me, did you?" He laughs. "Knew that wouldn't last."

My control, and probably my sanity, snaps. Killing him with kindness seems to be a losing battle. "You know what, David? Go to hell. You're a shitty excuse for a human." I shove past him and walk all the way home, hugging myself as I ugly cry. As I crawl into bed, I promise myself that, after tonight, I won't shed one more tear over Wes Reynolds. I will cry out all the sadness to make room for hope, but the only thing I'm hoping for is to turn back to a time where Wes and I were happy.

THIRTY

Wes

I wake up with my cell phone resting on my chest. Technology is awesome . . . until it's not. Having a way for someone to get a hold of you any time, any day makes it that much more painful when they don't.

I spent the past two days texting Blair, apologizing every way I could think of. I deserve to be ghosted after how I treated her, I get that, but it doesn't suck any less.

I give in to the temptation and check for missed texts that I know won't be there. My pessimism is on point, but I'm disappointed anyway.

"What the hell are you doing up?" I ask Nathan as he steps into the living room and pulls his hair back into a low ponytail.

He startles. "What the hell are you doing sleeping on the couch?"

"I'm not sleeping."

He drops onto the floor and starts repping out pushups.

"Dude, it's five in the morning."

I'm met with silence and the even exhale of his breaths.

"Fifty," he mutters quietly and jumps up. He moves to the wall and dips down into a wall squat. "You smell awful, man."

"Yep." I acknowledge the stench and the disgusting taste in my mouth from falling asleep after a night of drinking without brushing my teeth. "Feel just as awful."

Rubbing a hand over my forehead, I can practically feel the throbbing through my fingertips. I sit up slowly and grab the water I left on the coffee table, drain it, and then sit back, feeling a little more human.

"Since you're up, how about helping me with some band work?"

"Here? Now?"

"Nah, I'm meeting Shaw at the gym in five."

Lean back on the couch. "Pass."

"Come on, we need a third." He pushes off the wall. "And you know we could use the extra work. Got a lot of tough games coming up. Z's gonna need some help down low."

My better judgment hasn't had time to wake up or sober up, and he's played to my weakness—Z. "Yeah, fine. Let me shower quick."

It isn't until we're outside making our way across the street to Ray Fieldhouse that my stomach revolts and the alcohol in my system starts to seep out my pores. Haven't been back since I was carted out to the hospital with a broken foot. In fact, it's probably the longest I've gone without stepping into a gym since I started playing all those years ago.

To my surprise, Shaw is already here, running drills. His sweat-soaked shirt and wet hair tell me he's been here a while. I bite back my approval.

"Reynolds, nice to see you." The shock in Rookie's eyes combined with the pity dissolve all good feelings.

For the next hour, I basically play ball boy. Shaw and Nathan take turns. One wraps a resistance band around his waist and the other holds the ends of the band tight and pulls backward. When I set the ball on the floor a couple of feet away, they work against each other. The point isn't to keep the guy in front from getting the ball, it's to provide just enough resistance that he has to *earn* it.

My roommate has a good flow with Rookie. There's an ease to their routine like they've done it before.

"When did you two become besties?" I ask Nathan when Shaw takes a piss break.

He lifts one shoulder and lets it fall. "He needed someone to see beyond the multi-sport athlete thing. You know I don't give a shit about that stuff."

I do know that. Not much except silence during movie night gets Nathan riled up. He's able to leave the competitive nature and intensity of being a college athlete on the floor. Outside of the gym, he's just a chill dude looking for fun.

"Taking your spot, trying to do what you do? It isn't an easy job. If we're gonna have any type of shot in the tournament, he has to start mesh-ing with the guys. Some of the team resents him for splitting time, some are just frustrated that he isn't you, but no one feels good about where we are. It's a shitty place to be this far into the season."

I pull at my hair, hearing what he's saying and understanding the things he doesn't say. I'd been helping the rook until I realized I was done for, and now he has to find his way all on his own. Shitty for him, but I'm not in a mood to compare our tragic tales. "What do you want me to do?"

"Just show up, man. That's all anyone wants from you."

THIRTY-ONE

Blair

Vanessa sits at her desk across our small room. "Do people actually attend these workshops?"

My shoulders slump. If my friends' reactions are any indication, the answer to that is a big fat no. "I don't know. I hope so."

"Want me to come by for moral support?"

"No, no. It's fine. I just need to help one person. Then they'll tell their friends and so on and so forth. Plus, I think the real difference will be in the one-on-one sessions at the tutoring center. Goals are personal."

"Well, I'm really proud of you no matter what. And you've inspired me. Look, I bought one of those fancy paper planners." She holds up the spiral-bound planner like a proud elementary school student with coveted new crayons.

"Impressive."

"Well, it will be if I remember to fill the thing out."

I have my doubts. An electronic planner seems way more V's style, but far be it for me to keep her from attempting organization.

"Heard from Wes since the other night?"

"Yes."

"Yes?" She turns in her chair, which I only know because it squeaks. I've turned my attention back to my desk to study my own planner carefully. I've kept this information to myself because Vanessa is currently still seeing red when it comes to Wes. He may have a boot on his foot and a basketball shaped hole in his heart, but apparently, this doesn't save him from the wrathful blowback of hurting V's friend.

I sigh. "He texted to apologize again for the other night."

"Still hasn't apologized for being an ass for the three weeks before that?"

"No. Maybe I made too big of a deal out of it. We were nothing—we never put a label on it."

"Bullshit. Uh-uh. Don't you dare let his behavior make you feel like you don't deserve to be upset. That boy was falling all over you. I get that he went through some shit, but he doesn't get a get-out-of-jail-free card just because he suddenly grew a conscious. You deserve more."

"All right, all right. Point made. You may step down from your soap box now."

V smiles. "Good. What time is Gabby getting here?"

"Her mom is dropping her by after their campus tour."

She stands and rubs her hands together. "Perfect. That gives me time to dress myself and then you."

I don't bother fighting. A little bit of V pampering and a night out with my two favorite girls sounds perfect.

"People are staring at me!" Gabby hisses and ducks her head.

"Actually, they're staring at Blair." Vanessa gives me a once over and her glossy, hot-pink lips twist into a smile. "You should let me dress you more often."

I tug at the hemline of my dress as another guy openly checks me out in a way that does not make me feel beautiful. "It's like major creep alert tonight."

"Come on, let's go to the bar. Those legs are going to get us free drinks."

"Fine. I want to check my phone anyway."

I haven't given in and texted Wes back, but I'm anxiously waiting for each one he sends. It feels good to be on the receiving end of his attention, even if it's just to clear his guilt.

"Oh no. We are not texting Wes tonight. You need to stop being available to him until he mans up and claims you. If you let him, he's going to pull you back into that weird thing that's casual but not because you spend all your time together, and its bullshit. He either wants you for real or he can take a hike."

This coming from the queen of casual. At least before Mario. "I can see what you're thinking. You aren't me. You're in love with him, and I just don't want to see you get hurt if he decides to ghost. Again."

I look to Gabby for backup. She shakes her head. "I'm with her."

"I wasn't going to text him. I just like re-reading the ones he sent."

Okay, I've reached pathetic. I read it loud and clear on their concerned faces.

"You've made your point," I say, rolling my eyes and leaving my phone in my purse as we belly up to the bar.

"So, Gabs, are you coming to Valley next year?"

Leave it to Vanessa to cut right to the chase. I'd been hesitant to ask about how Gabby's day went. I knew this was hard for her and would be a big step.

"I'm not sure," she admits and plays with her hair, twisting and turning it around her fingers so it covers the left side of her face.

"You just need to own it. Pull that hair away from your face and hold your head up proudly. You're stunning, and people are going to stare. You show them that it doesn't bother you, and it won't bother them."

Gabby doesn't look convinced, but she does hold her head higher as the bartender comes to get our drink order.

"What can I get you ladies?" The bartender is a Valley grad student who Vanessa has dubbed the hottest guy on campus and also off limits. I can't argue with her reasoning unless I want the bartender at the most popular bar in town adding me to the no-serve list.

"Hey, don't I know you?" He points at me and narrows his eyes.

"Me?" I look around. "I don't think so. I mean . . . we come in occasionally. I'm Blair." I extend my hand to try to smooth over the awkward exchange.

He takes my hand and nods, recognition in his eyes. "You're one of the Valley Wild girls."

"The what?" V and I say at the same time.

"Yeah, your hair is pulled up in the photo, but I can tell it's you."

Bile coats my throat as he pulls out his phone, taps the screen a few times, and turns it toward us.

"Oh my God." V's voice is distant as I duck and push through the crowd to the bathroom. Everywhere I look, I see it now. The looks I've been getting all night aren't guys checking me out, they're guys picturing me naked in vivid detail."

Tears threaten as I close the door behind us and lock it. I pace the dingy, smelly bathroom, wishing I'd made my getaway to the car instead of here. This space does not help the downward spiral of my emotions.

"What the hell is going on?" Gabby asks, looking a bit shell shocked.

"Breathe, sweetie. It's gonna be okay. Mario is on his way. He'll get us out of here and take us home where we can figure this out."

"Figure this out? Ha! Everyone has seen me naked. Like, really naked, V."

"I know. Fucking David. I'm gonna kill him."

"David, your ex-boyfriend?" Gabby asks.

I stare up at the textured ceiling, feeling beyond humiliated as Gabby paces the floor and V scopes out the damage while filling Gabby in on the David drama from last semester.

"Why didn't you tell me?" The way Gabby looks at me makes me feel horrible for not confiding in her.

"I guess I was afraid it'd make you even more hesitant to come to Valley if you knew how shitty people can be here."

"Are you kidding?" She laughs. "There's so much drama here I think I'll fit right in. You had me believing Valley was filled with Ken and Barbie cutouts and I was going to be the weird scar girl. No one even noticed me out there. Which is probably in part because they were picturing my best friend naked." She scrunches up her face in an apologetic frown.

V sighs and tucks her phone away. "Well, in good news, it isn't just you naked on this horrible website."

"That isn't good news."

"We'll get them taken down, honey, I promise."

"It's too late. They'll be saved and shared forever."

They flank me and link their arms in mine. "What can we do to help?"

It's a role reversal. I'm usually the one offering sympathy and comfort, or in V's case, talking her down from cutting off someone's balls.

"Nothing. I just want to go home and hang with my best girls. I'm not letting David ruin our night. I'll deal with it tomorrow. Tonight, let's just forget about it. Well . . . once we get out of here."

"I think I have an old bottle of Apple Pucker stashed in our closet."

For some reason, that sends us all into a fit of giggles, and I think maybe it might just be possible to survive this. Just as long as we're together.

THIRTY-TWO

Wes

I'm standing next to Joel's car, huddling in my hoodie freezing my nuts off while I wait for him to come out of the fieldhouse. Coming to practice was a mistake. Watching the team struggle and not being able to jump in and do it myself is torture.

By the time he appears with Z and Nathan, I could have walked home and back twice. I've taken to blowing into my hands to keep them warm.

"I'm gonna walk," Nathan says and heads off toward the house before lighting a cigarette. Coach is gonna kick his ass if he sees him smoking. Not my problem now.

"What took you so long?" I ask as Joel unlocks the car and Z and I toss our bags in before squeezing ourselves into the small sports car. He starts the engine and then let's out a long breath. "We have a problem."

He hands me the phone, and I suck in a breath. "What the fuck is this?"

"It's everywhere. Like fifty different people texted me the site."

I read the title and scroll through the Valley Wild Girls website. What the actual fuck?

I pull out my own phone and dial Blair.

"She isn't answering." Panic laced with frustration and desperation fills my voice.

Joel's phone beeps, and I read the text from Mario. "They're at The Hideout."

I scroll back through the text exchange between Joel and Mario where

the latter outlines what transpired tonight. The short version: David is dead.
"I'm gonna kill that fucker."

Joel's grip tightens around the steering wheel as he flips a U-turn. I tap
restlessly on the dash until he screeches to a stop in front of The Hideout.

Mario and the baseball guys wait by the door.

"Where is she?"

"They're hiding in the bathroom. She hadn't seen it when they went in,
and well, you can guess the rest."

Mario steps in front of me, blocking my entrance. "You need to know
something else. David's in there. He was walking in as we pulled up. Thought
we better wait for you."

I push past him, and Joel grabs my arm to slow me down. "Easy, killer.
You have a gimp leg, and there's a bar full of people. Take a deep breath before you go in there and get yourself in trouble."

"Don't give a flying fuck, man." I pull free and keep going.

I spot David and see red. I manage to turn to Mario. "You guys should
go. Get the girls out of here."

I'm anxious to get to Blair. There's so much I want to say and so much
I have to apologize for. This is all my fault. I need to make sure she knows
I'll take care of it, but first, I need to deal with David. I made him a prom-
ise, after all.

Mario nods.

David has the audacity to look surprised as he watches me stalk across
the bar.

My hands ball at my side, and I don't give two shits about the guys
standing around him.

This asshole is gonna pay.

Before I can get to him, Vanessa flies across my vision and is up in his
face. Mario and his guys flank Blair and Gabby. Gabby's here? Blair doesn't
look up no matter how much I silently beg her to. I need to see her face. See
that she's okay. Vanessa's voice pulls my attention back to David.

"You're a worthless piece of shit." She grabs him by the shoulders and
knees him hard. So hard that my boys shrivel up and hide in fear. Damn, V
is savage.

"Douche canoe," she spouts as she flips her brown hair over one shoulder and marches back to Mario's side. Mario gets the girls out of the bar
just as it erupts in a collective groan. David doubles over in pain, but it isn't

enough. I want him lying on the ground. Joel and Z follow me to the table David and his cronies occupy. Z crosses his arms over his chest, displaying his massive size. Glad he's on my side.

David stands upright, but he doesn't see the punch coming, and as my knuckles meet his jaw, the pain feels fantastic. So good that I go in for another and another. My vision goes black.

"All right, all right. That's enough," Z says sternly, but I don't miss the humor in his voice. He catches my arm, and I still as awareness returns. David's buddies look torn between standing up for their friend and getting their own asses beat or letting me take my pound of flesh without their intervention. I'm almost hoping they're stupid enough to come at me. I don't have beef with them, but I'm looking for any reason to hit something else.

Z and Joel have other ideas. They pull me back and shove me down into a booth.

"Hope that was worth it." Z points outside where red and blue lights flash.

"Oh, it was worth it."

She's worth everything.

It isn't until Coach shows up that I feel even the tiniest bit of remorse. And even then, I don't regret hitting David, just getting the rest of the guys involved and making the team look bad.

He leans against the side of the cop car beside me. I've already given my statement, and so far, no one has put me in cuffs, so that's a good sign.

He's silent for a beat before he says, "What a shitty practice tonight."

Laughter shakes my chest, the sound foreign to my ears. When was the last time I laughed?

"Coming back tomorrow?"

I flex my hand. A sting of pain shoots up my arm. I search for words, an answer. Neither yes or no feels right. How can I be there? And how can I not?

Coach straightens. "Well, they aren't pressing charges, so get your ass home. See you tomorrow. Or not."

As he walks away, Joel steps up. "Come on. I'll take you to see Blair."

"Nah, somewhere else I need to go."

He raises both eyebrows, and I hold my hands up. "This stop doesn't involve the police. I promise."

Pulling up to the Morenos' estate is like pulling up to something out of the movies. The massive house sits on the side of a mountain and is lit up like an amusement park. When we finally reach our destination, Joel pulls up under the old-school carriage style covered awning in front of the house.

"Thanks," I say before we get out of the car. "I know you don't like going to your father for help."

He shrugs. "Guess there's no other way around this one. He probably already knows."

The Moreno house is organized chaos. Joel's mother brings coffee and then orders her daughters, Joel's sisters, to re-heat leftovers despite everyone's insistence they aren't hungry. Mr. Moreno sits at the head of a long dining table that looks out into the Rincon Mountains. A king on top of his mountain.

"Idiotic. This could end up splashed across every sports headline tomorrow. No respect for Coach Daniels." He mutters more to himself than us, but Joel, Z, and I stare shamefaced down at the table anyway.

Joel is the first one to speak. "Pa, the guy posted nude photos of several Valley students."

He slides his phone to his dad, who looks down at it and then slides it back. "I've already seen it. The site was taken down thirty minutes ago."

"So, that's it?" It's my voice that yells out.

"There'll be a formal investigation, and we're sending out a reminder email tomorrow morning about the campus policy on sexual harassment."

"You can't be serious. He just gets to walk around campus while these girls are humiliated? That's bullshit."

Mr. Moreno raises his eyebrows at me as the three women in his life enter the dining room with dishes of hot food.

"Sorry," I mumble an apology to Mrs. Moreno.

"I think it's noble." She pats my shoulder. "Too many young men thinking it's okay to treat women like sex objects these days."

Mr. Moreno sighs. "Without proof, I can't do anything. Hence, the investigation."

"But we know who did it," Joel says.

"You have hearsay." He shakes his head and stands. "We're going to do everything we can to resolve it quickly. You think I want something like this going unpunished?" He looks in the direction the women disappeared. "I have two daughters who are going to be at Valley in a few years. I want others to know it won't be tolerated, but there are appropriate channels to go through when dealing with stuff like this."

All I hear is that it will be weeks or months where David goes unpunished, and it isn't enough, but I can see resolve in Mr. Moreno's face.

Mrs. Moreno insists that we stay the night, and I think we're all too exhausted to fight her. I go to bed fully clothed and watch as the minutes tick by. I really screwed things up this time. I wonder what Blair is doing right now. Is she in bed, wishing she could rewind time and erase me from her life? I've made such a mess of things. I was too busy feeling sorry for myself to protect her. As the sun rises, I'm still staring at the ceiling and trying to figure out how the hell I'm going to make this right.

No grand gestures come to mind, so I settle for persistence. I'll win her back the same way I've won at every aspect of my life—hard work and dedication. And heart.

THIRTY-THREE

Blair

My alarm wakes me at the usual time, but instead of jumping right out of bed, I lie there and play back the last year of my life like a highlight reel. Surprisingly, the most painful memories aren't of David, but of Wes. David humiliated me, but his betrayal was expected and skin deep. Wes's dismissal cuts at the very core of me.

When I finally step outside to head to class, he's the last person I expect to see sitting on the front steps. Bags under his eyes, clothes rumpled, he's still the hottest guy I've ever seen. "What are you doing here?"

"I called last night. I—"

"I heard what you did. Thank you for standing up for me, but really, I'm fine. Go home."

Of all the times I wished he'd show up for me, he picks the moment I feel the least beautiful, the least deserving of him.

"Can't do that until I apologize and make up for how I acted. I'm so sorry, Blair."

"Apology accepted. Now go home."

I take off down the sidewalk toward campus, and Wes follows beside me. Wordlessly, he walks me all the way to Stanley Hall.

"See you in fifty-five."

I sigh. "Do you even have class right now?"

"Nope. My morning is wide open."

"Go *home*, Reynolds. You aren't doing me any favors by sitting outside my class like some sort of security guard."

He challenges me with a determined set to his jaw. "You're right. I'm coming in with you."

"That's not—"

"Up for discussion." He pushes past me and holds the door open. Whatever, Wes wants to waste his day, then so be it. I have no more secrets to be used against me, and I'm more determined than ever to rock my classes.

Most people don't even look up as I take a seat in the large auditorium, and the few guys who act like maybe they want to say or do something turn away when they see Wes glowering behind me.

I slump into my seat and breathe deeply as I pull out my phone and sit back in my chair, waiting for class to start. Wes silently does the same, and as I scroll through Reddit, a text flashes on my screen.

Wes: I want names of anyone who participated in what went down last night.

I roll my eyes as I respond.

Me: I don't need you to protect me. Let it go.

Wes: Not a chance.

When class is over, Wes stands and blocks me from leaving before he's stared down every single classmate. It's so obvious he's trying to make some sort of statement that I'm not to be messed with, and as annoying as it is, it's also so ridiculous that my heart betrays my resolve. The struggle is real when it comes to hardening my heart against this man.

And so goes the rest of my day. Wes walks me to every class and even back to the sorority house. He's limping and, as frustrated as I am, I'm touched too. But this is insanity. I don't need him acting as my bodyguard. He didn't want anything to do with me before, so why act like he cares now? I get that his loyalty makes him feel somehow responsible, but I don't want him around out of loyalty alone.

"Okay, as you can see. I'm safe and sound. No one said a word to me all day. I relieve you from your duty."

"They didn't say anything because I was with you."

That's probably true.

"Seriously, Wes. You don't need to do this. I'm fine. I can take care of myself. I don't need your pity."

"Pity? You think I'm doing this because I feel sorry for you? Fuck, Blair, this whole thing is my fault. I should have stopped him. I was supposed to protect you, and I didn't."

I shake my head. "That isn't accurate, and even if it were, I'm not yours to protect anymore."

My words cause him to frown and step back. "See you tomorrow," he says and gives me a salute.

I bite my tongue as Joel's car stops in front of the house. He waves from the driver's seat. I don't miss the grimace on Wes's face as he slumps into the seat. His foot has to be killing him.

The next morning, I sneak out an hour early to avoid any possible Wes run-ins and hole up in my new cubicle at the tutor center. I'm teaching my first workshop on goal setting and career planning today and, though the timing sucks with my peers all having seen me naked recently, I'm excited.

My excitement is short lived.

"That's it. Thank you so much for coming." The words are barely out of my mouth before the three people who stumbled in run for the door. I dig around in my backpack for a stray Spree. Certainly surviving that is cause for a reward. I exit the classroom, flipping off the light and pushing the door open with a hip, and stumble into a wall of muscle and my backpack lands with a *thud* next to a black boot.

Wes leans down and scoops up my bag.

Fingers brushing as I take it from him, I manage a mumble of thanks.

"How'd it go?"

"Only three people showed up. Luckily, they seem to be the only three people on campus who haven't seen me naked."

He pulls a bag of Chewy Spree seemingly from thin air, and I salivate like a dog in one of those Pavlovian experiments. "Now, how could you re-phrase that to better represent your achievements instead of focusing on the things you can't control?"

I balk, staring at him, delicious candy not forgotten but temporarily moved to second position of things of interest.

"You were listening?"

He shrugs. "We spent a lot of time together, some of what you said was bound to stick."

I quirk an eyebrow and cross my arms over my chest. "What are you doing here?"

He looks down at his shoes before meeting my eyes. "I wanted to make sure you were okay."

"I already told you, I'm fine." I move to step around him, but he's quicker and sidesteps with me.

"Also, I wanted to apologize again. Not for what happened with David. For everything before. I acted like an ass."

"Apology accepted." I take another step around him, but he cuts me off and shakes the bag of candy above my head.

I sigh. "Three people showed up today. That's three more people that I've helped and three people who might tell their friends."

"Good job." He pats my head. I'd love to be offended, but the goofy smile on his face makes him look young and carefree. Like the Wes I fell in love with.

I swipe the Sprees from his hand. We walk out of the university building together. I can feel him watching me, but he doesn't say anything.

"How'd you find me?"

He waves a hand as if it isn't a big deal, but there is a pleased grin on his face. "I follow all the happenings of the career resource center." His expression falls. "Actually, I probably should stop in now that it's time to start thinking about what I'm going to do after graduation."

"Where are you headed next?" I ask after he goes silent.

He points to Moreno Hall. "I have macroeconomics."

I scrunch my nose.

"Eh, it'll be fine. The professor doesn't mind if I sleep through class like Professor O'Sean."

"It's infuriating that you can sleep through and still manage to get an A."

"Wasn't so infuriating when I was saving your ass from failing."

He's flirting . . . I think. It's almost like the playful banter we used to have that kept me on my toes and gave me full body tingles. My head and heart are conflicted. I do forgive him, but it's too hard to be around him like this. Wes Reynolds isn't the kind of guy you can be friends with after you've had more.

"I hear tomorrow night's game is going to be a good one."

He nods and shoves his hands into his pockets. "Utah is tough. They run a combination defense that . . ." He stops himself, and I wonder how long it's been since he's talked basketball. Is he going to practices? Has he stopped sulking and started travelling with the team again? They're questions I want to ask, but I know it would be crossing some invisible line he's drawn.

"Thank you for the candy," I say instead. "I guess I'll see you at the game."

"Maybe. I haven't decided if I'm going to go."

"What? Why not? You have to go." I stop and stare after him. He can't be serious.

He lifts one shoulder and lets it fall. "They don't need me there."

"Maybe not in the way you want to be there, but they do need you. You're their leader. You said so yourself."

His jaw flexes. "Enjoy the candy. Congrats on your first workshop. Text me if anyone gives you any trouble."

THIRTY-FOUR

Wes

I can see the steady stream of people entering Ray Fieldhouse from the window in our living room. It's weird to watch people come to a game decked out in blue and yellow. They hurry from their cars to the front door as excitement and hope that the home team will pull through radiates from them.

A contradiction to the way the bus of Utah players walked in two hours earlier. Slow, taking it all in and adjusting to being in someone else's house. They walked into my house, but it isn't really mine anymore, and it's fucking weird and awful. I consider where I should be. Do I go to the game and sit on the bench like I somehow still belong? Sitting in the bleachers isn't fucking happening. That's my team but in a completely different way than the fans think it's their team. I built that team, and spent the last four years busting my ass. Z and I crafted a team that is strong and quick and smart.

When the parking lot finally calms, I step out onto the front porch, and the sounds assault me. The rise and fall of the crowd cheering is my score-board, the refs whistle a shrill sound that brings silence that is more nerve wracking than the noise. I'm sweating, and my foot throbs as I pace back and forth, picturing it all.

I remove my hat, pull at my hair and then stop. Gonna make myself bald with the amount of tugging I've been doing. I put the hat back on and pull out my phone, giving in to my temptation to check the score online. I've missed two texts from Blair.

Blair: Are you here?

Blair: Where are you? Get here NOW.

Well, fuck, now I'm even more curious about what the hell is going on. Do they need me like the game is going bad or it's going well and she wants me to see the team finally meshing? I'm not even sure which would hurt less.

Or, Christ, maybe someone is messing with her. So far, people seem to have gotten the message that I'm not playing around when it comes to protecting Blair, but maybe my absence has brought out the bullies.

I cross the street and slow down as I approach.

"Wes! Wes!"

I catch a mass of brown hair in my peripheral and turn. Blair is running toward me, waving her arms. We're the only two people out here, so it isn't like I could miss her.

"Hey. You're here." Her breaths are shallow, and she puts a hand at her waist like she has a cramp from the fifty-yard jog.

My eyes fall to her chest, where the number twelve is proudly displayed. Her eyes follow mine.

"Everything okay? Why aren't you inside?"

She's still panting as she says, "I came to find you. Why aren't *you* inside?"

"For what? I can't play." What about this is so fucking hard for her to understand?

"They need you. Z looks angrier than ever and Shaw is a mess. You may not be able to play, but they need you right now. You're still their leader."

"How bad is it?"

"Go see for yourself."

The buzzer goes off, and there is a surge of movement inside the fieldhouse.

"Halftime," she says. "I think they need a pep talk from you more than they do the coach. I can't even pretend to understand your role and how much this has to suck, but I can see they are struggling and looking for someone to step up. Go be that person."

"What the hell am I supposed to say?"

She grins widely, probably pleased I'm finally soliciting her words of wisdom. "I can't pull something from my canned inspirational quotes for this one."

"You could try," I grit out. Figures . . . the one fucking time I need her is the one fucking time she tells me she has nothing.

"How about pulling from your own material, maybe something about heart and talent? It helped me when I needed it, maybe it'll work for them too."

She leaves me standing there gawking after her. Even in this moment, I can appreciate how damn good she looks wearing my jersey. My name plastered across her delicate shoulders and number stretching down to her tiny waist.

Well, looks like this is it. I either have to get in there or get the hell out of dodge before I'm spotted.

It's doubtful anyone is going to recognize me without my jersey, but I'm not taking any chances. I'm here for Z. The idea that he might need me, that I let him down . . . again, is more than I can take. I should be out there making sure he gets the shots he needs. Making sure the team makes it to the tournament again and ensuring Z's name is called in the first round of the draft. That was my job.

Coach's voice booms down the hallway. A set of security guards blocking off entry to the locker room look me up and down, but before I have to do something embarrassing like explain who the fuck I am, the one on the right recognizes me.

"Sorry about the foot, Reynolds. Boys sure could use you out there tonight."

I nod and open the door before I can talk myself out of it. It creaks shut, announcing my arrival just as Coach finishes his halftime yelling spree with the usual pep talk about coming back and working as a team.

"Reynolds." Coach nods and places his clipboard at his side. "You gonna join us for the second half?"

My teammates eye me with a mixture of pity and hope.

"Yes, sir."

He tosses me the clipboard. "Shaw, see Wes before you head out see if he has any notes on Utah's defense."

My hands shake as I grip the board in one hand and uncap the dry erase marker with the other. I stand in front of Shaw and make x's to represent the defense that Utah typically runs.

"Utah runs a combination. Pressure up top and zone down low. The most important thing you need to know about their style is that they're a bunch of selfish pricks. Talented, but selfish. They're aggressive and they take risks, which tends to pay off because it rattles their opponents. You can't let them rattle you. You play your game, not theirs. They want to pressure you to take the shot or make a quick pass, but that isn't our style. Our game is slow and smart. If you find yourself feeling rushed, you're giving in to their game."

Shaw nods, but he looks as good as defeated. I sigh and give in to Blair's advice.

"You can do this. We can beat them. We're just as talented, and our team has more heart. We play as a cohesive unit and get the ball to whoever has the best look—no matter what. They don't understand how not to be selfish, and that's how you're going to beat them. Take your time and move the ball around to get the best look."

"Sounds so simple."

I pat him on the back, a real smile threatening at the corners of my mouth. "It is."

Everyone clears the locker room except for Z, who hangs back, waiting for the door to close behind Shaw.

"I'm glad you came. Know it must be hard being here."

"I think it's going to be hard either way. This way, at least I don't feel like I'm letting you down again. I'll do whatever I can to make sure Shaw plays the kind of ball that'll get you in that first round."

"Fuck the draft."

My eyebrows shoot up high enough to reach the Valley hat on my head.

"You think I care about all that more than I care about you?"

"I . . ."

Well, fuck, yeah that's what I think.

"Playing next to you these years has been an honor. God willing, I'll get picked up in the first round, but right now I just want to know my friend is okay. Whatever you need, I'm here, just say the word."

"What do you say we start with a win out there tonight?"

He smirks. "Guess that depends on the pep talk you gave rook. He ready?"

"I sure as shit hope so," I mutter as we exit the locker room together.

Sitting on the sidelines during the second half is less weird than I imagined. Or maybe I'm just too glued to the action to feel anything but anxious. I've spent very little time on this bench during my college career and never really looked around and enjoyed the view. The way the stadium is filled with blue and yellow, the way the fans are always ready to jump to their feet to defend a bad call or cheer us on. The way one particular girl wrings her hands as she watches me instead of the guys on the floor.

I smirk at her and give her a small nod. Her shoulders visibly relax. I'd give anything to be out on that floor, but the view from the sidelines definitely has its perks. I wonder what she looked like when she watched me play. Did she jump up and down and cheer for me? Did she watch me more than the other guys?

We pull ahead and win the game by two points. Too close for anyone to feel like celebrating.

"What made you decide to come?" Joel asks as we make our way back to the house. Despite Z's monologue earlier, he's back to quiet, headphones on and the bass pumping.

"Blair," I admit. "Chick's relentless."

"We owe her. Having you here made all the difference," Joel says.

And I know just how to repay her.

THIRTY-FIVE

Blair

I stumble into the tutor center Monday afternoon a little defeated and a whole lot undercaffeinated. In my first week at the tutor center, I had exactly two students stop by to see me. Honestly, I think those poor souls got bad information and thought I was going to look deep into a crystal ball and uncover top-secret job opportunities with a six-figure salary on a bachelor's degree education.

I'm trying to remain positive. I know I can help people, but it's harder than I expected it to be to spread the word about what I'm doing without making it sound hokey. The students who would be up for this type of thing are either hesitant about the benefit of chatting with a peer or simply don't have time to add another to-do to their schedule. And though no one has said anything, I'm pretty sure people are avoiding me because of the nude photo ordeal. I'd expected laughter or more slimy come-ons, but it's as if I don't exist.

Every passing minute is another chance to turn it all around.

Great, now I'm thinking in Tom Cruise movie quotes. Admittedly, I binged all the ones I hadn't seen over break. It made me feel somehow closer to Wes, which makes me officially pathetic since he spent the entire break avoiding me. Sigh. And I'm now thinking my sighs aloud.

I pull open the library door and hold my head high. I can do this. It's a brand-new week.

I frown at the line that twists around the main desk and out the door of the tutor center.

Everyone in line is tall and muscular, and each and every one of them looks underwhelmed to be here.

Tanner Shaw gives me a head nod as I study the faces of the guys in line. I know it's wrong to be hostile for something out of his control, but I still bristle at the sight of him.

I find the start of the line at the doorstep of my tiny makeshift cubicle. Wes is holding the front with the look of a proud boy scout.

Merit badge definitely earned.

"What is this?"

"I owed you for the other night. For lots of things. I've given you shit about all this"—he lifts his arms—"but the other night, I guess I realized I needed it more than I knew."

"So, you brought every jock you know for what? Creative hazing?"

He covers his mouth with a fist. "Admittedly, that's part of it, but I do think you have some things that could help each one of them. You're good at this. Better than I gave you credit for. I just wanted to show you I see it now. I get it, and I want to support you the same way you always supported me."

"Thank you." I place my backpack down beside my chair and eye the coffee cup on my desk. I pick it up and read the quote scribbled in messy penmanship. *Focus. Repetition. Heart.*

"Nice touch."

He beams back at me like a proud pupil. "That's a Coach Daniels' special."

A look around the tutor center reveals intrigued, if a bit annoyed, glances from the tutor stations. The commotion has disrupted any chance of concentration. "Well, looks like I have my work cut out for me. You gonna stick around and make sure they don't sneak out?"

"Nah. I gotta do some studying." He turns and raises his voice so the guys in line can hear him. "But I'll stop by later and get a full report on how it went."

I roll my eyes. "Get out of here, Reynolds."

Surprisingly, the guys are good sports. A few of them even take it seriously. And when the last ball player walks out the door, there's a new line that's formed. Gotta give the jocks props for that. Where they go, others follow.

Wes shows up as the tutor center is closing for the night. The last students are packing their bags and the tutors are tidying up the room. I lean back in my chair, completely spent.

Every eye in the tutor center follows his path from door to my desk.

"Got time for one more?"

I sit forward and narrow my eyes. I can't tell if he's serious or not. One side of his mouth pulls into a smile. "Then how about dinner instead?"

"I, uh . . ." I trip over my tongue. What even are words? Did he just ask me on a date? "Sure. Let me just grab my things."

Silently, Wes leads me to University Hall. We order food and then take a table in the far corner. "Brought you something," Wes says as he slides me a small gift covered in Christmas paper. On top is a handmade origami bow made from a Chewy Spree wrapper.

Nice touch, Reynolds.

"It's a little belated. I didn't get a chance to give it to you that night . . ." His words hold a hint of sadness.

"I see you got mine." I point to his gray T-shirt, and he looks down proudly at the black bold letters: *Smart is the new jock.*

"Open yours," he says and winks.

I tear open the paper to find a flat, rectangular box. My throat goes dry. I'm not prepared for whatever is in this jewelry box. I pry open the top slowly and hold my breath as I reveal the bracelet inside. It's similar to the ones Gabby and I make out of colored embroidery thread, but there are only two colors—orange and purple. My and his favorites. My heart thumps wildly in my chest as I lift it and study the letter beads that twist around the braided thread. *BLESS*

"No way," I say in complete disbelief. "Where did you get this?"

"I, uh, may have commissioned it?"

I lift a brow.

"Gabby," he says, looking a little guilty.

"Gabby was in on this?" I inspect the bracelet and see her in the smooth braid, the neat knots at either end. I can't believe she kept this a secret. "I love it. Thank you."

"I have one other gift. Though, it isn't from me."

I narrow my gaze, intrigued. "Okay. Who's it from? Did you get Vanessa to write me a poem?"

He shakes his head. "Let's call it a gift from the university. David was expelled today."

All the air leaves my lungs as he continues.

"The campus police received several anonymous tips leading them to him, and when he was questioned, he folded. All the evidence was on his laptop anyway."

"He's gone," I whisper. I expected to feel better, but the damage is already done. I'm glad I won't have to see him, but I guess I'd already eradicated him from my life.

"You know, if you pressed charges, he could be charged with a felony. Laws in Arizona are strict about this kind of thing."

A nervous laugh escapes at the scary expression on his face. Wes is pissed and ready to see David pay. Me too. "I haven't decided what to do yet. I made an appointment with a counselor for later this week and I need to tell my parents. That's going to be hard."

His jaw flexes before he speaks. "I'm really sorry I didn't stop this from happening. I failed you in so many ways."

The loyalty of this man never ceases to amaze me. "David's crimes aren't yours. It's not on you. I just want to move on. I let him hold me back for too long. Whatever I decide to do, it's going to be about me—what's best for me. Part of me thinks I just want to be free of him, but I don't know if I could live with myself if I don't see this through and make sure he never has the opportunity to do this to someone else."

"Obviously I'm a fan of the latter," he states dryly. "But I'll be here for you either way. Whatever you need."

Swallowing down the lump in my throat, I can only nod.

I steer the conversation to lighter topics. Between bites, we talk about classes and he tells me a little about how he's helping at practices. It's comfortable and easy to be with him, but there's the slightest tension in the way we interact. We're careful to keep our hands to ourselves, and the one time he bumps my leg under the table, I jump so high in my seat he apologizes like he's wounded me deeply.

We're us, but we aren't. This isn't Bless it's Weir—the weird, nonsensical version of our cooler couple alter ego.

"Thank you for—" I start to speak at the same time he does.

"Listen, I—"

"You first," we say at the same time and smile.

I open my palm toward him in a silent offering for him to go first.

"I owe you an explanation for the way I acted. After my injury, you were trying to be there for me and I wouldn't let you. I pushed you away. I destroyed what we had."

"You were dealing," I say simply. I always knew the why, but his apology doesn't fix the hurt it caused or the pain he inflicted when he removed himself from my life.

"It wasn't just that." He lets out a shaky breath and meets my eyes. His blue stare is melancholy and regret. "I wanted to hurt you. You pushed your way into my life, bringing your optimism and joy, and it changed me. I made room for something in my life besides ball. But then I was laying in that hospital bed, hearing your bubbly voice tell me to flip the negativity and see the positive, and I didn't want to. I wasn't ready to do anything but be angry and bitter."

"No one expected you to see the positive in this. Least of all me."

"I know." He shakes his head. "It was petty and childish. I'm sorry it took me so long to realize it. I miss you. Fuck, I miss you. I'm just not sure who I am or what I'm doing anymore. I don't want to be this miserable guy who is pissed at the world, not when I'm with you. You deserve better than that."

"You're allowed to have bad days or months. This isn't exactly my banner year so far." I wave my hands as I speak. "Relationships are ugly sometimes." I shrug and inwardly cringe because I just used the word relationship when we never put a label on whatever we were before.

He reaches across the table and takes my hand. The warmth of his fingers soothes something that's been aching without his touch. "I'm crazy about you, but I gotta be honest that I'm still going through some shit."

"Well, I can handle your grumpiness if you can put up with my optimism and spunk."

"Deal."

My heart swells with that one word. *Deal.*

It isn't until we've said goodnight that I realize I have no idea what we just agreed to. Are we in a relationship? Are we friends?

He didn't kiss me. We said goodbye with a long hug and a promise to hang out tomorrow afternoon, but did I just agree to a friendly hang out or Netflix and chill?

I'm still wondering as I sit on his bed the following day, watching him pack for a team away game.

Joel knocks on the door and pokes his head in. "You still have that Spanish textbook from last year?"

Wes nods toward his bookshelf. "Yeah, it's on the shelf. What's up?"

"I told someone I'd help her. Just want to get an idea of how much they're covering in introductory Spanish."

"You're tutoring someone?" Wes asks, his tone as disbelieving as the thoughts running through my head.

"Shut up," Joel grumbles.

Wes crosses the room and pulls the book from the shelf. He stops in front of Joel and holds the book, obviously using it as bait for more information.

Joel mutters, "I guess I promised her I'd help with Spanish to get her to sleep with me. There, happy now?"

We laugh at his expense. "Dude, that's low even for you."

"Shut the fuck up. I don't even remember saying it . . . or doing it for that matter." He shakes his head. "She says we hung out at the baseball party last week. I was so drunk that night I crashed on Mario's couch, so anything is possible." Joel looks at me. "This is your fault. You told me chicks dig the Spanish."

I hold my hands up. "Don't put this on me. I didn't tell you to use it as a bargaining chip for sex."

"Good luck." Wes tosses the book at him and Joel walks backward out of the door already flipping through the pages.

I turn to Wes. "You know you guys are sitting on an untapped gold mine. Women would"—I pause and point after Joel—"and apparently already do, go to great lengths to have a hot, smart male tutor."

"Whatever you're suggesting, hard pass."

"Come on, the marketing alone would be fantastic." I wave my hand in front of my face like I'm seeing it on a billboard. "Smart Jocks: Get an A while enjoying eye candy too."

"That's a terrible slogan."

"It was my first attempt. Oh! I have it! Smart Jocks: Their brains are as big as their—"

"Don't finish that statement." He holds a hand up. "I want to imagine the possibilities of that last word."

I toss a pillow at him.

"How about. Smart Jocks: Figure it out your damn self. I'm busy."

I tap my chin. "*Hmmm*. I dunno, I mean it certainly sounds like something you'd say, but it's a bit grumpy."

"I thought you agreed to put up with my grumpy ass." He leans down and places a kiss at the corner of my mouth.

It's the first time his lips have touched mine in a month, and my insides turn to total mush. Instead of responding, I grab his hand and tug him closer. He lets out a throaty chuckle as he brings our lips back together. The dam has broken, and our kiss becomes frantic and needy. He places two strong hands under my ass and lifts me, bringing me upright with him. I wrap my legs around his waist as he walks us to the door, shuts, and locks it. Crossing back to the bed in two long steps, he drops us to the bed and settles on top of me. He breaks away to stare down at me. "You're so beautiful. Don't think I'll ever get enough of looking at you or kissing you."

He steals another kiss, as if proving his point. "You always taste like sugar . . . so damn sweet."

He continues his worship and praise of my body, getting us undressed in record time. We're hot and sweaty and can't keep our hands off each other. Looks as if he didn't listen to Joel this time. Or maybe he just hadn't planned for this to happen.

"Gotta head out in ten." Nathan yells and knocks from the other side as Wes tears open a condom and covers himself.

"Sadly, I'm not gonna need that long," he says around a smile, just loud enough that I can hear.

The giggle that tickles my throat is lost when he enters me, stretching me and filling me completely. He stills, braced above me, his expression fixed in exquisite torment.

"Have to make this up to you when I get back on Saturday night."

But there's nothing to make up for. I'm as needy and close as he is. Each thrust threatens to push me over the edge. His breathing is labored and sweat beads on his chest. He's holding back, delaying his pleasure to get me there. If that isn't the most deliciously sexy thing a man could do in bed, I don't know what is.

"I'm close," I rasp. It isn't a warning. It's permission for him to let go.

Still, he waits until the orgasm takes over my body before he growls out, shuddering as he gives into his release.

He rests his forehead on mine. "Last thing I want to do is get out of this bed and get on a flight with a bunch of dudes."

But he has to, and I watch him as he slides from the bed, disposing of the condom and dressing quickly. He tosses my jeans and shirt onto the bed before he shoves stuff into his duffel bag.

"I gotta run. Stay as long as you want. In fact, if you want to be in that same spot when I get back, I won't complain." He winks and drops a hurried kiss on my lips."

"Good luck," I call to his back.

When I hear the faint sound of the front door slamming closed, I pull Wes's comforter around me and inhale. I'm in deep again. No, not again. My feelings never changed. I feel like I never left, but his feelings have bounced around, and I don't want to be on the bench, waiting for more time in the game. Yep, I'm in deep. Even my thoughts have converted to basketball analogies for his sake.

I've done exactly what Vanessa warned me against. I've fallen into old habits where Wes and I spend time together without ever really discussing the depth of it. Maybe it's positive thinking or maybe it's just plain idiotic to hope things will work out on their own. Pushing away the negative and focusing on being happy is the only real choice because my heart is already his.

THIRTY-SIX

Wes

We win our game in Oregon, which has everyone in good spirits on the way back. It's a long ass flight and then an hour bus ride to get back to Valley, and every minute feels like torture. I don't know where to sit on the bus. Ridiculous as it sounds, everything has changed, and I'm no longer one of them. If I were an injured sophomore or even junior, it'd be different, but I'm never gonna be a real member of this team again.

I settle next to Z, but his silence only makes my nervous energy feel more pronounced. The tension I usually release on the floor has built up, and I can't sit still. Shaw sits across the aisle and catches my eye. "You all right? Foot bothering you?"

"What?" It takes a second for his attempt at polite conversation to register. "Nah, just feel restless."

He nods as if he could possibly understand. "Look, I know we haven't always seen eye to eye, but I'm really sorry about the way things went down. You were a good player. The guys really respect and look to you. It's tough shoes to fill. I just want you to know I don't take the job lightly."

I resist an eye roll but can't stop the disbelieving grunt that escapes.

"What is your problem with me, anyway? You've been on my ass since I arrived at Valley, so I know it isn't just that I've taken your spot."

Count to five and consider keeping my mouth shut. The consideration is rejected. "I don't like that you're dividing your time. Pick a sport.

Coaches might be okay with it, but no one else is. It's damn risky, and it makes both teams feel like you aren't giving one hundred percent."

"That's such bullshit," he says and shakes his head. "I work my ass off to be a part of both teams. Twice as many practices, double the coaches and training routines."

"Why do that to yourself? Just pick one and give it your all. Save yourself and all of us a lot of heartache when you get burned out or injured."

"You just don't get it. I can't pick between the two of them like it's a choice of pizza or tacos. I love basketball. I love the sound of shoes squeaking on the floor and the echo of the ball in an empty gym. But I love baseball too."

"Yeah, sure. I loved football once upon a time, but I made the decision to put everything into one sport." Most of us played other sports as kids, but at one point or another we gave the others up and made basketball the primary focus.

"You didn't love football as much as basketball." He is adamant, and that pisses me off.

"Excuse me?"

"You couldn't have. There's no way I could pick between basketball and baseball. Come on, you know what it's like to love two things so much you can't give either up. How is my loving two sports different from you playing ball and having a girlfriend?"

"You're really comparing your situation to my dating life?"

His head bobbles like he's waiting for me to figure out the connection.

"It isn't the same," I finally say.

"Sure it is. You split your time between the two. They both consume your thoughts. Your main objective for both is to score."

I roll my eyes at his lame attempt at humor. "That is the weakest analogy I've ever heard, rook. We're done here."

I stand and move to the front next to Joel. He looks me over and nods appreciatively. "Nice work today. You have a knack for keeping Shaw and the bench ready to go. And you look damn good doing it. Getting laid agrees with you."

"Jesus H Christ," I mutter and stand again. The only other available seat is next to Coach.

He takes off his glasses and looks me over as if I've personally offended him by invading his bubble. "The guys are in rare form after that win."

"It was a good game. Shaw is finally finding his rhythm. Thanks to you."

"Please don't thank me." I scrub a hand along my jaw and around my neck. "I resent every second of it."

He laughs. "You won't after a while."

I narrow my eyes as if that'll help me understand him better.

"I wasn't always a coach," he says

"Yeah, I know," I say. "Baylor, player of the year in 1999."

"That's right." He nods with a proud look on his face, and I see a bit of that cocky player he had to have been back then. Z and I looked up old clips once; Coach was a beast. "I played all four seasons. Four great seasons. Still hurts just the same no matter when you have to give it up."

"Why'd you become a coach if you resent not playing anymore?"

He studies me. "Why'd you decide to come back and sit with the team?"

I shrug.

"The only thing that hurts more than not playing is losing it completely. They'll have to drag me off that court kicking and screaming when I'm ninety years old."

"I guess I came back because I didn't know what else to do. Who else to be."

He shifts in his seat and studies me. "You thought about what you might want to do after you graduate?"

"My dad has offered me a junior analyst job at his company." I shrug. I haven't really allowed myself to think beyond May.

"Coach Lewis is moving on, we'll have an assistant coaching spot if you're interested. Think about it. Pay is crap and you'd have to keep working with these knuckleheads, but for what it's worth, I think you have a real talent for it. You've already made a difference in Shaw. Maybe coaching at Valley, with guys you played with, is too much, but you say the word, and I'll make some calls to other programs."

Somehow, I manage to speak through the shock. "Thank you. I'll think about it."

Be a coach? We sit in an uncomfortable silence. It's already been a night out of bizzaro land, so I ask the question that's been floating around in my head since Shaw mentioned it.

"Do you think it's possible to love two things equally?"

He regards me seriously but waits for me to say more.

"Like two different sports or two different women or anything as much as I love basketball."

"If you find a penny today, are you more or less likely to find a penny tomorrow?" He shakes his head. "I don't know what the statistical likelihood is, but I think I'd worry less about trying to quantify it and grab on to anything that can even begin to compare to your love of the game. Especially now."

I mull that over for the rest of the trip, closing my eyes and faking sleep. Maybe quantifying love is a losing man's game. It doesn't matter if I love Blair the same way I love basketball, it just matters that I love her. She's been beside me for the worst year of my life, and when I try to picture it any other way, I don't know if I would have survived. She's breathed life into me again. I might still be bitter, but I'm no longer scared of what the future holds as long as she's by my side, forcing me to look at the positives and putting up with my grumpy ass.

The bus pulls into the fieldhouse after six. Been a long ass day, but I'm not tired. Ain't that a first. I gimp home, unable to wait for my roommates to shower and drop off their jerseys.

I've already texted Blair to give her an ETA on our arrival. So many times, I've come home to her waiting for me, giving up her life to be part of mine. I'm not selfless enough to think we'd be where we are today if she hadn't. She gave, and I took. I've always known what a badass chick she is, but I wouldn't have gone out of my way for her.

Not then, but I will now. I'll follow her around campus for the next four months, tell everyone that'll listen that she's mine, prove day in and day out that I'm not going anywhere.

I'm not happy that I can't play ball. There's no positive spin I'm putting on it today or any day in the future. Going out like this sucks, and I'll always wonder what-if and wish I'd been able to savor those last games knowing it was the end.

Nah, I'm not an optimist like Blair. I'm a grumpy motherfucker, and I probably always will be, but that's why I'm not letting go of her. She evens out my dark. Makes all the dull and gray seem polished and new.

Blair

Wes: Bus just got back. Where are you?

Me: Tutor Center. Want me to head over when we close?

Wes: Got some stuff to do first. I'll text ya.

My phone rings with a video call from Vanessa.

"What's up?"

Vanessa sets the phone down and steps back, turning side to side to show me her outfit.

"Mario is picking me up in fifteen minutes. Help!"

"Where's he taking you?"

"He won't say, which is why I can't figure out what to wear. All he'll say is it would be a night to remember."

"Maybe he's gonna propose."

She places a hand to her lips. "Oh my God, I think I just threw up in my mouth a little."

"You look hot, per the usual. Relax and have fun."

She picks the phone up, bringing it closer to her face. "What are you doing tonight?"

"Not sure. Wes just got back, but he said he has some things to do." Saying the words aloud makes my stomach flip—and not in a good way. I know I'm being overly sensitive, but it feels like the beginning of another brush off.

She bites at her lip and narrows her gaze. I wait for her to give me another lecture on being too available, but her phone beeps and her expression goes serious. "Shit, he's on his way. I gotta go."

"All right. Have fun and text me later. I can't wait to hear where he takes you."

When we hang up, I look around the empty tutor center and stand. It's ten minutes until we close, but no one has walked in the door in an hour.

I shift my attention to said door, and my eyes widen when Wes fills it. His arms are full of flowers and boxes and I start to make my way to him.

We meet in the middle, and his eyes scan the room. "Where is everyone?"

"Tutor sessions are over, and I told them I'd lock up. What are you doing here? What is all this?"

He shrugs, which is all he can manage with his arms full. "I was hoping for an audience, but I guess this will have to do."

I swallow a laugh when he begins to hand me the items he carries. A dozen red roses, a box of chocolates, a giant bag of Chewy Spree, a miniature stuffed pig, and a card that I can't wait to read later.

I'm stunned speechless, but manage to say, "Thank you."

"I know it isn't much, but it's all I could come up with on short notice."

"I don't understand."

"I'm in love with you. Been in love with you, and I've done a really shitty job of showing it. I wanted to storm in here and tell you and everyone else because you deserve that and so much more. Guess just telling you will have to do for now. I never asked the first time, just assumed. I don't want to do that this time. I want to be worthy. Want to be your choice. Be my girl?"

My heart is in my throat as this amazing guy stands in front of me looking more nervous than I've ever seen him. "You're in love with me?"

He nods.

"Dumb jock fell in love with the prissy sorority girl, go figure."

He grins. The cocky swagger is back as he closes the short distance between us and bends so we are eye to eye. "The smart jock fell for the hot sorority girl."

"She fell for him too," I say as I wrap my arms around his neck.

His lips slam down over mine, and I drop the gifts so I can jump him, wrapping my legs around his waist. "Probably should get out of here. I'd been prepared for an audience. Without one I'm likely to bend you over this desk."

I consider that, but ultimately pry myself off him.

"All right, boyfriend." I test the word, loving the way it sounds. "What's next?"

He chuckles. "I have no freaking clue. What do you say we start with a double date? Mario got tickets to some ridiculous K-pop band Vanessa likes."

"BTS?"

Wes shrugs. "Don't know, but I figure my best shot at winning over V is getting on her good side while she's happy . . . and maybe drunk."

I don't tell him what I already know—that all he has to do to win Vanessa over is keep me happy. It'll be way more fun to let him sweat this one out. And I can't wait to watch it unfold.

THIRTY-SEVEN

Blair

"A re you always this nervous at games?" Gabby asks, causing V to cover her mouth and suppress a laugh.

"I can't help it."

I wipe my sweaty palms on my jeans. It's the last home game of the season and Wes is taking the floor with his team one last time for warmups. Things have been great the past month. We're spending all our time together, and Wes seems to be back to his old self. I know he's still struggling to stand on the sidelines, but he's showing up. And he looks damn good doing it.

He looks over as he prepares to shoot, gives a wink, and then brings his right hand up to his mouth and kisses the blue sweatband. My heart does a pitter patter in my chest.

"Blair, why didn't you tell me how hot Wes's teammates are? Who's number thirty-three?"

"That's Joel."

She scrunches her nose. "The one that sleeps with everything that moves."

Vanessa doesn't get her hand over her mouth in time, and she spits the soda she'd just taken a sip of.

"One and the same," I confirm. "Nathan is number twenty-four, and Zeke is wearing jersey fifty."

Zeke picks that particular moment to glance up at us. His eyes narrow, brows furrow. A look of confusion and interest crosses his face and then disappears just as quickly. Gabby ducks her head and shivers. "He's hot too in a really intimidating way."

"We could set her up with Shaw. That'd drive Wes crazy." Vanessa grins.

The game starts, and I have a blast cheering on the team with my best friends. I haven't seen Gabby this happy in years, and it makes me think about how much fun we're going to have next year. And fingers crossed that Wes will be here too. He hasn't officially been offered the job yet, but Valley would be crazy not to keep him. He's their secret weapon even from the bench.

Valley is on fire, and we pull ahead by twenty early on and UCLA never recovers. Gabby and I have stopped watching the game all together and are planning out all the awesome things we're going to do when she moves to Valley. That is why I don't see Wes until he's standing right next to me.

"Hello."

The crowd around us is patting him on the back, and I swear I can almost feel the cameras zoom in on us. I wave my hands wildly in front of me and shriek over the noise, "What are you doing here?"

"I'm trying to watch the game. Move over." He leans in front of me. "Hey, Gabby. Good to see you."

I can't stop staring at him. I've never seen him up close like this in his jersey. He smells of leather and sweat and it's giving me a contact high.

"These seats really do suck. Good thing I'm gonna get to watch from the bench again next year."

"You got the job?" I yell and draw more attention to us, but I don't care. He nods, and I launch myself into his arms.

"Wes, that's amazing. Congratulations. You're going to be amazing.'"

The words are true. I can already picture it. Him standing on the sidelines with that confident and determined set to his jaw. Maybe I can convince him to wear a suit like Coach Daniels. I like this idea better and better.

As we pull apart, he leans down and rests his forehead against mine. "Didn't really have any other choice. This girl kept busting my balls about helping my team and being there, and turns out, I'm good at it."

"Of course you are."

I throw myself at him again and hug him tightly. The buzzer sounds, signaling the end of the game. Wes pulls back, but neither of us move as the commotion around us becomes background noise.

"I love you, Blair." He has to shout to be heard over the applause and cheers. "I thought not being able to play ball was my biggest fear. It isn't. I can live in a world where I'm not Wes Reynolds, college athlete, but I can't live without you. Or, if I can, I just don't want to. I should have locked you down the first day I met you. You're the best thing that's ever happened to me."

I lean up on my tiptoes and wrap my arms around his neck. "Stop. Just stop. You had me at hello."

"*Jerry Maguire?*"

I nod.

"That's what you're going with? In front of twenty thousand people, your friends, ESPN cameras, you're going with a cheesy Tom Cruise line?" He smiles despite his teasing.

Is this guy really busting my balls about this? And I thought he was a smart jock. "How about this? I love you, Wes Reynolds, you dumb jock."

"I can work with that. Convinced you once I wasn't dumb, I'll take that challenge again."

"Possible outcomes include convincing me and not convincing me."

"Nope. Not convincing you isn't a possibility. I have talent and heart and I know your weakness."

"Oh yeah?" I ask, wondering if he means the fact I'm absolutely insanely in love with him.

"Yep. Chewy Sprees and my reading glasses. I have both waiting for you as soon as we get out of here."

EPILOGUE

Wes
Four Months Later

L ess than one percent of college basketball players make it to the NBA. I've known the stats since I was a kid, but it didn't keep me from devoting my life to the game.

I averaged eight assists, three steals, and fourteen points per game. I ate, I slept, I balled. It wasn't enough. I'm not part of the one percent.

I prided myself on heart and dedication. I worked harder and smarter. I saw things no one else could see on the court. I made assists that not even I was sure how I pulled off. I saw through players twice as big as me. Managed to get the ball in the hands of guys before they even realized they were open.

I saw things before they happened—plain and simple.

As I stand at the back of the room and watch my friend and former teammate hold up his Suns's jersey and wear the orange-and-purple hat his agent thrust on top of his head when his name had been announced as the third pick in the NBA draft, I have nothing but the utmost love and respect for him. He's a one percent-er, and I'm not bitter about it.

I don't begrudge him the success because he worked as hard as I did. We sacrificed a lot to be elite college athletes. Championship titles and awards have been given to both of us, and I've accepted that my road ends here. I can rest easy knowing that everything I did helped in some small way to get him where he is today.

I saw this day happening. Always knew Z would be playing professional ball.

On the court, I saw everything. But off the court? I never saw *her* coming.

One day I was minding my own business, focused on my team, and the next, I was falling ass first for her determination and optimism. Getting the ball in the hands of an open player was my forte, but it wasn't until she came into my life that I made the ultimate assist. I helped her get an A in statistics, and she gave me everything in return.

As I cross the room to her, I take in my future. I couldn't figure out what it was I was meant to do with my life without basketball, until her.

I'll coach, and she'll finish school, but after that? I have no clue what we'll do next. I hope it involves more games of PIG that I *let* her win, more Chewy Sprees, a lot more sex. Hey, I'm just being honest. More of all of it with her.

Bless out

SWEET SPOT

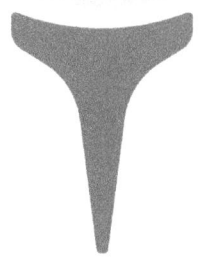

A grumpy golf pro coaches a hot-headed college golfer in this fun and sexy sports romance.

Lincoln Reeves may be a pro golfer and revered swing coach, but when I meet him, he is just one more person telling me I'm not good enough.

So, I do what any girl in my position would do. I tell him to get lost and take his arrogant, annoying smirk with him. I never expect to see him again. I certainly don't expect to run into him that same night after one too many tequila shots.

Turns out that he's kind of a big deal. Okay, fine, a really big deal. In fact, he might be the one person who can take my game to the next level.

Convincing him to help will be difficult.

Not throwing my club at his handsome face when he makes me work harder than I thought humanly possible will be excruciating.

But not falling for him will be the hardest thing of all.

Sweet Spot is a stand-alone sports romance set in the Valley U world.

For Craig
"Hitting a driver is easy, it's the size of a tennis racket."—Craig M.

ONE

Keira

I'm not good at very many things.

I never learned to play a musical instrument. I can't draw. I'm messy, unorganized, and hot-headed. Pop-Tarts are a staple in my diet so, obviously, maintaining a balanced diet isn't a talent of mine either. I don't understand classic literature, and I'm hopeless at video games. None of it ever mattered to me. Nothing but golf.

Wedge in hand, I bounce the ball off the clubface as if it's a paddle. Each time, the ball lands squarely in the center—right on the sweet spot—with a light tap.

Tap. Tap. Tap.

The noise soothes and excites me. Body poised, right forearm extended slightly in front of me, the tip of my tongue between my teeth. That last part isn't strictly necessary, but it's a habit any time I'm concentrating this hard.

My teammates stand to the side, watching my every move. I've done this trick a hundred times, but I know better than to look anywhere except at the ball. Even the trickle of sweat at the nape of my neck and the stray hair that's fallen in my face won't distract me.

Tap. Tap. Tap.

I move the club behind my back.

Tap. Between my legs. *Tap.* Club forward. *Tap. Tap. Tap.* Right foot hop and kick, letting the ball bounce off the sole of my shoe before catching it.

Tap. Tap. Tap. Deep breath as I track the ball, move into my final position, and swing.

A shot of pride zips through me as the ball sails through the air, a white dot in the bright blue sky. My teammates cheer, finally breaking their silence.

"That's incredible," Abby says, offering me a high-five. "And on the first try. Is this how you spent all of winter break?"

I shrug. "It didn't take that long to perfect it."

Erica stares at her phone, thumbs moving rapidly over the screen. "I'm posting it. Your trick shots get more likes and comments than anything else I post." She looks up at me. "You're more popular than I am on my own account. That's screwed up." She snickers and goes back to her phone.

The other girls are giving me the appropriate props when Coach's voice bellows from the clubhouse. "Ladies, hit the bunkers."

I swear he glares right at me as if I'm the only one standing here. I glare back, refusing to cower. He looks away first, and I call that a victory until he adds, "You too, Keira. Your fancy trick shots won't help you in a tournament."

I open my mouth to argue that we were on a water break, so it wasn't as if I had been wasting practice time, but Abby steps in front of me, blocking him from view. "Come on."

I grab my bag, and we head for the sand traps with the rest of the team.

"You have to stop letting him rile you. It throws you off all practice."

"He hates me."

"He hates everyone." Abby and I walk a few paces behind our teammates. She finger combs her silky, black hair into a ponytail and adjusts her visor. "He just picks on you the most because he knows he can get a rise out of you. Stop giving him what he wants."

I mumble my acknowledgment. It isn't that I'm argumentative by default, but Coach Potter pushes all my buttons. If the man were a Pop-Tart, he'd be the unfrosted kind—a total disgrace to the Pop-Tart brand.

"How was break?" she asks as we reach the group and set our bags on the ground.

"It was fine. Yours?"

"Good. What'd your dad get you this year?"

My dad's Christmas gifts are . . . entertaining. I raise my arm to show off the bright neon-pink unicorn scrunchie, which is one of twelve of varying colors he gave me this year. Last year, I got a pair of cat ear headphones. I'm convinced he thinks I will forever be thirteen years old.

Abby laughs. "Why doesn't he just get you a gift card or golf stuff?"

"Oh no, he never goes the gift-card route. And I have so much golf stuff that I'm sure he would have no idea what to buy."

"Let me guess, you told him you loved it?"

"He's always so proud of what he picks, how could I not? Besides, I could be into unicorns."

She snorts. "It's actually pretty cute. Maybe I need to get on the Christmas list next year."

We spend the next half hour hitting shots from the bunker and then Coach lays the pin down behind the hole and instructs us to keep going until we've each hit it three times in a row.

It takes a few minutes to stop overthinking it, but soon, I have two consecutive hits and am lining up for my third.

"Open the clubface a little more. Address it off the toe. You're looking rusty. Come on ladies, focus," he barks loud enough that I know it's advice meant for the entire team, but Coach's presence directly behind me makes me grip the club tighter. The man sets my every nerve on edge. His personality is completely abrasive, making me firmly believe either he hates coaching, golf, or maybe both. He certainly doesn't like me.

I'd rather swing the wedge at his head, but I breathe and refocus. Unfortunately, as soon as I make contact with the ball, I know it's going right. Coach walks off without a word.

I'm the last to finish and head back up to the putting green. The boys' team has already arrived. They practice right after us, but a quick glance at my phone tells me we still have more than thirty minutes left. They're never this early.

Abby's holding her putter, leaned over as if she's eyeing the line, but the only thing she's eyeing is her boyfriend Smith. He's on the driving range, staring right back at her.

"You two are ridiculous, sneaking glances at one another like you're in middle school," I say, dropping a few balls onto the green and joining her.

My friend blushes. "What? He's cute. Let me stare without your judgment."

I shake my head. "What are they doing here so early, anyway?"

"They have a clinic today with some big shot swing coach."

"Figures. Why do they always have people coming in to offer extra coaching? We've had a better record for the past two years, but do fancy swing coaches come to see us?" I don't wait for her answer. "No, they do not."

She shrugs, not the least bit bothered by it, and honestly, I don't know if I'd be upset if it weren't for the fact our coach barely speaks to me, let alone coaches me.

We've never seen eye to eye, but when I was holding my own in tournaments, he didn't seem to loathe me quite so much.

While we finish putting, Coach strolls over to review this week's schedule. We have a tournament upstate this weekend but only five will travel and play.

I keep my eyes glued to the ground as he says the first four names. Our top three rarely changes. Erica, Kim, and Cassidy are our most senior members and have earned their spots by consistently placing well in tournaments. Then there's Abby. She's streaky, but as of our last tournament in December, that streak is holding. That leaves only one spot. My spot. Or it was. One bad tournament last October and Coach was all too eager to replace me. I've been trying to claw my way back to his good graces ever since. Unsuccessfully, I might add.

"And finally, Brittany will join us."

I glance up in time to see his cold, gray eyes sweep over the team and lock on to me, waiting for a reaction. It's as if the man gets off on my anger. I plaster on a congratulatory smile and clap for my teammates. I will not let him see how much it hurts.

He places both hands on his hips. "Weak practice today, girls. Get your heads right and show up tomorrow ready to work harder."

After everyone separates, I approach him. "Coach, can I talk to you for a minute?" My big, fake smile is starting to make my cheeks hurt.

"What is it, Keira? I'm not going to change my mind on the girls going to the tournament."

Oh my God, why is he such a dick?

"I understand. I was just going to ask what I might do to improve so I can have my spot back? Or, at least, a chance to earn it back. Before break, I was consistently scoring with the top three in practice."

"I can't give you the answers. You have to prove it out there." He points toward the course. If it's some sort of voodoo mind trick, I'm clueless. He's the coach, the sole decider of who plays. Of course, he has the answer. And I *am* proving it out there.

"Right."

"Put the work in and give your best every time. And your attitude needs a serious adjustment." His brows raise, and his eyes widen as he waits for me to respond. He's expecting me to argue, I'm sure.

"Yes, Sir."

I'm screwed. I'm already the hardest worker on the team, and he knows it. Golf is my passion. I love it. I want to be the best, not just on our team but in the world. I don't think that's out of reach for me. I'm good—really good—but I can't prove that if I'm not playing.

Abby waits for me by our bags. "What did he say?"

"Nothing useful. Go ahead. I'm gonna stay and hit a bucket of balls."

"Seriously?"

"I have to get my spot back. I'll sleep here if I have to."

She chuckles. "Just don't sleep with him."

"Ewww." Bile coats my throat at the idea of seeing that vile man naked. He's young-ish, late thirties, and reasonably attractive, but his personality kills any and all sexual vibes.

I'm still swallowing my disgust when Abby elbows me. "Look, that must be the swing coach. *Damn.*"

Slowly, I scan until I locate him. He isn't hard to find. Tall, dark hair, bronzed skin set off by dress pants and a crisp white polo that he fills out nicely. His body language, even from this far, gives off an air of confidence.

He smiles at something the boys' coach, Coach James says, and it's hard to look away. So hard it's annoying. I'm totally annoyed by his good looks because *of course* he's good-looking. Probably a real jerk, too.

Okay, I might just be projecting my hatred for Coach Potter on all mankind, but I also really despise how the boys' team always seems to get the outside attention and help.

Abby pulls her hair from the ponytail. "We should go introduce ourselves."

"Why?"

"Because I want to see that man up close. Don't you?"

I laugh. "What about Smith?"

"See him; not jump him. Come on, it can't hurt to make nice."

"No thanks." I pick up my bag and shoulder it. "See you back at the dorm later."

"Don't forget that we're going out tonight with Erica and Cass."

"Oh, I haven't forgotten. The promise of alcohol is the only thing that got me through that practice."

"All right, well, I'm headed back to shower and get ready. Don't stay too long."

"Just long enough to work out my frustration."

"Please, it'll be dark by then." She smiles smugly and walks off toward the parking lot.

I head to the clubhouse, splash some water on my face in the bathroom and try to wash away my irritation from practice. I grab a bucket of balls and walk over to an open mat on the driving range. The boys team huddles off to the side, Coach James and hottie swing coach the center of their focus.

I don't need them, and I don't need Potter. I'm going to prove I deserve that spot all on my own. I bounce the ball on the clubface a few times, the concentration it requires and the familiar movements calming me instantly.

I can do this.

TWO

Lincoln

Starting a new business is hard. Exhausting. No, exhausting doesn't even cover the half of it. Travelling the world, a different city every week, early mornings, late nights, sporting event after sporting event. It's basically everything I ever dreamed of.

Except for the crappy jobs that need to get done but can't be pawned off on anyone else, which is my current state at the Valley University golf course. Ah, the joys of being the boss. I'm trying hard not to think about the box seats I had to turn down for today's Cardinals playoff game. A cold beer and a million-dollar view would be pretty great about now.

I find Coach James on the driving range, instructing his team to warm up and give each of their clubs a few swings. A few of the guys notice me, but I hang back until Mark lifts a hand.

"Hey, Mark. Long time. Good to see ya." I nod to toward the guys and smile.

"You too, Linc." We shake hands, and then he motions for me to follow him. "Let's chat before I introduce you to the team."

He leads me into the clubhouse and to a small office. "Thanks for coming."

"Thank you for inviting me," I say as we take our seats. "This should be fun."

He grunts a laugh as if he doesn't believe my optimism. Yeah, I don't either. The Cardinals haven't made it this far in the season in years, and instead of watching the game, I'm going to spend my Sunday afternoon giving pointers to a bunch of college kids who expect me to sweep in and make big changes to their game in two hours of work. Not even I'm that good.

I lean back and rest my interlocking fingers at my waist as I study my old friend. It's been almost twelve years since I've seen him, but he's the same arrogant kid I knew in high school—minus a little hair and plus a little weight around his midsection.

"It's fine. Happy to do it. You've been a big supporter of the new coaching site and I appreciate it."

"But?"

"How do you know there's a but?"

He arches a brow pointedly.

"But any one of my guys could have done it. Why am I here?"

"Because you're the best."

Well, I can't argue there.

"Look," I reason with him, "I'm glad to help how I can, but this isn't really what I do. Analyzing and fixing an entire team of kids' mistakes in a single afternoon . . . I'm not a miracle worker. Usually, I work with individuals over weeks, sometimes months or years. And the group clinics I offer cover a single aspect of the game like downswing sequencing or setup. A few hours giving pointers to ten kids isn't going to make the same kind of difference that I see with my personal clients. I want to make sure you understand that."

"Well, you're welcome to stay for as long as you need to get these boys on track. They're excited about meeting you. They're a young group, making all sorts of rookie mistakes, but I think they have potential. Smith Jacobson has a good, clean swing I think you'll appreciate."

"You can't afford for me to stay that long." I smirk. "Let's just focus on what you think would be the best use of their time for today."

Leaning forward in his chair, Mark grins back at me. "Fair enough."

After chatting about what he views as the biggest weaknesses of the team collectively, we decide the best use of everyone's time is for me to do a few quick drills on adding length and accuracy to their drives. Then I'll spend time with each kid before giving them targeted feedback.

We don't talk individual players because I don't want to walk out there with any preconceived notions about them. If I'm looking for a specific fault right off the bat, I might miss something else.

"All set?" Mark stands. "The guys are probably getting anxious to meet you. A few of them were here an hour before practice already stretching and warming up."

"Let's do it."

The bright blue Arizona sky is flawless, not a damn cloud as far as the eye can see. That, and the nonexistent breeze make it spectacular golfing weather for January.

A man approaches as we step onto the grass and Mark slows. "Lincoln, this is Wyatt Potter. He's the coach of the girls' team."

"Pleasure to meet you. I hear your record is pretty good this year."

"Top two consecutively since I took over three years ago."

"Impressive. I'm happy to include them in the clinic today or—" Before I can offer my services another day, he holds up a hand, which annoys the fuck out of me.

"No offense, but no one coaches my girls but me. Too many outside influences confuses them and makes it hard to keep them motivated."

I quirk a brow. Is this guy for real?

Mark jumps in, "Lincoln's a hell of a coach. He played professionally and—"

I clap a hand on Mark's shoulder to stop him from saying more. It's obvious this guy has no interest in my qualifications or background, no need to waste my time.

"Even still," Coach Potter says, voice and face full of condescension.

What a prick. I dig deep for some professionalism and manners, despite his lack thereof. "Well, the offer is always good if you need anything. Good luck on the season."

I step away, and luckily, Mark follows. When the boys spot us, they stop warming up and move in our direction, clearly ready to get started. There's so much excitement on their faces that I can't help but feel a little more energized myself.

Mark and I stand in the center as they form a half circle around us.

"Everyone, I'd like to introduce you to Lincoln Reeves. It's a real honor to have him here today. He knows more about golf than all of us combined, so if he tells you something, take it as gospel."

I bite back a laugh, knowing it probably cost Mark a little pride to give me that much credit. It isn't as if he doesn't mean it; I'm here because he wanted the best. But the relationship Mark and I had as kids included a lot more ribbing and jokes at one another's expense than flowery compliments. Blame it on growing up together, competing against one another, and knowing all each other's embarrassing childhood shit. Regardless, I appreciate him having my back with that asshole coach of the girls' team and with his guys.

After thanking Mark and saying hello to the boys, I lead the group to one end of the driving range and go over some tips on technique specific to the driver, demonstrating as I talk. It isn't overly complicated to understand, but putting it into practice is much more difficult.

When I'm done, I send them off to work on it, giving them about five minutes before I grab my camera and tripod. Going down the line, I film each of their swings from behind and the side, offer a few quick tips or corrections, and then move on. I don't have time to completely analyze each swing, but I can pinpoint fundamental issues on the fly, so I do my best to give each of them helpful, individualized feedback.

I keep it lighthearted and fun, knowing they'll perform better if they're relaxed instead of worried about being perfect. Clinics are supposed to be inspiring, otherwise, what's the point? I even find myself smiling and enjoying myself as I stand back and watch each kid take a couple of swings.

There's always this moment as a coach or a lover of any sport where you're holding your breath, hoping to be awed. I'd be lying if I said any of them succeed.

Smith Jacobson, Mark's star athlete, has a decent swing, but it lacks power, and he's missing confidence and tenacity. Every time he hits a bad shot, he takes five minutes setting up for the next, overthinking it and second-guessing himself. But, all in all, they're a good group of kids, and with some work and experience, they'll be all right.

"You're good with them." Mark nods toward his players. "If the site flops, I could use another good coach here." He elbows me so I know he's joking. "Love to have you back any time."

We're standing back twenty feet or so from the range. Time is up, but all the guys are still working, so I linger. I bet they've each hit close to two hundred balls. They have to be exhausted, but they're pushing through on fumes and dreams.

"I'll try to get the videos uploaded and sent to you tomorrow."

"No rush. I appreciate it," he says earnestly. "In a year or two, you're going to have so much business you aren't going to be able to keep up. Your grandfather would be proud."

I soften at the mention of Pop. "Thanks, Mark. That's a problem I'm looking forward to solving."

Mark extends his hand, and we shake. "It was good to see you, Lincoln. Don't be a stranger."

By the time I pack up, Mark and his team have moved down the first hole. The late afternoon sun has started to descend, casting the sky in pink and orange. I stop and take it in, trying to remember the last time I hit a few balls for fun.

Another year, maybe two, and then I will be able to find a better balance. I've already found more success than I ever could have imagined when I'd had a moment of drunken brilliance to take the business my grandfather started forty years ago and expand it.

It's taken longer, been harder, and required more sacrifice than expected, but it's also brought a sense of pride and accomplishment that is beyond anything golf alone has ever given me.

I step back, scanning the horizon and soaking up this feeling so I can pocket it for a reminder the next time I'm going on two hours of sleep and want to give up.

A pure, hard *thwack* snaps me from my daydream. I find and follow the ball as it sails beautifully high and straight down the line.

"Damn," I mutter and start toward whoever hit it. I need to shake this kid's hand and, more importantly, see if he can do it twice. Anyone can get lucky and hit a shot like that once, but great golf comes from consistency.

My pace slows as I get closer. Confusion sets in, not because I was wrong and a chick hit it but because this girl in particular looks nothing like I would have expected. For one, she's small.

The average woman on the LPGA is only five foot four, but I don't think this girl is even that tall. And she's thin. Toned, but not overly muscular like I'd expect someone driving the ball that far. Otherwise, she looks the part in a black golf skirt and matching long-sleeved shirt.

I don't know where she gets her power, but I'm intrigued. She's setting up another ball, so I hang back and watch. Crossing my arms over my chest, I wait to see what she can do.

She lets out a long breath as if she's trying to calm herself. Dark hair, which has a reddish tint under the remaining sunlight, hangs over her shoulders and falls in her eyes. She jabs at it twice with one hand, only to have it fall right back in her face.

Resting the grip of the club against her stomach to free her hands, she pulls the long mane back into a ponytail and secures it with a bright-pink scrunchie from her wrist. Her frustration is evident, but I don't think her hair is the problem.

Finally, she's ready, and I find myself holding my breath as she swings. She's more powerful than most the guys I helped today, swinging in a way that makes me wonder who the hell she's picturing as the ball.

I watch as she hits three more awe-worthy shots before I approach her. "Nice swing."

"Thanks," she says without looking back at me. She switches from a driver to a seven iron. This time, she doesn't hit the ball square on, and it hooks to the left. Her jaw tenses, and instead of taking her time and a minute to compose herself, she goes right for the next ball with a similar result. It takes five shitty shots before she growls her frustration. "Damn it."

"Can I offer you some advice?"

Her dark eyes lock on to me, and her brows rise as if I've totally offended her, but she doesn't speak.

Trying to diffuse the situation, I step closer and offer my hand. She stares at it but makes no move to take it, so I shove both hands into my pockets. "I'm Lincoln Reeves. I just finished a clinic for the boys' team. I'm a golf instructor and owner of an instructional sports website. You have power. Those shots you hit with your driver were really nice. Best I've seen all day."

Her demeanor softens only slightly. "Thank you."

"If you let me record a couple of swings, I think I can show you where it's breaking down and help you hit it more consistently." My body buzzes in anticipation. I really want to see what this girl is capable of. God, I love this job.

"No thanks. I got it." She brushes me off with a flick of her ponytail and tees up another ball.

Well, that's never happened before. Golfers tend to be open to feedback or will, at least, humor tips from pros at the driving range. It's such a complicated and yet simple thing, hitting a golf ball.

"Are you sure? It's no problem." I can't get a read on this girl. She's out here putting in the work, so I know she's determined, and her body language makes it clear she knows a good swing from a bad.

"On camera, it's easier to see the nuances. You're spinning your hips.

Your timing is good, so it isn't affecting every shot, but when it does, you're hooking it."

She stands tall, which isn't really that tall, but my spidey sense tingles, alerting me to danger. I've pissed this girl off, though I don't know why.

"Figures you're helpful now."

"Excuse me?" I smile, which is absolutely the wrong thing to do because she glowers back.

"Guys like you show up and offer all your wisdom to the boys' team like just because they have penises, they deserve all the advantages. Did it ever occur to you to offer a clinic for the girls' team?"

"I—"

"No, of course not. It doesn't matter that we have a better record, year after year, or that I can out drive most of them." She scoffs, tees up another ball, and gets into position. "So, no thanks. I don't need another man who thinks he's God's gift to golf to offer advice that he probably picked up from the Golf Channel."

Before I can speak, she draws back and smokes it. Chills run up my fingertips all the way to the back of my neck. "Holy shit," I whisper.

A pleased smile tips up her lips.

"You're right. Doesn't look like you need me at all."

She stalks off, that smug expression painted firmly in place. I watch her until she disappears from sight, the smile on my face so big and awestruck I think it might have been worth trading those Cardinal tickets for.

After leaving the golf course, I meet up with one of the guys who works for me, Heath, for a quick dinner before I head out of town.

"Can I get you guys anything else?" our waitress at The Hideout asks, her eyes not leaving Heath.

Amused, I rest an arm on the back of the empty chair next to me and wonder when she's going to realize she hasn't put down the beer she's holding on her tray. *My* beer.

"Just that Bud Light you got there," Heath says with a wink.

"Oh, right, of course." Flustered, she sets the pint in front of Heath, gives him one last awkward smile, and then scurries off.

Heath wraps his hand around the glass and lifts it.

"Give me that." I reach out and take it from him before he gets a drink. After a long pull of the cold beer, I ask, "You wanna get us both in trouble?"

"Relax, it's just a beer. Besides, I look twenty-one."

"Oh, well then, I guess it's perfectly fine since you *look* old enough."

"I've drank here lots of times. It's no big deal."

I'm about to lecture him, or at least tell him not to tell me shit like that so I don't have it on my conscience, as a couple of guys walk by the table and then backtrack when they notice Heath. He stands and the guys chat for a few minutes before he motions toward me and tells them he'll meet up with them later.

I officially feel like an old man. He's making plans to go out after dinner and the only thing I have scheduled is a night alone, probably working.

"Looks like things are going well for you. Try not to get yourself into trouble. You get caught drinking underage and—"

Heath groans. "Save it. Between you and my brother, I've had this same conversation nearly every day since I got here five months ago. *Five months.*" He holds up a hand and wiggles his fingers for emphasis. "I made it through one semester, didn't I?"

His sullen expression makes him look like the teenager he is, and I hold back a laugh.

"Noted. Tell me about the team."

Heath gives me the rundown on school and the Valley U hockey team while we eat. He's a good kid. Typical freshman looking to jump off the deep end and enjoy everything college has to offer.

I feel a sense of responsibility for him, almost like a kid brother. I met his real brother Nathan last year through a mutual friend.

He worked for me through his senior year of college, coaching aspiring basketball players. Their home situation wasn't the best at the time and they both needed some extra cash, so I hired Heath to field the hockey questions that come in from other athletes trying to get an edge.

Though my background is golf, my coaching website spans multiple sports and is growing faster than I can keep up with. Heath is just one of the many experts and stars in their field mentoring the next generation of great athletes.

Heath's a talented kid who won't need my help for long if he keeps himself out of trouble.

The waitress drops the bill on the table and slides it in front of me as she gives me a timid smile. It's the first time she's given me much notice. Her eyes flash to Heath and he gives her a wink as she hurries away.

"Thanks for dinner," Heath says. "You wanna meet some of the guys?"

Do I? A glance around the busy bar. Since we sat down, the college hangout has gone from a handful of empty tables to standing room only. Classes start back tomorrow, and everyone is ready to see their friends and party, totally undeterred by the chaos. I'm sure I was the same way, but that feels like a million years ago.

I suppress a groan. No, I definitely don't want to mingle in this crowd. Thirty isn't exactly old, but the years that separate me from these kids are dog years. However, if I'm looking out for him like a big brother would that probably includes hiking up my old man balls and tucking them into my waistband so I can meet the people he's spending time with.

THREE

Keira

Abby and I meet some of the team at our favorite local restaurant and bar. It's crowded, which isn't all that surprising. A new semester starts tomorrow and the best thing about going on break is coming back and catching up with friends.

And this is the perfect place to do that while also bumping into lots of other people. Frat guys, sorority girls, jocks, nerds . . . The Hideout is beloved by just about everyone. Greasy food and cheap drinks, you really can't go wrong.

We give up on finding a table, grab drinks from the bar, and then make our way over to Erica and Cassidy. The four of us stand in a tiny circle, basically shoulder to shoulder.

"It's so packed," Erica says as someone bumps into her from behind and sends her stumbling forward, her vodka and cranberry spilling over the side of the glass.

Abby grabs her elbow and steadies her. "You okay?"

She nods but still shoots a dirty look to the guy behind her.

"Be right back," Cassidy says. "I'm gonna do a lap and see if I know anyone sitting at a table. Maybe we can squeeze in."

After she disappears, Abby looks to Erica. "How was break?"

"It was good. I went to North Carolina with Cassidy. You guys should see her dad. Holy silver fox. I mean, I'd seen him a few times before at tournaments, but when he's at home in old concert T-shirts and sweatpants . . ." She tilts her chin toward the ceiling and sighs.

"You're ridiculous," Abby says. "And if Cass hears you, she's never going to invite you back home with her."

Erica just shrugs. "What about you guys?" She looks between Abby and me.

"Smith and I split the time between our families. He came to Texas for Christmas, and I went to Alabama for New Year's Eve."

Both girls glance to me expectantly.

"It was nice."

Erica snorts. "That's code for boring as hell because you spent the entire time playing golf instead of enjoying break."

She isn't wrong, but golf is what keeps me sane. Well, golf and nights out with my girls. But in their absence, I might have spent more time than usual with a club in my hand.

Before I can defend myself, Cassidy returns with four shots, and is grinning as she holds them out to us. "I didn't find a table, but if you can't beat 'em, join 'em."

Erica grabs one excitedly and Abby laughs as she takes one, eyes the lime wedge, and then sniffs the alcohol. "Tequila? This early?"

"I told the bartender to surprise me."

Cassidy dangles the last shot glass in front of my face. "Ready to get drunk enough we can't feel how much our feet hurt from standing in these heels?"

"Some of us were sensible enough not to wear five-inch heels to the bar." I lift a foot, showing off my chunky heel boots.

"Cute," she says, eyeing them with appreciation before holding up her shot glass. The rest of us join in, raising our glasses to the center and clinking them together before throwing back the strong liquor.

We all grimace, and Erica gags a little as she sucks on the lime.

"No more shots," Abby says, and we all agree.

Ah, the best laid plans.

One hour and two shots later, my face is flushed pink and I can't stop smiling. I'm holding on to Cassidy as we make our way back from the restroom. The place has only gotten busier, but the alcohol is doing its magic, and I'm less annoyed when people bump us from both sides like we're inside a human pinball machine.

Cass leads the way, a step ahead of me, her blonde hair swaying side to side with each short, bouncy step she takes. Every two seconds, she stops to say hello to someone. She's definitely the most social and outgoing of my teammates.

As the top-rated girl on our team, it should be easy for me to think of her as competition, but she's just too dang nice to dislike.

Tonight is exactly what I needed. A carefree evening with my girls. I've no sooner thought about how much fun I'm having when I spot Abby with Smith at the bar. I stop, and Cass looks back as our hands start to separate. She follows my line of vision.

"Awww, they're so cute." When I don't comment, she adds, "You don't think so?"

"No, they're perfect together. I was just having a good time spending the night with just us girls. Since they started dating, I barely see her outside of practice."

She gives me a reassuring smile. "Come on. Let's find Erica."

When we eventually find the missing member of our party, she's sitting at the end of a table with three of the golf guys.

"Hey," Erica says, "look who I found."

"What's up, Keira? Hey, Cass." Keith stands and offers me his seat. He smacks Griff on the shoulder as he's mid drink. "Get up, man."

Cassidy and I take their seats across from Erica and Chapman.

The guys somehow manage to find two free chairs and drag them up to the ends. Keith gets another pitcher of beer and more shots magically appear.

I can't have another drink. I'm already riding the line between puking in a public restroom toilet and passing out peacefully as soon as my head hits the pillow. The latter is my preference, obviously. But I know myself and one more shot and I'll think I'm invincible to the effects of alcohol.

"No," I say when all eyes fall to me and the last shot glass on the table. "I can't."

"Come on, one more shot and then we'll go dance," Cass pleads.

"Dance?" I ask and look around. "Where?"

"Anywhere and everywhere," she singsongs with a laugh.

I glance to Erica for backup, but she looks just as excited as Cassidy. I have no idea where these two are storing their liquor, but they don't seem nearly as drunk as I am. They're only slightly taller than me, and we have similar builds. I could toss either one of them over my shoulder like a rag doll.

Okay, actually that's a lie, I'm too scrawny to toss anyone like that except maybe an actual rag doll, but I'm definitely stronger than them so why am I the only one feeling it so hard right now?

Someone slides the shot glass from the center of the table to just in front of me. I open my mouth to protest again, but Cassidy looks at me with those big, brown eyes. The girl is some sort of sweet ninja with her ability to make me want to do things.

I don't usually care about going along with people just because I can stand on my own—maybe too much sometimes. But if Cassidy were holding a torch gun in one hand and a bottle of moonshine in the other, I'd probably want to tag right along to see what she was going to get into.

She's the scary type of friend who makes everything seem like a fun time until you're sitting in the back of a police car or holding your head over the toilet while you sit on the dirty floor of a frat house bathroom. That first thing hasn't happened yet, but the second has on more than one occasion.

I knew she had this effect on me within two hours of meeting her freshman year, so I shouldn't be surprised that right now as she tries to push a shot glass in my hand, my fingers curl around it and effectively sign me up for wherever the night might lead.

Cassidy squeals with victory as I raise the shot. "Cheers!" she exclaims merrily, making sure to clink glasses with everyone.

I give a little mini salute with mine and then bring it to my lips. I tip the shot glass back ever so slightly so just a taste falls into my mouth, and my stomach clenches in warning. Nope, not happening. Absolutely not.

As discretely as I can, I move the glass to the left and quickly toss the remaining liquid over my shoulder. I glance around to see if anyone noticed, but everyone is busy squeezing their eyes closed and grimacing. Freaking tequila.

I giggle at the ridiculousness and set my empty glass on the table at the same time Cassidy does.

"That wasn't so bad, right?" she asks.

"No, it really wasn't," I say with sarcasm that goes totally missed.

Success. I'll just tag along tossing my good intentions and my drinks over my shoulder with no one being the wiser.

FOUR

Lincoln

I hate to admit it, but I'm not having an awful time. I feel a little old as these kids talk about lounging around their parents' houses all break and how bummed they are to start waking up for eight a.m. classes again, but I can't remember the last time I had a night out that was this carefree.

Sure, I go to games and get to booze and schmooze, but I'm there to make connections, not to get shitfaced. As such, there's always a certain level of professionalism I have to maintain so when business talk slips in, which it always does, I'm ready to make my pitch.

I stand from the table of hockey players, which is more difficult than it should be thanks to the crowd. I sidestep at the same time as something wet hits my neck and trickles down the back of my shirt.

What the hell?

My hand instinctively wipes away the liquid, and I turn my head to survey the spot on my white shirt. The smell of tequila hits me, and a cold shiver runs down my spine. Tequila and I are not friends. That bitch screwed me over years ago, and I still haven't forgiven her.

I look up to find wide, brown eyes staring at me, horrified. I glance between the soaked fabric and the empty shot glass in her hand.

"You," I say at the same time she blurts out, "Oh my God, I'm so sorry."

The girl from the golf course yells at someone to hand her napkins, but no one at the table is paying attention, so she finally leans over to the holder, grabs a handful, and turns to shove them toward me. Seeing her flustered after she was all confidence and sass earlier is comical.

"If you were aiming for your mouth, I'd say you missed."

"My aim was dead on, but I wasn't expecting someone to walk into it."

Ah, there it is. I lied. Her sass is far more amusing than her fluster.

"You were trying to toss tequila on strangers?"

"Not on strangers, just anywhere but my mouth."

I chuckle at her response. I feel that.

"I can't take another shot," she adds with a wobble of her head.

I look to the group she's with. They still haven't noticed she's gone, and by the number of empty shot glasses on the table, I can assume they are all drunk.

I can't tell if she's in the same boat, but since she's chucking shots over her shoulder, I'd say it's likely she's either drunk or out of her mind. Someone bumps her from the side, and I reach out to catch her, cupping her small shoulders. Her long, reddish-brown hair falls forward, teasing my fingers.

There's no way for me not to check her out this close up. Tight jeans wrap around her legs and come up high on her waist, meeting a white sweater that seems twice as short as a normal shirt should be.

My lips twitch at the same hot pink scrunchie from earlier circling her wrist. And are those unicorns on it?

People have been bumping into me all night, but this is the first time I haven't minded the contact. I inhale, catching a whiff of raspberries and tequila.

Heath appears beside me, and her gaze momentarily flits to him before resting back on me. She steps back and tries again to hand me the napkins, but I shake my head. "I'll live."

Heath snickers. "Don't mind him. He could use a shot or two." Then he turns to me. "Linc, I'll be right back."

"Keira!" A girl in a tiny black dress appears at her side and hugs her arm. "I thought you ditched us and went home."

I test her name out, saying it in my head as I look her over. *Keira*. It fits.

"No, sorry, I just ran into . . ." She stops as if she's trying to remember my name. *Ouch.*

"Lincoln," I say, saving her.

"Hey, I'm Cassidy." She pulls her arm free from Keira's and smiles—one of those big, Julia-Roberts grins with so much teeth it's a little scary. "Come, both of you should sit before someone else tries to squeeze in."

Cassidy and Keira slide in, and I step up to the table.

"Holy shit. Lincoln Reeves." One of the guys at the table stands, runs a hand through his hair, and then thrusts his hand out, takes it back, and then smiles sheepishly. "Hello, sir, or Lincoln. Mr. Reeves? I mean, hey, man."

I'm having trouble remembering where I met the kid before until Smith Jacobson steps beside him and places a hand on his shoulder. "Hey, Lincoln. We weren't expecting to see you here."

Ah shit. Figures Keira would be sitting with a bunch of guys from the golf team.

I rub the back of my neck. "Hey, guys. Good to see you. I was just about to head out."

"No, no way," Smith says. "Stay and have a drink with us."

I don't see much of a polite way out, so I nod. "All right, one beer."

Smith grabs me a chair, which I pull up next to Keira, and a glass is filled and pushed into my hand. Then it's twenty minutes of constant questions before the guys take a break long enough for me to take a drink and glance at Keira.

She fidgets with the pink scrunchie on her wrist, tugging and twisting it. I keep staring and finally she looks up as if she can feel the weight of my gaze on her. Her lips curve up, not exactly in a smile, but she no longer looks like she's plotting my death.

Someone orders a round of shots, and I take the opportunity to slide my chair closer until my arm brushes the soft fabric of her sweater. "Let me know which way you're tossing so I can stay dry."

I raise a shot glass and a brow, daring her to do the same. Keira brings it to her lips first as if she's considering drinking it just to spite me, which wasn't my goal at all. If she says she's too drunk to have another, I believe it.

While she sits frozen, summoning the courage or whatever, I keep my eyes locked with hers and chuck the contents over my shoulder. Her pink lips tilt up into a relieved smile and then she does the same.

She holds my gaze as we both set our empty glasses on the table.

"Let's go to The White House!" someone exclaims, breaking the moment. "I heard they're having people over for after hours!"

Keira looks away first, and I shake my head, trying to make sense of the weird turn this night's taken.

There's some back and forth over it, but the general consensus is they're all ready to take the party elsewhere. Keira stands to let her friend out, and I unfold myself from my chair to make room.

She fiddles with that hot pink scrunchie on her right arm and peers up at me through dark lashes. "I'm sorry," she says when everyone else has gone to the bar to close out.

"What's that?" I ask, leaning down and holding back a smile. I'm totally messing with her, and she knows it.

She lets out a long breath. "I said I'm sorry. I was pissed at my coach, and I took it out on you."

"And the tequila?"

"*That* was an accident."

"Maybe we should start over." I grin and offer her my hand. "I'm Lincoln. Swing coach, business owner, non-creeper."

She stares at my hand for a beat before placing her palm in mine. A shot of pleasure races up my arm.

"Keira. Golfer, college student, skeptic."

A deep chuckle escapes from my chest. "Nice to meet you, Keira."

We stand smiling at one another, taking the other in, until someone bumps into her again. I motion for her to have a seat so we're out of the way and then take the chair next to her.

"I think you made a few lifelong fans," she says, and I follow her slight nod to where Keith and Chapman stand talking.

Chapman lifts his beer in a salute, and I wave before responding to Keira. "Believe it or not, most people were excited to see me today."

"I thought we were starting over."

"Fair enough. I won't mention it again, but just so you know, I did offer my services to your coach."

Her eyes widen in surprise. "Really?"

"He said no, obviously. My guess is that I'm not the first person he's said no to, if that helps your hatred toward all mankind any."

Her jaw clenches and her features go from gorgeous to glower, which also happens to be gorgeous—so long as she isn't glowering at me. "Why would he do that?"

"Some coaches like things a certain way and think bringing another person in messes with their system." Do I think it's bullshit? Yes. But I'm not about to admit that.

"I'm never going to get my spot back." She meets my gaze. "I was travelling with the team until last fall."

"What happened?"

"I had a bad tournament, lost my head." She shrugs. "Coach replaced me, and I'm pretty sure he's going to punish me indefinitely for it." Her dark lashes flutter closed as her voice softens. "I miss it. The early morning smell on the course just before the first group tees off and the buzz of energy as the last pair walks onto the green on the final hole." When she opens her eyes, her face flushes adorably.

I clear my throat and take a sip of my beer. "I'm sorry. That's tough."

"Are you speaking from experience or just being nice?"

"I got looked over plenty of times," I assure her.

"What did you do?"

"Worked harder, proved I belonged out there."

She rolls her eyes. "I could win the freaking US Open, and it wouldn't make a difference to Coach Potter. He hates me."

"So, do it. You don't need him to go the professional route."

She scoffs, but I'm not wrong. Playing college golf isn't the only way to go pro—or even the best way.

"No, but I do need coaching and experience, neither of which I'm getting. And now I know he isn't letting anyone else come in and help me either. What a prick."

"He really that bad?"

"He's a dictator, ruling with fear instead of respect. He makes the game less fun for everyone." She sits up a little taller and lets out a deep breath. "Anyway, not your problem."

"Still, he's managed to have some impressive seasons."

"That's because the team is crazy talented. Coach Hanson, the coach before Potter took over, was amazing. Everyone loved him. He's the reason the team is stacked. He recruited hard, and everyone wanted to play for him. He left to coach at a smaller school closer to family, and Coach Potter took over right before my freshmen year. Really regretting not going to Duke about now," she mumbles the last part.

Smith and his girlfriend appear at the table, interrupting what I'm sure was likely to be a much longer tirade.

"Hey, Lincoln," Smith says, near empty beer in hand. "I just wanted to say thanks for all your tips today. I worked on them all evening. My release is already looking better. I took video, just like you said. And I signed up for an account on your site."

"Good, I'm really glad it was helpful."

"Keira, are you ready?" Abby asks. "We're heading out."

She stands. "Yeah, can you guys drop me off on the way? I'm ready to crash."

Smith nods, finishes his beer, and places the empty glass on the table.

"Well, it was interesting," Keira says, hanging back as her friends start to leave.

"It was really good to meet you."

"Same." And with that, she moves to follow her friends out of the bar.

I call out before she gets lost in the crowd. "Keira."

"Yeah?" She angles herself between tables and groups of people on each side. Those brown eyes soften, and warmth spreads through my chest. I think about asking her to stay. I want to keep listening as she talks about golf with a passion that vibrates off every word. I understand it and respect the hell out of it.

Instead, I go with something much more appropriate. "Work hard, keep your head down, you'll be okay."

She seems to let my advice sink in for a moment before she gives a slight head bob and then ducks into the crowd.

FIVE

Lincoln

I sit up with a groan and look around the small, drab hotel room. I slept like shit. By the time I found Heath and got out of the bar, it was almost midnight.

I'd planned on going back yesterday afternoon as soon as the clinic was over, but Nathan found out I was at Valley and wanted me to check on Heath and then, well, the night slipped away.

I only had two beers but driving the nearly three hours home that late with any amount of alcohol in my system seemed like a bad idea. Then, I couldn't fall asleep because I was too busy thinking about Keira and her fiery hatred of her coach.

I don't pretend to know if she's a good golfer just from watching her swing, but I know she has the potential to be, and that's even more exciting as a coach. So, why isn't Potter playing her?

I looked through everything I could find on the guy. He jumped around a few junior colleges before landing at Valley, decent records at all of them. Really, nothing out of the ordinary.

I followed that with looking up Keira.

Keira Brooks. Twenty-one, junior. Played on her local Valley high school team with all-state honors her junior and senior years. Since coming to Valley, she's placed in a handful of tournaments, missed the cut at the championship last spring, and had her first individual win a few months ago.

After that, I could only find one more tournament she played where she led until the last day and then bombed with three bogeys in a row and tossed a driver into a water hazard. I laughed at that because I could totally picture it. And then saw it for myself when I found a clip on YouTube. Guess that was what she meant by losing her head.

By the time I drag myself through getting ready for the day and get in my vehicle to head back to Scottsdale, I'm behind schedule. But I can probably take care of most of the things I missed last night and this morning with a few phone calls during the drive. When I get home, I can get to my client emails, and shit, I need to check in with all my direct reports too.

There's really no escape. Anything I put off one day just gets piled onto the next. Still, I think last night might have been worth it; although, I need some caffeine.

At the end of the parking lot, I hesitate to turn right toward the freeway. I rub at the back of my neck and let out a sigh.

It's none of my business. I have better things to do. I shouldn't get involved. I have my own shit to handle. I absolutely shouldn't be angling for ways I can see Keira again. Not only would that be a bad business decision, but also a terrible personal decision.

Fuck.

I turn left.

At the Valley U golf course, I head through the clubhouse and out to the driving range, where I find Mark hitting a few balls. He leans on his driver and waits until I reach him before he says, "Hey, Linc. What are you doing back?"

Shifting awkwardly, I wonder if I made a mistake coming here without calling first . . . or just coming at all. I'm winging it, and I hate winging shit.

"I took a look at the videos from yesterday and thought it might be useful if I could sit with the boys and talk them through what I see."

"Yeah, of course." He gives me a weird look. "I don't have the budget to pay for another day."

I hold up a hand. "No, of course not, and in fact, I'm crediting you back for yesterday. We're friends—or, at least, we used to be. I just want to help. They seem like good kids, and like I said yesterday, I really appreciate that you've been such a big supporter of my business. I should have offered long before you reached out."

"All right, don't get too soft on me or I'll think too hard about why you're being so accommodating. The truth is that I don't care why. I need all the help I can get. Practice isn't for a few hours still though."

I nod. "I figured. Uh, one other thing. Do you think it would be okay if I offered my services to anyone that comes by today?"

His brows furrow. "You mean like a public clinic?"

"Sure. To anyone. Not all my clients are competitive athletes, you know?"

"Yeah, I don't see a problem with that. Just tell me what you need."

Mark and I drag a table and three chairs outside and he erects a sunshade over me while I setup my laptop.

I'm actually a little disappointed I didn't think to do this yesterday. Yeah, it takes more time, but it'll be easier to provide specific and hopefully helpful feedback when I can show them exactly what I mean on the video.

It's slow for the first hour. A handful of people come by the course, but only one is interested in help.

Lou is a retired Valley professor who, according to him, is trying to figure out what to do with his days now that he's no longer teaching. He's a nice guy, and I enjoy chatting with him, but I cringe as I watch his swing back on the screen. There are so many problems that all I can do is help with his setup and grip. Feels like a shallow victory when he masters that and heads off to the driving range.

Mark let his team know I was here again today, so they drop in early, which is nice since I'm twiddling my thumbs and triple guessing being here.

As I suspected, showing them slow-motion clips of their swings gives them a better understanding of what they are doing wrong and where they can improve. The real challenge comes from their ability to change habits that have been ingrained with thousands of golf balls. But it's a start.

I'm finishing the last review when she arrives with a few other girls she was with last night. Her eyes narrow in confusion and she slows her pace. The girl to her left, Erica, I think, says something that Keira waves off.

I meet her halfway.

A small smile tugs at the corners of her mouth. "You're back."

"So are you."

She tilts her head toward the girls she walked away from. "We have practice in fifteen minutes. What are *you* doing here?" She looks past me to my tent setup and smirks. "Another clinic with the boys' team?"

"No. Well, yes, but not them exclusively. It's a free clinic and it's completely open to the public."

"The public?" Her voice lifts an octave while she puts it together. A slow smile spreads across her face.

"Maybe you could let the *public* know? What time is practice over?"

"Five." She's still looking at me as if she maybe doesn't believe I'm for real. "You'll still be here?"

"I'll still be here."

The hopeful and pleased look she gives me makes my day seem not quite so wasted.

As the girls' team heads off to practice, the driving range gets crowded with locals. I'm too busy to watch the time pass, but two hours later, the Valley U women's golf team starts to fill my line. Though Keira is nowhere in sight.

I'm helping the first one of his players, when Coach Potter storms over. "What's going on here? I thought I said I didn't want you offering your services to my girls?"

The young girl in front of me, a freshman named Clarice, wilts in his presence.

"It's a free swing review. What could it hurt?"

"Clarice, go on now," Potter instructs. "Practice is over for the day."

I step to him, giving Clarice and the rest of the girls my back, and lower my voice. "I get that you want to be the end all be all to these girls, but you might consider that I have something to offer them, as do a lot of other people."

He scoffs, shoots me a glare, and then sends one over my shoulder to the girls as well. What a prick.

"My way. My rules," he grits out and pushes past me, telling his girls to go home and rest up.

One by one, they shuffle away, looking defeated. Once again, I look around for Keira, finally finding her on the driving range. Her gaze follows Coach and her teammates, eyes blazing with hatred I'm finding it hard to blame her for.

She walks toward us with purpose, ponytail swinging side to side with every determined step. She stops and briefly chats with one of the girls, jaw tightens, and then she marches toward me.

Her teammates watch her with something like admiration, and when she reaches the tent, she hesitates for only a second before walking in and taking a seat.

"Are you sure about this?" I ask quietly.

She meets my gaze and then lets it slide to the left so she's glaring at her coach. "Definitely."

I try to forget about everything else around us and focus only on Keira, which isn't really that difficult. Any hope I had that my fascination could be easily expelled by setting things right is shattered when I see her in action again. Everything about the way she moves with a golf club excites me.

It takes maybe two minutes to record her swing from every angle and upload it to my laptop so I can show her. In that time, her coach has disappeared, and her teammates have gathered back around.

I play her video as she sits in the chair on the other side of the table.

"You have a good swing . . . really good, actually. Nice and smooth. A few tweaks, and you'll be hitting greens all day long."

Her lips curve up as she laces her fingers together in her lap.

I freeze the video and then turn the screen so I can show her. "Right here, see how you're extending early? You're shifting your swing plane. I've seen much worse cases, but I think it's where your inconsistency comes from. It also looks as if you're holding back a little in a few of these."

"I've had issues in the past with opening my hips too quickly. Coach Potter doesn't want me swinging as hard as I can because I'm not consistent enough to control it."

I grind my teeth a little and bite my tongue. "Yeah, it's all related. But you have power, and you should use it. Let me show you something."

Standing, I come around the table and walk her through a drill I use on clients with the same issue. She watches, brown eyes following my every move with interest.

"You wanna try it?" I ask when I'm done.

Silently, she stands and gets into position with her club.

"Do a few without the club first to get a feel for it. Bring it back to the basics. Changing motor functions requires breaking it down to the simplest movements."

She tosses her club to the ground, and I step in front of her and get in position. Sometimes people are self-conscious, so doing the training with them helps remove barriers.

We move together, her mirroring me. I'm so close I can smell the fruity scent of her hair and a hint of sunscreen with each gust of wind.

"Nice, there you go. Can you feel the urge to push off that right leg?"

"Yeah, I really can." She does it again, mouth set in a determined line and the tip of her tongue between her teeth.

"Do that about a thousand times and then add in your arms." I extend my hands out in front of me and do the same motion. "And then you can add the club back to your swing."

She nods again, but this time, it's with a lot more enthusiasm. "Thank you."

"I didn't say anything any guy with a Golf Channel subscription couldn't have." I wink and grab a business card off the table. "I'd love to hear how it works for you or if you have any questions. You really do have a beautiful swing. Best I've seen in a long time. If I had a swing like that, they'd be fitting me for a green jacket."

The tips of her fingers brush mine as she reaches for my card. Neither of us makes a move to break the contact right away, and her pale skin dots with pink on her neck and cheeks. "Thanks, Lincoln."

She pulls away, tucking the card into her pocket and grabbing her club. As she walks backward out of the tent, I find myself holding her gaze. I can't seem to look away. With the flip of her ponytail, she's gone and the next girl steps through.

SIX

Keira

By the time I shower and scarf down a Pop-Tart, I have to sprint across campus to make it to my evening physical chemistry lab. I slip into my chair with only seconds to spare.

Professor Teague lifts a brow and glances at the clock. The head of the department is a huge stickler for attendance and being on time.

I catch my breath and hurriedly drink my Red Bull while he goes over the syllabus and then gives a brief lecture for today's lab. He removes his glasses and holds them in front of him as he says, "You may get started."

I swivel in my chair to face Keith. He's a chemistry major like I am, and we've been partners for nearly every lab since freshmen year. He's big on following the rules and does so to the point of basically brown nosing. Our friendship causes him great anxiety, I'm sure.

"Are you trying to get on his bad side on the first day?" he asks as he shakes his head. "You know he'll dock us points if you're late."

"Relax, I made it."

"I'm gonna get an ulcer if you cut it that close every week."

"Practice ran late."

"Oh, I heard," he says as he sets up.

I skim over the instructions and the questions we'll need to answer as we go along. "You heard what?"

"That you caused a scene after practice," Keith says, tosses me a disapproving smirk, and then tries to read the handout upside down. "Tell me, do you try to make waves everywhere you go, or is it just a special gift?"

I know he's mostly teasing, but I still bristle. "Coach Potter is a jerk. There is no reason we shouldn't get the same extra resources you guys do. How'd you hear about it already anyway?"

"Everyone was talking about it at the house before I left."

Keith lives in an off-campus house with Smith and Chapman. I'm pretty sure I have Abby to thank for Keith knowing, not that it wouldn't have gotten out anyway. But, screw it, I stand by my actions. I learned a lot from Lincoln, so it was well worth whatever punishment Coach plans on doling out.

"Look, I don't blame you. Lincoln Reeves is the best there is. I don't know if I'd have gone against my coach's wishes and made a scene like you did, but I get it."

"Your coach would never do that to you."

He shrugs and we start on the lab, easily falling into sync. We've worked together enough that we don't waste time deciding who does what, we both jump in and do what's necessary.

"What do you mean, he's the best there is?" I ask a few minutes later.

He looks up, the protective goggles on his face making it hard to tell he's raising his brows in question.

"Lincoln Reeves," I explain. "You said he was the best there is."

"Oh, right." He scribbles something on our paper before continuing, "You don't know who he is?"

"Just that he's a swing coach. Abby said he was a big deal." I lift one shoulder and let it fall. "He seems to know his stuff."

"Lincoln Reeves is going to be a legend. Reeves Sports, his online coaching website, is still new, but it's already one of the best out there. It has every sport you can imagine. Baseball, football, lacrosse, rugby, pickle ball, curling. And the athletes he has coaching?" Keith raises his goggles so they rest on the top of his wavy, brown hair. His blue eyes widen with excitement, and there's a faint outline from the goggles making him look funny. "He has pro-level coaches answering questions, providing tutorials, and creating training plans. When you sign up, you're getting the best of the best as your personal coach. If I had the funds, I'd totally sign up."

"Is it expensive?"

"Nah, but it's still out of my price range."

"Pretty cool," I say, but the excitement that hums through my veins makes me want to open my laptop right here and check it out. And maybe check out Lincoln some more while I'm at it.

He's . . . well, hot, of course, but there's something about his rare smile that makes my stomach flip. Mostly, those smiles seem to come at my expense, but I still can't help but admire them.

"Yeah, it really is."

"So, why would he come to Valley?" I ask, stopping any pretense that I'm working, and take a seat. "No offense, but you guys aren't exactly attracting media attention."

"He and Coach James played together in high school."

It's weird to picture Lincoln and Coach James as being in the same age bracket. Coach James is a younger coach. It's his fifth year at Valley and second as head coach. Still, that has to make Lincoln, what? Thirty? The way he holds himself and the experience that oozes off him make him seem like he could be that old. But last night at the bar, he seemed like one of us—a hot grad student maybe.

"Did he play college?"

"They both did; although, not together. Coach James went to ASU. Lincoln went to Texas for a couple of years before he went pro."

"He's a pro? How come I've never heard of him?"

"He didn't tour for long. He struggled the first year, missed a lot of cuts, and almost lost his eligibility. Then, as soon as he started placing and gaining momentum, he had some back issues that took him out for a year. They were speculating that when he returned, he'd be the next big thing, but when he resurfaced, it was as a swing coach for one of his friends on the tour. He worked with several pros before starting his company."

"Really? He coaches the pros?"

"Yeah, well, he did. I heard him say he only personally coaches a handful of clients now so he can focus on the business."

I nod, lost in my thoughts. Keith pulls his goggles back down over his eyes, and we get back to work.

After lab, Keith walks me back to the dorm on the way to his car.

"Thanks," I say as we approach the front of Freddy. "See you in class tomorrow."

"No problem, and, uh, maybe be on time. Need me to text you?"

I roll my eyes. "I got it."

Inside my room, I toss my bag on the bed, lie down beside it, and stare up at the ceiling, exhausted. My reprieve only lasts a few seconds before I sit up and grab my laptop and the card Lincoln gave me earlier.

Lincoln Reeves, Owner Reeves Sports. It lists the website URL, his email address, and phone number.

I place it on the bed next to my laptop and type in the web address. My pulse quickens as the logo appears in the left-hand corner. There's a video on the main page, Lincoln's build and those full lips of his are frozen on the screen.

Smiling, I click play and listen intently as he gives a thirty-second pitch for the site. His tone is serious, no smiles or enthusiasm—all business.

From there, I navigate to the golf portion of the site and watch another video, then two more. He holds a seven iron casually in his left hand, standing on a driving range, swinging the club lightly as he talks to the camera. He goes through a proper setup and then a few drills. It's an introduction video, beginner stuff, but his command speaks to the breadth of knowledge I now know he has.

He isn't saying anything I don't know, but it's the way he moves, and the memory of how being coached by him felt. Even now, my face warms like it had as his confidence and guidance wrapped around me earlier, making me feel as if I could do it—I could be exactly who I want to be. Nothing else mattered, only golf. I wish I could bottle that feeling.

There are a lot of videos. Some are by different coaches, and others feature current pros—men and women. I must view twenty videos, each one from start to finish, afraid I might miss the smallest piece of advice.

I click through every single one with Lincoln. He really is the best. His explanations are clear and concise, and he's able to break it down in a way that makes sense.

I press play on another. In this one, he's teaching the stinger. After a few minutes of explanation, he sets up to demo it. His swing is a beautiful, effortless thing. The ball rushes down the fairway, low and straight, before it bounces onto the green and rolls smoothly toward the pin and in.

His smile turns boyish with surprise at the hole in one he just caught on video. He treks down the green with the camera at nearly a run. When he pulls the ball from the hole, he holds it up and smiles with pride and excitement. Pressing pause, I smile back.

I open my email, type in his address, and then pause, going back and forth over how to address him. Lincoln? Mr. Reeves? Eventually, I decide to leave off all formalities.

Thanks for today. I've never seen Coach Potter so mad.
Keira
P.S. Sorry again for insinuating that you might be a creeper . . . and for throwing tequila on you.

After I press send, I get ready for bed and watch a few videos on my phone.

There's a nine-year-old kid in Florida who has his own golf channel where he does trick shots. It's one of my favorites, and I watch his newest video as my eyes get heavy.

He's blindfolded and stands in front of five golf balls teed up about a foot apart. He goes down the line, hitting each one dead on. It's impressive, and his young face beams as he removes his mask.

His love and joy for the sport leaves an uncomfortable ache in my chest. Coach Potter makes it easy to forget how much I love golf, but today was a good day, and I want to savor it before he ruins it tomorrow.

I loaded my schedule to take most of my classes on Tuesdays and Thursdays so that I can get in more practice time on my light days and so I can check in on Dad and take him to doctor appointments, as needed.

I'm eating a bowl of noodles for lunch when I finally check my email and see that Lincoln responded. I open it with a giddy smile.

You're welcome. I hope you aren't in more trouble with your coach. Working on the drills?
Lincoln

Still chewing, I type out a quick response.

Headed to the course early to practice. I'll find out what sort of punishment Coach has in store for me in a couple of hours. Whatever it is, it will be worth it. Are you still in town, maybe going around door to door to see if there's anyone else you can help?

Keira

"Dad," I call out as I come through the front door later that evening.

The television is on, but he isn't in his favorite recliner. I stop at the dining room table and strip off my jacket and place it on the back of a chair.

The floor creaks, and his cane knocks on the hardwood before he shuffles into view.

"Hey, kiddo. Wasn't expecting you."

He hobbles the rest of the way to drop a kiss on my forehead, pausing before his lips press to my skin. "You smell like golf."

I snort. "Like golf?"

"Yeah. Fresh-cut grass and sweat with a dab of Hawaiian Tropic." He drops the kiss, and I smile into his quick embrace. "How was practice?"

"Shot seventy-two." I smile for the first time in a long time when thinking about practice. Even Coach ignoring me all afternoon can't take away my excitement. "Best score on the team today."

He takes a seat in his chair and mutes the basketball game. "Proud of you."

"I thought I'd make dinner for us."

"Already ate," he says, not quite meeting my gaze.

"You didn't?" I ask and move toward the pantry. When I see the empty frozen meal box in the trash, I groan. "Dad, no one should eat those. Ever. Ever, ever."

"The Suns are playing. I didn't want to bother with cooking. Besides, they really aren't that bad. Tell me about golf. When's your next tournament?"

He's deflecting, but golf is always a good way to distract me. I tell him about the upcoming tournament. "I'm not going. Coach still hasn't moved me back to top five."

"You'll get there."

I shrug, not wanting to think too hard on what it'll take to get Coach to see that I deserve another chance. I change the conversation to school and fill him in on my class schedule this semester. He pretends to be interested while I take out ingredients for his favorite casserole.

My schedule, outside of golf is pretty short and uninteresting, and within a few minutes, we fall silent. With the exception of the occasional outburst at the television, neither of us speaks again until I cover the top of the dish in tin foil and set it in the fridge.

"Put it in the oven at three hundred fifty degrees for about thirty minutes. I'll be by later this week to take you to your doctor appointment."

He makes a dismissive grunt of acknowledgment. He hates feeling like he can't do stuff for himself, but since his accident, he needs me more than he's willing to admit.

A fall from a roof left him with a broken leg and a knee that needed extensive surgery to repair. It left me with a grumpy parent who is arguably the worst patient in all of history.

I tried to move back in with him at the end of last semester, but he wouldn't have it. He even went as far as to block my entry into the house when I'd arrived with an overnight bag.

I drop a kiss to his cheek. "Bye, Daddy. Stay away from the frozen dinners."

"You stay away from the junk food," he fires back.

I'd say it's unlikely either of us is going to heed the other's advice.

SEVEN

Lincoln

G ram hands me a New Balance shoebox. "Here are all his old client records, like you asked for."

I lift the top and laugh even as I cringe. "This is how he organized them?"

Index cards that don't appear to be in any kind of order take up most of the box. Underneath those are a yo-yo, a half-empty pack of Big Red gum, and a notebook my grandfather carried to jot things down during client sessions.

I shuffle through the cards, admiring his familiar handwriting. Some include addresses or phone numbers, but most don't. I take one out and read it aloud, "Mary Lou always wears purple."

I raise my eyes in question, and my grandmother smiles. "I remember Mary Lou. She was a snowbird and came down every year January through April from Wisconsin, I think. She passed a few years ago."

"Wears purple?"

She nods. "Always. Without fail."

I don't bother throwing out her card. My guess is they're all about as helpful.

My grandfather was a great teacher. People came from all over Arizona for lessons with him, sometimes farther. He was patient, encouraging, and smart, so freaking smart. And I'm not just biased because I looked up to him my entire life. He taught me the game, so I can attest to how much his teachings have stayed with me over the years. Everything I know about golf leads back to him in some way.

He wasn't as good of a businessman, it seems. Guess he didn't need to be. He was satisfied with the life he and my grandmother built here. If he were still alive, he'd probably balk at how much I've expanded the idea behind his small business. Reeves Sports is a tribute to the man I loved and a motivation to push harder, find success for myself, and ultimately, solidify my grandfather's legacy.

"These ought to be good for a laugh, if nothing else," I say and drop the box onto the dining room table. It's formally set with placemats, napkins, and dishes. And just like always, there is a bouquet of fresh flowers in the center. My gaze drops to the third setting. "Are we expecting someone else?"

Gram smiles. "I invited Patty's granddaughter, Autumn. You remember Autumn, right? She graduated and moved home."

I sigh. "Yeah, Gram, I remember her." I also remember that she dated my brother Kenton for two years. I use the word *dated* loosely, but either way—that's a hard limit for me. "I'm not interested in dating right now."

"Oh, you don't mean that. You're just scared after the way your marriage went up in flames."

I chuckle against my better judgment. Leave it to Grams not to pull any punches. "It isn't just that. I'm busy. The travel and long hours . . ."

"The right girl will make all of those excuses seem silly. You'll see."

No matter how many "right girls" Gram sends my way, I'll never be the *right* guy to be what they need. But I don't have the energy or headspace to try to convince my stubborn grandmother of that, so I accept defeat. "What can I do to help?"

"She'll be here in ten minutes, so go freshen up and let me worry about everything else." She cups my cheek lovingly and then darts off to the kitchen with more energy than I'd expect from someone her age. Energy that has been dead set on getting me a new wife since the day I signed the divorce papers a year ago.

Right on time, the doorbell rings. Gram shoos me to the door, and I drag it open with a forced smile.

"Hey, Lincoln." Autumn holds a bouquet of flowers in one hand and steps inside slowly.

"It's good to see you," I tell her and offer an awkward one-arm hug.

"You too." She looks around as if she's expecting someone else. "When your grandma invited me over to have dinner with her grandson, I assumed she meant Kenton."

Ah, well this makes more sense. No wonder she agreed to a setup.

"Sorry about that."

She smiles, and it eases some of the tension for the night ahead. Gram appears, and Autumn steps forward. "Hi, Milly. These are for you."

"Oh, how lovely."

"I remember how you always had fresh flowers out. I used to love that."

Grandma's eyes sparkle, and her gaze slides over to me. "Isn't that nice, Lincoln?"

Good lord, I'm sure she's already imagining the flowers at my and Autumn's wedding. Pump the brakes, Gram.

"It sure is." I reach for the flowers. "Let me take care of those."

"Nonsense, you don't know what you're doing. You kids grab a drink. Dinner will be ready in fifteen minutes."

We do as Gram instructed and head out on the patio. Maybe the fresh air will help me feel less like I might suffocate at any moment.

Autumn is exactly like I remember her. Tall and thin with long blonde hair. Back when we were kids she was all tomboy, but if her dress and high heels are any indication, I'd say she's given up playing in the dirt and chasing lizards.

Our grandparents have lived next to one another for as long as I can remember, so we've bumped into one another a lot over the years. She and Kenton spent lots of weekends exploring the neighborhood while I tagged along with Pop when he went to work. He'd take me to the range, get me a bucket of balls to hit, and when those were gone, I'd sit on the ground and watch as he worked with clients. If it rained or when he travelled, I'd be forced to stay behind and hang out with my little brother and the girl next door.

"Relax, Lincoln, it's just dinner," she says after we're seated. "You look like you're ready to take off in a dead run down the ninth hole." She inclines her head toward the golf course behind Gram's house.

"Just dinner?" I laugh quietly. "You don't remember my grandma as well as you think you do."

She rolls her eyes and settles back into her chair, obviously more comfortable than I am. "What have you been up to? It's been years. I was sorry to hear about you and Lacey. I always liked her, she was really nice."

"Still is." I take a long, *long* drink and then fill her in on the major milestones of my life, which takes an embarrassingly short amount of time. "What about you?"

"I went to school upstate. Graduated last May, spent some time travelling Europe, and now I've accepted a position teaching middle school. It's a long-term sub gig for now, but hopefully it'll lead to a full-time job next year."

"A teacher?" I ask in surprise. Then she shoots me a glare that I bet makes her pre-pubescent students wet themselves and wipes the look off my face.

As she's telling me all the reasons she chose teaching as a career path, my phone rings with a call from my IT guy. Gram walks out to let us know it's time to eat and eyes the phone in my hand with a disapproving scowl.

"It's work. I'll be right there."

"Work can wait."

"Five minutes."

"Two," she states firmly. "Come on, Autumn. I want to hear about your plans now that you're back."

"Yes, ma'am," Autumn says, and they disappear into the house.

I place the phone to my ear. "Hey, Will. What's up?"

"Hey, boss man. Site crashed."

"How long?"

"Just happened. Looks like it was an operating system update. I'll have it back shortly, just wanted to give you a heads-up."

"Okay. Send me more information when you have it. Anything else?" I ask, mostly to delay going inside. Will is one of those guys who needs minimal supervision, which I appreciate more than he knows. I barely have time to manage myself.

"All good. We're probably gonna need to add another server sometime in the next six months to handle the traffic, but we're okay for now." I can hear his fingers flying over the keyboard. "And we're back. A few emails came in at the same time, I'll put them in a zip file and re-send."

"Thanks."

"No problem. Later, boss man."

The call ends, and instead of hustling into the house like I should, I pull up my email. I really need to set up a filter to weed out the hundreds of spam messages I get every day. One from Keira Brooks catches my eye, and a smile spreads across my face as I open it. We've sent a few back and forth over the last couple of days as she's checked out the site and worked on the drills.

Saw your video with the hole in one. Impressive.
Keira

There's a video attached. Under any other circumstance, I might wait
or have a second of hesitation about opening an unsolicited video from
a girl I barely know, but since I'm avoiding dinner with my brother's ex, I
click play.

The camera faces a blank, white wall. Keira comes into view, long hair
pulled back into a ponytail. She glances back at the camera and smirks before holding up a red cup in her hand and then setting it on the floor.

She backs up about five feet, grabs a wedge and a ball, and stands side-
ways to the camera so I can see her profile. She takes a deep breath and then
tosses the ball with her left hand and catches it with the club in her right.

She bounces the ball off the clubface in a steady rhythm. After a few
bounces, she moves the club behind her and between her legs, keeping that
rhythm and holding command over the ball.

Then she goes into trickier moves, catching it on the top of her shoe
between bounces, kicking it with the sole of the other shoe behind her. It's
really something to watch. I've seen plenty of trick shots, but she has a
graceful, fluid control that most don't possess.

For the finale, she bounces the ball a touch harder, moves the club behind her back, taps the ball, and somehow hits it into the cup.

My eyes widen in disbelief. I watch it twice. If she somehow spliced
the video, I sure as hell can't tell.

I send her a quick email in response.

How many tries did that take?
Lincoln

I'm smiling at my phone, watching the video a third time when another
email from her comes in.

One.
Okay fine, three.
Keira

I kick my feet up and lean back, sending another reply.

Nice. How's the swing coming?
Lincoln

As if she's waiting for my email, the same way I'm waiting for hers, the reply is quick.

Just got back to my dorm. I'm going to work on the drills after I study.
Keira

The reminder that she is in college is a swift kick to the old man balls. She has a life outside of golf that I can't relate to anymore. I sit forward in my seat and send one last email.

Sign up for a free account on the site, there are a ton of videos that you'll have access to, and you can get one free swing review each month from someone on my team.

Even though I told myself the email was my final reply, I still wait for hers. It comes just as quickly as the others.

Your team, huh?
Keira

"Lincoln."

"Hmm." I raise my head slowly from my phone and find Gram scowling at me.

"I said your name three times before you answered. Put that phone away and come eat. Whatever it is, it can wait."

I place my phone in my pocket. "Sorry, Gram."

Dinner passes relatively quickly, and it isn't even that awkward because it's clear neither Autumn nor I are interested in the other. After thanking Gram, I walk Autumn out to her car.

"How is Kenton? Do you talk to him much?"

Hands in my pockets, I follow her slow pace. "He's good. Still in L.A. playing soccer."

"He always said he was getting out of Arizona. I guess I should have believed him." She looks a little sad, and I don't know what to say. Kenton is . . .

Kenton. Carefree and fun, incredibly hard working and successful but somehow still manages not to take himself too seriously. "Tell him I said hello."

I nod and open her car door. "It was good to see you. Congrats on graduating and good luck teaching."

"Thanks, Lincoln." She slips into the car and grabs a pen and scrap piece
of paper from the console. She scribbles on it and then hands it to me. "Call
me if you want to get together again."

A flicker of attraction in her eyes that wasn't present until just now surprises me and has me standing mute as she closes the door and starts the
car. Well, that was unexpected.

When I get home, I grab a beer from the fridge and head into my office.
I drop Pop's shoebox of contacts on my desk and open my laptop.

I check email first, curious as hell to reread the conversation with Keira,
then shoot her a quick response.

Did you sign up?
Lincoln

I switch over to the site and log in so I can check my messages and
swing submissions for the day. The notification for Keira's reply pops up in
the bottom of the screen, and I click on it.

Yes. I submitted a video and someone named Simon is reviewing it.
Keira

I search through Simon's inbox, something I alone have the site priv-
ileges to do. When new members sign up, their inquiries are routed to one
of three of my golf coaches. Simon has the least experience, but he's sharp.

I can see he's watched the video but hasn't responded yet. That isn't altogether surprising since it only came in an hour ago. We promise a response
in twenty-four hours, so I expect he'll get back to her tomorrow.

I watch her swing, noting that she's worked on her weight shift. It isn't
quite there, but the initial turn is better. My fingers itch to do her review
myself, but there just aren't enough hours in the day. I really shouldn't be
holding on to the few clients I have now, but coaching helps me remember
why I'm doing this in the first place.

My phone rings, and I go to silence it but pause at the name on the screen. *Lacey*. It keeps ringing while I decide whether or not to answer. It isn't like her to call or text unless it's absolutely necessary. We aren't on bad terms exactly; we just have nothing to say to one another.

"Hello?" I try to keep my tone totally neutral as I answer. Maybe it's a butt dial.

"Hey, Lincoln. It's Lacey," she says, voice tight.

I find it humorous she thinks I've deleted her contact. Even if I had, hers is one of only a few numbers I could recite by heart.

"Hey. Uh, everything okay?" I wince and try another approach. "How are you?"

She laughs, breaking some of the tension. "I'm fine. Sorry to call, but I wanted to remind you that we have to get everything out of the storage unit. We pre-paid through April, after that there are additional fees."

"Right. The storage unit." I think back, trying to remember what's in it. It felt like my whole life at the time, yet I've managed just fine without any of it.

"I'm going tomorrow if you want to meet me there. There are a few boxes we should probably go through together anyway."

"Tomorrow's no good for me." I rub at the back of my neck. "But feel free to go through them and take whatever you want. You know better than I do what's what anyway."

She's quiet, and I check the phone to make sure we didn't get disconnected. "Lace?"

"I spent our entire relationship taking care of things when you were gone or too busy or maybe just didn't want to be bothered, so don't take it the wrong way when I say that it isn't my job anymore to go through your shit."

That wasn't exactly what I meant, but years of guilt gnaw at me and keep me from lashing back. She isn't completely wrong, a lot of things did fall on her, and I guess I got used to depending on her. It's easy to slip back into those same roles, even now. "I can't tomorrow. Is there another day? Next week I'm travelling, but maybe the week after?"

She sighs, and it's a long, exasperated sound. "Yeah, sure. Give me a call when you're ready."

She disconnects first, leaving me with dead air and a thousand regrets. I drop my phone to the desk and stare at my computer screen.

The end of Keira's video is paused so that she's frozen in position. I hit play one more time, letting her swing bring a little bit of joy to this shitty night, and then force myself to get to work.

EIGHT

Keira

Wednesday's practice is nearly identical to Tuesday's. We break into groups to play eighteen holes and then spend some time with Coach working on individual drills. Well, except for me and a few freshmen he doesn't get to before time is up. I'm positive that isn't a coincidence that he somehow didn't get to me two practices in a row.

After everyone else leaves, I stay at the driving range, working on my swing until it's too dark to see the ball. I'm trying to incorporate the things Lincoln said, but I can't feel if I'm getting it right, and it's beyond frustrating.

I head back to the dorm, checking my text messages as I walk the stairs to the second floor. Abby is at Smith's apartment, per the usual. Since she started dating him last semester, she rarely sleeps here.

I shower and pick through clothes on Abby's bed. I've taken to using it as a storage area for my clean-ish clothes—the ones I've only worn once but am too lazy to hang back up in the closet. Erica and Cassidy texted that they were having people over, and since I'd rather go out than sit here alone, I get ready and call an Uber.

With eleven minutes to kill until my driver picks me up, I open my email. Simon from Reeves Sports has completed my swing review, and the write up has way more details than I expected. He's even attached a slow-motion video of my swing like the one Lincoln had done, and talks through what he sees. I'd been expecting something much more generic. This is really cool.

I grab my seven iron from my bag and hold it as I listen, pulling back and trying to get the feel of my weight shift like Lincoln had said that first time. Honestly, what Simon says is much the same, so either it's standard advice they give everyone or Lincoln was right. I don't know why that continues to surprise me. Everything about him radiates a confidence that can't be fake.

The thing is that, pro or not, it doesn't automatically mean he's qualified to give others advice. The best mentor I ever had was my high school coach, whose only qualification was that he loved golf. He worked hard and genuinely wanted his players to succeed. That, in turn, made us work hard.

The Uber driver calls to say he's pulling up outside of Freddy, and I grab my purse and hustle downstairs. When we're on our way, I send Lincoln an email.

Simon was more helpful than I expected. The site is really cool. I like the video feedback.
Keira

His response comes as the driver stops in front of Erica and Cass's place. I thank him and walk to the front door slowly, reading.

I just saw his feedback. It's pretty spot on with what I thought after watching it.

I can hear people inside the house, but I pause at the front door and email him back.

You watched it?
Keira

An unexpected thrill shoots through me at the thought of him taking the time to follow up on me. I wait out front for a minute, and when I don't get a new response, I head inside.

A lot of the guys and girls from the golf teams are here hanging out in the living room watching television and drinking. Erica and Cassidy are sitting at a table in their small dining area with Chapman, Keith, and a sophomore named Han.

"You made it," Cassidy squeals and hugs me.

"I did." I squeeze her back and smile at the rest of the group. "I'm surprised you two are drinking the night before a tournament."

"Tomorrow is just a practice round, plus we can sleep on the ride," Erica says. "Help yourself, we restocked the booze."

I'm pouring vodka and Red Bull into a cup when Brittany comes up to me in the kitchen. "Hey, Keira."

"Hey, Britt." I offer her the vodka. "Drink?"

"No, I'm not drinking tonight."

I nod in understanding. Of course, she isn't. She knows as well as I do what it's like to be left behind while the team travels. I wouldn't be drinking either.

"I'm sorry about taking your spot. I know how hard you've worked and—"

"Don't be sorry. You've worked hard too. Coach made his decision, and as much as I disagree with it, it's good for you. Take advantage of it. I know I would be."

She nods, and I step away before the conversation tanks my mood. "Good luck this weekend, Britt."

After a couple of drinks, we clear the table and set up for beer pong. Erica and me against Chapman and Han. Cassidy and Keith stand off to the side watching us. Cass has switched to water, and Keith holds a Natty Light in each hand.

Erica and I get smoked three games in a row. My bloated stomach can't take another loss, but I've managed to distract myself from thinking about the tournament this weekend. Well, sort of.

"We're getting thrashed. Do you have a couple of wedges around we could use so we have a chance in hell of winning the next one?"

Erica's eyes narrow and then widen with understanding. "Definitely."

She returns with a golf ball and two wedges.

"All right boys, ready to switch things up?" I go first, tossing the ball and catching it with the club. I bounce it a couple of times before hitting it into the air, flipping the club around, and tapping it toward the cups. The ball hits the rim and bounces away, nearly tipping over two cups in the process. Guess there's a reason we use ping-pong balls.

Han shakes his head but gives it a try. After each of us has taken a turn, we've managed to spill half the beer, but no one has made a shot.

"How about you use empty cups, and then the loser has to chug?" Cass suggests.

"Good idea," Erica says. We wipe down the table and re-start. Slowly, we garner a crowd, and they're watching me closely as I bounce the ball off the clubface. This time, when I send it sailing toward the cup, it goes in. I drop the wedge to the floor and throw my hands over my head in victory as Chapman and Han chug their beers.

"Oh, man. I'm glad you made that because I need to pass out." Erica holds a hand over her mouth as she yawns.

"What happened to sleeping in the van tomorrow?"

"Sorry."

"Han and I are going over to The White House if you want to come," Chapman says at the same time I look around to see everyone has left or is preparing to leave. My teammates are headed off to sleep so they can play well this weekend and that makes me want to keep right on drinking, so I don't have to think about how I won't be there.

"I'm in."

Chapman, Han, and I walk the block to The White House, an off-campus house where some of the basketball guys live. Parties at The White House are always big and crazy fun. They had a foam party in their backyard once. It was insane. I've never seen anything like it.

Loud music greets us inside and there are people everywhere. We head out to the back patio. Chapman grabs us beers, and we mill around.

I spot the guy who was with Lincoln the night I tossed tequila on him at the same time he does me. I leave Chapman and Han and walk toward him. He stares at me for a second as if he's trying to place me, and then one side of his mouth pulls up into a grin. "Tequila girl."

"Not tonight," I say as I lift the cup of beer I'm holding. "You play basketball?"

He scoffs. "Nah, I'm on the hockey team. Heath," he introduces himself. "I don't think I caught your name."

"Keira." I glance around hopefully. "Is Lincoln with you?"

"No way. Linc be caught at a college party?" He laughs. "He went back to Scottsdale, I think. He travels so much it's kind of hard to keep track of him."

I nod like I know. "How do you know him? Is he a friend of yours or ..." I'm trying to piece together how a college hockey player knows a pro golfer.

"Sort of." He bobs his head from side to side. "Friend, boss, pain in the ass. He's tight with my brother, so he's like a second big brother in some ways."

"Did you say boss?"

"Yeah, you know his site? Reeves Sports? I work on the hockey portion of the website and do the occasional in-person job. Last summer, he got me a gig coaching at a kids hockey camp."

"Wow. That's awesome. I've only checked out the golf stuff so far, but it seems pretty impressive."

"You play golf?"

"Yeah."

"Well, Lincoln is the guy to know then. He's the very best and a really decent guy on top of it. You know, when he isn't acting like an overprotective ass."

"Do you provide reviews like he does—perfect hockey puck shooting form or something?"

He barks a laugh. "Not a big hockey fan, huh?"

"I grew up in the desert."

"There's hockey here."

I raise a brow.

"All right, I get your point. And no, my job is to answer questions that come in. Like, which shot is the hardest for a goalie to stop or how does someone increase the speed on their slap shot?"

"That's pretty cool."

Heath nods and flashes a cocky grin that reaches his dark blue eyes. "Just until I make it pro."

He says it so matter-of-fact that I believe him. If he's half as good as he is cocky, I have no doubt.

Someone yells across the party, and Heath's head lifts. He nods to whoever was calling his name and then his eyes flit back to meet mine. "I gotta go. Nice seeing you."

"You too."

I find an empty chair in the corner of the crowded living room and pull out my phone.

I entered Lincoln's number from his business card into my phone. I'm not even sure why, I never intended to use it, but my finger hovers over his name in my contact list. I bite my lip, close my eyes, squeal quietly, and tap.

He answers on the third ring. "This is Lincoln."

A small giggle escapes my mouth at his tone, which is totally serious and not fazed in the least about the time. Makes me wonder if he's used to getting calls at one in the morning.

"Hello?" he asks, voice bordering on annoyed.

"Ah, much better. Do you really answer the phone at one in the morning without so much as a hello first?"

There's a beat before his deep baritone slides over the line. "Anyone who calls this late is delivering bad news. Might as well get right to the point."

"I guess that's true."

"What bad news are you delivering, Keira?"

Maybe it's the alcohol or maybe it's because it's late at night and I likely woke him, but my name on his lips sounds like straight sex and my body warms. "It's good news actually."

"Yeah?"

"Yep. I've decided that I want you to take over for Simon and be my swing coach. I signed up for the daily review plan." Saying the words aloud makes me realize just how much I want it. I want to remember how it felt when he was standing near me, scrutinizing, and coaching me like he believed in me more than anyone else ever has.

"I saw."

"You did?" I ask, pleased that he's keeping tabs on me.

"It's my job." He's silent for a moment before asking, "Did Simon do something wrong? We have other coaches if you don't think he's a good fit."

"No, he's been fine. But you're the best. Everyone says so. I want the best."

He chuckles softly. "I'm not taking new clients. I'm having a hard enough time keeping up with the three I do have."

"And I'm not taking no for an answer."

There's commotion in the entryway, and I look up to see some guy wearing a bear helmet riding a scooter. People are laughing and cheering, a few start chanting his name. "Datson, Datson, Datson."

"Where are you?" Lincoln asks.

"At a party. By the way, I ran into your friend Heath."

"Heath is there?" He grumbles something and then adds, "I hope he isn't drinking. Was he drinking? Never mind, don't tell me."

"You're changing the subject."

He sighs. "I'm sorry. I can't. It wouldn't be fair to you or my other clients.

I don't have time right now. I will get Roy to take over for Simon. He's the most senior of the staff, and he's just as good as I am."

"I highly doubt that." I was so sure I could convince him that the rejection stings.

"How's practice going? Did everything smooth over with your coach?"

"He added an extra thirty minutes of conditioning to our weekend workout, and he's basically ignoring me, but it's fine. Totally worth it."

"Keep your head up. You'll be okay."

"Yeah, all right." The alcohol and the late hour crash into me. "It's late. I should go."

"Be careful and don't call any other boys this late. It screams booty call."

I roll my eyes. "I assure you that if I call anyone else, it *will* be a booty call."

Another deep chuckle tickles my ear. "'Night, Keira."

NINE

Keira

I wake with a groan and find Abby standing at the side of my bed. "Wake up, sleeping beauty."

I groan louder.

"Your phone has been going off nonstop." She tosses it on top of the comforter. "You missed your eight o'clock. If you get up now, you can still make your next one. I'd suggest a shower first, though, you smell awful."

I hurl my pillow at her, but it misses by several feet.

Laughing, she hands me my water bottle from my desk. "Do you still have the black Adidas jacket I loaned you before break? I want to take it with me."

"On the bed," I croak out, ignoring the pang of disappointment that I'm not going.

My voice is scratchy, throat dry, and head pounding. I close my eyes and feel around for my phone. Wrapping my fingers around it, I turn onto my side and slowly open my lids again.

Curse vodka. Or maybe it was the beer. Maybe it was the mixing. Maybe it was the sheer volume. After Lincoln's rejection, I softened the blow with a game of flip cup, and then I think there were a few games of quarters. Groan.

I have a dozen texts from people I ran into last night, ranging from concern to laughing emojis at how drunk I was and calling me a lightweight. There are two from Keith—one asking where I am and the next assuring me that he'll take notes and we can meet up at lunch so he can fill me in.

The newest message, though, makes my already rolling stomach lurch.

Lincoln: I've sent over a training plan. We may need to tweak it based on your practices, so I'd like you to detail everything you do in practices for the next week. This morning get the run in and do the weight training. After your practice, we'll adjust the swing drills as needed.

The time stamp is from ten minutes ago. I read it several times before I notice the messages above his from me, sent early this morning. I scroll up, heat making my face burn. There are three of them just after four a.m.

Me: What do I have to do to convince you?

Me: I'll work harder than any of your clients. You say, "Jump," I'll ask, "How high?" Or in this case, you say, "Swing," and I'll ask, "How many times?"

Me: Please? This is important to me. It's all I've ever wanted.

Oh God. I throw an arm over my face to shield me from the blast of embarrassment. My head is pounding, and I squeeze my eyes shut.

"You okay?"

I moan in response, but then his text sinks into my foggy brain.

"He said yes." I sit up fast, too fast, and gag.

Abby sits on her bed folding the pile of clothes, mostly mine. "Who said yes?"

I check my email but don't see the training plan that Lincoln mentioned. My laptop is on my desk, so I swing my legs off the side of the bed and stumble the few steps to get it and bring it back to bed with me. Abby grabs her mug off the Keurig and joins me.

"You're acting weirder than normal. What's going on?" She crosses her legs and takes a sip of the coffee.

"Ugh. The smell of that coffee is making me want to gag."

"Don't blame the coffee. You're the one who lost three straight games of beer pong. For someone who deals in small balls, you have shit aim throwing them."

"I don't see it."

"I'm pretty sure I got some video of it if you want to see just how bad you were."

"Not that. Lincoln said he sent a training plan, but I can't find it."

"Lincoln? Lincoln Reeves, the swing coach? The one you threw tequila on?"

"Will no one let me live that down?"

"Why is he emailing you?"

I keep my eyes firmly on the screen as I admit the embarrassing truth. "I drunk dialed him last night. And then drunk texted him."

"Keira!" She laughs. "What did you say?"

"I asked him—no, I begged him to coach me."

Her eyes widen. "And he said yes?"

I log into the Reeves Sports website and see I have a message waiting from Lincoln. His profile picture makes me laugh—a stoic expression, ball cap on, blue polo shirt. He's still gorgeous but far too serious. "Ah, I found it!"

Abby stands. "I gotta get to the van, and you need to get to class." She picks up her phone. "Keith is texting me now. Will you put that poor boy out of his misery and tell him you're up and on your way?" She grabs her bag and heads to the door.

I tear my eyes away from the screen. "I will. Good luck this weekend. I put something in the side pocket of your bag."

She reaches in and pulls out the blue unicorn scrunchie.

"Go be a badass unicorn scrunchie-wearing superstar."

Her smile is sad. "It matches yours."

I lift my arm. I still haven't taken off the pink one. Maybe my dad knows me better than I think.

"Thank you." She slips it on her wrist and lingers in the doorway. "Part of me wishes we could trade places. I don't really feel like going, if I'm honest."

"You're just dreading the drive." Abby hates car rides. She doesn't even like going across town to run errands with me.

"You're probably right. Okay." She lets out a long breath. "I'll call you later and let you know how it goes tonight."

"Bye."

When she's gone, I read over the training plan with a huge grin on my face. It's detailed and a little intense. A two-mile run? And there are at least twenty different flexibility exercises in addition to weightlifting.

It all seems like overkill. We do conditioning and weights as part of our normal training, but it's nowhere near this much. Regardless, I'm excited to try some of it.

It'll have to wait though. I have to get moving if I'm going to get a shower and manage to stomach some food before my nine o'clock class.

I slide into a seat next to Keith just as class begins. My stomach cramps from the Pop-Tart I ate, and I'm sweating out alcohol from the half jog that was necessary so that I wasn't late.

Keith shakes his head disapprovingly, and I stick my tongue out at him. Then I regret it because it makes me gag.

Fifty minutes has never felt so long. When class finally ends what feels like a decade later, I have to go straight to my next class and sit through another lecture. I'm dragging when Keith and I make it to University Hall for lunch.

"Do you want anything? I'm gonna grab a sandwich?"

"No, definitely not. My stomach is still really angry." I look around at the food options and then end up changing my mind. "Well, maybe some chips."

He nods, and I place my head on the table until he returns. I do my best to pay attention as Keith catches me up on what I missed in organic chem.

"I'm going to email you my notes too since I know your brain is still foggy."

"You're a prince."

"I have to rush off to get my workout in before our next class. Don't skip measurements class. Professor Anolf docks a grade for too many absences."

"I won't," I assure him. "I have to take my dad to the doctor, but I should be done in plenty of time."

"Today?"

I nod. "It was their only available appointment all week."

When Keith leaves, I read through his notes and the accompanying chapters from the textbook. Since it's still the first week, one missed class won't kill me, but I can't afford to fall behind. The season is just about to pick up and study time will be hard to find.

An alarm on my phone goes off with a one-minute warning, and I silence it and continue to hold the phone until it rings.

"Hey, Mom," I answer.

"Hi, honey. How are you?" Her warm, upbeat voice makes me smile.

"I'm good. Between classes."

"Does this time still work for you this semester?" she asks.

"Yeah, it's fine."

"Good. I look forward to our calls every week."

"Me too."

I try not to think too hard about the fact I've been relegated to a time slot much like dropping off dry cleaning or grocery shopping.

I was sixteen when she and my dad divorced, and she moved back to Maryland where she grew up. Last summer she got remarried. My new stepdad (super weird to think of him as that), Bart, is a doctor at the same hospital where she works, and he seems nice. I've only met him a few times. Mom's happy, though, which is all that really matters.

"How's school? Busy schedule this semester?"

I give her a quick summary of my classes and then tell her about golf. I play down my disappointment in not being with Abby and the others at the tournament this weekend and give her my standard cheerful line, "I'll just keep putting in the work until I get my spot back."

"You will. I know you will," she says.

"How's everything else? Any boyfriends I should know about? Or girlfriends," she adds quickly.

I snort. "No, Mom. No boyfriends or girlfriends."

"Well, you'll find someone."

"I'm not worried."

"When I was your age, I was already married. Not that I'm rushing you."

I snort again and stop myself from pointing out the obvious—that it ended in divorce, but her thoughts must drift there anyway. "How's your dad?"

"Stubborn." I check the time. "Speaking of, I need to run so I can take him to the doctor."

"All right, honey. Call me if you need anything."

"I will." I pause before saying goodbye. "I miss you."

"You too, baby."

Dad's waiting on the curb when I pull up outside his house.

"You're late." Sweat beads on his forehead.

"I'm right on time. Your clocks are fast. I keep telling you that."

"If you aren't five minutes early, you're late."

"I don't think that counts for doctor's offices since they're going to make us wait at least fifteen minutes."

I get him in the passenger seat and drive over to the hospital.

"Wait here, and I'll grab a wheelchair to take you in."

"I don't need a wheelchair." He opens his door and swings his good leg out.

I hurry to help and bite down on my molars. Five very long and very exhausting minutes later, the sliding doors open and the air conditioning blasts my sweaty body. "We made it," I say breathlessly.

My dad's leaning on me, and my shoulder aches from the pressure, but he seems completely oblivious to my exertion. Damn, stubborn man.

"Mr. Brooks." One of the nurses rolls a wheelchair in front of us, shoots me a sympathetic smile, and then bats her eyelashes at my dad. He grins at her and lowers himself into the chair without complaint, and I try not to roll my eyes as I go to the reception and sign him in.

When I take a seat beside him in the waiting room, he finally looks more at ease. Depending on me and not being able to get around like he used to is harder for him than it is for me, and I feel guilty for all the frustration I felt. "I'm sorry I was late."

His mouth twists into a half smile that says bullshit. "You're a good kid. I know you have better things to do than cart your old man around. Hopefully this is the last appointment you need to drive me to."

"Optimism . . . I dig it." I raise my fist for him to bump, but he just stares at me confused.

He grabs my hand and squeezes tenderly. "Love ya, sweet pea."

<hr />

Since Coach Potter is with the team travelling to the tournament, it's a pleasant afternoon at the golf course. We divide into two groups and play eighteen holes and then work on some individual drills.

When I get back to my room, I face-plant onto my bed. I still have study group tonight before I can nap. Or maybe I'll just go to bed really early. Reluctantly, I sit up and open my laptop and send Lincoln a message through the website that details today's practice and the schedule through Sunday.

I've just started in on the swing drills he gave me when a message pops up.

Lincoln: How was the morning conditioning session?

Me: I didn't get to it. Just starting in on the swing drills now.

I take a step back from the laptop to start again just as a call request from him pops up on the screen.

Tentatively, I press accept. "Uh, hello?"

"What do you mean, you didn't get to it?" His voice is agitated and clipped. The screen is black, and I'm tempted to turn on the video so I can scowl at him.

"I didn't have time today."

"There's always time."

"I had classes all day, plus I had to go to the doctor, and I still have study group tonight, but I'm getting in what I can now."

A notification on the screen indicates he wants to turn on video for the call—guess he had the same idea—to turn on video to scowl at me. I tuck my hair behind my ears and do a quick scan around the room. There isn't much I can do about the mess, so I ignore it and press accept.

When his face appears, I forget to breathe for a second. His hair looks like he's been pulling at it, and he's frowning in a decidedly hot way—who knew that was possible? "Are you okay?"

"Yes?" I answer, a bit confused until I realize what I said. "I'm fine. I had to take my dad to the doctor. He can't drive."

His shoulders relax, but the frown stays firmly in place. "You have to make time for the training. You can't skip it because you stayed out too late and felt like shit this morning."

"That hardly seems fair since I didn't know about the training plan until after I made the decision to drink my troubles away." I smile at his ridiculousness, but he doesn't return it.

"No excuses. If you want this as much as you claim, then you'll make time. The next time you decide to skip the plan I line out for you, we're done."

I open my mouth to apologize or yell back, I haven't chosen which, when he asks, "How much time before your class?"

"An hour."

"All right, let's get to work then."

TEN

Keira

It's still dark outside when my alarm goes off. I don't bother changing clothes since I passed out in yesterday's workout leggings and tank. The last two days have been a blur. After Lincoln scolded me like a child on Thursday night, I was at the field house until midnight getting in the training he outlined.

I thought he'd be pleased, but yesterday, he was in the same pissy mood. And maybe it's delusional to think my getting up early on a Saturday morning to hit the gym will please him, but a girl can hope.

It isn't that I want to please *him* exactly, it's that I want him to know that I'm willing to do what it takes to be the best and he didn't make the wrong choice in taking me on as a client. I saw that look on his face at the clinic when he helped me with my swing. He believed in me. I want that look back.

I jog over to the field house with my eyes half open, hoping that by the time I get there my body will be warmed up and I'll be more awake. The weight room is basically empty. A few people are running on treadmills, but I have the free weights to myself.

I text Abby good luck on her second day of the tournament and then put my headphones on, trying to deceive my body into thinking I'm excited to be here by playing fun, peppy songs.

Today is upper body with a heavy focus on back, and apparently my *everything* is weak because every time I choose a weight to start, I have to go down by fifteen pounds and try again.

I note everything in the online workout journal Lincoln set up for me. Number of reps, amount of rest between sets, weight, and I add in my own notes of displeasure for certain exercises just for fun. Next to burpees, I let him know that it's a dumb exercise with a dumber name. It's too early to be clever.

I'm working my ass off for him, but I want to make sure he knows I think he's ridiculous and overbearing.

While I'm between exercises, I pull up the swing review he completed for me last night. His deep, clipped voice takes my breath away as he commentates through the video. It's gritty and raw, absolutely no frills. He goes right into it without so much as a hello.

He pauses at certain spots to highlight things I'm doing wrong and offer advice on how to correct it. Three minutes and twenty-five seconds of painfully honest feedback with absolutely no attempt to try to sugarcoat my weaknesses. It's a little hard to take, but I hang on his every word anyway.

The video ends as abruptly as it started, and I hit replay. Each time I watch it, which is basically every time I rest, I'm filled with the same overwhelming desire to do more, try harder, dig deeper.

As I'm finishing, Abby texts back to thank me and tell me she had a good warm-up and she's about to tee off. She also assures me that Coach is still a dick—as if there were any doubt. Sometimes, it's good to know I'm not the only one who feels that way though. Apparently, he spent most of day one with Cassidy and ignored the rest of the team.

I head to the outdoor track for a mile run. Today is supposed to be light conditioning, and I guess it is since I'm running one mile instead of two like yesterday, but it sure doesn't feel easy.

Two hours, a shower, and a quick nap later, I head to the driving range, only to have it start to rain. Big, cold drops soak my clothes and hair. I shoot a glare at the dark clouds that are ruining my training session.

Seriously? It couldn't have rained while I was running earlier?

I try to keep going even as my teeth chatter, but I can't video my swing in this condition, so I head to my dad's.

"Hey, sweet pea. You look like you ran over. Coming down pretty good out there." He glances out the window from the recliner.

"I got caught in it at the driving range." I take off my shoes and then go to my old bedroom to swap out my shirt for a dry one.

Back in the living room, I take a seat on the couch and wrap the throw blanket hanging over the arm snug around me. "Did you eat lunch?"

He nods to the counter. "Yeah, I ordered pizza a couple hours ago."

"Any left?" I stand and walk toward the kitchen.

"*Mm-hmm.* A slice or two."

It's cold, but I devour a slice of sausage pizza while I open the fridge and rummage around until I find a Diet Mountain Dew. I hide them in the vegetable drawer and behind condiments he rarely uses.

"Dad, do you still have my old golf mat and net?"

"They are in the garage, I think."

I take my soda with me and sigh as I see the disorganization of the garage. It's clear where I got my messy tendencies.

I manage to find them, and I'm standing on a ladder, hanging the net from the hooks in the ceiling, when Lincoln calls. I hesitate to accept the video call and seriously think about sending him to voice mail, but somewhere deep down (like really deep down), somewhere that can forget what a sadist ass he is and how sore I am, I know I need him.

"Hello?" I answer, putting it on speaker and setting the phone on the top of the ladder so I can continue to hang the net.

"Keira?"

I move my head in front of the phone so he can see me. "I'm here. One second."

"What in the world are you doing? And why do you look like a wet rat?"

I ignore the last comment because I totally do, and he looks perfect as usual. "I'm trying to hang my old golf net in my dad's garage. It's raining out."

"It is?" It sounds like he moves around before he speaks again. "Huh. It's raining here too."

"Where are you?" I ask, glancing at the screen and staring past him at the background. Blank, white walls that tell me absolutely nothing.

"At home. Let's see this net."

I get the last loop over the hook and step down the ladder. I switch the camera so it's front facing and show him the setup.

"How old is that mat?"

"I don't know. Maybe five years. I got it and the net for my sixteenth birthday."

"Well, you won't need either today."

"What do you mean? The training plan says two hundred reps."

"That's why I'm calling. Scratch that. I want you to go back to practicing without a club. And double the reps. That turn and weight shift need to be perfect. Your power is your best asset, but in order to swing as hard as you can, everything else has to be dialed in."

"But—" I start to object and think better of it. "All right, whatever you say."

For the next hour, I continue to bite my tongue and follow his instructions. Lincoln insists I need to slow down and rebuild my swing—something few people would dare try to do in the middle of a season.

But it's listen to Lincoln or keep hoping Coach Potter suddenly notices how much I deserve to be out there. And the latter seems as likely as Lincoln telling me to take tomorrow off and enjoy a nice bubble bath.

"Pause at the top of the turn and concentrate on using your legs—your arms are just levers."

It takes a few minutes of him nit picking every single part of my body.

"Your knees are bent too much."

"No, now not enough bend."

"You're tilting too much."

"Your pushing with your right."

"Your shoulders are too stiff."

But I listen, and soon, his commentary falls silent and I settle into a rhythm, focusing on the feeling of my body and trying to commit it to memory.

"I think I have it," I tell him once the correct way starts to feel natural. I stop and face the camera, waiting for the next step or maybe a compliment.

"Keep going. I'll let you know when to stop." He steps out of view, and I stick my tongue out at him.

The door from the house into the garage opens, and my dad smiles as he sees me standing on my golf mat.

"I'm gonna heat up a frozen dinner. Are you staying to eat, sweet pea?"

Oh God. I don't dare look at my phone to see if Lincoln is watching. "Oh, uh. I'll make dinner for us. Don't eat that garbage. Just give me a bit to finish up first."

He waves me off. "I'll cook two Hungry Man dinners so I can prove that they aren't garbage. Frozen packages of delight, those things are." He shakes a finger at me as he goes back in and then lets the door fall closed.

I glance at the phone and find Lincoln almost smirking.

"Don't say a word," I warn him.

"Wouldn't dream of it, *sweet pea*." He smiles, and I consider picking up a club and throwing it at his head, but don't want to destroy my phone. "Go, have a delicious dinner with your father and then get another three-hundred reps in. Message me later and let me know how it goes."

"Three hundred?" My eyes widen and my brows rise, but Lincoln's face remains completely serious.

"Take advantage of the setup at your dads while you're there. It's better than your space in the dorm. We really need to figure out how to make it where you can hit balls there when the time comes."

"Yeah, my neighbors would love that," I mutter quietly, but the man misses nothing.

"Enjoy your Hungry Man." He full-on smiles, and it looks good on him. I forget how annoying he is when he smiles like that.

"What are you having for dinner? Do you cook? Pizza delivery? Or are you more of a takeout kind of guy?"

"Actually, I'm having dinner with someone." He lifts his arm and checks the time on his expensive-looking watch. "I should get going. Have a nice night, Keira."

Irrational jealousy heats my face. He's going on a date and I'm having a microwavable dinner with my dad. Figures.

Focusing all my frustration, I set the camera up to record and do all three hundred reps. And then fifty more.

ELEVEN

Lincoln

I walk through Gram's door a half hour early. It's a first, and I catch her checking the time on the microwave before she speaks. "Lincoln, what are you doing here so early?"

"Can't a man show up early to help his grandmother with dinner?"

"He *could*, but I can't remember the last time he did."

"Well, I'm here now." I put the wine on the counter and push up my sleeves. "What can I do?"

She laughs. "Pour me a glass and grab the rose plates from the top shelf in the china cabinet."

I grab two wine goblets, fill them, and take a drink of mine before her request sinks in. "The rose plates? We only use those on special occasions."

They were a wedding gift from her mother, and I can count the number of times she's used them on one hand. Most notably her and Pop's fiftieth wedding anniversary and five Christmases ago when we first found out he had cancer.

"I made a vow this year that I would use the things that bring me joy more often. I'm not going to be around forever, you know?"

"Really, Gram? Playing the death card?" I cross my arms over my chest and wait for the real reason we're busting out her precious china.

"Also, I invited my friend Margie and her granddaughter over for dinner."

I groan.

She rolls her eyes, the second woman to do that to me today. "You act as if having dinner with a pretty young woman is the worst way you could spend a Saturday night."

She turns her back to me, stirring something on the stove, and I move to the china cabinet and pull down the rose plates.

"I'm in no position to date right now."

"You keep saying that, and I keep ignoring it."

I chuckle, well aware she's ignoring me. I can't figure out how to make her understand that I don't have anything to offer at the moment.

"Listen, honey, I know Lacey made you feel like it was all your fault that things didn't work out, but that's rubbish. She was just as much at fault."

"Eh . . ."

"She was. Marriage is hard work, but dating doesn't have to be. Have dinner with Sweetie and just try to enjoy yourself, that's all I'm asking."

"*Sweetie*? Her name is Sweetie?"

There's a knock at the door and Gram scans the place quickly. "Everyone's early tonight. Get the door, will you?" She turns back to the stove, and I shake my head.

"This is the last time," I tell her quietly over my shoulder. "No more setups. I mean it. I'll stop coming over."

She hums a response that I'm pretty sure is her total disregard for such a threat. And she's probably right. I'll keep coming back, hoping one of these times the girl at the door will make me believe Gram's optimistic outlook.

Sweetie turns out to be the perfect name for the woman sitting across from me. She's blonde with blue eyes and a soft, syrupy-sweet voice. Everything about her says feminine, right down to the light pink dress she's wearing and the pearls around her neck.

It's impossible to dislike her or not enjoy myself, but there's absolutely zero chance she and I would work out. I'm a grumpy asshole, and this woman looks as if she'd burst into tears if I so much as looked at her the wrong way.

If I do ever start dating again, it'll be with someone who can take my shit and call me on it. Like Keira does. Or did. Since we started working together, she's less vocal. The girl was holding back so many words today I thought she was gonna bite her tongue off.

My phone vibrates in my pocket, but I know Gram will be pissed if I take a call at the table. A few minutes later, though, Sweetie's phone rings.

"Oh, good gracious. I am so sorry. I forgot to turn this thing off," she says as she rummages through her purse and pulls out her phone. She bites her lip as she looks at the screen and then gives Gram and Marge big, puppy dog eyes. "I'm so sorry. I have to take this." Then she looks at me. "I'll be right back."

I wait until she disappears into the living room before I look at my phone.

Keira: 350 reps done. You're a sadist asshole. I can't feel my arms.

And another that came in a few minutes later.

Keira: I don't see anything on tomorrow's plan. Same as today?

I love that, even when she's calling me an asshole for putting her through the wringer, she's asking for more. And I don't have to ask if the extra fifty reps she did was a silent fuck you—I know it was.

"Lincoln," Gram admonishes.

I glance up from my phone as I tap out a text to Keira. Gram's expression changes from annoyed to something I can't place, curious maybe.

"Sorry, Gram." I fire off the message and pocket my phone.

After Marge and Sweetie leave, I help Gram clean up.

"Dinner was fantastic. As usual."

She smiles and hands me another plate to dry.

"And I saw Marge eyeing these dishes with envy."

She laughs softly, but the quiet surrounds us again. There is a look of melancholy on her face that makes me wonder, but not ask, if she's thinking of Pop.

After the dishes are done, Gram flips off the kitchen light and walks me to the front door.

"Same time next week?"

"*Mm-hmm.* And maybe bring whoever you were texting earlier. It'll save me a phone call or two to find your next date."

I try to picture Keira at dinner with Gram but shut down that train of thought fast. Do I think it would have been more fun, if not hazardous to my being, than sitting across from Sweetie all night? Yes. Is it highly inappropriate that I think that? Also yes.

"That was a client, Gram. I told you I'm not dating right now. Well, unless you count the blind dates you keep setting me up on, then I guess technically I am dating, but it's very solidly against my wishes."

She doesn't bother apologizing. I'm sure tonight's missed love connection has just made her that much more determined. "A female client?"

I hesitate to answer a second too long, and Gram smiles all too knowingly. I think back to texting Keira, but I don't see how anything I did or said could have made Gram think it was a woman. Maybe I'm not as good as I thought at hiding how much I'm enjoying working with Keira.

"Yeah, so? I have lots of female clients." Keira is my only *personal* female client, but the website has many, so Gram doesn't know any better.

"I saw that look in your eyes. You were smiling, for heaven's sake."

"I smile." Though as I say it, I realize I'm frowning.

Gram laughs and touches my cheek with her palm. "I love you. Don't work too hard. Have fun. Enjoy this time in your life. It goes fast."

I'm still thinking about Gram's words when I get home. I grab a beer, turn on ESPN, and open my laptop. Gram doesn't understand this is fun. I love my job. The pride and satisfaction I feel when a client succeeds is better than any high.

And, yeah, I miss having a woman to come home to sometimes, but any time that longing gets too heavy, I think about the look of disappointment Lacey wore like the latest fashion for the last year of our marriage.

Yeah, no thanks. I'd rather be single for the rest of my life than go through that again. Perpetually disappointing the person you care about the most chips away at you. Touching people's lives by making them better at something they love, inspiring them to be the best they can, isn't a bad way to spend my days.

It's late Saturday night, so I don't call or text Keira about tomorrow's training plan. I send instructions via the site, which will notify her by email.

I press send and reach for my beer, but as I'm setting it down, she messages me on the site's chat feature.

Keira: Are you feeling okay? Have you been body snatched? Did someone hack your account?

I chuckle as I respond.

Me: Sunday's are a recovery day. Stretch out, get a few turns in, and spend the rest of the day preparing for the week.

Me: And eat something besides a Hungry Man frozen dinner.

Keira: No worries on that. If I never eat another, it'll be too soon. How was your date?

It takes me a second to realize she misinterpreted my words earlier today when I told her I had dinner plans. I know I didn't say date, but seeing as how it ended up sort of being a date, I don't bother correcting her.

Me: It was fine.

Keira: Fine? *snort* Wow, lucky lady.

Me: If you go out tonight, take it easy on the alcohol and make sure you still get enough sleep. Don't derail all your progress.

Keira: Wow, you're a real conversation buzz kill. Do you ever stop thinking about training?

Me: It's my job to think about it. Every decision, no matter how minor you may think it is, plays a part in your success or failure.

Shit, I do sound like a buzz kill. It's true, though.

Keira: I have no plans to go out tonight, and I'm already lying in bed. Happy?

Well, no. Now I'm picturing her lying in bed. So, I'm not happy at all.

My thoughts run away from me for long enough that I picture her bare legs and that gorgeous sun-kissed hair splayed out begging for me to run my fingers through it. Perving on a client—super douche move.

Me: Good. Enjoy your day off.

I log out of the chat before she can respond and spend the next two hours working on her training plan for next week and trying hard not to be the creeper she accused me of being the first time we met.

TWELVE

Lincoln

Over the next week, I push her harder than I have pushed any other athlete I've ever coached. Ever. I need to know she's serious. That she'll work as hard as I will.

Adding another client might seem like a small thing, but I spend a minimum of fourteen hours a week on a client. That's an average client. I'm spending double that with Keira because of how much I believe in her. And if I'm spreading myself this thin and putting my *hope* in her, then I have to know that we're in this together.

On Tuesday night, I fly out to L.A. to see my brother and interview a woman to manage my tennis coaches. Kenton plays soccer for the L.A. Stars. Despite—or maybe because of—our family history with golf, he was never interested in it.

He's waiting at the bar near my gate. Turned in his seat so he can watch the passengers walking by, his hat is pulled low so he's hard to recognize. Not that it fools me; I'd recognize his tall, lanky ass anywhere. The slight tilt of his shoulders and the way he sits on the stool with one foot resting on the top rung and the other on the floor is all so familiar.

He stands as I weave through people to get to him.

"Linc." He embraces me and gives me a couple of good slaps before stepping back. "Been too long, brother."

Smiling, I nod and look him over. He's taller than I am by an inch, but his build is smaller—leaner from all the conditioning he does. I'm damn proud of him even if it means the time between seeing him seems to get longer each visit.

"You look good. Nice game last night."

We each take a seat, and he slides a beer toward me. "Thanks. You catch it or watch the highlights?"

I take a sip before I reply, "Come on, you really think I'd miss my little bro in action?"

He raises a brow.

"Fine, I caught the last twenty minutes or so."

"Did you see that header in the last minute?"

"I did." I hit the bill of his cap. "Should have picked a sport where you don't have to use your head so barbarically. Or at least one with a helmet."

He just grins.

We chat mostly about the team and what he's been up to in L.A. as we grab dinner and drink more beer. Then I fill him in on Gram and her latest setup attempts.

We're both dog tired so we make it an early night and head back to his house.

I chuckle as he leads me into his new place. It's the first time I've seen it since he moved in six months ago and it's as extravagant as I expected. "This place is ridiculous, Kent."

"I know, right? Check out the view."

I follow him through the entryway and into the living area with floor-to-ceiling windows that showcase the lights of the city at night.

I drop my bag to the floor and fall into the chair where I can appreciate the skyscape.

"I'm gonna shower. I got you all set up in the spare room." He motions with his head to the right and walks off toward the left. "Glad to have you here, bro."

I lean back in the chair and blow out a breath. Looking around the place, I smile. It's over the top sleek and modern, but in a way that is totally fitting for my baby brother. I'm proud as hell that he's been so successful.

My small apartment back in Scottsdale is a dump by comparison. I rented it after my divorce, not particularly caring about where I lived as long as it met two conditions: it was not with my ex and it was on a golf course.

With my business, I can live anywhere or everywhere. I travel a lot, but Scottsdale is home, and the weather is great year-round for golf.

Tired as fuck, I pull out my laptop and check email. I'm cc'ed on more than fifty emails, but there are only a few that require me to respond. I tackle those and then log into the website to check in with my clients.

Simon and Roy handle the majority of our golf clients, and I have a couple of team members who answer questions and do an occasional review if needed. It's a big market and we're growing faster than any other department.

Initially, I kept a few clients simply because we didn't have enough people to support the demand, but now, I keep a hand in it to remind me what fuels my desire and love for the company.

I have an up-and-coming pro golfer who'll be a household name soon, a twelve-year-old kid whose parents' ambitions are set on him being the next Tiger Woods, and a retiree who just wants to be able to show up his buddies on their weekly golf outings. And now, Keira.

I check in with my other clients first, leaving Keira for last. She sent her swing video, a detailed write-up of what they did in practice today, and notes on the morning training session I gave her.

I read over it, watch the video a handful of times. I'm watching her swing one last time in slow motion when Kenton appears. Hair wet, basketball shorts and a faded Nike T-shirt, he looks a lot more like my little brother like this.

"I thought I heard you still out here." He grabs two beers from the fridge, takes a seat on the couch across from me, and offers me one.

"Thanks," I say absently, staring at the screen.

"How are things going with Reeves Sports?" He crosses one leg over a knee and holds the neck of a Bud Light with his fingers.

"You should know." Kenton is a silent partner, so he's copied on all the executive reports, which he clearly doesn't read.

"You don't really want me sitting in on those long conference calls, do you?"

I huff a laugh, and he shakes his head.

"I didn't think so." He sits forward and cranes his neck to look at the screen. "Got any fun clients I can see?"

Turning the screen, I press play, and we watch Keira's swing. She took the footage at the driving range, so the scenery of Arizona and the sun setting over the mountains is the backdrop.

Even after seeing it so many times, I get a little rush and goose bumps dot my arms.

I glance over at Kenton. He doesn't look all that impressed, but I'm not surprised. It isn't Keira's ability alone that excites me; it's her potential. I wouldn't expect most people to see it. In fact, my career is as successful as it is because most don't.

"Not bad. Pro or amateur league?"

"Neither."

His gaze meets mine, and he lifts a brow in question.

"I did that clinic at Valley University for Mark James. He's the coach there now. Anyway, I met Keira there." I motion to the screen. "She's on the girls' team."

I press play again. "She's a little unfocused and impulsive, but she has a lot of promise."

"She's hot." Kenton continues to stare at the screen as he quickly drains the rest of his beer and places the empty on the coffee table.

I turn my laptop so he's no longer able to see her. "Anyway, I should get back to it."

"I can see it's a real hardship." He snorts. "Enjoy the view. I have to get to bed. I have an early workout in the morning. Lunch tomorrow?"

"Yeah, sounds good."

When he's gone, I play her video again feeling more protective than is rational. Keira's young and beautiful, any dude with a pulse could attest to that, but Kenton voicing something I can't bothers me more than I'd like to admit. I can't exactly be jealous of every guy that looks at her and sees the obvious, though that feels exactly like what just happened.

I carry my stuff into the spare room, change into fresh T-shirt and sweatpants, and grab another beer before I call her. Pacing the room, I stare out into the L.A. night while I wait for her to answer.

"Hello?" Her voice is groggy like I woke her up.

I check the time. "Sorry if I woke you. I assumed you'd still be up."

"It's fine. I must have fallen asleep reading my chemistry notes."

I snort. "Can't blame you there. We can talk tomorrow."

"It's okay. I'm awake now."

I should insist she go back to sleep, but our training has become something I look forward to every night. "All right. Grab your seven iron. I want to talk you through what I'm seeing."

"Hold on."

The website allows for video chat, though I've never used it with clients before her. Typically, the feedback I send is in email format. If I need to get more detailed, I record a video of my screen as I watch their swing in slow motion and talk through any issues I see.

We've used all those features, too, but with Keira, the live sessions together have proven to be invaluable.

"All right, I'm set."

I hang up the phone and start the video call on the website. She answers almost immediately, and her face appears. With no greeting, she steps away, checking back once to make sure she's in full view of the camera.

Her dark hair is pulled back in a messy ponytail and falls over one bare shoulder. She's wearing some sort of tank top with straps so small I can barely see the pink material against her skin. The tiny shorts she's wearing aren't any better.

I'm frustrated by my inability to ignore how gorgeous she is. Fucking Kenton. It isn't really his fault, he didn't tell me anything new, but now it's fresh on my mind.

"Lincoln?"

"Yeah, sorry." I slide my gaze away from her legs and hope she didn't catch me gawking like a perv. "Let me see what you worked on today."

She's set up in her dorm room, standing in the space between two beds. She has just enough space to swing. It isn't really ideal, but I can't very well ask her to head to the gym at this hour. Though, the thought did occur to me.

"So, what do you think?" she asks after she's done three swings.

"It's hard to tell. Your swing changes with a ball in front of you. Right now, it looks good, though. I can tell you've been working the drills. How's the weight training?"

She groans. "Awful. My legs are so sore I could barely walk up the stairs today. And who knew going *down* stairs would be worse?"

My eyes sweep over her legs again and up. "You're going to need to be stronger. It'll help with consistency, and it'll also allow you to trust yourself more when it comes to those big, key moments where you have to let go and just believe you've worked hard enough to pull off whatever the gods of golf throw at you."

"The golf gods." She smiles, tosses the ball in the air with her club, and begins to bounce it. She does it often between drills as we're chatting. The move seems to calm her. She barely looks at it, feeling the ball with the club-face and trusting the movement. It's sexy as hell.

"How'd you learn to do that?"

She stops as if she just realized what she was doing, and the ball drops to the floor. "Saw Tiger do it when I was a kid, and I practiced. A lot."

"Tiger, huh? He was your favorite?"

"Of the men." She abandons the club and sits on the bed, bringing the laptop closer to her face. She has a hint of sun on her cheeks, but the rest of her skin is smooth and flawless.

Keira on a bed, in a bed, or near a bed are all combinations that stir things I haven't felt in a long time.

"Who's your favorite?"

I consider just going with a canned answer. I looked up to Tiger a lot, but it was never him I was trying to emulate. "My grandfather."

"Did he play professionally?"

I shake my head. "No, but he played in college and taught me everything I know about the game. Coached a lot of other people too. He was a golf pro in Scottsdale."

"Is he willing to come out of retirement to take on a new client? I bet he would be nicer. Old people love me. I'm spunky." She yawns.

A chuckle escapes. "Sorry, you're stuck with me. He passed two years ago."

"Oh, I'm sorry." Her mouth falls into a frown, and her eyes lift from mine. "Where are you? Is that a different room in your place?"

I look behind me to the picture hanging on the wall over the bed. It's a black-and-white nude of Kenton's naked back and the top of his ass, holding a soccer ball at his hip. It's an artistic shot and probably (hopefully) not meant to be sexy, but it's still my damn brother's ass above the bed I'm supposed to sleep in.

I turn back to face her. "I'm in Los Angeles staying with my brother for a couple of days. He plays soccer for the Stars, and apparently, he likes to welcome his guests with uncomfortable artwork."

"Any other siblings?"

"No. You?"

"No, I'm an only child." She yawns again, and I check the time.

"You should get some sleep. Your body needs recovery time. Drink lots of water too."

She rolls her eyes, but her voice is soft. "Yes, Coach."

"'Night, Keira."

THIRTEEN

Keira

"You came!" Erica jumps up from her spot next to Chapman on the couch and rushes to hug me.

I laugh and try to speak, but she has a vise grip around my neck and shakes us from side to side. When she releases me, she links our hands and jumps with excitement. "You have been hiding away for weeks."

Cassidy joins us in the entryway and hands me a drink before nodding her agreement. "Seriously. The only time I see you anymore is at practice."

"I can't drink this," I say after smelling the contents of the cup.

"Just one!" Erica says. She and Cassidy share matching pouty expressions.

"Nice try. I'm not drinking tonight." I hand the cup back to Cassidy.

"Well, fine, as long as you'll still dance with me. The White House is having a party, and I need to dance it out." Cass closes her eyes and sways her hips from side to side.

"Dance what out?"

"She's waiting for Peter to call her," Erica supplies.

I glance between them for the story. "Peter?"

"Peter Kurtis, he's a hockey player Cass is crushing on ha-ard," Erica sing-songs the last word.

"I am not," she says but then smiles. "He asked for my number a week ago but hasn't called or texted."

Erica nudges me. "I have a class with Peter's roommate, Tiny, and he said they're going to The White House tonight."

"Will you come and be my dance partner?" Cass begs.

"Of course, I will." I fight a yawn. "Do you have any Red Bull?"

ⵙ

At The White House, Cassidy pulls me outside to where a DJ is setup and a few people are dancing on one side of the yard. Erica is sitting near the pool with Chapman.

The beat of the music relaxes my aching muscles and the caffeine temporarily makes me forget how tired I am. The last couple of weeks have been exhausting in the best way. Classes, practice, and hours of training with Lincoln.

Cass leans forward, her blonde hair falling around her face and shielding her from everyone but me. "He's here."

Casually, I glance around. "Where?"

"He just walked out onto the patio with another guy. White hat, gray sweater."

I find him easily enough. He's scanning the crowd in the way people do when they first get to a party to see who else is there. He finds Cass and turns to his buddy to say something. And as luck would have it, I know that buddy.

"Come on, I know his friend." I drag Cass with me.

Her hand grips mine hard, and I laugh a little at how nervous she seems. She's gorgeous, sweet, and super talented. I can't imagine any guy not being into her.

Heath notices me as I approach, and his mouth draws into a wide smile.

"Hey, Keira." He takes a sip from the beer.

"Hey, yourself." I yank Cass closer to me. "Heath, this is my friend Cassidy."

"Hi." She gives a small wave and steals a glance at Peter. "Hey, Peter."

"You two know each other?" I play dumb.

"Yeah, of course. Hey, Cassidy." I swear this big, hunky hockey player is blushing. "Can I get you a drink?"

She stares at him, frozen and mute until I elbow her, then she sputters out, "Yeah. Great."

Heath and I watch them disappear into the house.

"She likes him." I shrug.

"Yeah, him too. He's been talking about her all week, trying to figure out when to call her and what to say. I've never seen someone obsess so much over calling a girl." He looks at my empty hands and then asks, "You need a drink?"

"Nah, I'm not drinking tonight."

He raises a brow in question.

"I have to get up early tomorrow to work out."

"Me too." He looks around the party. "I'd wager half the people here have practice or workouts in the morning."

Cassidy and Peter rejoin us at the same time Erica and Chapman do. Once everyone is introduced, Erica tries to hand me another drink.

"No thanks," I say. "Still not drinking."

"Boooo." She gives me a thumbs-down and then holds her hand out. "Give me your phone."

"Why?"

"I'm going to call mister hottie swing coach and tell him that you need a night of drunken fun."

I keep a strong grip on my phone because there is no chance I'm letting her call Lincoln.

"You're still working with Linc?" Heath smiles.

"Yeah, he's helping me with my swing."

"That's cool." He takes out his phone as he continues to talk. "Do you like working with him? He isn't too tough? I met this kid he worked with last year, he said Lincoln had him running a mile every day and weight training three to four times a week, getting something like a thousand swings in. All that on top of his regular team practices."

Heath's eyes are wide with disbelief. "All that for golf? I mean, no offense, I know you gotta be in shape, but that seems like a lot of work just to walk along the golf course and hit the ball. Is that what he has you doing?"

I grind my teeth as I answer. "Yeah, something like that."

"Here, smile." He holds his phone out in front of us and takes a picture before I can do anything but stare dumbly ahead. He chuckles as he taps on his phone and then pockets it.

"What was that?"

"I was texting Lincoln."

"You told him I was here?" I look around like he can somehow see me from Scottsdale . . . or wherever he is today. I can't keep track of him and believe you me, I've tried.

"Well, no. I just told him I bumped into you at a party and that he should go easier on you."

"Great." I wince as my phone vibrates in my front pocket. One guess who that is.

I pull it free and show the screen to Heath. "You did this!"

He plucks it out of my hand and answers. "What's up, old man?"

I shoot a death glare at him, but he just gives me a wide, cheeky grin in return.

"Yeah, she's right here." He winks at me. "Nah, of course, I'm not drinking." He takes a big swallow of his beer. "All right. Sounds good. Talk to you tomorrow." He shoves the phone at me. "He wants to talk to you."

Yeah, no kidding. I knew I should have stayed in. Three weeks of non-stop training. I've pushed my body harder than I thought possible. I've made more progress than I have in two years with Coach Potter too.

Working with Lincoln is amazing. I don't want to screw it up, I just need a night out with my friends to unwind. Another tournament is coming up this weekend and Coach announced the starters today. I didn't make the top five, again, and it stung.

I'm trying not to think about it, but it's hard not to. And it isn't as if I'm planning to slack off on my training tomorrow. I already have three alarms set so I'll be sure to wake up with plenty of time to get in the run and weights before my first class. I might be tired, but I'll push through.

I plan to tell Lincoln all of this as I take the phone with a shaky hand and put it to my ear. "Hi."

"Are you all right?" he asks, the harshness I expected in his tone absent and instead he sounds genuinely concerned for my wellbeing.

I give Heath one last glare for good measure and walk away from the group to find a quieter place to talk. "Yeah, I'm fine. I just needed to get out of the dorm for a bit. I'm heading home soon."

"I saw the roster for the tournament this weekend. I'm sorry."

I sink into one of the patio chairs, embarrassed that he knows and that I hadn't been the one to tell him.

"Am I . . ." I start, and my voice breaks. I feel like I'm hanging on by a thread. "Am I ever going to be ready?"

"You've made huge strides already. We just keep working at it."

I nod.

"Keira?" His deep voice somehow sounds tender as he says my name.

"Yeah, I'm here. I heard you."

I lean my head back and stare into the night sky. The helplessness and defeat that I've been fighting all day finally hits me. I may never get my chance. I'm not even sure I deserve it anymore. Maybe Coach Potter is right.

"You have more raw talent than any person I've ever coached. Ever. I can't predict the future. I don't know if I can make your dreams come true, but I promise that I will do everything I can to make sure you get your shot. You may hate me for how hard I push you, but it's because I want to know we've done everything we can. We're a team. If you fail, I fail."

A lump the size of a golf ball lodges in my throat. I don't have to ask if he means it, I heard the sincerity of his tone and Lincoln has never, not once, tried to pad my ego. It's one of the many reasons I like working with him. But he fails if I fail? That seems like a lot of pressure for him to put on himself and on me.

Suddenly, my grumblings about his methods and how tired I am feel bratty. Although . . .

"I heard a rumor tonight that your usual training only includes a *one*-mile run and *three* days of weights per week."

He curses quietly away from the phone. "Heath has a big mouth."

I don't argue that.

"None of my clients ever have the same regimen. It isn't some generic thing I pass from player to player. You get what I think you need."

"And I need to do twice as much as the others?" I can't hide the note of hurt in my voice. Am I really that awful?

"The better the player, the harder they need to work."

I scoff. Really, that's the best he's got?

"I'll never ask you to do anything that isn't necessary to get you where you want to be. You're capable of so much more than you think. Get out of your own way. Can you do that? Can you just trust that I only want what's best for you?"

I'm nodding again like he can see me. "Yes, I trust you. Tell me what to do."

He lets out a sigh of relief. "Tonight, have fun with your friends. We'll get back to it tomorrow."

The next day at practice we split up into groups to play nine holes. I'm grouped with Abby and Brittany.

"You're quiet today. Everything okay?" Abby whispers as we stand back and wait for Brittany to tee off on the third hole.

"Yeah, I'm all right." I meet her gaze and find her staring back unbelieving. We may not spend as much time together as we once did, but she still knows me better than anyone. "I'm disappointed about the tournament and starting to wonder if I'll ever get back to the top five."

"You will."

"I don't know." Brittany swings, and the ball sails high and drifts slightly from left to right, leaving her in good position on the green. "She's good."

"So are you."

We make our way down the par five. Abby is lining up a five-footer while Brittany and I wait. She rests the club against her leg and grabs her right wrist with her left hand and winces. "Shit."

"Are you all right?"

"My wrist is achy today. I think I'm gonna walk back and see if I can ice it."

"Do you want us to come with you?" I offer.

"No, I'm sure it's fine. Can't be too careful this close to a tournament."

"Right." I try to smile reassuringly, but the reminder that she's playing and I'm not hurts, and I'm not good at faking anything It's one of the many things Coach Potter dislikes about me.

Golf is a country club sport where players are supposed to school their features and always appear completely dignified. But I've always felt too strongly about the sport to pretend to be unfazed by how I'm playing. If I'm happy with a shot, I'm going to show it. And if I'm so mad I want to throw a club . . . well, I throw a club.

"What's up with Brittany?" Abby asks as we head to the next hole without her. A par three with a wicked sand trap on the right side.

"Wrist is bothering her. She decided to call it so she's ready this weekend." I really try to keep my voice from sounding bitter, but I fail. Bad at faking *everything*.

Abby and I play better when it's just the two of us. We're comfortable,

we joke, and we egg each other on. We still play hard, our competitive spirits making everything a game, but it's way more fun. I miss her, spending
time just the two of us. Don't get me wrong, I'm happy for her and Smith,
but selfishly I want more moments like this.

We're laughing, and I'm lighter than I've been in weeks when we finish
the ninth hole and walk back to the clubhouse.

A group of our teammates are standing outside the door, and when
they spot us, they go quiet.

Erica smiles at me as we approach. "Looks like you're up."

Abby and I share a confused look.

"Brittany has tendinitis in her wrist. She's out, which means . . ."

My heart races. "I'm in."

FOURTEEN

Keira

"When do you leave?" His brows draw together in hard concentration, and his face shows none of the excitement I expected after telling him the good news.

"Thursday afternoon. The practice round is Friday and the tournament takes place Saturday and Sunday."

He stands and brings me with him to another room via the laptop in his hand. He sets me down and sits in a big office chair. There's a picture behind him—the first evidence of personalization I've seen in his house.

I stare at it, trying to make out more of the photograph while he does whatever it is he's doing and not paying attention to me. It's a picture of two people standing on a golf course. One is definitely Lincoln. There's no mistaking that dark hair and build. The man next to him looks like he could be his father or grandfather. I'm guessing the latter since he told me that's who taught him to play.

"I can move some things around, but I wouldn't be able to get to Valley until late Wednesday night." He frowns. "I'd really like to see you before the tournament. I suppose video will have to do. Can you clear Wednesday night to get a long session in?"

"Sure. I'm free after class on Wednesday. I'm done around ten."

He nods his approval but still looks disappointed and not directly at me. "I could come to you."

His focus finally snaps to me. "To Scottsdale?"

"That's where you live, right?" I shrug. "If it's easier, then sure."

He considers it for a few quiet seconds, but slowly, I see the agreement in the relaxing of his shoulders. "I'll send you the address. I have another client at three, but if you can get here early then we can get time in before and after."

A whole day of golf and Lincoln? "I'll be there," I say too eagerly.

I spent the morning in the hot seat while he watched my swing and offered critiques. It felt good, as if we were finally making real progress.

While I sit in the golf cart and eat a sandwich from the country club restaurant, Lincoln chats with Tommy, a local high school kid. He's different with Tommy than he is with me. More hands-on, nicer even.

Lincoln is hard to get to know. He's all business all the time. We've only had a few small moments where we've shared that personal connection, but I want more of it. And I want more of this shiny, fun Lincoln in front of me. I mean, the guy just laughed. Full-on, head back, laughed.

He left his phone in the cart with me. Light music he turned on earlier still plays and I'm starting to get an idea of his taste in music—mostly rock, like dudes with big hair screaming about drugs and rock and roll. It makes me giggle.

I'm enjoying being in his world and learning these small things about him. When he finally walks over to me, his demeanor changes with each step as if he's retreating back into himself and only allowing me to see the serious and professional side of him.

"I'm just gonna grab some water, and then I'll be ready."

"There's no rush if you want to get lunch." He made sure I ate but I haven't seen him eat anything all day.

"I'll grab something later."

He returns from the clubhouse with two waters and gets into the driver's seat of the golf cart. When we pull up to the tee box at the first hole, there's a hint of a smile on his face. "Let's see what you got."

"I get to play?" I'm giddy as I step out and grab my driver before he can change his mind.

This course, what I can see of it anyway, is breathtaking. Nicer than any other I've played.

Lincoln gets out of the cart but stays off to the side as I set up. For some reason, this is more nerve-wracking than having him pick apart my swing all day, every day. All our work will be graded here on the course.

"Just relax. It's going to take time to translate everything from practice to playing. There are more distractions and your old tendencies are still going to show up. Relax, focus on only one swing at a time."

I close my eyes and take a deep breath. When I open them, he's standing closer. His masculine scent and the smell of grass wrap around me, adding another distraction I should ignore.

"Let me see you at the top of the backswing."

Once in position, he walks a circle around me. "Good. Now pull with your lead leg. Focus here." He places a hand on my left thigh. "Here," he says again. "Got it?"

I'm holding my breath, the skin-to-skin contact doing funny things to me while he seems totally unaware and completely focused on golf. He removes his hand and stands tall. I realize I still haven't answered when he steps into my line of vision.

"I got it."

"All right." He steps back. "Show me what you got."

By the third hole, I finally relax, and by the sixth, I'm smiling at how much more consistent my drives are. I still have work to do, but I'm playing the best round of golf in my life.

We catch up to a couple of guys just ready to tee off at the seventh.

"Lincoln?" An old man in the standard-issued country-club getup of polo with khakis walks toward us. "I thought that was you." He flashes a smile under his Sam Elliott style mustache.

"Hey, Bob. Nice to see you."

"Are you playing today? Hank and I could use a little friendly competition."

"Nah, just working with a client. Bob, Hank, this is Keira."

"Pleasure to meet you, young lady." Bob's brown eyes twinkle as he smiles at me. Based on first impressions, he's impossible not to like.

"You too."

Hank shakes Lincoln's hand and then nods to me. "You two go ahead and play through. If I get back to the clubhouse before five, I'll have to go to dinner with my wife and her *sister*. That woman sends back everything.

The water is too warm. The burger is too rare. The vegetables are touching the rice." He rolls his eyes and puts the cigar in his left hand to his mouth.

I look to Lincoln for my cue on whether I should go ahead. He smiles, a crooked grin that makes my stomach flutter. "Go ahead, Keira."

As I'm grabbing my driver, I overhear Bob ask Lincoln, "How come you aren't playing today?"

"It's been a while. Maybe he can't hack it anymore, Bob," Hank says on an exhale of smoke.

I fight to keep my lips pressed together and laughter inside.

Lincoln shakes his head. "Today is just about Keira. She has a tournament coming up this weekend."

"Sounds likes she could use some competition then." Hank nods toward where I walk to the front tees.

Lincoln smiles but doesn't move. His clubs are in the back of the cart, so I know he doesn't have that as an excuse not to take the guys up on their offer. "I'm just here for some last-minute instruction."

"I think I'd feel better *supported* if a pro came up here and showed me how it was done."

Bob and Hank whistle and chuckle.

"I like her," Hank says.

I stare at Lincoln with a smug, challenging set to my jaw, but I don't really expect him to grab a club from his bag. He carries it under his arm and walks toward me as he puts on his glove.

The tiny victory I feel at goading him into showing me his swing disappears when he leans over to place a tee on the ground and then again to place a ball on top. It's hard not to check out his ass. Some women love football pants, some love baseball pants, but a man in dress pants swinging a golf club—that's my weakness.

With his eye on the fairway, he swings the club lightly just in front of him. "See that tree on the left side just before the sand trap?"

"Yeah."

"Closest ball wins."

"Wins what?"

A cocky smirk twists his lips. "When I win, we're going to finish nine and then head back to the driving range so you can do two-hundred more solid swings."

"What about if I win?"

"If you win, then you're done for the day. You can drive back to Valley in time to hang out with your friends or whatever it is you do when you aren't practicing."

As if there's time for anything else. Also, I don't want to go back. I want to stay here and play until it's too dark to see the ball.

And I want him to keep smiling at me like he is right now.

"All right. You're on, but if I win, you have to buy me dinner first."

A rough huff of a laugh rolls out of him. "I have dinner plans."

"Not if I win you don't."

"Ladies first." He raises both brows in a friendly challenge.

I step back. "Oh no, age before beauty."

Hank and Bob stand off to the side. It sounds like they're placing bets, but I focus only on the man next to me as he steps up to the ball.

His chest rises and falls with a long breath. He shifts his weight around until he's comfortable, and then he stills. I hold my breath as he pulls back and hits the prettiest shot I've ever seen in person.

My mouth is wide open when the ball drops near the tree and he turns to face me.

"That was . . . beautiful." I'm too impressed to be embarrassed by the awe in my voice.

He seems a little taken aback by my compliment, and there's an awkward beat of silence as he grabs his tee and pockets it. "You're up."

More so than any time he's watched me, I feel his gaze like a weighted blanket—though, not at all as comforting as people claim. I do my best to ignore everything but the club in my hands and the tree I'm aiming for, take a deep breath, and swing.

For the first time, I feel it. That elusive sensation that only comes from hitting the ball pure and exactly where I intended.

"Woooooweee," one of the guys—Hank, I think—calls as my ball sails through the air.

Chills run up my right arm, and Lincoln steps up beside me, driver held loosely in his right hand. "Nice shot." He rests the clubface on the top of his shoe. "It's gonna be close."

"She won. Pay up," Hank says to Bob as the two head for their cart.

"You can't see that far." Hank rolls his eyes and hops in next to Bob.

Lincoln and I exchange an amused smile and follow them. Even as the balls come into view, it's impossible to tell whose is closer.

I'm about to ask how we're going to determine the winner when Bob grabs a laser rangefinder from his bag.

"That thing won't work, it's too close. I'm going to walk it out," Hank starts counting his steps from Lincoln's ball to the tree while Bob continues pressing buttons on his rangefinder.

"That was the best drive I've seen from you yet," Lincoln says as we stand back and await the results.

"Thanks. Yours was really good too. I saw it on some videos, but they didn't do it justice. You have a great swing."

"I'm rusty," he says with a small chuckle. "I don't get a chance to play much anymore."

"Five steps on Lincoln's," Hank calls and moves to do the same for mine.

"I can't imagine not playing." I breathe in the smell and lift my head to the sky enjoying the way the late sun beats down on my face.

He's quiet, and when I look over, he's staring at me with a strange expression. Sometime this afternoon he's developed a five o'clock shadow that I find myself wanting to reach out and touch, see if it feels and sounds the way I imagine as I lightly run my nails along his jaw.

"She won! Four and a half steps!" Hank exclaims, breaking the moment. He walks over to me with extra pep in his step and hugs me and bounces us around, shaking laughter out of me. Lincoln watches, looking happy and young, and I think I fall a little in love with him.

⊤

"Where are we going? I'm starving." I sit in the passenger seat of Lincoln's SUV. It's nice; sparkling leather without a trace of dust, floors and compartments clean and tidy. He has one of those center console organizers where everything is put in its perfect place. It's so very Lincoln.

We left my car at the country club and I'm collecting my winnings before I head back to Valley.

He turns into a subdivision where the lawns are green, and the houses get bigger with each one we pass. "Wherever you want, but I need to make a stop first."

He slows in front of a beautiful tan-colored home with a large rose bush out front. It isn't the type of place I expected him to live. "Is this your house?"

"No." He laughs and pulls up behind a silver Mercedes. He puts it in park and sits back in the seat, making no move to turn it off. "Shit."

"What?"

"Gram did it again."

Knowing this is his grandmother's house makes more sense. "Did what again?"

He rakes a hand through his hair and squeezes his eyes shut. Seeing Lincoln irritated at something that isn't me is new and much better for appreciating how hot he looks when he's grumpy.

"Is that her?" I point to the woman coming out the front of the house. She's wearing a floral apron and looks an awful lot like Betty White with a head of big, white hair and bright pink lips.

Lincoln shuts the engine off and opens his door. "I'll be right back."

He embraces the woman, and they exchange words I can't hear. She looks past him to me, and a big smile lifts her lips up even higher and then falls. She focuses back on Lincoln and there's more back and forth.

Obviously, they're talking about me, and even though he told me he would be right back, it's completely rude of me to just sit here and not even say hello. Also, I kind of want to meet her.

I step out and walk a few steps toward them before either of them notices. Lincoln is telling her he'll call later when his grandma stops paying attention to him and looks to me.

"Hello." Her smile puts me at ease, and I close the remaining distance.

"Hi. I'm Keira."

FIFTEEN

Lincoln

"**I**t's lovely to meet you, dear. I'm Milly, Lincoln's grandmother."

"I was just telling Gram that we had dinner plans and can't stay." I place a hand at Keira's back and then remove it, flex it and try to rid the burning sensation working up my arm. I'm about to crawl out of my skin with all the ways this is fucked up.

I brought a client to my grandmother's house, which is unprofessional enough without all the ways my body is reacting to said client—none of which are the least bit professional. And now she's a door away from seeing the blind date Gram has waiting for me. I should have known. The woman never gives up.

Gram seems to really like Keira, or maybe she just likes that I willingly brought a woman over. Gram was never supposed to know. I was just gonna slip inside, tell her something came up with a client, and then Keira and I'd be on our way. I should have called.

"We have dinner together every week. He's a good boy."

"That's sweet." Keira smirks at me, obviously loving every second of my discomfort.

Ha! If Keira knew the thoughts going through my head, she wouldn't be calling me sweet. I scan the length of her. Her little golf skirts are going to be the death of me.

Gram nods. "I made tamales tonight. It's Lincoln's favorite, and I've invited my friend Jenny and her granddaughter."

"That sounds delicious," Keira says and presses a hand against her stomach, the movement lifting her shirt to show off the smooth skin just below her belly button. "I'm starving."

I can see the wheels turning under Gram's big hair.

"We can't. Keira has to get back to Valley." And away from me before I screw up and touch her again.

Keira shrugs. "It's okay. It's been a while since I've had a real home-cooked meal."

"Well, let's get you inside. The more the merrier. There are chips and guacamole you can snack on while I finish dinner." Gram herds Keira inside, and I shove my hands into my pockets so I don't rip the hair out of my scalp. Or touch her.

Keira turns her head as they enter the front door and smiles at me, sweet and playful. Gram continues inside, but Keira waits for me to come unglued from my spot.

"Come on." She rolls her eyes, steps to me, and takes my hand, pulling me along.

Her small fingers wrap around mine and squeeze before she leaves me in the entryway and heads toward Gram in the kitchen. She washes her hands and then snags a handful of chips.

I move to the dining room to say hello to Jenny, who's one of Gram's friends I actually remember; though, I've never met her granddaughter Whitney. I apologize to them both, fumbling over what exactly I'm apologizing for since I had no clue, but I did just bring another chick to a blind date, so saying something seems like the right thing to do.

"I'm sorry about this. Gram must have mixed up the dates." She definitely didn't mix up the dates, and anyone who knows her, knows she's still whip-smart. "Keira is a client, and she has an important tournament coming up this weekend."

"Your grandmother said you're a golf coach. Is that right?" Whitney asks.

I give her and Jenny a brief overview of the company. As I talk, my gaze randomly falls to Keira. She hasn't left Gram's side in the kitchen, and more surprising is that Gram hasn't shooed her out. That might be because she wants to keep Keira and Whitney apart, so her matchmaking wasn't in vain, but they're both smiling an awful lot.

I do my best to entertain Jenny and Whitney while only allowing myself small glances at Keira. Making conversation has always come easy to me. I'm not as charismatic as Kenton, but I like people and I'm generally good at making them feel at ease and welcome. It's part of the reason I travel so much. I'm more persuasive in person.

It's nice out, so Gram and Keira set the table on the back patio, and we all sit to eat.

"Anyone want more wine?" Gram asks, bringing bottles of red and white to the table.

I prefer beer, but since I know there isn't any in the fridge, I take the red and refill Jenny and Whitney's glasses before giving myself a small pour. I'd like to guzzle the entire bottle to make this less awkward, but since I'm driving Keira, I won't.

"Would you like some wine, dear?" Gram asks Keira, she's the only one without a wine glass in front of her. "There are more glasses inside. Lincoln, why don't you grab her a glass."

Keira holds up a hand. "Oh, no thanks. I have to drive back to Valley tonight." She takes a bite of her tamale and groans. "This is so good."

Gram smiles while I watch on amused. Keira has totally bewitched her. If Pop were here, he'd be smitten too . . . just as soon as he saw her hit a golf ball, anyway.

"Lincoln was saying you have a big tournament this weekend." Whitney passes a platter to me but speaks to Keira.

Keira glances at me while nodding. "Yeah, that's right." She squirms in her seat, pushes some food around her plate, and takes a drink of water, clearly uncomfortable with being in the spotlight. Put a golf club in her hand and she'd be giving them a show, but without one, she's less sure of herself.

"Keira plays at Valley University. She had back-to-back top ten placings at the Pac-12 Championships and NCAA Regionals, was named Player of the Month in September, made first team all-Pac-12, almost advanced to semifinals of the NCAA Championship, too." I finish and take a sip of wine. It's still silent when I place it back on the table.

Gram's smile couldn't get any bigger, and Keira looks dumbstruck, as if she didn't expect me to know her stats. Did the girl really think I took her on just because she begged and pleaded?

"Wow." Whitney is the first to speak. She looks between Keira and me a couple of times. "That's really impressive."

"It sure is," Gram says, eyes not leaving my face. I shake my head because I know exactly what she's thinking. Just because I know the girl's history, it doesn't mean I'm interested in dating her.

And even if I were, it's simply not possible. Putting aside the fact I'm her coach, I care too much about seeing Keira succeed to screw it up by getting in her way.

SIXTEEN

Keira

Lincoln went to walk Whitney and her grandmother to their car, but I stay on the patio with Milly, enjoying the light breeze and the last heat of the sun.

"Your house is beautiful. I can't imagine waking up to this every day." Lincoln's grandmother's house has a beautiful view of the golf course.

"George, my husband, had coffee out here every morning, and a lot of evenings too. I don't sit out here nearly as much now that he's gone, but it always makes me think of him."

"Lincoln talks about him a lot—or, as much as he talks about anyone."

"He started following George around as soon as he was able to walk and never stopped."

I pull my legs under me as I try to picture a young Lincoln.

"My parents moved out here from Maryland when I was little. My grandparents were always far away so I never really had that type of relationship with them. I think it's nice that he did. And nice that you two are still so close."

"That must have been hard."

I shrug. "They've passed now, but they would send cards, and we talked on the phone occasionally. I never felt like I missed out. Well, not too much. Seeing you and Lincoln together makes me think it would have been nice to have lived closer."

"I'm sure Lincoln would love to have me across the country right about now. He's one blind date away from never speaking to me again."

I giggle, which is something I'm finding I do a lot around Milly. "Why do you do it if you know he hates it?"

She sighs. "Because I'm afraid that, if I don't push him, he'll spend so much time fixing people's golf swings that he'll forget to fix his own issues and live his life. Eventually, you get old enough to realize work is the thing you do to afford a life, not to create one. And I don't mind admitting that I'd also like a great grandchild before I die."

Milly smiles and places her hand over mine on the table. "Don't misunderstand me, I'm proud of him, and I'm glad he's helping you. I just wish he'd take more time for himself." She taps her fingers over mine and then lifts her hand. "There's something about seeing you with him, though. You keep him on his toes, I can tell."

She stands just as Lincoln reappears. "I'm gonna clean up. Why don't you and Keira go for a walk along the course before it gets dark."

I expect Lincoln to offer an excuse, but when Milly goes inside, he waves a hand toward the gate at the edge of the yard. "What do you say?"

As we walk down the golf cart path, the only sounds are our footsteps and the birds chirping. Palm trees dot the horizon, and the ninth hole stretches out before us. We have this entire amazing course to ourselves and it's breathtaking.

"Your grandmother is . . ." I smile as I try to think of the right adjective.

"Overbearing? Bossy?"

"I was going to say wonderful, but those things too."

"Yeah. She's great minus the setup attempts at every turn. Last week, a woman emailed me and asked about having me out for a clinic at her high school, and when I called her to get more details, she told me she'd gotten my number from Gram, and oh, by the way, she was the librarian."

"A librarian with a passion for sports . . . or maybe just the man playing the sport." I bump my shoulder against his and then remain close. "You're a catch."

He arches a brow. "My gram tell you that?"

"Me and every other woman in the state probably."

"Thank you for being so nice to her. She likes you."

"I like her too."

He steps away to pick up a water cup in the path and toss it into a nearby trash can. "You ready to get back?"

I nod. "Yeah, I should probably get started home."

We turn around and head the way we came, walking up the ninth hole. I step closer again and this time he doesn't try to put distance between us. The sleeve of his shirt and the warmth of his arm tickles me. "Why does your grandmother keep setting you up so she can, in her words, fix your issues?"

He groans. "Can we pretend she didn't tell you anything that would make our whole client-coach relationship inappropriate and awkward?"

"Definitely not. I mean . . . I yelled at you and then threw tequila on you. It's only fair I have dirt on you too."

His lips twitch at the corners.

"So? What happened?"

He makes a strangled sound and I think his pace speeds up as if he's trying to speed walk away from this conversation.

"Come on, tell me. It can't be that bad."

"I was married and things didn't work out."

I motion with a hand for him to keep going, which surprisingly, he does.

"Since the divorce, Gram has been on my case to get back out there. I keep telling her I'm fine, but she keeps pushing and setting me up on blind dates. I know she means well, but the woman refuses to accept that my life doesn't lend itself very well to relationships. I'm on the road a lot, and even when I'm not, I'm working or thinking about work. Anyway, now that you know entirely too much about me, what about you?"

"It's really just me and my dad. My parents are divorced, and my mom lives in Maryland with her new husband. Since my dad is as likely to set me up on dates as he is to cheer for the Cubs, I have far fewer dates than you."

"They aren't breaking down the door, making him clean his guns, or whatever the cliché dad jokes is?"

"Is that what you're going to do someday? Answer the door on your daughter's dates with a shotgun, blaring eighties rock, wearing jorts?"

He shakes his head. "I don't own jorts, and you're avoiding the question."

"I've dated, nothing serious since high school . . . if you can count that as serious."

"How come?"

"I don't know." I shrug. "There isn't a lot of time. Plus, guys aren't as into the whole standing on the sidelines and cheering on their significant other as chicks are."

"You're young, beautiful, and talented. I'm sure that's intimidating for some guys. Trust me, plenty of guys would love to be there to cheer you on."

My stomach flips, and I ask, "You really think so?"

His dark eyes meet mine, and those full lips pull into a wide smile. "I know so."

SEVENTEEN

Keira

The university golf course at Stanford is beautiful. Bright green colors set against the mountain landscape. In some ways, it isn't so different from home, but in all the ways it matters in relation to golf, it's completely different.

The elevation is different, for one, and then there's the turf. One bad bounce on our hard, dry ground in Arizona, and I'd be swinging at dust. The grass here is lush and more forgiving. Every shot from the fairway is like hitting off a tee.

"You looked good," Abby says as we're finishing our practice round. "All those extra hours of practice are showing. How'd it feel?"

"I don't know."

She laughs, but I'm serious. I don't think I felt my body the entire time. But now that I am focusing on it, a sinking feeling settles in my stomach. I'm so screwed.

"Come on, let's go back to the hotel, shower, and then watch QVC before dinner."

"I don't think I'm gonna go to dinner."

"What? Why?"

"I think it'll just make me more nervous." The team dinner the night before a tournament is something that's supposed to be relaxing and uplifting, but it has the opposite effect on me. Maybe it's Coach Potter, maybe it's just me. Either way, I need to get my head right before tomorrow.

One thing is certain, if I screw this up, Coach Potter will make sure I never get another shot.

In our hotel room, I let Abby shower first and collapse onto the bed. I close my eyes and visualize the course. I see myself moving through each hole in best-case and worst-case scenarios.

Once it's my turn for the shower, I stand under the hot spray and let every negative thought or fear come to the surface, and then, one by one, I try to dismiss them. It's easier to let go of some than others.

"Are you sure you don't want to come? It might be good to get out and forget about tomorrow for a couple of hours," Abby asks as she grabs her purse.

I run a brush through my wet hair and pull the towel tighter around my body. "I'm sure."

"Do you want me to bring you back something?"

"Nah, I might order room service or walk downstairs to grab something from the market across the street."

"All right. See ya later."

I'm lounging on my bed in a T-shirt and jeans, watching the local weather channel, when my phone pings with a text.

Lincoln: How did your practice round go?

Me: Okay, I think. I shot one under.

Lincoln: Nice work. Eat a light dinner, drink lots of water, and get a good night's sleep.

Me: Does ordering pizza count as light?

Lincoln: Definitely not. Don't you have some sort of team dinner tonight?

Me: I didn't go.

Lincoln: Why not? You need to eat.

I roll my eyes but find myself smiling as the phone rings and Lincoln's name lights up the screen. "Hello?"

"What's wrong? Why aren't you eating with the team? Did Potter do something?"

The protective note in his tone makes me want to hug him simply for implying he'd be pissed if my coach had stepped out of line. "No, Coach Potter didn't do anything. Well, nothing out of the normal."

"Are you nervous for tomorrow?"

"Yes," I admit. "Terrified. What if I screw up?"

"You won't."

"You can't know that. I could go out there and bogey every hole. Or double bogey."

He laughs. "That's pretty unlikely."

"But I could!" I insist.

"Okay, fine. I'll play this game. Yes, you could go out tomorrow and double bogey every hole."

The sinking feeling grows in my stomach, making it hard to breathe.

"*Or* you could go out there and shoot sixty-two and let everyone know that you mean business. Either way, the plan remains the same."

"Coach Potter will never let me have another shot if I embarrass the team again."

"Fuck Potter," he clips and then his voice softens. "You're the best player on the team, Keira. Go out there tomorrow and act like it. Own that shit."

I'm nodding, that rush of excitement before a game finally thrumming through me. "Okay."

"Yeah?" He sounds surprised.

I nod again, more determined. "Yeah."

"Good luck tomorrow. Call me after and let me know how it goes."

A half hour after we get off the phone, my stomach is growling, and I'm considering moving from my spot on the bed to go find something to eat when there are three sharp knocks on my door. I look through the peephole and see a man carrying a tray of food.

I open it, prepared to tell him he has the wrong room, but then he smiles. "Room service for Miss Brooks."

"I didn't order anything."

He looks back at the paper in his hand. "Keira Brooks. Room three thirteen."

My stomach growls at the smell of something I can't place.

We're at an awkward standoff.

"Where would you like it?"

"On the bed, I guess." I go to my wallet so I can pay him.

"It's been taken care of."

"Like on a room charge?"

"No, it was paid for separately over the phone."

He leaves, and I remove the top off one of the plates. Salad.

I pop a crouton into my mouth, well aware of where the food came from now that I see the boring contents. The second plate has a grilled chicken sandwich with veggies. Still boring, but better.

Me: Thanks for dinner.

He doesn't respond, so I lift the top off the third plate. The smallest piece of chocolate cake I've ever seen makes me laugh. Such a complicated man.

ㅜ

I'm the first from Valley to tee off. While I warm up on the driving range, Coach Potter stands back, arms crossed, and watches. It feels good, and my accuracy has improved, but I try not to get overly confident.

There is a tenfold stress difference between warm-ups and taking that first swing to start the tournament, and that difference is responsible for talented players falling out of competition by the end of day one. Myself included.

I hit my last ball and turn around for any parting wisdom from Coach. "I think I'm ready," I say.

"No one is expecting much, so just go out there, do your best, and try to contribute to the overall team score. No matter what happens, keep your head. You represent us all when you're on that course. Understood?"

Anger vibrates under my skin, and a cool sweat makes me want to push up my sleeves even though it's barely fifty degrees. "Got it."

EIGHTEEN

Lincoln

I f determination were ever personified by a look, Keira would be wearing it. Determined and pissed—at the ball or at life, I'm not sure which. She's just off the fairway in the first cut rough about to take her second shot on this par five. It's her second round of the day, and I can tell she's in better condition than the other girls. While they're tiring, she still looks fresh.

Teddy, the coach from Stanford, spots me and weaves through the small crowd to where I'm standing in the back.

"Lincoln." He extends a hand, and we shake. "What are you doing here?"

"Watching." I nod toward Keira and one of his players, Wren Thompkins. "She's good."

He crosses his arms over his chest, and we stand shoulder to shoulder, watching as Keira takes her swing. It's long, and Keira's face shows her frustration.

Mine must show it too.

"That girl has power." He laughs as Keira shoves her club into her bag and shoulders it. "And spunk. Reminds me a little of you when you were fresh on the tour. Remember that time you almost took a swing at Johnson?"

I smile, but the memory makes me pissed all over again. He'd made a snide comment about Lacey and threw me off my whole game, which was exactly what he wanted. I should have punched him.

We walk behind the crowd as they move with the players. Thompkins looks indecisive as she tries to pick out the right club for her approach shot.

"Good to see you, Lincoln." He moves up to confer with his player, and I hang back because I'm fairly certain Keira hasn't spotted me yet.

I probably should have told her I was coming, but the truth is I didn't know I was until I found myself ordering her room service and then booking a plane ticket. Not being able to be here yesterday when she needed me ate away any concern of it being inappropriate.

We can practice every day, all day, but it's her ability to transfer that to competition that is important. She can do it, I know she can, but if she needs me to keep reminding her, I'll be here for those reassurances later.

Keira finds a rhythm on the back nine and ends the day one under and tied for fifth, though there are a lot of players who still have to finish. I find her in the clubhouse with one of her teammates.

The other girl elbows her when it's clear I'm headed toward them, and Keira's brown eyes fall to me. She does a double take and then a wide smile breaks out on her face.

"What are you doing here?" She steps forward and hugs me, taking me by surprise. She smells really good, and her body fits to mine a little too well. If I weren't her coach, I'd be all too happy to pull her against me and let her know I'm just as happy to see her.

"I came to watch you play, of course. Plus, my brother doesn't live far from here, so I wanted to stop in and see him." Kenton is in Seattle until tomorrow so it's unlikely I'll actually get to see him, but it makes me feel a little less weird about being here to add that tidbit.

Keira introduces me to Abby, or reintroduces me since we met once before, and then Abby excuses herself leaving Keira and me alone.

I motion for her to take a seat on a small bench next to the window and do the same.

"I can't believe you're here. I was just getting ready to text you."

"Yeah? What were you going to report?"

"One under." She makes a face that tells me it isn't as good as she hoped.

"How'd you feel out there?"

"Nervous, anxious, excited. By the second round, I was finally starting to calm down, but it's infuriating how good Wren Thompkins is. Her shots were chasing down the pin all day."

I chuckle. "You out drove her every single time."

She sits a little taller. "Yes, that I did." Her gaze turns to the window and out to the course. "I should probably get out there and watch, wanna come? Cassidy's on two."

I want to. I really do, but I know I have a dozen things I need to do, things I put off this morning to be here. "I can't. I need to do some work this afternoon. I'll check in later."

There's a hint of disappointment on her face that makes me seriously consider blowing off work, but she nods and stands to leave. "See ya later then."

I watch her go, each step she takes making the room feel a little less enjoyable.

"Keira," I call out before she's out of earshot.

She stops and turns her head, a hesitant smile on her lips. "Yeah?"

"Good job today."

That smile gets bigger, and she takes a step, still looking over her shoulder. "Thanks, Coach."

⊤

I'm on the phone with Heath for our weekly check in. All the other employees check-in with the manager of their division because there's simply too many for me to oversee all of them, but I do Heath's one-on-one every week.

Really, I just want to make sure everything's good with him, but we do chat work for the first ten minutes and getting his take on things I might not see from my position, is always interesting.

I lean back in the single chair in my room while he tells me about the most entertaining client of his week, a woman who is trying to win her man back by learning hockey via barraging Heath with questions on terminology and breakdowns of games she's watched on television.

"Look at you, hockey guru and relationship counselor."

I can almost picture him flipping me off through the phone as he says, "Fuck off. I'm going pro after this year. Watch and see, old man. Then you'll have to find someone else to be your hockey guru."

"In the meantime, how about you stop procrastinating and crack open a book. I have to make some other calls."

He mumbles something, but I'm distracted by the knock at my door.

I stand and speak as I cross the room, "Stay out of trouble. Call me if you need anything."

When I open the door, Keira holds up a bottle of wine in front of my face. I take it and open the heavy door wide so she can step in.

"How'd you find me?"

She walks in, taking in the space before sitting on the edge of the bed. "I asked. Nicely. And I might have batted my eyelashes at the cute guy at the front desk."

"Shameless." I put the wine on the dresser and lean my back against it, crossing one ankle over the other. "What's the plan for the night? Are you guys getting in some practice or taking the night off?"

"Night off. Coach was pleased with how things went today, and it was spitting rain as we left anyway, so . . . we have all night to prepare for the final round tomorrow."

"Is that right?"

She pulls her legs under her on my bed, and my thoughts go from golf to—fuck, I need a drink and to get out of this hotel room.

Keira and bed—two words I've already established don't need to be said or thought together. Seeing it, also real, reaaaal bad.

"Have you eaten?" I stand straight.

"Yeah." She bobs her head from side to side. "Well, sort of. I had a sandwich at the course."

"Come on, let's feed you something."

While Keira and I eat downstairs at the hotel restaurant, I give her a brief rundown of what I saw today. Then try to keep the conversation off golf so she can relax and have a few hours without stress.

I'm usually good at small talk, but I find myself struggling to say anything and simultaneously trying to keep it all inside. She doesn't need to know that I think it's beautiful how she lights up when she talks about golf or how I want to run my fingers along her smooth skin.

I'm on my third beer, which initially I thought was helping but now I'm wondering if sober state of mind was the way to go. A group of guys at the bar keep looking back at her. She's totally unaware and I'm not about to point it out to her.

Her phone vibrates on the table between us, and she glances at the screen. "I have to get upstairs. Curfew is in ten minutes." She lets out a long breath, all the nerves we chased away returning before my eyes. "Will I see you tomorrow?"

"I'll be there," I assure her. I've already paid our tab, so I down the rest of my beer and stand. "Let me walk you up."

She's quiet as we take the elevator up to her floor. I want to say or do something to make her feel confident. It's something I don't usually need to do with my clients because I build their self-confidence through months of training, but we've only been working together a short time, and she doesn't have that yet.

The doors open, and I step out with her.

"Thanks for dinner and for being here."

"No need for thanks. Does your dad make tournaments very often?"

"No. Don't get me wrong, he's my biggest fan, but he only comes to the home tournaments."

With my hands in my pocket, I linger in the hallway. "I have a call I can't miss tomorrow morning at eight, but I'll do my best to get to the course while you're warming up. Try to sleep tonight, I know how hard that is the night before the final day. No matter what happens tomorrow, you proved you belong out there today. They can't take that away from you."

"I don't want to just prove I belong; I want to win. I feel like I should stay up all night and visualize or practice my downswing. I can't just sleep when I could be doing something."

"I know." I free my hand from my pocket and take her fingers loosely in mine. It's only the lightest brush of skin, but I feel more connected by that small touch than I have felt fully naked with others. "Trust me when I tell you that the best thing you can do tonight is sleep. Tomorrow you can go back to conquering the world."

She nods, and I drop her hand and step back to the elevator. "'Night."

NINETEEN

Keira

Abby is on her bed texting Smith while I warm up with some light stretching in our hotel room. My alarm goes off, signaling the five-minute warning that the van is leaving.

"Ugh, I just want to lie here another hour," Abby says as she sits up.

It's still dark outside, but I don't understand why she isn't more excited. It's day two, the final day of this short tournament. Today we'll play our last round. Only eighteen holes to climb my way up the leaderboard.

"The guys say good luck." Abby stands and brushes her dark hair back into a neat ponytail and then grabs her visor and bag.

"Why are they up so early?"

"They have a special practice today to work on putting with another friend of Coach James."

"Why am I not surprised?" I chuckle lightly. It doesn't bother me quite as much as it used to . . . probably because I know I've already snagged the best coach in the world.

Abby and I are the last to load up in the van.

"Morning," Erica chirps.

Kim and Cassidy wave from the backseat. Kim has her headphones on, and Cassidy goes back to staring out the window. We all have our own ways of prepping on tournament days.

"Everyone ready?" Coach Potter asks from the driver's seat. His sunglasses dangle from a black cord attached to either side so they hang around his neck.

On the ride to the course, I re-read the texts from my parents. Both sent early this morning, within minutes of each other, which makes me wonder if Dad texted Mom to remind her. Normally, I'd think it was Mom who'd have it neatly scheduled in, but there's no way Dad forgot. He may not know what to buy me at Christmas and think Hungry Man makes gourmet food, but when it comes to supporting me and my love for golf, he's never let me down.

Dad: Good luck today, sweet pea.

Mom: Good luck, sweetie!! I'm cheering you on from afar.

My mom included a picture of her and Bart wearing the Valley U golf T-shirts that I got them for Christmas. It's funny because I'd bet my dad is wearing his too.

My nerves kick in as we arrive at the course and exit the van. The sun is still rising, and the morning air is brisk, so I zip up my Valley jacket higher on my neck.

"I couldn't sleep last night," Erica whispers as we walk a step behind the rest of the team.

"Me either."

"At least you're in placing position. The top half of the leaderboard has to choke for me to come anywhere near the top three."

After all the groups finished yesterday, I'd been bumped to ninth place. It isn't great, but I'm still in it. Abby and Cassidy are in fifth and second respectively.

The team splits to warm up. Kim, Cassidy, and Abby start with chipping while Erica and I go to the putting area. Our easy conversation turns to silence as soon as our feet touch the green. Anxiety creeps up my body making my grip sweaty and my arms shaky.

A few minutes later, Coach walks over with Cassidy. The expression on his face and the way they both nod seriously tells me he's giving her last-minute pointers. He's putting all his efforts into her, which isn't a bad bet. She's really good and continually places top five. Still, I can't help but feel annoyed that he's never given me that type of coaching.

My high school coach used to say that when I stop yelling, that's when I stop caring. Coach Potter stopped yelling the day I threw my club in the water hazard and blew the tournament. Actually, he started and stopped that day. I know he doesn't believe in me, but in moments like this, a little boost of confidence, even from him, wouldn't hurt.

"Erica," Coach calls and waves her over. She glances at me, rolls her eyes so only I can see, and then heads over to them.

Closing my eyes for just a moment, I inhale and will my body to relax. All around me people are quietly talking and shuffling around, stretching, or pulling clubs from bags.

Players down the line swing and hit balls, the *ping* coming every few seconds. It's usually my favorite sound in the world, so I try to focus on it and ignore everything else. I search for that sound, among all hits, that perfect ping of the ball being hit on the sweet spot of the club.

A gruff voice, not much louder than a whisper, breaks my attention, and I turn to see Lincoln off to the side, away from the coaches and players.

Two bottom fingers wrapped around his coffee cup lift in a wave. The rhythm of my heart speeds up, but there's something soothing about his presence too. He's here for me. Just me.

I sneak a peek at Coach, who may as well not even know I exist, and walk toward Lincoln.

"Hey," I say when I reach him.

The smell of soap and coffee hangs on him. A white Under Armour hat covers his dark hair, and his face is smooth, as if he shaved only minutes ago. He fits right in with gray slacks and a black polo, but there's something about Lincoln that always stands out.

"Morning. How are you feeling?"

"Nervous."

His smile lifts. "Relax, have fun, and don't throw anything."

An unexpected chuckle slips from my lips, garnering the attention of those around us, including Coach Potter. If looks could kill, then I'd be squished like a bug under my coach's shoe.

"Shit," I mutter under my breath.

Coach Potter waits until he's close enough he doesn't have to raise his voice before he speaks. "Keira, get back in line and pretend like you want to be here, for heaven's sake."

My jaw drops, and I scramble for words to spit at him, but Lincoln's hazel eyes meet mine, and his head shakes ever so subtly from side to side.

I walk back and stand next to Abby.

"What was that?" she whispers.

"Coach being an ass like usual. God, I hate that man."

Lincoln and Coach exchange words, neither looking happy. Eventually Lincoln nods, glances over to me, and gives me one last reassuring smile before he walks away.

Coach turns, doesn't spare me so much as a cursory glance, and shakes his head in disgust.

I'm paired with Mia Arnold, a freshman standout, from New Mexico State. She struggled yesterday, but as she walks over to stand beside me to wait our turn, she looks confident and ready to go.

"Good luck today." She pulls her driver. The smile on her face seems to sit there so securely.

"You too." There is no smile on my face. I feel like I might throw up or pass out.

Hole one is a par five at five hundred and five yards. Yesterday, I parred it both rounds, but if I want a chance at placing, I need to do better.

Mia tees off first. A nice start with a drive around two hundred and fifty yards. Not all that long, but it left her in a good position on the fairway.

When my name is announced, I step up and position my teed ball just right of the center of the box. I do a quick glance for Coach, but don't find him. It shouldn't surprise me, but it still does. I bet he'll be here to watch the others tee off.

There isn't time to be disappointed or to wish things were different. This is my moment, my time to prove I don't just belong here, I'm here to win.

Lincoln lingers on the sideline with a few other spectators. His eyes bore into me, silently communicating everything I need to hear. *Relax, have fun, you can do this.*

I can do this.

The hole fits my strengths perfectly. It has a wide fairway and a gentle right to left dogleg. I take aim dead center with the intention of letting my draw move the ball toward the left edge of the fairway, which will setup a perfect approach. I take a breath and swing hard.

The ball screams down the center of the fairway with a hint of a draw. Holy crap.

I'm stunned for a moment as the crowd claps enthusiastically because not only did it go exactly where I wanted but also ended up sixty yards past Mia's.

TWENTY

Lincoln

The crowd at the fourteenth hole is twice as big as the one that was at the ninth hole. And it's all because of the amazing show Keira is putting on. With each hole, she finds a little more confidence, and people are getting to see the version of Keira that only I've been privy to. Well, me and her dickhead coach who wouldn't know talent if it slapped him upside the head.

Speaking of, Potter walks up from wherever the fuck he's been, a big, proud smile on his face. Hands on hips, he hangs back while Keira takes her turn. It's another beautiful shot on the short par four, putting her in a great position close to the pin and beating Mia Arnold's drive by a good thirty yards.

The crowd claps and starts to walk, but I hang back, watching as Potter approaches her. A hesitant smile pulls her lips apart like she's afraid to believe he's actually there and praising her.

They walk toward her ball together, all the while he's talking to her, waving his hands and suddenly super involved. Trying to temper my annoyance, I move with the rest of the spectators.

Mia Arnold's coach smiles reassuringly and gives her a few small claps to get her going. Keira's intimidated her, out driving her on every single hole and flying by her on the leaderboard as if she's on a do-or-die mission.

My girl is focused but relaxed, having fun and kicking ass. It's a real pleasure just to be watching. And the energy of the crowd tells me it isn't my own personal bias speaking.

I bring my index finger to my mouth and bite my knuckle while I wait for her turn. After Mia takes her second shot, Keira goes to grab her wedge. Potter stops her, talks to her for a second, and then backs away as she switches her club to a nine iron, looking a bit hesitant.

It isn't a good move. The hole sits on a slope. Keira is longer than the average female player, and if she goes long, she's not going to have any green to work with. No coach I know would play this hole like he's instructing Keira to do.

Shit. I don't wanna watch, but I do because if there's a chance Keira's going to look over for support, I need to make sure she sees whatever reassurance she needs on my face.

The crowd is none the wiser. They watch with hope that they're going to see her move up another spot on the scoreboard. She's six under par for the day putting her in third place overall, but at the rate she's dropping birdies, she has a shot to win the whole dang thing.

As she gets into position, her demeanor is less confident than it's been all day. She doesn't glance at the crowd or her coach before she draws back.

I can tell as soon as she gets to the top of her swing that it's going to be long. I tense as it sails through the air, and stop tracking the ball and watch her instead. She knows it too and her eyes fall to the ground at her feet.

The heartbroken sigh of the crowd puts a voice to the pain in my gut. Potter doesn't show any sign of understanding the magnitude of his fuck up. His face settles into a serious expression that gives nothing away. He should be kicking himself for his utter stupidity.

He gives Keira a nod and a go-ahead signal to take her next shot, clearly not sensing her mood. She's freaked. It may only be one mistake, but an unforced error like that can mess with your head. Lifting my hat, I rake my hands through my hair.

"Look at me, Keira. Look up. Come on," I mumble under my breath, willing her to look at me. "Take a breath. You're okay."

The guy next to me furrows his brow, and I feel him staring, but fuck if I can give him a second thought. If I thought it wouldn't throw her off more, I'd be shouting it to her. Screw the rules, screw the man holding the quiet sign.

Everything inside me screams that this is all wrong. She's off, spiraling inside, and I can't stop it.

I cross my arms and squeeze them into my body to keep myself still.

The next shot isn't awful, but it doesn't redeem her, and she ends up one over for bogey.

Coach Potter visibly withdraws from her and even the crowd senses the shift in their favorite new underdog. Still, they hang around through fifteen and part of sixteen. But with each shot, they lose a little more hope, and so does she.

Potter leaves her at the start of seventeen. She's in eighth place and solidly out of the running for placing today.

She doesn't so much as side-eye anyone on those last two holes. Retreating deeper into herself until all signs of the confident, capable woman I know are gone.

I wait for her in the clubhouse. Two of her teammates flank her on each side. They offer hugs and high-fives, but Keira's grim expression doesn't change.

When she finally approaches me, she looks completely broken. I rub at the sharp pain in the middle of my chest and force a pep in my step as I close the distance between us.

Instead of speaking, I wrap my arms around her and cradle her head against my chest. Any anger she was holding on to turns to sadness, and she buries her face into my shirt and cries. My hands tremble as I run my fingers down her hair and caress the back of her neck.

"Hey, you're good," I whisper so only she can hear. "I've got you."

Her hold on my waist tightens and her entire body leans into me like I'm the only thing keeping her upright. She's a fragile, beautiful thing in my arms and I've never felt more helpless or more needed.

"I've got you," I repeat. "I've got you."

⊤

Keira is at dinner with the team, and I'm in my hotel room, shifting around my meetings for tomorrow morning. Originally, I planned to head out tonight, but there's no way I'm leaving now.

There will be other tournaments; she'll get more chances. I know it, she knows it, but that isn't the point.

It's after eight and my eyes are crossing from staring at financial reports when my phone pings.

Keira: Thanks for coming today. We just got back from dinner, and I'm gonna crash. You're probably already on a plane back to Arizona. Anyway, I'm sure you have notes for me from today's performance. I know I fell into some of my bad habits at the end. I can fix it. Please don't give up on me yet.

Jesus. What the hell did Potter say to her? She spent the last three hours with her teammates and coach, I assumed that was for the best. They could girl talk or whatever, maybe Potter would have some encouraging words. She sounds just as defeated as when I left her.

Me: I'm still here. Can you come down for a few minutes?

Keira: You're still here?

Me: Yes.

I'm holding my phone, waiting for her response, tapping my thumb against the device, when someone knocks lightly on my door.

I pull it open without checking, already figuring that it's her, and damn, maybe I should have. She looks every bit the young, beautiful college girl she is wearing cut-off denim shorts, a gray T-shirt, and orange flip-flops. Her hair is down, and her face is free of makeup. She steps inside and the door closes behind her.

The determination and focus she wears like armor on most days is totally stripped away. She walks to the center of the room and then turns to me. Her brown eyes glisten as if she's on the verge of tears. "If you're going to drop me as a client, just tell me now."

Um, what? My face contorts with confusion, but she doesn't allow me to get a word in.

"I get it. I screwed up today." She squeezes her eyes shut, and one tear slips from the corner. She swipes it away with the palm of her hand and then tilts her head up and bats her eyelashes as if she's annoyed that she's crying and trying to stop. "I embarrassed you, my team, my coa—"

My mouth is on hers, silencing the nonsense spilling out before I've decided I wanted to act. Though, it feels like the best decision I've made in a long time.

Her lips soften and mold to mine before responding. When she kisses me back, it's with her whole body. She steps against me and places her hands on my chest before breaking the kiss and looking up at me.

It's an unspoken question, a dare to do it again, or maybe a chance to change my mind. Fuck that. As hard as I've tried to keep her at arms-length, Keira has always been more than some client.

This time when I take her lips, there's no hesitation from either of us. My hands thread through her hair and tilt her head back. Deepening the kiss, my hands fall to her waist and around to cup her ass. She pulls her head back and peers up at me but doesn't break the contact of our bodies. I take a moment to drink her in. Lips wet, face flushed, her chest rises and falls with breathless excitement. She's stunning.

"You kissed me." Her voice hides none of the shock or want I can see on her face.

"Correction. I'm *kissing* you. I'm not even close to done."

TWENTY-ONE

Keira

"So, you aren't dropping me?" I ask, gliding my hands up and down his forearms, tracing the veins and enjoying his warmth and strength.

His back leans against the headboard, and I'm straddling him, knees bent underneath me.

A rough chuckle shakes his upper body, and he cradles my head and runs his hands down to rest lightly on my neck. "For what? You were amazing today."

One eyebrow cocks with disbelief. He can't be serious.

"Did you know you had the longest drive on every single hole today? Every single one. Not just against Mia, but in the entire tournament."

"I didn't, but even so, I lost. I totally fell apart. I should have placed."

"You stopped trusting yourself. You let Potter throw you off when he told you to switch to the nine, which was a garbage call, and then you couldn't recover. You should have trusted your instincts and smoked the wedge. You're comfortable playing power golf and when the situations get tight you need to play to your strength. Potter should know that. It's his whole job. Today's loss was a coaching catastrophe. You were the best player out there."

His words comfort me and light the fire of determination I lost earlier today. Lincoln has never fed me compliments when they weren't deserved.

"You mean that? It isn't just because you suddenly want to kiss me that you're saying that?"

"Suddenly?" His brows rise as a teasing smile plays on his lips. Slowly, he shakes his head. "I've thought about kissing you since you all but called me a creep and tossed tequila on me."

"Why didn't you?"

The playfulness falls away, and I wish I could suck in the question and keep it to myself.

"The business takes a hundred percent of my time and is my top priority. Yeah, I've thought about kissing you, but I also considered what that would mean for the relationship we've built. I don't want to mess with that or hurt you."

"I appreciate the honesty, but I just stopped plotting your death for making me run a thousand miles, so you can stop worrying. I'm not expecting anything. I have my own life."

Some of the tension in his body relaxes, but I can tell he isn't convinced. I look into his dark eyes. From far away, they look brown, but up close, they're more hazel. A myriad of beautiful, complicated colors that's fitting for this man.

I move my hands from his arms to his amazing pecs and the steady thump of his heart under the cotton shirt to the nape of his neck. I curl my fingers into his thick hair. "Tell me again how good I was."

His teeth glide along his bottom lip before he smirks. Slowly, he inches closer until his mouth hovers over mine. His breath tickles and heats my skin as he says, "You really have no idea how good you are, do you?" He searches my face for an answer. "Watching you play is inspiring. Being your coach and watching you see the rewards of working your ass off . . . it's a privilege. You're the most incredible person I know, Keira Brooks."

I close my eyes and smile, letting those words and his nearness heal the embarrassment and frustration of my loss. They become my truth, and I cling to them.

Removing the millimeter of distance between us, I kiss him. I pour all the passion of my hopes and dreams into him, knowing that, whatever else happens between us, he'll be the protector of those things.

Large fingers wrap around my waist on both sides. His thumbs circle at the hem of my shirt and slip under so the calloused pads run along bare skin. Those full lips leave mine only to find my neck and collarbone. His touch brings goose bumps to the surface, and we make out like two people who need connection more than air.

Moaning and tilting my head to give him better access, I'm not prepared for his words. "We should stop."

"What?" My eyes fly open. "Why?"

"Because I don't want to wreck what we have. I like you." His head rises slowly, kissing the sensitive skin on the way, as if he's convincing himself with his own words while enjoying a final taste.

"Turning down sex because you like me? Well, that's a first."

He lifts me from his lap with a groan and places me next to him where our legs still rest against each other. "I meant what I said earlier. That wasn't me feeding you a line or giving some bullshit excuse. I don't have a lot to offer. I can't be a boyfriend or even promise to be what you need tomorrow. I like and respect you too much to lead you on. I enjoy helping you and being around you. I'm not going anywhere, but there are limits to what I have to give outside of coaching."

"I get it," I reaffirm him. "But it's really cruel to offer all this up"—I gesture to him and his hotness—"and then take it away. Will you at least take your shirt off?"

He chuckles and brushes my hair back from my face. I can see his resolve to take this back to G-rated. No matter what he says, I know the lines he just drew are about him, not me. I'm perfectly capable of separating sex with Lincoln from our working relationship. But fine. I mean there are lots of things Lincoln and I can do fully clothed and not touching.

I enjoy him. Our connection with golf and our desire to push ourselves gives us a lot to talk about. Though talking naked is obviously my preference.

"Fine, but can I stay in here tonight?"

He tilts his head, and I raise both hands innocently. "I only want to talk golf. I'll keep my hands to myself."

And I do. Mostly.

I barrage him with questions. Silly things that don't touch on serious topics because tonight is about pulling back the curtain, getting to know him in a way that he's kept off-limits.

His favorite color is green, favorite food is tamales followed closely by Chicago style pizza, he doesn't care for sweets, he still uses a putter his grandfather gave him for his high school graduation, and so many more things that I file away for safekeeping. I know I'll never forget a single thing he tells me, no matter how small or insignificant he thinks it might be.

He lies on his back, an arm around me as I snuggle into his side. My head rests on his chest and I run my fingers across his stomach. Even through the soft material of his shirt I can make out the lines and dips of muscle.

My eyes are heavy from the physical and emotional toll of the past few days. I fight to keep them open so I can savor this moment. In his arms I feel invincible.

"Got any Red Bull?" I ask, stifling a yawn.

"For what?"

"To keep me awake."

His chest shakes with a silent laugh. "Go to sleep. It's been a long day."

"I don't want to sleep." I'm bolder with my exploration of his body this time and dip my hand lower on his stomach.

He makes a strangled groan of a sound, captures my hand in his, and rests them on his chest. "Sleep."

I try to keep my eyes open despite his bossy command, but his thumb moves in a slow circle on the top of my hand, and my lids droop.

"I'm staying up all night," I threaten, but even as I say it, I start drifting off.

The next morning as I'm getting ready to leave his room to catch the team van to the airport, Lincoln brushes his teeth in the open bathroom. He slept in a T-shirt and gym shorts, but that shirt is gone now, and I'm not shy about getting a good look at his chiseled upper body while he's showing it off.

He has a great chest. Not so muscular that he's beefy, but defined enough that it lifts and falls in all the right places, a light smattering of dark hair trimmed close.

"Talk to you later?"

He nods, leans over the sink, spits, and rinses his mouth out before standing and wiping his face with a towel. I watch the whole thing completely entranced. He's so comfortable in his skin, and that skin . . . well, it's sensational.

"Yeah, I'll update your training plan sometime today. I have a few meetings first."

"Okay."

A beat of awkwardness plays out between us before he strides forward and places a hand at my hip. The warmth and strength of his grip makes my breath catch. I want to go back to twenty minutes ago when we were in bed, every inch of my body touching him in some way, and stay there all day.

"What do you think about doing the sectional qualifier in April?"

"You mean the *Open* qualifier?" My voice quivers with excitement or maybe disbelief.

"Yeah." He pulls me against him. "That gives us a couple of months to work your swing out, and then you can go show everyone what you're capable of."

"You think I'm ready?" I hate the way my voice wavers with my lack of confidence.

"I think I'll make sure you are. You might hate me again. It's going to mean working twice as hard as before. More running and weights and—"

I stop him by pushing up onto my tiptoes and kissing him. When I step back, the excitement in his eyes matches mine. "Bring it on."

TWENTY-TWO

Keira

W e have a rare day off practice Tuesday, so I use the time to check on Dad. Over a sausage pizza, he grills me about the tournament.

Normally I'd be all too eager to talk golf, but I'm blushing and squirming in my seat as if Dad can tell by looking at me that I spent the night with my hottie swing coach. So, I give him a lightning speed overview and then ask about his scheduled doctor appointments and physical therapy this week.

He should be cleared to drive at this appointment, and I'm both looking forward to him regaining his independence and already missing the time together.

Dad retires to his chair and puts on the game, so I take that as my cue to head back to the dorm.

"Hey you." I nearly run into Abby as she opens the door to our dorm before I can.

"Hey." She smiles and backtracks into the room.

"Headed to Smiths?"

"Study group then Smith's." She points to a box next to my bed. "That came for you."

"To the room?"

"Yeah, they brought it straight up because it was taking up too much space in the mail area downstairs." She raises a brow and looks to me, expecting answers. "What in the world did you order?"

"I didn't." I try to lift the box, but it's heavy. Really heavy.

"All right, well the suspense is killing me, but I have to go." Abby heads to the door. "Text me later."

"I will. Bye," I call over my shoulder as I search for my scissors.

Once I find them, I sit on the floor next to the box, cut the tape, and peel back the flaps. I find a piece of plain, white copy paper on top.

For your dorm. Let me know if you need anything else.
Lincoln

I set his note on the floor and dig through the contents of the box. Foam golf balls, a chipping net, a hitting net, a small putting mat, and a much larger hitting mat. A nice one. It's way nicer than the one at my dad's. There's even a pair of ear plugs that I'm guessing are supposed to be for Abby. He thought of everything, because of course he did.

He calls as I'm working on a new trick shot. I place the phone on my desk so I can show him before grabbing my wedge and a ball. "Prepare to be amazed."

"What is it you're trying to do exactly?" Lincoln asks, dark brows raised and a smirk on his lips. Those lips . . . now that I know what they feel like against mine, I can't look at him without doing an instant replay of our make-out session.

"No look into the cup."

"I can't see the cup," he says.

"It's on the floor by the wall," I say as I bounce the ball off the clubface and turn so that my back is to the cup. I tap it into the air, flip the club, and hit it over my shoulder. I turn in time to see the ball hit the rim of the cup and bounce away. "If you didn't see it, I guess I can pretend that went in."

The ball continues to bounce around the room noisily, and we both laugh.

"I just need a little more practice." I grab the phone and my laptop. "You want me to log into the site?"

"Nah, it's fine as long as I can see you. I'm reviewing the videos you sent this morning now."

"Check out my new setup." I angle the phone so he can see how I've pushed my and Abby's beds farther apart and put the net between them. My mat is on the floor in the open space.

"I have just enough room to swing my club." I move the phone again so I can show him where I put the putting mat and chipping net. "Thank you. This is ridiculous, but I love it."

"Don't thank me yet. Now that you have a decent setup in your room, I'm going to up the intensity."

"Do your worst."

Lincoln shakes his head and laughs before going back to analyzing my swing videos from earlier. "Swing looks pretty good. I see what you're talking about with your arms not being at full extension past impact. Let me see it. Can you position the camera so I can see your swing from the front?"

I spend the next hour taking swings in my new makeshift training area while Lincoln coaches me. He tweaks and nitpicks, but he's encouraging as he does it.

"We have our home tournament in two weeks."

"Good. You could use another competition to work on playing under pressure."

He's in his living room. The computer sets in his lap, phone resting on the couch beside him. His brow's furrow, legs are kicked up on the coffee table.

We finished our training session fifteen minutes ago, and he's moved on to checking email while I force him into conversation. He is a willing, if a bit distracted, participant.

"Will you come?"

"Hmm?" He briefly glances at me and nods. "What days? Saturday and Sunday?"

"Yeah."

"I'll try. I'm supposed to fly out to L.A. to watch Kenton play on Friday. My parents are coming in from New York, so I can't skip it, but I'll see if I can get a flight back Saturday."

He says it casually, as if everyone jets off to amazing sporting events on the regular.

"Fair enough. I'd choose the Stars over me too."

He sets his phone down on his thigh. "You like soccer?"

"It's okay. My dad loves sports, so I spent a lot of time fighting over the television with him. Soccer and basketball I didn't mind so much."

"You guys ever been to a pro game? Soccer or basketball? Football?"

"No. My dad is pretty much a homebody. Always has been, but especially after the divorce and now that he's injured—forget about it."

He nods thoughtfully. "What does he do?"

"He is a roofer, but he's on leave until they clear him to go back."

We're quiet for a moment, him on his computer and me thinking about my dad.

"How long was it after your divorce before you started dating again?"

Lincoln pauses, and his eyes meet mine.

I pull my unicorn scrunchie out of my hair and slide it onto my wrist before combing my fingers through the tangled strands. "It's just that it's been years since my parents split, and as far as I know, my dad hasn't dated at all. I worry about him. When I graduate, he's going to be all alone, eating frozen dinners and watching the game in his old chair."

He rubs his jaw and sighs. "That sounds pretty good to me." I think that's all he's going to say, but then he adds, "It was nine months, but to be honest, every date I've been on since has been a Gram setup. I am perfectly content to sit in my chair and eat meals by myself."

"Really? Forever? Isn't that, I dunno, lonely?"

"I don't have time to be lonely. Plus, I have months of entertainment to look forward to with you while we get that swing of yours right." He winks.

"You'll never be lonely with me around."

"Definitely not."

Υ

Thursday night, Keith and I get permission from Professor Teague to do next week's lab early since Keith is travelling with the boys' team for a tournament in Texas and won't be back for our Monday night class. I show up to lab with a Pop-Tart in one hand and an energy drink in the other, still sweaty from weight training. There's another lab going on, but I find Keith set up in the back.

I fan my sticky shirt away from my body, and Keith gives me a questioning glance.

"Sorry, I came straight from the gym."

"Your coach lets you eat junk like that?" He motions toward my dinner.

I know he means Potter, but I think of Lincoln. "What he doesn't know won't hurt him. Besides, I had a protein drink on the way over. This is my dessert."

Professor Teague comes over to our table and gives us brief instructions before he starts his class. Keith and I fall into the work silently. I'm not sure how long we've been working before my phone starts vibrating in my pocket. As discretely as I can, I take it out and glance at the screen and then answer.

"Hey," I whisper. The only person who notices is Keith, and his brows pull down in disapproval.

Lincoln's serious expression slowly drags into a big grin. "What are you doing?"

Lifting the goggles off my eyes, I answer. "I'm in lab."

"Why the hell did you answer?"

Because it's him. Because I haven't talked to him all day and it's becoming my favorite part of the day. "What do you need?"

Behind him, it's dark, the sun setting on the golf course at his grandmother's house. "Are you trying to escape another blind date?"

He chuckles. "Nope. Just me and Gram tonight. Those goggles are charming as hell. You have adorable raccoon eyes."

I rub at my eyes in a weak attempt to make the marks go away. "Maybe you've already turned down every eligible bachelorette she knows."

He laughs. "I doubt it. Anyway, I called because I'm teaching a golf clinic tomorrow and I have to go to the Suns game tomorrow night, but I'm free between and was thinking of playing a round."

"Your life is bizarre."

A grin tugs up one side of his mouth. "But awesome, right? Come with me."

"What?" Did I just hear him right? Because it sounded like he invited me up to see him.

"The course here is tougher than the one you play at Valley. I think it'll be a good challenge for you."

I mull it over, though it really isn't a matter of if I want to go but rather if I can work it into my schedule. "What time?"

"Miss Brooks," Professor Teague addresses me from the front of the class.

"I gotta go," I say quickly and hang up on Lincoln's amused face before shooting my professor a sheepish smile. "Sorry."

Keith shakes his head, and I shrug. As I go to put my phone in my backpack, I get a text.

Lincoln: Sexy scientist, I dig it. 😉

After lab, I head back to the dorm. Abby sits on her bed facing Cassidy and Erica, who are on mine.

"Hey, what are you guys doing here?" I ask as I drop my backpack to the floor.

"Well, since you won't come to us, we decided to come to you." Cassidy smiles with her elbows resting on her knees and her chin perched on her palm.

"I just saw you guys at practice a few hours ago."

"Not the same and you know it," Erica says. "Get ready and let's go out. Wherever you want."

"Where's Smith?" I drop onto Abby's bed next to her.

"He's at the library. Thought I might try sleeping in my own bed for a change." She elbows me gently.

"Novel concept."

"We miss you," Cass says. "You haven't been out with us in weeks."

"I miss you guys too, but I'm exhausted. I don't feel like going anywhere tonight. Maybe this weekend?"

My phone pings, and Abby narrows her gaze. "Or maybe you'd rather spend the night talking to Lincoln. I mean, look what he did to this room?" She gestures to all my golf stuff.

"I'm sorry. I've been training nonstop."

"Hey, no need to apologize. He's seriously fine. I'd be glued to my phone too."

My face warms, and I shift in my seat. I haven't told anyone except Abby about staying with him last weekend. It isn't that I'm embarrassed or anything, but telling them leaves it open to scrutiny and I want to keep whatever is between Lincoln and me in a bubble.

"Oh my God. You're blushing, Keira." Erica tosses my pillow at me. "You absolutely slept with him!"

"What?" Cassidy screeches. "You had sex with Lincoln Reeves?"

"No." I toss the pillow back at Erica. "I didn't."

She catches it easily and holds it up as if she might toss it back. "I don't believe you. Your face is so red."

"We kissed. That's all."

Erica and Cassidy scream and laugh. They high-five, which I find particularly amusing.

"It isn't a big deal," I try to say, but they aren't listening.

"Tell me everything," Erica says when she's settled down. "It's been so long since I've kissed a guy. What were his lips like? Where did he put his hands? Have you seen his penis?"

"Oh my God." I laugh. "Let's talk about why you are on a self-imposed sex hiatus instead?"

"It isn't self-imposed, there's just a serious lack of options."

"What about Chapman or Han? Or Keith, he's sweet."

Erica shakes her head. "Does Lincoln have any hot, single friends?"

"Uh, I don't actually know. I get the feeling he doesn't do a lot of hanging if it isn't work-related. He does have an in with several pro sports teams, though, so I'd say the odds are good least one of them fits your criteria."

She claps excitedly. "Let's go to The Hideout and snag a corner booth and you can tell us every detail over cocktails."

"I have to get up early, and I don't really feel like changing out of comfy clothes." I've been living in leggings and golf skirts for weeks.

Abby stands and disappears into our closet only to pop out a couple of seconds later with a bottle of RumChata. "Fine. Then we'll just drink here. I've had this bottle stashed since before winter break and have been waiting for the perfect time to break it out." More than two months have passed. Between golf and school . . ."

"And you basically living at Smith's," I add.

"And that." She nods. "But, seriously, how many more opportunities are we going to have before Erica and Cassidy graduate?"

I look between my friends. Their faces are a mixture of excitement and sadness. I know they're right, and I do want to spend time with them.

Finding a balance has been hard, and okay, maybe spending every night working with Lincoln hasn't been the biggest burden. The man is seriously hot and smart, and being coached by him is probably the single most exciting thing that's ever happened to me. Still, putting in all this hard work won't mean much if I've alienated everyone along the way.

"Hand it over," I say finally.

TWENTY-THREE

Lincoln

I fumble for my phone on the nightstand and bring it to my ear, eyes closed and only vaguely aware of what I'm doing.

"Hello?" It comes out in a croak. My voice is groggy, and my throat feels like sandpaper, so I clear it a couple of times and try again. "Hello?"

"Hi!" Keira's bubbly sweet voice answers. "Did I wake you? What time is it?"

"I'm not sure." I bring my free hand to my forehead and rub it absently.

"You aren't sure if I woke you or of what time it is?"

"Both."

Her sweet giggles filter into my ear, and I hold the phone out so I can check the time.

"What are you doing up so late?" I ask, placing the phone back to my ear.

"I was hanging out with the girls."

"Oh, yeah? What was on the agenda tonight?"

"Boy talk, junk food, and now drunk dialing."

"*Mmmm.* Sounds fun."

"It was, but now that I'm in bed, I'm fading fast." She yawns. "Is the offer to come up tomorrow still good?"

"Yeah, of course. I checked the weather it's supposed to be really nice and—" I'm about to add to the list of reasons she should come, but she interrupts me.

"You should send me a picture?"

"Uh, what?"

"A picture."

"A picture of what?" I play back our conversation in my head. "The golf course?"

"Of you. Duh. What do you sleep in?"

I'm smiling as I answer, "Boxers, sometimes shorts or sweats."

"No shirt?"

"Not usually, no. Why?"

"I knew it!" she shouts, and I pull the phone from my ear for a second.

"What did you know?" Following this conversation is hard, and I don't know if it's because I'm half asleep or because she's tipsy. Either way, I like that it's me she's drunk dialing.

"The night at the hotel you slept with your T-shirt on. I got totally cheated. Show me."

"I'm not taking a picture of my chest."

"You're no fun."

I try to picture her on the other end of the phone. Smiling and face flushed from alcohol.

"What time will you be here?"

She yawns again. "We don't have formal practice tomorrow. I just need to get in eighteen holes with my group. We're meeting at eight. I'll call you on my way up."

"I was thinking, can you stay the night and go back Saturday morning?"

"Like stay at your place?" Her voice slows and the pitch goes up at the end of her question.

"Or I can get you a room at a hotel if you're more comfortable. I'd like to take you to the game, but it might be kind of late by the time we get back."

She's quiet for a second, and I wonder if she's trying to find a nice way to turn me down or maybe she passed out.

"Keira?"

"Will you sleep with your shirt off this time?"

It's just as beautiful as the weatherman predicted. The sky is a brilliant blue, the few clouds look as if they were painted on, and there is just enough of a breeze to need long sleeves. I do a lot of small clinics at my home course, and today, I'm teaching a bunch of Pop's old friends and students how to adjust their putting speed.

This kind of thing is far more laid back since most of the guys have known me since I was a kid following Pop around. The country club was my daycare and my playground far before it became my office, and these guys will never let me forget it.

"Hey, Linc, the wife said you turned down our Franny." Darrell raises his head to see my reaction before he takes another putt. "My granddaughter not good enough for you?"

"My Angel, too," Lance pipes in. "Something wrong with your equipment, son?" He uses the end of his putter to point toward my crotch.

"The wife says he's *brooding* after the divorce."

"I'm not brooding, and my equipment is just fine. Your lag putting, on the other hand, is shit. Focus on that, Darrell."

The guys snicker, and I shake my head.

As we are finishing, Keira arrives wearing a black skirt that shows off her toned legs and a blue zip-up that's skin-tight, highlighting her athletic curves without revealing any skin.

Her sunglasses sit on top of her head, hair still down, though I know from the many times I've watched her play or practice, she'll take the unicorn scrunchie from her right wrist and secure it back before she starts.

"Hey," she greets me and glances over at the guys and gives them a shy wave. They've all stopped what they were doing to check her out. Our clientele is very strongly in the sixty-plus age bracket, so they aren't shy about their interest in her. "I thought I'd hit the driving range if you're still working."

"It's all right. We're done here," I say loudly enough that the guys can hear me. "Nice work today, guys. See ya next time."

With a wave and a few personal goodbyes, I collect my stuff, and Keira and I head toward my golf cart. "Do you still want to hit a few balls or are you ready to go out?"

"I actually already hit a small bucket. I got here early and didn't want to disturb you," she says as she slides into the passenger side.

While we wait to tee off at the first hole, Keira takes a long drink from her water bottle.

"Hung over?"

She gives me a small, rueful grin. "A little. Sorry for the late-night call."

"Don't be. You can always call me. Besides, you're a funny drunk. What was the occasion anyway?"

"Just some girl time. Seems like I have less and less time every week. Not that I'm complaining," she adds quickly and then elbows me. "My coach is a real hard ass."

"Yeah?"

The wind blows her hair around her face, and I push it back with my fingers, resting my thumb on her cheek. When she leans into the touch, it answers the question I've had all week on whether or not I imagined the chemistry between us last weekend. Her eyes fall to my lips.

Another cart pulls up behind us at the tee box, and I let my hand fall away.

Forcing myself from the cart, I stand and grab my driver from my bag in the back, and then toss her a cocky smirk. "Your hard ass coach is about to kick yours."

We zip through the course, playing through other groups. I can't remember the last time I had so much fun. I don't coach her unless she asks for specific feedback, and instead, we take turns launching bombs down the fairway and enjoy being on the course together.

As we finish on eighteen and head into the clubhouse, Darrell and Lance are standing behind their cars while the kid from the pro shop puts their bags in their respective trunks for them.

"Well, look who it is," Lance says. He smiles at Keira. "Lovely day for golf."

"It was." She smiles back at them, sun-kissed skin alive with excitement.

"What about you, Linc? Did you have a good time?" Lance asks, a hint of humor in his tone. He places his white golf glove in his back pocket.

Darrell smirks. "Guess it wasn't your equipment after all, just reserved for someone else?"

I shake my head. "See you guys later."

⊤

"Oh my gosh!" Keira's eyes are wide with excitement as I guide her through the arena. "I feel like I should have changed or put on some fresh deodorant or something." She smooths a hand over her hair.

She looks beautiful in a golf skirt and spandex shirt. Her face is free of makeup but painted with a glow from the sun.

"I have you covered," I say and point to a table of Suns merchandise.

She looks over every item before she narrows it down between a hat and a T-shirt each with the team logo.

"She'll take both," I tell the guy and hand him the money for it.

"Thank you." She pulls on the T-shirt over the one she was wearing and then places both hands on her hips. "What do you think?"

I set the hat on her head. It's too big and nearly covers her eyes. "Perfect."

Stepping closer, I adjust the cap, tuck her hair behind one ear, and let my hand linger at her neck. She leans into my fingers, and the day of being around her with only small touches and no kissing has officially become too much. I've been itching to feel more of her, brush my lips against hers.

The thing is, I knew it'd be just like this once I gave in—an obsessive desire to touch her all the time. And as super as that sounds, Keira isn't just some girl I'm seeing. Lines have blurred, for sure, but I still have a job to do. And right now that job is to reward her for all her hard work.

"Come on, stinky." I let my hand fall away and take hold of hers, interlocking our fingers.

Seeing Keira's excitement as we sit behind the team is worth everything I own and then some. The team is still warming up, and Keira perches on the edge of her chair, one hand squeezing my thigh as she takes it all in. Zeke Sweets, the team's rising star, waves and walks over when he spots me.

"Hey, Zeke, how are you?" I stand and shake his hand.

"Good, good. Nice to see you." He glances at Keira and smiles timidly. For all his stardom, he's a pretty quiet guy.

"Zeke, this is Keira. Keira, this is—"

She stands. "Zeke Sweets, I know. You went to Valley, too. My dad and I have been following your career. You're amazing. Incredible. Really, I'm a big fan."

The big guy smiles for real at her cute rambling. "Thank you."

"Keira plays golf at Valley," I tell him and watch her face pink. She's freaking adorable all flustered in front of Zeke.

"That's great. I hear the team's pretty good." He holds the basketball at his side, giving Keira his full attention.

"You follow golf?" Her jaw drops, and I can't resist chuckling at how awestruck she is.

"I keep an eye on all the Valley teams. Gotta rep the alma mater." He glances over his shoulder. "I should get back out there. Good to see you, Linc." He smiles at Keira. "Really nice to meet you. Good luck on the rest of the season."

Keira turns to me when Zeke walks away, opens her mouth, and lets out a long, quiet scream. "I can't believe I just met Zeke Sweets. Your life really is awesome."

I nod and drape an arm around her shoulders. "It really is."

⊤

I pull into the garage, kill the engine, and turn to Keira, who slept almost the whole way back to my place.

"Rise and shine, beautiful."

She lifts her head slowly from the headrest and looks around.

"Where are we?"

"My place," I say before sliding from the car.

She's unbuckled and sitting up by the time I get around the vehicle to open her door. When she places her hand in mine and I start to lead her inside, a weird sensation pulses through my body. It takes me a second to decode the feeling. I'm nervous.

My apartment isn't big. Kitchen, living-dining room combo, two bedrooms, two bathrooms, and it's sparsely decorated. I'm sure it screams divorced, single man, but Keira walks into the middle of the living room and turns a circle. When her brown eyes land back on me, there's nothing but delight on her face.

"I love it. It's exactly how I pictured it. The space is great."

I chuckle and walk to her, wrap my arms around her waist. "I forget you've already seen most of my place."

"Only in pieces. Plus, I was distracted by you."

She tips up onto her toes, and I lean down to take her lips in a quick kiss.

"I'm not here often, but it's on the course and near Gram." It's on the tip of my tongue to tell her most my stuff is in storage, make excuses for how bland it is, but then that makes me think of Lacey and how I still haven't called her back.

"I like it. Honest. It suits you."

I'm not sure what that says about me, but I don't think on it too hard.

She goes to the couch and sits, making a big show of crossing her arms over her chest, leaning back, and putting her feet on my coffee table. Forcing a frown, she asks, "Who am I?" Her voice deepens in a shit impersonation of me. "One hundred more reps. Do it until you get it right, and then do it until you can't do it wrong. No, no, no. That's garbage! Who taught you how to swing a club?"

"I don't sound like that, smartass." I fall onto the cushion beside her and pull her onto my lap, remove my hat and toss it onto the table, then run a hand over my matted down hair. Her eyes follow the movement and then her fingers come up to take over, gently threading through the strands.

My scalp pricks at her touch, and a pleasant warmth spreads through my body. "That feels good."

She scoots farther onto my lap, knees inching toward the back of the couch. The black skirt she's wearing lays flat, so I'm not getting a show, but the position and all the ways our bodies are touching is almost as good. My eyes fall closed, and I relax into the leather as she continues to comb through my hair with her fingers.

I bring my hands to her thighs and run my thumb along the hem of her skirt. Her skin is smooth and taut, and even though I'm not looking, I can recall her legs in vivid detail from the hundreds of times I've seen them on video.

I'm tired. A bone-deep exhaustion that has nothing to do with lack of sleep and everything to do with the restraint I've been holding on to all day. There are a million really good reasons I should stop whatever this is between us, send her on her way, rub one out, and go to bed alone.

I don't have any delusions of this ending any way other than with Keira eventually finding her swing and us going our separate ways. Maybe we'll run into one another again or maybe I'll be at a pro tournament and get to watch her dominate, like I know she will, but we aren't skipping into the sunset holding hands after tonight.

I know this. She does too. Yet, here we are anyway.

"I love your hair." She tugs gently. "It's so soft and thick." Her voice is quiet and husky, straight-up phone-sex-operator style; though, I know it isn't intentional.

Weeks of foreplay, of staring at one another through a screen but not being able to reach out and feel the person on the other side, makes everything more intense than it would have been had tonight been a real first date.

I groan a reply, and her hands still. When I open my eyes, she's staring at me, tongue between her teeth in concentration.

"What?" I ask, suddenly a little self-conscious as her beautiful brown eyes dance slowly over my features.

Instead of answering, she brings her mouth down and presses her lips softly against mine. It's torture as I let her run the pace. Her nails sweep over the stubble along my jaw as she kisses me.

I hold out on taking control for as long as I can, but when she moves closer so that her sweet heat presses against my dick, I grip her hips and draw her hard against me.

We're a tangle of tongues and a clash of teeth as we press together as tightly as our clothing will allow. Her tits crush against my chest so that I can feel the rise and fall from her labored breathing. I bring my hands around her back and fist a handful of hair so that her face tilts up and I can reach her neck.

She tastes sweet, the slightest tinge of salt from a day golfing in the sun. A low moan escapes from her as I nip at the sensitive flesh.

"Lincoln." She says my name in a way that no one has in so long. As if she enjoys being with me. As if she wants me. As if right now is enough.

When I don't answer her, she pulls back until I look at her.

I lean forward and kiss her collarbone and then retreat so I can see her stunning face again. "Yeah, baby?"

She bites the corner of her lip and smiles. Her hands fist my shirt on either side, and she raises the material an inch. I love that she's so excited to see my body because that's a mutual desire. I sit forward and allow her to peel my shirt off for me. She holds it in her hands as her eyes greedily take in my chest.

I work out most days and have stayed in shape since I quit the pro tour because it keeps me in a good place mentally, but right now, it feels as if it were for this moment—for that look on her face.

She traces the lines in my upper body, flattens her palms and glides across my pecs and abs. Finally, after she's thoroughly explored my bare chest, her hands move down to the top of my belt.

That side of her lip goes between her teeth again as she seems to contemplate removing my pants. I move to stand, and she squeals and throws her arms around my neck so that she doesn't fall back.

I kiss her hard as I walk toward my bedroom. I don't bother turning on the lights, but she still gives a quick glance around the darkened space as I set her on the bed.

"A room I haven't seen before."

"I don't work in here."

"No?" she questions and removes her shirt and tosses it.

Black lace wraps around her, lifting her tits and teasing the shit out of me. I place a knee on the bed, forcing her onto her back. Bracing over her, I drop my mouth to one bra-covered nipple and gently bite.

"Separation of church and state."

She giggles, the sweet sound eliciting a smile from me as well. More clothes come off and are tossed to the floor between smiles and laughter. Getting naked with Keira is fun in a way I never knew it could be. I'm of two minds: wanting to worship and take my time with her and needing her quickly so I can finally take a real breath again.

It isn't until I'm grabbing a condom from the nightstand and covering myself, staring down at her gorgeous body, that the air shifts between us. All playfulness fades to hot desire.

"Are you sure you wanna do this? We can go back to making out or watch a movie, talk golf. I'll even keep my shirt off."

"Don't you dare try to talk me out of this." She reaches for me. Her fingers wrap around my throbbing dick and she strokes me slowly, hand gliding down until the girl literally has me by the balls. "I know what this is, and I still want you."

Nodding, my pulse races as she brings my dick to her wet entrance. Brown eyes lock on mine as I push inside. Her mouth drops open, and I can see the effort her breathing takes, the flush of her skin and the sheen of sweat from desire.

As I stare down at her, heart in my throat, I can't help but think that she might know what this is, but I'm not sure I do anymore.

TWENTY-FOUR

Keira

I t's still dark out when I wake up in Lincoln's bed alone. I check the time on my phone as I swing my legs over the side and place my feet on the cool, hard wood. I find my panties and new Suns T-shirt Lincoln bought me and pull them on before padding out of the room to find him.

The apartment is set up with the bedrooms on either side of the kitchen and living area. Light seeps out from the spare bedroom and a familiar sound draws me toward it.

Standing in the doorway, I lean against it and watch a shirtless Lincoln swing the golf club. He has quite a setup in here. There is a large floor-to-ceiling net that spans the better part of a wall, and a golf mat that matches the one he sent me.

A desk is pushed to one corner, his laptop, a shoebox, and some other random things spread across the top of it.

His muscles flex and turn as he takes another shot. He's focused and completely oblivious to everything else. I let him hit a half dozen more before I speak.

"Nice swing, Coach."

He hangs in the follow through a second longer before turning to look at me. "Morning." He leans his club against the wall and grabs his water bottle. "Did I wake you?"

"No, I slept like the dead." I walk fully into the room, checking it out. "This is amazing. Is that a simulator?"

He nods, picks up a remote, and an image of a golf course is projected onto the net with amazingly life-like details.

"Oh my God, you never need to leave your apartment."

He shrugs. "I don't use it much anymore, but when I was touring, it was nice to be able to get reps in at home."

"What was it like touring and getting paid to play golf?" I pick up his club. It's heavier than mine, grip still warm from his hands.

"It was hard, time-consuming, and stressful. I gave everything to it, and some days, it gave very little back."

As he talks, I take a few practice swings, stretching out my sore muscles. I get in position and then feel his body press up against me. Even after being in his arms all night, the feel of him this close is exhilarating.

His hands guide me slowly through the swing twice before he says, "But when it gave back, they were some of the happiest times of my life." He kisses my shoulder and his hands fall to my waist. "You'll see."

"How can you be so sure I have what it takes to make it?" I turn so I can face him. No one has ever believed in me the way he does, except maybe my dad, and that's mostly parental love bias.

"I've been watching people swing golf clubs my entire life, and you remind me a lot of myself when I was starting out. Hot headed and passionate with an incredible work ethic. Very few people are willing to do everything that's asked of them." He brushes my hair away from my face. "And you do it and then ask for more."

"Maybe it's just you who I'm good at pleasing."

His mouth pulls up into a smile. "That you are."

"You've never said why you gave it up."

"Not a lot to tell. I quit so I could coach and build my own business."

"Do you miss it?"

"I miss the pursuit, working toward a goal and then moving the bar higher. But, no, I don't miss touring. Getting hurt was a blessing. It made me realize it wasn't being out on the course that made me happy, it was the work I put in to get there. I spent an entire year training so hard to get back and then when it was time." He shrugs. "It didn't sound as appealing as what I'd been doing in the gym. And giving that to other people, the same way my Pop did, it's like I can feel him smiling down at me."

I'm nuzzling into him, enjoying the heat of his skin and the touch of his body, thinking about his words and how amazing he is, when he steps away. "I gotta hop in the shower before a call. I made oatmeal, and there's fruit in the fridge."

The grimace that turns my lips down makes him chuckle. "There are also Pop-Tarts. I couldn't remember if you said you preferred s'mores or brown sugar cinnamon." Now it's his turn to make a face. "I got both."

"Oh my God, you do listen when I talk."

He smacks my ass as he starts to the door. "Hmm? What'd you say?"

I'm still half-dressed and still playing with his toys when Lincoln returns, smelling of soap and dressed in slacks and a green polo. The ends of his black hair are wet, and he runs a hand through it. I'm not sure why I expected him to spend the day lounging in gym shorts and a ratty T-shirt since he's worked every Saturday since I've known him, and I'm disappointed as he takes a seat behind his desk like he's ready to settle in for the day.

"This thing is amazing. If they had these in arcades while I was growing up, I never would have left."

He smirks and opens his laptop.

"What do you have today? Jetting off to an NFL game? Calling up your Stanley Cup winner friends?"

"Lots of emails, checking in with my other clients, phone calls with . . ." He stops and raises his brows. "You really want to hear the details?"

I scrunch my nose and shake my head. "All day?"

He must read the disappointment on my face. "Yeah. I figured you'd need to head back to Valley this morning. You're welcome to stay as long as you want. I can take calls in the living room so you can hit balls in here or you can take the cart to the course."

I fake a smile as he goes back to his laptop. I leave the spare room, grab a Pop-Tart from the kitchen, and wander around his apartment while I eat.

His office is the only room that looks lived in. The living room is sparse—coffee table, couch, and television. He's tidier than I am, which isn't exactly a large feat, and there are no water rings on the coffee table or stacks of papers.

In his bedroom, I close my eyes and inhale his scent. It lingers from the open bathroom. He's made the bed, which earns a chuckle from me. Of course, he makes his bed every morning. I shower and get dressed, pack up the few things I brought, and then head back into his office.

He's on the phone, leaned back in his chair, brows furrowed, and the end of a pen between his teeth. I hang back until he sees me and motions me in.

I grab his club again and take a few swings in front of the simulator without a ball. His eyes track my swing, always dissecting and coaching. I half expect him to pass me a notebook filled with critiques, but he only watches until I give up and go to him.

Facing him, I sit on the edge of the desk. I don't touch him or speak; I just want to be near him.

His free hand palms my thigh, and his long fingers run absently across my skin. He doesn't look at me or acknowledge me in any way but with his touch. And he doesn't freaking skip a beat on the phone. He's all tech talk about maintenance times and backups. Still, it's pretty hot watching him be the boss man.

When he's finally done with his call, he blows out a breath, drops his phone onto the desk, and then puts a hand on either side of my legs. "I thought you were practicing."

"I am. I'm visualizing."

He smirks before his lips twist into a regretful frown. "I have to send feedback to a client and then hop onto another call."

"I know. I don't want to get in the way. I should head back soon anyway."

He tugs me down onto his lap, and his thumb holds my chin steady as he brings his beautiful, full lips to mine. His touch is soft, but his kiss is demanding. No warm up or interlude, just greedy desire to take what he can with the moments he has.

I don't know how we get there so fast, but I'm grinding into him and he's got both hands under my shirt when he mutters a string of curses. I'm breathless when he pulls back. It's only then I realize his phone is ringing.

He answers, sounding totally normal while I can barely form a thought in my lust-addled head. I start to stand to give him privacy, but he holds me in place.

"Sorry about that," he says when he hangs up a minute later.

"Is that a yo-yo?" I point to the open shoebox on his desk. His long fingers splay out over my ribs and he nods as his mouth covers mine.

His phone rings again, and he hums an annoyed sound as he inches back. His expression is apologetic but also resolved like he wants—or maybe needs—to answer it. I stand and step away. He doesn't let go of my hand like I expect him to, and I'm stuck an arms-length away. "Thanks for yesterday. Go be awesome, Coach."

Υ

"Your swings from the driving range looked pretty good. You still aren't releasing your hands at impact, though."

I nod and slowly rotate through my swing, focusing on keeping my right side from overpowering my left. Practice tonight has been beyond frustrating, and the tension, even through the screen, fills my room.

"I'm not seeing it with the foam balls. You have it here, but you gotta translate it to the range and course. There are more distractions out there, more pressure during a tournament." His serious tone and the furrow of his brow make me want to work harder, but I'm already working hard, and I still can't seem to get it.

I blow out a breath of irritation.

"Take a break. You have to give your brain time to piece it all together. We've thrown a lot at it. It's just time and reps."

"Time I don't have," I say and take another swing.

He lets me swing a dozen more times before saying, "Show me some of your fancy club work."

"Why?"

He shrugs and leans back in his chair. "I think it's cool. Come on, show off for me."

I think for a moment before I go into one.

Tap. Tap. Tap.

I fall into the rhythm easily and allow my breaths to even out as everything else falls away.

Tap. Tap. Tap.

On the last bounce, I push the ball higher into the air and then catch it, pause with it on the face of the club, and turn a quick circle, arm straight. I end with bouncing it a few more times on the clubface and then catching it behind my back.

I do a mock curtsy at the end, a little annoyed but not exactly at him. I can do tricks all day, but it won't fix my swing issues.

"That was awesome." The proud smile on his lips erases some of my frustration. "Wanna see one of mine?"

When I nod, he grabs the yo-yo that was on his desk last weekend. He stands and adjusts the screen so I can see him. With a wink in my direction, he loops his finger through the slipknot and begins. He's laser focused as he gets into it like he's remembering the feel.

After a few times up and down, he looks at me. "This one is called the sleeper." He tosses the yo-yo to the ground and keeps it there, allowing it to spin for several long seconds before snapping it back up to his hand.

"Walk the dog." He throws it back down and somehow moves it along the floor. "Around the corner. And . . . take the elevator." He finishes with some fancy handwork and a big, boyish grin.

"Wow. That is the nerdiest thing I've ever seen." Also, the hottest. Who knew yo-yoing was hot?

"Don't pretend you aren't impressed."

I fake a yawn and look away from the screen. "Eh."

When I glance back, he's pulling his shirt over his head.

I sit forward, and he grins. "More interested now, huh?"

"Show them to me again."

He does, and this time, at the end of them, he adds another, something he calls man on the flying trapeze.

"Why do you know all these?"

"My pop taught me. He kept it in his truck, and when I'd go with him to the golf course, he'd teach me a trick and then tell me to master it before I did anything else. Mostly, I think he was just trying to get me out of his hair for a while. A bucket of balls only kept me occupied for so long, and he spent four or five hours at a time with clients." He stops and looks at the yo-yo in his hand. "I'd actually forgotten about this thing until I found it in some of his stuff."

"Well, I never thought I'd say this about yo-yoing, but that was hot. Take your pants off and do it again."

He shakes his head, and a deep chuckle makes my insides turn to mush. Lincoln happy and laughing makes everything seem better. Well, almost everything.

He must sense my mood shifting back because his voice changes. "Get some sleep, Keira. You worked hard today. Tomorrow will be better."

TWENTY-FIVE

Keira

I t rains on and off all week. Practices are inside, and by Thursday, we're all sick of being cooped up inside the small, indoor practice room and ready to get outside and take some real swings outside.

Coach dismisses us, telling us to get over to the driving range either tonight or early in the morning. Teams will begin showing up tomorrow afternoon for our weekend tournament.

"Are you going over?" Abby asks at the same time Coach says my name.

"Not sure. Go ahead. I'll text you when I'm done."

Coach talks to Brittany, and I approach slowly. He and I have been getting along just fine since he mostly ignores me, sometimes muttering under his breath when I do things to annoy him, but I've stopped letting him rile me. He isn't worth it, and I don't need him now that I have Lincoln.

"You wanted to see me?" I ask when I reach him.

He nods, and Brittany opens her stance to include me instead of leaving. My gut twists with the look of apprehension on her face.

She drops her eyes to the ground as Coach speaks. "Brittany's been cleared to play at the tournament this weekend."

"But—" I glance between them. "How?"

"My wrist is better." She lifts her arm and smiles.

"But she hasn't practiced in weeks. I'm a better choice to play this weekend." I look to Brittany with what I hope is an apologetic smile. "I'm sorry, but it's true."

"You don't get to make the decision." Coach Potter yanks at his belt, hitching it higher on his hip. "I make the call, and I'm including Brittany in the lineup. I'm sorry, Keira. You're just not consistent enough in your tournament play."

I ball my fists in irritation. I don't know if I'm angrier with him or myself. I text Abby that I'm not going to the driving range, and I do something I haven't done in a long time, I crawl into bed before dark.

Lincoln texts around our usual time, but I tell him I'm exhausted and going to sleep early and turn off my phone. I need to tell him that I'm not playing this weekend so he doesn't bother trying to make it, but I don't want his, or anyone else's, pity or empty words of encouragement. I want to wallow.

I'm surprised when Abby shows up at our dorm, but one look at her face tells me it's solely for my benefit.

"You heard?"

She nods. "Brittany was over at the guys' house. Why didn't you tell me?"

"I just wanted to be alone."

She picks up an empty Pop-Tart wrapper and raises a brow.

"No judgment. I'm eating my feelings."

"Well, stop because you're playing this weekend." Abby sits on the edge of my bed.

"No, I'm not. Coach made it very clear that I was not in the lineup."

"That was before I quit."

She smiles at my reaction—jaw dropped and eyes wide. "What? Why?"

"I've been thinking about it for a while." She shrugs.

"But you're playing so well. Don't quit just because of me. You've earned that spot."

"I know I did. To be honest, standing up for you is only part of the reason I did it. Golf isn't fun anymore. It's become just part of my routine. I spend practices wishing I were doing just about anything else. Seeing how much you love it, I don't know, it made me realize how much I don't. I want to enjoy my last year of college without running to practice every afternoon or travelling to tournaments I don't want to play in."

"You could see the season out. Quit before fall semester."

"I could, but it felt much sweeter to do it this way."

"I don't know what to say."

"Say that you'll spend tonight hanging out with me, watching cheesy romantic comedies, eating Pop-Tarts or whatever other junk food you have stashed, and tomorrow morning, you'll get up and be ready to kick some ass in that tournament. Unicorn-scrunchie-wearing badass, remember?"

I laugh and glance down at my wrist. "Deal."

On Friday, the sun finally comes out from behind the clouds, drying out the course as teams start to arrive. Lincoln calls as I'm leaving my dorm to head over to the course.

"Hey," I answer with the phone between my shoulder and ear.

"Did I wake you?"

"No, I'm on my way out now. I want to get some extra swings in this morning."

"Don't tire yourself out before it starts," he warns. "Go through your usual routine, and if you still feel like you need more time, do some visualization and drills without the club."

"Okay."

He chuckles. "I'm serious. There's such a thing as being over prepared, and it usually goes hand in hand with too little rest. Remember, it's supposed to be fun."

"It'll be fun when I'm on the leaderboard."

We continue to talk as I drive over, and when I pull into a parking spot, I linger in my car because I'm not ready to say bye to Lincoln yet. Even though he's always miles away, it feels weird knowing he's boarding a plane and won't be within driving distance.

"When do you fly to Los Angeles?"

"This afternoon. I land around five, but text me when you're done with the practice round and let me know how hard you kicked ass today, all right?"

"Yeah, okay." I inhale a deep breath and let it out. "Will you be back tomorrow or Sunday?"

"I'm not sure yet what Kenton and my parents have planned for me this weekend. I'll do my best. Listen, I gotta go, my IT guy is calling. Give 'em hell today."

The first eighteen holes are a blur. I'm in a zone. A mixture of determination and anger. I only get a short break before I'm teeing off for my second round.

Coach Potter waits at the first par three, but his words don't even register. Part of not letting him negatively impact me anymore means I can't let him positively impact me either. So, I tune him out and focus on everything Lincoln's been telling me for weeks.

On the tenth hole, I hit a beautiful stinger that gets a lot of cheers. The girl I'm paired with steps up to take her turn, obviously shaken and in her head. I'm intimidating, who knew?

My heart beats wildly, and every step closer to the final hole feels a little more like I'm walking on a cloud. As I walk to eighteen, the crowd follows alongside me, and it sinks in. I'm leading. It's early, there are still a few groups to finish today and I have to get through tomorrow, but I'm freaking on top. By *five*.

A pang of something hits me. Lincoln. Lincoln knew. I glance over at the sidelines, hoping to see his dark head among the spectators. It's silly. I know he isn't here, but I wish he were anyway.

Abby catches my eye and waves. Her other hand is linked with Smith's, and they are wearing matching smiles that tell me they're proud of me. Keith and the rest of the guys are here too. I wait for it to fill me with the same burst of pride I get when Lincoln smiles at me, but it doesn't come.

It isn't just because of how much I respect him; though, that certainly helps, it's because I know he gets it. This hunger inside me to succeed. He's been in my shoes, and he knows what this feels like and what it's going to take to make it.

With my final putt on eighteen, I stand, ball in hand, and wave. Coach Potter grins like he's suddenly a proud and involved member of my success. I walk right past him and hug Abby hard. If it weren't for her, I wouldn't have this moment. We may not want the same things, but she's here and she believes in me.

My dad didn't want to try to crutch his way through so it's a little bittersweet playing in Valley without him here, but I know he'll be proud too.

"Oh my God, that was amazing." Abby refuses to let me go, squeezing me so hard I have to hold my breath.

"All right, babe, let her go, she's gonna pass out from lack of oxygen," Smith says.

"Sorry." She steps back. "I'm so proud of you."

"Thank you." I'm grinning so widely that my cheeks hurt.

"Congrats," Keith says and offers his fist for me to bump. The rest of the guys offer their similar praise.

"Thanks, guys."

Abby links her arm through mine. "Celebratory dinner, or are you planning to go back to the room to work with your hottie swing coach all night?"

"Hottie?" Smith questions with enough jealousy in his tone that we all laugh.

"We'll celebrate tomorrow *if* I win," I say, nerves already ramping back up. "I wanna swing by my dad's and tell him all about it. I'm sure he's going crazy not being here."

Abby hugs me one last time, and I say bye to the guys and thank them all for coming. I text Lincoln when I get to my car, but by the time I get a pizza and take it to dad's house, he still hasn't responded.

"Nice job, sweet pea." Dad hugs me in the doorway with one arm, the other holding on to his cane. He's getting around better, but I can tell by the way he hobbles that his knee still bugs him.

I babble on through an entire pizza, excitedly telling him every detail. He listens intently, smiling proudly.

"Did you call your mom? She'll be dying to hear all about it too."

"No, not yet. I came straight here. I haven't even showered yet."

"I thought I smelled something." He winks. "Go, call her, and then get some rest. Tomorrow is a big day."

"Thanks for reminding me. No pressure, right?"

He chuckles softly as I kiss him on the cheek. "Good luck tomorrow, kiddo, not that you need it."

TWENTY-SIX

Lincoln

"It was amazing. I was in a zone like I've never been before. I hope I didn't use all my awesomeness today."

I smile as I lie back on the bed in Kenton's spare room while Keira tells me about her day. She holds the phone out in front of her face, free hand waving wildly and smile so big it's contagious. Getting to listen as she relives it is almost as good as it would have been to be there. Almost.

"Did your dad go?"

"No." Her smile falls only slightly. "He still isn't getting around that well, but I went by and told him about it after."

She's quiet for a second and then goes back to telling me about the tournament. "Oh, and you should have heard Coach this afternoon. One of the local news stations was there, and Potter walked up in the middle of my interview like he was my number-one fan. He told them, and I quote, 'Keira's made a lot of really solid improvements this season, and our hard work is finally paying off.' *Our* hard work, like he had any part of it."

"Potter's a prick. He's going to take every opportunity he can to make it about him. You did this. Not him."

"*We* did this. You and me."

"No. This was all you. No one made you get up day after day and put in the work. I've coached a lot of people, especially when I was just starting out. They'd tell me how bad they wanted it, they'd fork over thousands of dollars for lessons, but when push came to shove, they wouldn't put in the work. So, no, *we* didn't do this. It was all you. Own it. Enjoy it."

She flops onto her bed, still holding the phone out so I can see her face. "Tell me about your day."

"Spent it with my parents, got to watch Kenton play, and then he had a few people over after the game."

"Did his team win?"

"Yep, it was a good day for both of you."

She settles back against her headboard. "What are your parents like?"

"They're cool. Dad was a high school history teacher and golf coach, and my mother worked in advertising. They retired a couple of years ago and primarily live in upstate New York. That's where my mother's from originally. I have a bunch of aunts and uncles out there."

"Do you see them often?"

"They come back to Scottsdale every few months, and Kenton and I go up there for Christmas every year. It's cold as fuck." She covers a yawn as I talk. "I should let you get some sleep."

"Fat chance of me sleeping tonight." She yawns again. "Are you coming back early tomorrow?"

"No. Kenton has another game tomorrow, so we're staying until just after it. I should be back to Arizona about the time you're finishing the tournament. I'm sorry I'm gonna miss you kicking ass."

"I understand." The tone of her voice says that may not be entirely true.

"All right, baby, get some sleep."

"Uh-uh. I wanna keep talking to you."

"Close your eyes."

Her brown, tired eyes widen in defiance.

"Just do it."

She gets up from the bed and walks across her room. A second later, it darkens. "Fine, but if I fall asleep, promise me that you'll hang up immediately. I don't want you watching me drool or snore." She makes a horrified face as she climbs back into bed and lies down, but then her long lashes flutter closed and fan out against her fair skin.

I turn on the television in my room to the sports channel and turn off the lamp on the nightstand.

"Are you going to tell me a bedtime story?"

I chuckle quietly. "Will it help you fall asleep?"

"Maybe." She turns onto her side and opens her eyes briefly to position the phone on the bed next to her. The angle has the top of her head cut off but gives me an eyeful of the cleavage popping out of her tank top—a darkened eyeful, but still an eyeful. "Tell me about your first pro tournament."

"You wanna talk golf right now?" I swear this girl never gets sick of the topic. She's more hardcore than I am.

"Well, I'm too tired for phone sex, and golf is the next best thing." Eyes still closed, her mouth tips into a sleepy smile.

Just the mention of sex makes my dick twitch, pleading with me to make her reconsider, sleep be damned. Ignoring the semi, I adjust myself with one hand and think back to my pro debut. "It was in Milwaukee. I'm sure I was scared shitless, but the only thing I can remember is how excited I was to be in the same place as guys I'd looked up to for so long—some my entire life."

"You don't look nervous in the videos and pictures online."

Her having watched the footage makes me smile, but I'm not really surprised. I looked her up the same way.

"I don't know. Maybe I was too dumb to be nervous. I don't really think it struck me how big of a deal it was until after. It took years of effort to get to that point, and once I was there, all I could think about was proving myself. That need and desire to get to the next level never really goes away. The goalpost moves every time, and you have to learn to celebrate the small wins. Like today for you. No matter what happens tomorrow, today you proved to yourself that you can do it."

"I really want to win tomorrow."

"I know." I close my eyes too. "Did you see that putt where I almost choked on the tap in?" I ask, still reminiscing about my debut tournament.

"*Mm-hmm.*" Her response comes on a hum.

"God, my heart was in my throat. It took three holes to calm down."

"I couldn't tell."

"Well, I knew I couldn't blow up and make a scene on my first day."

"I also saw the tournament where you broke your driver over your knee."

I groan. "Ah, man, I was really hoping you'd never know about that one."

"It's probably my favorite of all the videos I've watched of you."

"Really? Why? It's one of my worst rounds of golf ever."

"Because I can see the passion on your face. People who aren't dropping f-bombs or thinking of breaking their club while playing a round of golf are either having an incredible day or don't care enough. That video shows how much you care. You were frustrated and you let it show, but then you pulled it together and had an incredible round the next day."

"I had to after that."

"Golf is a lot like love, I think. If it isn't making you a little nuts, is it even real? Passion—good or bad, is how you can gauge what's really important to people."

We both fall silent, and I contemplate her words. It isn't an uncomfortable silence since the voices of the television provide white noise so we aren't listening to each other breathe. Still, doing shit like this with anyone but Keira would be weird, but with her, everything feels normal.

I'm just about to drift off when I can sense she's fallen asleep. I open my eyes to verify. There's an ache in my chest as I stare at her parted lips and the soft rise and fall of her chest as she breathes. After a few long moments, I move to end the call. "'Night, baby."

The last update I got on the Valley tournament was an hour ago, and Keira had a two-stroke lead with four holes left.

Pacing back and forth at my flight gate, I'm refreshing the website for the millionth time for final scores when my boarding group is called. I head down the jet bridge with my overnight bag, phone still in hand. After I take my seat, I continue hitting refresh.

"I'm just there." A man stands in the aisle and points to the empty window seat beside me. I stand, annoyed for the interference of hitting refresh, no matter how irrational it is, and let him pass.

The boarding process takes forever and every second delay in getting back to Arizona makes me more restless. I know I'm too late to make the tournament but I need to be back in the same state where I can comfort her, if needed.

I pray to God she won today, but if she didn't, she's going to need to talk it out. After the high of yesterday, a loss today would be brutal.

As the plane taxies down the runway, the flight attendant starts in on the in-flight safety procedures. I tune her out, hit refresh again, and freeze when the final tournament results load on my screen.

"She won," I whisper. I stare at her name at the top of the final leaderboard. Pride fills my whole body. I look over to the guy next to me and repeat it. "She won."

He smiles politely, clearly having no idea what I'm talking about. I show him my phone, and he humors me with a quick glance. "Keira, I mean my client won a golf tournament."

"Congratulations."

"Thanks." I tip my head back against the seat and shake it from side to side in astonishment. She did it. She freaking won.

There's a strange feeling as I sit there, heading up into the sky and a few hundred miles away from Keira. I'm so damn proud of her. Happiness tinged with regret for not being there to see the look on her face when she realized she'd done it. Not being the person she shared all of it with.

My life, my job, has always meant more to me than single moments like this. Even big moments. Hell, aside from the actual day my ex and I exchanged vows, I spent most of the days surrounding my wedding wondering why there had to be so many small celebrations involved. An engagement party, a bachelor party, dinner with the two families, a bridal shower, a rehearsal dinner, and on and on.

My job was always a point of contention with Lacey. The honest truth is that I worked harder at golf and then the business than I did at being a good husband. And while I have my regrets, I think I always knew that she and I would never work.

Selfish men don't get a happily ever after. They might get a significant other who deals with always being second priority, but that knowledge comes at a price. Lacey wasn't willing to pay it, not that I blame her, and I'm not willing to put anyone through that again. No one deserves that. Not Lacey and certainly not Keira.

I smile at the thought of Keira letting anyone put her second to anything. And then there's that pang in my chest again because, for the first time, I realize it isn't going to be me who walks away from Keira when we're done working together, it'll be her walking away from me. Because she deserves better, and she knows it.

TWENTY-SEVEN

Keira

C oming down off the high of my win today, I sit on my bed eating frosted animal crackers and watching Abby pack an overnight bag. Nothing like a post-celebration with a little sugar and bed crumbs.

"I'm heading to Smith's," she says, zipping her backpack and slinging it over one shoulder.

"Thanks for hanging out tonight."

After the tournament, she and the guys took me to The Hideout to celebrate. I'd been too amped up to eat then, but now I'm starving. I'm also a little tipsy, which probably isn't helping.

"Are you kidding me? There is no way I would have missed tonight. I'm so freaking proud of you."

"Thank you."

She points to the pile of clothes between our beds. "Can that disappear before I return?"

"I can't do laundry when I'm celebrating."

She laughs. "Well, then, at least move it to the other side where I don't see it. Out of sight, out of mind."

"Okay, Mom." I smirk.

She waves and heads out, shutting the door behind her. Silence floods the room and washes away the adrenaline from today.

I unlock my phone and open my texts. I haven't heard from Lincoln since the good luck message he sent this morning, and I'm desperately trying not to be upset that he hasn't checked in yet. It isn't like I expected him to be glued to his phone waiting for updates, but I thought he'd be more anxious to hear how it went. Even my mom has called to say congratulations.

I flip through Netflix for something to watch, but I'm too antsy or tired or some weird combination of both, so I give up and get out of bed to grab my wedge and a ball. The door to my dorm opens before I reach my bag, and I look up, pleasantly surprised to see Abby again.

"Hey, you're back. Thank God, I just realized, I have no idea what to do when I'm not—"

Lincoln steps in behind her, silencing me with his presence.

"Look who I found," Abby says around a grin. While Lincoln isn't looking in her direction, she mouths *oh my God* and fans her face.

I laugh, and Lincoln turns to see what's so funny.

Abby uses the hand she was fanning herself with to wave. "See you two later."

Once she's gone, he walks toward me slowly, offering a quiet, "Hey."

"What are you doing here?"

"I wanted to surprise you."

"Well, you succeeded."

I close the space between us with two skips and throw my arms around his neck. "I can't believe it. Seriously, not complaining, but why are you here? I thought you'd call."

He waits until I pull back. His hands frame my face, and the pad of his right thumb runs along my cheek. "You won today."

Three simple words that make pride and happiness swell inside me. "I did."

"So damn proud of you." His lips meet mine in a caress, and when he speaks again, his words drift to me softly. "I'm sorry I missed it."

"You're here now."

I make the move this time, smashing my lips against his. It feels better than any victory. Electricity courses through me as his hands fall to my hips and then swoop under my ass to pick me up. My legs wrap around his waist as my fingers sink into the dark hair at the nape of his neck.

Lincoln's lips pull into a smile against my mouth before he says, "Let me guess, yours is the unmade bed?"

"I was busy today. Hello, Valley Invitational tournament winner."

I kiss him again, so he doesn't look around at the rest of the mess.

He lays me on the bed and stands beside it staring down at me. "You're beautiful." He tosses a shirt off the foot of the bed and then a tube of mascara follows. "Messy as hell, but beautiful."

His sexy smirk stays in place until I sit up and take my shirt off. I toss it in the same direction as the others. That moves him to action. With one hand at the nape of my neck, he guides me back and then settles on top of me.

My hands go to the hem of his shirt and tug. We break apart only long enough to remove it and then he's back at my lips, tasting and teasing.

I yank at his thick, dark hair as his expert mouth explores mine and then lowers to my chest. He palms one breast and nips at the other as I arch into his touch.

He takes his time even as I trail my hands down and try to cop a feel by squeezing my hands inside his pants.

"Pants. Off," I finally mutter.

"I'm celebrating up here." His tongue circles my nipple and then his teeth clamp down on it.

"Can you celebrate with your penis inside me?"

He chuckles but doesn't relent. My orgasm is on a hair trigger when he finally kisses down my stomach and pushes my shorts and panties down past my hips. Every inch of my stomach gets kissed or licked or nipped before he finally removes my clothes completely and his lips descend to my pussy. He kisses it, and the small amount of friction pulls a long moan from me.

He settles between my legs and looks up at me. His dark eyes shine with mischief and my heart thumps wildly.

Finally, he pushes my legs apart wider and licks me. One long swipe of his tongue that makes me feel drunk and desperate.

"Lincoln," I pant as he presses a thumb to my clit and moves it in slow circles as he tastes me.

My body quakes, and the noises that pour out of me are porn-star worthy. He's porn-star worthy. I want him to stop and to never stop. The orgasm that builds is so powerful I'm sure it'll break me into a million pieces.

Stars dance behind my eyelids while he moans as if my pleasure is getting him off as much as it is me. My eyes fly open as I come. Our stares collide, and my heart squeezes as so many things I can't or won't say pass between us.

As I'm panting and trying to get my world to stop spinning, he undresses and grabs a condom. His fingertips slide across my cheek and tuck my hair behind my ear before he tears the foil opens and sheaths himself. He positions himself at my sensitive core and slowly eases inside.

The walls of my pussy squeeze him, and he hisses a breath as he buries himself completely. The rhythm is slower than the last time, and something about it makes my body soar faster.

This unhurried pace and the look in his eyes as he stares down at me seems to blur the lines we've drawn and all the rules we've set. Not that we set them exactly. He told me he couldn't be a boyfriend, and I accepted that. But tonight, I feel as if he's giving me more of himself, and I cling to it, taking it, savoring it, hoping for more.

I close my eyes, letting his touch be the sensation that overpowers all others.

"Look at me," he says, stilling until I comply. His lips hover over mine as he whispers, "Congratulations, baby."

He takes my mouth in a bruising kiss and pumps into me faster. Raking my hands along his back and lifting my hips to meet each thrust, I use my body instead of words to thank him for being here, for seeing something in me that no one else has, and for breaking the rules—whether he realizes he's breaking them or not.

ᵧ

Lincoln puts on his boxers and jeans while I lie naked in bed watching him. I grab his hand. "Stay."

I try to fight the yawn, but it's been a very long day and my body is like putty. "I missed you. Don't go."

"I don't think there's room in that bed for two of us." He turns his shirt right side out and puts it on before sitting on the edge of the bed. "I don't want to, but I have to get up early for work."

"You can work here." I motion to my desk, which is currently covered by books and clothes. Luckily, he doesn't actually look at the place I'm suggesting as his workspace.

"You brought your laptop, right?" I ask, knowing he never goes any-where without it.

I sit up and wrap my arms around him and he lets me wrestle him flat on his back while he wears an amused grin at my insistence. Lying on top of him, I pull the comforter around us. I don't expect him to give in, but when I wake up a few hours later, I'm still wrapped tightly in his arms.

TWENTY-EIGHT

Lincoln

"I'm not wearing that."

Keira looks from the button in her outstretched palm to me and back again. "Why not? Everyone else is wearing them."

When I still don't make a move to take it, she rolls her eyes and extends the poster board in her other hand to me. "Then you're holding this."

The Valley U hockey team takes the ice and the crowd stands and cheers. It's the last home game of the season—family night.

"It's a bummer Heath's family couldn't make it." She pins the button with Heath's face on it to her shirt and an irrational flash of jealousy surges through me.

"I don't like it."

"They probably don't either, but at least you're here. You're a pretty good guy, Lincoln Reeves."

"I meant I don't like other dudes touching your boobs." I cover the button with my fingers, so Heath's cocky smirk isn't staring at me and also because it's placed in just the right spot for me to be able to cop a feel.

She bats my hand away. "Look, there he is. Hold up the sign."

I groan but lift the "Feel the PAYNE" sign Keira made and insisted we bring. If Heath sees me holding this, he'll never let me live it down.

I'm only slightly relieved when I'm able to sit and put the sign at my feet. We're touching shoulder to knee in this packed arena, reminding me I haven't had sex in a week. Before Keira, I went . . . well, way too damn long without. But now, even a day of not being inside her, is a day too many.

For the past month, we've alternated driving back and forth between Valley and Scottsdale. Sex, golf, repeat. Life is great.

"He's really good," she says, leaning in so I can hear her and putting more of her soft curves against me.

"*Mm-hmm*." I slide my hand up her thigh an inch or two.

"Is he really good enough to go pro? He told me he was, but I don't really know anything about hockey."

Another inch. "Sure."

"Hockey players are hot, don't you agree?"

"Yes."

"So, what position does Heath play? Quarterback? Outfielder? Point guard?"

"Yeah." Another inch.

"Lincoln!" She grabs my fingers and twists.

"Ouch. Shit."

"You aren't even listening to me."

"Yeah, I was. Heath's good, yada yada."

"I mixed in terminology for three different sports, but you didn't even notice."

"I noticed. It wasn't important."

Not the right thing to say when she still has my hand in a death grip.

"Ow. Ow." I pull free. "What I meant was that it wasn't as important as being here with you."

"Awww." Her face softens and then she rolls her eyes.

"I mean it." I duck my head to press my mouth to hers as I drop my hand back to her upper thigh. "I missed the hell out of you. Touching you, kissing you . . ."

She hums a little needy sound. "You're vibrating."

"Damn right I am."

Her lips curve into a smile. "I meant your pocket."

She pulls away, taking all her soft, warm awesomeness with her, and stands with the rest of the crowd, which is now screaming, waiting for the puck drop.

My phone keeps vibrating, and I take it out to read through my messages. Nathan thanked me for being at the game and asked me to get a couple shots of Heath playing, Kenton sent a picture of the new ninety-eight-inch television he bought for his place, a couple work-related messages, and one from Lacey.

I wait to open hers last, already knowing what it will say. She's politely reminded me twice about the storage unit, but I can't ever seem to find the time to meet up. And okay, fine, I might be avoiding it.

I'm pocketing my phone as Keira takes her seat. Her expression morphs from happy to concern when she sees my scowl.

"Everything okay?"

"Yeah, just something I need to take care of tomorrow."

"Ominous."

"I have some stuff in storage I need to get."

"That's why your apartment is so bare. Need any help?" she asks, facing forward and following the action on the ice.

"No thanks, I've seen your hobo style. It isn't for me."

I get a playful glare before she's back to watching Heath. "Help cleaning out the storage unit, smartass."

"I thought you were going with your dad to an appointment tomorrow."

"I am, but I could come up after."

"How about I clean it out while you're with your dad so when you get to my place, we can just focus on getting naked?"

Finally, I get her full attention, and she crowds my space. Her eyes go to my lips—girl really likes my lips. She might have more restraint than I do, but I know she feels it too. This crazy chemistry and insatiable sexual desire between us.

Sex with Keira is awesome, obviously, but I've had awesome sex before and not been this . . . addicted. I don't think I'll ever get enough.

"Deal," she says, pressing her chest (and Heath's face) into mine.

I pull back suddenly. "Wait, did you say hockey players are hot?"

ϒ

The next day, I pull up outside of the storage unit and kill the engine. Lacey waves from the open doorway, an apprehensive look on her face.

"Hey," I say as I approach her. "Good to see you."

"Yeah, you too."

Well, this is as awkward as I imagined. Seeing Lacey and the hurt I caused her never gets easier. The girl who used to look at me as if I hung the moon, can now barely stand to look at me.

Maybe we were always doomed to fail. We married young without really talking about what kind of life we wanted together. But regardless of the reasons, I feel a deep sense of responsibility for the way it all ended.

"I'm sorry it took me so long to get out here."

"It's fine."

"All right. Should we get started?" I'm starting to sweat under my shirt.

"I already grabbed my things." She nods to her car and the packed back seat and then hands me the keys to our unit. "It's all yours. Just turn those in at the front desk when you're done. If no one is there, they have a drop box."

"Oh, okay. Thanks. Do you need any help unloading? I could follow you."

"No thank you. I've got it," she says and nods curtly.

The thing about divorce is you're either fighting or being too polite to one another. I'm not an asshole that wants to yell and scream, but her anger was easier to live with.

She takes a step toward her car and I call after her, "Lace."

She turns slowly, shoulders tensing as her guard goes up. "Yeah?"

"I really am sorry. For not taking care of this sooner and for . . . everything really."

She stares at me for a moment as if she's gauging my sincerity.

"I know that I've apologized before, and I don't know if you believed it then or if you'll believe it now, but not a day has gone by that I haven't been sorry for how things ended. You deserved so much more. I hope you find it."

"Thank you." A tight smile lifts her lips. Maybe she believes me, maybe she doesn't. Maybe the wound is too deep for my apology to make a difference either way. I don't think I'll ever know the answer, and I guess that's my punishment. "See you around, Lincoln."

I force myself to watch her go, waving as she pulls out of sight, and then with a deep breath, I turn toward the storage unit that holds my previous life. One side is empty where Lacey already grabbed her things, and the other contains boxes and colorful tubs, a few pieces of small furniture.

I load it all into my SUV, each item adding weight to the light feeling I walked in here with.

Since Keira came into my life, I've allowed myself small, indulgent thoughts. Not about the future exactly, but glimpses of what it might have been like with her instead.

But here, all around me, are the reminders that I can't change the past or escape the baggage I carry from it. The best I can do is shove it, like these boxes, from one dark corner to another so it doesn't touch what Keira and I have.

TWENTY-NINE

Keira

I head up to Lincoln's the weekend before the sectional qualifier to play a round on the course and attempt to settle my nerves. He answers the door with his phone glued to his ear.

"I hate Friday night traffic," I mumble.

Smiling as he talks to the person on the phone, he drops a quick kiss on my lips and then takes my bag from me and disappears toward his bedroom with it. He returns a second later, heading across the apartment to his office, talking on the phone the entire time.

I follow along behind him. Exhaustion from the long hours I've put in over the past few weeks mixed with excited anticipation makes me too frazzled to do anything else.

Lincoln takes a seat, and I climb onto his lap and wrap myself around him, hugging him tightly and breathing in his clean, familiar scent. We've seen each other almost every weekend over the past two months, and each time I miss him more between visits.

As he speaks, his chest vibrates under me. He scoots his chair closer to the desk, puts his phone on speaker, and sets it next to the keyboard. His arms circle around my waist so he can reach his keyboard behind me. I should probably move and let him work, but he doesn't ask, so I melt into him.

The man on the phone gives Lincoln numbers—stats on total registered members for the website broken down by area of interest. It hits me in a way that it hasn't before, how massive his company is and how much of a sacrifice he made when he agreed to coach me.

I lift my head and kiss his neck. Goose bumps pebble under my lips, and a thrill runs through me. Lincoln talks on, seemingly unaffected, but those little raised dots give him away.

I kiss my way up to his jaw, and he dips his head to take my lips. I smile into him as our mouths lazily linger and play.

The guy on the phone asks Lincoln a question, and he raises his head to respond. I nuzzle into him again, fully prepared to continue my seduction as soon as he's off the phone, but I must fall asleep because, the next thing I know, I'm being carried through the dark apartment to his room.

"What time is it?" My voice is raspy.

"After one in the morning."

"You let me sleep on you that long?"

He chuckles. "I was on the phone for most of it, but yeah. I could get used to working with an adorable sleeping woman on my lap, even if it makes simple things like using a keyboard a challenge. I love a good challenge." He kisses my forehead. "I'll be back in a bit. I just need to reply to a few emails."

Sleep drags me back under before I can protest, and when I wake again, he's wrapped around me and his breathing is a deep, even rhythm that lulls me back to unconsciousness.

The next morning, Lincoln wakes me holding a banana and a glass of water. He places them on the bedside table. "Rise and shine, gorgeous."

"Come back to bed." I reach out and take his hand and try to tug him down beside me. He doesn't budge.

"Can't. I need to stop by Gram's before we head to the course."

"Everything okay?"

"Yeah, she's just being stubborn and threatening to climb a ladder and pull down her boxes of Easter decorations on her own." He uses my hand to pull me upright. "It won't take long. Hopefully."

Truth be told, I don't mind at all. I adore his grandmother.

We've barely walked in the door when Milly pulls me against her soft, pillowy chest. "Keira, it's so good to see you again, dear." She smells of flowers and hairspray, and her embrace is so warm and loving that I instantly feel at ease around her.

She shows Lincoln and me to the garage and points to the boxes that contain Easter and spring decorations and then announces her plan to make us breakfast.

"We already ate, Gram."

She waves him off and disappears inside.

"That woman." Lincoln shakes his head. He grabs a ladder and moves boxes from the shelving along one side of the garage.

"She's amazing."

"I think she's a fan of yours as well."

"I think she'd be a fan of any woman you brought around."

"*Humph.*"

"Still no more blind dates?"

"Not yet." He hands me a box labeled "Spring Wreaths."

I take it inside to the living room and return to the garage to find he's pulled four more boxes with varying season-related labels: Easter Bunnies. Easter Plates. Spring Outdoor Decorations. Easter Baskets.

We take them all inside to the living room and then Gram calls us into the kitchen, filling our plates with eggs, turkey bacon, and toast before setting a bowl of fruit between us.

"Thank you."

She smiles lovingly between us. "Lincoln tells me you're doing the sectional qualifier."

"I am." I swallow a bite of eggs, but the reminder of the qualifier has my food settling like a brick in my stomach.

Lincoln lightly nudges my shoe with his under the table. "She's gonna do great."

His confidence in me helps a little, and I take a few more forkfuls of egg and a nibble of toast before I politely push it away. "That was delicious, but my stomach is too tied up in knots for me to eat another bite. I'm sorry."

Lincoln's grandmother doesn't miss a beat. She takes the plate in one hand and runs her free hand from the top of my head down my hair. "If Lincoln says you're ready, then you are. He isn't much of a bullshitter."

I laugh at her cursing, and she grins, pleased that she lightened my mood a bit.

Before we leave, Gram clutches me to her chest again and then reaches for Lincoln

"Thank you." She cups his face and smiles at me. "Take care of that one and make her eat something later."

One side of his mouth lifts before he drops a kiss to her cheek. "Will do, Gram."

"Good luck." Her arms grip me firmly with a freakish strength despite her age.

"Thank you."

Lincoln and I drive to the course in silence. I'm mulling over something he said earlier in an attempt to avoid thinking about golf.

"Does Gram know we're . . ." I wave between us.

He smirks. "Does she know we're what?"

"Don't make me say it."

He chuckles and then shrugs. "Maybe. She hasn't said anything, and I'm not in the habit of talking to my grandmother about my sex life."

We pull into the parking lot, and he kills the engine. He jumps out, and I'm slow to follow, while I try to sort through the emotions swirling around me. I can't help being disappointed even if it's unjustified. I haven't told my family about him, so why am I annoyed he hasn't mentioned it to his grandmother?

I'm still working through my feelings as we grab a large bucket of balls from the pro shop and head over to the driving range. Lincoln sets up his camera to capture my swing, and I stretch.

"Do you think she'll set you up on more blind dates eventually? It's been what, two months since the last one?"

"The one you crashed?" He smirks. "Probably. I'm sure there's someone at the country club she hasn't hit up for single daughters or granddaughters yet." He's all set up and faces me. "Ready?"

"Why don't you just tell her we're . . ." I tread carefully. I know he doesn't want anything serious, but whatever we are is more than fuck buddies. "Dating or hanging out or whatever you want to call it."

He doesn't respond at first, and I get my driver and tee up the first ball.

"Trust me, you don't want her knowing. She'd probably start picking out names for her great grandchildren."

When I'm silent for too long, he adds. "I'm not ready for that."

"I know, and I'm not asking for that, but we're *something*. I don't understand why you wouldn't say something to get her off your back."

"Is this about me seeing other people? Because I'm not sleeping with anyone else."

"No, it isn't that."

He lowers his voice and walks closer. "Then what is it?"

I shrug one shoulder. "Things are good between us, or at least they are for me. We're spending lots of time together, and I really like you. I guess I'm wondering what happens when we're done working together?"

He rakes a hand through his hair and doesn't quite meet my gaze. "I'm not sure."

The pit in my stomach grows.

"Come on," he says, "let's get you through the qualifier and then you can start thinking about the day you're gonna be free of me." He says it teasingly, but I'm hurt that he is so easy to dismiss whatever is going on between us.

I nod my agreement, and we get started. It's painful working together the rest of the morning. I go through the motions while Lincoln stands back, seemingly unaffected. Though I know he can tell the difference in me. I'm not exactly subtle about my dark mood.

"Nice. That looks really good," he says after my first drive off the back nine. Smiling, he raises his hand to give me a high-five, and I slap my palm against his softly. He captures my fingers, and I meet his gaze. "How'd that feel?"

Numb is what I think, but I say, "Okay."

He doesn't bring up my sour attitude until I miss the fairway on fifteen. "What's going on in your head? You're getting sloppier with each swing. If this is about anything but golf, push it away for later. Next week is it—everything you've worked for."

"Maybe you can compartmentalize your life like that, but I can't."

"Damn it, Keira, I won't let you sabotage yourself like this. You can do this, but you can't break down now. This is it."

"And then what? I go pro and live a lonely existence where I never let anyone get close like you do?" I brush past him and put my driver into my bag. I know I've gone too far when I turn and see the pain in his eyes. "I'm sorry, I didn't mean that."

He faces off with me, keeping a few feet between us. "I've never lied to you about who I am or what I want."

"I know. I just thought somewhere along the way things changed. I guess they only changed for me." I feel foolish. Not because of my feelings but because I never expected him to not be able to own up to his.

"Keira—"

"No. It's okay. You're right. This is my fault. I'm days away from the biggest event of my life, and I need to focus. Nothing else matters right now."

He nods. "Okay, let's get back to work then."

I unbuckle my golf bag from the cart and sling it over my shoulder. Acceptance, defeat, determination—they each take their turn forcing one foot in front of the other as I realize I'm responsible for what I allow or don't allow to mess with my head.

Lincoln was right about one thing; I have to push everything else aside and focus on golf.

"I think I need to do this on my own."

He looks as if he wants to argue, so I say the only thing I can think of to stop him and protect myself. "You're fired."

CHAPTER THIRTY

Lincoln

"Did you hear what I said?" Kenton asks, and I glance at my laptop.

"No, sorry, what?"

He chuckles. "Jesus. What in the hell is going on with you? I've never known you to be so disinterested in talking business before. You watching porn or something?"

"Sorry. Sorry." I shake my head and force myself to focus on the report we're supposed to be reviewing. "What was the question?"

"Doesn't matter. You don't really need me to review the business shit. Any questions I come up with are ones you probably already asked."

That is usually true, but today I'm not so sure about that, which is why I'd forced him on the phone to talk it out.

"Keira's qualifier is coming up, right?"

"How do you know about that?"

"Gram."

"Ah." I nod. "Yeah, it's on Thursday." I fiddle with the yo-yo on my desk.

"That's awesome. If she qualifies, it'll be great publicity for the company."

"That isn't gonna happen."

"Wow, bro, way to have confidence in your mad coaching skills."

"Not that. Keira's fantastic and has a good chance of qualifying, but we aren't working together anymore."

"Oooooh. Shit. I'm sorry. That's why you look like someone told you golf is for pussies."

"She'll be all right. She's ready."

"Yeah, but what about you?"

"There's no shortage of clients. In fact, I might have to hire another golf coach to handle the overflow."

"Come on, Linc, you and I both know she wasn't just some client. Even you aren't that much of a dumbass to believe that. You like her. She's different. Gram said you've brought her over a few times. The last person you brought to Gram's was Lacey."

"And you know how well that worked out," I say dryly.

"Fix it. Whatever you did."

"There's nothing to fix, so drop it, okay? It's for the best. I'm not looking to get involved beyond a certain point, and I passed that point with her a month ago. She wants things I can't give her." Every word burns like acid.

"Can but don't want to because Lacey was a giant bitch."

"I gave her a lot of reasons to be a bitch. The divorce was my fault. I'm not capable of shutting off work. When I was playing, it was all I thought about. Same with work. Lacey was a distant second. It wasn't fair, and I won't do it to Keira."

"So, don't. I'm not telling you to be a selfish prick. I'm telling you to get your shit together and do better. You're clearly upset about losing her, so do something about it."

"I have to jump on another call."

He shakes his head slowly. "I just wanna see you happy, bro. So does Gram. It's why she's always setting you up on dates. Since you brought Keira around, she moved on to me, and I'm loving it. I don't even have to leave my house anymore to find chicks."

"Oh yeah? She sending you dates in Los Angeles?"

"Sort of. One of her friends has a granddaughter out here, and they've been badgering us to meet up. Anyway, the point is, I'm happy with the setups. Someone else is doing all the work and I just get to date awesome women. Don't screw this up for me."

I laugh. "Good luck with that." My phone beeps with my next call. "Gotta go."

"Later, bro."

I click over to Heath. "Hey."

"Hey, old man, what's up?"

"The usual. What about you? Managing to fill your time since the season's over?"

"Eh." His response is about what I'd expect for bringing up their season ending. They finished with a brutal loss in the conference championship.

"I have a couple of camps looking for coaches again this summer, including Deerwood. You did a great job for them last year."

"When would I have to decide? I'm hoping to get invited to the Coyotes developmental camp in July."

I sit up straighter. "Yeah? Wow, Heath, that's awesome."

"Well, I haven't been invited yet, but Coach Meyers thinks it's likely."

"That's really cool. Best news I've had all week." I make a note to look for some other guys I can recommend to the camp should Heath not be available. "I can probably hold Deerwood off on finalizing staff until the end of the month."

"'Preciate it."

I can usually count on Heath to carry our conversations with his usual antics, but he seems to have as much on his mind as I do, and we wade through the usual business stuff in less than ten minutes.

"What else is new?" I ask before he can push me off the phone. "Still managing to show up to class?"

"They haven't kicked me out yet, so I guess I'm doing okay."

"That's encouraging."

"I'm kidding. Geez. Yes, grades are good. Everything is good. Next year, are you and Nathan gonna get off my case?"

"Not likely."

"Didn't think so. Well, on that note, I gotta go. I'm going to a party where there'll be booze . . . lots and lots of booze and opportunities for all sorts of shady decisions."

"Stay out of trouble." I can't help but add the one last order. "Where are you heading tonight?"

He hesitates a second, probably because I never ask specifics. "Why? Are you planning to stop by to check in on me, old man?"

"Just making polite conversation." And wondering if he's going somewhere that he might run into Keira, but I'm certainly not telling him that. I don't even want to admit it out loud to myself.

He laughs and disconnects without answering, and I spend the next few hours taking one call after another. When I'm finally able to toss my phone onto the desk and breathe a sigh of relief, I look up at the boxes from the storage unit lining the far wall in my office.

I'm tempted to throw all of it into the dumpster just to be rid of it, but I know there are probably a few mementos from my childhood I'd be sad to lose.

I stand and cross the room. I can't feel any worse, right?

Wrong. I pull back the flaps on the closest box and stare down at an eleven by fourteen framed photo of my wedding day. A young, happy couple stares back at me. Lacey's smile is big and genuine as I bend her backward in a kiss-the-bride pose. God, we look so happy and totally unaware of the shitstorm that lies ahead.

And that's why I need to let Keira stay pissed at me. She has her whole life ahead of her, a golf career and love. I choke on the last word, already bitter picturing her with someone else. She deserves it all.

My phone vibrates on the desk and I ignore it as I let the flaps fall closed and walk out of the office. I don't let my mind wander to what other treasures might be waiting for me in those boxes. I don't answer clients. I don't beat myself up over the work I should be doing instead of crawling into bed. I don't question it when I close my eyes and inhale her faint scent.

And I don't call Keira, though that one is much harder than all the others.

CHAPTER THIRTY-ONE

Keira

After our practice on Tuesday, a local reporter stops by the campus course to talk with Cassidy. Erica stands beside me as we watch Coach beam with pride next to Cass as she's being interviewed about her invitation to the amateur championship.

"You'd think they were recognizing him." I don't have to look at her to know she's rolling her eyes.

"Yep. I'm sure he's figuring out a way to make it all about him."

We grab our bags to head out. "Are you coming over tonight for Cass's party?"

"I can't. I'm heading up to Scottsdale as soon as I pack."

"Oh, right. The sectional qualifier is this week."

"Yep. It's Thursday, but I have an early morning practice round on the course tomorrow."

"I wish I could come watch. You're gonna kill it, you know that, right?"

"I wish I had your confidence. Practice this week has sucked."

"You're just in your head. When you get there and your handsome coach is by your side, you'll get your confidence back."

Thinking of Lincoln makes my heart hurt. I haven't told the girls we aren't working together anymore. If I did, they'd want to talk about it, and I definitely don't want to talk about it—at least not this week. Next week, I'll let them take me out, and I'll word vomit all my feelings. But not yet.

"Keira Brooks?"

I turn to find the reporter walking toward me.

"Um, yeah, that's me."

"I'm Ernie with the Valley Daily Newspaper. Do you have a few minutes? I'd love to talk to you about your season."

"Sure." I look from him to Erica.

"See ya later, superstar." She nudges my side and shoots me a big smile.

Ernie goes straight into his questions. "Congrats on your season. You've had a great showing recently with the win last month and a second place finish two weeks ago in Texas, how are you feeling?"

"I feel . . ." Heartbroken. Annoyed that I'm heartbroken. Determined. "I feel good."

"Rumor has it you're heading to the sectional qualifier in Scottsdale this week. Any truth to that?"

"Yes, I am." I force a big, excited smile.

"How have you been preparing for an event of this magnitude?"

"Wow. I don't know." My heart thumps wildly as I scramble for something coherent to say. "I've been focusing on taking each moment as it comes. Lots of practice and visualization to think through different scenarios."

Coach Potter walks up as I'm finishing my answer.

Ernie looks to him. "Keira was just telling me how she's preparing for this weekend. You must be pretty proud to have so many talented girls on your team this year. One headed to the amateur championship and another making a run for the US Open. Pretty exciting for Valley U golf."

"Yeah, of course. I'm extremely proud of Cassidy and of Keira too. It's brave of her to enter and get the experience. People are going to see a real difference in how far she's come this year."

My face heats at his wording. The pseudo compliment is his way of trying to take credit for Lincoln's work, which is total bullshit. He might as well tell this reporter I don't have a shot in hell of winning.

"You've done great work with them, Coach." He extends a hand, and I bite my tongue as they shake and say goodbye.

After Ernie leaves, Coach walks off without so much as a good luck to me. Screw him. I don't need him or his support.

I'm still seething as I get back to my dorm. Abby left a note wishing me good luck on my desk with a new box of Pop-Tarts. I dig into them as I pack my bag and that lifts my mood some.

I'm on autopilot as I drive up to Scottsdale and nearly make the turn to Lincoln's apartment without thinking. I miss him and I'm so freaking mad at him.

The hotel near the course is busy when I arrive. I spot a few golfers I know and others I just recognize as I make my way through the lobby and up to my room.

Once I'm settled, I call my mom.

"Hey, honey," she answers. "How are you?"

"Fine. Nervous. I'm playing the course tomorrow morning to get a feel for it."

"I know. Well, it slipped my mind but it's on the calendar and your dad sent me a text a little bit ago to make sure I remembered. The man doesn't have an organized bone in his body except when it comes to tracking your golf schedule. We're really proud of you, honey."

"Thanks, Mom."

I expel a breath and a little of the tension.

"Want me to sing to you like I did when you were little and scared to sleep in your own room? Do you remember that? I'd sing Twinkle, Twinkle Little Star."

"And then I'd make you do it over and over again in different funny voices."

We both laugh into the phone.

"Good luck tomorrow, Keira. I love you."

After we hang up, I order room service and turn on the television for noise. I'm too scatterbrained to focus on anything for long. The time passes as I alternate scrolling through my phone and flipping through channels. I ignore the part of me that wants to call Lincoln knowing he'd be able to soothe and comfort me in that way only he can.

I go to bed at eight, but I see every hour, dozing only in short increments before waking in a panic that I'd somehow overslept.

Needless to say, I'm tired during Wednesday's practice round. I take the course at a slow pace, trying to figure out the best way to play each hole. My anxiety grows with each swing, and by the time I make it back to my room, I'm a mess.

My phone rings, and Lincoln's name on the screen makes my weak heart race. I'm too tired to be angry.

I take a deep breath and force myself to wait until the third ring to answer. "Hello?"

"Hey." His deep voice rumbles, and I close my eyes, trying to fight off the emotions it stirs in me. One word, and it all comes crashing back. I want to be mad, but it's really a deep hurt and sadness I feel without him.

"How are you feeling?" he asks sounding upbeat and optimistic. "Ready for tomorrow?"

"I think so."

The awkwardness that hangs between us is unfamiliar and painful.

"You're gonna be great. Just go out there and have fun."

Fun.

I haven't had a lot of that over the last few days. For a guy who's so serious and work-focused, Lincoln became a big part of the joy and excitement I've had playing recently. Loving golf and having fun while playing haven't always gone together for me.

It's silent again while I struggle with what to say. I don't want there to be this weirdness between us. I respect him too much, and he gave me a lot. Too much and not enough.

"Thank you for everything. I wouldn't be here if it weren't for you. I hope I can do your coaching justice."

"You already have. It was my absolute pleasure, Keira." He sighs into the phone, and I can picture him running his fingers through his dark hair. "I just wanted to wish you luck and let you know that I'll be rooting for you. Gram too. She asked me to bookmark the live scoring website so she can follow along."

"She did?"

"Yeah, you made quite an impression on her. Keira, I . . ." He curses lightly away from the phone and then clears his throat. "I should let you get some sleep."

Disappointment and resolution center me, and I finally feel like sleeping. "Yeah, okay. Thanks for calling, Lincoln."

Ending the call, I curl into a ball on top of the scratchy comforter and fall asleep, wishing Lincoln's arms were wrapped around me. When my alarm goes off early the next morning, I rise like the dead, shower, and get ready.

Conditions aren't great today. It's sunny, but dark clouds in the distance threaten rain. It's also hot and muggy, making it hard to breathe. But I can't let that stop me. I've done all the work. Today is about battling my head. There's no room to wish or hope for any aspect of my life to be different.

Me, the ball, and my golf clubs. They're all I focus on. They are all I need.

I'm in a later starting group, so I'm able to watch some of my competition. Among them are girls I've played against, girls I've looked up to, and a few I've never heard of before.

A senior at Arizona State, Martha, is putting up a strong performance. Each swing looks better than the last. She's unbeatable, or that's what everyone whispers as they watch her dominate for the first hour of the day. She has skill and confidence that makes others feel timid and weak.

In hindsight, I probably shouldn't have watched her because, by the time it's my turn to tee off, even I'm shaken by her strong showing.

I step up, place my tee and ball, and let out a deep breath. I stare down the fairway to the flag, visualizing my ball exactly where I need it to be—where I know I'm capable of hitting it.

This is it.

I scan the crowd without realizing I'm looking for him, but when I don't see Lincoln's dark head, frustration and anger sets in. Not at him, but at myself for being disappointed about anything during the biggest moment of my life.

I'm angry for most of the front nine, but it works for me. I hone it into a focused desire to do well despite his absence, to do well for myself.

It's so disgustingly hot out and that pisses me off too, so I add it to the list and let it drive me to work even harder.

I first notice Coach Potter walking along the course at the tenth hole. I shouldn't be surprised he decided to deign me with his presence. He'll want to be here in case I pull off a miracle so he can pretend he's a loving and supportive coach.

I falter at twelve with a bogey, but I'm able to recover on the last five and finish five under and tied for second place.

I sign my card in the clubhouse and make my way toward the player rest area. I have a short break before my second round, and I need to eat and drink a gallon of water. It's only gotten more humid as the day progressed.

I check my phone, trying not to be sad that Lincoln hasn't texted. I know it's possible he isn't tracking the tournament, though some part of me refuses to believe that. That part is still hopeful and closely tied to my need to believe what Lincoln and I had went beyond obligation and a casual fling.

My body aches, and I'm so tired when I spot Potter waiting for me with a big pleased smile on his face that I don't bother to try to avoid him. I'm so hot, but my skin feels dry instead of sweaty when I wipe my hand across my forehead. I suck in a deep breath that doesn't do anything to get oxygen to my lungs.

Coach Potter rests an arm around my shoulders, and I try to move out of his hold, but there's nowhere to go and my legs are shaky underneath me. God, if he'd just stop touching me, maybe I could catch my breath.

My mouth is gritty, and my throat aches as I try to swallow. Dots blur my vision. I really need to eat something.

If I could just get to a quiet area and relax for a few minutes, then I would be okay. My stomach twists violently, stopping me in my tracks. Bile rises, and I heave. My throat is so dry it takes three attempts to bring up my breakfast.

I'm aware that I've puked on Potter's shoes, but the pain is so intense I can't even be happy about it. My legs give out, and I collapse.

I'm out only a few seconds, I think, but when I open my eyes again, two people in tourney polos are carrying me into a private room. Potter elbows his way into the room behind them.

A lady, who introduces herself as Mary, assures me she's a doctor and then asks me a bunch of questions. I answer in a daze. There's a real threat of puking every time I open my mouth.

"Can I have some water?" I croak.

One of the polo dudes hands me a bottle of water, even going as far as to unscrew the cap for me.

"Keira, I think you have heat stroke," Mary says. "I have a car waiting for you."

I lift my head and see the seriousness in her expression as she places a cool washcloth on the back of my neck. "It's just a precaution."

I want to put up a fight, but I can't seem to form the words. The room is spinning, and it feels as if I'm burning from the inside out.

I'm helped to my feet and taken out a back exit to a waiting car. I have enough wherewithal to realize I probably need to text my parents and let them know what's happening, but I can't remember if I actually do it.

Potter slides into the back of the car with me, and I can't help but think his presence isn't helping at all.

THIRTY-TWO

Lincoln

I'm on the phone with a client when I get the call about Keira. The fact that Gram knows before I do would be obnoxious if I weren't so pissed that I wasn't there. I wrestled with going all morning, finally deciding it was best for Keira if I didn't show. She didn't need any distractions.

"Is she okay?"

Gram does her best to sound calm, but I can hear the worry in her voice. "I'm not sure, but they took her to the hospital."

I grab my keys and head out the door at a run. "Which hospital?"

I jump into my SUV and am starting it and slamming the gear into reverse before the door is even closed. Dark clouds hang low and rain spits onto my windshield just hard enough that I have to use the wipers.

I don't remember the drive over, parking, or running through the hospital, but I'm panting when I get to the emergency room. The woman behind the front desk looks at me as if I might be the one in need of help.

"Keira Brooks."

"Are you family?"

"No." I grind my teeth.

Her flat smile tells me I'm not getting back there. "If you have a seat, I'll let the nurse know Miss Brooks has a visitor."

A woman in scrubs stands holding the door to the emergency room open as she calls the next patient. Fuck it. I run past her.

"Sir. Sir. You can't be back there, sir."

Over the intercom, they call for security, which means I have to find her fast.

"Keira," I call out.

Curtains are pulled, giving privacy to patients. There are a handful of nurses and doctors who have stopped what they were doing to stare at me, so I stop in front of them, asking, "Keira Brooks?"

My heart is pounding so hard I might need to lie down in one of these beds. But only after I find her.

A big dude in a security uniform approaches before anyone answers. "Sir. I'm gonna have to ask you to leave."

"Keira," I shout a little louder, desperation and panic clear in my tone. This time, she responds. "Lincoln?"

I run toward her voice and find a doctor giving me a disapproving look as he holds the curtain open. Keira's in the bed behind him, and Coach Potter in the chair beside her. I bypass the doctor and his dirty looks, ignore fucking Potter's existence altogether, and go to her side.

"Oh my God." I lean down and lightly run my hand across the top of her head, breathing her in.

"Sir." The security guard stands outside the curtain.

"I'm not leaving."

"Sir, we—"

"It's okay. He's okay," Keira speaks up. Her voice sounds small and weak, but the security guard reluctantly retreats.

"What happened? Are you okay?" She's hooked up to an IV, and her face is flushed red, but otherwise, she looks okay.

"I got overheated and dehydrated. I'm fine."

The doctor clears his throat. "Fine might be a stretch. Your potassium was dangerously low. Fortunately, everything else looks okay. We're going to move you up to a room so we can monitor you a little longer. If everything looks stable later tonight, we can get you discharged."

"No." She moves to sit up, but I can tell it pains her. "I have to get back to the course before I'm disqualified."

"Uh, actually, I just got word that there's a weather delay. So, everyone who was slotted for this afternoon will tee off first thing in the morning." Potter reads from his phone.

The doctor looks to Keira and speaks sternly. "You need time to recoup. We're giving you fluids, but you were severely dehydrated." He shakes his head. "Even for someone young and active, you aren't going to feel one hundred percent for a few days. Don't push too hard or you'll end up right back here."

"But she *could* play tomorrow?" Potter asks. "We have a chance to win."

"We?" I ask, not hiding my disdain.

He glares at me but doesn't answer, so I focus my attention back to Keira.

She lets me hold her hand for the next few hours while they pump her with fluids. She dozes on and off, but it feels like every time she gets comfortable someone wakes her up to check this or that.

It's after seven before the doctor releases her. A nurse makes her sit in a wheelchair so she can wheel Keira out to the parking lot, and Potter and I flank her on either side.

"I'll bring the SUV around."

She stands, and I lead her to a bench to wait while I get the car. Rain comes down in a steady pour and it doesn't look like it's going to break anytime soon.

"I already called a cab to take us back to the hotel," Potter says.

Keira looks between us. Even on my worst day, I'm a hell of a better option than Potter.

"You can't stay at the hotel. Come with me. You'll be more comfortable at my place, and I can keep an eye on you."

She stares at me blankly.

"Nonsense. I'm staying at the hotel too and I can keep an eye on her."

"Like you did today?" I step to him. I've easily got three inches on him and I use every single one to make him feel small and worthless. "Where the fuck were you? Why weren't you looking out for her?" I hate him for letting it happen, but only a fraction as much as I hate myself.

I can see the anger on her weak frame as she says, "I'll be fine at the hotel. I don't need either of you."

The weight of that statement slams into me. I kneel in front of her and take her hand. "Come with me. Please. I'll take you to Gram's if you prefer. I just need to know you're okay and that someone is there if you need anything."

Potter scoffs. "She just needs a little rest. She can do that at the hotel and I'll be there if she needs anything else."

I wouldn't trust this guy with a pet goldfish, let alone my favorite person in the world.

She bites her bottom lip but doesn't outright turn me down, so I take that bit of leverage and run with it. I dial Gram and put the phone to my ear. She answers on the first ring as if she were waiting for news. It seems right somehow that she's concerned too.

"Gram, I'm gonna bring Keira to your house for the night. That okay?"

"Yes. I'll get the spare room set up and make soup. Do you think she could eat some homemade bread? I'll make some anyway, just in case."

Keira watches my face as I smile and nod. "That'd be great, Gram. Be there soon."

"Ready?" I stand and hold out my hand. She puts hers in it slowly, and I lean down and sweep her legs out from under her so I can carry her to my SUV. I don't say another word to Potter before we leave him standing there to wait for his cab.

I hold her hand as I drive, but neither of us speaks. I want to tell her everything is okay, but nothing is okay, and I won't make things worse by lying to her.

When we get to Gram's house, she's standing at her door, waiting for us. Gram pulls her into a hug, and Keira surprises me by wrapping both arms around my grandmother and leaning into her. Her shoulders shake and sobs wrack her tired body.

Gram meets my eye and pats Keira lovingly. They stand that way for several long minutes before Gram leads her into the house. I follow, chest aching at not being the person she wants to lean on.

I don't want her to cry, but when she does, I want to be the one to wipe her tears.

"Lincoln, can you check the soup and the bread, I'm going to get Keira settled."

I stand alone in the hallway as Gram and Keira go into the spare room and shut the door. After checking the food, I grab a beer from the fridge, open it, and take a long swig before abandoning it on the counter.

Pacing the hallway, I wait for either of them to emerge or to call out for me. Anything would be better than standing here helpless.

When Gram finally comes out, she turns the light out and closes the door quietly. As I step forward, she stops me with a shake of her head. "She's resting."

"But—"

She shakes her head again, and I know my grandmother well enough to know she's as likely to let me through as she is to stop trying to find my next wife. I drain the rest of my beer, grab another, and follow Gram into the dining room. She instructs me to sit and then puts soup and bread in front of me.

"I'm not hungry."

She raises a brow and waits.

Grumbling, I pick up the spoon and take a few bites. I taste nothing, which is a real tragedy because I'm sure it probably tastes amazing.

"How is she?"

"She'll be okay. You did the right thing bringing her here."

"She wants to play tomorrow." I wave a hand outside. The rain has slowed, but still pelts the ground. "Assuming it isn't further delayed."

Gram nods. "She told me. I don't think anyone is going to be able to talk her out of that."

"I should have been there. If something happened to her . . ." It's hard to breathe as I contemplate that.

"Lincoln, honey, I don't know what happened between you and Keira or why you weren't there today when I know there's nowhere else you'd have rather been, but I have a sneaking suspicion it all leads back to one thing." She pauses to look me square in the eye. "Lacey."

I groan. Here we go again.

"You have to stop beating yourself up for things that happened in the past and start living your life. It wasn't your fault. I know it, Lacey knows it, heck, you're probably the only one who doesn't know it. But that isn't the point. You either need to believe that or decide to forgive yourself anyway so you can move on."

"I'm a workaholic with a schedule that makes it damn near impossible to date, let alone be in a serious relationship."

"Then why are you upset?"

I grind down on my molars.

"Keira isn't Lacey. Don't make the mistake of pushing her away because you're scared. You've never been a coward. Don't start now."

"What if I hurt Keira the same way?" I shake my head, the thought physically painful.

"You won't."

"How can you know that?"

"Because you're too smart and too stubborn to make the same mistake twice."

I wish I could believe that.

After dinner, Gram makes a plate for Keira and takes it into the spare room in case she wakes up hungry.

"Are you staying?" she asks as she turns out the kitchen lights.

"Yeah." I grab the throw blanket off the back of the couch, and Gram brings me a pillow. "Thanks."

She kisses my cheek, gives me a sad smile, and heads to bed.

Once I'm settled on the couch, I stare up at the ceiling as silence falls over the house. I think about what Gram said, trying to make it fact in my head and heart, but I know to my core I didn't do right by Lacey.

I didn't fight for her or for us. I was relieved when it was over because it was one less responsibility and distraction. That's a shitty realization—to know your marriage has gone up in flames and you're happy about it.

Nowhere near sleep, I throw off the blanket and quietly head down the hallway. I rest my hand on the wooden door and try to talk myself out of going inside. I rap my knuckles lightly and then push the door open just enough to see through a crack. The room is dark, save for the dim light coming from the lamp on the bedside table that casts her small frame in shadows.

She's turned away from it, and the comforter is askew and bunched up at her feet. Moving to the bed in two long strides, I settle in behind her and pull the blanket over us. Wrapping my arm around her, I breathe easy for the first time in days.

THIRTY-THREE

Keira

I already know he's gone before I open my eyes. His scent lingers, but the bed is entirely too cold and quiet without him. I don't know when he joined me, but I woke in the middle of the night with Lincoln wrapped around me like a cocoon.

I should have told him to go so I wouldn't have to feel the sadness of losing him all over again, but instead I let myself enjoy one more night in his arms.

A plate of food and two water bottles sit on the nightstand, and I down one of the waters before getting out of bed. I tear off a hunk of bread and chew it while I put on my shoes. My body is achy, and I definitely don't feel one hundred percent, but I'll survive. I have to. I need to block out the pain, swing by the hotel, shower, and get to the course.

"Good morning. I made breakfast," Milly says as I tiptoe through the living room, trying to make an escape.

I turn, plastering a thankful and convincing smile on my lips. "I have to get going. Thank you so much for letting me stay last night. I feel much better after a good night's sleep."

My eyes dart around the living room, kitchen, dining room, and then finally the patio, but I don't see Lincoln anywhere.

"He isn't here." She sets a plate on the dining room table. "Come on. You'll be dropping at the third hole without a good breakfast."

"Where is he?" I follow the scent of hash browns and eggs.

"Some sort of work emergency. He said to tell you that he'd see you at the course."

Work. Of course.

"You didn't need to do this but thank you. It smells delicious."

Milly doesn't linger in the dining room while I eat, which makes me insanely grateful. I don't really feel like talking or thinking about anything except golf. I cried ugly tears last night in front of this woman, letting all my fears about golf, Lincoln, life pour out of my eyeballs.

I eat slowly and manage to finish everything Milly puts in front of me. Now I'm ready, I tell myself ignoring the way my hands tremble as I carry my dirty dishes into the kitchen.

"The rain stopped early this morning, and it promises to be a beautiful day." She takes the plate and glass from me and hands me a brown paper bag. "Take this with you for later."

I look inside to see a banana, a sandwich that looks like it might be peanut butter and jelly, and a Gatorade. I reach out with one arm and wrap it around her neck, surprising us both with how tightly I hug her. When I pull back, there are tears in my eyes. "Thank you."

"I know that there's no talking you out of playing today, but listen to your body. There's no shame in taking care of yourself. There will be more tournaments. Your time is coming. I can feel it."

"I will," I promise.

"Let me grab my keys, and I'll drive you."

"No need, Uber's on the way."

She nods. "Good luck."

Once I'm in the back of the Uber and headed to the hotel, I call my mom.

"Honey, I'm so glad you called. I wasn't sure how long to wait before I worried. You sounded so tired last night. Are you okay?"

"Yeah, I am." I close my eyes and lean my head against the headrest. "I had a good night's sleep and a good breakfast. I'm going to try to play today."

I wait for her to chastise me or tell me that isn't a good idea, but she laughs lightly and says, "Of course you are. I wish I were there to see you. Bart and I'll be there at the Open though. He's already memorizing the course and checking out the local restaurants."

"You're coming?"

"Yeah, your coach sent us all the details, booked us flights and hotels.

Your dad, too. Honestly, honey, I didn't know how much you wanted us there, but he said it would make you happy if we were there to cheer you on."

"He did?" I'm confused as to why Coach Potter would call her and make these plans, but then I realize she's talking about Lincoln. "When?"

"Last week."

My heart clenches at the thought of him going to all that trouble for me because he was so certain I was going to make it.

What if I don't? I keep the question inside for fear that voicing them will somehow make it more likely.

"I can't believe you're really coming."

"Of course. Don't sound so surprised."

I nod and wipe a tear away. I'm a freaking faucet lately. "I know it's hard to get away. You have work and lives."

"I have some vacation time saved up, and I can't think of a better way to spend it than watching my baby go after her dreams. Also, I googled the event and I saw that sometimes celebrities attend. Maybe I can trade in Bart for a Ben Affleck look-alike."

We both laugh, and the weight I'm carrying lifts a little.

"I'm so proud of you, Keira. And I miss you. I don't know when you got so big on me."

I hear a page for a doctor in the background and can picture her walking the halls of the hospital in her scrubs. I used to love to curl up beside her on the couch when she'd get home from working late shifts. "Listen, honey, I have to go, but good luck today and call me when you can, okay?"

"I will. Thanks, Mom."

At the hotel, I shower and dress for the day and then head to the course. It's still early, but many of the players in the first tee time groups are already warming up. I stretch first, not even touching my clubs for the first fifteen minutes.

I avoid the questions about how I'm feeling and the sad looks from people who are already discounting my ability to play today. Their doubt wears at me, nicking away my confidence one sad glance and soft, condescending word of encouragement at a time.

I head to the putting green. The club feels cold and heavy in my shaking hands. Zipping up my jacket and flipping the collar up to block the breeze, I take a few deep breaths to get my focus.

I fall into my usual routine, but nothing goes right. I don't know if it's my body or my head, but I'm off, and it shows. My line isn't right on my short or long putts. I head to the bunker with similar results.

By the time I walk to the driving range, I feel as if I'm going to throw up. Coach Potter joins me as I take the first swing with my driver. His eyes light up with excitement as he nods to the lady with a microphone and the accompanying camera guy. "Keira, they want to ask you a few questions."

I step back, and the reporter introduces herself. "Hi, Keira. I'm Belinda with KTLR, how are you feeling today?"

"I feel good." My voice quivers, so I smile as big as I can to overcompensate and twist and turn the pink, unicorn scrunchie on my wrist.

"You've had an exciting month, winning the Valley Invitational tournament and placing second at the University of Texas tournament. What's contributed to your recent successes?"

Lincoln's face flashes before me, smiling back at me through the computer screen all those nights. I open my mouth to speak, but Coach interjects, "She's a hard worker. We had a rough start to the year, but she's really listened to the feedback, and I think it shows just how far a person can go with the right guidance."

My face heats at him trying to take credit for Lincoln's work. Belinda looks to me to verify his statement.

"I have a great coach," I say simply. "I wouldn't be here today without him."

That much is true. Potter smiles smugly, but it doesn't matter. If I win, I'll set the record straight, and if I don't, people can believe my failures are at the hands of Potter. Lincoln has never once tried to take credit, which is just one more reason in a long list of why he's a better coach and man.

"Do you think you'll be able to play at the level you need to today to win?"

I suck in a breath because, isn't that the question of the day? "I'm going to give it my best shot."

"Thank you, Keira. It was a pleasure to meet you. Good luck today."

I walk back to my spot on the range, Coach Potter standing behind me just like he did all those times for other girls on the team. I always imagined what it would be like to have his undivided attention before a tournament, but I have to say that it doesn't feel any better with him by my side.

His presence doesn't encourage or soothe me like Lincoln's does. In a moment of weakness, I look around for him. But even before I finish scanning the small crowd, I can feel he isn't here.

Focus. Only golf.

I tee up another ball, blow out a breath, and swing. I know I'm holding back, but I can't seem to access that gut-deep power and determination I usually can.

"That was short." Coach Potter's brows draw together, hands on hips. "Try it again."

I hit five more balls and then take a break since I'm already out of breath and sweaty.

Coach looks me over and shakes his head. "You can't do it. You don't have it today."

Then he just walks away. Now that I'm not performing at peak level, he isn't interested in standing beside me. It doesn't shock me, but it does hurt.

Of all the times he's doubted my ability, this is the only time I've ever believed him.

THIRTY-FOUR

Lincoln

"**A**ny update?" I pace the office with a club in my hand in case I decide to completely lose my shit and break everything in sight.

"Not since you asked thirty seconds ago." Will chuckles and then his voice is serious again. "I'm working as fast as I can to figure it out. We'll get it back up."

Four hours ago, our server crashed. The whole website down. *Kaboom*. I kept picturing it like a car explosion in an action movie, but instead of walking away like a badass, I'm in the car going up in flames.

I'd woken with Keira nuzzled into my side and so many voice mails it used up all my phone storage. Begrudgingly, I left because that's what you do when you own a business. You get out of bed or stop whatever it is you're doing and you deal with it.

I've already typed out an email to every member of Reeves Sports, letting them know we're aware of the problem and working quickly to get the site back online. I emailed my clients personally, as well as my staff, and now I'm helping Will any way I can, which is basically just staying out of his way. It's harder than it should be since all I want to do is to barrage him with questions as I pace.

We redirected traffic from the website to our dark site, which explains the outage, but with thousands of members waiting to hear back from coaches and hundreds of potential new clients not being able to sign up—this is a nightmare.

I click refresh on the browser again just for fun. The golf ball stick figure with a sad face frowns back at me. Once upon a time, I sat on a call and smiled at that graphic. How clever, I thought. That'll make people feel better when they can't access the site. Now I wanted to smash the cute cartoon figure in his adorable face.

Stand, pace, check the time, sit, click refresh, ask Will for update.

I shower, leaving my phone sitting on the counter and the ringer turned up so loud it'll likely let the whole neighborhood know if I get a call.

Keira's probably already at the course warming up. I know she's going to play—it just isn't in her to give up. I hate the way my skin prickles with guilt not being there with her. I'm not even sure she wants me there, but it doesn't change how awful I feel for missing it anyway.

Dressed so I can leave for the course as soon as I'm done working, I head back into the office. Will sends me an update that they think they've figured out the issue and I need to jump on a call with him and the rest of the team to lay out a plan.

I'm back to pacing with my club in hand, but with a slightly less ragey grip, while Will outlines the problem and possible solutions. Finding the issue was only step one.

We brainstorm, me mostly just listening. I hire the best, so I don't have to be an expert on everything, but right now I'd trade my left arm to be a computer engineer.

"Worst case scenario, how long until we're back up?"

Will takes his time answering. "I'm not sure. An hour, maybe longer."

I kick the closest thing to me, which happens to be one of the many boxes stacked up in my office. The box on top of it falls to the floor with a metallic clank, contents spilling out in my pacing path.

"Shit," I mutter and squat to clean it up.

Trophies and medals from tournaments dating back all the way to my first junior tournament are spread out in front of me. I pick up the closest one, a medal from a high school tourney, running my thumb along the raised lettering.

I right the box so I can put everything back and dig through the papers at the bottom. Receipts and warranties—stuff from our filing cabinets that Lacey must have found and put together for me. Most of it's trash, but Pop's familiar handwriting makes me pause.

A few days after my first pro tournament, when I was still wallowing in self-hate for all the stupid mistakes I'd made, he'd stopped by, told me he was proud of me and handed me this folded piece of paper.

"Focus on remedies, not faults."

Pop wasn't much for speaking his heart, but that single line said it all. It was everything he believed about golf and about life. When you screw up, take a moment to be sad or pissed, and then figure out how to fix it.

And I had. It was exactly what I'd needed to stop obsessing and get back to work.

"Lincoln? Boss man?" Will's voice brings my attention back to the call.

"Yeah, sorry, I'm here."

I carry the paper with me to my desk and sit behind my laptop to get back to work. I'm asking questions and taking notes, but my eyes continually drift back to Pop's words.

Focus on remedies. Simple advice that I'd put into practice in every aspect of my life.

Except one.

Fuck.

I'd let all my faults get in the way of the thing I wanted most. Keira.

And of course I want to be with her. Despite everything. Because of everything.

I want her more than I've ever wanted anything. Ever. Period.

I fold the paper and slide it into my pocket as I stand. "Will, I gotta go. You guys got this."

There's silence on the other end of the phone for two long seconds. "You're dropping off?"

"Yep. I have somewhere important I need to be." I smile as I picture their surprised faces. But no one is more surprised than I am. "I trust you to find the best solution. Do what you can and I'll check in later."

I just hope I can get there in time.

At the course, I park and run out to the area between the warm-up area and hole one. Fuck, I hope she hasn't already teed off.

I weave between players and spectators, tournament officials in their matching polo shirts. I finally spot her hanging back, all by herself.

"Keira," I call out. "Keira." I reach her, out of breath and shaky from adrenaline. "Thank God. I made it."

She shakes her head slowly. "It doesn't matter. I'm not playing."

"What?"

"I can't do it." She shrugs looking defeated. "Not like this. I'm not even close to one hundred percent, more like fifty. Weak, anxious, in my head—"

"I love you."

Her eyes widen, and her lips part in surprise, so I repeat it. "I love you so much. I'm sorry I didn't tell you before. I was scared that I'd fail you somehow and you'd hate me. Still am scared, if I'm being honest."

"But . . ." Her mouth opens and closes like an adorable baby fish.

"I was a bad husband. My priorities were fucked up, and I stopped trying. I gave up. It was easier than admitting it wasn't what I wanted anymore. I swore I'd never do that to anyone else. I tried to keep you at arm's length because I knew that, if I let you in here"—I place a hand over my heart—"I'd never be able to walk away. So, I pushed you until you walked away from me, and I've hated myself every moment since."

She smiles the tiniest bit. This stunning woman that's somehow become more important than anything else.

"You needed me to push you, to show you that you were capable of doing anything you set your mind to, but I wasn't expecting you to push me the same way. I'm in. All in. Without you, nothing else matters."

A guy in a white polo shirt with the country club logo walks up behind Keira and says her name. She looks from me to him and then back to me. I can see the panic on her face and feel the anxiety bouncing off her.

"If you don't feel up to this today, I'll spend every day for as long as it takes helping you get back here. Say the word and we're out of here. But, baby, you can do this. This is your destiny."

I take out the note from Pop, unfold it so she can read what it says, and hand it to her. "I want you to have this. My grandpa gave it to me after my disastrous pro debut. It's a Jack Nicklaus quote that he said fairly often. I carried it every time I played after that, but I never really felt the weight of his message until today. I have a hundred faults, but I promise I'll keep working to be better for you. So I can push you when you need it and help you get everything you want and deserve."

"It's almost time." Polo guy smiles and nods for her to approach the tee box.

"Just one more second," I tell him and take her gloved hand, running my thumb over the leather. "I love you. You can do this. You don't need me, you never did, but I'm glad as hell you found me anyway."

I can't read anything on her face but shock that I just dropped my heart at her feet and nerves that she isn't in any shape to play golf today.

"Keira," the tourney dude says again in a quiet, serious tone as he moves to stand at her side.

She nods to polo asshat. "I'm coming."

Lifting Pop's note, she glances back at me. "Thank you for this." She moves toward the tee box, turning before she steps onto the grass. "You're staying, right?"

"Nowhere else I'd rather be."

She smiles and marches up to the tee box as I move over to watch with the other spectators.

And it's exactly where I plan to stay, right here on the sidelines making sure she gets anything and everything she wants for as long as she'll let me.

CHAPTER THIRTY-FIVE

Keira

I find Lincoln standing to the side, exactly where he said he'd be, and he nods encouragingly. I wave to the crowd and then tee my ball. I stare down the fairway to the flag and visualize the flight of my ball and the exact spot for it to land that would put me in the best position for this par four.

I take a few practice swings back from my ball and exhale a long breath. With it, I push out all the negative thoughts that have plagued me. I'm not in top shape today. Everyone here knows it, but they don't know how much I want this.

Lincoln does.

I glance once more at him before I take my place. With him cheering me on, I feel unbeatable. He fuels my desire to push through, and I know that, win or lose, I'm going to give it everything I have.

The crowd quiets until the only sound is the whisper of a breeze and my own breathing. Lincoln's voice is in my head, encouraging and pushing me.

I check my line one last time and swing.

The crowd claps as I watch the ball flight. It's shorter than yesterday's drive and slightly off target, but it isn't awful.

My second shot brings me onto the green, but I have a slippery downhill twelve-foot putt. I miss it but manage to leave myself in decent position and save par.

The next three holes are about the same. I'm playing safe, but it still feels as if I've run a marathon, and my throat burns from sucking in air. I'm still tied for second place, but there is only one stroke that separates us.

Lincoln stands, hands crossed over his chest, white hat pulled low so I can't see his eyes with the shadow, but I still know he's looking at me.

Hole five is a par three at one hundred fifty-three yards. Yesterday, I hit my nine-iron low and controlled and then was able to make putt for birdie, but it was risky. The greens are playing fast today, and a bad bounce could put me in an awful spot. I can't miss long.

I waver between clubs, ultimately sticking with the nine-iron. My caddy nods. He's one the tourney provided for me, so we haven't chatted much, but he seems to approve.

I tee my ball and stare the flag down. I strike the ball flush, and it flies high and straight. The crowd claps heartily and then groans as it rolls off the green. I end up with bogey.

Going into the back nine, I'm tied for third place. The crowd builds at each hole. The earlier tee times are finishing, and there are only three groups left ahead of us.

Lincoln walks alongside me from the rough, looking just like the boy-friend on the sidelines I always wanted.

Coach Potter is in the crowd too, hanging back as he plays the role of supportive coach. One thing is certain, no matter how today ends, I've decided I'm taking a page from Abby's book and quitting the team. Four months working with Lincoln was more helpful than all the coaching Potter's done his entire career. Times ten.

After drinking some water and taking a few deep breaths in the shade, I pull out my scorecard and course map so I can study the tenth hole. I don't need to since I have it memorized, but it gives me something to focus on.

It's a par five with an elevated green. There are two bunkers running along the right side of the fairway, and trees line the left just beyond the rough. It's a beautiful sight, but there are so many ways to screw it up.

When I shove the scorecard back into my pocket, my fingers graze the piece of paper Lincoln gave me. I don't take it out, just hold it in my hand. I know how much his grandfather meant to him, and the fact he gave this to me touches me deeply.

I think about the words scribbled on it and how hard I've worked to get here, how hard Lincoln worked to get me here. He may be unwilling to take credit, but I wouldn't be here without him. I think he wants this for me nearly as much as I want it for myself.

My driver is heavy in my hand as I stare between two points on the fairway. One safe option and another fifteen yards beyond that, if I strike the ball pure, it should give me a chance to get home in two.

Oh god. I'm gonna go for it. I think this and try to talk myself out of it, but know it's as good as done. All out. Not just for me but also for the man who apparently loves me.

I haven't let the words sink in yet. They're too big coming from him.

The crowd's interest has waned, but Lincoln's still watching. He adjusts his hat, giving me a better view of the smile on his lips. It's encouragement in the exact moment I need it. If I don't make a move up the leaderboard now, it's going to be too late to make a run.

There are two spots, but I don't just want to qualify, I want to win today.

CHAPTER THIRTY-SIX

Lincoln

S omething changed in Keira on the tenth hole. She stopped holding back. There's no indecision in her club choice or her swing, and she moves down the course like a machine.

It's the most beautiful thing I've ever seen. I can't take my eyes off her, not even as the ball flies through the air. I judge the lay by the cheers and the hint of a smile on Keira's lips. Then she's all business again and practically sprinting up the course.

The energy of the crowd buzzes as she and the girl she's paired with arrive at the eighteenth hole. Keira only needs par to tie for first and secure a spot at the Open.

She glances around as if she's seeing her surroundings for the first time in a while, and the crowd roars as she scans it slowly, hopefully letting the moment sink in. I can see her exhaustion as her chest rises and falls with a deep breath.

She's tired. She has to be. The fact that she's pushed through after her body was so depleted yesterday is catching up to her. The adrenaline is probably wearing off too. You can only ride the high for so long.

"You got this, baby," I quietly mumble, lift my hat, and run my fingers through my hair before putting the hat back on. I'm more nervous watching her than I ever was for my own events.

I stay in her line of vision, always where she can find me if she needs a familiar face. I'm honestly not sure if my presence is helpful or a hindrance after I ran in and professed my love seconds before the biggest day of her life. Not my finest moment, but I couldn't hold it in a second longer.

The eighteenth hole is a straightforward par four. She needs to birdie in order to win outright.

The other girl, whose name I should remember but don't, drives the ball well. Not as long or consistent as Keira, but her short game is as good as anyone I've seen. She's made more saves with chips and putts today than should be humanly possible.

Weston? Waston? Watson? Yeah, that sounds right.

Keira goes first. Her drive is a little shorter than she's capable, but it lands just off the center of the fairway. Watson pulls out a monster, and for the first time today, her drive is the longer of the two.

Keira looks angry as hell as they walk down the course. The crowd keeps cheering them on because, no matter what happens in the next few minutes, it's been a great tournament and they're going to see more of these ladies.

Their approaches vary only on direction. Both of them get up just off the green, but in the fringe. Watson has a slightly better lie in that she'll be putting on a mostly flat area. Keira's closer but will be working downhill where the slightest miss can end up rolling to no-man's-land.

Watson takes her time lining up her shot, and we all hold our breath as her ball inches toward the hole. There's a collective "oooh" as the ball hits the rim but fails to fall in. She knocks it in for par, securing a tie unless Keira can make the next shot.

The pressure of the moment hangs in the air. Watson stands off to the side, and even those who have counted Keira out are watching. All eyes are on my girl.

Putter in hand, she walks to her ball and crouches behind it to get a good look at the angle. When she stands, she wobbles off balance, and the lady next to me gasps and clutches my arm.

"Sorry," she says and removes her hand as soon as she realizes what she's done. I nod my acceptance of her apology, but I kind of wish she'd keep squeezing my arm to distract me from how weak Keira looks.

I'm fighting every urge to charge onto the course to make sure she's okay. My pulse thrums and anxiety vibrates inside my chest.

Keira takes a moment to regain her composure, but her body's failing her and that's gotta be messing with her mind.

"Take your time, baby."

The forearm-clutching lady beside me doesn't look at me as she says, "You know Keira Brooks?"

"She's my . . ." Girlfriend? It doesn't seem like enough. "She's my everything."

I feel her eyes on me briefly, but when Keira gets into position to take her putt, everything else ceases to exist.

Keira stares at the line and adjusts her grip, but instead of taking the shot, she steps back. The indecision has us all worried. Everyone's rooting for her at this point, the underdog who didn't let anything stop her.

When her eyes lift and find mine, they are brimming with worry and nerves. I do my best to reassure her, nodding and smiling. If she had any idea how confident I was in her ability to make this shot, she wouldn't have any room for doubt inside her.

Win or lose, it doesn't matter, but I want her to win for herself. I want her to feel that ultimate satisfaction of having her hard work pay off in a big, big way. No client has ever made me this proud, no woman has ever made me want this much.

She holds my gaze for a few seconds more and then her eyes close and her chest rises as she takes a deep breath. When she opens them, she moves with purpose into position, allows a second to adjust, and then takes her shot.

I'm pretty sure the world stops. I know my heart does. The ball rolls along the green to the hole in no hurry. It teases us, drawing out the seconds and the suspense, until I feel like I might faint.

I switch my gaze to Keira just before the ball makes its final decision.

The crowd roars, my heart restarts, and Keira raises her hands in victory. Tears stream down her face as she tilts her head back and looks to the sky.

The woman next to me nudges me with an elbow. "Congratulations."

"Thank you."

Keira hugs her caddy, shakes hands with Watson, and then heads off the course. I walk along the rope just ahead of her. Though she doesn't see me right away, her eyes scan until she finds me. Her smile hits me in the gut, and we move toward each other at a jog. My hands wrap around her waist and hers find my neck.

"You did it."

She's still crying, happy tears that mark her face and slide down to her upturned lips. "Was there any doubt? What happened to all that *it's your destiny*?"

"That was before I realized some idiot rushed in here minutes before you were supposed to tee off and unloaded on you, not to mention the whole recent hospitalization thing."

"I had to win. It had to be today."

"Why?"

"Because I needed to make sure that when I told you that I love you too, you knew it wasn't because I needed you to coach me." Her hands cradle my face. "I love you so much."

My head falls back, and a laugh rumbles from my chest. "Nice try, we have a lot of work to do before June."

"Can you kiss me first?"

I crash my mouth down onto hers, holding nothing back. I don't know how I lived without her, but I don't plan on ever letting her go.

EPILOGUE

Keira
Two Months later . . .

I stand on the golf course at the ninth hole right outside of Lincoln's grandmother's house. What feels like a million people are gathered around me. Some talk to me and others only about me.

"Just act natural."

"But try to smile."

"I think she needs a little more blush."

"How's the black shirt? Should we have her in white instead?"

"Can I have a minute with Keira?" Lincoln's voice cuts through the others, and I want to fall into him the second everyone else walks off and it's just us.

"Nervous?" he asks.

"Yeah, when you said we were gonna shoot a video for the site, I thought it'd just be you and me." I gesture toward the people and equipment. It looks like we're shooting a music video. "Is all this necessary?"

"Nothing but the best for my star client. Ignore them and just show off for me, sweetheart." He hands me my wedge and a ball, drops a kiss to my cheek, and calls everyone back.

When I'm given the go ahead, I take a breath and start.

Tap. Tap. Tap.

The noise soothes and excites me. Body poised, right forearm extended slightly in front of me, the tip of my tongue between my teeth, and my man standing on the sidelines watching me. I move through the trick, forgetting about the cameras.

After five takes, the guy holding the camera calls, "We got it."

As the crew packs up, I stand off to the side and watch Lincoln thank everyone. He's so good at being in charge, at making people feel his thanks and respect, and ultimately getting them to do what he wants in the exact way he wants them to do it.

"Seems like a lot of manpower for fifteen minutes of shooting," I say when he walks over to me.

He takes my hand and leads me to the golf cart path. "Take a walk with me?"

"What about all our stuff? Shouldn't we help pack up?"

"Trust me, they don't want us touching their equipment. Leave your clubs here; we won't be long."

The sun sets in front of us, and we walk with our hands linked. It's the perfect ending to a chaotic week. The Valley semester ended, and school is out—forever for me. I'm going to finish my degree eventually, but since meeting Lincoln and realizing what's possible, it no longer feels like the right path for me. I have new goals and dreams, starting with playing in the US freaking Open next week.

Also, I moved in with Lincoln. A big step for us, but another one that just felt right. I'm attempting to hide the extent of my messiness for at least another month or two so he doesn't change his mind.

But so far, it's been bliss. He works a lot, but I've instituted a shirtless workplace, and that's helped morale a lot, if I do say so myself. And when he forgets to take a moment to breathe, I just crawl into his lap, wrap my arms around him, and remind him.

"I really love it out here. Think Gram will mind if I start sleeping on her patio every night?"

"No." He chuckles. "She'd probably be thrilled."

I close my eyes and breathe in the scent of jasmine and grass. "Someday I'm going to live on the golf course where I can just walk out and play golf any time I want. We can sit on the patio and you can critique swings of everyone who passes by."

"I bet they'd love that."

"Not to them, just to me. For fun."

"I can think of a lot of things to do in this hypothetical house that would be a lot more fun than that."

"Oh yeah? Like what?"

"Like surprising the hell out of you by telling you it isn't so hypothetical." He stops walking and turns to face the back of a house across the fairway from Gram's. It's down from the tee box a hundred yards or so and has a big For Sale sign hanging just off the course.

"Gonna buy me a house someday, sugar daddy?" I joke and lean against him. "That one is nice. Good patio. That pool is great too. Yep, one just like this will do. Got a cool million I could borrow?"

"It won't cost you quite that much."

I pull back and look up at his face because he's gone along with this charade far too long and sounds far too serious.

"What'll it cost me?" I ask tentatively, my pulse speeding.

He takes out his yo-yo, which makes me laugh.

"I have to learn a trick? You know I'm hopeless with that thing." He's tried to teach me a few basic tricks, but it seems that I can add yo-yoing to the list of things I'm not very good at.

He takes my left hand and guides my ring finger through the slipknot, still holding the yo-yo in his palm. "Ready?"

I nod. I have no idea what he's up to, but I'm ready for it all—anything he wants to throw at me.

"It'll cost you forever." He opens his palm, and a beautiful platinum ring slides down the string and onto my finger.

I gasp as Lincoln gets down on one knee. His lips are wrenched into a tight, nervous smile, and he looks at me with such hope and want that I'm utterly floored.

"You're sure?" I have zero doubts that the man loves me, but this? I'm stunned.

"I've never been more sure of anything." He pushes the ring down my finger. "I want us together in this house." He nods toward the home behind us. "I want your stuff strewn all around it, and I want to wake up every morning and try to figure out how to be the best husband and coach that I can be. I'll never stop wanting you. Never stop wanting to be better for you. Not in a million lifetimes together. Marry me?"

"Yes! Yes, of course, I'll marry you."

He stands and brushes a quick kiss against my lips before tipping his head back and screaming, "She said yes! She said yes!"

I'm laughing as he sweeps my legs out from under me and carries me back toward Gram's house, kissing me and telling me how much he loves me the whole way. When he sets me down, he does so in front of a bunch of people who are all smiling and holding champagne glasses.

"What if I'd said no?"

He smiles. "It was going to be a really lame party."

"Dad?" I spot him off to the side dressed fancier than I've maybe ever seen. I rush to him. "What are you doing here?"

"Heard my baby girl might be getting engaged."

Lincoln's at my side and extends a hand to him. "Good to see you again, Mr. Brooks."

"Now that you're getting married, I think Dan will do just fine."

I squeeze my dad and then pull back and check him out. Face clean-shaven, and I think I smell cologne. I pat the pocket on his button-down shirt. "You clean up well."

Leaving him was the hardest part of moving away from Valley.

"Dan," Milly calls as she walks toward us. A woman follows closely be-hind her. "Dan, have you met Addison yet?"

Addison blushes a bright red that almost matches the shade of her hair and holds her hand out to my dad. "Milly has told me a lot about you."

Lincoln leans down and whispers in my ear. "Looks like Gram found someone new to play matchmaker with."

I glance to her, and she gives me a mischievous wink, which has me grinning like a fool.

"Come on, my parents are around here somewhere."

He sweeps me away and we make our way through the small crowd until my eyes land on a man who looks like an older version of Lincoln.

"Keira, these are my parents, May and Jim."

"It's so nice to finally meet you," I tell them.

"You too. Welcome to the family." Lincoln's mom pulls me into a warm hug, and then his father does the same.

"What'd I miss? Did she say yes?" A man comes to a stop next to Lincoln's parents, adjusts his tie, and then finally looks between Lincoln and me. A cocky smirk pulls his mouth into a wide smile.

"Keira, this is my obnoxious little brother, Kenton," Lincoln says before grabbing him playfully and hugging him.

"Nice to meet you, Keira," Kenton says. "If you want embarrassing stories on this one"—he punches Lincoln in the arm—"I have you covered."

"Don't even think about it," Lincoln warns him.

"What? She can't agree to marry you without hearing about the time you peed the bed and blamed it on the dog."

Lincoln hangs his head and mutters under his breath. He wraps an arm around my waist and pulls me away, shouting over his shoulder, "Thanks a lot, man. Enjoy the party."

Abby, Erica, and Cassidy sit off to one side with Smith and Keith. After I've met all of Lincoln's family, I sneak away to join them.

"Congratulations." Abby stands and squeezes me hard.

The other girls do the same, and I take a seat next to Keith.

"Congrats," he says. "Senior year won't be the same without you."

"I *am* an awesome lab partner." I bump his shoulder with mine. "I got you a present to make up for all the stress I've caused you over the last three years."

He raises a brow in question.

"Reeves Sports all access, unlimited membership for life."

"No way?"

"Yes way. Thanks for always having my back."

"I, uh, have something for you, too." Keith stands and produces a folded newspaper clipping from his front pocket. He holds it out to me. "I thought you might want to frame it."

As I unfold the paper, Erica moves so she can see and busts out laughing.

"What is it?" Abby asks.

I hand it to her. "It's the correction the paper issued from that interview I did at the qualifier citing Lincoln Reeves as my coach instead of Potter." I smile at Keith. "Thank you. I knew you had a little rebellious streak in you."

It's hours before Lincoln and I get back to the apartment, and when we do, I drop onto the couch exhausted and happy. So freaking happy. I hold my left hand up, admiring the big rock on my finger. It's beautiful and a little heavy.

"Do you like it?" he asks, taking a seat next to me. "I've never seen you wear jewelry, so I had no idea what to pick."

"I love it."

"I'm glad. That ring belonged to Gram."

"It was your grandmother's?" I ask. "It looks brand new."

"Pop gave it to her for their fortieth anniversary. She wore it for a month or two and then went back to her original set. Sentimentality won out over the size of the rock, I guess. Anyway, when I asked her for help finding a ring, she offered me that. I thought you'd like having something that was hers."

"I do." I hold it against my chest. "It's perfect." Moving so I can face him, I ask, "You're sure about this? Really? I'm not sure you know what you got yourself into. I'm messy, and I get hangry. I like to eat in bed, and I—"

He presses his lips to mine mid-sentence, kissing me hard and making me forget what I was going on about. When he pulls back, it's to say, "Stop trying to scare me off. I know exactly who you are."

"You do?"

"*Mm-hmm.* You're the girl who's stuck with me. I'm not going anywhere." He stands and tugs me to my feet before leading me to the bedroom. "Well, except to bed so I can sex up my new fiancée."

Calloused fingers gently lift my shirt over my head and push my skirt and panties down to the floor. I step out of them and unhook my bra before he can get to it, tossing it to the ground.

Instead of throwing me onto the bed like it looks like he wants to do, he draws my naked body against him. "I love you so damn much."

"I love you too." We stand together, leaning on one another and soaking up all the feelings and things words can't say. "What's next, Coach?"

I feel the laughter from his chest, and his mouth descends close to mine. "Sex. Lots and lots of reps. I'll let you know when to stop."

Secretly hooking up with the team captain's sister was a bad idea.

In my defense, the first time I saw her I didn't know who she was.

Kind, gorgeous, a little naïve. Ginny brightened my world from day one.

I knew I was no good for her. She was just out of a relationship and I had a reputation for having a new girl in my bed every weekend.

I tried to do the right thing. Honest.

I'm the one who insisted we should be just friends.

That lasted about as long as you'd expect.

But Ginny? She's the best—best friend, best everything.

So yeah, hooking up with the team captain's sister wasn't a great idea.

Would I do it again?

In a heartbeat.

AUGUST

ONE

Ginny

"What are you doing here?" I ask my brother through a small crack in the door.

He leans his large frame against it, widening the gap and keeping me from closing it on him. "I'm checking on my favorite sister."

"I'm your only sister."

He pushes a big shoulder against it, and I give up on trying to keep him out. Crossing the small dorm room in three steps, I resume my position on the bed.

"Have you left the dorm at all this weekend?" He follows me and takes a seat at the end of my bed. "Hey, Ava."

My roommate Ava's on the phone with her boyfriend Trent, but waves and blushes when Adam acknowledges her.

"I'm enjoying my last days of summer vacation," I tell him as I pull my hair down from the messy bun and attempt to make it look like I haven't been rocking this same hairstyle for three days. It's the day before classes start and the only things going on around campus are parties and new student activities—neither of which have sounded appealing enough to get dressed and leave my room.

He picks up the package of cheese and peanut butter crackers I'd been devouring when he knocked. "This looks like the opposite of fun. And you bailed on my party last night."

"A party with a bunch of your teammates . . . yeah, no thanks."

"You can't sit in here moping forever. Bryan did you a favor. Long-distance relationships in college suck. Next to no one survives them. Plus, the guy was a tool anyway. Don't let it ruin college. College is awesome."

My heart cracks a little more at the reminder that my ex-boyfriend, who should be with me at Valley starting our freshman year together, decided at the last minute to go to Idaho instead.

It wasn't entirely his fault. He got the offer after they'd lost their second-string quarterback to an injury. Bryan became their new second-string and I was cut from his roster altogether.

Adam nudges my arm with his elbow. "Come on. Let's grab lunch, or come over and hang at the apartment, meet my roommates. *You don't need no man. There's plenty of fish in the sea.* What kind of pep talk are you feeling?"

I smile. "Of course you think there's plenty of fish in the sea. You have a new girlfriend every semester."

"Exactly. I speak from experience."

I don't think it'll be that easy for me. My brother is a hockey player, tall and muscular, and I guess objectively he's attractive. He certainly has no problem finding girlfriends if that's any indication. He has perfect hair; I'll give him that. I've had hair envy my whole life. Where my dirty blonde hair is stuck somewhere between straight and curly, his is lighter, thick, and the longish strands hang perfectly at the nape of his neck.

"How about lunch?" he asks.

It's tempting, really. If anyone can make me feel better, it's Adam, but I'm not sure I want to feel better yet.

Being single is a wonderful and liberating thing. "Single and ready to mingle." "I'm every woman." "Put your hands up." "Truth hurts". There are so many songs about it, I can't even list them all. But the thing about the single girl anthem . . . it's usually born out of a lot of tears from the last heartbreak.

The girl power and celebration of singledom only comes after you've cried your eyes out and burned every item that belonged to the last man who did you wrong.

I'm still somewhere between the two, but I catch Adam's drift—it's probably time to re-enter the land of the living.

I let out a cleansing sigh. "Tomorrow. Breakfast tomorrow, I promise. I need to help Ava get our room organized." I glance over to the boxes stacked on top of my desk that I still haven't unpacked.

Adam doesn't look convinced.

"I said I promise."

He holds his pinky out and I roll my eyes but link it with mine.

"I'll swing by on my way to the dining hall. You've got an eight o'clock, yeah?"

I nod and groan. I am so not a morning person. "Yeah, but you don't."

"Preseason workouts this week and next at six. I'll be heading over to eat around that time anyway."

"Six o'clock in the morning?"

"Yeah. In the morning." The deep chuckle that follows makes me smile. He stands and ruffles my already messy hair.

"Stop it." I swat at his hand. He knows I hate it when he treats me like I'm twelve. In his mind, a three-year age gap makes him *so* much wiser.

"Be ready at quarter `til," he says as he moves to the door. "I'd hate to have to bang on the door and wake up the entire hall."

"God, you're obnoxious," I say, but he's already gone.

I get up and shower, hoping it washes away some of the lingering sadness along with the cracker crumbs. Back in my room, I look around it with fresh eyes and cringe. Ava's side is organized and decorated with bright colors and then there's my side. Even I can admit it looks a little depressing. Okay, a lot. White concrete walls, gray bed frame, and desk. The only color is my pale-yellow comforter.

After I'm dressed, I finally unpack. I didn't bring a lot of personal items because so many of them reminded me of Bryan. I fill the closet with my clothes and shoes, organize all of my school stuff on the desk, and I tape up a few pictures of my family and friends from high school on the wall.

Standing back, I survey the results. It's a start, and I feel a little more ready to face the world tomorrow. I flip on the small bedside light and crawl under the covers to sleep. I pick up my phone out of habit. Nothing good ever happens from scrolling your phone after midnight.

All of my friends from high school are posting selfies and tours of their new college dorms. There's Bryan, handsome as ever, in blue and orange. The college campus is in the background and he's lined up beside a group of big guys I assume are other football players based on their size. They hold beers and smile looking at the camera. He's obviously having no problem enjoying college without me.

That same handsome face I've known my whole life. We were neighbors, childhood friends, and then high school sweethearts. I close my eyes and the last conversation I had with him replays in my mind.

"I don't understand. What do you mean you're not going to Valley? We're supposed to leave in three days." We lie on my bed and I'm still in that post-sex high, so it takes me a few seconds to realize he's serious.

His heavy weight on top of me suddenly feels claustrophobic. "I got a call from the coach at Boise State. One of their incoming freshmen got into a car accident. He's out all year, maybe longer."

"But we've been planning on going to college together for two years, and Idaho is like . . . a long way from Arizona. How is this going to work?"

He hesitates and runs a hand over his jaw while he studies me with an embarrassed look on his face.

"Oh my god. You're not just telling me you're going to Boise; you're ending this?" I motion between us.

"I don't think it would be fair to either of us to go to college with unrealistic expectations. You said it yourself, Idaho is a long way from Arizona. When we come back for holidays or summer vacations, we can pick up where we left off. You'll always be my perfect girl, Ginny." His gaze drops from my face to my cleavage and continues doing a long sweep of my naked body. The least a guy can do is avoid staring at your boobs while he breaks up with you. Or pull out. "But, I think we should give ourselves the freedom to explore and have fun while we're apart."

"Why would you break up with the perfect girl? That doesn't make any sense," I mutter quietly to the room, swiping a rogue tear. I didn't give him the satisfaction of seeing me cry then and I'm not going to let him ruin my first day of college tomorrow.

I force a smile as I reimagine all the amazing things college will bring without Bryan. For starters, I don't have to do anything I don't want to. I can be absolutely selfish with my time. Truthfully, I have no idea what that looks like anymore, but I'm ready to find out.

I put in my earbuds, hit play, and fall asleep with Beyoncé on repeat.

The next morning, Ava and I get ready for classes. She's got the TV hooked up and *Vampire Diaries* season one, episode one playing. Feels right somehow. The first season of everything starting today.

Our room finally looks like two excited freshmen live here. Ava's side is a little more personalized, photos of her and Trent, her boyfriend, take up most of the wall above her bed.

My roommate is in a serious relationship with her high school boy-friend, who is going to college upstate. It was something else we'd shared when we first connected over the summer, being in serious relationships. They don't seem concerned about the distance, although it's not nearly as far as Idaho.

Ava's been on the phone or texting him the better part of the last week since we moved in. She's nice and I think we'll be great roommates. I guess since she's in a relationship, at least I won't have to worry about her bringing random guys back to the dorm. Because I'll be starting college single and not exactly thrilled about the opposite sex, it'll be nice not to worry about that.

"Do you want to come to breakfast with us?" I ask as I'm preparing to leave.

"No thanks." She shakes her head, making her short, black hair toss around her heart-shaped face. "I'm going to video chat with Trent on our way to our first classes."

A little pang of jealousy hits me, but I push it aside and head down-stairs to meet Adam. Excited energy floats in the air. Blue and yellow ban-ners hang on the front of the dorms welcoming us to the new school year.

Students are already out in droves heading off to classes, backpacks strapped to their shoulders, coffees in hand. They walk mostly in groups to their destinations; those who don't have earbuds in or stare down at their phones.

The Valley campus is truly beautiful. When we dropped Adam off be-fore his freshman year and I got a look at the campus for the first time, I knew that it's where I wanted to go to college too. The buildings are mostly old and historic looking, green grass makes it feel a little less like the desert, and there's a huge fountain in the middle of campus.

"Ginny," Adam calls out, catching me by surprise while I'm lost peo-ple watching.

"Hey." I turn to see him and his friend and teammate Rhett with him.

"You remember Rauthruss?" Adam asks and runs a hand through his still-damp hair. Even wet it looks better than mine.

Rhett grins and steps forward with his hands shoved in his pockets. "Hey, Ginny. Good to see you again. Welcome to Valley."

Rhett Rauthruss is a giant man-boy. He's tall and built. His legs are like tree trunks. Seriously, his thighs could crush my head. But he's got this baby face and pouty mouth that keeps him from looking too intimidating. He's also got a really great Minnesota accent that I absolutely love.

He and Adam have been teammates and roommates since their freshmen year, so I've met him a few times over the years and he came home with Adam once last semester for a weekend.

"Hey, Rhett, good to see you too."

He grins a little shyly.

"Are we ready?" Adam asks. "I'm starving."

My dorm doesn't have its own dining hall, so we cross the street to Freddy Dorm to eat. I follow Adam and Rhett inside, and we fall into the long line of people entering the dining hall, scanning their student ID cards as they go.

The smell of burned toast hangs in the air as we shuffle inside the busy dining room. Rhett heads off at a near jog for food, but Adam hangs back with me. "Grab food and then meet us at the big table in the right corner. You can't miss us."

With that, he rushes off too.

I do a lap while I check out the food options. Five or six different stations are set up with varying breakfast foods ranging from yogurt to omelets and everything in between.

I decide on waffles, get at the end of the line, and pick up a tray. The guy in front of me drums his fingers on the back of his tray impatiently. His fingers are long and strong-looking . . . somehow just really attractive. I let my gaze move up to his forearms and appreciate them in the same way. Tan and toned. The gray T-shirt he's wearing hugs his back and the short sleeves are snug against his biceps. Muscular but not too beefy.

When it's finally his turn, he sets the tray down and grabs a plate. With his profile to me, I take in his straight nose and sharp cheekbones. Dark, messy hair that I have the ridiculous urge to run my fingers through, sticks up on his head.

I think maybe I spent too many days in my dorm room crying over Bryan. I'm flat out gawking at this point, but it's a little hard not to. This guy is attractive without even getting a front view. He has this whole look about him that feels like he didn't bother glancing in the mirror this morning. Actually now that I think about it, it's a little frustrating that I spent twenty minutes taming my hair while he rolled out of bed and managed to look like that.

Damn. Welcome to Valley, Ginny.

He proceeds to fill his plate with four waffles. These aren't the size of the small, frozen waffles that you pop in the toaster, they are huge, bigger than my head waffles. He grabs a second plate and fills that one with bacon and eggs farther down the line. He glances between his plates and the food still left on the warmers ahead like he might not be finished.

I chuckle and he glances back at me. My breath hitches when his blue eyes meet mine. Not blue, a thousand shades of blue. He gives me a sheepish smile.

"Can you hand me another plate?" His deep voice washes over me, vibrating my insides. He's a lot to take in, but I do, not able to stop myself. His hair isn't only dark brown, it has hints of lighter strands too. It's like no part of him could decide on being one thing and instead he's made up of varying shades and depths.

He has an athletic build, tall but not towering over me like Bryan did. My ex was six foot four, which made him a great height to see over a mass of bodies on the football field, but not so great for kissing without standing on my tiptoes. I'm standing here wondering if I could kiss this guy flat-footed.

Aaand he asked me a question.

"Are you serious?"

He doesn't bat an eye, so I grab another plate and hand it to him.

"Thanks."

I fill my plate with one waffle like a reasonable human and continue to scoot down the line behind him. He's added four pieces of toast and a handful of grape jelly packets to the third plate, and he's *still* eyeing the food ahead of us.

"Are you feeding a family of bears?"

One side of his mouth pulls up. "Just one very hungry dude."

We reach the end of the line and he slows like he's waiting for me. He eyes my tray. "Barely four hundred calories on that plate. How are you going to make it to lunch?"

"Somehow I think I'll manage."

We start walking, both in the same direction.

"Are you following me?" I ask when we've walked shoulder to shoulder for three steps.

"No. I think you're following me." We reach the table where Adam and Rhett are seated with a group of guys.

"Yo, Heath!" one of the guys calls to him.

It takes a couple of seconds for my brain to catch up.

"You're a hockey player?" I frown while I try to place him. I've only met a few of Adam's teammates, but I've been to several games, so I'm surprised I don't recognize him.

His brows pull together studying me, maybe trying to place me as well. "Not a fan of hockey? I think you're at the wrong table then."

Adam stands and puts a protective arm around my shoulders. "She's not a fan of any men at the moment."

Kill me now.

I stare down at my white tennis shoes as Adam introduces me. "Guys, this is my baby sister, Ginny. It's her first day."

The group offers their hellos and grunts of acknowledgment. They've all got several plates of food in front of them like Heath and are shoveling it in like they haven't eaten in days.

I take a seat and so does Heath, across from me.

"Did you come to the games last year?" he asks as he pours syrup over his waffles.

"Yeah, a couple. Why?"

"I don't recall seeing you."

This makes me laugh. In a crowd of cheering fans, how could he possibly remember? "I don't recall seeing you either."

He leans across the table with a cocky smirk. "I was the one doing all the scoring."

CHAPTER TWO

Ginny

I eat my breakfast, staying mostly quiet while the guys talk back and forth. They complain about the workout this morning and talk up the season. I've gotten good over the years at tuning out hockey talk.

I catch Heath staring at me an uncomfortable number of times. Uncomfortable because I only know he's staring at me because I'm staring at him too.

Oh, and he eats every one of the giant waffles, plus the rest of his food.

"Where's your first class?" Adam asks me as we're finishing up.

"Umm . . . the humanities building, I think."

He nods and sits back in his chair. "You know where it's at? Want me to walk you?"

I resist rolling my eyes. "Yes. I'll be fine."

"Humanities building?" Heath asks. "I'm walking that way."

Standing, I put on my backpack and then pick up my tray. "I've got it, really." I glance at my brother. "See you later." And then I give a little wave with my free hand to the rest of the table.

As I'm dropping my empty tray, Heath steps up beside me. "Adam Scott's sister . . . I don't see the resemblance."

"Thank you . . . I think?"

He's still following me when we get to the exit. "There's really no need. I know where I'm going."

"Okay." He shrugs one shoulder. "See you around, Ginny Scott."

The way he says my name is taunting and playful and has my tummy doing weird, excited things.

"Hopefully not if I want there to be any food left to eat," I say before he can leave.

I should walk away now, but there's a bizarre chemistry between us and something about him makes me feel the best I have in days. We stand a foot apart, grinning at one another and forcing people to go around us.

He snaps out of it first. "Better get here early for lunch then. That's when I get in my big meal for the day."

"Your big meal?" I can't help but laugh.

"That was nothing. I burned those calories before you woke up this morning."

"Presumptuous, much? Maybe I'm a runner or a soccer player."

His gaze sweeps over me slowly and I hold my breath. "Are you?"

"N-no."

He laughs and takes a step away. "Noon. That's what time I eat lunch, in case you want to get here early or join me."

He gives me his back before I come up with a witty response. I can't decide if that was flirty banter or him really asking me to have lunch with him, but I figure it's best not to dissect it too much and not to show up at noon. I might be ready to sing all the single girl anthem songs, but I am not ready to start planning my schedule around cute boys. No matter how very, *very* cute they are. The only thing I've made any sense of from my breakup with Bryan is that I need to figure out who I am and what I want, make my own friends. Over the two years Bryan and I dated I grew farther and farther apart from my other friends. To the point, I really don't have any good girlfriends to call up and cry on their shoulder.

This is my fresh start.

I find English Composition easy enough. It's a big class in a room with long rows of seats, many of which are already taken.

I take a spot in the middle trying not to appear too eager or too much like a slacker. I don't mind English, but I'm not a fan of being called on in class either.

After English I have algebra and I'm not quite as confident about where the building for it is located. The Valley campus is pretty big, and the number of people walking around makes it hard to get my bearings. I slip my thumbs around the straps of my backpack and fall into the crowd of students, hoping I look like I fit in and don't have FRESHMAN stamped on my forehead.

I'm backtracking to find Moreno Hall when my front pocket vibrates. I pull out my phone and move off the sidewalk onto the grass, so I don't get trampled.

Adam: Get lost yet?

I glance up at the building that is most definitely not Moreno Hall.

Me: Of course not, but say I was looking for Moreno Hall . . .

Adam: Hang a left just past the engineering building, it's on the corner—big fancy-ass looking building, can't miss it.

A minute later he follows up.

Adam: Find it?

Me: I would have found it on my own eventually.

Adam: I'm sure.

Hurriedly, I pocket my phone and head to Moreno Hall.

By the end of the day, I'm exhausted but even more excited about the semester. All of my classes seemed okay, I met a few girls on our hall, and Ava and I spent the late afternoon walking around campus and soaking in all the first-day excitement.

I don't even think about Bryan until we get back to the dorm and I'm lying on my bed listening to Ava and Trent share first-day stories. I consider texting him for all of a millisecond. I don't hate him. Maybe I should. It'd probably be easier to get over him that way, but despite the awful way he ended things, I don't totally blame him for taking a great opportunity. And I'm working on not blaming him for not even wanting to try to make it work. Of course, I don't text him. Mostly because I don't think I can handle hearing how awesome everything is on his end. Not when the most notable part of my day was watching a table of jocks devour food like they hadn't eaten in months.

Over the next few days, I don't have any more hockey team run-ins. Which might be in part because Ava and I stock up on noodles and have lunch in our room most days and when I do go to the dining hall, I avoid the back table. My brother's teammates all seemed nice, but I'm not interested in continually being referred to as Adam Scott's baby sister.

Adam texts me every day to check in and invites me over to his place to hang out. I finally give in and agree to dinner Thursday night.

"Are you going to the dorm social tonight?" Ava asks that afternoon as we're hanging out in the room. I'm watching a new makeup tutorial, and she's letting me practice on her. I know a lot of people like to use themselves as a model, but I've never been one for wearing much makeup. Putting it on other people, though, makes me insanely happy.

"Can't. I'm having dinner with my brother. Tomorrow night? I've heard several fraternities are having parties."

"Trent is coming to town this weekend. I meant to ask how you felt about him staying in the dorm? If it makes you uncomfortable, we'll get a hotel."

"He's coming to visit already?"

She grins wide and the raspberry red color I've put on her lips looks fantastic. "Yeah, we've worked it out so we can visit each other almost every weekend this semester."

I hadn't given much thought to what we'd do when he was visiting. I grab a gloss and she parts her lips to let me coat them with a little shine. "He should stay here, of course."

"Cool. Thank you. Trent was stressing about coming up with the money for a hotel. The only one in town that's reasonably priced looks like it also rents by the hour." She pulls her mouth down into a grimace. "But it'll be fun. You'll like him."

"I'm excited to meet him. What are you guys going to do?"

"I'm not sure. Maybe the football game, maybe skipping it to make out." She blushes.

I nod, suddenly imagining a weekend of trying to ignore the sex sounds coming from the other side of the room.

Adam picks me up after he's done with classes for the day. I smile when his familiar Jeep comes into view. He stops at the curb outside of my dorm and I hop in.

"How's the first week?" he asks as he drives toward his apartment.

"Good. I think I'm finally getting a feel for the campus. It's sort of con-fusing—all the old buildings look the same. And what's up with the floor numbering in Emerson?"

He chuckles lightly. "How long did it take you to figure out there are two second floors?"

"Long enough that I was late to class."

"You'll have it memorized in no time and then you'll be laughing at the newbies getting lost."

"You're laughing at us?"

"Of course, we are." He winks.

"I think I might need to find a group or join something." I didn't do a lot of extracurricular activities in high school. I hung out with friends, I attended sporting activities and was always happy to cheer on my school, but there wasn't anything I cared about enough to dedicate my hours before or after school.

"Why's that?" Adam asks as he pulls into the parking lot of the apartment complex.

"Everyone here seems to be into something except me. The girls on my hall are great and I've met a few people in class, but they've all got a clique of people interested in the same things. The girls rushing sororities, the jocks, the nerds . . . I swear it's worse than high school."

He nods. "I guess that's true. I never thought about it before."

"That's because you came to college already in one of those cliques and with an instant group of friends."

"What about your roommate?"

"Ava's great, but she has a boyfriend at another college. I get the feeling she'll be spending a lot of her weekends visiting him or him visiting us." I scrunch up my nose. "He's staying with us this weekend."

"Did you find somewhere else to crash?"

"No. Why? It's my room too."

"Ginny, trust me, you need to find someone on your floor who'll let you stay in their room this weekend. Your dorm room is tiny, and they're going to be naked and going at it—that sounds hella uncomfortable for everyone. Unless you're into that sort of thing." Now he scrunches up his face. "Don't tell me if you are. I'd like to continue to believe my baby sister is asexual."

I snort laugh, but then everything he's saying hits me. "You're right. I can't stay there."

He nods. "There's always someone leaving on the weekends. Ask around and see who's heading out of town and will let you crash in their room."

"This is a thing. Seriously?"

"I lived in a suite, so it wasn't that big of a deal. I'd just crash on the couch in the living room."

"Ugh. I should have been a jock. Then I would have a ready-made clique and I wouldn't be getting kicked out of my own room."

"You're welcome to stay at my place."

"I'll figure it out." I appreciate him, but there has to be another option.

Adam's apartment isn't far from campus and if the number of vehicles with Valley University bumper stickers and license plate holders is indicative of how many students live here, then I'd say it's a lot.

He leads me up the stairs to the second-floor unit.

"Where is everyone?" I ask as we walk into the quiet living room.

"Campus or the gym." He drops his backpack on the couch. "We have preseason workouts twice a day this week. I'm gonna change real quick." He heads into one of the bedrooms off the living room.

"Where do you want to eat?" he calls through the open door.

"I don't care. Wherever you want."

I walk around the apartment scoping out my brother's living arrangements. There are three bedrooms, Adam's and then two on the opposite side of the unit. In the middle is an open concept area that has a kitchen, dining, and living room.

The place isn't that big but it's a pretty nice setup and feels huge by comparison to my tiny dorm room.

In the living room there's a matching couch and chair in a light brown leather. A coffee table, its top made of old hockey sticks, sits in front of the couch. The only artwork on the walls are a few jerseys and a hockey poster of the Bruins—Adam's favorite team.

The entire apartment is cleaner than I would have expected. A few empty Gatorade bottles on the kitchen counter, a football and a hockey stick—which I can't help but note is a random combination of sporting goods—lying in the middle of the floor in the living room, and a couple of stray articles of clothing on the backs of the chairs at the dining room table.

Adam reappears as I'm looking inside their empty refrigerator.

"Where's all your food?"

"We haven't gone shopping yet."

"What do you eat?"

He fills a glass with tap water and chugs it before responding. "We mostly eat on campus or we go out. We have a small kitchen in the locker room too that is re-stocked every few days."

"Can I use your bathroom before we go?" I head toward the one that is near his bedroom.

"Use the other one." He points to the bathroom on the opposite side of the apartment. "The light is out in mine. I need to get new bulbs."

"How do you see to shower or pee?" I ask.

"I leave the door open."

Boys are weird.

●

Instead of going to a restaurant, Adam and I go through a drive through and eat in his Jeep while he takes me all around Valley showing me Frat Row and some of the popular college bars and restaurants.

"Have you heard from Mom and Dad?" he asks. "Are they back from their trip?"

"They get back tomorrow, I think." Our parents went on some fancy, romantic vacation to Mexico. Initially I'd been bummed that they weren't going to be able to drop me off at college, but I'm glad they missed seeing me all sad and teary. The day Adam and I arrived on campus, I dropped my things in my room and then fell onto my new bed and sobbed. Poor Ava must have thought I was nuts.

"I'm really glad you're here," I admit.

He grins. "Me too. I get to spend the last year of college with my baby sister."

"You have to stop calling me that. I'm not a baby."

His mouth pulls into a wider smile. "Come over this weekend and crash at my place. You'll avoid listening to your roomie's sex sounds, and I'll introduce you to everyone. People are always coming and going from our apartment. It'll be good to meet more people here. Hell, maybe I'll throw a party."

"You never let me come to your parties in high school and now you're practically begging me. I find this quite redeeming even though now I don't actually want to go. Back then I would have killed to hang with you and your friends."

"High school was different. No one here cares if you're a freshman or senior or if you go to college at all. Plus, I want to see that you're settled. I know the shit with Bryan was rough."

I groan and Adam laughs.

"Only one condition. Promise me that you won't get wasted and make an ass of yourself in front of my teammates. I'm captain this year, and I need them to respect me."

"I promise," I say as I roll my eyes and toss a fry in his direction.

CHAPTER THREE

Heath

"Carry me. My legs are dunzo." Maverick leans his sweaty, heavy frame against me.

"Get the fuck off. I'm barely standing on my own." I wobble and take a seat in my stall.

The first week of hell training is done and we survived . . . mostly. Coach Meyers likes to start out the year with a shit ton of conditioning and weight training. We won't even be allowed to step on the ice for another two weeks.

My buddy falls into the seat next to me and pulls a T-shirt over his head. "Wanna grab a drink at Prickly Pear?"

"I can't. Scott's called a house meeting," I say, annoyed and loud enough so Adam can hear me.

"Four-thirty. Don't be late," Adam says sternly. The rest of the guys are scared of him, being our team captain and all, but I know better. He's all talk. I push his buttons on a regular basis and I'm still standing despite him having a good three inches and fifteen pounds on me.

Maverick and I stop for alcohol to restock for the weekend. When we get back to the apartment, we settle into the couch for our house meeting.

I've only lived here for a month and this is the second meeting Adam has called. It looks to be a long year. At least I have Mav for entertainment. He lives downstairs in a single apartment, but he spends way more time here than his own place.

His French bulldog, Charli, lies at his feet, staring up at him with adoring eyes. Charli is pretty much the only one who looks at Maverick like that. He's a total jokester and softie, but his size and tattoos intimidate most people.

Adam and Rauthruss wander out of their respective rooms. Rauthruss grabs a wooden chair from the dining table and Adam takes a seat in our leather recliner. He eyes the bottle in Maverick's hand. "Dude, really?"

"Ah, ah, ah," Mav tsks. "You can't speak until you have the bottle. New house rule." He hands it to Adam with a smirk. "Take a shot, captain, my captain."

"You don't even live here." Adam takes a long swallow of the MD 20/20 anyway and grimaces. "That shit's nasty. I haven't had Mad Dog since high school."

"Ironically, that's the last time I got called to a family meeting, too," Mav points out, taking the bottle back.

"Yeah, well feel free to leave since, again, you don't live here, but this won't take long. Three things." He holds up his fingers like he's talking to children. I glance over at Mav as he runs a hand along his tattooed chest where he's spilled on himself and a trail of alcohol trickles down to his shorts. Okay, maybe we're more like overgrown toddlers than functioning men. Maverick and I like to have fun, so sue us. We show up on the ice where it matters.

"Number one," Adam goes right into it. "We looked like shit out there this week."

Mav holds up a finger, takes a drink, and then speaks. "We're not even on the ice yet. Give it time."

Adam starts to respond, but not before Mav hands him the bottle and he begrudgingly takes another sip. "No, it's my last year and I'm not taking any chances by waiting for ice time. I think we should invite the guys over."

"Party. Good call," I say and find the bottle thrust into my side.

As I'm taking a drink, Adam shakes his head. "No, not a party. Well, okay, a party, but no girls. Just the team."

"You want us to spend our nights with a bunch of sweaty guys now too?" We're already spending long days in conditioning together. The only thing that got me through the week was the promise of a weekend of fun. "I'm not sure more time together is the answer."

"Girls," Mav says. "The answer is always girls. Let's get the freshmen laid."

"That's actually not a bad plan," Rauthruss speaks up for the first time.

The bottle is passed to him and he fingers the label as he finishes. "Maybe they just need to let off a little steam."

Adam frowns and the vein in his forehead becomes noticeable—never a good sign. "We party all the time. The guys don't need our help finding chicks. This is about coming together as a team."

"You're going to go all weekend without your latest girlfriend?" Mav asks Adam pointedly.

Adam always has a girlfriend. I can't remember the current one's name. Hannah? Holly? I don't understand why he doesn't stay single. It isn't like he, or any of us for that matter, need the relationship label to get laid. But, no, Adam Scott is the full boyfriend experience. He doesn't only hook up or go on a few dates. He wastes months on these girls, going all in with dates and sleepovers . . . just not for more than six months or so at a time. He's an odd duck.

Rauthruss too. He's been dating the same girl since high school and she lives in freaking Nebraska. Why have a girlfriend you never see? The only perk of having a girlfriend is getting laid on a regular basis, right? I'm really asking; I have no idea.

"Maria and I broke up," he says with a shrug. "And it's just for tonight."

Maria. Wow, definitely off there.

"What happened to Heather?" Mav asks.

Ah, yes, Heather! My memory isn't failing me yet.

"They broke up in May. Keep up." Rauthruss reaches out for the Mad Dog again, but Maverick holds it up and shakes the empty bottle. Fuck, we went through that fast.

"Fine. Party tonight. No girls," Mav says and looks to me. I'm the last holdout. "It's one night, man."

"What are the other two things on the agenda. We'll circle back," I say with a smile and Mav chuckles.

"Nice. Circling back. I think my dad used that the last time we talked."

His dad is a big executive—suit and tie, phone permanently attached to his ear. Rich as sin, but kind of a prick, so we have a bit of fun at his expense with our corporate speak, or jargon, if you will.

Adam interrupts our joking, which to be fair is probably the only way to get us back on track. "Number two. Heath, you have to walk your dates out the door. Like personally see that they make it outside." He looks to Rhett who's turning a nice shade of red.

Mav gasps dramatically with a hand to his chest. Charli at his feet lifts her head to check on her owner. "Heath would never. He's a true gentleman."

"It was one time and I did walk her out." I glance at my flushed roommate. The memory of him all bed head and in his boxers kicking out a half-naked Kimberly still makes me smile. "I just didn't lock the door behind her. How was I supposed to know she was going to come back and try to work her way around the apartment?"

I mean, seriously . . . is it my fault that she broke into our place and slipped into bed with the guy? Apparently nothing is sexier or more challenging for a girl than a guy in a real committed relationship. And Rauthruss is as loyal as they come even though he barely sees his woman. It drives girls crazy. Seriously, he could have any chick he wanted. He might be onto something, not that I have any plans to try his method. Mine's working just fine.

Maverick sets the empty bottle on the coffee table and heaves a sigh. "Are there any items on your list that don't revolve around our dicks?"

No one speaks. Adam raises his brows and keeps his sharp stare on me.

"Agreed. I will walk them out." I'm almost positive I can remember to do that. Definitely can tonight since I'll be spending it with my hand apparently.

"Next item on the agenda," Mav prompts.

Adam looks a little nervous, pausing before he speaks. This can't be good.

"My sister is crashing here this weekend, so best behavior." He stands.

"What the hell? What happened to no chicks?" I ask.

"She's my sister, not the same thing."

"Depends. Is she hot?" Mav asks, totally serious, which makes the vein in Adam's head protrude.

Yes, yes she is. I keep that to myself. I'm not scared of Scott, but I'm not an idiot. If he knew my unfiltered thoughts on his little sister, I'd be neutered in my sleep. Nah, actually, he'd probably do it when I was wide awake. Can't really blame him. Ginny Scott is sexy as hell and all my thoughts about her are dirty.

Long, blonde hair, light brown eyes, and her legs . . . those long legs are the things dreams are made of.

"Best behavior." Adam pulls his phone out and walks toward his room.

"Meeting adjourned then, eh?" Mav says and then looks to me. "I'm gonna need a copy of the minutes on my desk by end of business."

"I'm right on top of that, sir," I say and give him the middle finger.

"What the hell are we going to do tonight?" Mav looks seriously defeated as he runs a hand through his dark hair.

"Halo?" Rauthruss lifts an Xbox controller.

"Why the fuck not." He pets Charli and grabs the controller with the other hand.

I get up and take a step toward my room. "I'm going to shower and touch base with myself."

Mav cackles. "Not as good as circling back, but good wordplay. Mariah or Ariana for inspiration music?"

"It's definitely a Mariah kind of day," I decide.

Mav hums as I walk by. "'Santa Baby' or 'Heartbreaker'?"

I shake my head. "'Fantasy.' Always 'Fantasy.'"

Later, I close my door so I can hear Nathan on the phone over the noise in the living room. A few guys have already made it over. I hope Scott's right, and this is what we need. He might be a pain in the ass, but he's not wrong about us needing to play better together. It's his last year, so I get the extra pressure to make it the best before he's done.

He's not interested in playing professionally, so this really is it for him.

"How does it feel to be back?"

"Not as good as it would feel to be practicing with the Coyotes right now," I say as I take a seat at my desk.

He snickers. "Soon enough."

"Eh," I grunt. I've never been much for living in the future. Even now that it's set. I signed with Arizona's professional team over the summer. Three more years at Valley and then I'll get paid to play hockey. It still hasn't really sunk in. "How's everything in Florida?"

"Good. Busy. Between the team and all the wedding plans, it's gotten nuts. Did you get the save the date?"

"I did." I pick up the thick paper invitation on my desk. "June, huh? You really think you can continue to not screw this up for another ten months?"

"God, I hope so. I don't know what I'll do if she wises up before then," he says in a teasing voice. I can hear his fiancée Chloe in the background taunting him back but can't make out her words.

"Tell her I said hey and thanks for the giant box of stuff. This one's got Chloe written all over it. A gift card to The Olive Garden?"

Nathan speaks away from the phone, "Busted. Totally called you out on The Olive Garden gift card."

"Take a nice girl to dinner," Chloe yells.

"You hear that?" my brother asks.

"Yeah, I got it."

They've been sending me packages every month since my freshman year. Each one is different and contains shit ranging from razors, body wash, homemade oatmeal raisin cookies (my favorite), to new clothes and cologne. And then there's the gift cards. Each month, a hundred dollars or more from random places.

Since I refuse to take money outright from Nathan, they find creative ways to be generous. I don't really need it. I have a full-ride scholarship for hockey and a part-time job that helps with anything else. But that's Nathan, always trying to take care of me.

"All right, well I won't keep you. Chloe and I are headed to the beach. Stay out of trouble."

I groan and tilt my head back.

With a chuckle, Nathan says, "I'm proud of you, but what kind of big bro would I be if I didn't remind you not to screw up? You've got more than ever on the line."

"Oh, I don't know, the cool kind maybe?"

"Have fun. I'll call you next week. Let me know if you need anything. Oh, and call Mom. She said she hasn't heard from you in two weeks."

"Been busy."

"Mhmm, weak excuse. Later, Heath."

"Bye, Heath," Chloe says in the background.

"Bye, guys, talk to you later."

FOUR

Ginny

Trent arrives late Friday afternoon and Ava is brimming with excitement. She introduces me and then recaps a list of facts about the guy. Facts she's already told me several times. I feel like I know him better than I know Ava at this point; she's told me *that much* about him. Maybe a little too much.

"I'm going to show him around campus and then we're going to the football game. Do you want to come with us?" She's practically beaming with happiness and I have a twinge of sadness that this could be me and Bryan if he weren't in freaking Idaho.

She leans into his side and Trent wraps an arm around her waist. His fingers slip under the hem of her T-shirt and he kisses her forehead.

It's obvious how much they've missed one another by the touchy-feely display in front of me, and I'm starting to understand just how imperative it is I get the hell out of here. I haven't even been able to bring myself to watch porn since Bryan broke up with me. I certainly can't handle a full-on romantic display with a side of orgasms.

"No, thanks. You two enjoy. My brother is having people over, so I'm going to go hang with them. You two will have the place all to yourself tonight. It was really nice to meet you, Trent."

I shower and get ready, hesitant to head over to Adam's before the party gets going. I appreciate that he always looks out for me, but I want to find my own friends at Valley, too, and if I run over there every time I need an escape, I'm going to spend the next year as Adam Scott's little sister instead of Ginny Scott. So tonight, I need to find some friends.

I text Adam to make sure he's there before driving over.

Adam: Yep. Just hanging out at the house. You coming over? I warned the guys to be on their best behavior.

Me: Yes, but please don't make it weird. I know you and your friends are disgusting. You don't need to warn them like I'm some sort of delicate flower.

I ignore the rest of his messages that pop up, telling me he's only looking out for me or whatever. Having an older, overbearing brother is a real pain sometimes.

The apartment is easy enough to find and I carry my backpack with a change of clothes and toothbrush up to the second-floor door and knock.

"You must be Little Scott." A guy with a shit ton of tattoos on full display thanks to his bare chest greets me with a goofy smile. "I'm Johnny Maverick."

"Ginny."

He pulls the door wide and I enter. A bunch of guys I don't recognize are standing around the apartment. For real, it's like I just entered the men's locker room with the way they all stop what they're doing and stare at me.

Adam's head pops up from the kitchen and he hustles forward. "Did you find it okay?"

"Yeah. I have this thing called maps on my phone."

I spot Rhett in the living room and he lifts a controller in greeting. "Hey, Ginny. Good to see you again."

I wave awkwardly. They're all still staring.

Adam shuts the door and I follow him into the living room. He points to the guy who answered the door. "You met Maverick. Ignore any and everything he says."

He scoffs. "I am hilarious and awesome."

"That's Liam, Jordan, and Tiny."

"Hey," they say in unison.

"Want something to eat or drink?" my brother asks and goes back to the kitchen.

"I'm okay for now." There's an empty seat next to Maverick, so I head for it and sit down.

"Where is Payne?" one of the guys asks him.

"Still showering and jerking it to Mariah, probably." Maverick stills, looks to me, and clears his throat. "Shit, sorry."

I laugh and wave him off. "Good for him. And Mariah."

"I like you." Maverick puts his arm around me on the back of the couch, but it's in a friendly way that doesn't feel like he's hitting on me.

"Hands off," Adam's deep voice bellows from the kitchen.

Maverick rolls his eyes and I'm glad he's not so easily intimidated by my brother. It was a real issue in high school before Adam graduated. He would look at guys the wrong way for talking to me and they'd scamper off too afraid of him.

He stands and looks down at me. "You need a drink? A smoke?"

"Yeah, I think I might need a drink after all."

The party, or what's arrived of it, moves outside on the deck off the kitchen of the apartment. It's nice out. Still hot like August nights always are in Arizona, but a nice breeze and the cold drink in my hand helps. Even Adam seems to relax as the guys kick back with their beers. It's still just the guys on the team, but it's early.

"I'm going to get another drink." I head inside to the bathroom and have to use the flashlight on my phone to see anything. Why my brother hasn't changed the light bulb is beyond me.

I can't really see much in the mirror, enough to make out my French braid is mostly still intact. In the kitchen, I rummage through the refrigerator looking for something besides beer, but it's that or Wild Turkey. Definitely no.

As I turn, movement catches my eye and I jump in surprise. "You scared me."

He grins, hand gliding through the wet hair sticking up on his head like he ran a towel through it and said fuck it. He looks me over carefully. I'm frozen, my tongue feels heavy or too wide for my mouth or something.

"Hey, Ginny."

"Hi." I look around dumbfounded. I'd expected to run into him, but not half-naked. "Do you live here?"

"Well, I don't usually walk around in my boxers at other dude's houses." He looks to the ceiling and a smirk pulls at his lips. "Well, not often."

I'd been actively avoiding the wall of nakedness in front of me, but now that he's acknowledged it, I can't look away.

The only thing he wears are a pair of gray boxer briefs that hug his huge thighs and—oh my god, Ginny, do not look at his crotch. Shit, too late. I tear my gaze away from the bulge and up to his abs. Forget a boring six-pack, Heath has ridges and lines that wrap around his midsection. I follow the line to his chest and biceps. It shouldn't be possible for someone to look this good naked.

And oh my God, stop looking already!

Adam comes through the door before I can make words come out of my mouth.

"Payne, fucking finally. We thought you drowned in there." Adam tosses his empty in the trash and grabs another beer, his face hardening as he gets a good look at him. "Dude, what the hell? Put some clothes on in front of my sister."

"Relax, I didn't know she was here yet." Heath's tone is agitated, rightfully so.

"Pants, dude. Now."

"Adam," I admonish.

"And no hitting on my baby sister." His demeanor relaxes slightly, and he punches Heath playfully in the arm, although it seems a little harder than necessary.

"Are you coming back outside?" Adam asks me, pausing at the door that leads to the deck.

"I'll be right there," I assure him.

Heath brushes by me, the heat of his body licking flames up my arm and grabs two beers from the fridge. He hands one to me. "So, I hear you're sleeping with me this weekend."

"Umm . . . what?"

"I hear you're sleeping at our place this weekend." He leans a hip against the counter and pops the top off the beer.

"Right. Yeah. My roommate's boyfriend is in town for the weekend."

"Lucky for us."

"I doubt you guys will even know I'm here."

"One chick among twenty-seven guys? Plus, it's you. You're kind of hard to miss." His eyes drop to my mouth.

"One chick? Please. Actually, I'm surprised there aren't girls over already. Are you hiding an orgy in your room?"

He laughs. It's a deep, playful tone that lights up my insides. "I wish."

He pushes off the counter. "Your brother has banned girls from the apartment tonight."

"What? Why?" That doesn't sound like Adam.

"Team building or some shit. Just you and the team, Ginny Scott."

"No. Absolutely not. Adam said he was going to introduce me to people, not hang with his bros."

With a light chuckle, he lifts his beer and takes a drink making me realize I haven't touched mine.

"I'm going to kill him."

"Well, that I want to see. I better get dressed." He winks and heads down the hall on the opposite side of the apartment from Adam's room. I'm finally able to take a breath again. Holy mother of all that is good, he's a lot.

I head outside and take a seat next to Adam. "No girls? What the hell? I thought you wanted to introduce me to people."

He looks conflicted on how to respond. "I will. I am." He motions around the party.

"People besides your teammates, Adam." I flail my hands around. "Girls."

"Yeah, let's get some girls over here," someone says and Adam scowls at them over my head and then drops his gaze back to me.

"Please?" I ask quieter. "I'm sure your teammates are great, but I don't want to hang with a bunch of dudes all weekend."

"Shit, Ginny, I didn't even think about Bryan and what it might be like to be around a bunch of guys . . ." He rubs at the back of his neck. "All right, yeah, let's have a real party."

That wasn't exactly what I'd meant by not wanting to hang out with a bunch of dudes, but if it gets girls over here, I will keep my mouth shut and let him think it's my sad, I hate all of mankind broken heart speaking.

"On it," Maverick says and pulls out his phone.

CHAPTER FIVE

Heath

A knock brings my attention to the door and Scott's head peeks in. "Hey, I'm going to run to the store to get more alcohol. You need anything?"

"Are you sure I'm allowed out of my room?" I ask. I still haven't bothered to get dressed. I sat down at my desk to check in with work and got distracted.

"Sorry, man, I'm a little protective of her. She's been through a lot."

I nod and open my top desk drawer and pull out the stack of gift cards. "Where are you going?"

"Dude, what all you got there?" He laughs and walks closer.

"Gift cards to pretty much every place you can think of."

His eyes widen. "You're coming with me. Bring your stash."

I don't know what his sister said to him, but in an hour's time, our place has become packed with guys *and girls. Good work, Ginny.*

Adam and I head out and make several stops getting booze and food. When we're on our way back, I finally decide to broach the subject on my mind.

"Soooo . . . your sister's smoking hot."

I'm messing with him, sort of. She is smoking hot, but I'm only sharing this information to get a rise out of him. As predicted, he pins me with a hard stare. I meet it and smile, letting him know I'm not intimidated.

"Off-limits, Payne."

"Relax, I'm giving you shit. I don't do the whole girlfriend thing like you. We've only talked a few times. She's nice."

"She is. I worry about her. She doesn't know a lot of people at Valley yet and I want to introduce her to everyone, but she's off-limits. Friend zone only, man. I know how you are."

Ouch. I'm a perfect gentleman, thank you very much. Just because I don't date the same girl for months at a time, doesn't mean I treat them any worse.

"Is there some sort of big brother gene that makes you all giant over-protective assholes?"

"I'm serious. She just got out of a relationship and she doesn't need another guy screwing her over."

We pull up to the apartment and grab the bags to carry inside. Before we enter the apartment, Adam stops and regards me seriously. "You'll help me keep an eye on her? Make sure the rest of the guys don't mess with her?"

"She doesn't need a babysitter, man, and I'm no nanny."

His mouth pulls into a thin line and I cave, some part of me understanding his concern. I can't imagine having a little sister around my teammates and friends.

"I will keep an eye out, but I'm not going to lord over her like some sort of protector. Normal, friendly, keep an eye out, not whatever you've got going on there." I lift one of my arms bringing the grocery bags with it and motion to him and his moody intensity.

"Good enough, I guess."

I barely get the beer to the fridge before people are grabbing for it. I take two and spot the object of my and Adam's conversation sitting on the couch watching Maverick and Rauthruss play Halo.

"Hey," I say as I take a seat next to her and hold out a beer. Her hair is in an elaborate looking braid, the end hanging over one shoulder.

She takes the can hesitantly. "Thanks."

"Where's mine?" Maverick teases.

"In the fridge."

He holds a hand to his chest and pretends to be appalled.

"When you're as hot as Ginny, I'll start being your beer bitch, too."

She rolls her eyes as she pops the tab on her beer, but there's a faint blush to her cheeks.

"Genevieve," Adam calls from the kitchen and lifts a beer in a silent offering. She holds up the one I gave her so he can see she's already got one.

"Genevieve?" Mav asks. "I thought your name was Ginny."

"Ginny is short for Genevieve."

"That's rad. Why would you ever go by anything else?" He says her name again slowly. "Genevieve."

"Adam couldn't pronounce it when I was born."

Mav and Rauthruss bust up laughing.

"He was three," she adds, sticking up for him.

Rauthruss wins, like he always does, and Mav looks to me. "I'm done getting my ass kicked. Do you want to play?"

Nodding, I hold a hand up and he tosses the controller to me. I nudge Ginny. "What do you say?"

Rauthruss holds his out to her and she takes it.

"Have you played before?"

"I grew up with Adam. What do you think?" She sits forward and places her beer on the coffee table and straightens her shoulders. She's taking this seriously, looking determined and sexy as hell.

I set out with the goal of taking it easy on her, but Ginny doesn't need it. A few of the guys on the team crowd around to cheer her on and voice their hope of me getting my ass kicked. I win, just barely, and everyone boos.

"Thanks a lot, guys. Real team spirit."

"Do over," she demands.

I'm not confident I can pull off a victory twice, so I hesitate. We lean forward and grab our beers at the same time. I take a long drink while she sips and then grimaces.

"What was that face?" I stare at her cute little mouth and pink lips wet from the beer.

"Do you actually like the taste of beer?" she asks.

"I wouldn't drink it otherwise. Why didn't you say something?"

"I'm trying to learn to like it. It seems to be what everyone drinks here." She takes a longer drink as if to prove her point.

"Be right back."

I find Jordan and trade a twenty-dollar gift card for a twelve-pack of his hard seltzers. Two more people have taken over the game, so I motion for Ginny to follow me and lead her out to the deck.

"Try this."

"Thank you." She takes it and I lean back against the railing. There are a lot of people out here, but no one is paying us any attention except her brother. Big brother radar, I guess. Dude needs to chill.

I turn so his big-headed scowl isn't in my peripheral. There's no pleasing the guy. He wanted me to look out for her. I am, yet he still seems displeased. "I don't remember seeing you last year. You were really at our games?"

"A few of them." This time when she takes a drink, she smiles. "Much better." She plays with the end of her braid. "I was at the Colorado game and Arizona State and whoever you guys played for Parent's Night."

I think back to that game for a second. "Western Michigan."

"Right." Her smile lifts higher.

"I can't believe I didn't see you." Her phone is stuck in the front pocket of her jeans and I nod toward it. "Let me see your phone."

She hands it over without question and I program my number in it and send myself a text so I have hers.

"A lot of people come to the games. Plus, it wasn't like I was sitting on the bench with the team. Do you guys notice anyone in the crowd?"

"We notice hot girls." Maverick butts into the conversation and puts an arm around her shoulders. "You're hot, Little Scott."

She blushes and I hand her phone back.

Mav holds on to her and takes a step away from me. "I'm stealing her. Ginny here has a lot of people dying to meet her and you're hogging her, Payne."

"I do?" Ginny asks, sounding a little hopeful.

"Oh yeah." Mav nods. "Come on. You need a tour guide."

"Okay, yeah, that'd be great." She glances at me. "You probably want to hang out with your friends anyway." She lifts her seltzer. "Thanks for this."

"Anytime, Genevieve." I wink and tug the end of her braid.

She follows Mav, and I head inside, grab another beer, and take a seat back on the couch next to Rauthruss's giant frame. "I've got winner."

CHAPTER SIX

Ginny

T rue to his word, Maverick introduces me to everyone. He has a shirt on now, but the tattoos that cover both arms, all the way down to his fingers, are still visible. And I can spot a hint of his chest ink peeking out of the top of his T-shirt.

He leads me to where Liam and Jordan are standing. Liam and Maverick look like polar opposites. Where Johnny Maverick is dark-haired and covered in tattoos, Liam is blond and clean cut. He's even wearing a polo shirt. Even though I met him earlier, this time when Maverick introduces me, Liam extends a hand for me to shake. "Ginny, really nice to meet you."

"Same." His politeness catches me by surprise, but I slip my hand into his giant palm and squeeze.

"Roadrunner?" Jordan asks, holding a blue shot glass out to me.

I take it and sniff. "What's a Roadrunner?"

"It's like a Blue Kamikaze," he says and continues passing out shots.

I don't bother asking what a Blue Kamikaze is. My experience with alcohol is pretty limited. My high school bestie always grabbed a bottle of white wine from her parents' wine refrigerator and we'd drink that when we went to parties or had sleepovers. I never paid much attention to the label—none of it was great, but it was better than beer.

Jordan lifts his and the rest of us mimic the movement. I watch the others drink first. No one grimaces, so I take a sip. It's good, sweet. I smile and then drain the rest of the glass.

"We're off to meet more people," Mav tells them, pulling me away. He stops every couple of steps to make introductions and share the bottle of Mad Dog he's carrying. He's funny and kind of ridiculous, saying whatever pops into his head. Or maybe not, but if he's holding back at all—I don't want to think about the thoughts left unsaid.

"Total douche," he says after we're done talking to one guy that I think he said was a neighbor.

I laugh. "Then why did you introduce me to him?"

"Gotta know which ones to stay away from."

The next time he stops, it's in front of a girl standing by herself, her face hidden behind her phone. "Dakota, baby, I missed you all summer."

"You missed having someone to bum laundry detergent and junk food from." She looks up and over the device at Maverick. She's pretty. Big, ice-blue eyes and strawberry blonde hair that hangs in loose waves around her shoulders. She looks sweet, but the playful glare she gives Maverick makes me believe she could cut a bitch with words alone. That gaze slides to me and softens. "Hey."

"Dakota lives in the apartment next door. I'm her favorite neighbor." He tips his head to me. "This is Scott's little sister, Ginny."

"Hey there." I wave three fingers around my drink.

"Where's Reagan?" Maverick asks. Then to me, "Her roommate. The nicer of the two."

Dakota flips him off. "She'll be here. She was still getting ready. Ginny, you're a freshman?"

"Did the seltzer give it away?"

She lifts her cup. "We've got a better variety at our place if you want something else. These guys only know cheap beer and hard liquor."

"Thank you. That's really nice."

"Of course."

Dakota's phone pings, and she smiles at the screen. "Wardrobe emergency. I should go make sure Reagan's not buried under a pile of dresses. Do you want to come with me and scan our booze?"

Maverick nods his approval and smiles like a proud parent who's set up their kid on a successful playdate. "You two have fun. Don't tell her any lies about us, Dakota."

"Lies would be less incriminating."

Dakota lets us into her apartment across the breezeway from the guys.

"Help!" a muffled voice calls from one of the bedrooms. A girl with hair the color of honey pulled up in curlers rushes out wearing a silky robe. "I don't know what to wear."

Dakota laughs. "This is Ginny. Ginny, that's my neurotic but lovable roommate, Reagan."

"Hey," she says, breathless, cheeks pink.

"Green's a good color on you," I tell her and motion to the emerald color of her robe.

"She's right. Put on that green dress with the crisscross back."

Reagan smiles, deep dimples popping out. "Oh, right. I forgot about that one." She disappears back into the room.

Dakota moves to the kitchen and I hang in the living room looking around.

"I like your apartment." It's decorated with lots of black and white with pops of dark pink. Old Hollywood movie posters and cute furniture. It's a smaller version of my brother's, but same basic setup with bedrooms on either side of the living area.

"Thanks," she says, and I join her in the kitchen area. "Pick your poison." A wide selection of alcohol is spread out on their kitchen counter. Wine— red and white, hard lemonade, vodka, Captain Morgan, and a bunch of mixers. I settle on half a cup of white wine. After all the mixing, I'm a little nervous to drink too much.

"So, you're Adam Scott's little sister?" she asks with a smirk once we both have a fresh drink.

"I am. Yeah. You know him?"

"Everyone knows him. He's Adam Scott."

Reagan reappears in green with her hair down, looking like she walked out of a salon. If I could make that sort of transformation in five minutes, I'd probably get dolled up more often.

"Do we have a winner?" Dakota asks.

Reagan holds her arms out to her sides. "I think so."

"You look great." I glance down at my jeans and tank top. I'm underdressed by comparison. Dakota's in a skirt and T-shirt with tennis shoes, but her makeup and jewelry give it all a much more put-together look than my casual outfit. "Do you guys always dress up like this for parties?"

Dakota responds first. "This is my basic uniform, but that one"—she nods toward her roommate—"has her eye on a boy."

Reagan makes a face at her but smiles.

"Oooooh. Someone at the party?" I ask. "One of the hockey guys?"

"Yeah." She takes a seat next to me.

"She won't say which one. I've got money on Liam. He's got that nice guy vibe, but something about him screams that he's probably not afraid to get down and dirty in the sheets." Dakota pours white wine into a cup and hands it to Reagan.

"Liam? Really?" Reagan asks with a shake of her head. "He's not my type. And I'm not saying who because I don't want to jinx it."

"Well, he'd be a fool to turn you down," I tell her honestly. Reagan is the kind of pretty that you wish only existed on the pages of a magazine or on TV.

She takes the drink and sighs. "I'm nervous, which is ridiculous, right? Who gets nervous about going to a party where their crush is? It's like junior high all over except without the zits and braces. Thank god. I've been trying to talk to this guy for . . . a long time. I get all weird and shy around him. Well, shier than normal."

"You're going to knock his socks off. Trust me." Dakota says. "And if not, you get to come home to me."

"Have you guys been roommates for a long time?" I ask. It's easy to see how close they are. They tease, but it's with a smile and none of the catty, fake compliments that some girls do to one another.

"Since our freshmen year in the dorms," Reagan answers. "Dakota was all fast-talking and no-nonsense, and I think I spent half of first semester completely terrified of her."

Dakota laughs. "It's true. She said maybe three full sentences until she saw me crying over *The Notebook*."

"She was *sobbing*."

"Those old people get me every time."

They smile at one another and then Reagan adds, "We moved out as soon as we could last year."

Even though Reagan and Dakota are two years older than me, we fall into an easy camaraderie. They tell me more about their time in the dorms together and they ask me about Ava and how my first week went.

When we finally fall silent, my cheeks hurt from smiling.

"I can see it," Dakota says looking me over closely. "You've got the same eyes and smile."

This makes Reagan look between us and when her brown eyes land on me, they narrow as she studies me. "Same eyes and smile as who?"

"Ginny is Adam's sister."

"Adam Scott?" she asks, eyes widening through thick, black lashes.

Man, it really pains me that even someone as beautiful as Reagan has this reaction about my brother. At least my high school friends hid their fascination with him better.

"That's the one." My phone buzzes in my front pocket and I pull it out. "That's him, checking in. He's a total pain in the ass." I type back a response letting him know I'm next door.

"Everyone ready?" Dakota asks.

Reagan and I nod.

Dakota leads the way. "Let's do this."

Hanging out with Dakota and Reagan is fun. They know everyone, and after the initial shock of finding out I was Adam's little sister, they haven't made me feel like the other Scott.

Speaking of the popular Scott, when I finally spot him, he's in the corner with his arm wrapped around a girl I haven't met. He leans down and whispers in her ear and she giggles and tips her mouth up to let him kiss her. Gross. Seeing my brother in action—really not cool.

"What do women see in him?" I huff. "I mean, honestly?" I turn to Reagan and Dakota.

"Dude, your brother's hot." Dakota shrugs. "Sorry."

I scrunch up my face and walk toward him. He comes up for air when I clear my throat.

"Ginny." He pulls the girl tighter to his side and then nods to Dakota and Reagan. "I see you two met my sister."

"Yeah, she's way cooler than you. What happened?" Dakota deadpans.

"Tough crowd." Adam tilts his head to the girl still clinging to him. "Guys, this is Taryn."

"Hey." Her red lips pull up into a big smile. "Your brother's told me so much about you."

"Oh really?" I ask, surprised since he's never mentioned her, but I smile because I'm not an asshole, and it isn't her problem my brother jumps from girl to girl. "Well, it's nice to meet you." I give Reagan and Dakota a *save me* look, which they interpret quickly and make excuses for us.

"How does he already have a new girlfriend?"

Neither of them answers, not that I expected them to.

"It's the hot thing," Dakota says. "And the hockey thing."

"We should hang out tomorrow," Reagan offers.

"Are you coming to the pool party?" Dakota asks.

"What pool party?"

"Oh yeah, you should definitely come." Reagan smiles. I freaking love her dimples. "It's at The White House. It's a big, back to school party they have every year. Everyone will be there."

"I'm in." And just like that, I'm pretty sure I've made two new friends here.

CHAPTER SEVEN

Ginny

The next morning, I'm sitting outside on the deck FaceTiming with Reagan and Dakota recapping last night. I had so much fun and I'm excited to hang out with them again today.

Adam comes out, shirtless, hair matted from sleep, and a giant bottle of Gatorade in hand. "'Morning."

"Hey."

He takes a seat next to me with a big, tired sigh and glances to the phone in my hand with a smile. Which reminds me . . .

"Reagan, what happened with that guy last night?"

"Oh, nothing." She bites at the corner of her lip, making one dimple dot her cheek. "It was stupid. He's dating someone else. I didn't realize until last night. Moving on."

"How is that possible? You're gorgeous. Did you tell him you were into him?"

She shakes her head.

I angle the phone so she can see Adam. "Would you tell her that she needs to tell this guy so he can break up with his girlfriend to date her?"

He chuckles and Reagan's eyes go wide. "Oh my god, Ginny. Adam, you absolutely do not need to—"

"She's right." He nods and smiles at my new friend. "Guy must be crazy."

"See. Told you."

She covers her face with her hands like she's embarrassed.

"I'm going to hang with Adam for a bit."

"Hurry up and get over here," Dakota says, popping her head in front of the screen for a second.

"I'll be over soon," I promise.

"Looks like you made some friends," Adam says as I hang up the phone.

"I did. Thanks for letting me crash in your room last night."

"No problem. The couch wasn't too bad."

"That might have had something to do with the girl that was on it with you."

"Probably so," he agrees. "Do you girls want to ride over to the party together?"

"Sure, sounds good." I stand and stretch. "See you later."

I knock at Dakota and Reagan's and then open the door. "Hello?"

"In my room," Reagan calls.

Dakota sits on the bed and Reagan tosses two giant handfuls of swimsuits onto the comforter.

"I pulled all my suits for you to choose from," Reagan says.

I didn't bring a bathing suit from the dorm, so I'm thankful she's letting me borrow one but holy crap. "That is a lot of options."

She nods happily.

I shower and pull my hair into a braid. I go for a low-cut pink one-piece suit and my own cut-off shorts and sandals.

I'm waiting on Dakota and Reagan's couch while they finish getting ready when I get a text.

Hottest guy on campus: Did you leave without saying goodbye? <sad face>

Me: Who is this and how did you get this number?

Hottest guy on campus: Name is self-explanatory.

It is self-explanatory, sadly. I met dozens of people last night, but Heath is the only one I can recall with any detail. There's a hotness about Heath that goes beyond types and is more universal truth.

Hottest guy on campus: Back at the dorm?

Me: No, actually I'm next door waiting for Dakota and Reagan so we can leave for the pool party. Are you going?

Hottest guy on campus: Depends. Are you going to be there in a bikini?

I glance down at my very covered midsection.

Me: Guess you'll have to come to find out.

Despite Heath's texts that sound anxious to see me, he isn't around when Dakota, Reagan, and I meet Adam and Rhett in the parking lot to catch a ride over.

We pile into Adam's Jeep and drive the few blocks to the pool party. Adam parks along the street and points. "That's Ray Fieldhouse. The student fitness facility is inside, and a lot of the teams have private workout rooms there, too."

"Where's the rink from here?" I ask, trying to get my bearings. The Valley U campus is big and I'm still not sure where everything is.

"Couple of blocks west," Rhett answers.

I sling my beach bag over my shoulder and follow the guys up the sidewalk. "Whose house is this?" I ask once we get to our destination. I was expecting an apartment with a community pool or an old house with a tiny yard and pool. This is none of that.

"This is The White House," Adam remarks. "Guys from the basketball team live here."

We walk around to the back of the giant white house, aptly named, to the pool party going on outside. The pool itself takes up half the large yard and the other side is grassy with a volleyball net set up. There are people everywhere. *Everywhere.* The scene looks like something straight out of a spring break video. Music pumping loudly, girls lounging on rafts, guys chilling with beers in hand, a coed volleyball game.

Even in my tiny shorts and my cleavage pushed up to my ears, I'm grossly overdressed. And where does one stow a bag in a place like this? Something tells me I'm not going to need any of the things I packed: sunscreen, towels, bottled water, three pairs of sunglasses.

On the plus side, there are entirely too many people in the back yard of The White House to feel uncomfortable or self-conscious about my giant bag. My thoughts only stray as far as my next step.

We squeeze through behind Adam and Rhett's large frames to the keg. I'm introduced to more guys from the hockey team, some I recognize from last night.

"Tiny?" I can't help but ask of the guy who is anything but. "Your name is Tiny?"

Tiny, I find out once I have a beer in hand, is a nickname because Tony Waklsinski is the shortest player on the team. And I guess in comparison with Adam, who's at least five inches taller, I can sort of see it. I know how sensitive boys are about inches.

Maverick finds us and joins the circle. Today he's wearing a brightly colored Hawaiian shirt left open to reveal his chiseled abs and tattoos. He lifts the bottle of Mad Dog in his hand. "Shot?"

The other girls pass, but I'm feeling adventurous, so I take it and tip it back, letting some of the sweet liquid slide down my throat. I grimace; it's so sickly sweet that I chase it with beer, which doesn't really help since I'm not a fan of it either.

"All right. Let's not get my baby sister shitfaced." Adam takes the bottle and takes a drink three times as big as mine as if he's trying to drink it all so I won't.

"Anyone seen Payne? He's supposed to be bringing reinforcements." Maverick reaches for the nearly empty bottle and gives it a shake.

"No clue," Adam says. "Thought he was with you."

When Taryn shows up with her friends, that feels like my cue to leave.

"Mingle?" I ask Dakota and Reagan.

We make a circle around the party and head inside to check out the drink selection. "This is not what I thought of when you guys said pool party."

"It's more bikini party unless you're brave enough to get in the pool," Reagan says.

"What's wrong with the pool?"

"Going into the pool is the equivalent of posting an *I'm here to get laid* sign on your forehead," Dakota says. "Which if you're into that, it's totally fine, but don't say I didn't warn you." She holds up the vodka in invitation. "Drink?"

After we swap out our beer for vodka and tonic, we head back outside.

We sit on lounge chairs on the patio near a mister and watch the people in the pool. Some love matches (or rather, hookups) are being made while other people are being hilariously blown off.

Dakota drills me with twenty questions while we people watch. Now that we've spent a little time together, she holds nothing back, but somehow the way she pries is endearing.

"So, no boyfriend?" Reagan asks, leaning forward with her elbows on her knees.

"No," I say with a scowl.

Dakota laughs. "Oooh, there's a story."

"Not a good one."

Water drips onto my toes and I look up to see Maverick leaning over and shaking his head on us.

"Bad dog," Dakota scolds him.

I'm laughing as I dodge him continuing to get us wet when my gaze falls to a guy approaching from behind him.

"Ah, there he is," Maverick says, taking a seat next to me. "Payne, where the hell have you been?"

"Been around." His dark blue eyes land on me. He's got a twelve-pack of hard seltzer under one arm and my stomach flips. He pulls a bottle of Mad Dog out of his pocket and hands it to Maverick.

"Trade you." He motions with his head and Maverick stands, giving up his seat and taking the bottle.

He smells like soap and sun and wild dreams. Dreams you shouldn't allow because they're so out of reach, but you can't help but want. Dreams you don't speak of, but that live in the darkest corner of your mind.

"Swim anyone?" Maverick asks.

I shake my head as does Reagan.

"Oh, why not." Dakota stands, looks to me and shrugs with a smirk

"I'm going to find the bathroom. Do you want to come?" Reagan asks me, then glances between me and Heath.

"I'm good."

Heath opens the case and holds out a can. "Drink?"

As I wrap my hands around the cold can, he holds tight and leans in. "You look good. Do you want to skip this party and go make out?"

I laugh, but heat rushes to my core at the thought. "Pass."

"You wanna not skip this party and just make out right here?"

"Definitely pass." I pull the drink from his hand and pop the top. After I've taken a long drink, I ask, "Does that usually work for you?"

"Honestly?"

I nod.

"Every time."

I roll my eyes. "What is wrong with women?"

"I'm really good at making out." His stare darts to my mouth. I have no doubt.

"You and I are going to be just friends."

"Friends?" His brows raise. "I don't have girl friends."

"You do now."

CHAPTER EIGHT

Heath

L ooks like the Scotts are on the same page, anyway. Friends? With Ginny?

I can't stop staring at her lips. That's not a thing friends do, I don't think.

When Reagan comes back from the bathroom, I'm disappointed at the prospect of sharing Ginny, but Reagan takes off her coverup and tosses it on the lounge chair. "I'm going in the pool. Anyone want to join me?"

"Really?" Ginny asks and she and Reagan share some sort of look I can't decipher.

"Only live once. Coming?"

Ginny shakes her head and Reagan heads to the pool

"You know it's a pool party, right?" I ask when it's just the two of us again.

She gives me an annoyed look and motions to her chest, covered by the swimsuit, but uh, I might get lost a little too long staring at her chest. Also, not something a friend does.

"Something against swimming?"

"No, I love to swim. But . . ." She pauses. "Dakota said the pool was where people go to find hookups."

I try real hard to keep from smiling too big. Sweet, innocent Ginny's not looking for a casual hookup. I could have guessed that. It shouldn't make me happy because it also means I won't be hooking up with her, but for some reason, I'm glad that no one else will be either.

"What do *you* want to do?" I ask her. "We've got people watching which we're perfectly positioned for now, we could play one of the many party games—flip cup, beer pong—all the usuals, there's volleyball, I'm still offering up making out in case you want to rethink that one, or we can go to the pool and I'll swat the swarms of boys away so you can swim without being harassed."

She rolls her eyes. "Swarms?"

"I mean, look at you. Yeah, *swarms*."

"And you're going to be my protector?"

"Totally self-serving," I tell her honestly.

"How's that?"

"I like spending time with you."

She glances to the pool, and I can see the longing there.

"Come on." I stand and take off my T-shirt. Her eyes flit over my chest and abs before she gets up and carefully removes her shorts and sandals.

The light pink suit she's wearing dips low in the front and cuts up on her hips. Ginny's thin and her frame is small, but her boobs did not get the memo because they're disproportionately bigger. Thank fuck for disproportions.

We enter the pool at the shallow end. A lot of people are swimming or hanging out near the edge, but I manage to snag a floatie for her.

She leans her upper body onto it and we go to the middle of the pool. The water comes up to my armpits and I dip down so it covers my shoulders and I'm at eye level with Ginny. Her gaze darts around taking it all in, but I see the exact second that she relaxes into the blue floatie and decides to be in the moment with me.

I grab a hold of the floatie and let my legs drift underneath me. Music pumps through the speakers and I close my eyes behind my sunglasses soaking it in. Good tunes and a bunch of people hanging out, talking and laughing. Not a bad way to spend a Saturday. Not bad at all.

"You look pretty comfortable in here," she says. I open my eyes to see her skim her fingers across the water. "This your typical hang out?"

"Are you trying to ask if I use the pool to find my hookups?"

"Do you?"

"Don't knock it `til you try it."

She laughs, her lips pulling wide and flashing her straight white teeth.

"Maybe I will. Anyone you suggest?" She lifts her head and glances around the pool.

"Just say the word." I find myself staring at her lips again. They're full, the lower one so plump I want to trace it with my thumb and my tongue, and they're this perfect pink color.

"I'm not dating for a while. Boys suck."

"Why is it when girls get their heart broken, they go off men entirely? A guy gets his heart kicked in and he moves on to the next. Chicks aren't like that."

"Well, women are smarter. It takes you guys longer for your small brains to catch up and be brokenhearted."

A chuckle escapes from my lips and she smiles.

"I got out of a relationship right before I came to Valley."

"Might have heard something about that."

"Ugh. Really? Adam told you about Bryan?"

"Not by name, but he did mention that you'd recently gotten out of something. He's worried about you, wants me to look out for you."

Her mouth gapes and her shoulders tense. "Is that why you're . . ."

"No. Fuck no." Her hair is in another braid today and I finger the end and tug it gently. "I thought we established that I like hanging out with you."

"Same." Her body melts back into the raft and those perfect pink lips pull apart. "How'd you and my brother become roommates? I get the hockey connection, but you don't seem like the best of friends."

"Cheap rent," I tell her honestly. "I wanted to move out of the dorms but couldn't afford a place on my own. Your brother and I are cool. We're not the best of friends, as you said, but we get each other. He's a good captain."

It's hot out and there's really no escape from the sun in the middle of the pool, so we get out when Ginny's shoulders start to burn. Inside the house, we find Adam and his new girlfriend sitting with Maverick and a brunette he introduces as Maddie. Rauthruss is there too with his phone in hand, no doubt texting his girlfriend.

"Little Scott," Maverick greets her as we take a seat. She bristles at the name, which I totally get. Since Nathan went to Valley too, I've often been called Baby Payne and that shit gets old really quick.

"She has a name, man," I tell him.

His brows raise slightly, but he nods. "Yeah, I know, just messing around."

"Do you want something to drink?" I ask her and stand. She nods and I head outside to where we left our stuff.

Dakota and Reagan are sitting in the lounge chairs we abandoned.

"Where's Ginny?" Reagan asks.

I grab the alcohol and all our clothing. "Everyone's inside." I motion with my head and they follow.

"Got a crush on Ginny?" Dakota asks with a tease to her voice.

"It's not like that."

"What is it like?" she presses as we walk toward the house.

"She's cool."

"Cool? So you don't want to sleep with her?"

Of-fucking-course I want to sleep with her. She's beautiful and fun and if I had standards . . . she'd exceed them.

"She's Scott's sister."

She nods in understanding. "He would kill you. Better get your shit on lock then. It's written all over your handsome face."

Inside, Liam has slid into my spot and a few others have crowded around the table. When Ginny sees me approaching with her things, she stands. "Oh, thank you."

I take her seat while she pulls on her shorts and steps into her sandals. The end of her braid swings forward into my face. Back and forth all hypnotic-like. Reminds me of that movie *Office Space* and I'm going deeper and deeper, way down into Ginny.

When she's ready to sit, I crowd Liam and make room for her on half the seat. As she settles in, I wrap an arm around her to keep her from falling off.

She smiles at me all sun-kissed skin and smelling like chlorine and something twists in my gut.

"Heath."

My name being called draws my attention to a group of girls walking up to the table.

"Hey, Kimberly. How are you?"

"Good, good." She glances around the table, stopping on Rauthruss for a few seconds longer than the others. He gets real busy staring at his phone. I don't get it. I get loyalty. I respect him for that, but if he wants a girlfriend, why not find one he can actually see . . . and fuck?

Kimberly's stare finally finds its way back to me. "What have you been up to? You didn't call."

Ginny giggles quietly next to me and I squeeze her waist playfully as I answer. "School, hockey . . . the usual."

"Well, let's hang out later."

I give her a noncommittal head bob. "See ya."

"Friend of yours?" Ginny asks with a smirk when she's gone.

"Never seen her before in my life." I wink and she giggles again.

Her face is soft and sincere when she pulls away. "Go, you don't need to keep an eye out for me just because my brother asked you to. I'm good."

"I thought I told you—"

"I know what you said, but it's a party and . . . we're friends." Her insinuation is clear. She and I aren't happening. "Go." She shoves at my shoulder playfully.

I stand, though I don't know why. I don't want to hang out with Kimberly. "All right, you know where to find me." I tug her braid one last time and head off to the pool.

CHAPTER NINE

Ginny

T he more I drink and the darker the sky gets, the more relaxed I feel. We moved back outside now that it's cooled off. I can feel the slight burn on my skin from earlier and the breeze makes goose bumps dot my arm.

Adam and Taryn are sharing a lounge chair next to me and Reagan. Dakota and Maverick are both in the pool. Maverick's tossing a beach ball back and forth with the girl he's been hanging out with all afternoon and Dakota's full-on making out with some guy Reagan tells me is a basketball player.

Liam sits on the ground between us. He's attached himself to my side. I can't tell if he's hitting on me or if he's another one of the guys Adam's asked to keep an eye out for me. His approach is much more subtle than Heath's, and dammit if I don't prefer Heath's cocky, playfulness to Liam's politeness.

I find him in the pool. He's leaning against the side and the girl I all but pushed him into hanging out with is next to him. She's facing him, her back to me, but I have a clear view of Heath.

He smiles and holds a beer in one hand. They're not touching, at least that I can tell, but they're standing close. He laughs and his stare moves past her to me. It isn't the first time he's caught me staring in the last hour.

I know he's all wrong for me. Dakota and Reagan have filled me in on all the guys and what they said about Heath is exactly what I expected. He hooks up, he's all for the fun, but he doesn't date, and he's never had a girl-friend that they're aware of.

The reasons to not hook up with him are many, not the least of which is him being my brother's roommate and teammate. And if I'm totally honest, I'm not one hundred percent over Bryan. I think it's mostly turned into anger at the way he ended things and missing the idea of what I thought college would look like. We were supposed to be doing all of this together, but if we had, I wouldn't have met Dakota and Reagan and I already can't imagine that.

"You're staring," Reagan says, nudging me with an elbow.

"I know. It's pathetic. She's beautiful. Do you know her?"

"No, not really. I've seen her around."

"With Heath?"

She nods. "If it's any consolation, I don't think it's serious. I think it's lack of options and similar goals."

"Is the goal not going home alone?"

She laughs. "Yeah, pretty much. And Heath's a hot commodity, especially now that he's been drafted."

"Drafted, like to the NHL?" It clicks before she answers. "I remember Adam saying something about one of his teammates being drafted, but I didn't realize it was Heath."

"Heath and Maverick both already signed with teams." Standing, she slips into her shoes. "Come on, I see Rhett playing flip cup."

I take one last look at Heath and our eyes catch again. I tear my gaze away first this time and stand. "Let's do it."

"College is awesome. A-W-E-S-O-M-E awesome."

Reagan and Dakota's laughter is a hazy sound as they help me into Adam's bed.

"I put a glass of water on the nightstand and your phone on the desk. Do you want help getting changed or at least out of those shoes?" I think it's Reagan who asks.

My eyes are shut, and their voices are surprisingly similar.

"No, it's fine. This way I'll be ready to go to classes in the morning. No getting ready. Voi, voile, I mean voila!"

"Tomorrow is Sunday, sweetie."

"How did you get so drunk?" Dakota asks. I can tell it's definitely her this time, the little snort laugh she does gives her away.

"I'm not drunk. Just tipsy and tired."

"Now I see the family resemblance. You're as stubborn as your brother. Last time Adam got drunk, he swore he was fine until he fell down the stairs on the way to the bar."

I'm too tired to laugh, but the image in my head of my bossy and always in control brother tumbling down a flight of stairs is hilarious.

"Okay. Night, Ginny. Sleep tight."

Their footsteps retreat and one of them flips the overhead light off before the door shuts.

"Wait," I call, not loudly enough. I groan and sit up, prying open my eyelids. A small strip of light underneath the door is the only thing saving me from total darkness. I get up and look for my phone, but I can't see anything. I flip the light on and take a deep breath. I still don't see my phone, but now I need to pee.

I stumble out into the empty living room. Rhett came back at the same time as we did, but he must have gone to bed. I hurry into the bathroom and close the door, then fumble with the light switch.

Only nothing happens. Damn Adam and his inability to change a freaking light bulb. It's really dark in here and my pulse quickens. I find the door handle, turn and yank, but nothing happens. It's a standard turn lock, but no matter which way I turn, it doesn't seem to do anything and my breathing gets more erratic with each failed attempt.

Oh my god, this can't be happening. I close my eyes to try to trick myself into believing it isn't as dark as it is, but I'm already panicking too much to fool myself.

I bang on the door. "Little help in here."

I wait for a few seconds before I try again, this time louder. Rhett's room is all the way across the apartment, and I have no idea if anyone else is home. I didn't see Heath when we left, and Mav was going to catch a ride with Adam and Taryn. "Help!"

I slide down onto the floor before my legs can give out and continue banging with both fists. I try counting to focus on something else. One. Two. I'm fine. Everything is fine. Three. Four. Someone will come home any second now.

My hands fall to my lap and I suck in deep breaths. All the fuzzy edges from the alcohol are gone and I'm entirely too sober and aware that I'm trapped in a very dark, small room.

Hot tears roll down my face. I yell as loud as I can through the crying. "Help!"

"Ginny?" Heath's voice on the other side of the door makes me cry harder. "Are you okay?"

"I can't get the door open."

The handle rattles. "It's locked."

"I know. It's too d-dark to see, but I can't get it open either way I turn it. Could you get Adam?"

"Ginny, I'm going to kick the door open, but I need you to move back out of the way. Maybe step into the shower."

"O-okay." I crawl on my hands and knees and sit inside the tub, hugging my knees.

"Are you away from the door?"

"Y-yes."

A second later the cheap wood door slams in and against the wall and the light from the living room pours in. Heath stands in the doorway frozen as he takes me in, then rushes toward me. "Are you all right?"

I nod even as I shiver and hug my knees tighter. He's quiet and I'm all too aware of my ragged breaths filling the silence between us. I close my eyes and concentrate on taking slow and even breaths. One, two, three . . .

"Everything okay?" Rhett asks in that heavy Minnesota accent.

I'm so embarrassed. I wonder if it's possible to never see any of Adam's teammates ever again.

"Can you get her a glass of water?" Heath asks Rhett.

My eyes fly open as my space is invaded and Heath climbs into the tub in front of me. He doesn't exactly fit, and his long legs are bent and flank me on either side. His hands raise to my shoulders and he strokes me gently. "Deep breaths in through your nose."

Yep, epic proportions of embarrassment.

"Here ya go." Rhett reappears with water in a big green plastic cup.

Heath takes it and thanks him, while I smile awkwardly.

"Uh, you guys good?" Rhett shifts uncomfortably. "Should I call Adam? I think he went with Maverick and Taryn on a taco run."

Heath's fingers continue to stroke my arms and back. "I've got her."

That's all the convincing Rhett needs to get the heck out of my bubble of crazy.

"I'm fine. Really. You can go now," I say, chest still rising and falling too fast. "Go back to the girl in your bed."

"You're not fine. You're having a panic attack. And there's no one in my bed. I left right after you." He hands me the cup of water. "Try to take a sip or two. Sometimes forcing your brain to do something else helps."

I do as he instructs, and the cool liquid does seem to help a tiny bit. Enough that I can better appreciate the man in front of me. He's shirtless, his ab muscles defined even as he sits. Blue basketball shorts hang on his hips, but his bare calves press against my back.

When I finally feel the sharp edges of my fear dissipate, I finish the water and let out a long, cleansing breath. "I'm sorry."

"For what?" A ghost of a smile tugs at the corner of his mouth. His arms wrap around me again and he rubs my back softly.

"For getting myself locked in and for that." I point toward the busted door. The trim hangs away from the wall where the lock pushed it away from the frame.

"That's nothing. Don't even worry about it. Are you feeling better?"

I nod. "I want to go to bed."

"Okay." He moves his legs and groans. "I think I might be stuck."

Standing, I offer him my hand. He smiles goofily as he places his calloused palm in mine, and I attempt to help him up. Somehow, we manage to get him upright and he's so close my breathing picks up all over again, but for a completely different reason.

He notices and his brows furrow. "Are you sure you're okay?"

"I'll be fine."

"This kind of thing happen before?" he asks and then adds, "When you've been drinking."

I nod, refusing to meet his concerned blue eyes. "I just need some sleep." And to wake up and pretend this never happened.

As gracefully as one can in this situation, I step out of the tub and glance at the burned-out light bulb over the vanity. "How many hockey players does it take to change a lightbulb?"

He follows me out of the bathroom. I walk to Adam's open bedroom and face him. "Well, this was humiliating and awful. Pretend it never happened?"

His lips twist into a playful smile and he reaches out and squeezes my hand. "Night, Ginny."

In Adam's room I flip the overhead light on and shut the door. And then I climb into bed and somehow sleep through the night.

When I wake up, Adam is on the couch sleeping with Taryn curled up next to him. The rest of the house is quiet. I tiptoe to the bathroom and reach for the light before I remember. Except this time, the bathroom floods with light and the doorframe is fixed.

It turns out it only takes one hockey player to change a light bulb, and I have a very good idea which one it was.

CHAPTER TEN

Heath

I'm lying in bed fully dressed when Maverick sticks his head in my room. "Time to stop touching yourself and go get fondled by the elderly instead."

I sit up and swing my legs onto the floor.

"Was that Mariah I heard while I was playing Xbox with Rauthruss?" he questions, dark eyebrows raised and a playful smile on his lips.

"It's weird when you listen in, man."

"Just looking out for you."

"How thoughtful."

We meet the rest of the team at the assisted living home. Coach's mom lives here. As such, this is where a good portion of our community service hours are done. At least once a semester, he drags us out here. Today we're doing some outdoor landscaping. Manual labor shit that sucks balls, but in truth, I enjoy it more than going inside the place.

It smells like old people, which makes sense, but I don't need reminders that we are all going to die and, if we are lucky, get to stink up the world on our way out. I learned that lesson the hard way when my dad died at forty-one. He didn't even get a chance to enjoy that mothball and shit stench. He'd gone out looking fit and healthy and smelling like Acqua di Gio. I was fourteen and thought he was invincible.

Desert Rose is a massive place. So many residents that I have to wonder if there are any old people left in Valley who aren't living here. The grounds are well cared for, flowers and shrubs trimmed to make Mother Nature look like a Monet painting.

We're probably more of a hindrance than a help to the crew since they clearly have it under control, but the old people enjoy watching us work hard. The old men come to sit outside in lawn chairs and regale us with tales of their youth, sleight-of-hand reminders at the end of every tale to enjoy being young and stupid.

Done and done.

Scott and I are spreading rock with rakes along a pathway to a gazebo. I'm tired and a little hungover. It's hot work, no reprieve from the sun blasting down on us.

"Rhett said Ginny got locked in the bathroom last night," he says, breaking the silence.

I'm really not sure how much to say. She was in a full-blown panic, but I don't want to freak out Adam. However, it sounds like Rauthruss filled him in.

"Yeah, she got in there with no light and couldn't get the door open to get out."

"Oh shit." He stops raking and stares at me with wide eyes. "Ginny's got a thing with the dark. She okay?"

"It took a few minutes to calm her down, but she seemed all right when she went to bed. I put a fresh bulb in, just in case." She was gone this morning before I woke up and she hasn't answered my texts.

"That must be why she left so early this morning. I'll check on her after we're done here. Thanks, man, I appreciate you looking out for her."

I swallow thickly and nod. His request to look out for her wasn't even a factor in it or really any of the times I've hung out with her. I like her. I like being with her. She makes me be in the moment more deeply. I'm not looking for hookups or to get drunk, I want to sit beside her, pull her hair, and tease her. Basically, I'm five again. I was thankful that I was there last night when she needed me. Last semester me wouldn't have been. He'd have been wasted or with a girl.

I take my shirt off and tuck it in my back pocket. It's so damn hot out. It's nice not to have the material sticking to my sweaty back, but now I can practically feel the sun turning my back into a barbeque grill.

Adam looks past me. "The old women at six o'clock are not so subtly undressing you with their eyes."

I pause and lean against the rake. Sure enough, three ladies with snow-white hair are walking toward us in monochromatic cotton ensembles and thick Dr. Scholl's sole-type shoes.

"Take it off. Scott, give the ladies something to live another day for," I taunt him. "I get it if you don't want them comparing our bodies and finding you lacking."

"Good morning, ladies," he says as they approach. He stands straight, lifts the hem of his shirt, and wipes his face. The ladies pause, taking in his abs, and when he drops the material, he tosses me a smirk. Fucker.

"You boys are doing a wonderful job." The one in the middle drops her gaze. As she brings it back to my face, I wink.

"Just trying to make this place as beautiful as you," Mav appears out of nowhere. The guy has a freaky ability to find the center of attention.

I hand him my rake. "I'm going for water. Make yourself useful."

I take my empty water bottle inside to the water fountain and fill it. Burt's in his usual spot sitting in front of the TV watching CSI or ESPN. I only know his name because someone is always yelling at him. He's a grumpy old prick, always sitting alone, and always pissing someone off. He's beating the remote on the arm of the chair, cursing under his breath. No one pays him any attention. A nurse walks by and sighs. I can't really blame her for not rushing to his aid. I've only been here a few times and even I'm tired of his shit.

"Goddamn remote." He tosses it across the room and it skips along the white tile floor, coming to a stop in my path back outside.

I lean down and pick it up and walk it over to him. He frowns as I hold it out.

"Trouble with the remote?"

"Trouble with everything," he grumbles as he punches at the buttons with his thumb.

"Maybe it's the batteries."

"Already changed them out, twice, to be sure they weren't dicking me around. That Sharon's got it out for me." He twists his body in his chair and hollers over his shoulder. "Are you sure this is the right remote?"

Sharon, I presume, doesn't even look up as she calls back. "Yes, Mister Thomas, I'm sure. I'll send Louie over to help as soon as he gets done with bedpans."

Burt snarls. I wouldn't want Louie's nasty hands on my remote either.

"I could give it a try if you want," I offer.

He holds it out with another sigh as if I am the last person he really wants to put his trust in. Again, can't say that I blame him. But a man should at least have TV if he's going to sit around in this depressing place all day. I test it out, pressing the channel up button with the same result Burt had.

"It's on the wrong input," I tell him and hold it so he can see. I press TV and then the channel button again, this time with success.

He keeps frowning as he takes it back in a liver-spotted hand and tries it for himself. I don't get a thank you or even an acknowledgment before I leave him to CSI.

If the options are going out young and unaware or old and hating the world . . . I think I'm in favor of the first. Live hard and die happy.

Desert Rose treats us to lunch after we're done. The guys are all in good spirits. Everyone's talking and laughing as we go through the buffet line set up for us. We're starting to get a nice camaraderie among the group, and I hope it translates to the ice when we get out there.

We spread out under the pavilion, sweaty and dirty but so hungry. Mav and I sit across from one another. The place goes silent as we eat. Even Mav barely speaks as we devour everything on our plates and then grab seconds. I finish and then guzzle what remains of my water.

"You want to grab a beer after this?" Mav asks.

"Nah, not today."

"Xbox?" he asks as we stand to leave.

I shake my head and we walk to his car. I need a shower and to find Ginny. She still hasn't responded to my text from earlier.

"Movie?"

"No." I slide into the passenger seat and Mav opens the driver's side door and gets in.

"Running out of options, buddy." He starts the car and taps his thumb on the steering wheel as he thinks. "Girls?"

"Now you've got it, but just one girl."

"Sharesies?" He seems surprised, but dare I say a little excited about the idea.

I lean back against the headrest. Tired laughter slips out. "Really, man?"

I don't have an exact plan. Find Ginny, make sure she's good, then convince her to spend more time with me.

"You wouldn't share with me? What if I sing Mariah and promise to keep my hands to myself?"

I don't know if he's kidding or not, but I wouldn't put anything past Maverick.

"Absolutely fucking not." I don't want to share one second of my time with Ginny. Not with anyone.

CHAPTER ELEVEN

Ginny

"And that's the story of why I'm never going back to my brother's apartment."

"I'm sure it wasn't that bad." Reagan gives me a hopeful smile across the table. I snuck out of Adam's early this morning and went straight to Dakota and Reagan's. They're consoling me over brunch at a cute little café they like.

"I was having a full-on panic attack in the bathtub. I have an issue with dark, enclosed spaces." I wave it off, hoping they don't ask more about that piece because I don't really feel like going into the specifics. "It was absolutely that bad."

Dakota snickers and takes a bite of her bagel.

"It's kind of romantic," Reagan insists. "Crawling into the tub with you and calming you down. I'm impressed, although not all that surprised that Heath was the one to come to your rescue. He's got that cocky but capable look about him. Still, I'm not sure I would have known what to do, so you were really lucky."

"It wasn't romantic. It was pity." I groan and bury my head in my arm on the table for a second. When I lift it back up, they're both smiling at me. "It's too bad. I liked Heath. Now I'm going to have to avoid him until I can look at him without wanting to disappear into the ground."

"Are you a drama major like this one?" Dakota asks and points her bagel toward Reagan.

"No, why?"

She smiles and I toss a crumpled napkin at her. "Ha. Ha. Very funny."

"We've all made fools of ourselves one time or another. It's college. It's fine." Dakota finishes her bagel and grabs her coffee. "Do you need to get back to the dorm or do you want to hang out today?"

"I need to shower and change, but I don't have anything after that."

"You'll want to shower after, but we can swing by the dorm on the way because you need sneakers."

"On the way where?" I ask, standing and following them out of the booth.

I gasp as we jog around the Valley U campus track. "When you said hang out, I was picturing Netflix or mani-pedis."

"Two more laps and then we switch to speed walking," Dakota says, sounding far too comfortable talking while jogging.

The Scott pride and competitive nature keeps me pushing on, but when we finally begin walking, I'm a lot more sweaty and tired than these two.

"Do you guys do this often?"

"Three times a week," Reagan says, sounding only slightly out of breath.

"Why?"

"I like to run," Dakota says.

"She was on the track team," Reagan adds. "I let her drag me along because it justifies the really big slice of cheesecake I'm going to have later while I make Dakota watch Lifetime movies."

"What's Ava, your roommate, like?" Dakota asks, swiftly changing the subject.

Ava and Trent hadn't been at the dorm when we'd stopped by, but Trent's things were still there. I can't wait to sleep in my own bed tonight.

"She's really nice. Her boyfriend goes to school at Northern. That's why I was at Adam's this weekend. He was visiting, and I wanted to give them some privacy. Hopefully next weekend she goes to his campus because I'm going to need a few weeks while I'm in hiding."

"You can always crash with us. The bathtub is all yours," Reagan teases.

"Thanks a lot, jerks," I say with a smile.

Trent's gone and Ava's asleep in her bed when I get back. I shower and then get into my own bed to nap, but last night plays over and over in my mind. Adam and Heath have both texted, but I only responded to my brother and with a quick—**I'm fine, it was nothing**—that will hopefully keep him from asking more.

A knock at our door gets me out of bed and I'm half expecting it to be Adam. It would be just like him to skip texting back altogether and want to check on me in person, but it's Heath standing in the hallway.

"What are you doing here?"

He smirks and adjusts the baseball hat on his head. "It's nice to see you too."

"Sorry. Hello, how are you today? Great weather we're having. What the heck are you doing at my dorm? And how did you know where I lived?"

His rough chuckle pulls a smile from my lips. "Good. Agreed. I wanted to see you and . . ." He leans in closer. "I can't reveal all my secrets." He's full-on grinning at me with a mocking glint in his eyes. "Come on, take a walk with me."

"A walk?"

"Sure. You got something better to do?"

"I was planning on taking a nap."

"Sleep's boring. Come on, am I really having to talk you into this? It's gorgeous outside and we can stop at the dining hall to feed you."

"Me?"

"Now that you mention it, I could eat."

He doesn't move and I relent. "One minute."

I leave him in the hallway, shut the door, and change out of my comfy yoga pants and into a pair of shorts. I swipe on lip gloss and a dab of mascara. When I pull the door open, he's leaning against the wall, one ankle crossed over the other and hands in his pockets.

"Ready?"

He pushes off the wall and motions for me to go first. "If you are."

We cross the street to the dining hall in silence. Heath seems perfectly at ease with the quiet, while I have a million questions on the tip of my tongue. He holds the door out for me.

"I should have assumed spending time with you would mean eating."

"Always," he says. "Plus, it's where we met. We have history here."

I huff a laugh and grab a tray. Now that we're here, I am kind of hungry. Heath gets a much smaller portion of food than normal and I raise a brow.

"I already ate lunch once," he admits.

We take our food to our usual table.

"What time did you sneak out this morning?" he asks.

I hesitate with a chip up to my mouth. "I didn't sneak out."

His left brow rises as he takes a bite of food.

"Okay, fine. I very quietly left at a ridiculously early time. Happy?"

"Obviously not since I tracked you down."

"I'm fine, okay?"

He shrugs. As we eat, he tells me about his morning with the team doing community service and I tell him about running with the girls.

"Congrats on being drafted, by the way. Adam mentioned it this summer, but I didn't piece together it was you until Reagan mentioned it last night."

"Thanks." He sits back in his chair, drinking his water and studying me.

"What?" I ask self-consciously.

"Trying to figure you out. What are you into?"

"Everything and nothing. I didn't play sports in high school or anything like that."

"Had to have been into something."

"I was into socializing. Turns out you can't make a career out of that unless your parents are rich and famous."

"Damn those Kardashians."

"Right?"

"Genevieve, Genevieve, Genevieve."

I love the way my full name sounds when he says it. I was always sort of embarrassed by it. Teachers would comment on how beautiful it was, which to a middle schooler, is super humiliating. Kids would taunt me with it, at least until I got boobs, then it became some sort of bad pickup line. *"Genevieve, huh? Cool name."*

Cue swooning. Not.

Except, I'm sort of swooning now and all he did was say my name. And I'm also staring at him when I'm supposed to be saying something. Anything.

"Heath, Heath, Heath."

His playful smile makes my stomach flip.

"I'm going to get ice cream." I stand before he can comment and take my time at the dessert bar creating a perfect sundae.

He's picking at the chips on my tray when I get back. "I assumed you were done."

"They're all yours."

"What is that?" he asks, face twisted in disgust as he eyes my bowl of ice cream.

"Neapolitan with sprinkles and gummy bears."

"All the flavors are touching."

I laugh and bring a big spoonful of all three flavors to my mouth. He continues to watch on horrified.

"I don't understand Neapolitan flavor. It's ice cream for people who can't make a decision."

"Not true. The decision is we want all three and don't want to settle for one boring flavor." I offer him my spoon. "Wanna try it?"

His mouth pulls into a tight line and he shakes his head.

"Come on." I sit forward and lean over the table to get the spoon closer to his mouth. He opens and I feed him, which turns out to be a surprisingly intimate thing. His throat works, eyes locked on mine, as I sit back and study his reaction to the food.

"Well?"

"I think I swallowed a gummy bear whole," he says, voice tight.

We finish the rest of my ice cream and if Heath eating more than half of it is any indication, I'd say he likes my Neapolitan sundae just fine.

After, we take a walk around campus. It isn't as busy as it is during the week, but lots of other people are out walking, hanging out in the shaded areas, playing frisbee, and some are even going in and out of buildings.

Eventually we take a seat on the ledge of the fountain in the center of campus. It's one of my favorite spots.

"So, you're all right?"

"What?" I try to play it off like I don't know what he's talking about, but his serious expression says it all. "Oh, yeah, I'm fine."

I dig through my pocket for a penny, close my eyes, and toss it into the fountain.

"What'd you wish for?"

"I can't tell you or it won't come true."

It's quiet and I hope we've successfully avoided talking any more about last night until he asks, "You've had them before, right? Panic attacks? Adam said you had a thing with the dark."

I consider lying, but it feels as if it couldn't get any more embarrassing with the truth.

"Really, I'm fine. I don't like being trapped in dark places. And, sure, I've had them before, but it isn't like a common occurrence." I quit talking and hope I've said enough to make me seem less crazy.

"My mom used to have them. The first time she thought she was dying or having a heart attack. Scared the shit out of both of us."

I finger the hem of my shorts and avoid meeting his gaze.

"It's okay. I didn't bring it up to make you embarrassed. I just wanted you to know it's nothing to be ashamed of."

"I'm not ashamed. I'd just prefer not to need to be rescued by my brother's insanely hot friend." I slap a hand over my mouth. "Forget I said that. Clearly there was something wrong with those gummy bears and it's making me say crazy things."

He quirks a brow. "You think I'm insanely hot?"

"Did I say insanely? That was the gummy bears talking. I mean, objectively yes, you're hot. But it isn't like *I* think you're hot."

His hand comes up and brushes my hair back from my face. His thumb traces my bottom lip. He leans in and the seconds while his lips descend on mine seem to happen in slow motion while my pulse quickens.

My eyes flutter closed and finally his mouth covers mine. His lips are soft, but his scruff is scratchy against my smooth skin. His hand at my face slides to the back of my neck, cupping it with his large palm as his mouth widens and his tongue asks for entrance.

His tongue feels divine. Kissing Heath feels divine. He's a great kisser, and even though it's only my neck and lips he's touching, I feel it everywhere.

When he pulls back, I'm breathless and turned on. Jesus.

"I'm sorry. I shouldn't have done that."

His words are like a bucket of cold water dumped over my lady parts. "Why not?"

"Because maybe you were right. You're off men, I'm not capable of being more than your friend without ruining everything else, your brother is my teammate, pick a reason I guess."

"Those gummy bears are making you do crazy things too."

He smirks. "Friends?"

Is he serious? He wants to be friends after that kiss? But I did just get out of a relationship and it's probably not the best idea to jump into something one week into college, so I nod. "Friends."

SEPTEMBER

TWELVE

Heath

Ginny takes the seat across from me with her bowl of ice cream. "I'm ready for fall. My boobs are sweaty just from walking across the street."

"I totally get it," Mav says. "My balls—"

"All right. Too much information, man," I tell him.

"I don't see how it's any different than Ginny's boobs." Mav shrugs and goes back to his homework laid out on the table in front of him.

"Boobs, Mav. It's different because boobs."

Ginny giggles, not the least bit offended by my buddy or me and slides the bowl along the top of the table to me without asking if I want any. The chemistry between Ginny and I is hard to ignore. I thought friend-zoning myself would take away the tension, but even when she says things like sweaty boobs, I find I'm wishing the clock would move a little slower so we could spend more time together.

There are too many complications. For one, I don't need the team captain having it out for me. And then there's the fact that I don't want to stop hanging out with Ginny. If that means being friends instead of kissing her so I don't screw things up, then so be it. Better friends than nothing at all.

I smile as I stare down at her bowl of ice cream. She never gets gummy bears on top anymore. I don't know if she really believes it was their fault she admitted I was hot and let me kiss her or not, but the loss of them makes me a little sad. Hard, awful little things.

I take a small bite and push it back.

"That's all you're eating?"

"Gotta get the season diet back on track. We're taking the ice today."

I can barely keep from jumping out of my skin I want to be out there so badly.

Mav looks up and nods, but then groans. "It's going to be short-lived for me if I fail this British literature test." He hits his head on his book several times and then sits up and closes it. He barely scraped by with grades good enough to play last year and Coach is watching him closely. "You still have Tonya's number? I think she tutors."

"Uhh . . . yeah, maybe." I pull my phone up and find her and hand the phone to Maverick. "I wouldn't tell her you got her number from me though, she's not my biggest fan."

"Did she *tutor* you?" Ginny asks.

"No, she did not." What we had was much more honest—a quickie in a bathroom at a party last year. She wanted to continue the fun and I didn't.

"Maybe I can help," Ginny says. "I love literature."

"Really?" Mav looks hopeful.

"Sure. Tonight?"

While they make plans, I sit back and watch Ginny. She's nice, interesting, funny, and a little naïve. But naïve in that way that she still believes in the good of people and situations, and being around her makes me believe a little more too. There isn't anything I don't like about her. Every little detail. It's safe to say Ginny Scott's grown on me just like Neapolitan ice cream.

I look forward to our meals together. She's never mentioned the gummy bear induced illicit kiss, and neither have I, but we both show up at the same time for breakfast and lunch every day to eat together. Sometimes Maverick and the guys are with us, sometimes not, but the two of us never miss.

Lunch friends. I can think of worse things to be. I can think of better things, too.

After lunch, I head to the rink for practice. I'm early, but I can't wait another minute to get out on the ice. The weeks of preseason workouts on the football field are hot and grueling, but I'd do it three times a day if it meant stepping on the ice sooner.

Adam's in the locker room already dressed when I walk in.

"Hey," he says when he sees me. "Couldn't wait either?"

"I barely slept last night," I admit.

He chuckles and heads toward the door. "Guess it'll be easy to stop you from scoring today."

"You wish," I call after him.

As I walk to the ice, I feel a sense of peace and an unbridled excitement. One month without skating and I feel like I'm regaining a limb. I respect Coach's idea that a month of practice on the turf learning to work as a team makes us stronger before we step out onto the ice, but man, how I've missed it.

I breathe in the cool air as my skates glide over the fresh ice. I nod to Adam, who's skating with that same look of joy on his face. We skate in silence for a few minutes before he juts his chin for me to join him. We take turns passing and shooting. I'm sweaty and breathless but in the best way.

When the rest of the team arrives, Coach Meyers and Coach Kelley start us with speed drills and then some power play scenarios.

My heart races and adrenaline courses through me as I skate hard.

"Move your feet," Coach Meyers bellows from his spot in the opposing side fan section. "There you go. Nice."

"I'm gonna puke," Maverick says on a raspy breath as I fall back into line.

"How are you out of shape? We spent the last month running our asses off."

"Can't run this sweet ass off," he says straight-faced. "Beautiful genetics, but not great for speed."

I laugh. "You're blaming your ass for being slow? Really?"

He smirks and takes off as Coach blows the whistle for the next person to go.

Practice goes by entirely too fast. The girls' team practices in thirty minutes, so I can't even linger like I want to.

Not everyone is so sad to be done.

Jordan's face is red and splotchy and he mutters, "Oh thank god. I was burping ham and cheese. I swear it was coming up in the next five minutes."

I'm the last one off the ice. Adam notices and laughs at what I'm guessing is close to a pout on my face. I'm totally not beyond kicking and screaming and throwing a tantrum if I thought it'd work instead of Coach Meyers making me run laps around the football field.

"Come on, Payne, I'll buy you a beer."

At The Hideout, Adam pays for two pitchers and sets it down on the table before handing out glasses.

Mav's filled his glass and taken a long drink before the pitcher even makes its way to me. "Dude, maybe it's the beer gut and not your ass that's the problem."

He flips me off, continues drinking and then says, "Hey man, how much do you think Coach Meyer will pay you to babysit Liam and Jordan this year? Minimum wage?"

I grimace and he laughs, knowing he's hit a sore spot. Coach had me on a line with two freshmen forwards today, both need a lot of work.

"It's going to be a great season," Adam insists, always wearing his captain hat. "Frozen four this year. Last chance to secure my legacy as a frozen four champ before graduation."

I lift my glass.

Ginny is waiting at the apartment when we get back.

"What are you doing here?" Adam asks and takes a seat on the couch next to her.

"Maverick and I are studying Shakespeare."

Adam looks to Mav. "You know, you don't live here, man."

"I ordered pizzas," he says, standing in the doorway. "Gotta take Charli out. Back in five."

When he's gone, Ginny looks from Adam to me. "How was it being back on the ice?"

"Amazing," we say in unison.

Ginny giggles.

"I'm going to shower," Adam says, standing and pulling off his shirt. "Save me some thin crust."

"Come keep me company while Mav is gone." I motion for Ginny to follow me back to my room and she does.

She walks in and scans the room before taking a seat on the bed, feet dangling off the side. I drop my bag and then pull out a pair of basketball shorts and T-shirt. I take off the shirt I'm wearing and toss it in the hamper without thinking about it. Ginny's eyes are fixed on my chest. I wait for her to catch herself, but she's full-on checking me out.

"Hey, friend?"

"Hmm?"

"Eyes are up here," I say with a wink.

She rolls her brown eyes, but then they land back on my bare upper body. "You're seriously cut. Maybe I should give up ice cream."

"Don't you dare. You're perfect."

Charli zips into my room, jumps onto the bed, and covers Ginny with slobbery kisses. She smiles and leans away but pets her behind the ears.

"Down, Charli."

Mav appears in the doorway and Charli goes to his side. "Ready, Ginny?"

"Yeah." She scoots off the bed. "See you out there?"

I nod and watch my friend and the object of my fascination walk out of my room. I might need a shower and some Mariah first.

CHAPTER THIRTEEN

Ginny

The following night Reagan's sitting at her vanity with the laptop open in front of her while I stand off to the side doing her makeup. "I can't believe how much it looks like the girl on the video. I swear I've tried a few of these and it never looks anything like it's supposed to."

"Ava's been letting me practice on her." I glance at the girl on the screen and back to Reagan. "The winged eye looks really good on you."

Putting makeup on Reagan is fun. She's so naturally beautiful I probably couldn't make her look bad if I tried, but she's right, I managed to get it pretty close to the girl on camera.

"You're hired. Someday when I'm a big well-known actress, I'm going to force you to do my makeup every day. In fact, I wish you could do my makeup for the winter play."

Reagan is a theater major, and according to Dakota, she kicks ass in the school plays.

"Doesn't the department hire someone to do makeup for the performances?"

"Yes. The previous stage director's mother, Ms. Morrison. She's lovely and nice and has been doing makeup for the university performances for something like twenty years, but last spring she had me looking like a clown. There's stage makeup, and then, there's straight-up too much blush."

I brush a little shimmer powder along her cheekbones. "Well, I'm happy to do it anytime. Seriously, doing your makeup every day is my dream job."

"Why aren't you going to school to be a makeup artist?" Dakota asks from the bed. She's lying on her side looking at her phone.

"Unless you work in a salon or store, it's a lot of freelance gigs like wedding days and special occasions. Plus, there's so much pressure to get it perfect so they feel beautiful and confident."

"Well, I feel both right now, so I think you'd be great at it." Reagan purses her lips and then smiles.

"Speaking of jobs, I need to find one if I'm going to be able to move out next year. Do you guys know of anything on campus or off? I was thinking about checking local restaurants and cafés." Rooming with Ava's been great. We get along well, and she doesn't have any crazy habits like leaving out old food or rummaging through my things without asking, but I don't want to do dorm life again next year.

"The Hall of Fame is always looking for guides," Dakota says.

"Guides?"

She sits up and abandons her phone. "Yeah, we do tours for local groups like schools and other organizations, but we also get to help with recruitment. I can ask my boss if you want."

"Just like that?"

"Well, I'm not going to lie, the fact that you're Adam Scott's little sister will probably help. My boss has a giant crush on him."

"What?" I ask at the same time Reagan mutters, "Who doesn't?"

Dakota and I look to her. "What? Come on, he's hot. No, not only hot, he's nice and . . ." She trails off. "I'm just saying, it isn't totally ridiculous that she has a crush on him."

Dakota shakes her head. "Well, whatever, but every time he's around, she gets all flustered and blushes."

Gross. "That's so weird, but whatever, the job sounds fun."

"Great. I'm working tomorrow, so I'll ask."

I get up and pull my phone out of my pocket so I can take pictures of my work. "Stand against the wall." I point to a blank section of white wall in her room and Reagan moves in front of it. "The guy you were crushing on earlier this year, it wasn't Adam, right?"

"What?" Reagan freezes. "No, of course not. I only meant I could understand it."

"Is it Heath?" Seems like a long shot since he's not dating anyone, but I need her to rule him out anyway. It would be too weird if she was into him.

"Definitely no."

"Why 'definitely no'? Heath is great."

"Rhett?" Dakota asks.

"Would you two stop trying to guess. I'm not telling you and it doesn't matter anyway. Every time I'm around him, I go stupid shy. I need a guy more on my level. Plus, I have a new crush and he is single and he asked for my number."

My phone pings as I take a few photos of Reagan's makeup. "That's Maverick. I'm going over to study with him again."

"Can you do this for my date?" Reagan makes a circle in front of her face.

"Absolutely, but you don't need my help to look gorgeous." I grab my stuff and wave as I head out.

Maverick is already at Adam's apartment when I get there. He's on the couch with Charli next to him. Rhett and Heath are playing video games.

"Did I miss Adam?" I sit in the chair next to Heath.

He bumps my shoulder. "Yeah, he left for Taryn's a few minutes ago."

"Does she ever come here?"

"Nah, not really."

I get up and haul my backpack to the table and pull out my laptop and a copy of Shakespeare's sonnets I borrowed from the library. Maverick follows and takes the chair across from me. Charli lies at his feet.

"Do you want me to take a look at your notes or should we jump into the study questions?"

He heaves a dramatic sigh. "My notes might be shit."

He hands over a notebook filled with three pages of his small penmanship.

"Did you write down everything the professor said?" I ask, baffled as I scan over them. The amount of detail he's captured is crazy.

"Uh, yeah. I wasn't sure what was important and what wasn't, so I wrote down damn near everything."

"I'm not sure either. Wow okay. The test is an essay?"

"Yeah. Payne, phone's going off in your room," Maverick calls to him.

Heath stands with the controller, backing out of the room. "Ah, ah, fuck. I'm cornered. Pause, one second." He rushes into his room and out of view, but I hear him answer the phone.

His voice lowers and softens, that tells me immediately he's talking to a girl. A surge of white-hot jealousy heats my face. He comes back out, phone to his ear, and tosses the controller on the couch.

"Sorry, man, gotta take this," he says to Rhett and then disappears back into his room, shutting the door behind him.

"So, what do you think?" Maverick asks, bringing me back to the present.

"These notes are great." We spend the next fifteen minutes picking out things we think he can use. Maverick is detailed and thorough in his studying. It surprises me he's failing actually. At least until I start asking him questions about it and his attention is about as focused as Charli's.

"What was the question again?" he asks.

I laugh and he gives me a sheepish grin. "I really fucking hate this class."

"Why are you taking it?"

"I thought it would be an easy A. I breezed through American Literature."

"Okay, well, how did you study for that class?"

"I don't know." He leans over and pets his dog and a smile pulls at his lips. "Heath and I read the books out loud to each other in funny accents."

"Heath helped you study? Did you have the class together?"

"Not together, but we were both taking it, different professors. Most of the reading was the same though."

"Were you roommates?"

"Yeah, we lived in the dorms together last year."

I'm suddenly less interested in studying than I am hearing about Heath helping Maverick study. What I would give for a peek into the past of those two reading Hemingway.

"Okay, well, we can try that." I grab the book off the table between us. "The first five sonnets?"

"I've already read them."

"But now that you know the form and themes, I think you'll be able to pick them out easier. Maybe they'll make more sense."

"Yeah, all right."

I clear my throat and open it to the first page and start reading.

As I'm finishing it and handing the book over to Maverick for a turn, Heath's door opens and he steps out.

"Payne! Sit your sexy ass down and read me some Shakespeare."

Heath takes a seat and to my surprise takes the book. "You're reading it out loud?"

"It helped last year. Worth a try, right?"

Heath crosses one ankle over the other. "What do we have here?"

"Sonnets," Maverick says.

A deep laugh rolls out of him as he brings the paperback up and starts reading. His voice is crisp, and the gravelly timber is easy to slip right under. His pitch varies and practically sings along the stanzas. I'm falling into it so deeply and I'm not even the one who needs to be paying attention.

Heath looks up as he's flipping the page and our eyes meet over the top of the book.

"Do it in your British accent," Maverick begs.

Heath looks like he might object, but then Maverick sticks his bottom lip out like he's pouting.

Heath looks to me again quickly before he starts again. I giggle at his accent, but my stomach flips. Shakespeare will never be the same.

As I'm packing up to leave, Maverick thanks me.

"I'm not sure how much I actually helped, but it was fun. Do you feel good about it?"

"Yeah, Shakespeare's the shit."

I laugh.

"Next week, then?"

"Sure. Also, I was thinking, if listening helps, you could try audiobooks."

"Maybe, but then I'd miss out on Heath reading to me." He winks at Heath and then whistles to get Charli's attention. "I'm out. See you tomorrow."

The man has a point. My body still tingles from Heath's voice reading such beautiful words.

Rhett went to his room earlier, so it's just me and Heath as I shoulder my backpack. "He's right—you have a really nice voice."

One side of his mouth pulls up into a boyish smile. "Thanks. I have no idea what I was reading."

"I won't tell Maverick."

"Do you have to run off or do you want to stay and hang out?"

"I can stay for a bit."

"Yeah?" He smiles wider like he'd been expecting me to say no, then takes my backpack off my shoulder and carries it to his room.

He puts my bag on the floor and then clears the clothes and books off his bed so we can sit. There's a box addressed to him at the end, still unopened. "What's that?"

"Oh, uh, my brother and his fiancée send me these care packages every month." He looks a little uncomfortable to admit it.

"My mom did that for Adam his first semester." Now that I think of it, she hasn't sent me one yet, although she has been distracted with all the fabulous trips they've been taking. The last time I talked to her, she and my dad had just returned from one trip and she was already planning another with her girlfriends. "Every month?"

"Yeah, pretty much without fail."

"What's inside?"

"Random shit, different every month." He pulls at the tape and dives in, looking more excited than he'd seemed a few seconds ago.

"Gift card." He sets it on the bed. "Granola bars, gum. Nathan must have put this one together."

"You guys are pretty close then?" I ask as I watch him pull out more stuff (all food-related, shocker) and lay it on the bed.

"Yeah, we're cool, but it makes me crazy how he's always trying to take care of me like I'm still a kid."

"I get that. Man, do I get that, but this is really nice." I motion to the gifts laid out on the bed.

"But I don't need him to send me stuff. I could buy all this on my own. Our dad passed when I was in middle school, so I think he feels like he needs to step into those shoes and make sure I'm okay."

"Or maybe he just wants to show you he cares with stuff he thinks you might need or want."

"Yeah, maybe." He laughs lightly and picks up a Ziploc bag filled with quarters. "What do you suppose he was trying to say with this?"

"I have no idea." I take the bag. It's heavy and must have at least ten dollars' worth of quarters in it. "Enjoy the vending machines?"

CHAPTER FOURTEEN

Heath

A knock at the door breaks my concentration and I rub the back of my neck as I call, "Come in."

Adam steps into my room with a beer in each hand. He holds one out to me. "You know there's a party out there, yeah?"

I accept the drink and set it on the desk. "I'm just finishing up work."

He takes a seat on my bed. "You're still working for that sports website?"

"I am. Jon in Texas wants to know how many hours a day he needs to practice in order to make his high school team."

Adam pauses with the beer up to his lips. "Depends on how bad he is."

"Yeah, I'm gonna need a more polite way to say that."

He considers for a moment. "Tell him to focus on quality sessions, practicing until he masters small skills instead of focusing on time. Quality over quantity."

"Not bad."

"I won't even charge you for using it." He stands. "Hurry up, someone needs to beat Rauthruss at Halo and you're the only one that can. It's a matter of life or death, man. His ego is going to make his head explode."

I pop the top of the beer and take a long drink before answering Jon. Nathan got me a job working for Reeves Sports, an instructional sports website owned by pro-golfer Lincoln Reeves, the summer before I started college. Linc has become a good buddy, so even though things aren't so destitute anymore that I need to have a job, it's nice to have extra cash. And the job itself is fun. I answer questions from hockey players all over the world looking to up their game.

The party is loud, and Maverick is louder when I finally close my laptop and head out to the living room. I grab another beer and make a lap to see who came. It's mostly the usual suspects, the team, their girlfriends, puck bunnies, but the sight of Ginny on the deck playing flip cup makes me smile.

It's her turn, and she chugs her beer and then sets her cup on the edge of the table, flipping it over on the rim her first try. She squeals and the next person goes.

I step up behind her. "What happened to the girl who didn't like beer?"

"I guess she's getting used to it."

"I guess you are." Her hair is braided in pigtails and I tug one end.

"Excuse me." Dakota pokes her head between us. "I need my girl here for the next game. She's our secret weapon."

Ginny smiles as Dakota pulls her back toward the table.

"See you later, Genevieve."

I head inside where Rauthruss is still dominating anyone who dares to take him on. He's got a puck bunny on either side, but I swear the guy doesn't even realize it. Or if he does, he's really good at acting disinterested.

Jordan groans as he takes his turn losing. "I give up."

I hold out my hand for the controller. "Don't take it so hard. Any kid with a name like Rhett Roger Rauthruss would be good at video games."

Rauthruss grunts a laugh. "He's not wrong. Kids are assholes. At least until I got big enough they were scared to mock me."

"That's awful," Jordan says. "Why would your parents name you that?"

Rauthruss stares blankly at him and doesn't answer.

"Move over, freshman, let me show you how it's done."

An hour or two must pass while I refuse to give up my seat, waving off anyone else who wants a turn. "This is personal," I tell them. "From one weird kid to another."

The girl sitting next to me drapes her hand on my thigh. I have no idea how long she's been there or how long she's been touching me. I guess now I understand why Rauthruss was oblivious to the two hanging next to him earlier.

"You were a nerd?" she asks. "I don't believe it."

"Not a nerd just weird." She looks at me unbelievingly, so I add, "Dead dad, non-functioning mom."

The words have barely left my mouth before I regret them. I don't talk about my family shit ever, but drunk Heath is a very sharing Heath. I don't usually drink so much, but I ran out of beer several games ago and instead of getting up to get another, I switched to sharing gulps of the Mad Dog bottle Maverick is passing around.

I glance around and notice the party is starting to die down. Inside it's me, Mav, Rauthruss, and the girls between us. Voices still carry from the deck outside.

"I'm gonna get some air." Standing, I'm much more aware of how drunk I am. My legs feel a little too light and kind of wobbly.

The group outside is almost as small as the one inside. Adam and the girl he's been seeing, Taryn, a few guys from the team, plus Reagan, Dakota, and Ginny.

Adam spots me first and his loud laughter barks into the night. "Gumby legs is back! Heath's druuuunk."

I lean against the railing beside Ginny. Her sweet smile hits me in the gut.

"Hi, Genevieve."

"Hi, Heath," she says, still smiling at me. "You look happy."

"I feel pretty happy."

"We should play sardines tonight," Dakota says. "Is Maverick still inside?"

I nod. "Yep."

"You guys in?" She looks around to everyone.

"What's sardines?" Taryn asks.

"I don't think that's a good idea," Adam says, arms wrapped around Taryn's waist, but his gaze is on Ginny.

"It's kind of like hide and seek," Dakota answers Taryn.

Ginny looks uncomfortable under her brother's scrutiny, but her words are enthusiastic. "Yeah, let's do it!"

The walk to campus in the dark with the fresh air sobers me up a little. Ginny's still smiling like something's funny as I walk beside her.

"What?"

"You're lifting your knees so high. It's adorable."

"You're adorable," I fire back.

She giggles, links her arm through mine, and leans in. Her boob presses into my forearm and all I can think about is reaching over and squeezing it like a stress ball. I completely understand that this is not acceptable behavior for friends—drunk or not, so I don't, but I think about it anyway.

At the edge of campus, Adam turns so he's walking backward. "Ginny, you good?"

"I'm fine." Her tone is playfully annoyed. "Seriously, Adam."

He waits a beat as if he expects her to change her mind. When she doesn't, he nods and says, "All right. We split into pairs. One couple hides and the rest of us try to find you. When you find them, you have to hide with them. The tighter the space, the better. No going inside buildings, no going on roofs." He looks at Maverick, who busts out laughing.

"Took you guys fucking forever to find us."

"So, wait," Taryn speaks up. "We're hiding on campus in the middle of the night? Campus is huge."

"There are some boundaries. You're with me. I'll show you." He winks and then looks to Ginny and me. "Heath, stay with Ginny. You can show her the boundaries."

"I'll be your guard, guardian, I mean guide, I think."

She smirks.

Adam points to Mav and Dakota. "It's your turn to hide and you get to make up a rule."

"We got this," Dakota says beside him. "Tonight's rule is that one partner has to carry the other by piggyback."

Everyone laughs.

Adam holds up his phone. "Five minutes and go."

While Dakota and Mav head off to hide, I lead Ginny over to the bottom of the economics building stairs and sit.

"You guys play this often, I take it?" she asks as she takes a seat next to me.

"It's fun. You'll see."

"I'm not really a fan of games where you have to hide in small, dark spaces."

It's then I notice she's staring down at her fingers and rubbing her thumb along the inside of the palm on her opposite hand.

I slide my hand in between hers and link our fingers. Shit, of course. Adam's words make sense now. "Do you want to go back? We can tell them we're going to go make out instead."

"Like they'd believe that." She huffs. "No, it'll be fine. Just don't leave me."

"I won't."

She pulls her hands away and glides them up and down her thighs. I don't really want to stop touching her, so I reach up and touch the end of her braid, rubbing the blonde ends between my fingers. "Adorable."

"You're a flirty drunk."

"I'm an honest drunk. Too honest. Don't ask me anything embarrassing."

"How'd you get so drunk?"

"Alcohol."

She giggles and then falls quiet. All around us, our friends are chatting and laughing, but we're in our own little bubble, which is nice. A Genevieve and Heath bubble that I kind of dig.

"Hmmm. What kind of dirt can I get on you while you're drunk?" She narrows her gaze and smirks. "What's your favorite color?"

"Pink." I get the reaction I hoped for and then chuckle. "Kidding, it's green. What's yours?"

"Mine actually is pink, but not *pink* pink. Like a really dark pink. Cerise."

"That's cute."

"What is?"

"That you think I know what color cerise is."

She reaches over, catching me by surprise, and runs a thumb along my chin. "Did you get this scar from hockey?"

She's barely touching me, but I like it, so I lean in a bit and tilt my chin up so she can see it better. "No, I had a confrontation with a coffee table. It won."

Her hand falls away. "Ouch."

"Time," Adam calls, breaking the moment. He holds up his phone. "One-hour time limit."

"One hour?" Ginny squeaks.

"We're really good hiders," Rauthruss says before Reagan climbs on his back and he jogs off. Dude is super competitive.

Ginny and I move at a much slower pace. I manage to get her on my back, the feel of her pressing up against me is way too nice, but my legs aren't cooperating.

"Maybe I should carry you?"

"I got this," I say but then stumble a few feet.

"Which way, ya think?" she asks when we get to the first turning point. Everyone else is going right, so I head left.

"I heard you got a job." I slow my pace. I'm not all that interested in searching for Maverick and Dakota, or generally being around anyone, but Ginny.

She smells like gummy bears which makes me think about kissing her again.

"I did. Dakota hooked me up with it actually. I start next week. I'll be leading tours of the Hall of Fame and athletic facilities, even doing recruitment tours once I get the hang of it."

"That's cool. I still remember mine."

"You do?" I pause when we come to another spot where we need to decide which way to go. "You decide."

She waves to the left, which really doesn't go anywhere and we're real close to being out of the borders of the game, but I keep that to myself. "Yeah, I had this guy named Clint. Wasn't nearly as cute as you."

Her light laughter tickles my ear. "You're incorrigible."

I'll be honest that I'm not really looking for Mav. I just want to keep talking, so I'm especially surprised when Ginny yells, "There they are!"

Dakota and Maverick are crouched down inside a fancy looking rectangular water fountain that's currently empty. It's a good spot and I don't see them myself until we're basically on top of them.

"How did you find us?" Dakota asks. "This spot is amazing. I've been waiting for weeks to use it."

"Maverick's shoes were reflecting in the light." Ginny points to his shoes.

Dakota throws her hands up.

Reluctantly, I set Ginny down.

"Now what?" Ginny asks, dropping off my back.

"We get in and wait for the others."

I hop down, not so gracefully, and then help Ginny down beside me. It's dark but not total blackout due to the lights around campus.

The space is really only big enough for us to sit side by side, but the more we spread out, the easier we are to see. Dakota and Maverick are sitting facing one another legs stretched out in front of them. I sit and pull Ginny down in front of me so her back is at my chest.

Maverick passes me the half-empty bottle of Mad Dog. Do I need another drink? Definitely not. However, we might be here for a while.

After taking a small drink, I tap Ginny on the shoulder with the bottle. Her fingers brush mine. They're cold and seem to tremble as she twists the cap off.

I wait until she passes it to Dakota before pulling her against me.

"Are you okay?" I whisper. Somehow the end of her braid gets stuck in my mouth in the process.

"Did you just eat my hair?" She runs her hand along her braid and flips it, so it lands in front of her.

"Unintentionally."

"Shh. I think I can hear someone coming," Dakota whispers.

Since I can't soothe her with words, I take her in a vise grip snug against me. Her shoulders are rigid, and I feel her take in a deep breath.

I hum the first song that comes to mind, 'Fantasy', and after a few minutes, she melts into me. She turns her head, so her lips are close to mine. "Thank you."

I'm frozen, staring at her mouth. The cupid's bow, the fullness of her bottom lip, how soft it feels under the trace of my thumb. I don't know when I touched it, but I keep doing it. Her eyes fall to my mouth and her tongue darts out, the warm tip wetting my thumb.

I lean in but hesitate to see how she reacts first. She nods her head a fraction, almost as if she's giving me permission to kiss her.

Adam's voice calls out, breaking the moment as the other four find us. "Twenty-five minutes. Mav, dude, your shoes are shining like a flashlight at anyone that walks by."

"Ow! Ow!" Mav yells and shields himself as Dakota pelts him and says, "Worst partner ever."

FIFTEEN

Ginny

"This is the coolest thing I've ever seen." I turn a circle. Flat screens cover every inch of the walls, floor to ceiling, all the way around.

Dakota grins and taps on the tablet in her hands. "Wait for it. It gets way cooler."

We stand in the middle of the room. It's cozy, not really meant for more than a few people comfortably. The recessed lighting above us dims and the screens all come alive at once.

Hype music pumps into the room and images and videos of the Valley U hockey team play like a highlight reel. My heart races as if I were sitting front row in a playoff game. My brother is shown a lot, which makes sense because he's been a big contributor to the team since his freshman year.

Sometimes the clips are of the players in action and sometimes it's media type posed images. One of the latter of Heath fills the screens. His face, jumbo-sized, stares back at me and my stomach does a somersault. He's so damn hot.

It goes on and on, a good five minutes of film, but when it ends, I want to watch it all over again.

"Awesome, right?" Dakota asks as the screens go black and the overhead lighting returns.

"This is just for recruits?"

"Hockey, specifically. Each team has their own recruitment video and there's a generic one too that combines pieces from all the videos. We do tours for the community, local schools, and alumni too." She shows me the tablet where I can select and play the videos and then how to get in and out of the room because it's a very fancy coded system that seals you in and won't open while the video is playing.

I follow her out of the room, still a little awestruck.

"That's the last stop on the tour. Once you're finished in the hype room, you'll walk them to the front desk and the coach from whichever team they're here for will take over."

"I didn't realize how much effort they put into getting athletes to come to Valley."

"They recruit hard. Basketball and hockey especially. So, do you have any questions? Feel ready to lead one on your own?"

"No, I'm probably going to totally botch it. How long have you worked here?"

"Since my freshman year. I quit the track team, but I still wanted to be a part of something that was sports-related. They like to hire student-athletes since we're familiar with a lot of the facilities and can answer questions they might have."

She must read the panic on my face because she laughs and adds, "You'll be fine. It isn't that hard. You probably know more than you think from Adam."

"I'm not so sure about that."

Dakota smiles. "We're just here to get them excited about Valley. You're one of the few people they'll meet outside of the team. It's fun. You get to meet a lot of top athletes from all over the country, and if they come to Valley, you'll see them again and know you were part of getting them here. I'm doing two tours today, volleyball and hockey, so you'll shadow me and see how easy it is."

We take a break to grab lunch before our afternoon of leading recruits around campus.

I sit across from Dakota at an outdoor table outside of University Hall.

"So, you and Heath looked pretty cozy last night."

"He was drunk."

"Drunk Heath is hilariously honest. One time, he told me I was really pretty, but not his type because I was too bossy." She takes a sip from her straw and then adds, "Which is totally true. But you and him, I could see it."

"We're just friends."

"Except that time you kissed." She raises a brow pointedly and takes another bite of her sandwich.

"It was the gummy bears."

"Would it really be the worst thing to admit you like him?"

"Even if I did, Heath made it clear that he isn't interested in dating and that Adam's little sister was off-limits."

"Your brother shouldn't be giving anyone orders on being single. The man goes from one relationship to the next."

"He's always been like that. He got his first girlfriend in seventh grade and probably hasn't been without one for more than a week since."

"Taryn seems nice. I like her better than the last one, Heather."

"Heather wasn't the last one. He dated Maria over the summer." I shrug. "Taryn's okay. I try not to get attached anymore."

"Makes sense. Probably especially hard given Taryn's history with Heath."

My head pops up. "She dated Heath?"

"Dated might be a stretch. They were more like fuck buddies. Those two were going at it all the time loudly and everywhere."

My face heats and the food in my mouth turns to paste.

Dakota busts up laughing. "I'm totally kidding. I'm sorry; I couldn't resist." She points a fry at me. "I knew you liked him."

The first tour is a local high school volleyball player. She towers over me and I keep pushing up onto my tiptoes, so I don't feel so small. I barely say a word after introducing myself, and instead let Dakota take charge while I try to memorize every detail she says. I really don't want to screw this up when it's my turn to lead a tour on my own.

The hype room is just as cool the second time around and as we hand her off to the coach of the volleyball team, I'm feeling better about the job.

"The next one should be here in five." She reads from the tablet and then passes it to me. "Nick, a senior from Newburg High in Boston."

I look over Nick's information at the front desk while we wait. The scouting reports are detailed and makes me appreciate how much effort goes into recruiting athletes to Valley.

Maybe Adam and our parents downplayed it, but hockey was just sort of this thing he did. Adam never made a big deal out of touring colleges or getting a full-ride scholarship. Even when he had NHL teams inviting him to summer camps and agents asking about his plans after college, he waved it off like it was nothing. I'm not sure why he doesn't want to go pro, but he's wanted to be a doctor for as long as I can remember.

My thoughts briefly go to Bryan. He came to Valley and did a tour that probably looked a lot like this, too. He hadn't made a big deal out of it either. Maybe the jocks in my life are used to being fawned over like this. Freaking jocks.

I'm only checking Bryan's social media every other day now, a real step in the right direction from the hours I spent obsessing after we first broke up. Since I've started hanging out with Dakota and Reagan, I'm less jealous of his happy photos with new friends. He likes every single thing I post as if he truly believes we're cool and going to step right back into the way we were when we see each other again.

"There he is," Dakota says, breaking my thoughts. I look up to find Adam and Heath walking Nick through the front doors. Heath and my brother are wearing matching Valley Hockey T-shirts and jeans.

I smile and stand beside Dakota while we wait for them to approach the desk.

"Hey," Dakota says cheerily. "You must be Nick."

Dakota introduces me and then gives Nick a chance to use the restroom and grab a soda or water before we start. When he's gone, Adam leans against the desk. "Hey, Ginny. First day?"

"Yep."

"Anything we should know about him?" Dakota asks. It's good one of us is still thinking about the job because I'm ridiculously distracted by Heath. His hair looks like he tried to manage it into a style, but the long top curls and flips in every which direction.

Adam and Dakota talk and Heath smiles at me and takes a step to the side of the desk, motioning for me to follow.

"Look at you." His eyes scan my blue polo and khaki pants.

"Look at you," I toss back.

He runs a hand through his hair and his smile turns sheepish. "Missed you at lunch. Guess I'm going to have to find a new lunch buddy."

"It's only a couple of days a week."

He nods. "Tomorrow then?"

"Yeah, I'll be there tomorrow."

Nick rounds the corner and we all stop talking to give him our attention.

"Ready?" Dakota asks him with a big smile.

"Later, Genevieve." Heath winks and then he and Adam say their good-byes to Nick.

I watch him leave and then blow out a long breath. Holy gummy bears.

OCTOBER

SIXTEEN

Ginny

We're decked out in Valley blue and yellow for the first home game of the season. Dakota, Reagan, and I sit in my parents' season ticket seats.

"I feel bad for not inviting Taryn," I admit as the team takes the ice.

Dakota waves me off. "She's fine. She said she was going to sit with her sorority sisters and meet up with us after."

"I think I'm going to have to get to know her."

"Why do you sound so defeated? She's nice," Reagan says, eyes forward watching the guys.

"Every time I get attached to one of Adam's girlfriends, they break up and it's like I lose them, too. I always wanted a sister."

Dakota and Reagan put their arms around my shoulders. "Well, now you have us and neither of us plans on banging your brother. Right, Reagan?"

Reagan's jaw drops. "Of course not. He's with Taryn."

When the game starts we cheer like crazy. It's nothing like being at a game with my parents and I feel so much more invested being a Valley student now.

And my brother is good. Really good. I spot Taryn jumping up and down in the front row of the student section as he scores a goal. Ugh. I really am going to have to make an effort with her. She seems to really like Adam and not be one of the crazy ones, but first I need to talk to my brother and make sure he isn't already thinking about breaking up with her.

There's a line switch and Heath and two other guys come off the ice. They sit not far from us. Jordan, a freshman I think, is drinking out of a water bottle. Heath shakes his head when someone tries to hand him his own water. Stick in hand, he's practically bouncing with untapped energy to get back out there.

He turns his head to follow the action on the ice, giving me a view of his strong profile. Dark hair peeks out around his helmet. His nose is straight, jaw sharp, nice lips that are soft despite all the ways the rest of him is hard.

I press two fingers against my lips remembering how it felt to be kissed by Heath. I've done my best to avoid going down this particular memory lane because I don't want to ruin the friendship we have, but I don't think I'll ever forget that kiss.

Valley wins and the girls and I head to The Hideout. The local restaurant and bar is a favorite among college students, and we have to push our way through a mass of people to find a table.

There's a collective cheer in the place when the guys arrive. Adam and Taryn lead the pack, Rhett, Maverick, and a few other guys from the team not far behind.

"Congratulations." I stand and hug my brother. "You were amazing."

"You've seen me play before."

"I know, but it was different this time. I can't explain it. I'm so proud of you."

One side of his mouth pulls up into a smile. "Thanks, Ginny."

We pull a couple of tables together so we can all sit. Pitchers of beer and shots arrive at the table, some the guys ordered and others that people buy for them.

My gaze falls to the front entrance every time someone new appears. I just assumed Heath would be coming, but now I'm not so sure and I'm disappointed. A friendly disappointment. We're friends—I'm allowed to be disappointed when a friend doesn't come out for the night.

I'm sitting at one end between my brother and Jordan. Adam's turned toward Taryn which kind of leaves me hidden behind his giant back from the rest of the table.

I'm leaning in and listening to a Celine Dion cover that Jordan promised would change my life when Heath's voice washes over me.

"Thanks for saving my seat, J."

Jordan looks from me to Heath and he nods slowly. "You two are . . .?"

"Friends," I say at the same time Heath says, "Yep."

"I'll send you the link," Jordan says as he stands to give Heath his seat. "I wasn't sure you were coming."

"Came with the rest of the guys, but my brother called as we were walking in."

"You've been outside on the phone this whole time?"

He nods and reaches for one of the pitchers and a glass. "Yeah, what'd I miss? Other than Jordan hitting on you."

"He wasn't hitting on me."

Heath's brows rise and he takes a long drink from his glass then leans back and places his arm around the back of my chair.

"Five minutes talking with him and anyone would know he's totally hung up on his ex-girlfriend. He was playing me videos of her singing some Celine Dion song."

"That's why he picked that sappy-ass song."

"Picked it for what?"

"On game days, we do a light skate in the morning and we each get to pick one song that Mav compiles into a playlist for us."

"That's cool. What's your song?"

He smirks and instead of answering pulls out his phone. Like with Jordan, I have to lean in close to hear it. As the music plays I can see how it affects him, getting him pumped up. But unlike when I was this close to Jordan, I'm acutely aware of everything about Heath. The way he smells like soap and something masculine—sandalwood, I think. The fit of his shirt, tight around his chest and biceps but looser at his tapered waist. And the way my body reacts—heart racing and breathless.

Friends schmends. I want to kiss him again.

When the song ends, he pockets his phone and leans back, and I can think a little clearer without him so close. I push my chair back and stand. "I'm going to use the restroom."

I catch Dakota's gaze as I walk by the table and motion for her to come with me. She and Reagan tail me into the ladies' room.

"What's up? You were flashing panic eyes. Do you need a tampon?" Dakota asks as she checks herself in the mirror.

Reagan sets her giant purse on the counter and pulls out a tampon.

I wave her off. "No, I'm good."

Next, she pulls out lip gloss which I take.

"I like Heath," I admit after I swipe on the shiny pink gloss.

Dakota snorts. "Duh. What's the problem?"

"We're friends. He's one of my best friends here. He's already told me that he isn't interested in dating me. If I make a fool of myself, then I'll have to stop hanging out with you guys, and that would be a real bummer."

"First of all, we're not going anywhere. Second, don't be a pussy." Dakota meets my gaze in the mirror.

My mouth tingles and I rub my lips together. "What is this gloss?"

"Lip plumper," Reagan says, putting it back in her purse and pulling out mascara and adding a coat to her lashes.

"It stings. Holy crap." I grab a paper towel and wipe it off, but the burn only subsides a little. "That's awful. Do you have something else that will dull the pain?"

Reagan hands me another gloss, this one I inspect more closely before applying.

Dakota holds out her hand for the lip plumper. "I like the pain," she announces as she puts it on, turning so her back rests against the counter. "Listen, if you're sure that nothing is going to happen between you and Heath, then stop torturing yourself."

"She's right," Reagan says. "You guys spend a lot of time together which makes it hard to get over him."

"Or find someone else." Dakota's icy blue eyes bore into mine. "Come on. Let's go back out there. Sit with us and forget about Heath for tonight. There are a ton more guys at Valley, and we're going to introduce you to all of them."

"The ones out there anyway," Reagan says with a light laugh.

Not a terrible idea. I'm done being angry and sad about Bryan, and spending my time wondering what college would have been like if he were here. I'm ready to have fun, date, maybe even hook up with someone new. And if that's not Heath, then there are other people out there.

Heath is at the bar getting another pitcher when we make our way back to the table which makes my transition to sitting next to Reagan and Dakota less awkward. When he spots me down the table, he raises both hands in question, but I just smile at him like it's nothing.

Reagan and Dakota are true to their word and they casually introduce me to so many guys they start to blur together. I feel like I'm on a covert version of The Bachelorette.

"Okay, point taken. There are a lot of guys at Valley. You don't need to introduce me to any more." My gaze flits to Heath across the bar. He's talking to Maverick but looks up and smiles when he catches me staring.

"Hey, Ginny." Liam approaches with his hands in his pockets. "Are you going over to Adam's . . . I mean, your brother's after this?"

"Uhh." I look to Reagan and Dakota, who both nod eagerly. "I think so."

"Cool, I'll see you there."

I watch him walk off and then look to Reagan. "I think I'm going to need more lip gloss."

She digs into her purse and hands it to me. "Keep it. You may need to reapply many times."

SEVENTEEN

Heath

I get a ride back to the apartment with Maverick. I'm riding shotgun while Taryn and Adam sit in the backseat sucking face.

"Is that Liam's truck?" Adam asks as Mav parks and we get out.

"Yeah, I think so," I answer, looking over the silver F-150. There's like a million of these trucks and they all look the same, but this one has a Valley University Hockey license plate.

His brows draw together, and he has a weird look on his face as he passes it. Adam isn't one to care who comes over—it's one area he's actually chill about. He's got the whole, "everyone's welcome" mentality when it comes to the apartment.

"Something wrong with Liam being here?"

"He asked for permission to ask out my sister." He makes a little grunt of annoyance and Taryn smiles and pats his arm.

"Ginny?"

Now I'm the one getting the weird look from Adam. "I only have one sister, dude."

"Right."

I hang back, trailing the guys up to our apartment. I pull out my phone and text Ginny.

Me: Where'd you go? You coming by? Halo rematch?

I cringe a little at my borderline needy message, slide my phone back into my pocket, and force myself to chill the fuck out.

After grabbing a beer, I look for Ginny. I don't see her or Dakota and Reagan. The three of them are inseparable these days. I check my phone, but she hasn't texted back.

Liam is outside and I head toward him.

"What's up, Liam?" I tip my chin up in acknowledgment to the other guys on the team standing with him.

"Hey, Payne. Nice assist tonight."

"Thanks."

I spot Dakota walking out the back door to the deck first. Ginny and Reagan follow.

They go to the opposite side, stopping to talk to Taryn and Adam.

"Heard you asked Scott for permission to ask out Ginny?" I go for a teasing tone, but don't quite hit the mark.

Liam nods. "She seems like a cool chick. You two are friends, right? Any advice?"

Back the fuck off. Find someone else. Anyone else.

But that's not really fair. Ginny *is* a cool chick and Liam is a decent guy and hockey player.

I avoid his question altogether. "Scott gave his blessing?"

"He didn't seem all that happy about it, but he said Ginny could make up her own mind who she dated."

Jordan laughs and elbows Liam. "And threatened to beat your ass if you hurt her."

"And that," Liam admits. "But I'd never screw over a teammate's sister."

God, I hate that he's such a nice guy.

"I think it's a terrible idea," Tiny says with a shake of his head. "It's messy. If things don't work out, then you're on the outs with the team captain. No chick is worth that much trouble."

I watch Liam's face to see if he agrees. Part of me hopes he does and backs off.

"Some girls are worth the risk," he says, and I grind down on my teeth.

Of-fucking-course Ginny is worth it, but Liam and Ginny? I can't see it.

"Well, good luck, man."

I go inside, do a shot, and grab another beer.

"Everything okay?" Mav says as he gets two beers from the fridge.

"Fine."

He lingers as he pops the top on the first can. "You sure? You look . . . off."

"Off?"

"Yeah, like at practice that time Coach tried to switch you to the left wing. You do this weird thing with your face." He looks like a deer caught in headlights in some shit imitation of me.

"I don't look like that. Fuck off. I'm fine." I run a hand through my hair.

"Seriously, man, what's up?"

"It's nothing. Liam is interested in Ginny, and I can't see it."

"Because—"

"Adam asked me to look out for her, and I don't know, it doesn't feel right."

"Because you like her."

"I don't . . . it's not . . ."

He waits for me to string a complete sentence together, a smug expression on his face. "It isn't a big deal. Ginny's cool. Just tell Liam you're interested and ask her out yourself."

I tap my foot on the linoleum, consider it, and shake my head. "She probably isn't even interested in him like that."

Mav clears his throat and points with a finger wrapped around the beer can to Ginny and Liam standing in the doorway between the deck and dining area. They're both smiling. Liam leans a hand above her, and she doesn't look at all uncomfortable.

I take off in their direction without a plan and hear Mav mutter behind me, "Yeah, that's what I thought."

Four steps. Four, big, hurried steps is all it takes to get to her. I grab Ginny's hand, mumble an apology I don't really mean to Liam, and pull her through the party to my room.

She laughs, obviously not concerned that I'm dragging her to my bedroom like some sort of caveman. "What's going on?"

"We need to talk," I say once I close the door.

"About?" she asks, sounding concerned but still smiling.

"Do you like Liam?"

"Sure. He's nice."

"Nice like you'd let him feel you up or . . ."

She laughs. Loudly and I think at me. She walks forward and pokes me in the chest. "You're jealous."

"Am not." I don't know why I bother denying it. Gut reaction, I guess.

She laughs again and moves to sit on my bed, digging through her purse. "I'm sorry I didn't respond to your text earlier. I thought we needed a little space. We're friends, but we've kissed, and I know you've probably already forgotten, but I haven't and sometimes things with us feel messy. So, yes, I think Liam is nice like maybe someday I'll let him feel me up, but I'm not going anywhere. You and I will still be friends, no matter what. You don't need to worry about me dating Liam or anyone else and forgetting about my favorite cafeteria buddy."

I grunt at being called her fucking cafeteria buddy. She pulls out a long tube of pink gloss and coats her lips. I'm mesmerized by the action and the way her lips catch the light. She rubs her lips together and puckers them and all I can imagine is her walking out there and every guy in the place wanting to kiss her and smear that perfect, pink outline.

She stands. "I promise not to be one of those people who ignores her friends when she meets a guy, or, in our case, another guy."

"Don't date him."

"Why not?"

"He's not good enough."

"Good enough for what?" She rolls her eyes. "Thank you for wanting to look out for me, but I'm a big girl. I can take care of myself. I swear, if it were up to you and my brother, I'd spend the next four years alone while everyone else hooks up and pairs off. I want to do those things too, go on dates and make bad decisions, and I know it's possible that he'll hurt me or he'll be a total bore, but I won't know unless I go out with him."

"Don't date him."

She looks like she's going to start arguing again, but I keep going before she can get a word in. "Don't date him. We could . . ."

"We could what?"

"You know."

"Date?" She fights a grin. "You can't even say the word."

I close the space between us and drop my mouth to hers. Her lips part in a surprised squeak and I take full advantage, sweeping my tongue inside. She tastes so good and so right. I'm breathless when she takes a step back.

Breathless and filled with so much energy, my steps feel light as I fill the gap again.

"Wait." She puts a hand at my chest. "I don't understand. You don't date. You told me that you weren't interested in dating anyone, especially me."

"I never said 'especially you.'"

"It was implied."

"Fuck no, it wasn't. We already hang out more than I ever have with any other chick, so let's do that and make out. That's basically dating, right?"

She gives her head a little shake. "I'm confused. Is this some trick to keep me from dating Liam?"

"Hell no. I don't care who Liam dates as long as it isn't you."

My mouth tingles. Fucking tingles. This girl . . . fuuuck.

"I said we shouldn't date because you had just gotten out of a relationship and in the past, dating hadn't really been my thing. Enjoying college has been my top priority. I only have a few years before I'm going to be married to hockey. I didn't want us to hook up and then never talk again, and I wasn't sure I was capable of more. I like hanging with you and I don't want to mess that up."

"Oh."

"But I was overthinking it. If what you're looking for is the same thing I am—to have fun, hang out, hook up." I pull her against me so she can feel how hard I am. "Then of course I want to date you."

"Really?" Her eyes light up.

I swipe a hand over my mouth. It's on fire and sticky from her lipstick.

"Really, but I should talk to your brother first."

She groans. "You don't need his permission."

"I know." I give in and press my lips to hers again. It's almost painful with how much my mouth aches to be on hers. I kiss her harder and the burn intensifies. "Fuck, baby, your lips are on fire."

Her hand flies to her mouth. "Oh no."

"Oh yes. Don't move. I'm going to talk to your brother."

"Right now?"

"I promised him I'd look out for you. I don't want him to feel like I took advantage or . . . I don't know, maybe it's stupid, but I respect your brother and you, and I can't kiss you like I want to until I talk to him."

"Kiss me like you want to?" she asks with a laugh.

I walk to the door and pause with my hand on the doorknob. "Naked."

Adam's in the living room. I call his name and motion for him, going to the kitchen where I can pour a couple shots just in case one, or both of us, needs it.

"Dude, what's going on with your face?"

I rub absently at my face, which still stings. Since I can't very well tell him my body is having some sort of physical reaction to kissing his sister, I avoid his question altogether.

"I need to talk to you about Ginny."

I slide one of the shot glasses in front of him. He looks but doesn't touch it. "What about her? Is she okay?"

"Yeah, she's fine."

Reagan picks this inopportune time to join us. "Hey, have either of you seen Ginny?"

I glance at her. "She's—"

"Oh my god, Heath, what happened to your face." Dakota appears next to Reagan and steps forward and inspects my face. "I think your body is rejecting whichever random bunny you were making out with."

I swipe a hand over my mouth.

"Pink's not really your color." Adam laughs.

I grab a paper towel and wet it so I can wipe his sister's lipstick off my face. It can't be helping the situation. "I think I'm allergic to this shit. It stings."

Reagan starts giggling, and within a few seconds, it's full-blown hysterical laughter that has tears coming from her eyes.

"The lip plumper," she manages to get out and that sets Dakota off.

"What the hell is going on?" Adam asks.

"I was kissing—"

My body is yanked to the right by Ginny as she pulls me away. "Sorry, I need to borrow him for flip cup."

I hear Reagan say, "I must have given it to her again by accident." And then Adam's gruff voice asks, "What the fuck is lip plumper?"

CHAPTER EIGHTEEN

Ginny

I don't stop until we're in the corner of the deck outside, far away from my brother. "We can't tell him."

Heath's rubbing at his lips. "Why not?"

"Because he'll freak out and make a big deal out of it. And any chance of low-key and fun will go right out the window with it."

"I don't know. He was pretty cool about Liam asking to date you."

"Liam asked to date me?" Ugh. I hate that they all feel like they need to ask permission. He's not the boss of me.

Heath puts his hands in his pockets and nods.

"Just trust me on this. He might have said he was cool with it, but he'll interfere somehow. We don't need his okay."

"I don't relish the idea of going behind his back. We may not see eye to eye on everything, but we're teammates."

"I know and it isn't forever, only until we decide if there's anything even worth telling him."

Heath raises a dark brow.

"You know what I mean."

"All right. If that's what you want."

I let out a sigh of relief. "Thank you."

"What the hell did you do to my lips?" He rubs at them again and I bite back a laugh and run a thumb over the tender skin. It's red and irritated, but his lips look nice and full, so I guess the stuff works.

I press my lips to his. A chaste kiss, but I linger, enjoying the feel of him being so close and his mouth against mine. Thirty seconds into this, and I'm already having a hard time keeping my hands off him around other people. He makes a little humming noise when I pull back.

"You expect me to keep this a secret?" He shakes his head. At least I'm not alone in wanting to jump him.

I take a step back as Maverick approaches.

"Hey, you two." He looks from Heath to me with a big smile and then sniffs the air. "Is that . . . romance I smell?"

Heath smirks at me. Busted.

"Well, so much for keeping it from everyone." I huff a laugh.

We do a slightly better job of staying apart after we make Mav swear to secrecy. With a butt squeeze and a whispered promise to find me later, Heath goes with Maverick to play Xbox and I find Reagan.

She's sitting in a folding chair in a circle of people, but she's quiet, playing with the label on the beer bottle in her hand. I grab a chair and pull it up beside her.

"Hey, are you okay? You look a little bummed."

"Sam, the guy I went out with last week, was supposed to meet up with me tonight, but he flaked."

"Oh, babe, I'm sorry."

"It's fine. He was kind of boring, but it still hurts to be blown off." Her shoulders rise and fall with a big sigh. "And the worst part is I'm still not over . . ." She pauses and fidgets with her beer again.

"Are you ever going to tell me who it is?"

"No, probably not."

"Well, at least tell me what it is about him that has you so spun up?"

"He's smart and caring." She bites her lip. "And so hot. Have you ever been totally into a guy and no matter how hard you try to move on, you can't stop hoping he notices you?" She groans. "I just realized how pathetic I am. God, I hate being the girl who can't even enjoy the party because of a boy."

"No, I totally get it. Been there."

"I think you're there now." She smiles, dimples popping out. "At least with you and Heath, it's mutual. You kissed again, right? He had gloss all over his face."

"Listen, can we keep that between us for now? I don't want my brother all up in my business with this."

"I won't tell him, but good luck hiding it—you've got a ridiculous grin on your face just talking about him."

"I do?"

She nods.

"You know what? You helped me earlier by introducing me to guys, let's do the same for you now."

"I already know all of these guys."

"Humor me? Maybe you were too caught up in this other guy to notice how great some of these other boys are."

"You think?" She looks so hopeful.

I stand and hold my hand out. She takes it and gets out of her chair. "Okay, but you're sleeping over tonight. I need a safety net, so I don't do something crazy and end up having sad, forget-you sex."

"You never know," I say as we head inside. I make eye contact with Heath and my stomach flips.

Later after everyone else leaves and it's just a handful of us left, Adam convinces us to play sardines.

Heath and I walk just ahead of the group toward campus. I'm holding his arm in a friendly way that we've done a hundred times before, but this time is completely about touching him any way I can.

"Which pair was the first to find Maverick and Dakota last time?" Adam asks when we arrive.

"Me and Heath," I speak up, briefly catching my brother's eye. I hold my breath to see if there's any indication from his expression that he knows. Maybe it really is written all over my face.

"All right, one of you gets to make the rule."

Heath looks to me. "You pick."

I think for a minute. "Partners have to swap shirts."

Heath eyes my white tank top and nods his approval.

"That's kind of easy, Ginny," Adam says, but then Rhett groans loudly and we all look to him and Reagan, who's wearing a dress.

Heath and I start our search for the perfect hiding spot, but only make it as far as the first corner away from the group before he backs me up against the building.

His lips take mine, and his body presses into me. I'm stuck in between a rock and a hard place quite literally. The brick building bites into my back and the rigid swell in Heath's jeans presses into my hipbone.

My body hums with excitement. I drop my hands to his waist and slip my fingers under the hem of his shirt. He keeps kissing me as I glide my palms over his abs and chest. His muscles tighten under my touch, and he grinds into me harder.

Who knew secret relationships were so hot?

Removing my hands from his body, which is exceedingly difficult, I take off my shirt, letting the breeze and his gaze pebble my skin.

"Fuck, Ginny," he rasps.

"We're supposed to swap shirts," I say, voice a little too breathy.

"Oh, right." Without taking his eyes off me, he pulls his shirt off and we trade. He tucks my shirt into the front pocket of his jeans and runs his fingers up the curve of my waist, stopping when his thumbs brush against the sides of my bra.

I don't make any move to put on his shirt because he's looking at me with so much admiration and hunger, I don't want it to end.

Wrapping my arms around his neck, I lift up on my toes to kiss him. The skin to skin contact feels better than anything I've ever experienced. Kissing down his jaw, which flexes under my lips, I move to his neck and chest.

He holds my hair back with one hand as I learn the contours of his body with my hands and mouth. I'm circling his nipple with my tongue, which he seems to like very much, when he curses and flattens me against the wall.

Footsteps approach and Adam and Taryn come into view holding hands. Adam's wearing Taryn's strapless top around his neck and she's in his oversized T-shirt.

Our only saving grace seems to be that we're so close they aren't looking for us yet. My chest rises and falls, and I fight to slow down my breathing as the others go off in search of us.

"Shit, that was close," Heath says when they're out of sight. He steps back and looks me over again, hunger flashing in his gaze and a smile on his lips. "We should hide." He takes his shirt from me and slowly pulls it down over me. His scent covers me, warmth still clinging to the material.

"Now? They're already looking for us."

He glances around and clicks his tongue. "I got it. Come with me."

"Is this in bounds?" I ask after he leads me back around the corner to the spot the seekers usually wait.

He shrugs and takes a seat on the top stair so we're as far out of sight as we can be while still pretty much being in plain view of anyone who walks by. He pulls me down into the space between his legs. "Technically it is, but no one has ever hidden here as far as I know."

"Probably because it isn't a very good hiding spot."

"I disagree. It'll take them at least ten minutes to double back, and in the meantime, I have you all alone." His mouth brushes against my neck. His shirt is baggy on me, giving him more access and his lips trail along my collarbone.

I start to turn around so I can touch him, but he stops me. "If you get any closer, they're going to find us naked."

Naked sounds great, but not in front of my brother, so I don't move.

There's something about holding still and just receiving his affection that is hotter than anything I could have imagined. Fingertips tease my waist and occasionally dip down to the top of my jeans, but he doesn't slide his hand lower to rub the ache between my legs like I desperately want.

This time, I'm the one who hears our friends approaching and I squeeze his calf hard enough it gets his attention. He hunkers down like he's hiding behind me, and we sit still until Rhett wearing Reagan's dress, a sight I'll never be able to unsee, spots us.

"What the hell, man?" he asks as he and Reagan take a seat on the stairs beside us. "You had to have switched hiding spots after we started. Is that legal?"

He's heated about it, talking loudly, and it isn't long before the others find us.

It turns out that it isn't legal, but I don't even feel a little bit bad about it when Heath and I get chastised for ruining the game. Totally worth it.

Taryn's chatting with Dakota on the walk back, so I take advantage of her not being attached to my brother's side and fall into step beside him.

"Sorry I ruined your game."

Hands in his pockets, his long stride is slow. "Eh, it's fine. Rauthruss takes games of any kind real serious. For me, it's just fun getting out and doing it."

"Taryn seems nice. Should I get to know this one?"

He shoots me an annoyed glare.

"What? Come on, your track record isn't stellar. It can't surprise you to know I'm hesitant to get attached to one of your girlfriends."

"Taryn's great." He shrugs. "Get to know her if you want or not, whatever."

"So it isn't serious?"

"I didn't say that."

"You're not saying anything." Good god, sometimes I want to shake him.

He huffs a quiet laugh. "Look, I like her. She's nice and a lot of fun, but I have no idea where it'll go. Dating in college isn't like it was in high school. People don't go into it thinking they've found their forever person or at least I don't."

I wonder if that's a universal thing or just my brother. Heath basically summed it up the same way. Seems a little depressing if I follow their logic too deep, but fun—fun I'm in for.

When the apartment building comes into view, I fall back beside Heath.

"I promised Reagan I'd stay over tonight to talk boys."

He smirks and his eyes darken. "You could come over later when you're done talking."

"I'd like to, really, but sneaking into your place with Adam there . . . I don't know."

He nods and I can't tell if he's disappointed or not. I'm glad he doesn't push any harder to get me to change my mind though. I'd probably cave, and some part of me knows I'm not ready to get naked with him yet.

I'm not a virgin, but my experience is pretty limited. And if what Adam says is true, that this isn't a big deal, I need to capture the butterflies in my stomach and give them a good pep talk about slowing their flutter every time Heath is near.

"Breakfast tomorrow?" I offer.

"Yeah. Text me and we can go over to campus together in the morning."

"Are you coming, Ginny?" Dakota asks when we reach the top of the stairs. She and Reagan are headed into their apartment, and the rest of the group has already gone into the boys' place.

"Yeah, I'll be there in just a minute."

As the doors close, Heath's mouth finds mine. He kisses me like he's begging me to reconsider going inside with him. His large hands frame my face, and he walks me backward until I'm trapped between him and the wall.

Heath likes to be in charge, and my body doesn't mind one bit. His lips find the sensitive flesh at the curve of my neck and I sigh. "How many hours until the dining hall opens?"

"Five or six." The words are spoken against my skin between nips.

"That's a long time to wait."

"Hungry, baby?" His deep baritone rumbles.

I don't answer, not even sure I'm capable of stringing words together as his face nuzzles in between my boobs. We didn't bother switching shirts back, so I'm still in his. Even through the cotton material, the scrape of his scruff provides a delectable friction. His hands fall to my ass, and he pulls me against him. He's hard again, or maybe still, and I rub myself on him desperate for more.

He growls and pushes his hips forward, slamming me back to the wall.

"Yo, Heath—woah, sorry, man." Maverick covers his eyes but doesn't leave as I duck my head, embarrassed.

"What the fuck?" Heath asks, not moving. Even in my embarrassment, I can't resist moving just slightly so I can recapture the delicious friction. At my movement, he moves his hand lower on my ass and his fingers dig into me through my jeans. Deep circles giving me just the right amount of pressure.

Maverick can't see what's going on, but I nearly cry out as the orgasm hits. I stop myself by biting down on Heath's bare shoulder.

I miss whatever exchanges between them and I'm coming down, body still shuddering, when the door closes. My head falls forward into his chest as I catch my breath.

Heath pulls me into a hug and kisses the top of my head.

"Did that really just happen?" I squeak, apparently out loud though not intentionally.

He chuckles, deep and throaty. "God, I hope so, but we can try again if you need to be certain."

I lift my face and wrap my arms around his neck. "I should go before Dakota comes looking for me."

He steps back and adjusts himself.

"Are you going to be okay?" I bite my lip. Maybe there's time. Hand jobs for him and her.

"Go. I'm fine. I'll see you in the morning. I'll still be hard then—don't worry. Seems to be a constant thing around you."

NINETEEN

Ginny

"My brother will be home any minute." I squirm as Heath's hands slide up my shirt and his hot mouth sucks on my collarbone.

"All the more reason to get naked quicker then."

The door opens and I sit up straight and elbow Heath inadvertently. He groans and leans back in his chair as Adam and Rhett walk into the house.

"Hey guys," I say cheerily and reach for a pencil on the table.

"Ginny?" Adam's brows pull together. "What are you doing here?"

"Studying with Maverick."

Adam quirks a brow.

"He's on his way over. He had to let Charli out."

"Oh, cool. You wanna stay for dinner?"

"Actually, I promised Reagan and Dakota we'd grab food when I was done."

"Invite them too. Mav can grill."

"You cook?" I ask the always shirtless Maverick as he walks in the front door with Charli.

"I grill."

"Is that different?"

"It's manly and awesome."

"Which is different than cooking?"

He grins. "Open flame."

Dakota and Reagan agree to come over to the guys' place for dinner and the seven of us sit around the outdoor table.

My brother might be oblivious to me and Heath, but my friends are not. Dakota corners me when I go inside to grab ketchup.

"What is going on with you and Heath? More kissing since last weekend?"

Reagan is right behind her, shutting the door and joining us.

"It's no big deal," I try, but I'm sure the smile on my face gives me away.

Reagan's dimples pop out and Dakota shakes her head. "You absolutely slept with him!"

"No, we haven't yet, but you cannot tell anyone that we're . . . whatever. Promise?"

Dakota looks to Reagan. "She's talking to you."

Reagan tries to look offended but then rolls her eyes. "I already knew. Besides, I'm good at keeping secrets of the heart. I won't say anything."

"Do you really think your brother would care?" Dakota asks. "I mean, he's one to talk."

"I'm not sure, but I don't want to cause a big thing. Heath and I are just . . . hanging out. If Adam finds out, he'll be all overbearing about it, and I don't want that. Judgment free fun."

"And hot, dirty sex?" Dakota smirks.

I feel my face warm.

"How are you planning on keeping it from him? They live together, G," Reagan reminds me.

"I don't know. I haven't thought that far ahead." I don't like the idea of outright lying to my brother and I hope it doesn't come to that.

Dakota snickers. "Well, you better figure it out because the two of you are beyond obvious. He's going to catch on."

There's no reason to worry tonight, though. As soon as dinner is over, Adam leaves to go to Taryn's and Rhett goes to his room to call his girlfriend. Maverick already knows so when Heath pins me against the counter in the kitchen, I let him kiss me like I've been dying to for the past two hours.

He hums into my mouth as his hands come up and wrap around the back of my neck. My fingers fly to the hem of his shirt, craving the feel of his skin against mine.

"I need to get you naked," he mumbles into my mouth.

"You two want to watch a movie?" Maverick asks.

Neither of us answers as we keep on kissing. Heath's hard and he presses into me with a groan. A pillow flies by our head and hits the cabinet door to my left.

"What the hell, Mav?"

"You two are a major bummer. Everyone's getting laid but me. Come hang out with me. Let me feel up your girl a little. Seems fair."

"Like hell," Heath growls, but he pulls me to the living room.

I can tell by Maverick's smile that he's just trying to get a rise out of Heath. Not that I doubt he'd like to feel me up because I think Mav is game to feel up just about anyone, but there are zero sexual vibes between us.

Heath's possessive side is hot though, so I follow him. He sits in the chair and pulls me on top of him. I hesitate to get comfortable, knowing Rhett could catch us at any moment. Heath doesn't seem to give it a second thought.

We watch the first half of some action movie. Heath teases me, fingers absently roaming over my skin. He doesn't seem all that affected, minus the huge erection poking me, until suddenly he stands and carries me to his room, calling out to Mav as we leave, "Sorry, buddy, you're on your own."

I giggle as he lays me down on the bed and stands tall to remove his shirt. "What if I wanted to watch the rest of the movie?"

He unbuttons my shorts and pulls them and my panties down before he answers. "Say the word and we can move this back out to the living room." His head dips and then his tongue flattens over my center, sending a jolt through my body. He glances up, eyes dark and taunting. "What do you say, baby? Wanna watch the movie while I lick you? Maybe you want Mav to watch as I eat your sweet pussy."

I arch into him wanting more. More of his mouth and more of the dirty, obscene things coming out of it. I don't know how much of it he's actually serious about, but the idea of him going down on me like this not giving one single fuck that people might watch is hot. Not that I actually want to give in to the fantasy.

He wraps his arms around my legs spreading me wider and lifting me to his mouth. His moans and grunts rival mine as the orgasm builds. I come once, crying out and trying to move away. It's so intense and my body can't decide if it wants more or to curl up in a ball and let the sensations slowly disappear. Heath doesn't give me an option. He keeps his grip tight on my legs, holding me in place.

He eases the pressure on my sensitive clit. His tongue laps slowly and tenderly until another orgasm begins to build and I start to writhe beneath him. He adds a finger, ever so slowly, matching the tempo of his mouth.

I reach for him, for any part of him to cling to like a lifeline as the second wave slams into me. I pull at his glorious hair and his ears, his shoulders. I'm not sure I've ever maimed a guy while he went down on me before.

I roll away from him as my body quivers and I try to catch my breath. Heath chuckles and lets me loose this time. He lies beside me and wraps his arm around my waist.

I shiver at the contact. "Even that feels like I might get off another time."

"Cuddle orgasms. I don't think that's a thing."

"There's nothing cuddly about you. Even your cuddles feel like foreplay."

"Oh, it's foreplay. It's all foreplay."

"I need like two minutes for my soul to float back inside of me and then it's your turn."

"Your soul floated away? Damn, girl, can I get that in a Yelp review?"

"Five orgasmic stars," I mumble as I wiggle back against him and his thick erection. I must doze off because when I wake up it's to Heath pulling on his T-shirt and answering the bedroom door. He talks so quietly I can't make out who he is talking to or what they're saying. He shuts the door and locks it and returns to bed.

"Who was that?"

"Rauthruss. They're playing Xbox, asked if I wanted to join."

"I haven't made good on my end of the bargain yet." I yawn again as I reach for him, which makes Heath chuckle.

He wraps me in his arms, and I tip my head up to look at him. "It's okay. I'm getting used to you leaving me with blue balls."

My jaw drops and he shakes his head. "I'm kidding, baby doll. Come on, I'll distract them while you make a getaway."

As I get to my feet, Mav's deep voice shouts from the living room. I can't make out his words, but it's his presence that makes me pause. "Oh, crap. I totally forgot about helping Maverick with his literature class."

"I'll help him."

"You're gonna read aloud to him in that sexy British accent?" Swoon. Maybe I can stay for that.

"Don't look at me like that Genevieve or I'll never let you out of here."

He goes first while I hide in his room, peeking out the crack of his mostly closed door. He calls for Rhett and then walks into the bathroom.

Rauthruss's tone sounds confused as he asks why he's going into the bathroom, but I don't stick around to figure out what Heath says to keep him in there while I hurry out of the apartment.

●

When Ava and I get to the dining hall the next morning, Heath is waiting outside, leaning against the wall, his phone in hand. He looks up as I approach and a smile spreads across his face.

"Took you two long enough. I'm starving."

I hadn't asked him to wait for me, so I find it particularly endearing that he did. Especially when I know how important food is to him.

"I'm going to grab something quick and sit outside to call Trent," Ava says before we split to grab breakfast.

"You don't need to do that. We can all sit together."

"Eh, it's fine. I get all tongue-tied around your brother and his hockey friends anyway and end up feeling like a bumbling idiot."

I fill a tray and find Heath at our usual table, already digging into his first plate of food.

He raises his brows and smiles around a big mouthful as I sit. His long legs find mine under the table and he spreads them to frame mine from either side.

We eat in silence. Heath somehow devours all his food before I do, and he leans back and eyes my tray as if he's hoping I might leave him some.

"Stop eye fucking my food, Payne."

"That strawberry jelly looks good."

"Should have gotten some then," I say and take a big bite of my jelly toast.

I'm teasing him, but now that he's watching my mouth while I chew, I'm a little turned on. Leave it to Heath to turn cafeteria breakfast into foreplay. In his words, it's all foreplay.

TWENTY

Heath

"Has anyone seen my hat?" Rauthruss walks around the living room moving cushions and checking under the couch.

"Bathroom," Mav and I say at the same time.

He narrows his gaze. "Why the hell is it in the bathroom?" He disappears and returns with the faded Bruins hat on his head.

"Hell if I know. You and Heath went in there and you came back with a frustrated scowl and without a hat. Did he violate you? You could tell me, you know?"

"I needed him to rub a little Icy Hot on my back," I say

"Mhmmm. And he took his hat off for that?" Mav grins big and looks to me. He knows damn well why I called Rauthruss in there yesterday. Getting Ginny in and out of our place without being seen is a great source of entertainment.

"I couldn't reach it!" I protest, playing along.

"The ol' reach-around." Mav hands me a controller as I take a seat next to him. "Where's Adam? I haven't seen him since practice this morning."

"Probably at Taryn's," I offer.

"He was having dinner with Ginny." Rhett sits in the chair messing with his phone, most likely texting his girl. Which is good because he misses the way my head pops up at the information.

"Dinner . . ." I look to Maverick. "I could eat."

"You could always eat." He sets down the controller. "I'm in. Any idea where they went?"

When we walk into The Hideout and crash the Scott's family dinner, Adam laughs. "Miss me, guys?"

"Nah, man, missed your sister," I say jokingly. Ginny turns red and Mav goes into a coughing fit. I slide in next to her and drape my arm over her shoulder.

Adam rolls his eyes, not taking me serious for a second, which is hilarious since I'm not kidding.

Rauthruss takes a seat next to Adam, and Maverick grabs a chair for the end.

"Smells good." I lean in close as she bites the end of a fry.

She elbows me. "Get your own."

We order food, but I continue to sneak fries off her plate while we wait. Ginny's so much nicer than I am. I'd never let anyone get away with taking food from me. *Heath doesn't share food.* I totally said that in my Joey from *Friends* voice. He had the right idea.

After dinner we linger. Maverick grabs a pitcher of beer and a few guys from the team show up. All the extra commotion means it's easier for me to flirt with Ginny without anyone noticing.

I place my hand on her leg under the table and she pins me with a playfully annoyed smirk. "Whatcha doing?"

She glances around.

"No one is paying us any attention," I tell her without looking. "Do you want to go into the bathroom and make out?" I waggle my eyebrows, and she laughs.

"No, thanks." She scrunches up her nose.

"I knew I should have gone with the dumpster out back."

"So much better." She leans in and my heart rate picks up. Sneaking around is hot. It isn't something I ever planned on doing. My sexcapades have never been secret but moving my hand up her thigh and brushing two fingers against her jean-clad pussy with no one being the wiser while Ginny tries hard not to react is awesome. I may never go public with a chick again.

"Seriously, though, I drove. Meet you at my car?" I motion with my head to the door.

She studies my face. "You're serious?"

"Hell yeah, I'm serious." I scoot out of the booth. "Are you coming?"

Her mouth opens and she looks around. This time I do too, but no one is staring at us. I mean, honestly, who'd picture us together? Ginny is sugar and spice and everything nice, while I'm the dude who propositioned her for a quickie in the public bathroom thirty seconds ago.

She nods. I put cash on the table to cover my food and a portion of the alcohol. I text Maverick that they are under no circumstance to come outside until I return, and I wait for her just outside the door. Maybe it'd be safer to wait inside the vehicle so that no one sees us walking together, but I'm not making her do the walk through the parking lot to my SUV for sex by herself. I'm a gentleman like that.

She pushes out of The Hideout and scans the parking lot, stopping when she finds my SUV and giving me a perfect opportunity to sneak up behind her and lift her at the waist.

"Oh my gosh," she squeals as I do an overhead press with her in my arms. When I bring her back down, she grabs hold of my neck. "What if you'd dropped me?"

"Such little faith." I unlock my car and open the back door.

"I can't believe I'm doing this."

She climbs in and I follow. I'm quick to shut the door and finally have her alone.

For whatever hesitation she had before, she attacks my face as soon as I turn my head. Her hands go to my hair and her mouth is on mine. I pull her onto my lap the best I can in this back seat, slouching down so our heads aren't bumping against the roof of the car.

God bless tinted windows. My fingers slip under her shirt and lift. I enjoy the way her skin pebbles at my touch. I push up the fabric so I can access her bra, pull the cups down and press my lips to one nipple. She arches into me and rubs herself against my crotch.

"Do you put something on your skin? Edible lotion?" I pop off just long enough to ask and then move to the next nipple.

"Edible lotion?" She giggles and then moans.

"You always taste so good." I lick and bite. Seriously, Ginny-flavored nipples are my favorite food and I am starving.

"It's just me." She pulls away, scrambling onto the seat beside me and unbuttoning my jeans. She smiles up timidly at me as she frees my dick.

I hiss as she licks the dot of precum. "Fuck, Ginny. Do that again."

She does, except this time, she takes me all the way in.

Dead. Gone. Rest in peace. Thought I was going to hell, but this is heaven.

I hit the back of her throat, and she gags, but does she stop? Hell to the no.

I place my hands on her head, running my fingers through her hair. Gently, I guide the tempo, but I let her decide how much to take. I'm a big guy—no one has dared to deep throat me before, and she's the last person I expected to try.

I'm getting dangerously close with each swirl of her tongue and hollowing of her cheeks. I hold her hair back from her face like a ponytail. One blonde strand hangs in her eyes, the ends brushing my stomach as she bobs.

"I'm close," I warn her. "I think there are some napkins in the glove box." Unless her hearing is broken or she's in some sort of blow job focused trance, she hears me, but she doesn't stop until I've come in her pretty mouth.

I lean my head back against the leather. My whole body is trembling. "That was . . . holy shit."

She laughs. "And I thought the way to your heart was through your stomach."

"Only one thing I enjoy more than food, baby."

Fifteen minutes later, after returning the favor, we head back into The Hideout. She runs a hand over her hair and then her mouth.

"Relax, you look gorgeous."

"I should probably go in first." She takes out her phone. "I'll pretend like I was on my phone."

As she pushes through the door holding her phone up to her ear like she's on a call, mine buzzes in my pocket.

"Hey, I'm just walking into dinner," I say, taking a step away from the door.

"Hello, Mom. How are you?" she mocks and then chuckles, and that light sound makes me smile.

"Sorry. Hey, Mom. How are you?"

"Well, I'm good now that I finally hear your voice."

"Sorry," I say again. Not just for being a dick with how I answered, but for not calling her sooner.

"Can I assume no news is good news?"

"Yeah, everything's good. How are you? How's Kevin?"

"I'm good. Kevin's good too. He's actually why I'm calling."

My brows draw together. Oh shit, if she's calling to tell me she's getting remarried or some shit, it's going to be a real bummer to my night. I want her to be happy, but . . . "He is?"

"I was talking about coming down for your home games next weekend, and he offered to come with me."

I'm speechless, letting the information sink in. My mom hasn't been to a game since before Dad died. I stopped asking years ago. Now she's coming willingly and bringing the guy she's seeing?

"Heath? Are you there?"

"Yeah." I clear my throat. "Yeah, I'm here."

"Well, what do you think? I know I haven't—"

"Sounds great," I interrupt before she can finish that statement. "Can I text you later to hash out the details? I'm with some friends."

"Of course. Have fun and be safe."

"I will."

"Love you, honey."

I click end and blow out a breath as I head inside.

NOVEMBER

TWENTY-ONE

Ginny

"It's nice." My mom steps into my dorm and smiles. Dad hangs in the doorway and gives a tentative glance around.

"Dad, you can come in."

He moves only an inch farther inside. Since my parents were in Mexico when I left for college, this is the first time they're seeing my dorm outside of the pictures I've sent.

"Where's Ava?" my mom asks now inspecting her side. *The Vampire Diaries* poster and the collage of pictures that is basically a shrine to Trent.

"She's visiting her boyfriend."

Dad frowns. "You stay here by yourself on the weekends?"

"Not every weekend. Besides I'm not exactly alone." I motion behind him where people are moving up and down the hallway.

I set the bag of new towels Mom brought me on the floor by my desk. "Should we head over to the arena?"

Riding to the game with my parents feels a little strange like I'm back in high school and reminds me of the times Bryan and I rode down to Valley with them. It's a fleeting feeling of sadness at the thought of my ex, but as soon as Valley U takes the ice and I see Heath, Bryan is completely forgotten. I sit forward in my seat to get a better look.

He and Adam skate out next to one another. Adam scans until he finds us in the crowd. He smiles and lifts a hand to greet my parents. Heath notices and follows the movement to our family. I wave back as I stare at Heath.

He smiles, drops his gaze, and then does his own scan of the crowd. His mom and her boyfriend are in for the weekend too. And though he didn't tell me, I know it's the first time she's come to a game. I heard Adam and Rhett asking him about it earlier this week when I was hiding in his room.

Grand Canyon is the worst team in the division, and they didn't bring their A game tonight. Valley leads by two after the first period. On the plus side, Adam is playing great, so my parents don't care that the game is a snooze fest.

I head to the bathroom during intermission and run into Taryn as I'm going back to my seat.

"Hey." I pause and move out of the flow of traffic. "I wasn't sure if you were here tonight."

"Yeah, of course, I am. Wouldn't miss it." Her red hair is pulled back in a high ponytail with blue and yellow ribbons. Adam's number is painted on her face. I have a flash of jealousy at how proudly and openly she displays her loyalty and fandom for my brother.

"Are you going to meet up with us for dinner after?"

She twists her hands in front of her and nods. "Yeah, Adam asked me to come. I'm a little nervous about meeting your family."

"Don't be. They'll love you. Do you want to come meet them now and get it over with?"

"I don't know."

"Come on. Let me introduce you, and by dinner, you'll be sharing embarrassing Adam stories with my mom."

A slow smile spreads across her face. "Yeah, okay."

As I predicted, my parents love Taryn. By the time the game ends and we get to The Hideout, they're completely enthralled with catching up on Adam and learning more about his girlfriend. I'm able to half-listen and stare across the restaurant to Heath and his table.

Maverick is with him, and they sit across from a woman with light brown hair and small features. I catch her smile as she turns her head to the man sitting beside her. He has a thick head of gray hair and a strong jawline and muscular arms that defy his age. They look happy. Heath looks . . . well not uncomfortable exactly, but like the outsider. To a bystander, you'd think Maverick was the one related. He looks far more relaxed and like he's enjoying himself. That's just Maverick though—he's always comfortable in his skin.

Rhett's girlfriend Carrie is here this weekend too. They're celebrating their five-year anniversary and the two of them sit up at the bar. She's nothing like I expected. Rhett is so nice and sweet, and Carrie is a little harsh and rough around the edges. When he introduced us, she didn't even fake a smile. Maybe she has resting bitch face?

I glance back at Heath. He's got RBF right now too.

"Right, Ginny?" Adam asks, breaking my surveillance of the Payne family.

"Sorry, what?"

My brother smiles like he's onto me and my cheeks warm. Shit, was that just totally obvious I was staring at Heath?

"I was telling Mom and Dad that you hang out at our apartment pretty often too. That it's nice and not the pigsty they are imagining."

"I wouldn't say often, no." I shake my head. "I've been over a couple of times."

"What? No way. You're over at Reagan and Dakota's all the time." He looks to my parents. "Our neighbors are cool, and we hang out a lot."

I'm slow to nod and my pulse is thrumming much too quickly as I realize he isn't talking about the times I've been over at his place and hidden in Heath's room.

"Right. Yes. We've become good friends. I'm actually considering moving in with them next year."

"Out of the dorms?" My mom frowns.

"Yeah. Just like Adam did his sophomore year."

"That's not exactly the same," my dad points out.

Adam smirks, knowing how it rankles me when our parents give him differential treatment for being a guy. Yes, I get that some things are safer for him because he's male, but I don't think this is one of those things. I could probably pull up statistics for crime in dorms versus apartments, but can't they just trust me?

I don't argue for now. It's a year away, and I don't want to spend this weekend annoyed with my parents.

Heath's table finishes with dinner first, and they get up and head toward the door. We're just out of their path to the exit, but Maverick moves to us with a big grin.

"Hello, Scott family."

"Mom, Dad, you remember Johnny Maverick?" Adam asks, dropping an arm around the back of Taryn's chair. "And Heath Payne?"

My parents say their hellos. Heath doesn't introduce his mom, and there's an awkward beat before she steps forward. "Hello, I'm Lana Payne. Heath's mom."

"It's nice to meet you," my mother responds with a warm smile. She's always been good at making people feel at ease.

"Are you guys heading out already?" Adam asks.

"We can pull up more chairs," my dad offers.

Mav looks to Heath, who glances to his mom. "You guys probably want to get back to the hotel?"

I'm not sure if it's a question or statement and neither is she. Lana nods, though I detect maybe the slightest disappointment. "It has been a long day." She smiles stiffly. "If you two want to stay with your friends . . ."

"Nah, I'm tired too. Mav?"

Mav's brows pull together. "Sure, man, let's go back. I'm beat."

"Catch you guys later," Heath says, finally meeting my gaze and letting it slide around the table. "Good meeting you Mr. and Mrs. Scott."

They walk off from the table and out of The Hideout.

After they're gone, my attention and desire to be out wanes. Don't get me wrong, I'm enjoying seeing my parents, but I talk to them almost weekly, so there's not a lot to add. And . . . I might also be thinking of a certain boy. I don't know his family dynamics. I know his father died when he was young and I know his mother hasn't visited him at Valley, but I don't know the why or how and if the two are related.

Heath isn't very chatty about his family, and okay, we haven't done a lot of talking lately. When we decided to date, we caved to months of sexual tension and haven't come up for air yet.

Mom and Dad drop me off in front of the dorm and I head up to my room. I unlock the door, push it open, and flip on the light. Movement catches my eye and my heart goes to my throat. "Oh my gosh, you scared me."

Heath sits on my bed, his back against the wall, and his long legs hanging off the side.

I glance back to the door. "That was locked, right?"

"Your RA let me in."

My brows raise up toward my hairline. "She did?"

Rachel, my RA, isn't known for being all that lenient on rules, which hasn't ever really bothered me since I don't spend that much time here.

"I told her I was surprising you for our one-year anniversary." He looks a little embarrassed which makes me laugh.

"Have you ever had a one-year anniversary?"

"Nah." He chuckles. "It was the first thing that came to mind with Rauthruss and his girl's big anniversary this weekend."

I move to the bed and sit next to him. "Six-month anniversary?"

He shakes his head. "I've never even had a one-month anniversary." A small shrug of his shoulders and then he leans into me. "What about you?"

"Bryan and I were together for two years. We didn't really celebrate the milestones. For one, we could never agree on the date. He thought it was March third and I swore it was the seventh."

Heath's chest moves with a silent laugh and he takes my hand, running his thumb along the inside of my palm.

"How was dinner?" I ask.

"Weird."

I scoot back against the wall and lean my head against his shoulder. "How so?"

He lets out a breath and brings our joined hands to his thigh. It's a few moments of silence before he answers. "I knew meeting Kevin would be weird. He seems nice, but he's just like this stranger who is the center of my mom's world now, and I don't know her life like I used to. Even Maverick's random jokes and comedic commentary couldn't push past the awkwardness."

"I'm sorry."

He sits tall and I do the same so I can look at him.

"It's over. Besides, she seems good so that's worth something." He clears his throat. "So, back to this anniversary thing. Why do people get hung up on the number of years or the exact date?"

I want to ask him more about his mom but can sense his need to talk about something else. "I'm not sure. I think people like to have milestones to celebrate or maybe it makes them feel like their relationship is the gold standard if they can slap an award on it."

He grunts a response.

"But also, it's just sort of nice to look back on a year or twenty of your life and reflect on how it might have been different if you hadn't been together."

He studies me carefully, and I feel like I've gone too girly on him. It's a romanticized version, I admit.

"What would you do if you made it an entire year with the same girl?"

His eyes widen, playfully exaggerating as if he's horrified by the idea of a relationship that long—maybe he's not exaggerating, but he grins. "I'm not sure."

His mouth finally captures mine. Maybe it's because we aren't in danger of being caught or maybe he's just exhausted from the day, but our kisses are lazier. We take our time just kissing without rubbing up on one another, no hands roaming beyond the face and neck. It's unexpected but nice. Soft and sweet in the sexiest way.

When we finally lay down on my bed, he removes my clothes between kisses dropped on my lips and body. I tug at the hem of his shirt and he lifts it and tosses it to the floor. We've never been completely naked at the same time. My heart rate skitters when I finally get the full skin to skin contact I'd only imagined until now.

Whether it's because he hasn't wanted to or because he's read my hesitation, I'm not sure, but Heath and I haven't had sex. We've done practically everything but.

The largest part of me wants to, but something inside of me still screams for me to hold back. I hate to acknowledge that something because I think it has everything to do with the way I held out on having sex with Bryan for years and then as soon as I did, he broke up with me. I get that it wasn't the sex, and maybe I still would have slept with him even if I knew it was going to end. But the fact of the matter is, it scares me that the same thing might happen with Heath.

His dick twitches between us and heat pools at my center. There's a lump in my throat as I find my voice. "I don't think I'm ready. Is that okay? I mean, I want to do other stuff, just not that."

His hands frame my face, and his blue eyes stare deeply into mine. "Of course, it's okay."

He savors my body in a way I'll remember forever. Taking sex off the table only makes him more creative, and he gets a well-deserved A plus in that department.

We fall asleep still naked and I take note of a different type of anniversary—the first time you realize you're falling for someone.

TWENTY-TWO

Heath

My mom wants to go to breakfast Saturday morning before I head to the arena. Mav is still sleeping when I get back from Ginny's, so I'm on my own when I push through the door of the café.

She waves from a booth, her other hand wrapped around a coffee mug.

"Hey," I say as I sit across from her. "Sorry I'm late."

"It's okay. You know I like to have my first cup of coffee in silence anyway."

I smile at the reminder that something is still the same.

The waiter stops by to pour me a cup of coffee and take our order. After which, I lean back in the booth. "Kevin isn't joining us?"

"No. Just the two of us." Her smile is warm and genuine as she studies me. "I've missed you."

There's an uneasy ache in my chest as the sincerity of her words hit me. Maybe our bond wasn't always the healthiest—me taking care of her more than the other way around, but in some ways, it's good to know I'm still missed, if not needed.

I spent the first year of college trying not to fuck up. If I'm honest, I didn't even want to come to college. I mean, I did. Of course, I did. College is fucking awesome. But I was so scared. My mom was barely hanging on by a thread after my dad died. I'd lost one parent and the panic was real that I'd leave and the other one would disappear without me watching over her like I'd done for the past four years.

I was the one who made her smile when no one else could. The person she relied on to remember things like paying the electricity bill and mowing the grass.

And I wasn't perfect. I found a release for my teenage angst with other things. Fast cars, easy chicks, occasionally getting high. But I did my best to never bring any more burdens inside the four walls that were already crashing in on us.

So imagine my surprise when I go away to college and nearly give myself a fucking ulcer with worry only to return home this past summer and see she's fine.

No, not just fine. Fine is the word she used when she was wearing last week's clothes lying on the couch and staring at the TV in a comatose state. She wasn't fine. She was good. She didn't need me to walk around the house singing Disney songs or brush her hair while we watched *Friends* on repeat.

I should be happy that she is doing well. I am happy. I'm just also bitter. Where was this woman when I needed her to hold me and tell me everything was going to be okay?

It isn't fair. I know that. There's no right way to mourn, and my dad's death rocked us all to the core.

You don't get to tell people how to feel. Fuck. You don't even get to tell yourself how to feel. It's a real bitch of the human condition to be in control of everything and also nothing.

"Is everything going okay? You look good."

"I am." She reaches across the table and squeezes my hand. I can't bring myself to return the gesture. Her fingers linger and each second that passes feels like an eternity. I don't know why I can't just accept and enjoy her company.

She gives me one last squeeze and then pulls back. "You looked good on the ice last night, too. I still can't believe how talented you and your brother both turned out. I can barely walk a straight line. You got your athleticism from your father. He would be so proud."

"Can we not?"

She flinches and I wince.

Dammit. Why can't I just sit here and let her talk about him? Partly it's because I'm afraid that conversation leads to me telling her how bitter I feel. And what good would that do? She's finally on her feet and I knock her down with memories of how she hurt me when she was drowning? No way.

"Can we talk about something else?" I try again.

She nods. "Sure."

We suffer through breakfast talking about stupid shit like the weather and repairs she's having done on the house back in Michigan. My mood sours with each bite, and I'm all too eager to head to the arena when it's time.

Adam walks in just after I do. "Hey, man. Where were you this morning?"

"I'm sorry. Did I need to check in before I left?"

His brows raise.

"Shit, I'm sorry. I'm in an awful mood. Had breakfast with my mom this morning."

He nods and takes a seat on the bench, setting his bag on the floor. "Are you two not close?"

"We are . . . we were. I don't know. When my dad passed away shit was fucked up for a while."

"Sorry, man. I can't imagine what it'd be like if something happened to my parents. Anything I can do to help?"

"Nah. I just need to get on the ice."

One side of his mouth pulls up into a smile. "All right."

After the best game of my life (apparently bitter frustration works well for me), I find my mom waiting for me outside of the locker room with some of the other families, including the Scotts. Ginny smiles and approaches me.

"That was incredible. Congratulations." She hugs me, taking me by surprise given all the onlookers, but it feels too nice to pull away.

"Thanks. Hopefully not the last time I get a hat trick." Then I lean down close to her ear. "Maybe we can celebrate with a hat trick of our own."

She blushes and pulls back. I accept a hug from my mom and a handshake from Kevin and from Mr. Scott.

"We should celebrate." Adam claps me on the shoulder. "What do you feel like doing?"

Your sister.

Mav steps up, his bag slung over his body. "Party at our place. Invite the 'rents. Let's get weird."

"I think we'll pass. Let you guys celebrate on your own." Mr. Scott wraps an arm around his wife, who nods her agreement. "We have reservations for dinner." She looks to my mom and Kevin. "Would you like to join us?"

"I think that sounds great," Kevin says. "What do you say, Lana?"

More of the parents make plans and the guys start heading out.

Ginny's still standing by my side, and I have the strongest urge to grab her hand.

"I'm going to find Reagan and Dakota. See you later?"

"Ride over with me."

"But?" She glances around. "Are you sure?"

"Yeah, no one will notice or care. Just give me a couple minutes to say goodbye to my mom."

"Okay."

My mom walks over to us before I get the chance to go to her.

Ginny smiles at her and then me. "See ya."

Mom watches her leave, only speaking once we're alone. A sad expression on her face as she lowers her voice. "I should have come alone and not brought Kevin. I wanted you to meet him to see that I'm happy. I thought it would give you some peace, but I see now that was my own selfish reasoning and I'm sorry. This isn't how I wanted this weekend to go."

"It isn't Kevin. It's us. I don't know how to do this with you." I motion between us. "Everything is so different."

"I know. But I still love you just the same. I'm so proud of you."

Love. I hate that damn word. Why does it always feel like it's an excuse? When she says it, all I hear is, I love you, so it's okay that I screwed up.

"Thanks, Mom. I am glad you came."

Kevin steps up behind her. "Nice game, Heath."

"Thanks."

The hall has cleared, and we start toward the door. Mom hugs me tightly before we head our separate ways. "Be safe."

I hug her back. She's heavier now, no longer the small, fragile thing she once was. "I will. I'll call next week."

She nods and smiles, maybe a little disbelieving that I really will.

Ginny leans against my vehicle, her phone in hand. It's dark and she's all alone and I feel like an ass for making her wait for me out here like this.

I hit the unlock button and she looks up, those light brown eyes meeting mine under the fluorescent parking lot lights. Instead of going to the driver's side, I go to her, kissing her hard out in the open where anyone might see us.

She doesn't seem to care either, though, because she wraps her arms around my neck and presses her body to mine. And it's the best damn part of the day. Well . . . unless she lets me hat trick her later.

TWENTY-THREE

Ginny

T he following weekend the guys are gone for two away games. I sit on the floor in Reagan and Dakota's apartment. Reagan brings two bags of chips and a platter of dips and sets it down between me and Dakota.

Dakota stands. "I'm going to grab the bottle of wine so I don't have to get up again. You're staying over, right?" she asks.

"Yeah, might as well. Ava's out of town visiting Trent," I say before digging into the queso.

She grabs the wine and we all settle in.

"Does Heath stay with you then on the weekends or are you two getting it on with your brother on the other side of the wall?" Dakota asks.

I make a face and toss a chip at her. "Gross, and Adam isn't on the other side of the wall, thankfully. Maverick is always hanging in the living room, though, and sometimes has girls with him. I have no idea why he doesn't go to his own place."

Reagan scrunches up her nose.

"Yeah. I've heard entirely too much of his sex talk for my liking."

"Dirty talk? Maverick?" Dakota asks. "That surprises me for some reason."

"Not dirty exactly. And I think he might be talking to himself." I make a face. "He's a weird dude."

"Come on, give us something. Anything. We're dying for details. You've

barely said anything about this new hot thing between you and Heath."
Dakota pulls her red hair over one shoulder.

I look between my friend's eager faces. "There's not much to tell."

"I don't buy it," Reagan says. "You two looked like you were gonna rip each other's clothes off playing video games last night."

"Some clothes have been ripped off, but we haven't had sex yet."

"Interesting."

She says it like "interesting" means bad or weird. Is it? We're making out every chance we get. He's given me more orgasms fully clothed than I would have thought possible. Technically we haven't slept together yet, but it's been fun and hot. None of it seemed odd before, but now I'm nervous that maybe he thinks it's weird too.

"Is that bad? Should I be worried?"

"Sounds sweet," Reagan says.

Dakota takes a sip of her wine. "Sounds very unlike Heath."

"Dakota," Reagan says in a shrill voice.

"What?" She looks to me. "You know he's not some innocent guy, right? I mean, I wouldn't call Heath a slut because I'm not into label shaming, buuut . . . he's not been shy about hooking up with chicks. And by hooking up, I mean sex."

"No, I know."

Reagan places a hand on my knee and squeezes. "But he hasn't dated anyone else as far as I know."

"When did dating become more romantic than sex?" I ask and then, "If I tell you guys something, will you promise not to laugh?"

"Yes," Reagan says at the same time Dakota says, "No way."

"Kota," Reagan admonishes.

"What? If it's funny, I won't be able to hold back. I will try."

"Good enough, I guess." I take a drink of the wine. "My last boyfriend, Bryan, broke up with me after."

"After?"

"After we'd had sex. Like still inside of me."

"Oh shit." Dakota's eyes widen.

I hide behind my hands stretched out over my face. "Now I wished you'd just laughed."

"Wait, wait, wait. We need the full story," Reagan says.

So, I tell them. How Bryan and I had planned to go to Valley U together, but then he'd received an offer to play football in Boise and how he'd broken the news to me after we'd had sex for the first time.

"What an asshole."

"He really isn't though. It was my idea. I was ready, and I thought it would bring us closer before we headed off on this great adventure together. After, he told me he wasn't going to Valley and that he thought it would be better if we broke up instead of trying to make it work."

I've gone over that day a million times looking for cues I missed, but I was ready and excited, and I think he could have shown me a million red flags and I would have ignored them.

"Sorry, babe." Dakota rubs my arm. "For what it's worth, even Heath's not that cold."

"No, I know. And I'd had sex before Bryan. Just one other time with a guy I met at summer camp. It was right before Bryan and I started dating. Neither were great. I made Bryan wait because I wanted it to mean more than the first time. And, I think I'm doing it again with Heath. Does that make me too idealistic?"

Reagan shakes her head. "No, of course not, but holding out doesn't mean that it will mean more . . . it just means you build it up to an impossible standard."

"I hadn't thought about it like that," I admit.

We go through two bottles of wine and watch a movie before calling it a night.

Reagan brings me a blanket and pillow from her room. "Thank you."

The TV is muted, but I lie down and watch *Golden Girls* reruns with subtitles. I'm just about asleep when my phone buzzes.

Hottest guy on campus: You awake?

Me: No

Hottest guy on campus: Me either.

Me: Don't you have a big game tomorrow or something?

Hottest guy on campus: Maverick snores.

Me: I don't snore, and I miss you.

Hottest guy on campus: Now I really wish you were in this hotel room with me instead.

Me: Oh yeah? Need a cuddle buddy?

Hottest guy on campus: Yeah, just don't tell Mav—he thinks I only cuddle with him.

Me: Your secret is safe with me.

Hottest guy on campus: What'd you do tonight?

Me: Hung out with Reagan and Dakota at their place. You'll be back tomorrow night?

Hottest guy on campus: Yeah, but it'll be pretty late.

Me: Can I come over and stay the night?

Hottest guy on campus: You never need to ask, baby.

I smile and close my eyes. My phone buzzes with another text.

Hottest guy on campus: Hat trick?

I type out a dozen different responses trying to decide if I should go along with his playful banter or take this opportunity to confide in him. He takes the decision out of my hands by sending another when I've been quiet too long.

Hottest guy on campus: Shit. I'm sorry. Did I freak you out?

Me: Honestly? A little maybe. I mean, I want to do all those things. A LOT. But I'm nervous too. My experiences are . . . limited and were just blah.

Hottest guy on campus: I find it very hard (pun intended) that any form of sex could be blah with you.

Me: That might have more to do with you than me. You're fun and hot.

Hottest guy on campus: Right back at ya, baby doll.

CHAPTER TWENTY-FOUR

Heath

I drop into the seat next to Rauthruss as my phone buzzes in my pocket.

"Payne, how are your ribs?" Coach Meyers stands in the aisle, hands on the seats in front of me. "That was a nasty hit."

"Fine. Nothing's broken." I laugh and then wince as my side screams. I adjust the ice pack strapped around my waist.

"Try to take it easy tonight. Check in with the trainer first thing tomorrow."

I nod and he walks off. I wait to make sure he's not watching before leaning back with a groan. I dig my phone out, breathless by the maneuvering that's required.

I read Ginny's text asking me to give her a heads up so she can sneak into my room before we get home. She added three hat emojis and fuck my life . . . I don't think I can even make good on that tonight.

I text her back the tongue, peach, and eggplant emojis because I'm not an idiot and I think it might be worth dying for.

Another win under our belt and it feels good, even if my body aches. I took a hard hit in the last minute of the game, and my ribs hurt like a bitch.

"You all right?" Rauthruss asks from the seat next to me.

I grunt a response as I close my eyes. Somehow that seems to make the pain lessen.

"I'm gonna video chat my girl. Cool?"

I wave my hand to let him know I don't mind.

Rauthruss is the kind of guy who doesn't care who hears his conversations with Carrie, so he doesn't even bother putting in headphones.

"Hi, baby." She answers. "Congrats on the win."

I've only met Carrie a couple times. Seems okay. I don't get why Rauthruss is so hung up on her, but he didn't ask my opinion, so I don't give it.

"Thanks. How's your editorial coming?"

She sighs and goes into a long explanation. Rauthruss listens intently with his *mhmm* and *oh yeah* at all the right times. He's good at listening. Has to be, apparently. She barely takes a breath between sentences.

I doze off and when I wake up again, we're pulling off the freeway to Valley and the dude is still on the phone and she's still doing most of the talking.

I sit up with a wince and check my phone, but only have a couple of texts from my mom and Nathan congratulating me on the game and checking in on my wellbeing. I tap out responses to both of them in the time it takes Carrie to get out a single run-on sentence.

How do two people have so much to talk about? It isn't like they haven't talked in weeks or something. She was at Valley visiting just last weekend.

As the bus pulls into the campus lot, they say their goodbyes with promises to talk later tonight before bed. When he hangs up, I ask, "Seriously? You're going to talk to her again later?"

His hard, steel-blue eyes study me and then he chuckles. "You don't get it, but someday you will."

When I don't respond, he clarifies. "Some girl is going to make you so crazy that you'll want to talk to her all day, every day."

"What in the world do you have to talk about after being together so long? Not even Scott talks on the phone as much as you." I look across the aisle to where Scott is staring out the window.

"It's different for him. He's going to get off the bus and go see Taryn. I gotta take what I can get for now."

"Sounds pretty awful," I say truthfully. What's the point of being in a relationship if you have to do it through an electronic device?

We file off the bus, me much slower than the rest of the guys. Mav's got an energy drink in hand as he steps up beside me. "Hey, buddy, how ya feeling?"

"Like I got hit really fucking hard in the ribs."

He grins. "Need me to drive?"

I toss him the keys and manage to get myself into the passenger seat with a lot of wincing.

"Text Ginny," I tell the Bluetooth once Mav is headed to the house.

When prompted for the message, I say, "Back. On our way" and send.

Her response pings over the speakers and the feminine British voice asks if I'd like her to read it aloud. I glance at Mav. "Earmuffs." And then, "Yes."

"Already here," the British voice reads the text, but I hear it in Ginny's bubbly voice.

I blow out a breath. Tired, but excited to see her.

"Ginny's at your place waiting?" Mav asks. "How'd she get in?"

"Her brother gave her a spare key." I grin. Wasn't that nice of him? And super convenient for me.

"I hate to be the one to rain on anyone's parade, bro, but don't you think you oughta tell him?"

"What? No. Why would I do that?"

"Look, at first, I understood you guys wanting to keep it from him while you figured out what it was, but it's been weeks and you're spending a shit ton of time together. He's going to figure it out."

"Ginny doesn't want to. Besides, he won't understand. You know what he's like in relationships. All in. Balls to the wall." I squeeze the phone in my hand. "He won't understand," I repeat.

"Maybe not. I still think it should come from you."

"Hey, Scott, guess what? I'm hooking up with your sister, but don't worry, it isn't that serious." I glance at Maverick with an annoyed glare. "That what you had in mind?"

He laughs. "Maybe work on the delivery."

A bead of sweat has formed on my forehead by the time I make it into the apartment, and that's with Mav carrying my bag.

"Just set it there." I point to the spot in the living room where our bags usually end up. "I'll get it tomorrow. Thanks, buddy."

He grins, knowing exactly why I don't want him to bring it to my room. Adam went straight to Taryn's, and Rauthruss heads to his room while I limp to mine. The light's off, and I wonder how she's handling the dark. I push open the door and find her sitting on my bed with her laptop; the screen is dimmed but providing a decent amount of soft light.

I flip on the overhead light and she closes the laptop and sits up. As I walk, her eyes narrow in concern. "What's wrong with you?"

"Bruised ribs."

She gets on her knees and lifts her hands to touch me.

"Easy."

"Why didn't you tell me you were injured?"

"I'm fine."

"Lay down." Bossy. I can dig.

Gingerly, I sit and then fold over. "I'm pretty sure I'm stuck this way." I kick off my shoes, and she lies beside me.

"Shit, I forgot the ice pack."

"Where is it?" she asks, angling like she's about to grab it for me.

"I left it in my car."

"I can get it."

"Nah, I got it. There's another in the freezer." I inch up, but not before Ginny is to her feet and padding to the door.

"Be right back." She opens it and peers out into the hallway.

"It should be all clear," I tell her, knowing Rauthruss is almost certainly still on the phone.

She nods and smiles back at me. "Okay. Be right back."

I manage to get out of my jeans although I think the shirt's going to have to stay because raising my arms hurts too damn much. I'm adjusting the pillow behind my head when she returns.

She hovers over me, lifts my shirt up to reveal my stomach, and gasps at the angry red and purple skin.

"Don't think I'm gonna be able to follow through on the hat trick tonight." I try to laugh, but my ribs dislike that a lot.

"It's fine. I've got my laptop for porn. Can I borrow your hand though?" She holds a serious gaze long enough that my dick starts to get ideas. "Oh my god, I'm kidding."

"Not a terrible idea though," I say and then have to clear my throat a few times. Not a terrible idea at all.

However, when she settles the ice on my skin, those ideas disappear pretty quickly.

"Want to watch a movie?" she asks as she gets up and takes her pants off.

Dammit, now I'm getting hard again. My body is so confused. She settles next to me and opens her laptop between us.

"Which one?" She scrolls between two. I'm starting to feel the exhaustion for the day, so I let her pick.

Once the movie is going, she places her head on my chest. Her hair smells like apples and tickles my face. This is nice, I'll admit. Maybe I can kind of see Rauthruss's point about wanting to talk to Carrie all the time. Though I can't really picture having an entire relationship through a phone. For Ginny though? My mind starts to conjure all types of ideas for phone sex.

Hanging out with Ginny is always nice. I'm not even disappointed we didn't have sex. Okay, I'm not *too* disappointed. When I finally get inside of her, I want full range of motion. Especially knowing her past experiences were blah. Seriously, what the fuck? How is that even possible?

There's so much passion in Ginny. Kissing her is a trip. Just lying next to her, there's an energy that flows through my veins that doesn't exist when she's not with me. Sex with Ginny blah? If I weren't so tired, the thought would be laughable.

TWENTY-FIVE

Ginny

Thursday night, Heath and I ride over to The White House with Maverick and Dakota. We're in the backseat and Heath's big palm is stretched out over my knee. He's texting with his other hand.

"Sorry, he's getting married next summer, and for some reason, I need to decide what kind of tux I want right this second." His fingers keep flying over the screen as he and his brother text back and forth.

"A tux. Hmmm." The image of Heath in a nice suit or tux does not suck.

He glances up and winks. "Tuxes do it for you, huh?"

"*You* do it for me."

Mav groans. "You two are a real buzzkill. Should have stayed home and boned, left the party to the single people."

"Don't be a dick to my girl," Heath tells him, still staring at his phone.

Maverick turns in his seat. "You are ruining it for the rest of us. Girls see you two together, and you give them hope and ideas about what the rest of us want. And all I want is a good blow job."

"I hope that's not your best pickup line," I tell him.

Heath and Dakota laugh. Maverick shakes his head but smiles.

"You're such a liar," Heath says, finally putting his phone in his pocket. "Some girl gets her mouth anywhere near your junk and you'll be proposing marriage."

"Probably true." Mav sighs. "I'm a romantic at heart."

From the front of The White House it looks like a nice, respectable family home, but one foot inside the door, and it's college madness. Though, thankfully, not quite so mad as the pool party. I can actually see two feet in front of me tonight.

As we walk through the entryway, I look around to take it all in. The last time I was here it was so packed, it was hard to appreciate.

"I know, right?" Heath takes my hand. The other two have already gone ahead of us. "My brother lived here."

Since my interactions with Heath have mostly been limited to the hockey team and the dining hall, I didn't realize just how many people he knows. Guys on the basketball team call out to him, "Baby Payne!"

They ask him questions about Nathan and a few girls ask about Chloe, his brother's fiancée. With each group of people we talk to, Heath introduces me, we chat, and we accept drink after drink. Heath more so than me.

The end result is a very Gumby-like drunk Heath by the time we've made it outside where the main party is happening.

He wraps an arm around my shoulders and leans into me. "I think I might be drunk."

I stutter step my way to where our friends are sitting. Dakota's found Reagan and they've pulled lounge chairs together. They're sharing one and facing Maverick.

When they spot us, more specifically me desperately trying to unload a very heavy Heath, Mav moves to sit with Reagan and Dakota, and I manage to get Heath and I seated.

"The Oversharer is here!" Maverick lifts his cup with a smile. "How ya feeling, buddy? Feeling good? Feeling like you want to tell all your deepest secrets?"

Heath makes a motion like he's zipping his lips and tossing the key, nearly loses his balance and falls off the back of the chair.

"How do you get so drunk when you're this heavy?" I groan as I pull him upright.

"I wanna take you to The Olive Garden." He sways a little, staring at me. "You deserve The Olive Garden."

Our friends are laughing, but even drunk and out of his mind, I can't take my eyes off Heath.

"I'm pretty sure they're closed right now, but food isn't a terrible idea." I look to Reagan. "What do you have in that purse of yours to soak up the alcohol?"

As she pulls out snacks, everyone suddenly gets very interested in eating. I manage to snag a granola bar and a mini bag of pretzels for Heath.

"I think you might be my dream woman," Maverick says to Reagan as he opens a peanut butter cookie and takes a bite. He finishes that off and then downs two granola bars. "Let's go eat. We can hit IHOP or get Jack in the Box and head back to the apartment. Ooooh Jack in the Box tacos." He closes his eyes and moans.

"Can't," Heath interrupts. "I'm showing my girl a good time." He throws his arm around me again.

"You can show her a good time back at the apartment. Naked." Maverick stands and everyone else follows his lead.

"It isn't about sex," he says and looks at me dreamily. My stomach does a thousand backflips.

We aren't having sex, so even though our friends are reacting with a series of "aww" and laughter, he's only stating facts. It isn't about sex, but I think that needs to change soon.

I get to my feet and pull him up. "Come on."

"Are we going to The Olive Garden?"

●

The next morning, Heath wakes as I'm getting dressed to sneak out of his room.

"Where do you think you're going?" He pulls me down and hugs me against his chest.

"I have to go to class."

"In three hours." His eyes are barely open, but apparently he knows the time.

"I want to get out of here before the guys wake up."

The apartment is still silent, but it's game day, and I know the guys will be getting up soon to go skate.

"It'll be fine. Go to sleep," he murmurs against the top of my head.

I turn so we're facing one another and trace tiny circles on his chest. "You have to get up in thirty minutes."

I decide to try another approach. Sliding a leg over him, I scoot on top of him. He makes a strangled sound between a groan and a sigh. I pepper him with kisses—his jaw, his neck, his chest. His hands move to my back, and one comes up and fists my hair. He pulls back just hard enough to lift my chin.

"Whatcha doing, Ginny?"

Instead of answering, I close the space between our mouths and kiss him hard. I can feel him smiling, that is until I roll my hips against the bulge in his sweatpants.

In one smooth motion, he has me on my back and he holds himself over me. He dips his lower body to brush against me.

"This what you want, Genevieve?"

My cheeks flame. It is, but suddenly, I feel really shy about it.

He tips my chin up with a finger. "No need to be embarrassed. You can feel how much I want you, but what do you want, Genevieve?"

I'm having a hard time finding my voice.

"There's no rush." His sweet words comfort me, but man, do I wish I were ready. It isn't that I don't want to have sex with Heath. I do. Very much. But it's a big deal to me, more so maybe because I know in the past it hasn't been to him. And because of my previous experiences.

I nod and his thumb glides across my lower lip before he kisses me again. My head may have reservations, but my body does not. Fifteen minutes later, we're basically dry humping when Heath's palm slides up my leg. His fingers brush against the lacy material between my thighs and a shiver wracks my entire body.

His thumb rubs the tiny bundle of nerves over my panties while one finger slips underneath. I cry out and then slap a hand over my mouth.

Heath pries my hand away. "I want to hear how good I make you feel."

He pumps in and out of me a few more times before he decides my underwear are hindering him too much and he yanks them down to my ankles. I think he's moving to free them and toss them to the ground, which he does, but then his large shoulders nudge my legs farther apart and he wraps an arm around me to open me wide.

I arch into his mouth, wanting more as his tongue flattens against my throbbing core.

He gives it to me, sucking and licking. Slow at first, but as I get louder and the orgasm draws closer, he pushes my legs wider and increases the pressure. As I start to go over the edge, I fist his hair in my hands and ride his face.

When one ends, another builds. He rumbles something that vibrates against my pussy and clamps down, sucking on my clit as the second wave hits.

My body melts into the mattress. Heath's head is still between my legs and he places chaste kisses along the inside of my thighs and along my hips. I reach for him, pushing my hand under his sweats.

He's not wearing any underwear which means I have easy access to wrap my fingers around his hard shaft. He hisses a breath and moves his hips. A slow pace that quickly turns into him fucking my hand, hips pumping fast. He growls out as his release fills the inside of his pants.

We lay shoulder to shoulder as we catch our breath.

"Shower with me?" he asks, brushing my hair away from my neck and kissing me there.

We pad down the hall to the bathroom quietly. He starts the shower while I stare at my wild hair in the vanity mirror.

He turns back and drops his pants. I'll never get over seeing him naked. My throat closes and I just stare. He steps forward and kisses me then pulls the T-shirt I'm wearing over my head.

"You're beautiful."

I reach out and touch his once-again-hard dick. "You're huge." I swallow.

He chuckles. "Come on."

He lets me get in the shower first and then follows and pulls the curtain.

I wash and condition my hair and then Heath covers the both of us in his body wash. It's somehow fun and silly showering with him. He looks adorable with his hair matted down. His very hard penis keeps poking me, but he doesn't make any move to do anything about it.

We dry off and get back to his room before I hear other people in the house starting to move around.

I sit on the bed and finger comb my wet hair while I watch Heath pull on a gray Coyotes hockey T-shirt. "What was it like when you got drafted?"

"It was cool."

"Cool? That's the best you've got?"

He flashes a sexy smirk. "Really cool?"

"I'm serious."

"It was incredible and surreal. Easily one of the best days ever."

"I'm jealous that you have it all figured out. I can't even decide what classes I want to take next semester."

"I think you're missing the best part of college."

"And that is?"

"Having fun and not thinking too hard about the future."

I snort. "Says the guy who knows his future."

"Maybe, but there're no guarantees that when the time comes, I'll play. A million things might happen between now and then to fuck it all up."

I never considered that Heath would worry about his future when he has it mapped out. I don't stress about life beyond college, only planning for it. I guess once you have it figured out, the only thing to worry about is how things might go wrong.

"You just got here. Give yourself time to just be and let life happen. You don't need to have the next three years or beyond all planned out. What fun would that be? Four months ago, I didn't know you and now I do." He steps into my space and places his hands on the mattress on either side of me. "Not knowing can be exciting."

A knock at the door is followed by Maverick's voice. "Yo, Payne, let's go."

Heath brings his mouth to mine and kisses me softly.

"I think I'll wait for you guys to leave," I whisper.

"How are you going to get to the dorm?"

"I'll walk."

"No."

"No?"

He finds his keys on top of his desk and tosses them to me and then kisses me one last time before he heads out.

TWENTY-SIX

Heath

W e're sitting around the apartment before we head to the arena for tonight's game. Rauthruss is FaceTiming Carrie, and it doesn't annoy me quite as much as usual. Mav's sharing his pre-game peanut butter sandwich with Charli, and Adam's staring at the TV with a look of hard concentration.

I know he wears the weight of the world on his shoulders before games, worrying about how we'll play. He takes a lot of that pressure on himself, most I think isn't really necessary, but I guess that's why he's the captain.

"Scott, what are you going to do after graduation?" I ask him, surprised I don't know.

Mav's already signed with the Cats and Rauthruss's family runs a hockey camp that he plans to take over.

"I'm premed, man. Going to medical school."

"Really?"

The other guys look to me with equally surprised faces.

"I didn't know." Or maybe I did and forgot it already. I don't spend a lot of time thinking past next week. Even my own future feels weird. Pro hockey is like this thing I've agreed to but doesn't really feel like it's going to happen. Two and a half years feels so far away.

"We're gonna be busting people up and he's going to be putting them back together," Mav says, mouth full of peanut butter.

"I can see you being a team doctor or something; that'd be cool."

He laughs and says sarcastically, "Thanks. I hadn't thought of that."

"I'm sorry. You probably mentioned it before, and I let it go in one ear and out the other. Making plans isn't really my thing."

"Speaking of plans, is it okay if I crash here tonight?" Maverick asks. "I'm meeting up with that girl Holly later and I don't want her to know where I live."

"Dude, gross, stop hooking up on our couch. You have your own apartment for that." Adam's laughing as he says it though, the mood light before we have to get serious and ready for the game.

He looks to me. "What about you? I haven't seen any girls running out in the mornings."

"You're never here," Rauthruss points out, somehow managing to follow two conversations—his with Carrie and ours.

"Okay, well, fine, but I don't see them zipping through to your room at night before I leave to go to Taryn's either."

Mav's smile is big and mocking. "Yeah, Heath, what's up with that?"

Well, now I know why I don't try to make small talk with Adam.

I stand and start toward my room. "Just focused on hockey." I come back with my bag. It's a little early, but I need out of this conversation. "You guys ready to head over?"

None of them mention the time. They're all just as ready to get out of here as I am.

"Hey, can I catch a ride over to The Hideout?" Maverick asks after the game.

I'm pulling on a shirt and jeans, but I glance over to make sure Adam is out of earshot before I answer. "I can drop you off, but I'm not going."

"Why not?"

"Taking Ginny out."

"A date?" he asks, louder than I'd like.

Adam's still not paying us any attention, so I nod. "Yeah, a date, hanging out, whatever."

"Where are you going?"

"I don't know. Maybe Prickly Pear since all the guys will be at The Hideout." The Prickly Pear is our second favorite local hangout, but on the weekends. It's often taken over by townies, so we aren't likely to run into anyone we know there.

"That's a lame date."

"Then I guess it isn't a date."

"Yo, Scott," Mav calls and I fight the urge to pummel him. "What's the best spot in Valley to take a girl on a date?"

"On a Friday night?" Adam asks, eyebrows drawn together in consideration. "The drive-in up on Mount Loken or pretty much anywhere downtown. Araceli's has a nice outdoor patio and good food."

"Didn't take you for the romantic type, Mav," Jordan says.

"People are surprising, aren't they?" He chuckles. "Thanks, Scott, knew you'd come through for me." Maverick closes his locker and turns to me with a smug look. "Ready?"

I pick up Ginny at her dorm. She slides into the passenger seat in a short dress smelling like apples and cinnamon and I can't help but kiss her while sitting in the no-parking zone. Someone honks and I reluctantly pull back and then guide the car back on the road.

"Where are we going?" Ginny's beaming at me and I'm suddenly glad I have some better suggestions than Prickly Pear.

"You'll see." I rest a hand on her thigh and head out of town.

I drive to the outskirts where the houses get bigger, set up on the base of the mountain, and are placed farther apart.

The roads are mostly quiet with as many people biking and walking as cars driving along it. It's still nice and warm in Arizona. A few trees have leaves that are changing colors, but mostly it's the usual dull greens and browns—nothing like what I'm used to from growing up in Michigan.

Even in the coldest part of the year, the days are too warm in Arizona to consider it real fall weather.

It takes almost an hour to get up to the top of the mountain. The road curves through the trees, and we follow a long line of cars all with the same idea.

I park and we get out to get food before the movie starts.

"It's so much cooler up here," she says, wrapping her arms around her body as the wind whips through the lot.

Ah, shit. Something I hadn't thought of. I double back and grab a sweatshirt from my car. She pulls it on over her dress. It's nearly as long and she looks freaking sexy as hell. I smooth her hair away from her face and drop a kiss to her lips. "Hungry?"

She presses her mouth to mine and nods. I tug her behind me to the concession stand. We order hot dogs and popcorn, soda, and more candy than any two people should eat (Ginny's words obviously) before walking back to the vehicle. The movie is just starting, and I open the back and help her into the cargo area of my SUV.

"How do you of all people know about this place?"

"Me of all people?"

She grins. "I said what I said."

Chuckling, I admit, "Actually, from your brother."

Her nose wrinkles up. "My brother? Ewww. He brings dates up here, doesn't he?"

"It's a good spot, gotta admit." I lay out a blanket and we sit, her nestling into my side. "Come on, it's gonna be fun."

We dive into the food while watching the first half hour or so. It's some old Cary Grant movie that I'm not really into, but Ginny is smiling and practically in my lap, so I'm dealing just fine.

When the movie fails to keep our attention any longer, we lie down flat in the bed of the SUV with our heads at the end so we can stare up at the stars.

"It's really nice up here," she says.

"Yeah, I think I'll start bringing more of my dates up here."

She turns her head to face me. We're both smiling. "Jerk."

Her eyes are lit with humor and a contentedness fills my chest as I slowly bring my mouth to hers.

Kissing Ginny is better than just about anything. She's fun and sexy, and when we're together, everything just feels good. Her nose is cold, and I pull the blanket around us and hug her tight against my chest.

"What's your major?"

She chuckles a little, caught off guard by the question as my dick poking her tells her just how much I'd like to be inside her. "I haven't decided yet. Why?"

"Just curious. I realized today I'm not great at asking people about themselves. I didn't even know your brother was premed."

"Adam's weirdly quiet about that. He is about everything he does, really. He takes things on and just holds it in so no one else can feel responsibility for it. I know I gripe about him butting into my life, but he's always looked out for me, always ready to save me from trouble. He'd do anything for me, no questions asked."

Am I trouble he'd try to save her from? The pit in my gut tells me yes.

Her hair blows into my face and she tries to tame it.

"The way you talk about Adam reminds me a lot of Nathan. Always looking out for me even when I didn't want him to."

"Maybe we're just good at giving them reasons to worry about us."

"That's probably accurate." I think back to all the times I gave Nathan reason to worry.

"What about you? You're going to be a big hockey star when college is over. Is it weird to have your future all mapped out?"

"Feels so far away it doesn't seem real yet, I guess."

"Will you get me tickets so I can come cheer you on?"

I like the vision of her being there even if it's unlikely to happen. "We might be able to work out some sort of barter system."

"Oh yeah? What'd you have in mind?" That sexy glint is back in her eyes.

"Nothing appropriate for the kids sitting in that minivan next to us," I tell her and sit up. I take her hand and pull her up next to me, drop a kiss to her forehead, and say, "We can discuss it back at my place."

TWENTY-SEVEN

Ginny

O n Sunday, I drag Heath over to my dorm to hang out. Ava's still
gone, so we sit on my bed and watch TV, make out, watch TV, nap,
make out—it's the perfect ending to a great weekend.

"You could stay the night," I offer as he's getting dressed to go.

"I wish I could, but I promised Maverick we'd work on Shakespeare.
His test is tomorrow."

I let out a sigh. "I should probably do some homework too. Someone
distracted me all weekend."

He leans down to kiss me. "You didn't seem to mind so much when
you were riding my face."

Fresh desire blooms, and he must read it all over my expression because
the next thing I know, I'm flat on my back and he's on top of me kissing me
like the world will end if he doesn't.

A squeak and the slamming of a door breaks us apart.

I give Ava an apologetic smile. No matter how many times she sees
Adam or Heath, she still gets shy around them.

"Hey, Ava," he says to my roommate and then slowly rises off me,
but not without another quick kiss. "Bye, baby. See you at the dining hall
tomorrow?"

"Umm . . . yeah." I think through my schedule. "Only for breakfast,
though, I'm working at the Hall of Fame in the afternoon."

"Too bad." He winks and then heads out.

Monday afternoon I have three tours in a row. It's only my second time working by myself. Usually we do them in pairs, but today, I'm the only one available.

I have a junior high class, a soccer recruit, and then finally a hockey recruit. Knowing I might see Heath before or after the last tour makes the time go by at a snail's pace. It's nice out today, though. Perfect Arizona weather with blue skies and a light fall breeze. I take Andi, the soccer chick, over to the practice field and we sit while I let her ask me questions and soak up the experience.

We return just in time for my last tour. I hand her off to a girl on the Valley team as Rauthruss and Maverick walk in the hockey recruit, Tom.

"Genevieve!" Maverick calls, his voice echoing in the big, open space.

I wave and step forward. "Hey, nice to meet you." I smile and extend my hand to Tom.

"You're in good hands," Mav assures him. "Ginny is Adam's sister and Heath's—" He catches himself in time, but my blood pressure still rises. Mav coughs. "Friend."

"Thanks, guys." I bypass the weirdness by stepping away and inviting Tom to follow me with a head tilt in the opposite direction.

Tom is a quiet guy who doesn't say a lot as I show him around. We go by all the usual places on the tour, but I still can't get a read on him until we get to the last stop.

"And this is the hype room." I do my best Vanna White as he stares into the darkened room with wide eyes and an excited smile. Upbeat music already pumps into the space, and with the press of a button, the TVs come to life with the standard Welcome to Valley message splashed across the entire room.

Tom walks in, slowly giving it the appropriate amount of awe. "This is so dope."

"Right?" I follow behind him and close us inside.

I cue up the hockey team video and scoot to the back to let him enjoy the five-minute segment in as much privacy as I can.

The hype room is still my favorite part of this job. I could sit in here all day. Even I feel like a badass after watching the videos and I did not inherit the athleticism my brother did.

I wait for the bits with Heath in them, having practically memorized when his face or an action clip appear.

Things have been great. While I don't love keeping it from my brother, it's been nice to spend time with Heath without the judgment or questions from anyone. I love my brother and I understand why he wants to protect me, but I don't need it in this scenario, and I'm not willing to gamble that he'll be cool with it. Heath and I are having fun. A lot of it. And yes, maybe my feelings have gone beyond that, but I refuse to get swept up in analyzing it. But as Heath's face displays on the screen, flashing a cocky and disarming smile, my body melts.

Fine, I like him a lot. Who knew dating could be so much fun? I've never laughed so much or felt so wanted. And I don't mean his obvious appreciation for my body. We spend a lot of time together and only half of that is naked. Seventy percent tops.

As it gets to the end sequencing, I step closer and get my tablet ready. It's the last tour of the day, and there's a whole different set of steps for shutting down for the night that I haven't done before. Dakota's shown me a few times and she texted me instructions earlier today as a backup.

This room is worth a very pretty penny to the university and I don't want to break anything.

When it finally freezes on the end frame, Tom turns to me.

"Awesome, right?" I ask at his captivated grin. I've seen this look before. He's totally sold. "Let me just shut everything down and some of the guys should be waiting at the desk outside to take you over to the arena."

I tap the screen and begin to shut things down. I'm sweating a little with Tom staring at me while I try to juggle my phone and the tablet. "Sorry, it's my first time closing it out for the night."

"No problem." He shoves his hands in his pockets, and I turn slightly and walk toward the door. It isn't pitch dark in here, but it isn't exactly a comfortable light level either. Dakota is much better at sequencing everything, so it happens seamlessly.

"Okay, I think I got it," I say as I tap the final button. Except instead of opening the door it shuts off all the TVs and now we really are in the pitch black.

Shit. I forgot to open the door before shutting down.

No problem. I've got this. With trembling hands, I try to turn on the TVs, but they won't come back on until the system's reset. I search for another button hoping to find one labeled lights.

Oh shit. Shit, shit, shit, shit, shit.

"One second. I'm so sorry." My breaths come in quick, short gulps as I text Dakota and then press buttons at random on the tablet hoping I get lucky. I'm sure there is a very simple solution, but I'm panicking. Oh my god.

"Are you okay?" Tom asks.

I think I nod, but it isn't exactly believable because I cower against the wall retreating into myself.

One, two, three . . .

TWENTY-EIGHT

Heath

When Adam and I get over to the Hall of Fame, it's chaos. There's a crowd hanging out in the back of the main area, and a couple of security guards stand outside of the hype room.

"What the hell?" Adam asks.

My pulse accelerates and adrenaline swells as we head toward the commotion.

"What's going on?" I ask one of the football guys hanging out watching the security guards talk into their walkie talkies.

"Two people got trapped in the hype room."

At that moment, the doors open and a frazzled Ginny pushes out. Her breathing is so labored I can see the rise and fall of her chest, eyes wild, clutching the tablet to her stomach. Adam and I move to her, and when she sees us, her pace quickens.

"Oh, fuck," I hear Adam mutter quietly under his breath.

He's a step ahead of me and I'm so thankful he's here because she looks like she needs him. She's on the brink of a complete meltdown. But when we finally get to her, it isn't him she throws her arms around. It's me.

Her body is limp as she sucks in air with ragged breaths. My throat is tight, and my chest cracks open, letting her slip inside. I feel her fear with the force of a Mack truck slamming into me and then dragging me a mile down the road. I can't find the oxygen to speak, so I wrap my arms around her and pull her head under my chin.

I glance at Adam, feeling his presence like a dark cloud hovering over us. His glare goes from confused to pissed, but this isn't the time or place to have this conversation.

Adam senses the same thing, and I shield her while he gets us some privacy, calling for everyone to get lost with only slightly more polite words.

"Ginny." When his attention is back on us, his voice is softer than I expected for the rage rolling off him. "G, are you okay?"

She pulls herself away from me, not meeting my gaze, and hugs him instead. He looks relieved as she glues herself to his side.

"What happened?" he asks gently, cupping the back of her head.

She tries to speak, but her voice is shaky, and he shushes her. "Later, G. Just relax." He's calm and loving with her, and I feel a sense of relief that he's here with all the right words, even if it means he's going to kick my ass later.

Adam's jaw flexes and he nods over my head. "Can you see Tom to the arena?"

Ginny's face is buried in his side, giving me her profile. She's not crying, but her eyes are closed, and her dark lashes fan out against her smooth skin.

"Heath," Adam says again, voice as sharp as razors.

I take a step back. "Yeah. Yeah, okay."

Adam doesn't show up to the arena while I'm showing Tom the locker rooms and team training facilities. The guys who are free this afternoon are hanging around, including Maverick and Rauthruss. They both question me on Adam's whereabouts. I shrug it off and focus on getting through the quick tour.

When Coach shows up, I hand off Tom and decide to do a quick skate to clear my head. I assume Adam is going to show up and slam me into the boards at any moment, but he doesn't.

I trudge home with dread and guilt weighing down each step. No matter how many times I tell myself it's none of his business, I can't find any solace in it.

Adam's sitting on the couch with his phone to his ear when I walk into the apartment. I hesitate, but ultimately decide a shower is what I need before he goes nuclear on me. When I'm clean and dressed, he's still sitting in the same spot—sans the phone to his ear. He doesn't even look at me as I join him in the living room.

I'm already sweating again with uncertainty on how to navigate this. Quick and honest, rip off the Band-Aid.

"It's not what you think."

A growl escapes from his chest and his eyes turn to angry slits. Fuck. Okay, that wasn't the best opening, I admit.

"Okay, it's what you think," I backtrack.

"Of all the girls, man. You can have any other one, but not her. Not my baby sister."

"I'm sorry if it pisses you off. Maybe I should have told you. Not because I think I need your permission, but out of respect. I'm sorry for that, but I'm not sorry for digging your sister. She's awesome and I like her a lot. I don't need your permission," I repeat. "And Ginny doesn't need it either, for any guy she decides to date."

"Ginny said as much." He stands. He's a good three inches taller than me and he uses every single one. "You can honestly tell me you think you're good enough for her? Fuck man, I see how you are with women. I don't want that for her, is that so hard to understand?"

He doesn't wait for my answer before heading to his room and slamming the door.

"He and Taryn are sitting guard in the living room," I tell Ginny on the phone later.

The two of them never hang out at our apartment. That's part of the Adam Scott boyfriend experience—bending over backward for his girl and always staying at their place. Or that's what I hear. Since this is my first year living with him I don't really know, but Rauthruss made an offhanded comment once that Adam hardly ever has girlfriends sleep over.

"So, I'll just come over. What's he going to do? Kick me out?"

"No, but he might kick me out."

She groans. "This is stupid. I can date whoever I want."

"He's just looking out for you."

"I don't need him to look out for me." She sighs into the phone. "I guess it's best to give him a couple of days to cool off."

My chest tightens, and I wonder if in a couple of days she'll decide it isn't worth making waves. Maybe that'd be for the best.

The next morning, though, she's waiting outside of the dining hall for me and a goofy grin pulls at my lips.

I hug her and she laughs. "Miss me?"

"Yep." I take her hand and follow her through the line for omelets.

"I need my hand back," she says, and I realize I'm still holding her palm in mine.

We take our usual table. Mav drops into a chair beside her a few minutes later. "Hey there, Romeo and Juliet."

Ginny laughs. "Their families were enemies—this isn't really that sort of thing."

"Well, it *is* a Shakespearean tragedy, anyway. What are you going to do?"

I shrug. Thought about it all night long and I still don't have an answer.

"I'm heading home tonight. I'm sure by the time I get back on Sunday, he'll be over it."

I'm not so sure.

After my morning classes, I head back to the apartment. Ginny's on her way home for the long weekend, and the prospect of spending that many days without her is a real bummer.

Rauthruss is on the phone with Carrie. Mav and Adam are still on campus. I've got my newest package from Chloe and Nathan, so I grab it and walk to my room.

I call him as I cut open the tape.

"Hey," he answers on the second ring.

"Hey. Got your latest box."

"And?"

As soon as I pull back the flaps, a deep chuckle escapes from my throat. "This one is all you, bro."

"What? How can you tell?"

"It looks like you went down the aisles at Target and just threw random things in." I pull out deodorant, body soap, condoms (major eye roll), toothpaste, pencils, a giant tub of my favorite protein, and an Xbox gift card. "Plus it's all just shoved in here. Chloe's boxes are packed a lot nicer than yours."

"I knew I should have had her wrap it all up."

I chuckle again. "Thank you. I appreciate it."

Sitting in my desk chair, I lean back as he catches me up on the latest wedding details. Getting married takes an awful lot of planning, apparently.

"So, spill," he says eventually when he's done with the rundown on dinner entrees and cake tasting. "What'd you think of Kevin?"

"He was fine." I shrug even though Nathan can't see it. "Mom's happy so that's good, right?"

"Yeah, I guess so. It's weird seeing her with someone else though. No matter how nice he is."

I hum my agreement.

"Are you still calling her and checking in to see how she's doing?"

"Nah. I mean, we chat every other week or so, but she doesn't need me to do that anymore. She's got Kevin, plus Uncle Doug is still checking on her."

"Yeah, I guess. Chloe and I are going to fly up to have Thanksgiving with her. Bummed you can't make it."

"I'm sure you guys will make the most of it." We've got a game on Saturday, so it'll just be another Thursday around here, although the extra days off school are nice.

"I could never make her smile like you could. Remember that time we went to the water park in Wisconsin?"

I smile, knowing exactly where he's going with the story.

"She got up on the top of that big slide and she wouldn't budge. The line was backed up and people were yelling for her to hurry up. There were six-year-old kids going down that thing."

"She hates heights," I say.

"Yeah. I'm not even sure why she attempted it in the first place."

"Because I was too scared to go on my own and you were whining about me tagging along with you and that guy you used to hang out with . . ."

"Lee," he fills in.

I nod. "She came up there for me. I knew she was scared too but I didn't care."

"Dude, you were like nine."

"I still knew it was a bad idea."

"You sang to her, at the top of your lungs, the whole way back down the line."

"I had to scream so she could hear me over all the people yelling at us."

He laughs.

I'm smiling now, but I was so embarrassed at the time and Nathan made fun of me for weeks.

"You were always good at calming her down, being her rock. You still are. She might be doing better, but there's no one that can make her as happy as you. Call her."

When I get off the phone with Nathan, I send her a text checking in and promise myself I'll call her tomorrow. With my gift card in hand, I walk out into the living room. Everyone's back from campus, and Adam has parked himself back in his guard dog position between the door and my room.

I toss the gift card on the coffee table. "I was going to order pizza and get the new Call of Duty. You guys in?"

"Oh, no way." Rauthruss picks up the card. "Rad, man. I'm in."

We both look to Adam and he shrugs his big shoulders. I guess that's a start.

TWENTY-NINE

Ginny

Hottest guy on campus: Hey, gorgeous. Why aren't you in my bed?

Me: Better offer.

Hottest guy on campus: Damn, woman. That's cold.

Me: I figured you would understand better than anyone. My mom's been cooking for days. SO MUCH FOOD.

Hottest guy on campus: My stomach just growled, for real. Also, my dick's hard just from texting you.

Me: Proof or it didn't happen.

Hottest guy on campus: Dick pics . . . always a bad idea, Genevieve.

Me: Like vag pics *shudders*

Hottest guy on campus: Not the same at all. Speaking of . . . feel free to send some my way.

Me: Tit for tat.

Hottest guy on campus: Tits okay too, I guess. Make sure you get front and side view . . . I very much enjoy a little side booby.

Me: How's Valley?

I don't want to ask specifically about how things are with Adam, but he must read between the lines.

Hottest guy on campus: Okay. We stayed in tonight and played video games. Adam hasn't punched me yet.

Me: I heard my mom say you guys are having a team dinner to celebrate Thanksgiving. That's nice.

Hottest guy on campus: Beats the dorm food. Don't tell Brenda.

Me: Brenda?

Hottest guy on campus: My favorite lunch lady.

Me: Of course, you have a favorite lunch lady.

Hottest guy on campus: Eyes keep closing. Gonna sleep. Don't forget (o) (o)

The following night I'm lying on the couch watching TV when there's noise outside. A car door followed by deep voices. I get up and peer out the window. Adam's Jeep is in the driveway, and I see his big frame climbing out of the driver's side. Heath, Rauthruss, and Mav follow.

I run to the door and fling it open as they approach. "What are you doing here?"

I hug Adam first. As excited as I am about the man behind him, it's been three years since Adam and I have celebrated a Thanksgiving together. He always stayed at Valley because of his hockey schedule.

"Decided to come up for the night, enjoy Mom's sour cream apple pie. We have to go back tomorrow night to have dinner with the team."

"Figures you found a way to have two Thanksgiving dinners."

Adam heads inside, so do Mav and Rhett. Heath lingers with a sexy smirk. "Hey, Genevieve."

I throw myself at him.

"Couch, Payne." Adam's voice comes from behind me. "Mav and Rhett, you guys can take the guest room."

Adam gets Heath a pillow and blanket, and I stay downstairs as Heath spreads out on the couch bed.

"Why didn't you tell me you were coming?"

"I wanted to surprise you. Also, I didn't know until about three hours ago. Your brother said he was heading up and asked if we wanted to come with him." He shrugs. "I was half expecting him to stop on the freeway somewhere and kick me out of the car."

"So you're here because of my brother?" I sneak a hand inside his shirt and up his chest.

"Yep. He really does it for me." He winces. "Shit, I can't even joke about it while I'm hard."

"Come up to my room." I start to stand, but he doesn't budge.

"I don't think I should."

"Because of Adam? He's had more girls in his room than Sephora on sale day."

"I don't know what that means, but I'm guessing it's a lot."

"Yes." I pull again, but he shakes his head.

"It's not just Adam. I'm a guest and I don't want your parents to think I came up to get in their daughter's pants.

"Oh my god, when did you turn into this good guy?"

"Don't worry, baby. I'm still bad." He pulls me down on top of him and quickly has me pinned underneath him on the couch bed.

He doesn't kiss me, though, just stares down at me.

"I'm so excited you're here."

He grins. "Me too."

I wake up to the smell of pumpkin and turkey and am instantly giddy. A real Thanksgiving with the whole family. And Heath.

Adam and the guys are already up, their doors open and rooms empty as I pass by on my way downstairs. I slow as I get to the last step. Heath's pulling a gray T-shirt over his head and holding his phone up to his ear.

When he spots me, he smiles, and my insides turn to mush.

"All right, I should go. The guys are waiting on me." He continues staring at me as he says goodbye to whoever he's talking to. I meet him halfway as he pockets his phone.

"Was that your mom?"

"Yeah."

"She must miss having you home for the holidays. My mom's ecstatic Adam's here. She's been in the kitchen all morning making extra pies."

"Hope she doesn't mind we came along."

"Are you kidding? She's thrilled. My mother's happiest when she has lots of people to dote on."

He wraps his arms around my lower back. "What are you up to this morning? Can you save me from some lame football game outside?"

I gasp. "Lame? It's an honored tradition." I take his hand and pull him to the door. "You can be on my team. I've never lost."

The neighborhood football game on Thanksgiving morning is a tradition as far back as I can remember. When I was little, I'd sit along the sidelines and cheer on my dad and Adam and whatever boy I had a crush on at the time. But sometime in middle school I decided to join the other brave girls out there. I love it.

"Morning, sunshine." Mav jogs up to us.

"Morning," Heath says, voice cracking. He clears it a few times. His gruff morning voice is my favorite.

"Glad you got your sexy ass up; we need a QB."

Heath shakes his head. "I never played football."

Mav punches him. "I know, but you've got those QB good looks like Tom Brady."

"Did they already pick teams?" I ask.

"Nah," Mav says. "They're fighting over Adam."

"You four are the most athletically inclined people we've had in a while." I scan the yard to see who made it to play this year, and my gaze snags on someone I didn't expect. "Bryan's here?"

The question is more to myself than the guys, but Heath asks, "Who's Bryan?"

"My ex." Bryan and I make eye contact and he starts toward me. Seeing him for the first time in three months has my emotions whipping around like I'm on a merry-go-round.

"Hey, Ginny." Bryan envelopes me in a hug, pressing his large body against mine and squeezing tightly. Apparently he feels none of the awkwardness I do. I can't decide if that's comforting or not. "It's so good to see you."

"I didn't expect you to be home for break."

"Just for the day. I fly back tonight."

"Oh." I shift uncomfortably and wring my hands to have something to do. "How's Idaho?"

"Eh . . . you know."

"Actually, I don't."

"Well, it's not Arizona. How's Valley?"

I sneak a glance at Heath out of my periphery. He's got his arms crossed and a hard expression on his face. "It's great. I really love it."

"Yeah?"

I nod.

"That's awesome." He does a blatant once over of my body. "You look amazing."

"Thanks." I smile politely. He looks good too, but not in that way where I want to rip off his clothes. And the guy who I do want to do that to is standing beside me. I turn to him. "Bryan, this is my friend Heath."

"Hey, man." Bryan juts his chin in acknowledgment. "You play hockey with Adam, right?"

"That's right."

"The guys were talking about you earlier. Sounds like you're going to be the opposing QB. I'll try not to make you look too bad." He takes a step back and winks. "Good to see you, babe. I'll call you. Maybe we can hang while we're both in town for winter break."

I wait until he's gone to face Heath, prepared to stroke his ego, but he's . . . smiling?

"Your friend, huh?"

"Did you want me to introduce you as my make-out buddy?"

He chuckles and winces at the same time. "Guess not. You dated that douche?"

"He's . . . not so bad." I play down any lingering resentment because the last thing I need is Heath or my brother to make a scene. And honestly, it's not so much resentment as just dislike for the guy. Sure, he had his own reasoning for how things ended, but let's be real, he did it in a super shitty way. I can see that so much clearer now.

"He's a douche."

"Is this jealous Heath?" I wave a hand in front of his broody frame. He glares toward Bryan's retreating back.

"What? No, of course not." But he continues to stand close while we set up the game.

We've got enough people to play with two full teams and a couple alternates. Rauthruss and Heath end up on my team and Adam and Mav on the other with Bryan.

"We're just waiting on my dad," Adam says and glances toward the house. "Ginny, did you see him when you came out?"

"No, I haven't seen him this morning."

Adam's brows scrunch together. "That's weird."

"He probably had to run to town for something Mom forgot. Let's just start, I'm sure he'll show up."

Adam doesn't budge.

"I will go check on him." I nudge Heath playfully. "Don't screw up my winning streak, Payne."

I hurry back up to the house and to the kitchen where I can hear Mom and her sister, Zoe, talking and cooking. Mom's wearing a half apron chopping onions while Zoe sits on a stool peeling potatoes.

"Hey."

They both look up as I enter.

"Morning. Game over already?" Mom asks.

"No, we haven't started yet. We're waiting on Dad. Do you know where he is?"

Mom and Zoe exchange a look.

"What?" I ask when neither of them immediately answers.

Mom shakes her head. "I don't know where he went, but it's not like him to miss the big game. Start without him, and I'll text and let him know the team's missing him."

I grin. "Okay. Thanks, Mom. Are you staying for dinner, Aunt Zoe?"

"No, your uncle Wyatt and I are heading to his mom's. I'll stop by Sunday before you head back to school."

As I go out, Dad's pulling into the driveway. I run to him, pleased to see he's dressed to play in an old T-shirt and shorts. "You're late."

"How's the team looking, kid?" He gives me a one-arm hug as we walk toward the game.

"We've got a few ringers thanks to Adam and his friends."

At the next break in play, Adam finds us on the sidelines, and he and my dad hug. Adam's taller and broader than him now, which is just another way things have changed over the last three years.

"Good to see you, son."

"You ready to get your ass kicked, old man?"

Adam and my dad smack talk like they're both twelve, but it's so good to see them together. Our whole family home at the same time.

"You're on Ginny's team," Adam tells him.

Our team huddles up, and Dad and I substitute in.

As we play, I have this sublime feeling of total completeness. Like I've never been this happy. Maybe it's just nostalgia and the sense that this is a rare moment. Adam will graduate, become a doctor with insane hours, and get married or move far away and who knows when we'll all be here again. Maybe another three years. Maybe longer.

Heath isn't as good of a QB as Bryan, as painful as that is to admit, and Adam is way better than I remember. While we grab water, Heath gives me a rueful smile. "You might want to think about a trade if you want to keep that winning streak."

"I would never leave my team in the final quarter," I say, faking shock then wrapping my arms around his sweaty neck. He grins and I kiss him in front of everyone. I definitely got the better QB and I'm not shy about letting the other team know it.

THIRTY

Heath

Ginny's ex is a piece of shit. *Hello, jealousy, nice to meet you.* But come on, this guy? I don't miss the way he tries to flirt with her or the little inside jokes he tosses out. I want to throw the football in a perfect spiral directly into his face . . . or maybe his balls.

I remind myself that Ginny referred to sex with this guy as blah. My jealousy? Petty as hell.

Adam makes the game winning touchdown and his team celebrates as I approach Ginny with a rueful smile.

"Sorry, baby doll."

My girl has a competitive streak I find as amusing as I do sexy. Her mouth pulls down in a disappointed pout. "It's fine. I was due for a loss. Besides, I was distracted more than normal."

I worry for a second that she means because of Bryan, but then her lips twist up and she fists my shirt to pull me closer. "You threw me off my game, Payne. Usually you're covered in layers of padding and I can't really see *you* when you're on the ice, but out here I could see every drip of sweat."

"That padding keeps me alive."

She brings her lips to mine and hums against my mouth. "Necessary evil."

"QB looks but missing that QB arm." Maverick places both hands on his hips when he stops beside us.

"Yeah, well, I'd like to see you get a pass through Adam and Rauthruss," I grumble.

Ginny drops another quick kiss and then steps back. "I better go check on my mom in the kitchen."

After everyone else leaves, the guys and I sit in the yard drinking beer. Adam and his dad are tossing the ball back and forth. They have this easy way about them. Like I can tell Adam respects him, but his dad has stopped being the hard-ass parent now that his son is older, and they just seem to enjoy being around one another.

I never got that. Never even knew it was a thing until now. I had lots of good times with my dad, but I was still a kid—we didn't talk girls or life, none of that. Losing a parent is one of those things that as soon as you think you're over it, something stops you in your tracks and the wound is as fresh as if it just happened. I have a feeling it'll be like that the rest of my life. But as sad as it makes me for what I missed out on, I enjoy being around Ginny's family. It's the first holiday I've had in years where my worries are only the limitations of my stomach and how much food I can stuff in it.

"We're eating in thirty minutes," Ginny says as she rejoins us outside. She's freshly showered and dressed in jeans and a ruffly shirt with a deep V-neck that's going to make it impossible to keep my eyes off her boobs while I feign the role of respectable friend.

She hasn't held back with the PDA since I showed up last night, but I still want to respect that Adam's not exactly on board. She takes a seat on my lap and I glance around to see if anyone shoots daggers at me, but Mr. Scott and Adam barely seem to notice.

"I should shower." I'm dirty and sweaty and probably not presentable for a Thanksgiving table.

"Yeah, we all should get cleaned up," Mr. Scott says as he tosses the ball to Adam one last time and heads for the house.

"Adam, do you have some clothes I could borrow?" Mav asks. "I was so excited when I packed all I managed to grab were socks and boxers."

Adam chuckles but nods. "I'll see what my dad has."

They all head in, but Ginny doesn't budge to let me up.

"I can think of a few things to do while you wait for the shower."

"Oh yeah." I put my finger in the V of her shirt and pull the fabric away from her chest so I can look down it.

"Mhmm."

She presses her lips to mine and then pulls back so we're nose to nose. "I, uh, decided something last night."

"What's that?" I ask and kiss her again.

"I don't want to wait anymore."

"Wait for what?"

"Sex, dummy. I'm ready."

A few months ago, I would have thought going without sex this long would have been a real sacrifice, but Ginny's sexual appetite is ravenous . . . just without the actual sex. When we first started hooking up, I couldn't wait to get inside her, but Ginny's creative and I can't pretend to have been anything but satisfied with our hookups. However, now that she's giving me the green light, I am ready to skip dinner and just have her instead.

All the blood is rushing to my cock with all the new things this opens up for us. I can't freaking wait. I kiss her hard, giving her a taste of how excited I am about her news.

"Payne," Adam bellows from the house. "Quit sucking face with my sister and get in here."

I smile into her mouth as our kiss stops.

We walk up to the house and Ginny goes to the kitchen to help her mom. I grab my overnight bag and Adam and I head upstairs.

"You can take a shower in my room. Should have everything you need in there." He stops outside his room and motions for me to go ahead.

"Thanks, man."

"No problem. Lock the door on both sides."

"What?" I ask, confused.

"You'll see."

I walk in and set my bag on the floor and then wander to the bathroom. There's another bedroom on the other side and I grin as I get my first peek at Ginny's childhood. I go all the way in and turn a circle. The walls are painted teal and the bed has a white comforter with a thousand throw pillows piled on top. Framed photos line the top of a desk. Even without walking closer, I can tell Bryan is featured in a lot of them.

Her ex-boyfriend might be better at football, but Ginny barely even looked at him the entire game. I know it sounds conceited to say she's totally into me, but I know she is. I'm totally into her too. Still, I turn the largest frame around so I don't have to stare at their happy faces.

As I'm coming back through the bathroom, Adam walks in his room with brows furrowed. "Do you have any extra clothes Mav could wear?"

"Nah, man, I just brought the one change of clothes."

He goes to his dresser and rummages through the few items inside. "My dad doesn't have a single item of clothing in their closet."

I shrug and so does he as he says, "Guess Mav will have to wear some vintage duds of mine."

By the time I shower and head back down, the Scott's dining room table is filled with food and the guys are already sitting around practically salivating. There's an empty chair between Ginny and Mav, and I take it.

Mrs. Scott sets a final dish on the table and smiles. "I think that's everything. Dig in everyone."

For five minutes no one speaks except to compliment the food between bites. Even my sweet little Ginny, who barely fills a plate most days, eats her weight in mashed potatoes and turkey.

I feel like I can't eat another bite, but then Mrs. Scott brings pies to the table and I can't help myself.

"I think I'm gonna be sick," Mav says after his second piece, leaning back and rubbing his stomach.

"What are you wearing, Mav?" Ginny asks. "Is that Adam's high school homecoming shirt?"

He looks down and shrugs.

Adam speaks from across the table. "Yeah, Dad. I went in your and Mom's closet to loan Mav a shirt, but I couldn't find anything. Did she finally take over the entire closet and ban your clothes to the basement?"

Adam laughs at the idea, but then an uncomfortable silence follows as Mr. and Mrs. Scott share a nervous glance.

My skin prickles with awareness even before I've put it together. I'm good at reading bad news. Ginny's confused expression is heartbreaking, and I rest a hand on her leg under the table.

Mrs. Scott frowns and then says, "We wanted to wait until after the weekend to tell you."

"To tell us what?" Adam asks, his tone hardened in anticipation.

Uncomfortable silence falls over the room.

"Your mother and I have separated," Mr. Scott answers finally.

Mav goes into a coughing fit, unable to hide his surprise and I elbow him hard in the ribs. He grunts loudly, but no one is paying him any attention anyway.

"Separated?" Adam questions. "You're getting divorced?"

Mrs. Scott looks around the table. "Maybe we should talk about it later."

"Mom?" Ginny's voice wavers and my chest . . . my chest fucking aches.

Mrs. Scott's mouth pulls up into a smile, but it's sad as hell. "We love you both very much. That hasn't changed and it won't. We're still a family."

Rauthruss clears his throat. "Maybe the guys and I should give you some time to talk." He glances to me and Mav, and we start to stand only to have Adam beat us to it.

"No, you guys stay. I need some air."

Ginny pushes back her chair so quickly it scrapes against the wood floor. "Me too." She disappears after him.

"Holy uncomfortable Batman," Mav whispers.

"I'm going to talk to them," Mr. Scott says and looks to his wife, maybe for approval. She nods and he follows them out.

It isn't until Mrs. Scott stands and excuses herself that the guys and I take a breath.

"Fuck, man, that was rough." Rauthruss grimaces. "What do we do?"

"No clue," I tell him honestly.

THIRTY-ONE

Ginny

Adam and I sit in the garage after Dad leaves to go back to his place. "He has his own apartment. How weird is that?" I ask, mostly to myself.

"You really had no idea?" Adam looks to me again like I should have known and warned him. Maybe I should have, but I didn't.

I shake my head. "I didn't know. Dad was in Scottsdale for work when I got here earlier this week." I think back, not only to the days since I got home for Thanksgiving break, but over the last few months. "They were going on trips and . . ." It hits me then that those trips were probably a last-ditch effort to save their marriage, and I feel like throwing up.

At some point, my brother grabbed a bottle of wine from the kitchen and we are well on our way to finishing it off. Adam's drunk the lion's share. He seems to be taking this harder than me. I feel numb, but he . . . well, I haven't seen my brother so devastated since the day I got locked inside the pantry. He'd been nine then and took on the big brother protector role with a dedication second to none. Since then I'd thought of him as unbreakable.

He can't protect me from this though, and I can't protect him. Everything is going to be different whether we like it or not.

Rauthruss walks outside with his hands in his pockets about the time Adam is tossing the empty wine bottle in the trash. "Are you guys okay?"

"Getting there." Adam holds up his wine glass and takes a healthy drink.

"We thought you might want to stay another night, head back in the morning?"

Adam nods and his expression softens. "Yeah, thanks, I appreciate it. Sorry for the family drama."

Mav and Heath walk out. Heath's blue eyes fixate on me.

"You guys wanna go out?" Adam asks. "I need to get away from here for a bit."

They all agree, and I stare down into my wine.

"You coming, Little Scott?" Mav asks.

"I think I'm going to stay."

Heath hangs back as the rest of the guys head for Adam's Jeep. Rauthruss climbs into the driver's side, thankfully. I know he'll make sure they're safe.

"Do you want me to stay?" Heath offers.

"No. I think Adam needs you more than me right now. I'm going to check on my mom."

He squeezes my hand and drops a kiss to my forehead. "Sorry, baby doll. Text me if you need me and I'll come back."

I offer the biggest smile of appreciation I can, which probably isn't that big. He jogs off, hops into the Jeep, and I watch them pull away.

I find Mom in the kitchen wiping down the counters. She stops when she sees me and offers a sad smile. "Are you okay?"

I slide onto the stool in front of her. "Funny, I was going to ask you the same thing."

She lets out a sigh and nods. "Yeah, it's the best thing for your dad and I, but I know that's not easy for you and Adam to understand."

"What happened? Is that weird to ask?"

Her smile is soft and warm, and she holds her arms out. I hop off the stool and go to her, stepping in and letting her wrap me into a reassuring embrace. "It wasn't one big thing, honey. We grew apart and started seeing our futures differently."

I tilt my head up to look her in the eye and she runs a hand along the back of my head like she did when I was a little girl. "I love you. Your father loves you. We're still a family, even if it looks a little different now."

"It'll be weird to go back to Valley and not think of you and Dad together here."

"I so get that. It's taken some getting used to being here by myself."

I glance around the kitchen wondering if she'll even stay here in this big house without him. I'm not brave enough to ask. I can't take another blow today.

"I promise that we'll both still be there for you and that we won't be those awful parents who can't be in the same room together."

My heart hurts imagining any scenario that looks different than what I'm used to. Everything's changing.

"Adam's wrecked."

"Your brother is a romantic."

I huff a small laugh. "Adam?"

"It's true. He is. From the time he was old enough to talk, he'd tell everyone he wanted to be a husband when he grew up, just like his daddy."

"I don't remember that."

"Middle school happened, and that's when he decided he wanted to be a doctor, but he hasn't changed."

"But he goes through girlfriends faster than anyone I know."

"He's a romantic, but he's still a young man." She smiles and I notice how tired she looks and wonder how I didn't see it before. "I should talk to him."

"They went to the bar."

"Even Heath?"

"Yeah, he offered to stay, but I figured Adam needed him more than me."

She touches my face. "You're a good sister. I'll talk to him before he leaves, but he'll be okay. We all will."

I hope so.

"I was going to have some pie in bed and watch *It's a Wonderful Life*. Want to join me?"

"Is there any pumpkin left?"

"You didn't really think I put all the pies out on the table earlier?" She smiles and shakes her head as she goes to the oven and pulls out a pumpkin pie.

I barely ate earlier and my stomach growls at the delicious smell of pumpkin and nutmeg. "In that case, I want two slices."

Mom and I eat pie curled up on her king-size bed. As I lay there, I can still smell my dad in their room and wonder if she can too. I'm sad, but I know my parents didn't come to this decision lightly, so I do my best to not let it show too much.

Mom falls asleep right after the movie, and I head to my own room. The guys aren't back, and the last text Heath sent said he thought they were in for a late night.

Adam's always been my protector. I never thought I'd need to repay the favor, but it seems like now might be the time. I can be the strong one this time.

I doze off sometime after one and wake up to the bed dipping with Heath's weight. His familiar scent mixed with alcohol wraps around me.

"You're back," I say, voice thick with sleep. "How's Adam?"

"Took all three of us to get him upstairs. Rauthruss is sleeping on the floor in there to keep an eye on him."

"I'm really glad you were here."

"Me too." He pulls me tight against him and rubs my back in long, soft strokes. "How are you doing? I hated not being here for you tonight."

"Well, I've had better Thanksgivings, but I ate my weight in pie, so I'm okay for the moment. It doesn't feel real yet. Twenty-three years . . . can you imagine?"

His head shakes almost imperceptibly. The TV is still on and his face illuminates with flashing colors. His warmth heats the space between us.

"You can turn off the TV if it bugs you," I tell him.

"It doesn't bother me, and I know you prefer it."

"Being scared of the dark is embarrassing. Maybe even more embarrassing than my parents announcing they're separating over Thanksgiving dinner, but I've gotten used to sleeping without the TV since going to Valley."

"I realize it probably doesn't help, but you don't need to feel embarrassed in front of me. Not for any of it."

"It does help, actually. Thank you. What also might help is knowing your deepest darkest secrets and fears."

He chuckles. "I'm scared of all kinds of things."

"Like?"

"Worms."

"What?" I laugh. "Why worms?"

He shudders. "We used them for bait when fishing. I never liked touching them and once Nathan noticed, he started chasing me around dangling the little slimy fuckers in front of my face." He shudders again.

"Worms are gross but not scary."

"Fears don't have to be rational."

"That's true."

"Why are you scared of the dark? Did something happen or have you always been?"

"When I was five or six, me and Adam were playing at my grandparent's house. It was this old house with creaky wooden floors and doors that somehow no longer fit the frame, so you had to put all your weight into them to close. They had this great back yard with a treehouse and a trampoline. Before my grandmother passed away, the whole family on my dad's side would get together. The adults would sit outside in lawn chairs and the kids could run wild."

"Sounds like something out of a fifties TV show."

"Well, it wasn't quite that idyllic. Uncle Walter showed up stoned more often than not, and my cousin Tillie was always teaching us Urban Dictionary slang. My mom almost had a stroke with some of the words I learned. Anyway, one day, the whole family was over there, I think it was one of my cousin's birthdays. Everyone was outside and the cousins decided we would play hide and seek. I'm the baby of the family and I really wanted to prove that I was a good hider, so I'd been scoping out places for weeks and finally found the best hiding spot. In the pantry there was this extra closet where grandma kept brooms and mops. It was really small, and I knew I was the only one who could fit in it and that no one else would think to look there. So, when everyone took off to hide, I hung back so not to give away my spot and then went and shut myself in."

Heath strokes my arm as my voice wavers. Part of the memory is so real I can almost smell the dust and Pledge mixture of that tiny closet. Other things I only remember like I watched someone else go through it, like the way I wrapped my arms around myself, squeezing tight and sobbing through the screams.

"I don't know how long I was in there. For a while I was so careful to be quiet. I didn't want to give myself away. I could hear Adam calling my name and I just felt so proud, you know? He's always been a total know-it-all. Cocky and just better at everything, so I was really excited to have beaten him at something. Anyway, eventually my cousins grew bored of the game and when I was certain I'd waited long enough that they were never going to find me, I pushed the door open ready to show off my awesome hiding skills, only I couldn't get out. The outside of the door had one of those hook latches and it'd fallen in place when I shut the door. I screamed and screamed until I lost my voice. It was so dark and so small."

"Fuck, Ginny."

I nod. "By everyone's best guess, I was in there for two hours before my mom noticed she hadn't seen me in a while and went looking for me. They called an ambulance because I couldn't get my breathing under control. Adam freaked. He knew I was missing but didn't think it was a big deal, so it really hit him harder than anyone. He didn't leave my side for weeks." Heath's hold tightens around me and I snuggle into him. "I know I probably should have gotten over it by now."

"I don't think fears work like that. I think they hang on until you face them in one way or another, poking holes in the pain and letting good shine through." He pulls the sheet up over our heads and smiles at me in the near darkness. "Let's make some good memories in the dark."

The thin sheet doesn't really block out the light of the TV, but it's a step and I take it.

THIRTY-TWO

Heath

I disappear from under the covers long enough to grab a condom and then hurry back underneath where a very eager Ginny is wiggling out of her clothes. I had big plans for undressing her with my teeth, but I'm too busy appreciating the view to complain.

"You're so beautiful."

Her smile, even in the near dark, is bright and genuine. She eyes the condom in my hand. "I'm on birth control. We can . . ." She hesitates. "I mean, if you're comfortable going without, so am I."

My already throbbing cock is now harder than it's ever been. I pull my shirt over my head and Ginny works on unbuttoning my jeans. Together we push them and my boxers down and before I can kick them off, Ginny's mouth is covering the head of my dick.

"Oh Jesus. Slow down, babe. I'm never gonna last, like that," I tell her, guiding her head up and down my length. Her warm mouth is heaven. She comes off with a pop and I groan at the loss. I pull her up and swipe a hand over her lips. She looks a little uncertain and I tuck a strand of hair behind her ear.

"You sure you wanna do this?"

"I do, but I'm a little nervous. I might suck at it."

"Well, in that case, you can just keep sucking me with your hot as fuck mouth." I wink so she knows I'm joking and shift so I'm on top of her, holding most of my weight off her slender frame. "Babe, don't take this any other way than I mean it—a compliment—but there's no way you're bad at sex. You're the sexiest, most enthusiastic partner I've ever had."

That earns me a grin and I take her mouth in a bruising kiss. And just like that, the wild Ginny I've come to know is back. The blanket falls, but she doesn't seem to notice or care. She pulls at my hair and rakes her nails down my shoulders. I swear I could make this girl orgasm from kissing alone, if I could ever bring myself to only kiss her.

There's no single part of her that I like better than the rest. I like it all and I show her so with a dedication to touching and kissing every inch.

She squirms underneath me as I move down her body, tracing a single finger along the middle of her stomach, past her belly button, and down to her slick pussy. She raises her hips to give me better access and I dip my head.

Her hands find my hair and her fingers slide along my scalp and tug the strands as I taste her. She writhes and moans and it's so fucking hot my dick leaks with desperation. I wait until she's so close she's panting my name before I finally line up at her entrance. I inch in slowly, her tight pussy squeezing me.

I'm worried about hurting her and making it good for her for all of two seconds before pleasure wraps around my spine and zaps my brain.

"I'm okay," she says when I don't immediately move.

"That makes one of us."

She laughs and the slight movement of her body nearly sends me over the edge, and I have to close my eyes and grind down on my back molars for a second to regain my composure. I move at a pace meant to keep me from coming, but that somehow tips Ginny over the edge. She looks up at me wide-eyed and gorgeous as she rides out her first orgasm.

Damn, she's beautiful.

I pull out and place a kiss to her lips and then turn her onto her stomach and lift her hips.

I bite one ass cheek and then kiss it before nudging the head of my cock inside her pussy. She pushes back into me. "Hold on, baby. This won't be as gentle."

She flashes me a grin over her shoulder. With one hand on her hip and the other at the base of her neck, I bury myself inside of her sweet heat.

We both shudder. My balls are heavy, and I resist the urge to pound into her like a jackhammer. Slowly, I ease in and out, finding a nice rhythm.

"Harder," she whispers so quietly it takes me a second to realize what she's asking.

"You're sure?"

She nods. "Fuck me hard like I know you want to."

Stars dot my vision and my voice is gruff. "Grab the headboard."

Her fingers find it in an instant. Her eagerness and the new angle gives new meaning to torturous pleasure. *Ermahgerd.*

I fuck her as hard as I've dreamed of doing, but with every thrust and every slap of skin against skin, it somehow feels more meaningful too. It's never felt this all-consuming before. I know Ginny in a way I've never known anyone else and that makes this better in so many ways. I can read her body and the emotions on her face.

She owns me as she falls apart beneath me for a second time. I fight to hold off my orgasm so that I can keep watching her, but with two more hard thrusts, my eyes slam shut and I follow.

I wrap an arm around her waist and fall onto the bed with her tucked into my front. We're gasping for air together. I feel like I've landed in another dimension. This girl . . . fuck, *this girl.*

I really don't want to move, but I need to clean up and I know she'll want to, also.

I start to pull back and she grabs onto my forearm. "Don't go. Not yet."

"Just going to clean up. I'll be right back."

I slide out of bed and pad to the bathroom to wash up, grab a wet cloth and bring it back to her. She sits up and reaches for it.

"I got it."

She leans back on both elbows while I take care of her; she watches me with a sleepy smile. After getting rid of the rag, I climb back into bed with her.

Neither of us speaks as we lie there drifting off. A peacefulness I wasn't expecting after the day's events settles in.

"Heath," she says as I'm just about asleep.

"Yeah?"

"I don't think I'm bad at sex anymore."

"No, baby doll." I snicker. "You definitely aren't."

She yawns, snuggles into my side, and falls asleep in my arms.

The next morning I wake up before Ginny and head downstairs. Rauthruss is already in the kitchen with a cup of coffee. He looks tired, hair sticking up everywhere.

"Long night?"

"Yeah, man. Real long night."

"How's Adam?"

"Sleeping hard. We've gotta get out of here soon though."

I nod and grab some coffee too.

His phone pings and he lets out a sigh. "What a weekend."

"That Carrie?"

"Yeah, she's pissed because I forgot to call her last night."

"Had a few things going on."

"No shit." He sighs. "I should call her, let her yell at me, and get it over with so I can start groveling."

"Sounds awesome." I chuckle as he heads outside.

I try to conjure an image of Ginny and me like that but can't summon it.

I take my coffee upstairs ready to wake my girl and enjoy the last moments before we head back. As I walk into Ginny's room, her voice carries through the bathroom from Adam's room. I glance in and see her legs hanging off the end of his bed and the bottoms of Adam's feet.

"Are you going to be okay?" she asks him.

"Yeah, I just can't believe it. They always seemed so solid. My whole life feels like a lie."

"That's a little dramatic."

"But seriously, if they can't work things out, what hope is there for anyone?"

"Oh, come on. You and Taryn are great. Me and Heath . . . it can work out."

"You and Heath." A deep, sarcastic laugh follows.

"Look, I know you're all anti-love right now, but don't rain on my parade. Heath is great."

"Sure, of course he is, Ginny. My issue with you two was never about him being a bad guy—he's not. Heath's fun and always up for a good time, but I've seen him go through a lot of women. Some he hooked up with more than once, most he didn't, but ultimately he moved on from all of them as easy as changing his underwear. I just don't want to see you get hurt again."

He's not wrong, but he's missing the thing that makes it different now. Ginny.

"Relax, we're good. Heath and I are . . ."

I'm holding my breath waiting for her to finish that sentence, but Adam lets out a long groan interrupting her.

"Oh, Jesus, you're in love with him."

"Stop it," she says playfully. It sounds like she tosses a pillow at him as her light laughter trickles from the next room. "But since you're being nosey, yes, I am. I love him, and I truly think what we have is special."

My hand tips forward and coffee spills on my bare toes. *Fuck.* I place the mug on Ginny's dresser, clean up the mess, and get dressed quickly. I manage to grab my stuff and head downstairs, heart in my throat, before either Ginny or Adam notices me.

THIRTY-THREE

Ginny

I walk out with the guys as they load up in Adam's Jeep. My brother looks as hungover as he smells. He slides into the passenger seat, Rhett gets behind the wheel, and Maverick hops into the back.

I follow Heath to the other side.

"Let me know how he is?" I ask, motioning with my head to Adam.

"We'll keep an eye on him," he promises. "We've got practice this afternoon. Hopefully that'll help."

"If he doesn't throw up all over the ice."

He makes a disgusted face and shifts from one foot to the other. I lean into him and close my eyes, and his arms wrap around me. Despite all the awful things that happened this weekend, I enjoyed being with Heath.

The Jeep starts up, and I know the guys need to get going.

"Later." He kisses my forehead and I step away.

The rest of the weekend is uneventful, a welcome change. Mom and I watch movies, I see a few of my friends from high school, I text with Heath between his practices, and I even have lunch with Mom and Dad together on Sunday before I head back.

After dropping my things at my dorm, I go to Reagan and Dakota's apartment.

"And all I did was eat turkey and watch college football," Reagan says when I've finished giving them the rundown of my crazy weekend.

"I saw Adam earlier," Dakota says from the kitchen where she's putting away groceries while Reagan and I sit in the living room. "He and Taryn looked like they were having a serious and depressing talk outside of the apartment. Trouble in paradise?"

"Oh no. I should probably check on him. I hope he didn't do anything stupid."

"Well, it has been what . . . three or four months? He's about due for a new girlfriend." Dakota smirks.

Maybe I'm turning into the new romantic of the family, but I really thought he and Taryn were a cute couple.

Reagan nudges my foot. "I want more details on you and Heath. So, he met the whole family?"

"Technically, yes. But it wasn't really like that. He was there as Adam's guest, not mine. Plus, with everything else going on, I don't think my parents even realized he snuck into my room at night."

"Ooooh. A sleepover! Fun." Dakota's eyes lit up from across the room. "Did you two finally . . ." She waggles her eyebrows.

A slow blush creeps up my face and I glance from friend to friend.

"Awww," Reagan says and tilts her head with a dreamy look on her face. Okay, maybe she's the romantic.

Dakota joins us in the living room. "You're totally gone for him."

There's little point in denying it. "Totally." I bury my head in my hands. "He's just so . . . perfect."

Dakota's eyebrows jump.

"Okay fine, not perfect, but the way I feel when we're together—*that's* perfect. Don't worry. Adam's already given me the 'Heath doesn't do relationships' talk."

"That was before you," Reagan insists.

I look to Dakota. I know she won't bullshit me. She shrugs. "If you'd asked me before you, I would have laughed in your face. Now, I'm not sure. Only one way to find out."

"You think I should tell him?" I squeak.

"Why is that so crazy?" Reagan laughs.

"I don't want to ruin what we have. What if it's too soon?"

"You'd be okay continuing to hook up even if you knew that's all it was to him? That he didn't feel the same way?"

A heavy pit settles in my stomach. "No, probably not, but things are great. I don't want to ruin it."

Dakota snorts. "Isn't love supposed to make everything better?"

"Yeah, yeah." I lean back and wave a hand of indifference.

"Well, I think you should tell him and soon." Reagan stands. "Do I look okay?"

I nod. Even if I couldn't see her, I'd know she does. Reagan always looks beautiful. "Date?"

"Yeah, a guy from my speech class. We're going to dinner." Her dimples pop out.

"You look gorgeous, as usual, babe," Dakota tells her. "Condoms in the purse? Phone charged in case you need to make a getaway?"

Reagan rolls her eyes. "I'm all set." Her phone buzzes. "He's here. Bye!"

Dakota and I watch her go and then I let out a sigh and lay my head on her shoulder.

"Wanna watch a movie or are you heading over to Heath's?" she asks.

"Nope, he has team stuff this evening. They're working out or watching film or something. I'm all yours."

The next day I corner Adam outside of his last morning class. He gives me a half-hearted smile that tells me everything I need to know about how he's doing.

"What are you doing here?" he asks as he wraps me into a one-armed hug.

"You didn't respond to my texts." I extend both arms around his middle and squeeze tightly.

"Sorry." He doesn't bother offering an excuse.

"It's okay." We walk down the sidewalk slowly. "Have you talked to Mom or Dad since you got back?"

"Not yet. Mom called while I was in class."

It's a weird switch of roles for us with me worrying about him, but I want to be there for him the same way he's always been for me. I nudge him. "It's going to be okay. I know it won't be the same, but they'll still be here for us. Plus, you've got me."

He grins.

"Anyway, the real reason I came to find you was to see what you were doing tonight. We need a night out. A fun night with all our friends to let loose and forget about parent drama."

"I don't know. Maybe. Let me see what's going on tonight. It is a Monday night after all."

"Monday is a perfectly good day to drink. Live a little, bro."

"Bro?" He hitches the backpack higher on his shoulder. "You sound like Heath."

We get to his car and he quirks a brow as I open the passenger side door.

"I mean, since you're going home anyway, can you give me a ride?"

He shakes his head. "Get in."

At the apartment, I walk back toward Heath's room. He's sitting at his desk in front of his laptop.

"Hey," I say cheerily as I enter.

One side of his mouth pulls up. "Hey. Did I forget we were hanging out?"

"Nope, thought I'd surprise you. I didn't hear back from you last night after your hockey stuff."

"Yeah, sorry, I crashed."

I go to him and he swivels to make room for me on his lap. "Let's go out tonight."

"It's Monday."

"Why does everyone keep using that as an excuse?"

He chuckles softly.

I take a deep breath. The girls are right. I need to make sure we're on the same page. "Also, I have something I want to talk to you about later."

He stiffens under me. Okay, that was probably not the smoothest. "Don't worry, it's nothing too crazy. A proposition if you will."

God, now he probably thinks I want to chain him to the bed and peg him.

His phone pings on his desk, Maverick's name flashes on the screen with a text. "All right, sure. I'll text you later. I've gotta check on Maverick. He didn't make conditioning this morning. He's got the flu or something. He hasn't been by all day."

I stand to let him up. "Well, then he really must be sick."

He takes a step toward the door and then backtracks and brushes his lips against mine before hurrying out to go check on Maverick.

THIRTY-FOUR

Heath

"Mav? Buddy, where are you?" I call as I enter his apartment. He's got a one-bedroom ground level unit. On a normal day it's already darker than ours upstairs, but today all the lights are off, the TV too, so it's like a cave.

The place is awesome. Nice leather furniture, a huge TV that takes up the better part of one wall, he's even got throw pillows. Why he always wants to hang at our place is beyond me.

Charli barks and I follow the sound to the bedroom where my buddy is on his back with the comforter and blanket thrown off the bed and an arm over his eyes. Charli lies at the end of the mattress near his feet.

"You don't look so good." I step closer and then back. "Or smell so good."

"I think I threw up a kidney." His voice is raspy and pained.

"What can I do? Do you need water? Soup? I can make a call about getting you a new kidney."

A knock at the door has me looking back through the living room to the front door. "Are you expecting someone else?"

"It's food. Can you grab it?"

I cross through the apartment and open the door, taking a deep breath of clean, uncontaminated air. After thanking the delivery guy, I take the bag of food back to the sick room.

"Here ya go."

"Not for me." He heaves. "Oh, just the smell makes me want to hurl again. It's for you, so you'll stay with me."

"You didn't need to bribe me."

"Look, I know I'm your favorite person, but eventually your stomach would have convinced you to leave me."

I chuckle and take the bag back out to the kitchen. "There is a lot of food in here."

"You're a hungry bitch."

He's in the same position, but Charli has moved up to his hip and Maverick strokes her with the hand closest.

"What do you need?"

"I just want to lie here until the room stops moving. Tell me a story."

I take a seat on the floor near the door and lean my back up against the wall. I like the dude, but he smells, and I don't want whatever he has. "A story?"

"Anything to distract me." He peeks out from under his arm and then reaches over to his nightstand and tosses me his Shakespeare textbook. "Read to me. Do the funny voices."

"I thought you were done with Shakespeare."

"I am. We're on Shelley now, but that book is all the way in my backpack." I hesitate.

"Come on. Pleeeease? I dig the rhyming shit; it's beautiful."

"All right, all right." I open the book and start.

Maverick falls asleep about five minutes in, which is good because reading sappy words about love is the last thing I want to be doing. I go out to the living room and eat, feed Charli, and then take her out for a quick walk.

Back inside, I take my spot in his room sitting on the floor and I must pass out because the next thing I know, Charli is licking my face, and Maverick is standing in front of me with a grin.

"Feeling better?" I ask, nudging Charli away and wiping a hand across my slobbery cheek.

"I think so. I'm gonna try to eat."

I follow him out to the kitchen, and he heats up some of the Chinese he ordered. We sit on stools at the counter. The smell of food has me heating up a plate too a few minutes later. Ginny texted while I was asleep to let me know the plans for tonight, meeting up at The Hideout with our friends.

I'm real nervous about whatever she wants to talk to me about, but I do my best to push it out of my mind for now.

Mav finishes about half the food on his plate and then pats his stomach. "Thanks for hanging."

"Yeah, of course."

"You're not as hot as Nanny Laura, but it did the trick."

"Nanny Laura?"

"She was my favorite. Had these gigantic boobs that were like pillows." He nuzzles his head to the side like he's remembering it. "She'd sing to me when I was sick or when I was upset—which was a lot because Dad was always flaking on shit. I think I got more hugs from her in the year or so that she was my nanny than I have from him my entire life. Parents are bullshit."

I'm quiet. Don't really know what to say. For all the shitty things that happened growing up, physical contact was never in short supply. Sometimes my mom clung to me all day as if I was the only thing keeping her connected to the planet.

My stomach twists and I push away my plate.

"Sorry, man, didn't mean to go dark."

"Nah, it's fine. I don't feel so well." I stand and I break out in a cool sweat, my mouth waters.

"Ah shit," Mav says right before I take off in a dead run toward the bathroom.

●

After puking for the better part of three hours, I join Maverick in the living room. I stripped down to my boxers—everything else is wet from sweat.

"God, you weren't kidding. All my organs feel like they've shifted. Is that a thing?"

"No clue." He nods with his head toward the kitchen. "Ginny brought soup and Jell-O."

"Ginny was here?"

"Your phone was going off, so I texted her."

I find my phone on the counter and see that she did text several times about tonight and then to tell me to feel better and let her know if I need anything.

"She wanted me to tell you that she'd be by later to check in." He shakes his head. "That Ginny, she's a peach."

"She's the best," I say because even though I'm a little freaked out, I know it's true.

I text her back to thank her for the food and tell her not to bother coming again until we're on the mend. The last thing she needs is to catch whatever this is. I feel like I've been run over by a bus. I take a seat in the recliner. The cool leather feels nice against my skin. I'm pretty sure I have a fever.

"I need a Ginny." Maverick sighs and Charli whines.

"I think Charli would take issue with getting kicked out of your bed for a chick."

We spend the late afternoon and evening watching TV. Just when I think things are taking a turn for the better, one of us gets sick again. We reek. The whole apartment probably does, but I've lost the ability to smell it.

Ginny continues to text, but I don't respond. Nobody needs to be around this. I miss her though. Weird to admit to myself how much I've gotten used to having her around. That even though I'm freaked about her loving me, I still want her.

I've had girls that I hung out with, not exactly friends but ones that were part of my circle of friends, and girls I've hooked up with for a month or two, but I've never had one that ticks both those boxes. I'm delirious enough I think about calling her and telling her that, but something tells me I'd fumble up the message. *Thanks for letting me do you, and also for being cool enough I want to be with you even when we're not naked. Let's keep things like they are. Cool?*

Shakespeare, I am not.

As I lie there, alternating sweating and then shivering, I think about her and what I'm going to say when she tells me she loves me. That's what she wants to talk to me about, right? Is she expecting me to say it back? And if I don't, what does it really change? Nothing? Everything?

My mom was quick to tell me she loved me, still is. And, yeah, I believe she means it, and even meant it then when she barely knew what day of the week it was, but it always felt like the words *I love you* came as a substitute for *I'm going to do right by you.*

Things with Ginny are amazing, and I don't want this pure and good thing we have to become an excuse to hurt one another when we could do better.

Fuck, I don't even know if I'm making sense. My head is fuzzy and my stomach aches.

I wake up sometime later that night, stuck to the recliner. Mav must have thrown a blanket over me and gone to bed because he's not here and I'm tucked in like a child.

The next forty-eight hours is much the same. I wake up Thursday morning finally feeling like I might be able to get up, but my entire body hurts. I'm laying here staring up at the ceiling when I notice Ginny on the couch.

"You're alive."

"Barely."

She sits up. "I tried to text a few times to check on you."

"My phone died. I wasn't in much shape to talk anyway."

"Do you want me to stay with you? I brought some more soup and Jell-O. It's in the kitchen." She jabs a thumb in that direction. "Do you want some?"

"You didn't need to do that. I'm fine. I just want to lie here for a minute before I go to practice."

"You're going to practice? Can't you take another day off?"

"Could, but I've played in worse shape. I'll be fine." We've got Vermont this weekend and I don't want to miss it.

She smiles and it hits me in the gut. Either that or I'm gonna be sick again.

"Okay, well, I'm going back to my dorm before class. Call me later?"

She looks uncertain and I hate that. Hate it but can't seem to bring myself to reassure her. I also don't want to get much closer in case I'm still contagious.

"Yeah, of course, I'll call you later tonight. I have a feeling after practice I'm going to need a nap."

"Okay." She steps back and gives me one of those sweet, Ginny smiles. "Feel better."

DECEMBER

THIRTY-FIVE

Ginny

I'm sitting at the bar at The Hideout waiting for my friends and brother. Reagan's the first to show.

"Hey." I stand to hug her. "Where's Dakota?"

"She wasn't done studying for her biology test. She said to tell you she was sorry and that she'd make it up to you."

"Well, boo. I was hoping she'd come. Adam's running late and the rest of the guys didn't feel like going out. It feels like everyone is bailing." Monday night was a bust after Maverick and Heath got sick, but I was hoping tonight we could all finally hang out.

"Actually, I'm glad I have you alone. I need to talk to you."

"Okay." We sit and when the bartender comes over, she orders two shots of RumChata.

"You're making me nervous, Rea."

The shots come and she downs one without waiting for me.

I start to chuckle. "Woah, there, it can't be that—"

"I like your brother."

Her words hit me slowly, but she doesn't give me time to respond anyway.

"I'm sorry I lied, but we'd just met, and I didn't want you to think I was some weirdo or that I was pretending to be your friend because of Adam."

His name makes it all finally click.

"Your crush, the hockey player, is my brother?"

"Yes, and I'm going to tell him tonight, but I wanted to tell you first." She eyes the second shot. "Do you need that or do I?"

"I'm not upset. Adam would be lucky to have someone like you, but you can't tell him tonight."

"Why not?" Her brown eyes crinkle at the corners as she draws her eyebrows together.

"Because I invited Taryn and she just walked in. I'm sorry. I didn't know." As I stand to greet my brother's girlfriend, I see Reagan down the last shot.

"Hey," Taryn says tentatively.

"Hi, Taryn," I say and we hug. "Thanks for coming."

She laughs lightly. "You didn't leave me much choice. You said it was life or death."

"Maybe that was a little dramatic, but it is important." I glance to either side of me, but there's nowhere for her to sit.

Reagan hops out of her seat. "Here, you can have mine. I'm going to . . . go. I just realized I need to be somewhere."

"Are you sure?" I ask. I feel awful, not that I could have predicted this.

"I'll call you later."

Taryn takes a seat and I blow out a long breath. Best to just dive right in. "Whatever my brother did or said . . . he's an idiot. He's going through some things right now, so he's not to be trusted."

Her face twists into a surprised expression. "You mean your parents separating?"

"He told you?"

"Yeah, of course. He's really torn up about it."

"Exactly. Don't let him push you away because of it. I think he just needs some time."

She smiles sweetly. "I agree, but that's not why we broke up."

"It's not?"

"No." She shakes her head. "It probably was the catalyst, but it wasn't the reason."

Well, shit. I guess this is what I get for meddling. "Oh." I slump in my chair. "You're sure? You two seemed great together."

"We are. Your brother is fantastic, and I really like him, but I'm transferring at semester and neither of us really wanted to try to manage a long-distance thing."

"Oh." Well, shit. "I didn't know."

"I just decided before Thanksgiving break. I got into a really competitive design program at my dream college." Her face lights up.

"Wow, well, congratulations."

"Thank you."

For the next half hour, I listen as she tells me about her plans and the program at her new school. The more we talk, the more I like her and the sadder I am that she's leaving. We part with a hug and a promise to keep in touch. I don't know if we actually will, but it's more than I can say for my relationships with most of Adam's ex-girlfriends.

I've got a bunch of texts from Adam apologizing for not being able to make it. This night is a giant failure.

I call Heath on my way to his apartment, but he doesn't answer. Since he got sick, he's been keeping me away for fear I'd catch it, but right now, I'm willing to risk it to lay in his arms.

Noise filters out, laughter and loud voices, as I head up the stairs to their door. I knock twice before walking in. Rhett, Maverick, and Heath are in the living room. All eyes are on the TV and whatever video game they're playing. Beer cans line the coffee table. It's far from the scene I was expecting.

When they finally notice me, Maverick and Rhett's glassy stares and big smiles give me some idea of just how drunk they are. Heath doesn't look drunk, but I'm still a little irritated that they're all hanging out together when I tried to plan a night out with all of us.

"Genevieve!" Maverick calls. He's got a bottle in one hand and a controller in the other. "Come be on my team. They're kicking my ass."

Rhett puts his controller down and runs a hand through his dirty blond hair. "You can take my place. I'm out, boys. I need to call Carrie." He stands and heads to his room, leaving me with Heath and Maverick.

"Need another?" Mav stands, sways, and then walks to the kitchen. He grabs a beer and holds it up.

"No, thanks," Heath says. He motions me over to him and holds his arms out.

I go to him and climb into his lap. As he wraps his arms around me, I snuggle in close and breathe him in.

"Hey," I whisper into his jaw. He's unshaven and I love the way his scruff feels against my smooth skin. "Feeling better?"

"Mhmm." He places a thumb under my chin and lifts my mouth to his and places a quick kiss on my lips. I melt into him. "I only had two beers and look at me, I'm a lightweight now. Sorry that we didn't make it out. How was it?"

"A total bust. You didn't miss anything."

"You two wanna cuddle?" Maverick asks. "Make a little Mav sandwich?"

"No chance," Heath says and stands, holding me in his arms. He's unsteady on his feet, but somehow he carries me without falling or dropping me.

"Night, Mav," I call over Heath's shoulder.

He kicks the door closed and deposits me on his bed and lies on top of me, burying his head in my neck. He kisses the spot. "You smell nice."

"You feel nice," I say, lifting my hips into the hard bulge in his pants.

I slip my hands under his T-shirt and up over his pecs. He leans up enough for me to pull the material all the way over his head. I love Heath's body. Every muscle and every ridge. The light smattering of hair covering his chest and the defined abs and V that disappears into his jeans.

A shiver of pleasure shoots through me as he kisses my neck and collarbone, first on one side and then the other.

I unbutton his jeans and slide the zipper down. As my palm meets skin, I chuckle.

"Had to freeball it," he says and leans up to give me a sheepish grin. "Haven't done laundry since I got back."

I free his cock from his pants. "Convenient."

He hisses and then moans as I slide my hand down his length. "I may never wear boxers again. Fuck. I missed you."

My insides are total mush when he voices his feelings. Even if I am touching his dick while he's saying it.

"It's only been a few days."

"And your point is?" he asks, eyes closed and hips bucking into my palm.

I pause and his eyes open and lock onto mine. It's an opening to tell him how I feel, but instead of taking it, I slide down the bed and wrap my lips around the head of his cock.

Afterward, we're lying on the bed curled up together. Heath's eyelids keep shutting even as he tells me he's not tired.

"Let me get you some water and Tylenol." I start to stand, but he captures my hand and tugs me back down.

"No. I don't need you to do that. People are always trying to take care of me. I just want you to lay here with me."

"You are very stubborn."

His mouth pulls up into a smile, eyes still closed.

"You know, it's okay to let people do nice things for you. It doesn't mean you're incapable. That's how relationships work." I bite at the corner of my lip. "Speaking of, I've been trying to talk to you since we got back from break, but with everything that's happened, we haven't had a chance. Maybe tomorrow we can hang out, just the two of us?"

His lids flutter open and those dark blue eyes focus on me. "It's okay, Ginny, I already know. I overheard you talking to Adam."

"You know what?"

"At your parents' house. I was in your room that morning before we left, and I overheard you tell Adam that you . . . how you feel about me."

"Oh." *Crap.* Embarrassed, stilted laughter slips out and I sit up. "Why didn't you say anything before?"

"I didn't know what to say." His lips turn down at the corners and then his tongue darts out to wet them. "Ginny . . . I like you a lot."

All the blood drains from my face. The way he says it and his expression—it's excruciating. *Like.* He didn't tell me because he doesn't feel the same.

I'm absolutely horrified, and fleeing is the first thing that comes to mind. Get out of here before I start crying.

"I forgot how honest you are when you've been drinking." I try to laugh it off, but tears sting my eyes. I stand and look for my clothes. "I'm going. Let's talk tomorrow when you're sober."

"Please don't go. This is why I didn't bring it up before. I didn't want you to say it and be hurt if I didn't say it back. What we have is great and it's just a bullshit word." He runs a hand through his hair, making the dark strands stand up, then the other hand joins it. I love his hair. It's always such a beautiful mess. Even now when he's breaking my heart.

"Love is a bullshit word?" I shake my head in disbelief. "This is why I told Adam and not you. I thought it might be too soon and I didn't want to pressure you or make things weird. I had no intention of telling you that I love you." I swallow. I can't describe how much I hate that the first time I utter those three words to him, it's like this. I feel completely shattered that I've been his unknowing pity case while he's been secretly trying to figure out how to let me down easy.

"No, that's not what I'm saying. It isn't that you . . ." He pauses. "Wait, you weren't? But you said that you wanted to talk. I just assumed that's what it was about. I've been worrying about it all week."

"Oh my god." I glance to the ceiling and try to calm the anger rising. When I look back to him, I can no longer keep my eyes from welling. Hot, angry tears.

"Fuck, that came out wrong," he says.

"I was going to ask you to be my boyfriend, you big jerk."

His brows draw together. "Oh."

"But it's really nice to know you've been stressing about me using the L-word, heaven forbid. What an awful thing for you to cope with."

Anger. Yes, I need more anger to keep from feeling the sadness.

He gets to his feet. His jeans are on but unbuttoned and they slide down on his hips as he starts toward me. "Fuck, Ginny. I thought I already was your boyfriend."

"Yeah, well, we've never talked about it. Hence, *the talk.*"

"I'm sorry."

"For what? Not loving me or thinking the whole concept of it is ludicrous?" My voice cracks.

He groans and he runs those big hands through his hair again while he struggles to find the right words. But it's too late. What could he possibly say now? Any illusion I had that he might feel the same way, today or someday in the future, is now gone. Dating a guy who isn't ready for a serious commitment is one thing, but once you tell them you love them (even by accident), there's no going back and pretending it's just a casual fling.

"This isn't going to work."

"Don't say that. Forget everything I said in the past five minutes. Start over. Ask me to be your boyfriend." He closes the distance between us and frames my face with his hands. "Ask me, Genevieve," he pleads.

He makes a strangled sound deep in his throat as I pull away and finish getting dressed, tossing the T-shirt of his I was wearing on the bed, yanking on my own clothes, and slipping into my shoes. I think he might say something else to try to stop me, but he doesn't. He just watches me prepare to leave, looking helpless. Before I go, I have to say it at least once—out loud and to him, if only for myself.

"I love you, Heath." He flinches. "I'm sorry if that's too much for you to deal with, but I do, and I don't want to just forget it."

THIRTY-SIX

Heath

"I haven't been this hungover in years." Mav drops on the couch and chugs half the Gatorade bottle in his hand with one long drink. "Getting drunk after being sick and hardly eating all week, I've basically got the tolerance of a high school chick."

I'm silent and he nudges my foot on the coffee table. "What's up with you? You've been quiet all morning."

"I'm fine."

"Girl fine or really fine?"

"I said I was fine."

His brows lift and he smiles, but he drops it. He finishes off his drink and stands. "Ready to go to campus? I'm starving."

"Let's go out for breakfast today instead of the dining hall."

"Yeah, that sounds rad. I want pancakes. Text Ginny and we can swing by and pick her up."

"She doesn't want to come."

"What? Of course she does. I'll text her."

"No, don't. We're not . . . she's . . ." Jesus, I can't even finish a sentence that puts an end to whatever we were.

Maverick stops and the hand holding his phone falls to his side. "What the fuck did you do, Payne?"

I'd like to resent his automatic assumption that I'm at fault, but of course I am. I let out a giant sigh. "I'll tell you over pancakes."

He doesn't press me to talk until we've both got a heaping stack of pancakes on our plates. Only then does he ask what happened. I fill him in on last night, unable to eat more than a bite or two.

"That's cold."

"What was I supposed to say?"

"I'm not sure." He shrugs and takes a large bite of his food. He looks thoughtful as he chews and then swallows. "You really think love is bullshit?"

"Don't you?" If anyone would understand, I figured it'd be Maverick. His childhood was as fucked up as mine, just in a totally different way.

"No, man. Love is beautiful."

"How the fuck would you know?" Damn, I need a muzzle lately. "Sorry, that came out wrong, but you know what I mean. Who's ever said it to you and not screwed you over?"

"Well, you've never said it, but you love me and you've never screwed me over."

"That's not the same."

"Isn't it?"

"Not unless you're over there thinking about me naked."

His lips part and pull into a smile. "Relax, you're not nearly kinky enough for me."

"But seriously, man. You think there's someone out there that's capable of speaking the words to you and really meaning it? No strings, no ulterior motives, two people who care deeply and want to support one another?"

"Isn't that basically what you and Ginny had before you blew it up?" He sets an elbow on the table and waves his fork around. "I'm not much for trying to live up to other people's expectations. I know what it means to me and yeah." He shrugs. "At least I hope so. Otherwise, it's going to be me and you heading to the Early Bird special together. The only question you need to ask yourself is, do you believe Ginny means it?"

"Yeah, I think she does. She's never given me any reason to doubt her." I toss my napkin on the table. "I'm not hungry."

He takes my plate and I watch as he inhales my food and then sits back with a contented sigh.

"I don't know what to do. I want to be with her, but I can't tell her I . . . you know, when the words make me want to throw myself off a cliff."

"But you do?"

"If I didn't hate the word and everything in my past associated with it? Yeah, that's probably how I'd define it."

"Big gesture. Huge. I'm talking Kanye-antics."

"I think I'll just try to talk to her first."

"Talking got you into this mess," he points out.

When we get to campus, Maverick starts toward class. I'm going by the dorm first to see if I can find Ginny. Something tells me she didn't show up at the dining hall this morning either.

"Good luck, buddy. Try not to use the word like."

I flip him off. He turns and I call after him. "Hey, Mav."

My buddy glances over his shoulder.

"You can always count me in for the Early Bird special. No matter what."

I move at a clip across campus and jog up the stairs to the second floor. I knock on the door and wait. No answer. Knock again.

"Ginny? Are you there? It's Heath. Open up if you're there. Please." It's quiet on the other side and I rest my head against the door. "I'm so sorry."

A few people pass by in the hall and give me weird looks, and the door continues to mock me by staying shut. I blow out a breath, the magnitude of how badly I screwed this up makes my whole body ache something fierce.

I'm caught off guard when the door finally opens, and I stumble forward. My heart soars and then plummets when it's Ava's face that appears and not Ginny's.

"She's not here," Ginny's shy roommate says, her cheeks turning pink.

"Right, okay, could you give her a message?"

She nods, prompting me. Shit, what's the message? I'm sorry that I'm a giant prick doesn't really tell her anything she didn't already know, even if it's accurate.

"Just ask her to call me." I step back and then add, "Please?"

THIRTY-SEVEN

Ginny

"Thank you for doing this one with me," I say to Dakota as the group of local elementary students line up for a tour of the Hall of Fame. It's my first day back working after being locked in the hype room. I'm already a mess from last night and the idea of being in there by myself again is scary.

"Of course. These guys might look little but trust me, it's going to take two of us plus their teacher to keep them in line." She gives me a reassuring smile and steps forward and introduces herself.

I fall back and let her do the majority of the talking. I'm not feeling particularly chatty, but I answer questions and help keep the kids from wandering off. It's a totally different experience than the recruits get, less focused and more about letting the kids walk around awestruck by catching glimpses of college athletes working out or walking around campus. They look up to them like celebrities and it's pretty heartwarming. But since it's less intense than our recruit tours, I'm able to fade into the background, and today I'm extremely thankful for that.

When we walk into the hype room, Dakota goes first, the kids follow, and I bring up the end of the line. She glances to me as I enter. I nod to let her know I'm okay. Maybe the anxiousness I thought I'd feel coming in here again is dulled by the deep aching pain I've had since I walked out of Heath's apartment last night, but I'm able to stand and watch the video without panicking. It's a generic video, encompassing all sports, but since hockey is such a big deal at Valley, there are still lots of times that Heath's face splashes on the screen. Each and every time it feels like someone's pouring alcohol into an open wound.

I'm sad and mad, flipping between the two so frequently even I don't know which one is the prominent emotion. Does he really think we can keep dating like nothing happened? Even if I could get over the idea that he doesn't feel the same, and likely never will, I'd be a wreck waiting for the day he freaked out again or decided to move on. There's really only two ways a relationship can go, and he took one of those options away. When you know how something is going to end, it's harder to enjoy the moment.

As the video stops on the final frame, a drone shot overhead of campus, the kids' faces are lit up with joy and wonder. I step to the door so I can be the first out.

Dakota and I take them to the football field and let them loose to run around in the big, open space.

"How was it?" she asks as we stand on the fifty-yard line.

"I don't know if I'll ever feel the same about that room, but it was okay."

"Listen, I've got it from here. Take off, go see Heath, or go lay in bed and cry . . . whatever you need to do."

"You're sure?"

"Definitely. Five more minutes of them sprinting up and down the field and I can hand them back to their teacher."

I hug her. "Thank you."

I take off for my dorm with the intent of trying to nap. Needless to say, I spent last night tossing and turning, so I'm not only emotionally exhausted, but physically too. However, as soon as I fall into my bed and pull up the covers, I get a 911 text from Reagan.

I get back up and trudge across campus. I find her in the back of the theater in their dressing room. Her hair is in curlers and she's wearing her green silky robe.

"Hey, what's going on?"

"Ms. Morris fell and broke her wrist. She's out and now I don't have anyone to do my makeup. Can you help? We have our dress rehearsal in thirty minutes."

I'd gotten the first part from her text message and had come prepared to do her makeup, but dress rehearsal? The look on her face is pleading, though, so I suck it up. "I've never done stage makeup like that, but I can try."

"Thank you!"

The dressing room in the theater is a large open room with a long counter that extends on two walls with lighted mirrors. Stools are around the room in disarray. Some tucked under the counter, others have clothes and makeup bags on them, and the rest are occupied by girls as they get ready.

Reagan sits; her cosmetics litter the space in front of her. "So, what happened with Heath? Dakota heard from Rhett that Heath was not looking great at their morning skate."

I set down my backpack and add my makeup to the counter. "It was a very long night after you left."

I fill her in while I add primer to her face.

"All of this happened last night? And you haven't heard from him since?"

"Ava said he came by the dorm looking for me."

She smiles and tries to shoo me off. "Go. I can do my own face."

"No way. I've got you. Let's just talk about something else."

"Okay. Like what?"

"Like how nervous I am right now."

"What? Why? You've done my makeup lots of times. It always looks great."

"But the lights and the people . . ." My hands tremble. "I'm nervous and I'm not even the one who has to go out there."

Her sweet laughter relaxes me. "It's only a dress rehearsal."

As I work, she studies the script in front of her. I've heard her running lines with Dakota enough that I know she's already got it memorized, but I decide it's best not to mess with whatever process she has.

When she finally looks up, I'm ready to add another coat of mascara.

"Oh, wow, Ginny."

"Is it too much?"

"It's amazing." She turns her face to look at each side more closely. "You're a miracle worker."

"I don't know about that but thank you." Mascara wand in hand, I tell her, "Look down."

⬤

Instead of heading back to my dorm or going to class, I stay for the rehearsal. The play is a modern take on *A Christmas Carol*, and Reagan plays the Ghost of Christmas Present. The green gown she wears could have been made specifically with her in mind. She looks exquisite. That's my first thought, but the longer she's on the stage, the more I fall into her character.

I smile as the clock strikes midnight, she bows her head and slowly walks backward until she disappears behind the curtain.

After the rehearsal, she comes down off the front of the stage and finds me in the third row.

"What did you think?"

I pull her into a tight hug. "You are so talented, Reagan." I let her go to look her in the eye, so she knows how much I mean it, and then I hug her again.

A woman who'd been sitting in the row ahead of me turns and walks toward us. Her blonde hair is pulled up into a tight bun and she wears red-framed glasses that she takes off when she reaches us. She has an air of sophistication and also looks like she might cut a bitch if necessary. "Really well done, Reagan. You found the lighting up there really well." She steps closer and inspects my friend's face. "Your makeup . . ." She makes a little humming noise in her throat. "Who did you use?"

"Oh, uh, I did it. I'm sorry if it isn't—"

"It looks amazing," she assures me. She tips her head to Reagan. "It needs to be a little darker to read at the back of the house, but it suits you. Great job today. See you tomorrow."

"Thank you, Dr. Rossen."

When she's gone, Reagan grabs my hand and squeals. "You did it."

"That woman is scary. Who is she?"

"She's the director."

"Well, she is not someone I want to cross."

"She's made more than one person cry since she took over last year. Come on, let me buy you coffee as a thank you."

We stay on campus and go to University Hall. It's busy with a late afternoon rush, but we order from the café and find a small table near the door.

"I'm so relieved that's over."

"Don't you have two real shows this weekend?"

"Yes, but the rehearsal is the only time I really get nervous. It's harder to be on when you're staring out into an empty theater."

"I so don't get that."

She smiles. "Thank you again. You might have been fleeing the Heath situation, but it benefited me greatly."

"Anytime." I take a sip of my coffee. "So, are we going to talk about that thing you said last night?"

She looks down to the table. "I was hoping we could pretend I never said a peep."

"Like you've been trying to pretend you don't have a thing for my brother all semester?"

"Longer than that," she mumbles.

I'm grinning ear to ear when she finally looks up at me. "I think you should go for it. He and Taryn are done for good. She's transferring at the end of the semester. Now's your shot."

"I don't know. Now that you and I are so close, wouldn't it be weird?"

I consider it for a few moments. "No, I don't think so. Not unless we make it weird."

"It's probably not even worth worrying about. Honestly, he hasn't noticed me in the three years we've known each other. I don't think he sees me like that."

"Only one way to find out."

"Listen to you, dishing out advice while you're hiding from your boyfriend."

"I'm not hiding . . . I'm giving us some time to breathe."

"And?"

"I prefer breathing his air."

●

I turn my phone on silent, stuff it in a desk drawer, and bury myself in schoolwork all afternoon. I don't allow myself to think about anything else. That is until a pounding on my door breaks my concentration. My heart is in my throat waiting for Heath's voice on the other side, but it's Adam that calls, "Ginny, open up."

I scramble off my bed and fling the door open. "Hey, what are you doing here?"

"I've been calling you all day."

"Oh, uh, I turned my phone on silent while I caught up on schoolwork. What's up?"

"I heard about last night."

"Oh, that."

"Yeah, oh that." He moves my books out of the way and sits on my bed. "I'm sure it's payback for meddling in your relationship with Heath, but I still can't believe you went to so much trouble to get Taryn and me back together."

Oooooh, right. *That.*

I sit and pull my pillow into my lap. "I know I overstepped. I thought you were having a reaction to Mom and Dad and I wanted to help. You've always looked out for me and I wanted to do the same for once."

"Taryn said as much."

"Are you mad?"

"No, I get it."

"I'm sorry about you and Taryn."

"Yeah, me too."

"On the plus side, I know lots of girls who will be thrilled you're single again." One in particular, but that's not my secret to tell.

His chest lifts and falls with a quiet chuckle. "I think I'm going to try being single for a change. With everything going on, I think the universe might be sending me a sign."

"Single, huh? I can't picture it."

"Me neither." He leans so his back rests against the concrete wall.

"I don't think I'm doing as well with Mom and Dad as I thought either. I came back and threw myself into making plans with our friends because I wanted so badly to pretend everything was normal. But it's not. I think it's going to be weird for a while no matter what. Plus, uh, Heath and I are . . . I don't even know."

"Yeah, that's actually why I'm here, but I figured that wouldn't get me in the door."

"You know?"

"One look at Heath this morning and I think we all knew something was up. Wanna tell me what happened?"

"The short version? He overheard me telling you that I loved him, freaked out, told me love was bullshit, and I ran."

"Why did you run? That's not like you."

"Because I was embarrassed. Do you know what it's like to tell someone you love them and have them not return the sentiment?"

"No." He shakes his head. "But I'm sure I've had a lot of people say it and not mean it. It's a risk either way."

"You know, I never thought about it before, but you're like the bravest person I know. You jump from girlfriend to girlfriend—"

He groans.

"Let me finish." I punch his leg. "You keep putting yourself out there no matter how many times it doesn't work. Maybe it's a *little* excessive, but definitely brave."

He rubs at the back of his neck. "Well, I guess that's one way to look at it."

We fall silent and I lean my head on his shoulder. The alarm on his phone sounds and I sit straight.

"I gotta go," he says. "Are you coming to the game?"

"I'm not sure. Probably."

"It's funny how even when you're pissed, you can't help but show up to support him."

"It's *you* I'm supporting."

"Mhmmm."

I roll my eyes.

"Are you gonna be okay?" He stops at the door and regards me seriously.

"Yeah, I will." I blow out a breath. "I was perfectly happy with our fun, college fling until he found out I love him. Freaking love."

He scrunches up his face. "And on that note, I'm out." He opens the door and winks back at me. "Later, G."

THIRTY-EIGHT

Heath

W hen we take the ice, I automatically look for Ginny in her usual seat. She's not there and the knife in my gut twists.

Vermont is tough. They've got a freshman, Lex Vonne, who's almost as fast as I am, and their defense is big and mean.

"I played against Vonne in high school," Adam says. "He was just a skinny kid who could barely stay upright back then."

We watched tape last weekend on Vermont and Jordan and Adam filled us in as best they could. All three of them are from Arizona, and Jordan went to high school with Vonne, playing together all four years. No one can believe the progress he's made. It seems the New England air agrees with him because every game he just gets better.

"Yeah, well, looks like he's improved. A lot."

"No shit." Adam laughs as we watch him warm up, looking steady and sharp.

The game matches our pace, a brutal intensity that's exactly what I need tonight. Neither team scores in the first period. I've skated nearly half of those twenty minutes and I'm sucking air, but the burn of my lungs is nothing compared to the feeling I get when I glance at Ginny's empty seat.

Coach gives us his usual quick and straightforward pep talk between periods. He's not big on grand speeches, but his words are always effective.

Vermont's goalie is one of the best in the country, not that we're making it hard on him. We're losing the puck before we can even do anything with it. I get a pass from Maverick and use some of my aggression on a mean slapshot. It's wide and I swear I feel him grin underneath that fucking mask.

The second line comes in and I get a breather and a moment to collect myself.

"You good?" Mav asks.

"Good enough to finish this," I grunt out. And then go find Ginny.

"Let's go then."

When we jump the boards it's another minute of skating my ass off before Vermont scores and the Valley crowd groans their disapproval.

We go into the third period down by one. Like some sort of masochist, I continue to glance to the spot Ginny's occupied at every home game. Every time I look is like another punch to the gut, but I can't stop myself.

"Payne!" Coach calls from the bench. "Are you standing still out there?"

I skate like the pain doesn't matter. I deke out a defenseman, pass to Jordan on the left side, and fly by two more players, just as he sends it back. I get a decent look at the net that's denied. At least this one requires the goalie to use a little of that all-star athleticism, but the end result is the same—with Valley losing. A shutout in front of our home crowd.

After our loss, no one feels like going out and the guys and I head back to the apartment.

I take a seat on the couch with my phone in hand. I haven't heard from Ginny and I don't think it's because her roommate didn't give her the message. I tap out a bunch of texts but don't send any of them.

Rauthruss is playing video games. "Wanna play?"

"Yeah." I lift my hand and he tosses me a controller.

We play in silence for a few minutes.

"Can, uh, I ask you a question?"

"Sure," he says, not looking away from the screen.

"You and Carrie. How'd that come about?"

"We went to high school together."

"Right, but I mean, how did you make it official?"

"She told me we were no longer seeing other people."

"And that was it?"

He pauses the game and looks to me. "I probably said something real eloquent like 'uhh okay.' She was popular and I wasn't. I'd have done anything she asked."

Adam's bedroom door opens, and he walks out and drops into the armchair and blows out a long, exaggerated breath.

Rauthruss looks to him. "Not going to Taryn's?"

Adam waves a hand. "Nah, that's over."

"Another one bites the dust?" Rauthruss jokes then looks to me. "You want advice on getting a girlfriend." He nods his head to Adam. "Scott's the one to ask."

"You want to ask Ginny to be your girlfriend?" Adam asks.

Yeah, this would be a lot less awkward if I weren't having this conversation with her brother. He hated the idea before I made her cry, so I doubt he's pumped now.

I tread carefully. "To be honest, I thought she already was, but I guess that's a thing people talk about first?"

Adam's face slowly transforms from a stony wall of indifference to amusement and he laughs. "Have you ever had a girlfriend, Payne?"

I clear my throat and wipe a hand over my brow. Jesus, it's hot in here. "Clearly not."

He studies me and lets out another one of his new broody sighs. "Ginny doesn't need a big gesture, just tell her how you feel. Well, no, actually first, you need to convince her to speak to you again."

"Yeah, thanks a lot. Good talk."

Mav walks through the door. "Honey, I'm home." He plops down and reads the room. "What's going on?"

"Heath is gonna ask Ginny to go steady." Rauthruss smirks.

"Fuck off," I tell him but smile. Dammit, I should have known better than to ask him. Nothing is ever taken seriously around here.

"I take it *talking* didn't go over so well?" Mav asks with a knowing smirk.

I flip him off. "Are you guys going to help me or what?"

Maverick claps his hands together. "Let's brainstorm on the whiteboard."

"We don't have a whiteboard," Adam points out.

Maverick shakes his head, smiling. "Real oversight, minion. Task one, find something to write down ideas."

Surprisingly, Adam does get up and appears to search for something to write on. Maverick goes to the fridge and grabs four beers and then hands them out.

Adam comes back with a scrap of paper and a pen. "All right, ideas to ask a girl out. I feel like I'm back in middle school."

"I would have guessed you started more pre-K age," Rauthruss says and twists the cap on his beer.

Adam flips him off and then looks to me, poised to write down our ideas.

"You're on board with this?" I ask him.

He shrugs. "If it's what she wants. Besides, it's going to be fun as hell to watch you try to pull this off."

Maverick takes the lead and I let him. For as much shit as he talks about his dad, I can see the family resemblance. When he sets his mind to it, he's a good leader.

An hour later, we've got a handful of ideas and they're all pretty awful. Rauthruss is the straightforward one—take her to dinner, buy her roses. Maverick is elaborate and has so many suggestions only about half are being written down. They range from renting out a movie theater to hiring a Mariachi band and everything else you can imagine in between. Adam has some good insight since he knows Ginny the best, but none of his suggestions feel right either.

I'm probably overthinking it. I don't know anything about love or being a good boyfriend, but I know Ginny and I know that I'm better when I'm with her.

"Well?" Rauthruss asks once we're out of new suggestions and beer.

"Maybe dinner?" It isn't the most creative, but a lot easier than renting out a movie theater. I have no idea how to pull off the latter and I feel like that kind of thing might take days or weeks, and I don't want to wait that long.

"Dinner?" Maverick's face twists up in clear disappointment. "Dinner is so . . . dinner. Unless . . ." He sits forward, elbows on knees. "You buy out the restaurant so it's just the two of you and then—"

I cut him off. "Let me stop you right there, buddy. 'Preciate your dedication, but I don't want it to feel like I'm being someone else for the night."

Some of my favorite memories with Ginny over the past semester have been hanging out with our friends or chilling just the two of us. None of that was elaborate or over the top, but maybe this is different? Maybe big and bold is what I need.

I scrub a hand down my face and then look to Adam. "Does anyone know her favorite song?"

"You're going with *that* one?" Rauthruss's eyebrows shoot up. "This I gotta see."

Maverick fist pumps. "Yeah, I love that one."

"Of course, you do. It was your idea."

THIRTY-NINE

Ginny

Dakota and Reagan sit on one end of my bed, their concerned faces staring back at me. Ava's gone for the weekend visiting Trent, and when I'd told my friends I was going back to my dorm alone after the game, they insisted on coming with me.

My phone pings on my desk and Dakota reaches to get it for me.

"Read it for me."

"It's Adam. He says he didn't see you at the game and wants to know if you're in your dorm watching *Notting Hill*?"

She looks up to me for an explanation.

"When I was in like seventh grade, my first boyfriend broke up with me and I was so devastated I watched *Notting Hill* on repeat for an entire weekend. Something like twenty times. It became my go-to breakup movie." I could so go for watching that movie on repeat about now.

"I love that movie," Reagan says. "Julia Roberts is a goddess."

Dakota sets my phone on the bed. "Guess they didn't see us. That's good."

"Yeah," I agree. I mean, I think it's good. I'm not sure what difference it would have made, but there was no way I could sit in my usual seat so close to the bench where he could read the sadness on my face. The game was brutal enough as it was.

Instead, the girls and I sat at the top of the student section blending in with the sea of blue and yellow. It was hard to watch them lose, but it fit my depressing mood nicely.

My phone pings again, and this time I reach for it.

Adam: Are you okay? Just let me know you're at the dorm and that all is well and I'll leave you alone.

Me: Yes, I'm safe and sound in my dorm.

He doesn't respond right away, and I toss my phone back onto the bed. Holding it reminds me I haven't talked to Heath. "Well, should we watch *Notting Hill?*"

We're just cueing up the movie when there's noise outside of my window. My window faces a parking lot, so it isn't unusual that it's noisy, but this noise is . . . well, it's different.

"Do you hear that?" I ask.

"Sounds like a bunch of drunk guys heading out to party. It's too early to be so obnoxious, must be freshmen. No offense." She stands and goes to look. "Uh, Ginny, I think you need to see this."

I scramble from the bed to look. There's shrubbery along the edge of the building, so the aforementioned obnoxious guys aren't directly under my window, but they're as close as they can get.

Adam and Rhett are on all fours on the ground and Maverick is on top of them on his hands and knees and then Heath stands on his back. They've built a freaking pyramid. Reagan and Dakota laugh. We open my window as far as it goes, which is only a couple of inches.

Heath holds his cell phone over his head and sings along with the music.

"What in the world is he doing?" Dakota asks.

"Shh! He's serenading her," Reagan says.

"Why Mariah Carey?" Dakota asks in a whisper.

A few other residents have opened their windows and call out or sing along. People walking by in the parking lot are stopping. Some have their phones out videoing it, no doubt.

Heath wears a shy expression, one I wasn't sure he possessed, but he belts out the song confidently. When he's through the chorus for a second time, he stops.

Rhett calls, "Did she hear us? What's going on? I can't see shit down here."

"The whole dorm heard you, asshole," someone calls.

"What are you doing?" I ask through the crack. My heart hammers in my chest. Hope and excitement claw at the hurt and anger.

"I didn't think this all the way through. I don't know what to do now," he admits with a sheepish grin.

"Tell her how you feel," Mav urges. He looks up to me and lifts a hand to wave, which makes Heath wobble on his back.

"Maybe you should get down first," Adam prompts.

Heath jumps down and the rest of the guys get up. Heath walks closer and stares up at me. "I miss you."

"You could have said that over the phone."

"I was afraid you wouldn't answer."

"Trying to watch a movie in here!" someone else calls out a window not far from mine.

Heath looks toward the voice. "Sorry, man. Almost done."

Mav pushes forward. "Go fucking watch it then. Guy's trying to pour his heart out." He nods to Heath as if to say, *I've got you covered.*

Heath tilts his head to the side and speaks a little quieter. "Can we talk somewhere else, not through the window?"

I hesitate and he adds, "Doesn't have to be tonight. Tomorrow? Next week? Next month? You name it and I'll be there."

Reagan whispers beside me, "Go down there."

My heart is beating so fast, but the rest of me is frozen in place. "I'll call you, okay?"

He nods, a look of resignation taking over his features and he takes a step back.

"Come on, boys," Adam says.

Every one of them looks disappointed, but I can't bring myself to run down there and throw myself into his arms. Of course, that's what I want to do, but then what?

They head toward the parking lot. Adam's Jeep is parked in one of the fifteen-minute spots closest to my dorm.

"Heath," I yell out my window. They all turn with matching hopeful expressions. "I miss you too."

Last night, Reagan and Dakota stayed through the movie. They didn't ask if I was going to call Heath or say anything really, and I'm glad because I didn't know the answer. I still don't.

After they were gone, I laid in bed with my phone scrolling through our text history and then my pictures. He's become such a big part of my life and I know that I can't cut him out completely. At least for another semester, he'll be living with my brother, but even if that weren't the case, I'd see him on campus. A glimpse across the crowd or maybe we'd run into one another at a party.

I've started a dozen different text messages, but I haven't been brave enough to send any of them.

I go to the game Saturday afternoon with Dakota and this time we sit in our usual seats. We're in our blue and yellow, and I do my best to plaster on a happy face as the team takes the ice.

Heath looks straight to my seat, and when he sees me, a hint of a smile pulls at his lips. Tonight's game is as fast-paced as last night's and we're on our feet, hands clenched in nervous excitement for most of it.

Vermont's defense is big and mean and they seem to have it out for Heath in particular. He takes hit after brutal hit.

I cringe when Maverick's slammed into the boards. In front of me, Adam and a guy from Vermont collide and both go down, but not before Adam passes the puck to Heath. It's like a wrestling match on skates, but Heath races to the net, past defenders, and finds the net. The horn blares and we go crazy with the rest of the crowd.

The goal seems to shift things and Vermont is sloppier, not quite recovering their composure. Valley holds on to win by one.

I decide to wait for Heath by the locker rooms. I have no idea what I'm going to say, but avoiding him forever isn't an option.

The guys are slow to come out and I'm pacing and wringing my hands when his dark head finally comes through the door. He pauses when he sees me and Maverick runs into the back of him. I start toward him and meet him halfway.

"Hey," he says tentatively.

"Congratulations."

"Thanks."

We both shift awkwardly, and I step forward and hug him. He hugs me back but hisses through his teeth.

"Oh, shit, sorry." I step back as he winces. "You got tossed around like a rag doll out there tonight."

"Yeah, it got a little rough."

"Are you headed to The Hideout?"

"That was the plan, unless . . ."

"Yeah, you should go. It was a big victory."

"You're not coming?" There's obvious disappointment on his face.

"Not tonight. Dakota and I are going to watch Reagan's play. It's opening night. But maybe we can talk tomorrow?"

"Really?" He looks so excited about it, I can't help but smile.

"Yeah, really. We should talk. It isn't like we can avoid each other forever."

"Wouldn't want to even if I could." I'm at a loss for words and he takes my hand. "Just give me a chance to explain."

I nod and take a step away, breaking our contact. "Tomorrow."

Seeing Reagan perform a second time is just as amazing as the first, and bonus that I get to watch as Dakota and the rest of the crowd react.

"She's so damn talented," Dakota says when it's over. She wipes an honest to goodness tear from her eye. "I don't even like theater."

"Let's go find her. She said she'd meet us out in the lobby."

I'm surprised to see my brother and Rhett as we crowd into the lobby with everyone else. Their tall and muscular frames make them easy to find, but getting to them takes a few minutes. When we do, I ask the obvious question, "What are you two doing here?"

A quick scan of them, and I can tell they're in their travel suits for away games.

Adam hugs me. "She always comes to support us, so we thought we'd return the favor."

"That's really nice of you. What'd you think?" I ask Rhett.

"I don't really like theater, but Reagan's part was cool."

"Maybe you could leave out the first part when you see her," I tell him as I spot her. "She's over there. Come on."

FORTY

Heath

After having a beer with some of the guys on the team at The Hideout, I head back to the apartment. My latest care package from Nathan and Chloe is waiting for me and I open it (definitely Chloe put this one together—it's covered in gold tissue paper) and call my brother.

"Thank Chloe for the package." I lie down on my bed and stare up at the ceiling.

"You can thank her yourself in three weeks. We're flying up to watch you play the weekend before Christmas."

"For real?" I ask and sit up.

"Yeah, Mom too. She didn't tell you?"

"Uh . . ."

"You haven't talked to her, have you?"

"She's my next call." I pull the phone away from my ear and look at the time. "Or tomorrow, maybe, it's kind of late there."

"She'll be up. You know what a night owl she is. Call her."

"I will, I will," I say begrudgingly.

"I get it," he says. "Trust me, I do. I did the same thing. I got to Valley and tried to live like the past hadn't happened. I barely talked to you or Mom my first two years of college."

"I know, I remember." I'd been sad at first and then pissed. Dad died, then Nathan left, Mom got worse, and before I knew it, everything had changed except me.

"She's trying. I know it doesn't magically make up for everything, but you can't be pissed at her forever if you really want to move on."

"I'm not pissed," I say and then backtrack. "Okay, maybe a little pissed."

"If it helps, the more I talk to her now, the easier it gets and the less I find myself thinking about the past."

"Yeah, all right."

"Well, I've gotta get to bed. We're flying to New York early tomorrow, but I'm really excited to see you in a few weeks. Also, Chloe started Christmas shopping two months ago, so be prepared—her level of excitement is intense."

"Can't wait," I say honestly. It's been a long time since we've had a holiday together or really any time together.

After we hang up, I call Mom, but she doesn't answer, so I shoot her a text and then change into sweats.

She returns my call as I fall back on my bed. "Hey, sorry I missed your call, my hands were covered in cookie dough. I'm doing some late-night baking."

"No problem. I'm about to head to bed."

"Have you talked to Nathan? Did he tell you we're coming to Valley?" Her voice is upbeat, and I realize she's excited, which makes me more excited.

"Yeah, I just got off the phone with him. I can't believe you guys are all coming."

"Visiting you at college and then your brother and Chloe coming home for Thanksgiving reminded me how much I miss my boys. I was so focused on myself and getting healthy that I've let us all go too long without getting together."

"You're doing great, Mom." She really is and it only takes her voicing her own regrets to make me feel like a giant douche for holding the past against her. I haven't magically forgiven her, and I don't know how long it'll be until I do, but I know Nathan is right—I've gotta meet her where she is now if I want any type of relationship with her.

The thing is I don't avoid calling her because I don't want her in my life. I'm just having a hard time figuring out what that looks like now while I try to let go of years of hurt I didn't even realize I was harboring until she was well enough for me to take a breath.

"I am," she says confidently. "And so are you. I'm so proud of you."

I clear my throat. "Thanks, Mom."

"Three weeks! I can't wait. I'm making a test batch of oatmeal raisin cookies now."

My stomach growls. "Those are my favorite."

"I know. I haven't made them in years."

The more we make plans, the more excited I am, but also cautious. "I'm excited too, but if it doesn't work out, then we'll still all be together next summer. Assuming they go through with the wedding."

"Of course, they'll go through with it. Your brother is head over heels for Chloe."

"Yeah, it's not her I'm worried about screwing it up," I joke. Honestly, I know my brother would gnaw off a limb before doing anything to sabotage his relationship with Chloe. And she's awesome, so I get it. I'm happy for them.

"Oh, hush. Your brother is doing great. I'm proud of both my boys. I'm really glad you called. The house is still lonely without you. Especially at night."

I yawn and she laughs in my ear. "Get some sleep, honey. I'll call you this week."

"Okay, sounds great, Mom."

"I love you."

I try not to react to the word, but my muscles tighten, waiting for the thing that comes next . . . which used to be disappointment. It doesn't come, but it's too many years of hurt built up. I don't know if there'll ever be a day it doesn't fill me with a sense of dread coming from her lips. Or a day I'll be able to say it to her or Ginny or anyone else. "Thanks, Mom."

Sunday I'm practically glued to my phone waiting to hear from Ginny. I texted her as soon as I woke up, but by mid-afternoon, I'm starting to worry she's blowing me off.

"Give me your phone," Maverick prompts and holds out his hand.

"No way."

"Payne, give me the fucking phone before you do something stupid."

"Why can't I text her again?"

"Because it's pathetic," Rauthruss says.

"That's really something coming from you. You're on your phone constantly with Carrie."

"Yeah, but she wants to talk to me."

Ouch, but okay, point made. I place my phone in Mav's palm and not two seconds later, her name flashes on the screen. I swipe it back with a giant smile on my face.

"And?" Mav asks.

"She's been at the theater all day. Apparently they asked her to do the makeup for Reagan and a few other girls at the show today."

"Oh, right." Adam's in the kitchen making food. "Yeah, I think I heard them talking about that last night. Reagan looked as hot as she always does, but I guess it was too subtle for the stage or the lights or, fuck, I don't know."

"You're just telling me this now?"

"I didn't think of it until now."

I take my phone into my bedroom and dial Ginny.

"Hey," she answers, sounding out of breath. "I'm just now heading back to my dorm. Sorry about that. I didn't realize that I'd need to stay through the whole performance."

"Stage makeup, huh?"

"Yeah, they even offered me a job for future performances."

"That's great, Ginny. Congratulations."

"Thank you. So, today was kind of a bust. I need to shower and then head to the library. I have a group meeting for one of my classes. I'm not sure when it'll be done. Can we talk tomorrow?"

Tomorrow. Shit, that sounds so far away. "Breakfast?"

"Yeah, I'll meet you at our usual time."

"So," Mav starts as we're walking into the dining hall. "Which one did you decide to go with?"

"What are you talking about?" I scan the room for Ginny.

"Which big gesture is next? Rent out a theater? Dinner?"

"I decided to go with something that's more . . . me."

"You?"

I slap Mav on the back. "Yeah, but it's not because I didn't enjoy your suggestions. You save those for when you find the perfect girl and screw it up."

"Good luck, buddy." He gets in line for food.

I don't see Ginny yet, so I head to the back where I find Brenda. She smiles when she spots me.

"How's my favorite lunch lady?"

She snorts. Brenda is the no-nonsense lady who manages the dining hall. I won her over last year. It started with a lot of flattery. Much deserved flattery. She works hard to keep us fed and I appreciate that more than most people. Then I got to know her a little and found out she's a huge hockey fan.

"Sam and the kids good?"

She softens at the mention of her husband and children. "Matty is graduating high school this year, and Sophia is all about boys, God help us all."

She hands me a tray and quirks a brow. "Coach Meyers approve of this?"

"What he doesn't know won't hurt him." I wink. "Thanks, Brenda. I owe you."

"Mhmm. How about paying me back with another win next weekend?" she calls as I walk off.

My steps are light as I head to my usual table. Ginny waits, looking around for me. When she spots me, a shy smile tips up the corners of her lips. Aaand, I'm suddenly really nervous.

"Hey," she says tentatively. She looks as anxious as I feel.

I'd planned to say a lot of things, but fuck words. I drop the tray on the table, frame her face with both hands, and bring my lips to hers. She lets out a yelp of surprise, but then her body melts and she kisses me back. I've missed her so much. Not just this. *Her*.

I don't want to stop kissing her, but the sound of people bustling around us going about their usual morning routines makes me pull back. That and I know there are things she needs to hear.

"I missed you so damn much, baby doll."

"Same."

"And I'm really sorry."

"I know you are."

I sit and guide her to take the seat beside me. "I want to explain, but I'm sure I'm going to say it all wrong." I blow out a breath. The way she watches me, willing to hear me out even when I know I've hurt her, pushes me forward.

"The other night was six years of frustration coming out at once, but it shouldn't have been you I was saying all that to. For a big part of my childhood, my mom used the words like a Band-Aid. Every time I took care of something for her—paid the bills or made dinner—the repayment I got was with a string of 'I love yous.' It changed how I felt about it. Her love felt like an excuse to not show up any other way." I squeeze my eyes shut. "Trust me, I know that's fucked up. I know she was grieving; I know she was depressed, but it didn't change the fact that all I wanted was for my mom to act like everyone else's. I didn't want *I love you*. I wanted her to take care of me."

"Oh, Heath, I'm sorry." She squeezes my hand. "I won't pretend to understand what that must have been like. I'm certain that she loved you the best she could. That's all anyone does. It isn't perfect."

"I know. Knowing it and accepting it aren't the same." My heart's beating like a drum in my chest. "The thought of my feelings for you being tainted by the past . . . I hate it. I don't want anything bad to ever touch you. You are my favorite person. You're the only person I'd skip food for or that could convince me to eat Neapolitan ice cream or . . . a thousand other things. You. It's only you. And when I walked in here, I fully intended to stand firm on my stance of never speaking the words, of keeping the best thing in my life away from my worst memories, but then I saw you and I realized that it doesn't matter what it's meant before. If loving you is wanting to spend every day with you, laughing and having fun, supporting you, and having your back, then I do. I love you, Ginny. Of course, I do."

"Really?"

"Really, really. I love you. I love you. I freaking love you."

She smiles and closes her eyes like she's trying to savor the moment. When her brown eyes meet mine again, it's such a punch to the gut I wonder how it took me so long to realize it.

"We don't need to use the word. Not if it bothers you. I just want to know that you're as crazy about me as I am you. That we're in this together."

"Did I mention I'd skip food for you?" Her lips part into a happy grin and my chest tightens. "One last thing."

I hop up onto the table and clear my throat. "Genevieve Scott, will you be my girlfriend?"

People are staring and snickering. Ginny's cheeks go red with embarrassment, but she nods. "Of course I will. I'd skip food for you too."

I jump down and kiss her again, then pull back so my forehead rests against hers. "I had no idea it was ever unclear that you were my girlfriend. I've always thought of you as my girl. I'm sorry that I left any room for doubt, but I won't make that mistake again. I'll stand on this table and ask every day if you want me to."

"I'll consider that. Could be entertaining." She laces her fingers with mine. "Speaking of food though, is that for me?" She tips her head to the bowl of ice cream.

I push the tray toward her, a huge bowl of Neapolitan ice cream topped with gummy bears.

"That is a lot of gummy bears. How did you get ice cream at this hour?"

"I know people."

Her gorgeous smile will be the death of me. She picks up the spoon and brings a big bite to my lips. I take it and then kiss her again.

Maverick appears at the table. "Awww, look at you two, all smiles." He drops his tray and then drapes an arm around each of our shoulders. "Bring it in, you two crazy kids. I'm so dang happy I could cry. Way to go big, buddy." He nudges me with an elbow and then squeezes Ginny into his massive frame. "I love you two."

And I know he does. Whatever it means to him, he means it with his whole heart. It's freeing to know I get to make it mean whatever I want to, too.

"Love you too, Mav," I tell him.

He gives me a toothy grin. "Damn straight."

FORTY-ONE

Ginny
One week later

"I have to go to class, I'm going to be late," I protest, but make no move to actually go anywhere. Heath's arms are wrapped around me and I nuzzle into his chest, stealing some of his warmth. "It's so cold."

"This isn't cold."

"It's like forty degrees outside."

"Like I said, this isn't cold. Wait until you come to Michigan sometime in the winter. You'll need real winter clothes, not these cute accessories you have." He pulls my beanie down farther, so it completely covers my ears.

"It would be fun to see snow. It almost never snows here and when it does, it's gone too quickly to appreciate it."

Another chilly breeze whips through campus and I shiver.

"Come on, baby doll," he says. "Let's get you to class where it's warm."

As we're crossing to the humanities building, a guy headed toward us slows and a big smile tips up his lips. Heath stops, as does the guy.

"Heath, hey."

"Wes!" Heath steps forward and they hug.

Wes is a few inches taller than Heath with lighter hair and a leaner build. He looks familiar, but I can't place him until Heath turns to me and introduces him as one of the coaches of the basketball team and an old teammate of his brother's.

Heath comes to stand beside me again. "And this is Ginny, my girlfriend."

My insides light up every time he calls me that.

Wes nods his head to me in greeting. "Nice to meet you, Ginny."

"You too."

"What are you doing on campus, old man?" Heath asks. "Shouldn't you be at the gym making guys run sprints or something?"

"Not for another hour." His smile is big, and his eyes crinkle up at the corners. "I'm meeting Blair for lunch." He takes a step past us and turns. "Hey, nice season, by the way. I'm hoping to make another game soon."

"Nathan's coming up in two weeks for the game against Western Michigan."

"Yeah? I'll have to call him and give him shit for not telling me himself. I'll see ya later."

He heads off in the opposite direction and Heath and I continue across campus. I slide my glove-covered hand around his and squeeze.

"Coming over tonight?" he asks, swinging our arms lightly between us.

"Yeah, but I need to do some laundry first. I've barely been at my dorm all week."

"I don't see a problem. Should just pack your stuff and bring it to my place."

I slow. "You'd give me a drawer?"

"I'll give you as many as you want."

I laugh lightly at how easy it is for him to share himself and his space. Although that's not really new. Heath may not have experience in being a boyfriend, but he's always gone out of his way to give me anything he thought I might want. But all I really want is him. No one has ever made me happier and I've never had more fun than when I'm with him.

It wasn't exactly my plan to fall for someone first semester, but I can't wait to see what new adventures the next one will bring.

"Mav, these burgers are amazing," Reagan says with a groan of pleasure.

"They really are," Rhett adds. "I bow down to the grill master."

Mav waves his hand and dips his head in a mock bow.

The guys bought a patio heater and we're outside having dinner. Me, Heath, Adam, Rhett, Maverick, Dakota, and Reagan—we're like our own little dysfunctional family.

My brother is leaned back, beer in hand, smiling as everyone eats and talks. He seems happier. I know our parents' separation hit him hard, but I think he's coming to terms with it. So am I. Things will look different now, but at least we've got each other.

It's so weird to think that if I'd come to college with Bryan, so many things would have been different, but the thing I'm the most thankful for is how close Adam and I are again.

Heath and I huddle under a blanket, eating and bumping shoulders occasionally since our hands are full.

"We should play sardines tonight," Rhett says as he crumples his napkin and sets it in the middle of his plate.

"We've got an odd number without Taryn," Adam says. "You guys play, I'll hang back."

"What, no way," I protest. "We can have three on a team."

"Mav needs two people to keep him in line anyway." Rhett nudges him. "Who's going with Adam?"

"Reagan," I say too quickly, and my friend's eyes get large as if she's afraid I'm going to out her. "Mav helps cancel out some of Rhett's hiding skills."

It's perfectly good logic and Adam nods. "Yeah, that makes sense. What do you say, Reagan?"

"Sure, I guess that's okay," she says, barely looking at him.

We head to campus. Heath and I are slower than the others, stopping to kiss every few steps and generally being the obnoxious happy couple.

"Who's hiding tonight?" Dakota asks.

"Should be Rhett and Reagan, so let's go with Adam and Reagan," I say.

Everyone nods their agreement. Playing matchmaker is way too much fun.

"What's the rule?" I ask Reagan and Adam.

They share a look as they try to decide.

"You pick," Adam says to her.

"One person has to close their eyes and be led by their partner or partners," she says the last part looking at our group of three.

"All right. Let's do this." Adam's breath shows in the cold air, and he claps his hands together before he and Reagan head off to hide.

"I've got the time," I call as we all settle in to wait. The ground is cold, so we stay standing and form a small circle sharing our body heat. Heath's arms wrap around me from behind and I lean back into his chest.

"You two are annoyingly adorable," Dakota says as Heath leans down to kiss my cheek.

While our friends make fun of us, good-naturedly of course, Heath keeps right on hugging me and I soak it up. Him, our friends, all of it.

"Don't be jealous, Dakota," Heath says, speaking near my ear. "You've got two. Ginny only gets one."

Rhett and Maverick attack her from each side, hugging her tightly between them. She squeals and bats at their chests, but she's laughing as they bounce up and down, jostling her around.

"Okay, okay." She finally gets free. "Let's go find Adam and Rea."

"Close your eyes, Dakota. We'll lead you," Mav says.

"Not a chance." She shakes her head, making her light red hair toss around her shoulders.

Rhett takes a step. "Mav, close your eyes. Dakota and I will make sure you don't run into anything."

Dakota gets on the opposite side of Mav from Rhett. "No promises from me," she says before they start to guide him away.

Heath sweeps my feet out from under me. "Close your eyes, baby doll, I got you."

I wrap my arms around his neck and let him carry me. I close my eyes, playing along, though I hardly see the point.

"Are you really leading me to find the others or taking me somewhere to make out?"

"That last one sounds real tempting, but the sooner we find the others, the sooner I can take you home and make out with you in my warm bed."

His lips graze against mine and I lean forward to kiss him harder. He stops, wherever we are, and his tongue sweeps into my mouth, warm and demanding.

He pulls back way sooner than I want, but he doesn't move.

"Ginny, open your eyes." His voice is filled with wonder and excitement.

His head's thrown back and he stares up into the sky. A tiny snowflake falls onto his nose.

"It's snowing!"

The small white flurries fall around us, slowly at first. Heath sets me down and I hold my arms out to the side. "I love the snow. It always feels so magical."

I can just make out Dakota's laughter and the guys shouting and know they're excited about it too. Heath and I walk toward them in the snow, joining them at the same time Reagan and Adam have abandoned their hiding spot.

"This is amazing," I say as I reach Adam.

"Right? I can't remember the last time it snowed like this in December."

"It won't last," I say sadly. Even by morning, it'll probably be gone.

"But it's here now." Rhett smiles and takes a seat on the ground.

One by one, we all drop to the cold grass in the middle of campus. Maverick goes into his coat pocket and brings out a bottle of Mad Dogg. "I came prepared."

It hits me, sitting here with my friends—people I can no longer imagine not being in my life—I found this amazing group of people in the hardest five months of my entire life when I needed them the most. And amidst my brother's friends. Who would have thought?

But, if I've learned anything since coming to Valley, it's that we can only really prepare for the small things. What to wear, what to bring on a trip, which direction to go. The rest is fate and luck. And I feel like the luckiest girl of all.

JUNE

EPILOGUE

Ginny

"Do I look okay?" I smooth a hand down my dress and turn in the mirror. Heath's sitting on the bed waiting for me as patiently as one can while his girlfriend changes clothes five times.

"You look gorgeous." He stands and wraps his arms around me, meeting my eyes in our reflection. "You don't need to be nervous. You've already met my family."

"I know, but it's not just your family—there are a bunch of people here this weekend and I don't know any of them."

"You know me. Besides, I only know half of them myself." He brings his lips to mine in a quick kiss. "Come on, I promise I won't leave your side."

The hotel is huge and right on the beach in California where Nathan's fiancée Chloe is from. Later tonight, we have the rehearsal dinner and tomorrow they'll say I do.

Down in the lobby, Heath guides me to a long table where his brother Nathan sits with a group of guys. Nathan and Heath look a lot alike, same nose and same eyes. Heath's hair is darker, and his build is bigger, although Nathan is a little taller. Nathan stands when he sees us, and he and Heath hug.

"You guys made it," Nathan says and smiles at me over Heath's shoulder.

When they separate, Heath comes back to my side. "We got in about an hour ago."

"This is gonna be fun." Nathan looks around at all the people and grins.

"Are weddings allowed to be fun?" Heath asks, earning a playful glare from his brother. "We're going to grab a drink."

"Baby Payne!" one of the guys calls as we start to walk off. "Grab me one too." He holds up his empty glass. He has deliciously dark hair and a cocky smirk. He turns that smirk on me and I go stupid.

"Who is that?" I whisper as we get to the bar.

"Hey now, no creeping on my brother's friends."

"I wasn't creeping, but *damn*. Is he a model?"

"He is happily married, young lady."

"I wonder if his wife gives him hall passes."

Heath chuckles. "Well, your boyfriend does not."

I bite back a laugh as he pulls me into his side possessively. Heath and I grab a drink and head back to the table where I meet Nathan's friends, Joel, Wes, and Zeke.

Watching Nathan with his friends reminds me a lot of Heath and his. They have the same easy way about them with all the teasing and competitiveness I've come to love. When their wives and girlfriends join us, I sit next to Heath, his hand around the back of my chair, missing our friends and wondering what we'll look like in five or ten years when the whole group of us gets together. I hope it looks even half as happy as this.

Nathan and Chloe are the picture of excitement and love as she sits on the edge of his lap and absently plays with the hair at the nape of his neck. I don't think she's stopped smiling since she sat down.

Joel, the one I'm pretty sure could have a second career in modeling, looks at his wife Katrina like she's the center of his world. And she looks at him the same way. Every time he looks at me I blush, I can't help it, he's stupid hot.

Zeke and his oh so very pregnant wife Gabby are possibly the cutest couple I've ever seen. She's all big, blonde hair and tiny body except for her bump. Zeke's at least twice her size and keeps reaching over and touching her stomach. I don't even think he realizes he's doing it.

Wes, who I've met before, and his girlfriend Blair are currently in the hot seat. They're the only couple of the group that isn't married and their friends are poking at Wes to get on the ball. Blair doesn't seem to mind. She leans over and kisses Wes, and they share some sort of private exchange.

I'm fighting a yawn and Heath notices. He sits forward. "I think we're going to take a nap before the rehearsal. We were up at dark-thirty this morning to get here."

Heath takes my hand and we start toward our room.

"Don't be late," Nathan calls after him.

Heath rolls his eyes and yells back, "I know how to tell time and work an alarm."

I pull him to the elevator and up to our floor.

"How long do we have?" I ask, climbing into bed and grabbing my phone to set an alarm.

Heath takes the device out of my hands and places it on the bedside table. He pulls his dress shirt out of his pants with a wicked glint in his eye.

"I thought we were napping," I say as I unbuckle his pants.

"We will, but first . . ." He shrugs out of his shirt and my hands slide up his abs, enjoying the way the muscle cords and dips. Yeah, I'm suddenly not tired either.

His body covers mine and he kisses me hard. He rolls us so I'm on top. Making quick work of undressing me, his hands come up to palm my breasts. They ache. My entire body does. That's the way it is with Heath. One touch is never just one touch. He touches me and I feel it in my soul. It's all foreplay, he said once and I think he was right. My body sings when he's near. I keep waiting for the newness to wear off, but the more time we spend together, the more convinced I am that what we have is a once in a lifetime type of love.

I guide him inside of me and we both groan. This . . . this feeling. It's completeness, it's connection, it's everything.

●

The next morning, I shower and get ready to meet up with the girls. Chloe and Nathan's mom, Lana, invited me to join them for hair and makeup.

"You're leaving now? It's barely noon," Heath protests, arms wrapped around my waist as I comb out my wet hair.

Last night's rehearsal dinner went late. I'm not sure how many people they invited, but with their family and friends and Nathan's teammates . . . there are a lot of guests here to watch Nathan and Chloe exchange vows. In a whirlwind of excitement and drinks, I met a lot of them after the rehearsal dinner. We closed down the hotel bar and then continued to hang out on the outdoor patio for well into the early morning hours.

So, the only thing we've done this morning is lie in bed—not that I'm complaining. Spending all day in bed with Heath is one of my favorite activities.

"Yes, I'm leaving now. Don't make that face—I don't want to be late."

"Fine." Reluctantly, he loosens his grip. "You're lucky I didn't tell Chloe you're a better makeup artist than the one she hired."

My jaw drops. "I would maim you, Heath Payne. It's the biggest day of her life!" My pitch rises with the panic I feel just imagining it.

"Relax, baby doll. You're secret's safe with me." He drops a kiss on my lips. "I guess I should find Nathan and see what he needs from his best man."

I kiss him again quickly and make my way to Chloe's suite. It's intimidating walking into the chaos. Chloe and her friends are chatting excitedly and fawning over her dress which hangs in the corner.

Gabby spots me from the chair she's sitting in and waves. She and the other bridesmaids are wearing matching pink robes, but Gabby's is shorter where it hitches up to cover her baby bump.

"I would get up, but the longer I sit today, the less chance that I'll have cankles when I stand up next to the blushing bride."

"You look beautiful. You totally have the whole glow thing going on."

She rubs at her stomach. "Thank you."

"Do you know if you're having a boy or girl?"

"Girl." She winces. "And I think she's dribbling a basketball in there."

"Ginny, hey." Chloe hugs me tightly. "Let me introduce you to everyone and then you're first up for hair and makeup."

Heath

The guys are kicked back in Nathan's room, a bottle of Jack on the table between them.

"Couldn't spring for something a little nicer?" I ask as I take a seat next to them and pour myself a glass.

"Old school, Baby Payne," Joel says. "It was this or Everclear, and I don't think Chloe would appreciate your brother passing out before the ceremony."

Nathan wears a sheepish smile as he tips back another small sip. A knock at the door gets him to his feet.

"Linc," Nathan calls as he holds the door wide and my boss walks in.

I stand to greet him as well with a hug. "Hey, I didn't know you were coming."

"Wouldn't miss it." He steps back and looks me over. "How've you been?"

"Good. Great."

"He met a girl," Nathan says as if that clarifies why everything is great. I guess it does.

"Man, I hand you over to Wally for weekly check-ins and I miss all the good gossip."

When I first started working with Lincoln and his sports coaching website, we talked weekly. I reported directly to him. But the busier he's gotten, the less frequent our calls have been. I'm also pretty certain that the only reason I was reporting to him was so he had an excuse to check in on me. I'd like to think he and Nathan have finally started to trust that I can take care of myself and are giving me more credit.

"Is Keira here too?" Nathan asks. "She killed it at the tournament last weekend."

"She is." He beams with pride talking about his pro-golfer wife.

The room becomes a back and forth of questions and cross conversations as everyone catches up. When Nathan gets up to get another bottle of liquor, I follow him.

"Hey, I have something for you."

"Yeah?" He abandons the bottle on the wet bar and takes the box I hold out for him.

"Wrapped it myself," I say as he pulls back the flaps of a battered box I re-used from my collection of care packages he's sent.

Grinning, he pulls the items from the box. Gum, breath mints, sunscreen, condoms, earplugs.

"What is all this?" he asks with a chuckle and holds up the earplugs.

"A little honeymoon care package from me to you. Those are for Chloe so when she's tired of your shit, she can tune you out."

"Thank you."

I take out the smaller gift from my pocket. "Your real present."

He tears off the white paper and a ghost of a smile pulls one side of his mouth. "Is this—"

"Yeah, it's the same cologne Dad wore. I was walking through the store and the scent just hit me. I don't expect you to wear it. I thought you might like to have a reminder . . . especially today."

His hug is unexpected and tight. It takes me a moment to return the gesture, but when I do, there's a feeling like Dad's really here with us, or at least looking down and watching.

Thirty minutes before the wedding is scheduled to start, we put on our tuxes and prepare to head down.

"Yo, Heath, can you do me a favor?" Nathan approaches me, looking sharper than I can ever remember seeing him. "I need to give Chloe her wedding gift before the ceremony, but I'm not supposed to see her."

I take the present covered not in wrapping paper, but in college-ruled notebook paper with his writing all over it. I give it a little shake. "What is it?"

"It's not for you." He blushes and now I really want to know what's inside. "Can you get it to her or not?"

"Yeah, of course."

I find the girls' suite and knock. When it swings open, my heart squeezes in my chest. "Holy shit, babe."

"Heath." Ginny looks around. "What are you doing?"

I'm still staring slack-jawed. Listen, Ginny, on an average day, is a knockout. She's generally casual—not a lot of makeup, hair straight or pulled away from her face in a braid . . . she doesn't need all the extra stuff to be the hottest girl I've ever seen, but right now . . . hair in big waves, eyes lined with black, wearing a dress that pushes her boobs up and shoes that make her legs look twice as long . . .

"Heath?"

I shake my head. "Fuck, you look . . . fuck."

She giggles. "You look nice too. I've been waiting for this day." She runs a hand along the lapel of my jacket. "You in a tux is really something."

"Yeah?" I step into her. "I'm starting to see the appeal of weddings."

"What's that?"

"Open bar and a night of fun while I try to figure out how to sneak you away without anyone noticing."

"You're ridiculous."

"You're beautiful."

"Five-minute warning!" someone yells from inside the room.

"Can you give this to Chloe? I don't want to go in there. It looks like a bomb went off."

"Yeah, I'll see you down there."

She turns, but I catch her wrist and pull her back to me, taking her lips in a much quicker kiss than I'd like. Someday I'm gonna marry that girl, but today it's all about Nathan and Chloe.

The guys and I head down first. The hotel restaurant has a huge patio that extends out onto the beach and there are flowers everywhere. In pots, hanging from the doorway, lining the wall. It's nuts.

People are seated and waiting for the ceremony. The other groomsmen bring Chloe's mom and grandparents up the aisle.

"What do you say?" I hold out my arm for my mom. Her eyes are already glassy. She's for sure going to cry, probably in the first thirty seconds. She lets out a breath and flutters her lashes a few times as if she's trying to stop the tears.

Turning to Nathan, she regards us both. "I'm so proud of the both of you. If your dad were here, he'd give some speech about baseball or fishing that somehow related back to life, but since he's not, you're going to have to make do with the girl version."

"Which is?" Nathan asks, hands in his pockets.

"Just be happy. Life's too short." Her eyes are tear-filled again, but she smiles. "He loved you two more than anything and so do I."

Nathan leans forward and kisses her cheek. "I love you too, Mom."

She slips her arm in mine and lets out a long breath. "Okay, ready."

I guide her up the aisle and to the groom's side. Ginny's sitting two rows behind the family. I shoot her a wink as we pass. Kevin stands from his seat when we approach.

We shake hands, and he smiles at Mom. He's a good guy and I'm coming to enjoy having him around. If nothing else, I know he's been good for Mom.

Today is one of those happy days when I can practically read Mom and Nathan's thoughts, all of us wishing Dad was here for our own selfish reasons. It's moments like these that will always remind us our family looks different now.

She squeezes my arm and then slips hers out to take her seat next to Kevin.

"Mom, wait." Her brows raise as she looks to me expectantly.

"I love you." My chest aches with emotion. Fuck, maybe I'm going to cry today, too.

Her eyes well with tears again and this time, one slips down her cheek. I've waited too long to say the words to her, but I mean them now in a way I didn't before. Acceptance, forgiveness, or maybe it just took me growing the fuck up. She hugs me tightly. I clear the lump from my throat and take my place at the front.

As the processional music starts and all eyes go to the back, mine go to Nathan, my mom, and then Ginny—my family. I couldn't imagine life without them. If that's not love, then I don't know what is. Maybe it's not supposed to mean the same thing to everyone or maybe it is and it's about finding someone whose meaning matches yours. I don't plan on giving it a lot more thought. It is what it is and that's good enough for me.

Ginny glances at me and it hits me in the gut, like it does every single time she's near. Our love matches, plain and simple, and it's the best thing to ever happen to me.

Life is short. Be happy and enjoy every moment.

ALSO BY
REBECCA JENSHAK

Campus Nights Series

Secret Puck

Bad Crush

Broken Hearts

Wild Love

Campus Wallflowers Series

Tutoring the Player

Hating the Player

Smart Jocks Series

The Assist

The Fadeaway

The Tip-Off

The Fake

The Pass

Wildcat Hockey Series

Wildcat

Wild About You

Wild Ever After

Standalone Novels

Sweet Spot

Electric Blue Love

ABOUT THE AUTHOR

Rebecca Jenshak is a *USA Today* bestselling author of new adult and sports romance. She lives in Arizona with her family. When she isn't writing, you can find her attending local sporting events, hanging out with family and friends, or with her nose buried in a book.

Sign up for her newsletter for book sales and release news.

www.rebeccajenshak.com

www.ingramcontent.com/pod-product-compliance
Lightning Source LLC
Chambersburg PA
CBHW051053030726
47504CB00006B/1612

* 9 7 8 1 9 5 1 8 1 5 3 7 0 *